PRIVATE
GAMES

JAMES PATTERSON is one of the best-known and biggest-selling writers of all time. He is the author of some of the most popular series of the past decade – the Alex Cross, Women's Murder Club and Detective Michael Bennett novels – and he has written many other number one bestsellers including romance novels and stand-alone thrillers. He lives in Florida with his wife and son.

James is passionate about encouraging children to read. Inspired by his own son who was a reluctant reader, he also writes a range of books specifically for young readers. James has formed a partnership with the National Literacy Trust, an independent, UK-based charity that changes lives through literacy. In 2010, he was voted Author of the Year at the Children's Choice Book Awards in New York.

Also by James Patterson

PRIVATE NOVELS

Private (*with Maxine Paetro*)
Private London (*with Mark Pearson*)
Private: No. 1 Suspect (*with Maxine Paetro*)

A list of more titles by James Patterson is printed at
the back of this book

JAMES PATTERSON
AND MARK SULLIVAN

PRIVATE GAMES

arrow books

Published by Arrow Books in 2012

3 5 7 9 10 8 6 4 2

First published in Great Britain in 2012 by Century

Arrow Books
Random House, 20 Vauxhall Bridge Road,
London SW1V 2SA

www.randomhouse.co.uk

Addresses for companies within The Random House Group Limited can be found
at: www.randomhouse.co.uk/offices.htm

The Random House Group Limited Reg. No. 954009

A CIP catalogue record for this book
is available from the British Library

ISBN 9780099568735
ISBN 9780099568742 (export edition)

The Random House Group Limited supports The Forest Stewardship Council
(FSC®), the leading international forest certification organisation. Our books
carrying the FSC label are printed on FSC® certified paper. FSC is the only forest
certification scheme supported by the leading environmental organisations,
including Greenpeace. Our paper procurement policy can be found at:
www.randomhouse.co.uk/environment

Typeset in Berkeley by Palimpsest Book Production Limited, Falkirk, Stirlingshire
Printed and bound by CPI Group (UK) Ltd, Croydon, CR0 4YY

For Connor and Bridger,
chasers of the Olympic dream – M.S.

Acknowledgements

We would like to thank Jackie Brock-Doyle, Neil Walker and Jason Keen at the London Organising Committee of the Olympic Games for their willingness to be helpful, candid and yet under-standably circumspect regarding a project like this one. The tour of the park construction site was incredibly instructive. We would not have got anywhere without Alan Abrahamson, Olympic expert and operator of 3Wire.com, the world's best source of information about the Games and the culture that surrounds it. Special thanks go out as well to Vikki Orvice, Olympic reporter at the *Sun* and a wealth of knowledge, humour and gossip. We are also grateful to the staff at the British Museum, One Aldwych and 41 for their invaluable aid in suggesting settings for scenes outside the Olympic venues. Ultimately, this is a fictional story of hope and an affirmation of the Olympic ideals, so please forgive us a degree of licence regarding

James Patterson

the various events, venues and characters likely to dominate the stage during the London 2012 Summer Games.

This book is not authorised or endorsed by the London Organising Committee of the Olympic Games or the London Olympic Games.

It is not possible with mortal mind to search out the purposes of the gods
– Pindar

For then, in wrath, the Olympian thundered and lightninged, and confounded Greece
– Aristophanes

Prologue

THERE ARE SUPERMEN and superwomen who walk this Earth.

I'm quite serious about that and you can take me literally. Jesus Christ, for example, was a spiritual superman, as was Martin Luther, and Gandhi. Julius Caesar was superhuman as well. So were Genghis Khan, Thomas Jefferson, Abraham Lincoln, and Adolf Hitler.

Think scientists like Aristotle, Galileo, Albert Einstein, and J. Robert Oppenheimer. Consider artists like da Vinci, Michelangelo – and Vincent Van Gogh, my favourite, who was so superior that it drove him insane. And above all, don't forget athletically superior beings like Jim Thorpe, Babe Didrikson Zaharias and Jesse Owens.

Humbly, I include myself on this superhuman

1

spectrum as well – and deservedly so, as you shall soon see.

In short, people like me are born for great things. We seek adversity. We seek to conquer. We seek to break through all limits, spiritually, politically, artistically, scientifically and physically. We seek to right wrongs in the face of monumental odds. And we're willing to suffer for greatness, willing to embrace dogged effort and endless preparation with the fervour of a martyr, which to my mind are exceptional traits in any human being from any age.

At the moment I have to admit that I'm certainly feeling exceptional, standing here in the garden of Sir Denton Marshall, a snivelling, corrupt old bastard if there ever was one.

Look at him on his knees, his back to me and my knife at his throat.

Why, he trembles and shakes as if a stone has just clipped his head. Can you smell it? Fear? It surrounds him, as rank as the air after a bomb explodes.

'Why?' he gasps.

'You've angered me, monster,' I snarl at him, feeling a rage deeper than primal split my mind and seethe through every cell. 'You've helped ruin the Games, made them an abomination and a mockery of their intent.'

'What?' Marshall cries, acting bewildered. 'What are you talking about?'

I deliver the evidence against him in three damning sentences whose impact turns the skin of his neck livid and his carotid artery a sickening, pulsing purple.

'No!' he sputters. 'That's . . . that's not true. You can't do this. Have you gone utterly mad?'

'Mad? Me?' I say. 'Hardly. I'm the sanest person I know.'

'Please,' he says, tears rolling down his face. 'Have mercy. I'm to be married on Christmas Eve.'

My laugh is as caustic as battery acid: 'In another life, Denton, I ate my own children. You'll get no mercy from me or my sisters.'

As Marshall's confusion and horror become complete, I look up into the night sky, feeling storms rising in my head, and understanding once again that I *am* superior, a superhuman imbued with forces that go back thousands of years.

'For all true Olympians,' I vow, 'this act of sacrifice marks the beginning of the end of the modern Games.'

Then I wrench the old man's head back so that his back arches.

And before he can scream, I rip the blade furiously back with such force that his head comes free of his neck all the way to his spine.

Part One

THE FURIES

Chapter 1

Thursday, 26 July 2012: 9:24 a.m.

IT WAS MAD-DOG hot for London. Peter Knight's shirt and jacket were drenched with sweat as he sprinted north on Chesham Street past the Diplomat Hotel and skidded around the corner towards Lyall Mews in the heart of Belgravia, one of the most expensive areas of real estate in the world.

Don't let it be true, Knight screamed internally as he entered the Mews. Dear God, don't let it be true.

Then he saw a pack of newspaper jackals gathering at the yellow tape of a Metropolitan Police barricade that blocked the road in front of a cream-coloured Georgian town house. Knight lurched to a stop, feeling as though he was going to retch up the eggs and bacon he'd had for breakfast.

What would he ever tell Amanda?

Before Knight could compose his thoughts or quieten his stomach, his mobile rang and he snatched it from his pocket without looking at the caller ID.

'Knight,' he managed to choke. 'That you, Jack?'

'No, Peter, it's Nancy,' a woman with an Irish brogue replied. 'Isabel has come down sick.'

'What?' Knight groaned. 'No – I just left the house an hour ago.'

'She's running a temperature,' his full-time nanny insisted. 'I just took it.'

'How high?'

'One hundred. She's complaining about her stomach, too.'

'Lukey?'

'He seems fine,' Nancy said. 'But—'

'Give them both a cool bath, and call me back if Isabel's temp hits one oh one,' Knight said. He snapped shut the phone, swallowed back the bile burning at the base of his throat.

A wiry man about six foot tall, with an appealing face and light brown hair, Knight had once been a special investigator assigned to the Old Bailey, England's Central Criminal Court. Two years ago, however, he had joined the London office of Private International at twice the pay and prestige. Private has been called the Pinkerton Agency of the twenty-first century, with premises in every major city in the world, its offices staffed by top-notch forensics scientists, security specialists, and investigators such as Knight.

Compartmentalise, he told himself. Be professional. But this felt like the last straw breaking his back. Knight had already endured too much grief and loss, both personally and professionally. Just the week before, his boss, Dan Carter, and three of his other colleagues had perished in a plane crash over the North Sea that was still under investigation. Could he live with another death?

Pushing that question and his daughter's sudden illness to one side, Knight forced himself to hurry on through the sweltering heat towards the police barrier, giving the newspaper crowd a wide berth, and in so doing spotted Billy Casper, a Scotland Yard inspector he'd known for fifteen years.

He went straight to Casper, a blockish, pock-faced man who scowled the second he saw Knight. 'Private's got no business in this, Peter.'

'If that's Sir Denton Marshall dead in there, then Private does have business in this, and I do too,' Knight shot back forcefully. 'Personal business, Billy. Is it Marshall?'

Casper said nothing.

'Is it?' Knight demanded.

Finally the inspector nodded, but he wasn't happy about it, and asked suspiciously, 'How are you and Private involved?'

Knight stood there a moment, feeling stunned by

the news, and wondering again how the hell he was going to tell Amanda. Then he shook off the despair, and said, 'London Olympic Organising Committee is Private London's client. Which makes Marshall Private's client.'

'And you?' Casper demanded. 'What's your personal stake in this? You a friend of his or something?'

'Much more than a friend. He was engaged to my mother.'

Casper's hard expression softened a bit and he chewed at his lip before saying, 'I'll see if I can get you in. Elaine will want to talk to you.'

Knight felt suddenly as if invisible forces were conspiring against him.

'Elaine got this case?' he said, wanting to punch something. 'You can't be serious.'

'Dead serious, Peter,' Casper said. 'Lucky, lucky you.'

Chapter 2

INSPECTOR ELAINE POTTERSFIELD, in charge of the crime scene, was one of the finest detectives working for the Metropolitan Police, a twenty-year veteran of the force with a prickly, know-it-all style that got results. Pottersfield had solved more murders in the past two years than any other detective at Scotland Yard. She was also the only person Knight knew who openly despised his presence.

An attractive woman in her forties, the inspector always put Knight in mind of a borzoi dog, with her large round eyes, aquiline face and silver hair that cascaded round her shoulders. When Knight entered Sir Denton Marshall's kitchen, Pottersfield eyed him down her sharp nose, looking ready to bite him if she got the chance.

'Peter,' she said coldly.

'Elaine,' Knight said.

'Not exactly my idea to let you into the crime scene.'

'No, I imagine not,' replied Knight, fighting to control his emotions, which were heating up by the second. Pottersfield always seemed to have that effect on him. 'But here we are. What can you tell me?'

The inspector did not reply for several moments, then finally said, 'The maid found him an hour ago out in the garden. Or what's left of him, anyway.'

Thinking of Marshall, the learned and funny man he'd come to know and admire over the past two years, Knight felt dizzy and he had to put his vinyl-gloved hand on the counter to steady himself. 'What's left of him?'

Pottersfield gestured grimly at the open French window.

Knight absolutely did not want to go out into the garden. He wanted to remember Marshall as he'd been the last time he'd seen him, two weeks before, with his shock of startling white hair, scrubbed pink skin, and easy, infectious laugh.

'I'll understand if you'd rather not,' Pottersfield said. 'Inspector Casper said your mother was engaged to Marshall. When did that happen?'

'Last New Year,' Knight said. He swallowed, and moved towards the door, adding bitterly: 'They were to be married on Christmas Eve. Another tragedy. Just what I need in my life, isn't it?'

Pottersfield's expression twisted in pain and

anger, and she looked at the kitchen floor as Knight went past her and out into the garden.

The air in the garden was motionless, growing hotter, and stank of death and gore. On the flagstone terrace, about five litres of blood, the entire reservoir of Sir Denton Marshall's life, had run out and congealed around his decapitated corpse.

'The medical examiner thinks the job was done with a long curved blade that had a serrated edge,' Pottersfield said.

Knight once more fought off the urge to vomit and tried to take in the entire scene, to burn it into his mind as if it were a series of photographs and not reality. Keeping everything at arm's length was the only way he knew how to get through something like this.

Pottersfield said: 'And if you look closely, you'll see that some of the blood's been sprayed back toward the body with water from the garden hose. I'd expect the killer did it to wash away footprints and so forth.'

Knight nodded. Then, by sheer force of will, he moved his attention beyond the body, deeper into the garden, bypassing forensics techs gathering evidence from the flower beds, to a crime-scene photographer snapping away near the back wall.

Knight skirted the corpse by several feet and from that new perspective saw what the photographer was focusing on. It was ancient Greek and one of Marshall's prized possessions: a headless limestone statue of an Athenian senator cradling a book and holding the hilt of a broken sword.

Marshall's head had been placed in the empty space between the statue's shoulders. His face was puffy, lax. His mouth was twisted to the left as if he were spitting. And his eyes were open, dull, and, to Knight, shockingly forlorn.

For an instant, the Private operative wanted to break down. But then he felt himself filled with a sense of outrage. What kind of barbarian would do such a thing? And why? What possible reason could there be to behead Denton Marshall? The man was more than good. He was . . .

'You're not seeing it all, Peter,' Pottersfield said behind him. 'Take a look at the grass over there.'

Knight clenched his hands into fists and walked off the terrace onto the grass, which scratched against the paper slip-ons he wore over his shoes. Then he saw what Pottersfield had indicated and stopped cold.

Five interlocking rings – the symbol of the Olympic Games – had been spray-painted on the grass in front of the statue.

Across the symbol, partially obscuring it, an X had been smeared in blood.

Chapter 3

WHERE ARE THE eggs of monsters most likely to be laid? What nest incubates them until they hatch? What are the toxic scraps that nourish them to adulthood?

So often during the headaches that irregularly rip through my mind like gale-driven thunder and lightning I ponder those kinds of questions, and others.

Indeed, as you read this, you might be asking your own questions, such as 'Who are you?'

My real name is irrelevant. For the sake of this story, however, you can call me Cronus. In old, old Greek myths, Cronus was the most powerful of the Titans, a digester of universes, and the Lord God of Time.

Do I think I am a god?

Don't be absurd. Such arrogance tempts fate. Such hubris mocks the gods. And I have never been guilty of that treacherous sin.

I remain, however, one of those rare beings to appear on Earth once a generation or two. How else would you explain the fact that, long before the storms began in my head, hatred was my oldest memory and wanting to kill was my very first desire?

Indeed, at some point in my second year of life I became aware of hatred, as if it and I were linked spirits cast into an infant's body from somewhere out there in the void. And for some time that was what I thought of as me: this burning singularity of loathing thrown on the floor in a corner, in a box filled with rags.

Then one day I began instinctively to crawl from the box, and within that movement and the freedom I gained thereby I soon understood that I was more than anger, that I was a being unto myself, that I starved and went thirsty for days, that I was cold and naked and left to myself for hours on end, rarely cleaned, rarely held by the monsters that walked all around me as if I were some kind of alien creature landed among them. That was when my first direct thought occurred: *I want to kill them all.*

I had that ruthless urge long, long before I understood that my parents were drug addicts, crackheads, unfit to raise a superior being such as me.

When I was four, shortly after I sunk a kitchen knife into my comatose mother's thigh, a woman came to where we lived in squalor and she took me away from my parents for good. They put me in a home where I was forced to live with abandoned little monsters, hateful and distrustful of any other beings but themselves.

Soon enough I grasped that I was smarter, stronger, and more visionary than any of them. By the age of nine I did not know exactly what I was yet, but I sensed that I might be some sort of different species – a super-creature, if you will – who could manipulate, conquer, or slay every monster in his path.

I knew this about myself for certain after the storms started in my head.

They started when I was ten. My foster-father, whom we called 'Minister Bob', was whipping one of the little, little monsters, and I could not stand to hear it. The crying made me feel weak and I could not abide that sensation. So I left the house and climbed the back fence and wandered through some of the worst streets in London until I found quiet and comfort in the familiar poverty of an abandoned building.

Two monsters were inside already. They were older than me, in their teens, and they were members of a street gang. They were high on something, I could tell that about them right away; and they said I'd wandered onto their turf.

I tried to use my speed to get away, but one of them threw a rock that clipped my jaw. It dazed me and I fell, and they laughed and got angrier. They threw more stones that cracked my ribs and broke blood vessels in my thigh.

Then I felt a hard blow above my left ear, followed by a Technicolor explosion that crackled through my brain like lightning bolts ripping through a summer sky.

Chapter 4

PETER KNIGHT FELT helpless as he glanced back and forth, from the Olympic symbol crossed out in blood to the head of his mother's fiancé.

Inspector Pottersfield stepped up beside Knight. In a thin voice, she said, 'Tell me about Marshall.'

Choking back his grief, Knight said, 'Denton was a great, great man, Elaine. Ran a big hedge fund, made loads of money, but gave most of it away. He was also an absolutely critical member of the London Organising Committee. A lot of people think that without Marshall's efforts, we never would have beaten Paris in our bid for the Games. He was also a nice guy, very modest about his achievements. And he made my mother very happy.'

'I didn't think that was possible,' Pottersfield remarked.

'Neither did I. Neither did Amanda. But he did,' Knight said. 'Until just now, I didn't think Denton Marshall had an enemy in the world.'

Pottersfield gestured at the bloody Olympic symbol. 'Maybe it has more to do with the Olympics than who he was in the rest of his life.'

Knight stared at Sir Denton Marshall's head and returned his gaze to the corpse before saying, 'Maybe. Or maybe this is just designed to throw us off track. Cutting off someone's head can easily be construed as an act of rage, which is almost always personal at some level.'

'You're saying this could be revenge of some kind?' Pottersfield replied.

Knight shrugged. 'Or a political statement. Or the work of a deranged mind. Or a combination of the three. I don't know.'

'Can you account for your mother's whereabouts last evening between eleven and twelve-thirty?' Pottersfield asked suddenly.

Knight looked at her as if she was an idiot. 'Amanda loved Denton.'

'Spurned love can be a powerful motive to rage,' Pottersfield observed.

'There was no spurning,' Knight snapped. 'I would have known. Besides, you've seen my mother. She's five foot five and weighs just under eight stone. Denton weighed nearly sixteen. There's no way she'd have had the physical or emotional strength to cut off his head. And she had no reason to.'

'So you're saying you *do* know where she was?' Pottersfield asked.

'I'll find out and get back to you about it. But first I have to tell her.'

'I'll do that if you think it might help.'

'No, I'll do it,' Knight said, studying Marshall's head one last time and then focusing on the way his mouth seemed twisted as if he'd been trying to spit something out.

Knight fished in his pocket for a pen-sized torch, stepped around the Olympic symbol and directed the beam into the gap between Marshall's lips. He saw a glint of something, and reached back into his pocket for a pair of forceps that he always kept there in case he wanted to pick something up without touching it.

Refusing to look at his mother's dead fiancé's eyes, he began to probe between Marshall's lips with the forceps.

'Peter, stop that,' Pottersfield ordered. 'You're—'

But Knight was already turning to show her a tarnished bronze coin that he'd plucked from Marshall's mouth.

'New theory,' he said. 'It's about money.'

Chapter 5

WHEN I RETURNED to consciousness several days after the stoning, I was in hospital with a fractured skull and the nauseating feeling that I had been rewired somehow, made more alien than ever before.

I remembered everything about the attack and everything about my attackers. But when the police came to ask me what had happened, I told them I had no idea. I said I had memories of entering the building, but nothing more; and their questions soon stopped.

I healed slowly. A crablike scar formed on my scalp. My hair grew back, hiding it, and I began to nurture a dark fantasy that became my first obsession.

Two weeks later, I returned home to the little monsters and Minister Bob. Even they could tell I'd changed. I was no longer a wild child. I smiled and acted happy. I studied and developed my body.

Minister Bob thought that I'd found God.

But I admit to you that I did it all by embracing hatred. I stroked that crablike scar on my head, and focused my oldest emotional ally on things that I wanted to have and to happen. Armed with a dark heart, I went after them all, trying to show the entire world how different I really was. And though I acted the changed boy, the happy, achieving friend in public, I never forgot the stoning or the storms it had spawned in my head.

When I was fourteen, I began looking secretly for the monsters who'd broken my skull. I found them eventually, selling small twists of methamphetamine on a street corner not far from where I lived with Minister Bob and the little monsters.

I kept tabs on the pair until I turned sixteen and felt big and strong enough to act.

Minister Bob had been a steelworker before he found Jesus. On the sixth anniversary of my stoning, I took one of his heavy hammers and a pair of his old work overalls, and I slipped out at night when I was supposed to be studying.

Wearing the overalls and carrying the hammer in a satchel harvested from a rubbish bin, I found the two monsters who'd stoned me. Six years of their drug use and six years of my evolution had wiped me from their memory banks.

I lured them to an empty lot with the promise of money, and then I beat their brains to bloody pulp.

Chapter 6

SHORTLY AFTER INSPECTOR Pottersfield ordered Marshall's remains bagged, Knight left the garden and the mansion consumed by far worse dread than he'd felt on entering.

He ducked beneath the police tape, avoided the newspaper jackals, and headed out of Lyall Mews, trying to decide how in God's name he was going to tell his mother about Denton. But Knight knew that he had to, and quickly, before Amanda heard it from someone else. He absolutely did not want her to be alone when she learned that the best thing that had ever happened to her was—

'Knight?' a man's voice called to him. 'Is that you?'

Knight looked up to see a tall, athletic man – mid-forties and wearing a fine Italian suit – rushing towards him. Below his thick salt-and-pepper hair, anguish twisted his ruddy, square face.

Knight had met Michael 'Mike' Lancer at Private London's offices twice in the eighteen months since the company had been hired to act as a special security detail during the Olympic Games. But he knew the man largely by his reputation.

A two-time world decathlon champion in the 1980s and 1990s, Lancer had served with and in the Queen's Guard, which had allowed him to train full-time. At the Barcelona Olympics in 1992 he had led the decathlon after the first day of competition but had then cramped in the heat and humidity during the second day, finishing outside the top ten finishers.

Lancer had since become a motivational speaker and security consultant who often worked with Private International on big projects. He was also a member of LOCOG, the London Organising Committee for the Olympic Games, and had been charged with helping to organise security for the mega-event.

'Is it true?' Lancer asked in a distraught voice. 'Denton's dead?'

'Afraid so, Mike,' Knight said.

Lancer's eyes welled with tears. 'Who would do this? Why?'

'Looks like someone who hates the Olympics,' Knight said. Then he described the manner of Marshall's death, and the bloody X.

Rattled, Lancer said, 'When do they think this happened?'

'Shortly before midnight,' Knight replied.

Lancer shook his head. 'That means I saw him only two hours before his death. He was leaving the party at Tate Britain with . . .' He stopped and looked at Knight in sad reappraisal.

'Probably with my mother,' Knight said. 'They were engaged.'

'Yes, I knew that you and she are related,' Lancer said. 'I'm so, so sorry, Peter. Does Amanda know?'

'I'm on my way to tell her right now.'

'You poor bastard,' Lancer said. Then he looked off towards the police barrier. 'Are those reporters there?'

'A whole pack of them, and getting bigger,' Knight said.

Lancer shook his head bitterly. 'With all due loving respect to Denton, this is all we need with the opening ceremony tomorrow night. They'll blast the lurid details all over the bloody world.'

'Nothing you can do to stop that,' Knight said. 'But I might think about upping security on all members of the organising committee.'

Lancer made a puffing noise, and then nodded. 'You're right. I'd best catch a cab back to the office. Marcus is going to want to hear this in person.'

Marcus Morris, a politician who had stood down at the last election, was now chairman of the London Organising Committee.

'My mother as well,' Knight said and together they headed on towards Chesham Street where they thought there'd be more taxis.

Indeed, they'd just reached Chesham Street when a black cab appeared from the south across from the Diplomat Hotel. At the same time, farther away and from the north, a red cab came down the near lane. Knight hailed it.

Lancer signalled the taxi in the northbound lane, saying, 'Give my condolences to your mother, and tell Jack I'll be in touch sometime later today.'

Jack Morgan was the American owner of Private International. He'd been in town since the plane carrying five members of the London office had gone down in the North Sea with no survivors.

Lancer stepped off the kerb, and set off in a confident stride heading diagonally across the street while the red cab came closer.

But then, to Knight's horror, he heard the growl of an engine and the squeal of tyres.

The black cab was accelerating, heading right at the LOCOG member.

Chapter 7

KNIGHT REACTED ON instinct. He leaped into the street and knocked Lancer from the cab's path.

In the next instant, Knight sensed the black cab's bumper less than a metre away and tried to jump in the air to avoid being hit. His feet left the ground but could not propel him out of the cab's path. The bumper and radiator grille struck the side of his left knee and lower leg and drove on through.

The blow spun Knight into the air. His shoulders, chest and hip smashed down on the vehicle's bonnet and his face was jammed against the windscreen. He glimpsed a split-second image of the driver. Scarf. Sunglasses. A woman?

Knight was hurled up and over the cab's roof as if he were no more than a stuffed doll. He hit the road hard on his left side, knocking the wind out of him, and for a moment he was aware only of the sight of the black cab speeding away, the smell of car exhaust, and the blood pounding in his temples.

Then he thought: A bloody miracle, but nothing feels broken.

The red taxi screeched towards Knight and he panicked, thinking he'd be run over after all.

But it skidded into a U-turn before stopping. The driver, an old Rasta wearing a green and gold knitted cap over his dreadlocks threw open his door and jumped out.

'Don't move, Knight!' Lancer yelled, running up to him. 'You're hurt!'

'I'm okay,' Knight croaked. 'Follow that cab, Mike.'

Lancer hesitated, but Knight said, 'She's getting away!'

Lancer grabbed Knight under the arms and hoisted him into the back of the red cab. 'Follow it!' Lancer roared at the driver.

Knight held his ribs, still struggling for air as the Rasta driver took off after the black cab, which was well ahead of them by now, turning hard west along Pont Street.

'I catch her, mon!' the driver promised. 'Dat crazy one tried to kill you!'

Lancer was looking back and forth between the road ahead and Knight. 'You sure you're okay?'

'Banged and bruised,' Knight grunted. 'And she wasn't trying to run me down, Mike. She was trying to run *you* down.'

The driver power-drifted into Pont Street, heading west. The black cab was closer now, its brake lights flashing red before it lurched in a hard right turn into Sloane Street.

The Rasta mashed the accelerator hard. They reached the intersection with Sloane Street so fast that Knight felt sure they'd actually catch up with the woman who'd just tried to kill him.

But then two more black cabs flashed past them, both heading north on Sloane Street, and the Rasta was forced to slam on his brakes and wrench the wheel so as not to hit them. Their cab went into a screeching skid and almost hit another car: a Metropolitan Police vehicle.

Its siren went on. So did its flashing lights.

'No!' Lancer yelled.

'Every time, mon!' the driver shouted in equal frustration as he slowed his vehicle to a stop.

Knight nodded, dazed and angry, staring through the windscreen as the taxi that had almost killed him melted into the traffic heading towards Hyde Park.

Chapter 8

BRIGHTLY FLETCHED ARROWS whizzed and cut through the hot mid-morning air. They struck in and around yellow bullseyes painted on large red and blue targets set up in a long line that stretched across the lime-green pitch at Lord's Cricket Ground near Regent's Park in central London.

Archers from six or seven countries were completing their final appointed practice rounds. Archery would be one of the first sports to be decided after the 2012 London Olympic Games opened, with competition scheduled to start mid-morning on Saturday, two days hence, with the medal ceremony to be held that very afternoon.

Which was why Karen Pope was up in the stands, watching through binoculars, boredom slackening her face.

Pope was a sports reporter for the *Sun*, a London tabloid newspaper with six million readers thanks to a tradition of aggressive bare-knuckle journalism and publishing photographs of young bare-breasted women on page three.

Pope was in her early thirties, attractive in the way that Renée Zellweger was in the film *Bridget Jones's Diary* but too flat-chested ever to be considered for the *Sun*'s page three. Pope was also a dogged reporter, and ambitious in the extreme.

Around her neck that morning hung one of only fourteen full-access media passes granted to the *Sun* for the Olympics. Such passes had been severely limited for the British press because more than twenty thousand members of the global media would also be in London to cover the sixteen-day mega-event. The full-access passes had become almost as valuable as Olympic medals, at least to British journalists.

Pope kept thinking that she should be happy to have the pass and to be here covering the Games at all, but her efforts this morning had so far failed to yield anything truly newsworthy about archery.

She'd been looking for the South Koreans, the gold-medal favourites, but had learned that they had already finished their practice session before she arrived.

'Bloody hell,' she said in disgust. 'Finch is going to kill me.'

Pope decided her best hope was to research a feature that with lively writing might somehow make the paper. But what sort? What was the angle?

Archery: Darts for the Posh?

No – there was absolutely nothing posh about archery.

Indeed, what in God's name did she know about archery? She'd grown up in a football family. Earlier that very morning Pope had tried to explain to Finch that she'd be better off assigned to athletics or gymnastics. But her editor had reminded her in no uncertain terms that she'd only joined the paper from Manchester six weeks before and was therefore low-person on the sports desk.

'Get me a big story and you'll get better assignments,' Finch had said.

Pope prodded her attention back to the archers. It struck her that they seemed so calm. It was almost as though they were in a trance over there. Not like a cricket batsman or a tennis player at all. Should she write about that? Find out how the bowmen got themselves into that state?

C'mon, she thought in annoyance, who wants to read about Zen in sports when you can look at bare boobs on page three?

Pope sighed, set down her binoculars, and shifted her position in one of the blue grandstand seats. She noticed, stuffed down into her handbag, a bundle of mail that she'd grabbed leaving the office and started going through the stack, finding various press releases and other items of zero interest.

Then she came to a thick Manila envelope with her name and title printed oddly in black and blue block letters on the front.

Pope twitched her nose as if she'd sniffed something foul. She hadn't written anything recently to warrant a nutcase letter, most definitely not since she'd arrived in London. Every reporter worth a damn got nutcase letters. You learned to recognise them quickly. They usually came after you'd published something controversial or hinting at diabolical conspiracy.

She slit the envelope open anyway, and drew out a sheaf of ten pages attached by paper clip to a folded plain paper greeting card. She flipped the card open. There was no writing inside. But a computer chip in the card was activated by the movement and flute music began to play, weird sounds that got under her skin and made her think that someone had died.

Pope shut the card and then scanned the first page of the sheaf. She saw that it was a letter addressed to her, and that it had been typed in a dozen different fonts, which made it hard to read. But then she began to get the gist of it. She read the letter three times, her heart beating faster with every line until it felt like it was throbbing high in her throat.

She scanned the rest of the documents attached to the letter and the greeting card, and felt almost faint. She dug wildly in her bag for her phone, and called her editor.

'Finch, it's Pope,' she said breathlessly when he answered. 'Can you tell me whether Denton Marshall has been murdered?'

In a thick Cockney accent, Finch said, 'What? *Sir* Denton Marshall?'

'Yes, yes, the big hedge-fund guy, philanthropist, member of the organising committee,' Pope confirmed, gathering her things and looking for the nearest exit from the cricket ground. 'Please, Finchy, this could be huge.'

'Hold on,' her editor growled.

Pope had made it outside and was trying to hail a cab across from Regent's Park when her editor finally came back on the line.

'They've got the yellow tape up around Marshall's place in Lyall Mews and the coroner's wagon just arrived.'

Pope punched the air with her free hand and cried: 'Finch, you're going to have to get someone else to cover archery and dressage. The story I just caught is going to hit London like an earthquake.'

Chapter 9

'LANCER SAYS YOU saved his life,' Elaine Pottersfield said.

A paramedic prodded and poked at a wincing Knight, who was sitting on the bumper of an ambulance on the east side of Sloane Street, a few feet from the Rasta's parked red cab.

'I just reacted,' Knight insisted, aching everywhere and feeling baked by the heat radiating off the pavement.

'You put yourself in harm's way,' the inspector said coldly.

Knight got annoyed. 'You said yourself I saved his life.'

'And almost lost your own,' she shot back. 'Where would that have left . . .' She paused. 'The children?'

He said, 'Let's keep them out of this, Elaine. I'm fine. There should be footage of that cab on CCTV.'

London had 10,000 closed-circuit security

cameras that rolled twenty-four hours a day, spread out across the city. A lot of them had been there since the 2005 terrorist bombings in the Tube left fifty-six people dead and seven hundred wounded.

'We'll check them,' Pottersfield promised. 'But finding a particular black cab in London? Since none of you got the licence number plate that's going to be near-impossible.'

'Not if you narrow the search to this road, heading north, and the approximate time she got away. And call all the taxi companies. I had to have done some damage to her bonnet or radiator grille.'

'You're sure it was a woman?' Pottersfield asked sceptically.

'It was a woman,' Knight insisted. 'Scarf. Sunglasses. Very pissed-off.'

The Scotland Yard inspector glanced over at Lancer who was being interviewed by another officer, before saying, 'Him and Marshall. Both LOCOG members.'

Knight nodded. 'I'd start looking for people who have a beef with the organising committee.'

Pottersfield did not reply because Lancer was approaching them. He'd wrenched his tie loose around his neck and was patting at his sweating brow with a handkerchief.

'Thank you,' he said to Knight. 'I am beyond simply being in your debt.'

'Nothing that you wouldn't have done for me,' Knight replied.

'I'm calling Jack,' Lancer said. 'I'm telling him what you did.'

'It's not necessary,' Knight said.

'It is,' Lancer insisted. He hesitated. 'I'd like to repay you somehow.'

Knight shook his head. 'LOCOG is Private's client, which means you are Private's client, Mike. It's all in a day's work.'

'No, you . . .' Lancer hesitated and then completed his thought. 'You shall be my guest tomorrow night at the opening ceremonies.'

Knight was caught flat-footed by the offer. Tickets to the opening ceremony were almost as prized as invitations to the marriage of Prince William and Kate Middleton had been the year before.

'If I can get the nanny to cover for me, I'll accept.'

Lancer beamed. 'I'll have my secretary send you a pass and tickets in the morning.' He patted Knight on his good shoulder, smiled at Pottersfield, and then walked off towards the Jamaican taxi driver who was still getting a hard time from the patrol officers who'd pulled them over.

'I'll need you to make a formal statement,' Pottersfield said.

'I'm not doing anything until I've spoken with my mother.'

Chapter 10

TWENTY MINUTES LATER, a Metropolitan Police patrol car dropped Knight in front of his mother's home on Milner Street in Knightsbridge. He'd been offered opiate painkillers by the paramedics, but had refused them. Getting out of the police car was agonising and an image of a beautiful pregnant woman standing on a moor at sunset kept flashing into his mind.

Thankfully, he was able to put her out of his thoughts by the time he rang the doorbell, suddenly aware of how dirty and torn his clothes were.

Amanda would not approve. Neither would—

The door swung open to reveal Gary Boss, his mother's long-time personal assistant: thirties, thin, well groomed and impeccably attired.

Boss blinked at Knight from behind round tortoiseshell glasses, and sniffed. 'I didn't know you had an appointment, Peter.'

James Patterson

'Her son and only child doesn't need one,' Knight said. 'Not today.'

'She's very, very busy,' Boss insisted. 'I suggest—'

'Denton's dead, Gary,' Knight said softly.

'What?' Boss said and then tittered derisively. 'That's impossible. She was with him just last—'

'He was murdered,' Knight said, stepping inside. 'I just came from the crime scene. I need to tell her.'

'Murdered?' Boss said, and then his mouth sloughed open, and he closed his eyes as if in anticipation of some personal agony in the near future. 'Dear God. She'll be . . .'

'I know,' Knight said, and moved past him. 'Where is she?'

'In the library,' Boss said. 'Choosing fabric.'

Knight winced. His mother despised being interrupted when she was looking at samples. 'Can't be helped,' he said, and walked down the hall towards the doors of the library, readying himself to tell his mother that she was now, in effect, twice a widow.

When Knight was three, his father Harry had died in a freak industrial accident, leaving his young widow and son a meagre insurance payout. His mother had turned bitter about her loss, but then turned that bitterness into energy. She'd always liked fashion and sewing, so she took the insurance money and started a clothing company that she named after herself.

40

Amanda Designs had started in their kitchen. Knight remembered how his mother had seemed to look at life and business as one long protracted brawl. Her pugnacious style succeeded. By the time Knight was fifteen, his mother had built Amanda Designs into a robust and respected company by never being happy, by constantly goading everyone around her to do better. Shortly after Knight graduated from Christ's Church college, Oxford she'd sold the concern for tens of millions of pounds and used the cash to fund the launch of four even more successful clothing lines.

In all that time, however, Knight's mother had never allowed herself to fall in love again. She'd had friends and consorts and, Knight suspected, several short-term lovers. But from the day his father had died, Amanda had erected a solid shield around her heart that no one, except for her son, ever managed to breach.

Until Denton Marshall had come into her life.

They'd met at a cancer fund-raiser and, as his mother liked to say, 'It was everything at first sight.' In that one evening, Amanda transformed from a cold, remote bitch to a schoolgirl giddy with her first crush. From that point forward, Marshall had been her soulmate, her best friend, and the source of the deepest happiness of her life.

Knight flashed on that image of the pregnant

41

woman again, knocked on the library door, and entered.

An elegant woman by any standards – late fifties, with the posture of a dancer, the beauty of an ageing movie star, and the bearing of a benevolent ruler – Amanda Knight was standing at her work table, dozens of fabric swatches arrayed in front of her.

'Gary,' she scolded without looking up. 'I told you that I was not to be—'

'It's me, Mother,' Knight said.

Amanda turned to look at him with her slate-coloured eyes, and frowned. 'Peter, didn't Gary tell you I was choosing . . .' She stopped, seeing something in his expression. Her own face twisted in disapproval. 'Don't tell me: your heathen children have driven off another nanny.'

'No,' Knight said. 'I wish it were something as simple as that.'

Then he proceeded to shatter his mother's happiness into a thousand jagged pieces.

Chapter 11

IF YOU ARE to kill monsters, you must learn to think like a monster.

I did not begin to appreciate that perspective until the night after the explosion that cracked my head a second time, nineteen years after the stoning.

I was long gone from London in the wake of the thwarting of my first plan to prove to the world that I was beyond different, that I was infinitely superior to any other human.

The monsters had won that war against me by subterfuge and sabotage, and as a result, when I landed in the Balkans assigned to a NATO peace-keeping mission in the late spring of 1995, the hatred I felt had no limits to its depth or to its dimensions.

After what had been done to me I did not want peace.

I wanted violence. I wanted sacrifice. I wanted blood.

So perhaps you could say that fate intervened on my behalf within five weeks of my deployment within the fractured, shifting and highly combustible killing fields of Serbia, Croatia and Bosnia-Herzegovina.

It was July, a late afternoon on a dusty road eighteen miles from the Drina Valley and the besieged city of Srebrenica. I was riding in the passenger seat of a camouflaged Toyota Land Cruiser, looking out the window, wearing a helmet and a flak vest.

I'd been reading about Greek mythology from a book I'd picked up, and was thinking that the war-torn Balkan landscape through which we travelled could have been the setting of some dark and twisted myth; wild roses were blooming everywhere around the mutilated corpses we'd been spotting in the area, victims of one side's or the other's atrocity.

The bomb went off without warning.

I can't recall the sound of the blast that destroyed the driver, the truck and the two other passengers. But I can still smell the explosive and the burning fuel. And I can still feel the aftershock of the invisible fist that struck me full force, hurling me through the windscreen, and setting off an electrical storm of epic proportions inside my skull.

Dusk had blanketed the land by the time I regained consciousness, ears ringing, disorientated, nauseated and thinking at first that I was ten years old and had just been stoned unconscious. But then the tilting and whirling in my mind slowed enough for me to make out the charred skeleton of the Land Cruiser and the corpses of my companions, burned beyond recognition. Beside me lay a sub-machine gun and an automatic pistol, a Sterling and a Beretta that had been thrown from the truck.

It was dark by the time I could stand, pick up the weapons and walk.

I staggered, falling frequently, for several miles across fields and through forests before I came to a village somewhere south-west of Srebrenica. Walking in, carrying the guns, I heard something above and beyond the ringing in my ears. Men were shouting somewhere in the darkness ahead of me.

Those angry voices drew me, and as I went towards them I felt my old friend hatred building in my head, irrational, urging me to slay somebody.

Anybody.

Chapter 12

THE MEN WERE BOSNIANS. There were seven of them armed with old single-barrel shotguns and corroded rifles that they were using to goad three handcuffed teenaged girls ahead of them as if they were driving livestock to a pen.

One of them saw me, shouted, and they turned their feeble weapons my way. For reasons I could not explain to myself until much later I did not open fire and kill them all right there, the men and the girls.

Instead, I told them the truth: that I was part of the NATO mission and that I'd been in an explosion and needed to call back to my base. That seemed to calm them somewhat and they lowered their guns and let me keep mine.

One of them spoke broken English and said I could call from the village's police station, where they were heading.

I asked what the girls were under arrest for, and

the one who spoke English said, 'They are war criminals. They belong to Serbian kill squad, working for that devil Mladic. People call them the Furies. These girls kill Bosnian boys. Many boys. Each of them does this. Ask oldest one. She speak English.'

Furies? I thought with great interest. I'd been reading about the Furies the day before in my book of Greek mythology. I walked quicker so that I could study them, especially the oldest one, a sour-looking girl with a heavy brow, coarse black hair, and dead dark eyes.

Furies? This could not be a coincidence. As much as I believed that hatred had been gifted to me at birth, I came to believe instantly that these girls had been put in front of me for a reason.

Despite the pain that was splitting my head, I fell in beside the oldest one and asked, 'You a war criminal?'

She turned her dead dark eyes on me and spat out her reply: 'I am no criminal, and neither are my sisters. Last year, Bosnian pigs kill my parents and rape me and my sisters for four days straight. If I could, I shoot every Bosnian pig. I break their skulls. I kill all of them if I could.'

Her sisters must have understood enough of what their sister was saying because they too turned their dead eyes on me. The shock of the bombing, the

47

brutal throbbing in my head, my jet-fuelled anger, the Serbian girls' dead eyes, the myth of the Furies, all these things seemed to gather together into something that felt suddenly predestined to me.

The Bosnians handcuffed the girls to heavy wooden chairs bolted to the floor of the police station, and shut and locked the doors. The landlines were not working. Neither were the primitive mobile-phone towers. I was told, however, that I could wait there until a peacekeeping force could be called to take me and the Serbian girls to a more secure location.

When the Bosnian who spoke English left the room, I cradled my gun, moved close to the girl who'd spoken to me, and said 'Do you believe in fate?'

'Go away.'

'Do you believe in fate?' I pressed her.

'Why do you ask me this question?'

'As I see it, as a captured war criminal your fate is to die,' I replied. 'If you're convicted of killing dozens of unarmed boys, that's genocide. Even if you and your sisters were gang-raped beforehand, they will hang you. That's how it works with genocide.'

She lifted her chin haughtily. 'I am not afraid to die for what we have done. We killed monsters. It was justice. We put back balance where there was none.'

Monsters and Furies, I thought, growing excited before replying: 'Perhaps, but you will die, and there your story will end.' I paused. 'But maybe you have another fate. Perhaps everything in your life has been in preparation for this exact moment, this place, this night, right now when your fates collide with mine.'

She looked confused. 'What does this mean, "fates collide"?'

'I get you out of here,' I said. 'I get you new identities, I hide you, and protect you and your sisters for ever. I give you a chance at life.'

She'd gone steely again. 'And in return?'

I looked into her eyes. I looked into her soul. 'You will be willing to risk death to save me as I will now risk death to save you.'

The oldest sister looked at me sidelong. Then she turned and clucked to her sisters in Serbian. They argued for several moments in harsh whispers.

Finally, the one who spoke English said, 'You can save us?'

The clanging in my head continued but the fogginess had departed, leaving me in a state of near-electric clarity. I nodded.

She stared at me with those dark dead eyes, and said, 'Then save us.'

The Bosnian who spoke English returned to the

room and called out to me, 'What lies are these demons from hell telling you?'

'They're thirsty,' I answered. 'They need water. Any luck with the telephone?'

'Not yet,' he said.

'Good,' I replied, flipping the safety on the submachine gun as I swung the muzzle around at the Furies' captors before opening fire and slaughtering every one.

Part Two

LET THE GAMES BEGIN

Chapter 13

AS THE TAXI pulled up in front of a sterile-looking skyscraper deep in the City of London, the UK's main financial district, Peter Knight could still hear his mother sobbing. The only other time he'd ever seen her cry like that had been over his father's body after the accident.

Amanda had collapsed into her son's arms after learning of her fiancé's death. Knight had felt the racking depths of her despair, and had understood them all too well. She'd been stabbed in the soul. Knight wouldn't have wished that sensation on anyone, least of all his own mother, and he held her through the worst of the mental and emotional haemorrhaging, reliving his own raw memories of loss.

Gary Boss had come into her office finally, and had nearly wept himself when he'd seen Amanda's abject sorrow. A few minutes later, Knight received a text from Jack Morgan telling him to come directly to Private London's office because the *Sun* had hired the firm to analyse a letter from someone who claimed to be Marshall's killer. Boss said he would take over Amanda's care.

'No, I should stay,' Knight had replied, feeling horribly guilty about leaving. 'Jack would understand. I'll call him.'

'No!' Amanda said angrily. 'I want you to go to work, Peter. I want you to do what you do best. I want you to find the sick bastard who did this to Denton. I want him put in chains. I want him burned alive.'

As Knight took a lift to the top floors of the skyscraper, his thoughts were dominated by his mother's command, and despite the steady ache in his side he felt himself becoming obsessed. It was always like this with Knight when he was on a big case – obsessed, possessed – but, with his mother's involvement, this particular investigation felt more like a crusade: no matter what happened, no matter the obstacles, no matter the time needed, Knight vowed to nail Denton Marshall's killer.

The lift door opened into a reception area, a hyper-modern room containing some works of art that depicted milestones in the history of espionage, forensics and cryptography. Though the London office itself was seriously understaffed at the moment due to the recent tragic loss of personnel, the lobby bustled with Private International agents from all over the world, here to pick up their Olympic security passes and assignments.

Knight circled the mob, recognising only a few people, before heading for a tinted bulletproof glass wall, passing on his way a model of the Trojan horse and a bust of Sir Francis Bacon. He looked into a retina scan while touching his right index finger to a print reader. A section of the wall hissed open to reveal a scruffy freckle-faced, carrot-haired man with a scraggly beard and wearing cargo jeans, a West Ham United football jersey, and black slippers.

Knight smiled. 'G'day, Hooligan.'

'What the fuck, Peter?' Jeremy 'Hooligan' Crawford said, eyeing Knight's clothes. 'Been having sex with an orang-utan, have you?'

In the wake of Wendy Lee's death in the plane crash, Hooligan was now the chief science, technology, and forensics officer at Private London. Early thirties, caustic, fiercely independent, and unabashedly foul-mouthed, he was also insanely smart.

Born and raised in Hackney Wick, one of London's tougher neighbourhoods, the son of parents who'd never finished secondary school, by the age of nineteen Hooligan had nevertheless obtained degrees in maths and biology from Cambridge. By twenty, he had earned his third

degree in forensics and criminal science from
Staffordshire University and had been hired by MI5,
where he worked for eight years before coming to
work at Private at twice the government salary.

Hooligan was also a rabid football fan with a
season ticket to West Ham United's matches.
Despite his remarkable intelligence, as a youngster
he'd been known to get out of control watching the
club's big games, at which point his brothers and
sisters had given him his nickname. While many
would not boast of such a moniker, he wore it
proudly.

'I scuffled with the bonnet and roof of a cab and
lived to tell the tale,' Knight told Hooligan. 'The
letter from the killer here yet?'

The science officer brushed past him. 'She's
bringing it up.'

Knight pivoted to look back through the crowd
of agents towards the lift whose door was opening
again. *Sun* reporter Karen Pope came out, clutching
a large manila envelope to her chest. Hooligan went
to her. She seemed taken aback at his scruffy
appearance, and shook his hand tentatively. He led
her back into the hallway and introduced Knight to
her.

Pope instantly turned guarded and studied the
investigator with suspicion, especially his torn and
filthy coat. 'My editors want this to be done

discreetly and quickly, with no more eyes than are necessary. As far as the *Sun* is concerned, that means you and you alone, Mr Crawford.'

'Call me Hooligan, eh?'

Knight had instantly found Pope both abrasive and defensive, but maybe it was because he felt as though his entire left side had been beaten with boat oars and had gone through the emotional wringer of his mother's collapse.

He said, 'I'm working the Marshall murder on behalf of the firm – and on behalf of my mother.'

'Your mother?' Pope said.

Knight explained, but Pope still seemed unsure.

Running out of patience, Knight said, 'Have you considered that I just might know something about this case that you don't? I don't recall your byline. Do you work the city desk? The crime beat?'

Chapter 14

THAT HIT A nerve. Pope's face flushed indignantly. 'If you must know, I work sports normally,' she said, thrusting out her chin. 'What of it?'

'It means I know things about this case that you don't,' Knight repeated.

'Is that so?' Pope shot back. 'Well, I'm the one holding the letter, aren't I, Mr Knight? You know, I really would prefer to deal with Mr, uh, Hooligan.'

Before Knight could reply, an American male voice said: 'It *would* be smart to let Peter in on the examination, Ms Pope. He's the best we've got.'

A tall man with surfer good looks, the American stuck out his hand and shook hers saying, 'Jack Morgan. Your editor arranged through me for the analysis. I'd like to be there as well, if possible.'

'All right,' Pope said without enthusiasm. 'But the contents of this envelope cannot be revealed to anyone unless you've seen it published in the *Sun*. Agreed?'

'Absolutely,' Jack said, and smiled genuinely.

Knight admired the owner and founder of Private. Jack was younger than Knight, and even more in a hurry than Knight. He was also smart and driven, and believed in surrounding himself with smart, driven people and paying them well. He also cared about the people who worked for him. He'd been devastated at the loss of Carter and the other Private London operators and had come across the Atlantic immediately to help Knight pick up the slack.

The foursome went to Hooligan's lab one floor down. Jack fell in beside Knight who was moving much more slowly than the others. 'Good job with Lancer,' he said. 'Saving his ass, I mean.'

'We aim to please,' Knight said.

'He was very grateful, and said I should give you a raise,' Jack said.

Knight did not reply. They had not yet talked about any salary upgrade that might be due in light of his new responsibilities.

Jack seemed to remember and said, 'We'll talk money after the Games.' Then the American shot him a more critical look. 'Are *you* all right?'

'Feel like I've been playing in a rugby scrum, but I remain chipper,' Knight assured him as they entered Private London's science unit, a cutting-edge operation in every respect.

Hooligan led them to a far corner of the area, to

an anteroom off a clean lab where he told them all to don disposable white jumpsuits and hoods. Knight groaned, but once in the suit and hood he followed Hooligan through an airlock and into the clean room. The science officer moved to a workstation that included an electron microscope and state-of-the-art spectrographic equipment. He took the envelope from Pope, opened it, and looked inside.

He asked, 'Did you put these in sleeves or did they come to you like this?'

Knight heard the question over a headset built into his hood, which made all their ensuing conversation sound like transmissions from outer space.

'I did that,' Pope replied. 'I knew right away that they'd need to be protected.'

'Smart,' Hooligan said, wagging a gloved finger at her and looking over at Knight and Jack. 'Very smart.'

Despite his initial dislike of Pope, Knight had to agree. He asked, 'Who touched these before you protected them?'

'Just me,' Pope said as Hooligan removed the sleeve that contained the letter. 'And the killer, I suppose. He has a name. You'll see it there. He calls himself "Cronus".'

Chapter 15

SEVERAL MOMENTS LATER the weird flute music from the card played, irritating Knight and making him feel as though the killer was toying with them. He finished scanning the letter and the documents.

The strange sound must have got to Jack as well because he slammed the card shut, cutting off the music, and then said, 'This guy's off his rocker.'

Pope said, 'Crazy like a fox, then, especially those bits about Marshall and his former partner, Guilder. The documents back his allegations.'

'I don't believe those documents,' Knight said. 'I knew Denton Marshall. He was a supremely honest man. And even if the allegations were true, it's hardly justification for cutting the man's head off. Jack's right. This guy is seriously unbalanced, and supremely arrogant. The tone is taunting. He's telling us that we can't stop him. He's saying this is not over, that it could be just the beginning.'

Jack nodded, and said, 'When you start with a

beheading, you're taking a long walk down Savage Street.'

'I'll start running tests,' Hooligan said. He was looking at the card that played the music. 'These chips are in a lot of greeting cards. We should be able to trace the make and model.'

Knight nodded, saying, 'I want to read through the letter one more time.'

While Pope and Jack watched Hooligan slice out the working components of the musical greeting card, Knight returned to the letter and began to read as the flute music died in the lab.

The first sentence was written in symbols and letters that Knight did not recognise but guessed was ancient Greek. The second and all subsequent sentences in the letter were in English.

The ancient Olympic Games have been corrupted. The modern Games are not a celebration of gods and men. They are not even about goodwill among men. The modern Games are a mockery, a sideshow every four years, and made that way by so many thieves, cheats, murderers, and monsters.

Consider the great and exalted Sir Denton Marshall and his corpulent partner Richard Guilder. Seven years ago, Marshall sold out the Olympic movement as a force for honest competition. From the documents that accompany this letter, you will see that they suggest that in order to ensure that London would be selected to host the 2012 games, Marshall and Guilder cleverly siphoned funds from their clients and secretly moved the money into overseas bank accounts owned by shell corporations that were in turn owned by members of the International Olympic Selection Committee. Paris, runner-up in the selection process, never had a chance.

And so, to cleanse the Games, the Furies and I found it just that Marshall should die for his offences, and so that has come to pass. We are unstoppable beings far superior to you, able to see the corruption when you cannot, able to expose the monsters and slay them for the good of the Games when you cannot.

– Cronus

Chapter 16

AS HE FINISHED READING the letter a second time, Knight felt more upset, more anxious than before. Thinking of the letter in the light of what had been done to Marshall, Cronus came across as a madman – albeit a rational one – who made Knight's skin crawl.

Making it worse, the creepy flute melody would not leave Knight's thoughts. What kind of mind would produce that music and that letter? How did Cronus make it work together to produce such a sense of imminent threat and violation?

Or was Knight too close to the case to feel any other way?

He got a camera and began shooting close-ups of the letter and the supporting documents. Jack came over. 'What do you think, Peter?'

'There's a good chance that one of the Furies, as he calls them, tried to run Lancer down this afternoon,' Knight replied. 'A woman was driving that cab.'

'What?' Pope exclaimed. 'Why didn't you tell me that?'

'I just did,' Knight said. 'But don't quote me.'

Hooligan suddenly brayed, 'Big mistake!'

They all turned. He was holding something up with a pair of tweezers.

'What've you got?' Jack asked.

'Hair,' Hooligan said in triumph. 'It was in the glue on the envelope flap.'

'DNA, right?' Pope asked, excited. 'You can match it.'

'Gonna try, eh?'

'How long will that take?'

'Day or so for a full recombinant analysis.'

Pope shook her head. 'You can't have it for that long. My editor was specific. We had to turn it all over to Scotland Yard before we publish.'

'He'll take a sample and leave them the rest,' Jack promised.

Knight headed towards the door.

'Where are you going?' Pope demanded.

Knight paused, not sure of what to tell her. Then he gave her the truth. 'I'm guessing that first sentence is written in ancient Greek so I'm going to pay a call on that bloke James Daring – you know, the fellow who has that show *Secrets of the Past* on Sky – see if he can decipher it for me.'

'I've seen him,' Pope snorted. 'Nattering boob thinks he's Indiana Jones.'

Hooligan shot back, 'That "nattering boob", as you call him, holds doctorates in anthropology and archaeology from Oxford and is the bloody curator of Greek Antiquities at a famous museum.' The science officer looked at Knight. 'Daring *will* know what that says, Peter, and I'll wager he'll have something to say about Cronus and the Furies too. Good call.'

Through the glass plate of her hood Knight could see the reporter twist her lips, as if she was tasting something tart. 'And then?' Pope asked at last.

'Guilder, I suppose.'

'His partner?' Pope cried. 'I'm coming with you!'

'Not likely,' Knight said. 'I work alone.'

'I'm the client,' she insisted, looking at Jack. 'I can trot along, right?'

Jack hesitated, and in that hesitation Knight saw the weight of concern carried by the owner of Private International. He'd lost five of his top agents in a suspicious plane crash. All had been integral players overseeing Private's role in security at the Olympics. And now Marshall's murder and this lunatic Cronus.

Knight knew he was going to regret it but he said,

'No need for you to be on the spot, Jack. I'll change my rules this once. She can *trot* along.'

'Thanks, Peter,' the American said, with a tired smile. 'I owe you once again.'

Chapter 17

IN THE DEAD of night, forty-eight hours after I opened fire and slaughtered seven Bosnians sometime in the summer of 1995, a shifty-eyed and swarthy man who smelled of tobacco and cloves opened the door of a hovel of a workshop in a battle-scarred neighbourhood of Sarajevo.

He was the sort of monster who thrives in all times of war and political upheaval, a creature of the shadows, of shifting identity and shifting allegiance. I'd learned of the forger's existence from a fellow peacekeeper who'd fallen in love with a local girl who was unable to travel on her own passport.

'Like we agree yesterday,' the forger said when I and the Serbian girls were inside. 'Six thousand for three. Plus one thousand rush order.'

I nodded and handed him an envelope. He counted the money, and then passed me a similar envelope containing three fake passports: one

German, one Polish and one Slovenian.

I studied them, feeling pleased at the new names and identities I'd given the girls. The oldest was now Marta. Teagan was the middle girl, and Petra the youngest. I smiled, thinking that with their new haircuts and hair colours, no one would ever recognise them as the Serbian sisters that the Bosnian peasants called the Furies.

'Excellent work,' I told the forger as I pocketed the passports. 'My gun?'

We'd left my Sterling with him as a good-faith deposit when I'd ordered the passports. 'Of course,' he said. 'I was thinking just that.'

The forger went to a locked upright safe, opened it, and took out the weapon. He turned and aimed it at us. 'On your knees,' he snarled. 'I read about a slaughter at a police barracks near Srebrenica and three Serbian girls wanted for war crimes. There's a reward out. A large one.'

'You stinking weasel,' I sneered, keeping his attention on me as I slowly went to my knees. 'We give you money, and you turn us in?'

He smiled. 'I believe that's called taking it coming and going.'

The silenced 9mm round zipped over my head and caught the forger between the eyes. He crashed backward and sprawled dead over his desk, dropping my gun. I picked it up and turned to

Marta, who had a hole in her right-hand jacket pocket where a bullet had exited.

For the first time I saw something other than deadness in Marta's eyes. In its place was a glassy intoxication that I understood and shared. I had killed for her. Now she had killed for me. Our fates were not only completely entwined, we were both of us drunk on the sort of intoxicating liquor that ferments and distils among members of elite military units after each mission, the addictive drink of superior beings who wield the power over life and death.

Leaving the forger's building, however, I was acutely aware that more than two days had passed since the bomb had hurled me from the Land Cruiser. People were hunting for the Furies. The forger had said so.

And someone had to have found the blown-up and burned vehicle I'd been thrown from. Someone had to have counted and examined the charred bodies and figured out that I was missing.

Which meant that people were hunting for me.

Maybe, I decided, they should find me sooner rather than later.

Chapter 18

AT THREE-TWENTY that Thursday afternoon, Karen Pope and Peter Knight crossed the courtyard and climbed the granite front steps of the venerable British Museum in central London. As they entered the museum, Knight was grinding his teeth. He liked to work alone because it gave him enough silence to think things through during the course of an investigation.

Pope, however, had been talking almost non-stop since they'd left Private London, feeding him all sorts of trivial information he really had no need to know, including her career highlights, the creep Lester she'd dated in Manchester, and the travails of being the only woman currently working on the *Sun*'s sports desk.

'Got to be tough,' he said, wondering if he could somehow ditch her without adding to Jack's problems.

Instead, Knight led them to an older woman at the information desk, where he produced his identification and said that someone from Private had called ahead to arrange a brief interview with Dr James Daring.

The woman had sniffed something about the curator being very busy, what with his exhibit about to open that very evening, but then she gave them directions.

They climbed to an upper floor and walked towards the rear of the massive building. At last they came to an archway above which hung a large banner that read *The Ancient Olympic Games: Relics & Radical Retrospective.*

Two guards stood in front of a purple curtain stretched across the archway. Caterers were setting up for a reception to celebrate the opening, with tables for food and a bar in the hallway. Knight showed his Private badge and asked for Daring.

The guard replied, 'Dr Daring has gone to take a—'

'Late lunch, but I'm back, Carl,' called a harried male voice from back down the hallway. 'What's going on? Who are these people? I clearly said no one inside before seven!'

Knight pivoted to see hurrying towards them a familiar handsome, ruggedly built man wearing khaki cargo shorts, sandals and a safari-style shirt. His ponytail bounced on his shoulders. He carried an iPad. His gaze jumped everywhere.

Knight had seen James Daring on television several times, of course. For reasons Knight did not quite understand, his son Luke, almost three years old, loved to watch *Secrets of the Past*, though Knight suspected that the appeal lay in the melodramatic music that accompanied the man in virtually every programme.

'My kids are big fans,' Knight said, extending his hand. 'Peter Knight, with Private. My office called.'

'And Karen Pope. I'm with the *Sun*.'

Daring glanced at her and said, 'I've already invited someone from the *Sun* to view the exhibit along with everyone else – at seven. What can I do for Private, Mr Knight?'

'Actually, Miss Pope and I are working together,' Knight said. 'Sir Denton Marshall has been murdered.'

The television star's face blanched and he blinked several times before saying, 'Murdered? Oh, my God. What a tragedy. He . . .'

Daring gestured at the purple curtains blocking the way into his new exhibit. 'Without Denton's financial support, this exhibit would not have been possible. He was a generous and kind man.'

Tears welled in Daring's eyes. One trickled down his cheek. 'I'd planned to thank him publicly at the reception tonight. And . . . what happened? Who did this? Why?'

'The killer calls himself Cronus,' Pope replied. 'He sent me a letter. Some of it is in ancient Greek. We'd hoped you could translate it for us.'

Daring glanced at his watch and then nodded. 'I can give you fifteen minutes right now. I'm sorry but . . .'

'The exhibition,' Pope said. 'We understand. Fifteen minutes would be brilliant of you.'

After a pause, Daring said, 'You'll have to walk with me, then.'

The museum curator led them behind the curtains into a remarkable exhibition that depicted the ancient Olympic Games and compared them to the modern incarnation. The exhibit began with a giant aerial photograph of the ruins at Olympus, Greece, site of the original Games.

While Pope showed Daring her copy of Cronus's letter, Knight studied the photograph of Olympus and the diagrams that explained the ruins.

Surrounded by groves of olive trees, the area was dominated by the 'Altis', the great Sanctuary of Zeus, the most powerful of the ancient Greek gods. The sanctuary held temples where rituals and sacrifices were performed during the Games. Indeed, according to Daring's exhibit, the entire Olympus site, including the stadium, was a sacred place of worship.

For over a thousand years, in peace and in war, the Greeks had assembled at Olympus to celebrate the festival of Zeus and to compete in the Games. There were no bronze, silver, or gold medals given. A crown of wild olive branches was sufficient to immortalise the victor, his family, and his city.

The exhibit went on to contrast the ancient Games with the modern.

Knight had been highly impressed with the exhibit. But within minutes of reaching the displays that contrasted the old with the new, he began to feel that the ancient Games were heavily favoured over the modern Olympics.

He'd no sooner had that thought than Pope called to him from across the hall. 'Knight, I think you're going to want to hear this.'

Chapter 19

STANDING IN THE exhibition hall in front of a display case featuring Bronze Age discuses, javelins, and terracotta vases painted with scenes of athletic competitions, Dr Daring indicated the first sentence in the text.

'This *is* ancient Greek,' he said. 'It reads, "Olympians, you are in the laps of the gods." That's a term in Greek mythology. It means the fate of specific mortals is in the gods' control. I think the term is most often used when some mortal has committed a wrongdoing grave enough to upset the residents of Mount Olympus. But do you know who it would be better to ask about this sort of thing?'

'Who's that?' Knight asked.

'Selena Farrell,' Daring replied. 'Professor of Classics at King's College, London, eccentric, brilliant. In another life she worked for NATO in the Balkans. That's where I, uh, met her. You should go and see her. Very iconoclastic thinker.'

Writing down Farrell's name, Pope said, 'Who is Cronus?'

The museum curator picked up his iPad and began typing, saying, 'A Titan – one of the gods who ruled the world before the Olympians. Again, Selena Farrell would be better on this point, but Cronus was the God of Time, and the son of Gaia and Uranus, the ancient, ancient rulers of earth and sky.'

Daring explained that, at his enraged mother's urging, Cronus rebelled eventually against his father and ended up castrating him with a scythe.

A long curved blade, Knight thought. Wasn't that how Elaine had described the murder weapon?

'According to the myth, Cronus's father's blood fell into the sea and re-formed as the three Furies,' Daring continued. 'They were Cronus's half sisters – spirits of vengeance, and snake-haired like Medusa.

'Cronus married Rhea and fathered seven of the twelve gods who would become the original Olympians.' Then Daring fell silent, seeming troubled.

'What's the matter?' Pope asked.

Daring's nose twitched as if he smelled something foul. 'Cronus did something brutal when he was told of a prediction that his own son would turn against him.'

'What was that?' Knight asked.

The curator turned the iPad towards them. It

showed a dark and disturbing painting of a dishevelled bearded and half-naked man chewing on the bloody arm of a small human body. The head and opposite arm were already gone.

'This is a painting by the Spanish painter Goya,' Daring said. 'Its title is *Saturn Devouring his Son*. Saturn was the Romans' name for Cronus.'

The painting repulsed Knight. Pope said, 'I don't understand.'

'In the Roman and Greek myths,' the curator replied testily, 'Cronus ate his children one by one.'

Chapter 20

'ATE THEM?' POPE said, her lip curling.

Knight glanced at the painting and envisioned his own children in a playground near his home. He felt even more revolted.

'It's a myth – what can I say?' Daring replied.

The curator went on to explain that Rhea hated her husband for devouring their children and she vowed that no more of her unborn children would suffer the same fate. So she snuck off to have the son she named Zeus, and hid him immediately after birth. Then she got Cronus drunk, and gave him a rock wrapped in a blanket to eat instead of her son.

'Much later,' Daring continued, 'Zeus rose up, conquered Cronus, forced him to vomit up his children, and then hurled his father into the darkest abysmal pits of Tartarus, or something like that. Ask Farrell.'

'Okay,' Knight said, unsure if any of this helped or not, and wondering if this letter could possibly be a ruse designed to take them in a wrong direction. 'You a fan of the modern Olympics, doctor?'

The television star frowned. 'Why?'

'Your exhibit strikes me as a bit slanted in favour of the ancient Games.'

Daring turned coolly indignant. 'I think the work is quite even-handed. But I grant you that the ancient Games were about honour and excelling in celebration of the Greek religion, while the modern version, in my personal opinion, has become too influenced by corporations and money. Ironic, I know, since this exhibit was built with the assistance of private benefactors.'

'So, in a way, you agree with Cronus?' Pope asked.

The curator's voice went chilly. 'I may agree that the original ideals of the Olympics could be getting lost in today's Games, but I certainly do not agree with killing people to "cleanse" them. Now, if you'll excuse me, I must finish up and change before the reception.'

Chapter 21

SEVERAL HOURS AFTER Marta killed the forger, the four of us were staying in a no-star hotel on the outskirts of western Sarajevo. I handed the sisters envelopes that contained their passports and enough money to travel.

'Take separate taxis or buses to the train station. Then use completely separate routes to the address I put in your passports. In the alley behind that address, you'll find a low brick wall. Under the third brick from the left you'll find a key. Buy food. Go inside and wait there quietly until I arrive. Do not go out if you can avoid it. Do not be conspicuous. Wait.'

Marta translated and then asked, 'When will you get there?'

'In a few days,' I said. 'No more than a week, I should imagine.'

She nodded. 'We wait for you.'

I believed her. After all, where else were she and

her sisters to go? Their fates were mine now, and mine was theirs. Feeling more in control of my destiny than at any other time in my life, I left the Serbian girls and went out into the streets where I found dirt and grime to further soil my torn, bloody clothes. Then I wiped down the guns and threw them in a river.

An hour before dawn I wandered up to the security gate at the NATO garrison, acting in a daze. I had been missing for two and a half days.

I gave my superiors and doctors vague recollections of the bomb that tore apart the Land Cruiser. I said I'd wandered for hours, and then slept in the woods. In the morning, I'd set off again. It wasn't until the previous evening that I'd remembered exactly who I was and where I was supposed to go; and I'd headed for the garrison with the fuzzy navigation of an alcoholic trying to find home.

The doctors examined me and determined that I had a fractured skull for the second time in my life. Two days later, I was on a medical transport. Cronus flying home to his Furies.

Chapter 22

AT FIVE MINUTES to four that Thursday afternoon, Knight left One Aldwych, a five-star boutique hotel in London's West End theatre district, and found Karen Pope waiting on the pavement, looking intently at her BlackBerry screen.

'His secretary wasn't putting you off. The doorman says he does come for drinks quite often, but he's not in there yet,' Knight said, referring to Richard Guilder, Marshall's long-time financial partner. 'Let's go and wait inside.'

Pope shook her head, and then gestured across the Strand to a row of Edwardian buildings. 'That's King's College, right? That's where Selena Farrell works, the classical Greek expert that Indiana Jones wannabe told us to talk to. I looked her up. She *has* written extensively about the ancient Greek playwright Aeschylus and his play *The Eumenides*, which is another name for the Furies. We could go and chat with her and then swing back for Guilder.'

Knight screwed up his face. 'In all honesty, I don't know if understanding more about the myth of Cronus and the Furies is going to help us get any closer to catching Marshall's killer.'

'And now I know something you don't,' she said, shaking her BlackBerry at him haughtily. 'Turns out that Farrell fought against the London Olympics tooth and nail. She sued to have the whole thing stopped, especially the compulsory purchase orders that took all that land in East London for the Olympic Park. The professor evidently lost her house when the park went in.'

Feeling his heart begin to race, Knight set off in the direction of the college, saying, 'Denton ran the process that took that land. She had to have hated him.'

'Maybe enough to cut off his head,' Pope said, struggling to keep up.

Then Knight's mobile buzzed. A text from Hooligan:

1st DNA test: hair is female.

Chapter 23

THEY FOUND SELENA Farrell in her office. The professor was in her early forties, a big-bosomed woman who dressed the part of a dowdy Earth child: baggy, faded peasant dress, oval black glasses, no make-up, clogs, and her head wrapped in a scarf held in place by two wooden hairpins.

But it was the beauty mark that caught Knight's eye. Set above her jawline about midway down her right cheek, it put him in mind of a young Elizabeth Taylor and made him think that, given the right circumstances and manner of dress, the professor could have been quite attractive.

As Dr Farrell inspected his identification, Knight glanced around at various framed pictures: one of the professor climbing in Scotland, another of her posing beside some Greek ruins, and a third in which she was much younger, in sunglasses, khaki pants and shirt, posing with an automatic weapon beside a white truck that said NATO on the side.

'Okay,' Farrell said, returning Knight's badge. 'What are we here to discuss?'

'Sir Denton Marshall, a member of the Olympic Organising Committee,' Knight said, watching for her reaction.

Farrell stiffened, and then pursed her lips in distaste. 'What about him?'

'He's been murdered,' Pope said. 'Decapitated.'

The professor appeared genuinely shocked. 'Decapitated? Oh, that's horrible. I didn't like the man, but . . . that's barbaric.'

'Marshall took your house and your land,' Knight remarked.

Farrell hardened. 'He did. I hated him for it. I hated him and everyone who's in favour of the Olympics for it. But I did not kill him. I don't believe in violence.'

Knight glanced at the photo of her with the automatic weapon. But he decided not to challenge her, asking instead: 'Can you account for your whereabouts around ten forty-five last night?'

The classics professor arched back in her chair and took off her glasses, revealing amazing sapphire eyes that stared intently at Knight. 'I *can* account for my whereabouts at that time, but I won't unless it's necessary. I enjoy my privacy.'

'Tell us about Cronus,' Pope said.

The professor drew back. 'You mean the Titan?'

'That's the one,' Pope said.

She shrugged. 'He's mentioned by Aeschylus, especially during the third play in his Oresteia cycle, *The Eumenides*. They were the three Furies of vengeance born from the blood of Cronus's father. Why are you asking about him? All in all, Cronus is a minor figure in Greek mythology.'

Pope glanced at Knight, who nodded. She dug into her bag. She came up with her mobile, which she fiddled with for several seconds as she said to the professor, 'I received a package today from someone who calls himself Cronus and who claims to be Marshall's killer. There's a letter and this: it's a recording of a recording, but . . .'

As the reporter returned to her bag, looking for her copy of Cronus's letter, the weird, irritating flute music began to float from her phone.

The classics professor froze after a few notes had played.

The melody went on and Farrell stared at her desk, becoming agitated. Then she looked around wildly as if she was hearing hornets. Her hands shot up as though to cover her ears, dislodging the hairpins and loosening her headscarf.

She panicked and raised her hands to hold the scarf in place. Then she leaped to her feet and bolted for the door, choking: 'For God's sake turn it off! It's giving me a migraine! It's making me sick!'

Knight jumped to his feet and went out after Farrell, who clopped at high speed down the hall before barging into a women's loo.

'That set off something big,' Pope said. She'd come up behind him.

'Uh-huh,' Knight said. He went back into the office, headed straight to the classics professor's desk and plucked a small evidence bag from his pocket.

He turned the bag inside out before picking up one of the hairpins that had fallen before Farrell bolted. He wrapped the bag around the pins and then drew them out before dropping them back on the desk.

'What are you doing?' Pope demanded in a whisper.

Knight sealed the bag and murmured, 'Hooligan says the hair sample from the envelope was female.'

He heard someone approaching the office, slid the evidence into his coat chest pocket and sat down. Pope stood, and was looking towards the door when another woman, much younger than Farrell but with a similar lack of fashion sense, entered and said: 'Sorry. I'm Nina Langor, Professor Farrell's teaching assistant.'

'Is she all right?' Pope asked.

'She said she's suffering from a migraine and is going home. She said if you'll call her on Monday or Tuesday she'll explain.'

'Explain what?' Knight demanded.

Nina Langor appeared bewildered. 'I honestly have no idea. I've never seen her act like that before.'

Chapter 24

TEN MINUTES LATER, Knight followed Pope up the stairs into One Aldwych, looking questioningly at the hotel doorman he'd spoken with earlier and getting a nod in response. Knight slipped the doorman a ten-pound note and followed Pope towards the muffled sounds of happy voices.

'That music got to Farrell,' Pope said. 'She'd heard it before.'

'I agree,' Knight said. 'It threw her hard.'

'Is it possible she's Cronus?' Pope asked.

'And uses the name to make us think she's a man? Sure. Why not?'

They entered the hotel's dramatic Lobby Bar, which was triangular in shape, with a soaring vaulted ceiling, pale marble floor, glass walls and intimate groupings of fine furniture.

While the bar at the Savoy Hotel along the Strand was about glamour, the Lobby Bar was about money. One Aldwych was close to London's legal and financial districts, and exuded enough corporate elegance to make it a magnet for thirsty bankers, flush traders, and celebrating deal-makers.

There were forty or fifty such patrons in the bar, but Knight spotted Richard Guilder, Marshall's business partner, almost immediately: a corpulent, silver-haired boar of a man in a dark suit, sitting at the bar alone, his shoulders and head hunched over.

'Let me do the talking at first,' Knight said.

'Why?' Pope snapped. 'Because I am a woman?'

'How many allegedly corrupt tycoons have you chatted up lately on the sports beat?' he asked her coolly.

The reporter grudgingly made a show of letting him lead the way.

Marshall's partner was staring off into the abyss. Two fingers of neat Scotch swirled in the crystal tumbler he held. To his left, a bar stool stood empty. Knight started to sit on it.

Before he could, an ape of a man in a dark suit got in the way.

'Mr Guilder prefers to be alone,' he said in a distinct Brooklyn accent.

Knight showed him his identification. Guilder's bodyguard shrugged, and showed Knight his. Joe Mascolo worked for Private New York.

'You in as backup for the Games?' Knight asked.

Mascolo nodded. 'Jack called me over.'

'Then you'll let me talk to him?'

The Private New York agent shook his head. 'Man wants to be alone.'

Knight said loud enough for Guilder to hear: 'Mr Guilder? I'm sorry for your loss. I'm Peter Knight, also with Private. I'm working on behalf of the London Organising Committee, and for my mother, Amanda Knight.'

Mascolo looked furious that Knight was trying to work around him.

But Guilder stiffened, turned in his seat, studied Knight and then said, 'Amanda. My God. It's . . .' He shook his head and wiped away a tear. 'Please, Knight, listen to Joe. I'm not in any condition to talk about Denton at the moment. I am here to mourn him. Alone. As I imagine your dear mother is doing, too.'

'Please, sir,' Knight began again. 'Scotland Yard—'

'Has agreed to talk with him in the morning,' Mascolo growled. 'Call his office. Make an appointment. And leave the man in peace for the evening.'

The Private New York agent glared at Knight. Marshall's partner was turning back to his drink, and Knight was growing resigned to leaving him alone until the next morning when Pope said, 'I'm with the *Sun*, Mr Guilder. We received a letter from Denton Marshall's killer. He mentions you and your company and justifies murdering your partner because of certain illegal activities that Marshall and you were alleged to have been involved in at your place of business.'

Guilder swung around, livid. 'How dare you! Denton Marshall was as honest as the day is long. He was never, ever involved in anything illegal during all the time I knew him. And neither was I. Whatever this letter says, it's a lie.'

Pope tried to hand the financier photocopies of the documents that Cronus had sent her, saying, 'Denton Marshall's killer alleges that these were taken from Marshall & Guilder's own records – or, to be more precise, your firm's *secret* records.'

Guilder glanced at the pages but did not take them, as if he had no time for considering such outrageous allegations. 'We have never kept secret records at Marshall & Guilder.'

'Really?' Knight said. 'Not even about foreign currency transactions made on behalf of your high-net-worth clients?'

The hedge fund manager said nothing, but Knight swore that some of the colour had seeped from his florid cheeks.

Pope said, 'According to these documents, you and Denton Marshall were pocketing fractions of the value of every British pound or US dollar or other currency that passed across your trading desks. It may not sound like much, but when you're talking hundreds of millions of pounds a year the fractions add up.'

Guilder set his tumbler of scotch on the bar, doing his best to appear composed. But Knight could have sworn that he saw a slight tremor in the man's hand as it returned to rest on Guilder's thigh. 'Is that all the killer of my best friend claims?'

'No,' Knight replied. 'He says that the money was moved to offshore accounts and funnelled ultimately to members of the Olympic Site Selection Committee before their decision in 2007. He says that your partner bribed London's way into the Games.'

The weight of the allegation seemed to throw Guilder. He looked both befuddled and wary, as if he'd suddenly realised he was far too drunk to be having this conversation.

'No,' he said. 'No, that's not . . . Please, Joe, make them go.'

Mascolo looked torn but said, 'Leave him be until tomorrow. I'm sure that if we call Jack he's going to tell you the same thing.'

Before Knight could reply there was a noise like a fine crystal wine glass breaking. The first bullet pierced a window on the west side of the bar. It just missed Guilder and shattered the huge mirror behind the bar.

Knight and Mascolo both realised what had happened. 'Get down!' Knight yelled, going for his gun, and scanning the windows for any sign of the shooter.

Too late. A second round was fired through the window. The slug hit Guilder just below his sternum with a sound like a pillow being plumped.

Bright red blood bloomed on the hedge fund manager's starched white shirt and he collapsed forward, upsetting a champagne bucket as he fell and crashed to the pale marble floor.

Chapter 25

IN THE STUNNED silence that now briefly seized the fabled Lobby Bar, the shooter, an agile figure in black motorcycle leathers and visor helmet, spun away and jumped off the window ledge to flee.

'Someone call an ambulance,' Pope yelled. 'He's been shot!'

The bar erupted into pandemonium as Joe Mascolo vaulted over his prone client and bulled forward, ignoring the patrons screaming and diving for cover.

Knight was two feet behind the Private New York operator when Mascolo jumped over a glass cocktail table and up onto the back of a plush grey sofa set against the bar's west wall. As Knight tried to climb up beside Mascolo, he saw to his surprise that the American was armed.

Gun laws in the UK were very strict. Knight had had to jump through two years of hoops in order to get his licence to carry a firearm.

Before he could think any more about it, Mascolo shot through the window. The gun sounded like a cannon in that marble and glass room. Real hysteria swept the bar now. Knight spotted the shooter in the middle of the cul-de-sac on Harding Street, face obscured but plainly a woman. At the sound of Mascolo's shot she twisted, dropped and aimed in one motion, an ultra-professional.

She fired before Knight could and before Mascolo could get off another round. The bullet caught the Private New York agent through the throat, killing him instantly. Mascolo dropped back off the sofa and fell violently through the glass cocktail table.

The shooter was aiming at Knight now. He ducked, raised his pistol above the sill and pulled the trigger. He was about to rise when two more rounds shattered the window above him.

Glass rained down on Knight. He thought of his children and hesitated a moment before returning fire. Then he heard tyres squealing.

Knight rose up to see the shooter on a jet-black motorcycle, its rear tyre smoking and laying rubber in a power drift that shot her around the corner onto the Strand, heading west and disappearing before Knight could shoot.

He cursed, turned and looked in shock at

Mascolo, for whom there was no hope. But he heard Pope cry: 'Guilder's alive, Knight! Where's that ambulance?'

Knight jumped off the couch and ran back through the shouting and the gathering crowd towards the crumpled form of Richard Guilder. Pope was kneeling at his side amid a puddle of champagne and a mass of blood, ice and glass.

The financier was breathing in gasps and holding tight to his upper stomach while the blood on his shirt turned darker and spread.

For a moment, Knight had an unnerving moment of déjà vu, seeing blood spreading on a bed sheet. Then he shook off the vision and got down next to Pope.

'They said there's an ambulance on the way,' the reporter said, her voice strained. 'But I don't know what to do. No one here does.'

Knight tore off his jacket, pushed aside Guilder's hands and pressed the coat to his chest. Marshall's partner peered at Knight as if he might be the last person he ever saw alive, and struggled to talk.

'Take it easy, Mr Guilder,' Knight said. 'Help's on the way.'

'No,' Guilder grunted softly. 'Please, listen . . .'

Knight leaned close to the financier's face and heard him whisper a secret hoarsely before paramedics burst into the Lobby Bar. But as Guilder finished his confession he just seemed to give out.

Blood trickled from his mouth, his eyes glazed, and he slumped like a puppet with its strings cut.

Chapter 26

A FEW MINUTES later, Knight stood on the pavement outside One Aldwych, oblivious to patrons hurrying past him to the restaurants and theatres. He was transfixed by the sight and sound of the wailing ambulance speeding Guilder and Mascolo to the nearest hospital.

He remembered standing on another pavement late at night almost three years before, watching a different ambulance race away from him, its siren's fading cry accompanying a feeling of misery that still had not lifted entirely from him.

'Knight?' Pope said. She'd come up behind him.

He blinked and noticed the double-decker buses braking and taxis honking and people hurrying home all around him. Suddenly he felt disjointed in much the same way that he had on that long-ago night when he'd watched the other ambulance speed away from him.

London goes on, he thought. London always went

on even in the face of tragedy and death, whether the victim was a corrupt hedge fund manager or a bodyguard or a young—

A pair of fingers appeared in front of his nose. They clicked and he looked round, startled. Karen Pope was looking at him in annoyance. 'Earth to Knight. Hello?'

'What is it?' he snapped.

'I asked you if you think Guilder will make it?'

Knight shook his head. 'No. I felt his spirit leave him.'

The reporter looked at him sceptically. 'What do you mean, you felt it?'

Knight sighed softly before replying: 'That's the second time in my life I've had someone die in my arms, Pope. I felt it the first time, too. That ambulance might as well slow down. Guilder is as dead as Mascolo is.'

Pope's shoulders sank a little and there was a brief awkward silence before she said, 'I'd better be going back to the office. I've got a nine o'clock deadline.'

'You should include in your story that Guilder confessed to the currency fraud just before he died,' Knight said.

'He did?' Pope said, digging in her pocket for her notebook. 'What'd he say, exactly?'

'He said that the scam was his, and that the money did not go to any member of the Olympic Site

Selection committee. It went to his personal offshore accounts. Marshall was innocent. He died a victim of Guilder's scheming.'

Pope stopped writing, her scepticism back. 'I don't buy that,' she said. 'He's covering for Marshall.'

'They were his last words,' Knight shot back. 'I believe him.'

'You have a reason to, don't you? It clears your mother's late fiancé.'

'It's what he said,' Knight insisted. 'You have to include that in the story.'

'I'll let the facts speak for themselves,' Pope said, 'including what you say Guilder told you.' She glanced at her watch. 'I've got to get going.'

'We're not going anywhere soon,' Knight said, feeling suddenly exhausted. 'Scotland Yard will want to talk with us, especially because there was gunfire. Meanwhile, I need to call Jack and fill him in, and then speak to my nanny.'

'Nanny?' Pope said, looking surprised. 'You have kids?'

'Twins. Boy and girl.'

Pope glanced at his left hand and said in a joking manner, 'No ring. What, are you divorced? Drove your wife nuts and she left you with the brats?'

Knight gazed at her coldly, marvelling at her insensitivity, before saying, 'I'm a widower, Pope. My wife died in childbirth. She bled to death in my arms two years, eleven months and two weeks ago. They took her away in an ambulance with the siren wailing just like that.'

Pope's jaw sagged and she looked horrified. 'Peter, I'm so sorry, I . . .'

But Knight already had his back turned and was walking along the pavement towards Inspector Elaine Pottersfield, who'd only just arrived.

Chapter 27

DARKNESS FALLS ON London, and my old friend hatred stirs at the thought that my entire life has all been a prelude to this fated moment, exactly twenty-four hours before the opening ceremony of the most hypocritical event on Earth.

It heats in my gut as I turn to my sisters. We're in my office. It's the first chance the four of us have had to talk face to face in days, and I take the three of them in at a glance.

Blonde and cool Teagan is removing the scarf, hat and sunglasses she wore while driving the taxi earlier in the day. Marta, ebony-haired and calculating, sets her motorcycle helmet on the floor beside her pistol and unzips her leathers. Pretty Petra is the youngest, the most attractive, the best actor and therefore the most impulsive. She looks in the mirror on the closet door, checking the fit of a chic grey cocktail dress and the dramatic styling of her short ginger hair.

Seeing the sisters like this, they're each so familiar to me that it's hard to imagine a time when we weren't all together, establishing and projecting our own busy lives, while staying completely unaligned in public.

And why wouldn't they still be with me after seventeen years? *In absentia* in 1997, a tribunal in The Hague indicted them for executing more than sixty Bosnians. Ever since Ratko Mladic – the general who oversaw the Serbian kill squads in Bosnia – was arrested last year, the hunt for my Furies has intensified.

I know. I keep track of such things. My dreams depend on it.

In any case, the sisters have lived under the threat of discovery for so long that it pervades their DNA, but that constant cellular-level menace has made them all the more fanatically devoted to me, mentally, physically, spiritually and emotionally. Indeed, ever so gradually over the years, my dreams of vengeance have become theirs, along with a desire to see those dreams realised that burns almost as incandescently as my own.

Over the years, in addition to protecting them, I've educated them, paid for minor plastic surgery, and trained them to be expert marksmen, hand-to-hand fighters, con artists and thieves. These last two skills have paid me back tenfold on my investment, but that is another story altogether. Suffice it to say that, to the best of my knowledge, they are the best at shadow games, superior to anyone save me.

Now the jaded might be wondering whether I am similar to Charles Manson back in the 1970s, an insane prophet who rescued traumatised women and convinced them that they were apostles sent to Earth for homicidal missions designed to trigger Armageddon. But comparing me to Manson and the Furies to the Helter-Skelter girls is deeply mis-guided, like trying to compare a true story to a myth of heaven. We are more powerful, transcendent and deadly than Manson could ever have imagined in his wildest drug-induced nightmares.

Teagan pours a glass of vodka, gulps it down, and says, 'I could not have anticipated that man jumping in front of my cab.'

'Peter Knight – he works for Private London,' I say, and then push across the coffee table a photograph that I found on the Internet. In it Knight stands, drink in hand, beside his mother at the launch of her most recent fashion line.

Teagan considers the photograph and then nods. 'That's him. I got a good look when his face smashed against my windscreen.'

Marta frowns, picks up the photograph, studies it, and then trains her dark agate eyes on me. 'He was with Guilder too, just now, in the bar, before I shot. I'm sure of it. He shot at me after I killed the one guarding Guilder too.'

I raise an eyebrow. Private? Knight? They've almost foiled my plans twice today. Is that fate, coincidence, or a warning?

'He's dangerous,' says Marta, always the most perceptive of the three, the one whose strategic thoughts are most likely to mirror my own.

'I agree,' I say, before glancing at the clock on the wall and looking at her ginger-haired sister, still primping in front of the mirror. 'It's time to leave for the reception, Petra. I'll see you there later. Remember the plan.'

'I'm not stupid, Cronus,' Petra says, glaring at me with eyes turned emerald green by contact lenses bought just for this occasion.

'Hardly,' I reply evenly. 'But you have a tendency to be impetuous, to ad lib, and your task tonight demands disciplined adherence to details.'

'I know what I have to do,' she says coldly, and leaves.

Marta's gaze has not left me. 'What about Knight?' she asks, proving once again that relentlessness is another of her more endearing qualities.

I reply, 'Your next tasks are not until tomorrow evening. In the meantime, I'd like you both to look into Mr Knight.'

'What are we looking for?' Teagan asks, setting her empty glass on the table.

'His weaknesses, sister. His vulnerabilities. Anything we can exploit.'

Chapter 28

IT WAS ALMOST eight by the time Knight reached home, a restored red-brick town house that his mother had bought for him several years before. He was as exhausted and sore as he'd ever been after a day at work: run over, shot at, forced to destroy his mother's dreams, not to mention being grilled three times by the formidable Inspector Elaine Pottersfield.

The Metropolitan Police inspector had not been happy when she arrived at One Aldwych. Not only were there two corpses as a result of the shoot-out, she'd heard through the grapevine that the *Sun* had received a letter from Marshall's killer and was incensed to learn that Private's forensics lab had had the chance to analyse the material before Scotland Yard.

'I should be arresting you for obstruction!' she'd shouted.

Knight held up his hands. 'That decision was

made by our client, Karen Pope of the *Sun*.'

'Who is where?'

Knight looked around. Pope had gone. 'She was on deadline. I know they plan on turning over all evidence after they go to press.'

'You allowed a material witness to leave the scene of a crime?'

'I work for Private, not the court any more. And I can't control Pope. She has her own mind.'

The Scotland Yard inspector responded by fixing Knight with a glare. 'Seems as if I've heard that excuse before from you, Peter – with deadly consequences.'

Knight flushed and his throat felt heated. 'We're not having this conversation again. You should be asking about Guilder and Mascolo.'

Pottersfield fumed, and then said, 'Spill it. All of it.'

Knight spilled all of it: their meetings with Daring and Farrell as well as a blow-by-blow account of what had happened in the Lobby Bar.

When he finished, the inspector said, 'You believe Guilder's confession?'

'Do dying men lie?' Knight had replied.

As he climbed the steps to his front door, Knight considered Guilder's confession again. Then he thought of Daring and Farrell. Were they part of these killings?

Who was to say that Daring wasn't some kind of

nut behind the scenes, bent on destroying the modern games? And who was to say that Selena Farrell wasn't the gunman in black leather and a motorcycle helmet? She'd been holding an automatic weapon in that picture in her office.

Maybe Pope's instincts were spot on. Could the professor be Cronus? Or at least involved with him? What about Daring? Didn't he say he'd known Farrell from somewhere in his past? The Balkans back in the 1990s?

Then another voice inside Knight demanded that he think less about villains and more about victims. How was his mother? He'd not heard from her all day.

He'd go inside. He'd call her. But before he could get his key into his front lock he heard his daughter Isabel let loose a blood-curdling cry: 'No! No!'

Chapter 29

KNIGHT THREW OPEN the front door into the lower hallway as Isabel's cry turned into a cutting screech: 'No, Lukey! No!'

Her father heard a high-pitched maniacal laugh and the pattering of little feet escaping before he entered the living area of his home, which looked as though a snow tornado had whirled through it. White dust hung in the air, on the furniture, and coated his daughter, about three years old, who saw him and broke into sobs.

'Daddy, Lukey, he . . . ! He . . .'

A dainty little girl, Isabel went into hiccupping hysterics and ran towards her daddy, who tried to bend down to comfort her. Knight gritted his teeth at the throbbing ache all down his left side, but scooped her up anyway, wanting to sneeze at the baby-powder. Isabel's tears had left little streams of baby powder paste on her cheeks and on her eyelashes. Even covered in talc like this, she was as beautiful as her late mother, with curly fawn-coloured hair and wide cobalt-blue eyes that could cleave his heart even when they weren't spilling tears.

'It's okay, sweetheart,' Knight said. 'Daddy's here.'

Her crying slowed to hiccups: 'Lukey, he . . . he put bottom powder on me.'

'I can see that, Bella,' Knight said. 'Why?'

'Lukey thinks bottom powder is funny.'

Knight held onto his daughter with his good arm and moved towards the kitchen and the staircase that led to the upper floors. He could hear his son cackling somewhere above him as he climbed.

At the top of the stairs, Knight turned towards the nursery only to hear a woman's voice yell, 'Owww! You little savage!'

Knight's son came running from the nursery in his nappy, his entire body covered in talc. He carried a bonus-sized container of baby powder and was laughing with pure joy until he caught sight of his father glaring narrowly at him.

Luke turned petrified and began to back away, waving his hands at Knight as if he were some apparition he could erase. 'No, Daddy!'

'Luke!' Knight said.

Nancy, the nanny, appeared in the doorway behind his son, blocking his way, powder all over her, holding her wrist tight, her face screwed up in pain before she spotted Knight.

'I quit,' she said, spitting out the words like venom. 'They're bloody lunatics.' She pointed at Luke, her whole arm shaking. 'And that one's a pant-shitting, biting little pagan! When I tried to get him on the loo, he bit me. He broke skin. I quit, and you're paying for the doctor's bill.'

Chapter 30

'YOU CAN'T QUIT,' Knight protested as the nanny dodged around Luke.

'Watch me,' Nancy hissed as she barged right by him and down the stairs. 'They've been fed, but not bathed, and Luke's crapped his nappy for the third time this afternoon. Good luck, Peter.'

She grabbed her things and left, slamming the door behind her.

Isabel started to sob again. 'Nancy leaves and Lukey did it.'

Feeling overwhelmed, Knight looked at his son and shouted in anger and frustration: 'That's four this year, Luke! Four! And she only lasted three weeks!'

Luke's face wrinkled. He cried: 'Lukey sorry, Daddy. Lukey sorry.'

In seconds his son had been transformed from this force of nature capable of creating a whirlwind to a little boy so pitiful that Knight softened.

Wincing against the pain in his side, still holding Isabel, he crouched down and gestured to Luke with his free arm. The toddler rushed to him and threw his arms so tight around Knight that he gasped with the ache that shot through him.

'Lukey love you, Daddy,' his son said.

Despite the stench that hung around the boy, Knight blew the talc off Luke's cheeks and kissed him. 'Daddy loves you too, son.' Then he kissed Isabel so hard on the cheek that she laughed.

'A change and a shower is in order for Luke,' he said, and put both his children down. 'Isabel, shower too.'

A few minutes later, after dealing with the soiled nappy, they were in the big stall shower in Knight's master bath, splashing and playing. Knight got out his mobile just as Luke picked up a sponge cricket bat and whacked his sister over the head with it.

'Daddy!' Isabel complained.

'Clonk him back,' Knight said.

He glanced at the clock. It was past eight. None of the nanny services he'd used in the past would be open. He punched in his mother's number.

She answered on the third ring, sounding wrung-out, 'Peter, tell me it's just a nightmare and that I'll wake up soon.'

'I'm so sorry, Amanda.'

She broke down in muffled sobs for several

moments, and then said, 'I'm feeling worse than I did when your father died. I think I'm feeling as you must have with Kate.'

Knight felt stinging tears well in his eyes, and a dreadful hollowness in his chest. 'And still often do, Mother.'

He heard her blow her nose, and then say: 'Tell me what you know, what you've found out.'

Knight knew his mother would not rest until he'd told her, so he did, rapidly and in broad strokes. She'd gasped and protested violently when he'd described Cronus's letter and the accusations regarding Marshall, and now she wept when he told her of Guilder's confession and his exoneration of her late fiancé.

'I knew it couldn't be true,' Knight said. 'Denton was an honest man, a great man with an even greater heart.'

'He was,' his mother said, choking.

'Everywhere I went today, people talked about his generosity and spirit.'

'Tell me,' Amanda said. 'Please, Peter, I need to hear these things.'

Knight told her about Michael Lancer's despair over Marshall's death and how he'd called the financier a mentor, a friend, and one of the guiding visionaries behind the London Olympics.

'Even James Daring, that guy at the British

Museum with the television show,' Knight said. 'He said that without Denton's support, the show and his new exhibit about the ancient Olympics would never have got off the ground. He said he was going to thank Denton publicly tonight at the opening reception.'

There was a pause on the line. 'James Daring said that?'

'He did,' Knight said, hoping that his mother would take comfort from it.

Instead, she snapped, 'Then he's a bald-faced liar!'

Knight startled. 'What?'

'Denton did give Daring some of the seed money to start his television show,' Amanda allowed. 'But he most certainly did not support his new exhibit. In fact, they had a big fight over the tenor of the display, which Denton told me was slanted heavily against the modern Olympics.'

'It's true,' Knight said. 'I saw the same thing.'

'Denton was furious,' his mother told him. 'He refused to give Daring any more money, and they parted badly.'

Definitely not what Daring told me, Knight thought, and then asked, 'When was this?'

'Two, maybe three months ago,' Amanda replied. 'We'd just got back from Crete and . . .'

She began to choke again. 'We didn't know it, but Crete was our honeymoon, Peter. I'll always think of it that way,' she said, and broke down.

Knight listened for several agonising moments, and then said, 'Mother, is anyone there with you?'

'No,' she said in a very small voice. 'Can you come, Peter?'

Knight felt horrible. 'Mother, I desperately want to, but I've lost another nanny and . . .'

She snorted in disbelief. 'Another one?'

'She just up and quit on me half an hour ago,' Knight complained. 'I've got to work every day of the Olympics, and I don't know what to do. I've used every nanny agency in the city, and now I'm afraid that none of them will send anyone over.'

There was a long silence on the phone that prompted Knight to say, 'Mother?'

'I'm here,' Amanda said, sounding as composed as she'd been since she'd learned of Marshall's death. 'Let me look into it.'

'No,' he protested. 'You're not . . .'

'It will give me something to do besides work,' she insisted. 'I need something to do that's outside myself and the company, Peter, or I think I'll turn mad, or to drink, or to sleeping pills and I can't stand the thought of any of those options.'

Chapter 31

AT THAT SAME MOMENT, inside the British Museum, upstairs in the reception hall outside his new exhibit about the ancient Olympics, Dr James Daring felt like dancing to his good fortune as he roamed triumphantly among the crowd of London's high and mighty gathered to see his work.

It has been a good night. No, a *great* night!

Indeed, the museum curator had received high praise from the critics who'd come to see the installation. They'd called it audacious and convincing, a reinterpretation of the ancient Olympics that managed to comment in a completely relevant way about the state of the modern Games.

Even better, several impressed patrons had told him that they wanted to sponsor and buy advertising on *Secrets of the Past*.

What did that dead arsehole Sir Denton Marshall know? Daring thought caustically. *Absolutely nothing*.

Feeling vindicated, basking in the glow of a job

well done, a job that had gone better than according to plan, Daring went to the bar and ordered another vodka Martini to celebrate his exhibit – and more.

Much more.

Indeed, after getting the cocktail – and fretting sympathetically yet again with one of the Museum's big benefactors about Marshall's shocking and horrible passing – Daring eagerly cast his attention about the reception.

Where was she?

The television star looked until he spotted a delightfully feline woman. Her hair was ginger-coloured and swept above her pale shoulders, which were bared in a stunning grey cocktail dress that highlighted her crazy emerald eyes. Daring had a thing for redheads with sparkling green eyes.

She *did* rather look like his sister in several respects, the curator thought. The way she tilted her head when she was amused, like now, as she held a long-stemmed champagne glass and flirted with a man much older than her. He looked familiar. Who was he?

No matter, Daring thought, looking again at Petra. She was saucy, audacious, a freak. The curator felt a thrill go through him. Look at her handling that man, making what were obviously scripted moves seem effortless in their spontaneity. Saucy. Audacious. Freak.

Petra seemed to hear his thoughts.

She turned from her conversation, spotted Daring across the crowd, and flashed him an expression so filled with hunger and promise that he shuddered as if in anticipation of great pleasure. After letting her gaze linger on him for a moment longer, Petra batted her eyelids and returned her attention to the other man. She put her hand on his chest, laughed again, and then excused herself.

Petra angled her way towards Daring, never once looking at him. She got another drink and moved back to the dessert table, where Daring joined her, trying to seem interested in the crème brûlée.

'He's drunk and taking a taxi home,' Petra murmured in a soft Eastern European accent as she used tongs to dig through a pile of kiwi fruit. 'I think it's time we left too, don't you? Lover?'

Daring glanced at her. A freak with green eyes! The television star flushed with excitement and whispered, 'Absolutely. Let's say our goodbyes and go.'

'Not together, silly goose,' Petra cautioned as she plucked two fruit slices onto her plate. 'We don't want to draw attention to ourselves, now, do we?'

'No, no, of course not,' Daring whispered back, feeling wonderfully illicit and deceitful. 'I'll wait for you down the street, near Bloomsbury Square.'

Chapter 32

JUST AFTER NINE that evening, not long after Karen Pope's article appeared on the *Sun*'s website, London radio stations began to pick up the story, focusing on the Cronus angle and rebroadcasting the flute music.

By ten, shortly after Knight had read the twins a story, changed Luke's nappy, and tucked them both into bed, the BBC was whipped into a frenzy, reporting on the allegations about Sir Denton Marshall and the Olympic site-selection process, as well as Guilder's dying confession that it had all been his swindle.

Knight cleaned and vacuumed talcum powder until eleven, and then poured himself a beer and a whisky, swallowed more pain medication, and crawled into bed. Jack Morgan called, distraught over Joe Mascolo's death, and insisted on Knight describing in detail the gunfight that had unfolded at One Aldwych.

'He was fearless,' Knight said. 'Went right after the shooter.'

'That was Joe Mascolo all the way,' Jack said sadly. 'One of Brooklyn's finest before I hired him away to run protection for us in New York. He only got here a couple of days ago.'

'That's brutal,' Knight replied.

'It is, and it's about to get worse,' Jack said. 'I have to call his wife.'

Jack hung up. Knight realised that he had not told Private's owner that he, Knight, had lost his nanny. Better that way, he decided after several moments' worry. The American already had too much on his plate.

He turned on the television to find the Marshall and Guilder slayings splashed all over the nightly news and cable outlets, which were luridly portraying the broader narrative as a scandalous murder-mystery, a shocking allegation about the Byzantine world behind the Olympics site-selection process, as well as a slap against London and indeed the entire UK on the eve of the Games.

Despite Guilder's dying words to the contrary, the French in particular were said to be very unhappy with Cronus's allegation about Olympic corruption.

Knight switched off the television and sat there in the silence. He picked up his whisky glass and drank deeply from it before looking at the framed photograph on his dresser.

Very pregnant and sublimely beautiful, his late wife Kate stood in profile on a Scottish moor lit by a June sunset. She was looking across her left shoulder, seeming to peer out from the photograph at him, radiating the joy and love that had been so cruelly taken from him almost three years before.

'Tough day, Katie girl,' Knight whispered. 'I'm badly beaten up. Someone's trying to wreck the Olympics. My mother is destroyed. And the kids have driven another nanny from the house and . . . I miss you. More than ever.'

He felt a familiar leadenness return to his heart and mind, which triggered a sinking sensation in his chest. He wallowed in that sensation, indeed let himself drown in it for a minute or two, and then did what he always did when he was openly grieving for Kate late at night like this.

Knight turned off the television, took his blankets and pillows and padded into the nursery. He lay down on the couch looking at the cots, smelling the smells of his children, and was at last comforted into sleep by the gentle rhythm of their breathing.

Chapter 33

Friday, 27 July 2012

THE PAINKILLERS STARTED to wear off and Knight felt the throbbing return to his right side around seven the next morning. Then he heard a squeaking noise and stirred where he lay on the couch in the twins' nursery. He looked over and saw Isabel on her belly, eyes closed and still. But Luke's cot was swaying gently.

His son was on his knees, chest and head on the mattress, sucking his thumbs, rocking side to side, and still asleep. Knight sat up to watch. For much of the last two years, Luke had been doing this before waking up in the morning.

After a few minutes, Knight sneaked out of the nursery, wondering if his son's rocking must have something to do with REM sleep. Was it disturbed? Did he have apnoea? Was that why Luke was so wild and Bella so calm? Was it what made his son's

126

language development delayed, and kept him from being toilet-trained when his sister was months ahead of the norm? Was that why Luke was a biter?

Knight came to no solid conclusions as he showered and shaved while listening to the radio, which was reporting that Denton Marshall's murder and the threats from Cronus had resulted in Michael Lancer and representatives of Scotland Yard and MI5 jointly announcing a dramatic tightening of security at the opening ceremonies. Those lucky enough to have tickets were being told to try to arrive at the Olympic Park during the afternoon in order to avoid an expected crush at the security stations.

After hearing that Private would be given a role in the increased security, Knight tried to call Jack Morgan. No answer, but the American was probably going to need him soon.

He knew that his mother had promised to help, but he needed a nanny now. He got a bitterly familiar file from a drawer and opened it, seeing a list of every nanny agency in London, and began calling. The woman who'd found Nancy and the nanny before her laughed at him when he explained his plight.

'A new nanny?' she said. 'Now? Not likely.'

'Why not?' he demanded.

'Because your kids have a terrible reputation and

the Olympics are starting tonight. Everyone I've got is working for at least the next two weeks.'

Knight heard the same story at the next three agencies, and his frustration began to mount. He loved his kids, but he'd vowed to find Marshall's killer, and Private was being called on to contribute more to Olympic security. He was needed. Now.

Rather than getting angry, he decided to hope that his mother would have better luck at finding someone to care for the twins and started doing what he could from home. Remembering the DNA material he'd taken off Selena Farrell's hairpin, he called a messenger to come and take the evidence to Private London and Hooligan.

Then he thought about Daring and Farrell, and decided that he needed to know more about them – about where their lives had crossed, anyway. Hadn't Daring said something about the Balkans? Was that where the photo of Farrell holding the gun had been taken? It had to be.

But when Knight went online and started searching for Farrell, he came up only with references to her academic publishing, and, seven years back, her opposition to the Olympic Park.

'This decision is flat-out wrong,' Farrell had stated in one piece published in *The Times*. 'The Olympics have become a vehicle to destroy neighbourhoods and uproot families and businesses. I pray that the people behind this decision are made to pay some day for what they've done to me and to my neighbours at the public's expense.'

Made to pay, professor? Knight thought grimly. Made to pay?

Chapter 34

ALMOST TWENTY-FOUR HOURS after the flute music had triggered a brutal migraine and a violent bout of nausea, the melody still played as a cruel soundtrack to Selena Farrell's thoughts as she lay in bed, the curtains of her bedroom drawn.

How was it possible? And what did Knight and Pope think of her? She had all but given them a reason to suspect her of something when she'd fled the scene like that. What if they started digging?

For what seemed like the thousandth time since bolting from her office and fleeing home to her tidy little flat in Wapping, Farrell swallowed hard against a burning in her throat that would not leave her. She'd drunk water all afternoon, and taken a handful of antacid tablets. They had only helped a bit.

She'd been dealing with migraines since she was a child, however, and a prescription medicine had blunted the agony of the electric head-clamp, leaving a dull aching at the back of her skull.

Farrell tried to fight the urge to ease that feeling. Not only was it a bad idea, given the medicine she was on, but when she drank alcohol she tended to become another personality, an almost completely different one.

I'm not going there tonight, she thought before the image of an exotic woman sitting deep in the corner of a pink tufted couch flashed into her head. At that, the decision was made for her. Farrell got out of bed, padded to the kitchen, opened the freezer and took out a bottle of Grey Goose vodka.

Soon the classics professor was on her second Martini, the ache at the back of her head was gone, and she believed she'd erased the memory of the flute melody. It was a syrinx melody, actually. The syrinx or Pan pipes featured seven reeds bound side by side. Along with the lyre, the Pan pipes were one of the oldest musical instruments in the world. But their eerie, breathy tonality had been banned from the ancient Olympics because it sounded too funereal.

'Who cares?' Farrell grumbled, and then gulped at her drink. 'To hell with the Olympics. To hell with Denton Marshall. To hell with the lot of them.'

Buzzing on the vodka now, becoming another person, Farrell vowed that with the migraine behind her she wasn't going to dwell on loss or injustice, or oppression. It was Friday night in London. She had places to go. People to see.

The professor felt a thrill go through her that deepened into a hunger when she swayed down the hall, went into her bedroom closet and unzipped a garment bag hanging there.

Inside was a dramatic hip-hugging A-line black skirt slit provocatively up its right flank, and a sexy sleeveless maroon satin blouse designed to show plenty of abundant cleavage.

Chapter 35

AT FIVE O'CLOCK that Friday afternoon, Knight was in his kitchen making the twins dinner, resigned to the fact that he would not witness the opening ceremony of the Games live and in person.

Knight felt spent, anyway. All day long, from the moment Luke had awoken crying, he had been consumed by the needs of his children, his frustration with the nanny issue, and his inability to push the Cronus investigation forward.

Around noon, while the twins were playing, he had called his mother and asked her how she was holding up.

'I slept two hours,' she replied. 'I'd nod off and all I could see in my dreams was Denton, and every time I'd feel such joy that I'd wake up and then face heartbreak all over again.'

'God, how horrible, mother,' said Knight, remembering the insomnia and anguish he'd suffered in the immediate weeks after the birth of the twins and

Kate's death. Many nights he'd thought he was going crazy.

He thought to change the conversation. 'I forgot to tell you: Mike Lancer invited me as his guest to sit in the organising committee's box for the opening ceremonies. If you find me a nanny, we can go together.'

'I don't know if I'm ready for that volume of pity quite yet. Besides, no memorial service has been planned. It would be unseemly for me to look as if I'm celebrating.'

'The Olympics are part of Denton's legacy,' Knight reminded her. 'You'd be honouring him. Besides, it would do you good to get out of the house and help me defend Denton's reputation to one and all.'

'I'll consider it.'

'And by the way: no nanny, no work on Denton's murder investigation.'

'I'm not a nincompoop, Peter!' his mother snapped.

Then Amanda Knight hung up on her son.

Around three, when the children were napping, Knight reached Jack Morgan. Private's owner was usually laid back and very cool, but even over the phone Knight could sense the pressure that Jack was under.

'We're doing everything we can to find a nanny,' Knight said.

'Good,' Jack said. 'Because we need you.'

'Bollocks,' Knight fumed after he'd hung up.

His doorbell rang at around five-thirty. Knight looked through the security peephole and saw his mother in stylish black slacks, shoes and blouse, grey pearl necklace and earrings. Dark sunglasses. He opened the door.

'I arranged a nanny for the evening,' Amanda said, and then stepped aside to reveal a very unhappy Gary Boss, resplendent in pedal-pusher khaki trousers, argyle socks, loafers, and a bow tie with barber-pole stripes.

His mother's personal assistant sniffed at Knight as if he were the purveyor of all things distasteful, and said: 'Do you know that I personally spoke with Nannies Incorporated, Fulham Nannies, the Sweet & Angelic Agency, and every other agency in the city? Quite the reputation, I'd say, Peter. So where are they? The little brutes? I'll need to know their schedules, I suppose.'

'They're in the living room, watching the telly,' Knight said. Then he looked at his mother as Boss disappeared inside. 'Is he up for this?'

'At triple his exorbitant hourly wage, I'm sure he'll figure out a way,' Amanda said, taking off her sunglasses to reveal puffy red eyes.

Knight ran up the stairs to his bedroom and changed quickly. When he came down he found the twins hiding behind the couch, eyeing Boss warily. His mother was nowhere to be seen.

'Her highness is in the car,' Boss said. 'Waiting.'

'I done one, Daddy,' Luke said, patting the back of his nappy.

Why couldn't he just use the loo?

'Well, then,' Knight said to Boss. 'Their food is in the fridge in plastic containers. Just a bit of heating-up to do. Luke can have a taste of ice cream. Bella's allergic, so digestive biscuits for her. Bath. Story. Bed by nine, and we'll see you by midnight, I'd think.'

Knight went to his children and kissed them. 'Mind Mr Boss, now. He's your nanny for tonight.'

'I done one, Daddy,' Luke complained again.

'Right,' Knight said to Boss. 'And Luke's had a BM. You'll need to change it straight away or you'll be bathing him sooner rather than later.'

Boss became distressed. 'Change a shitty nappy? Me?'

'You're the nanny now,' Knight said, stifling a laugh as he left.

Chapter 36

AS KNIGHT AND his mother made their way to St Pancras Station and the high-speed train to Stratford and the Olympic Park, Professor Selena Farrell was feeling damn sexy, thank you very much.

Dusk was coming on in Soho. The air was sultry, she'd got vodka in her, and she was dressed to kill. Indeed, as she walked west from Tottenham Court Road towards Carlisle Street, the classics professor kept catching glimpses of herself in the shop windows she passed, and in the eyes of men and women who could not help but notice every sway of her hips and every bounce of her breasts in the skirt and sleeveless blouse that clung to her like second skins.

She wore alluring make-up, startling blue contact lenses, and the scarf was gone, revealing dark-dyed hair cut in swoops that framed her face and drew the eye to that little dark mole on her right jawline. But for the mole no one, not even her research assistant, would ever have recognised her.

Farrell loved feeling like this. Anonymous. Sexual. On the prowl.

When she was like this she was far from who she was in her everyday life, truly someone else. The illicitness of it all excited the professor yet again, empowered her yet again, and made her feel magnetic, hypnotic and, well, downright irresistible.

When she reached Carlisle Street, she found number four, its sign lit in pink neon, and entered. The Candy Club was the oldest and largest lesbian nightclub in London, and was Farrell's favourite place to go when she needed to let off steam.

The professor headed towards the long bar on the ground floor and the many beautiful women milling around in it. A petite woman, quite exquisite in her loveliness, caught sight of Farrell, spun in her seat, mojito in hand, and threw her a knowing smile. 'Syren St James!'

'Nell,' Farrell said, and kissed her on the cheek.

Nell put her hand on Farrell's forearm and studied her outfit. 'My, my, Syren. Look at you: more brilliant and delicious than ever. Where have you been lately? I haven't seen you in almost a month.'

'I was here the other night,' Farrell said. 'Before that I was in Paris. Working. A new project.'

'Lucky you,' Nell said. Then she turned conspiratorial and added, 'You know, we could always leave and . . .'

'Not tonight, lover,' Farrell said gently. 'I've already made plans.'

'Pity,' Nell sniffed. 'Your "plan" here yet?'

'Haven't looked,' Farrell replied.

'Name?'

'That's a secret.'

'Well,' Nell said, miffed. 'If your secret is a no-show, come back.'

Farrell blew Nell a kiss before setting off, feeling anticipation make her heart beat along with the dance music thudding up from the basement. She peered into the nooks and crannies of the ground floor before heading upstairs where she scanned the crowd gathered around the pink pool table. No luck.

Farrell was beginning to think she'd been stood up until she went to the basement where a femme kink performer was pole dancing to the riffs and dubs of a disc jockey named V. J. Wicked. Pink sofas lined the walls facing the stripper.

The professor spotted her quarry on one of those sofas in the far corner of the room, nursing a flute of champagne. With jet-black hair pulled back severely, she was elegantly attired in a black cocktail frock and a pill hat with a black lace veil that obscured the features of her face except for her dusky skin and ruby lips.

'Hello, Marta,' Farrell said, sliding into a chair beside her.

Marta took her attention off the dancer, smiled and replied in a soft East European accent. 'I had faith I'd see you here, my sister.'

The professor smelled Marta's perfume and was enthralled. 'I couldn't stay away.'

Marta ran her ruby fingernails over the back of Farrell's hand. 'Of course you couldn't. Shall we let the games begin?'

Chapter 37

BY SEVEN THAT evening the world's eyes had turned to five hundred-plus acres of decaying East London land that had been transformed into the city's new Olympic Park, which featured a stadium packed with ninety thousand lucky fans, a teeming athletes' village, and sleek modern venues for cycling, basketball, handball, swimming and diving.

These venues were all beautiful structures, but the media had chosen British sculptor Anish Kapoor's *ArcelorMittal Orbit* as the park's and, indeed, the Games's signature design achievement. At three hundred and seventy-seven feet, the Orbit was taller than Big Ben, taller than the Statue of Liberty, and soared just outside the east flank of the stadium. The Orbit was rust red and featured massive hollow, steel arms that curved, twisted and wove together in a way that put Knight in mind of DNA helices gone mad. Near the top, the structure supported a circular observation deck and restaurant. Above the deck, another of those DNA helices was curved into a giant arch.

From his position high on the west side of the stadium, at the window of a lavish hospitality suite set aside for LOCOG, Knight trained his binoculars on the massive Olympic cauldron, which was set on a raised platform on the roof of the observation deck. He wondered how they were going to light it, and then found himself distracted by a BBC broadcaster on a nearby television screen saying that nearly four billion people were expected to tune in to the coverage of the opening ceremonies.

'Peter?' Jack Morgan said behind him. 'There's someone here who would like to talk to you.'

Knight lowered his binoculars and turned to find the owner of Private standing next to Marcus Morris, the chairman of LOCOG. Morris had been a popular Minister of Sport in a previous Labour government.

The two men shook hands.

'An honour,' Knight said as he shook Morris's hand.

Morris said, 'I need to hear from you exactly what Richard Guilder said before he died regarding Denton Marshall.'

Knight told him, finishing with, 'The currency scam had nothing to do with the Olympics. It was greed on Guilder's part. I'll testify to that.'

Morris shook Knight's hand again. 'Thank you,' he said. 'I didn't want there to be any hint of impropriety hanging over these Games. But it does nothing to make any of us feel any better about the loss of Denton. It's a tragedy.'

'In too many ways to count.'

'Your mother seems to be holding up.'

Indeed, upon their arrival Amanda had been showered with sympathy and was now somewhere in the crowd behind them.

'She's a strong person, and when this Cronus maniac claimed that Denton was crooked she got angry, very angry. Not a good thing.'

'No, I suppose not,' Morris said, and smiled at last. 'And now I've got a speech to give.'

'And an Olympics to open,' Jack said.

'That too,' Morris said, and walked away.

Jack looked out the window at the huge audience, his eyes scanning the roofline.

Knight noticed and said, 'Security seems brilliant, Jack. It took more than an hour for my mother and I to get through screening at Stratford. And the blokes with the weapons were all Gurkhas.'

'World's most fearsome warriors,' Jack said, nodding.

'Do you need me somewhere?'

'We're fine,' Jack said. 'Enjoy the show. You've earned it.'

Knight looked around. 'By the way, where's Lancer? Poor form to miss his own party.'

Jack winked. 'That's a secret. Mike said to thank you again. In the meantime, I think you should introduce me to your mother so I can offer my condolences.'

Knight's mobile buzzed in his pocket. 'Of course. One second, Jack.'

He dug out the phone, saw that Hooligan was calling and answered just as the lights in the stadium dimmed and the audience began to cheer.

'I'm at the stadium,' Knight said. 'The opening ceremony's starting.'

'Sorry to bother you, but some of us have to work,' Hooligan snapped. 'I got results on that hair sample you sent over this morning. They're—'

A trumpet fanfare erupted from every speaker in the stadium, drowning out what Hooligan had just said.

'Repeat that,' Knight said, sticking his finger in his ear.

'The hair in Cronus's envelope and Selena Farrell's hair,' Hooligan yelled. 'They fuckin' match!'

Chapter 38

'WE'VE GOT CRONUS!' Knight said in a hoarse whisper as he hung up. A powerful spotlight broke the darkness, fixing on a lone figure crouched in the middle of the stadium floor.

'What?' Jack Morgan said, surprised.

'Or one of his Furies, anyway,' Knight said, and then described the match. 'Farrell's house was razed to make way for this stadium. She said publicly that the people who did it to her were going to pay, and she completely flipped when we played the flute music for her.'

'Call Pottersfield,' Jack advised. 'Have her go to Farrell's house. Put her under surveillance until they can get a warrant.'

Out in the stadium a clarinet solo started and from the corner of his eye, Knight saw the figure on the stadium floor rise. He wore green and carried a bow. A quiver of arrows was slung across his back. Robin Hood?

'Unless Farrell's in the stadium,' Knight said, anxiety rising in his chest.

'They've got names attached to every ticket somewhere,' Jack said. He started moving away from the window towards the exit, with Knight trailing after him.

Behind them the crowd roared as a spectacle designed by British film-maker Danny Boyle moved into high gear, depicting through song and dance the rich history of London. Knight could hear drums booming and music echoing in the long hallway outside the heavily guarded hospitality suite. He speed-dialled Elaine Pottersfield, got her on the third ring, and explained the DNA evidence linking Selena Farrell to Cronus's letter.

Beside him, he heard Jack giving the same information to whoever was the watch commander of the moment inside the Olympic Park.

'How did you come by Farrell's DNA?' Pottersfield demanded.

'Long story,' Knight said. 'We're looking for her inside the Olympic stadium at the moment. I suggest you start doing the same at her home.'

He and Jack Morgan both hung up at the same time. Knight glanced at the four armed Private operatives guarding the entrance to LOCOG's hospitality suite.

Reading his thoughts, Jack said: 'No one's getting in there.'

Knight almost nodded, but then thought of Guilder and Mascolo, and said, 'We can't consider LOCOG members as the only targets. Guilder proved that.'

Jack nodded. 'We have to think that way.'

The pair entered the stadium in time to see Mary Poppins launch off the Orbit, umbrella held high as she floated over the roof and the delirious crowd towards a replica of the Tower of London that had been moved onto the floor. She landed near the Tower, but disappeared in smoke when lights began flashing red and white and kettledrums boomed to suggest the London blitz during the Second World War.

The smoke cleared and hundreds of people dressed in a multitude of costume styles danced around the replica of the Tower, and Knight thought he heard someone say that they were depicting modern London and the diverse citizenry of the most cosmopolitan city in the world.

But Knight was not interested in the spectacle: he was looking everywhere in the stadium, trying to anticipate what a madwoman might do in a situation like this. He spotted an entryway on the west side of the venue.

'Where does that go?' he asked Jack.

'The practice track,' Jack replied. 'That's where the teams are getting ready for the parade of nations.'

For reasons that Knight could not explain he felt drawn to that part of the stadium. 'I want to take a look,' he said.

'I'll walk with you,' Jack said. They crossed the stadium as the lights dimmed yet again except for a spotlight aimed at that Robin Hood figure who was now perched high above the stage at the venue's south end.

The actor was pointing up at the top of the Orbit, above the observation deck where more spotlights revealed two armed members of the Queen's Guard marching stiffly towards the cauldron from opposite sides of the roof. They pivoted and stood at rigid attention in their red tunics and black bearskin hats, flanking the cauldron.

Two more guardsmen appeared in the stadium at either side of the main stage. The music faded and an announcer said, 'Ladies and Gentlemen, Mesdames et Messieurs: Queen Elizabeth and the Royal Family.'

Chapter 39

THE LIGHTS ON the stage came up to reveal Queen Elizabeth the Second in a blue suit. She was smiling and waving as she moved to a microphone while Prince Philip, Charles, William, Kate, and various other members of the Windsor family flanked and followed her.

Knight and Jack slowed to gawk for several moments while the queen gave a short speech welcoming the youth of the world to London. But then they moved on towards that entryway.

As more dignitaries gave speeches, the two Private operatives reached the grandstand above the tunnel entry and had to show their corporate badges and IDs to get to the railing. Teams of armed Gurkhas flanked both sides of the tunnel below them. Several of the Nepalese guards immediately began studying Knight and Jack, gauging their level of threat.

'I absolutely would not want one of those guys

pissed-off at me,' Jack said as athletes from Afghanistan started to appear in the entryway.

'Toughest soldiers in the world,' Knight said, studying the traditional long, curved and sheathed knives several of the Gurkhas wore at their belts.

A long curved knife cut off Denton Marshall's head, right?

He was about to mention this fact to Jack when Marcus Morris shouted in conclusion to his speech: 'We welcome the youth of the world to the greatest city on Earth!'

On the stage at the south end of the stadium, the rock band The Who appeared, and broke into 'The Kids Are Alright' as the parade of athletes began with the contingent from Afghanistan entering the stadium.

The crowd went wild and wilder still when The Who finished and Mick Jagger and the Rolling Stones appeared with Keith Richards' guitar wailing the opening riff of 'Can't You Hear Me Knocking?'

With a thousand camera flashes, London went into full Olympic frenzy.

Below Jack and Knight, the Cameroon team filed into the stadium.

'Which one's Mundaho?' Jack asked. 'He's from Cameroon, right?'

'Yes, indeed,' Knight said, searching among the contingent dressed in green and bright yellow until he spotted a tall, muscular and laughing man with his hair done up in beads and shells. 'There he is.'

'Does he honestly reckon he can beat Shaw?'

'He certainly thinks so,' Knight said.

Filatri Mundaho had appeared out of nowhere on the international track scene at a race in Berlin only seven months before the Olympics. Mundaho was a big, rangy man built along the same lines as the supreme Jamaican sprinter Zeke Shaw.

Shaw had not been in Berlin, but many of the world's other fastest men had. Mundaho ran in three events at that meet: the 100-metre, 200-metre, and 400-metre sprints. The Cameroonian won every heat and every race convincingly, which had never been done before at a meet that big.

The achievement set off a frenzy of speculation about what Mundaho might be able to accomplish at the London Games. At the 1996 Atlanta Games, American Henry Ivey gold-medalled and set world records in both the 400-metre and 200-metre sprints. At Beijing in 2008, Shaw won the 100 and 200-metre sprints, also setting world records in both events. But no man, or woman for that matter, had ever won all three sprint events at a single Games.

Filatri Mundaho was going to try.

His coaches claimed that Mundaho had been discovered running in a regional race in the eastern part of their country after he'd escaped from rebel forces who had kidnapped him as a child and turned him into a boy soldier.

'Did you read that article the other day where he attributed his speed and stamina to bullets flying at his back?' Jack asked.

'No,' Knight said. 'But I can see that being a hell of a motivator.'

Chapter 40

TWENTY MINUTES LATER, with The Who and the Stones still counterpunching with songs from their greatest-hits collections, the contingent from the United States entered the stadium led by their flag-bearer Paul Teeter, a massive bearded man whom Jack knew from Los Angeles.

'Paul went to UCLA,' Jack said. 'Throws the shot and discus – insanely strong. A really good guy, too. He does a lot of work with inner-city youth. He's expected to go big here.'

Knight took his eyes off Teeter and caught sight of a woman he recognised walking behind the flag-bearer. He'd seen a picture of her in a bikini in *The Times* of all places the week before. She was in her late thirties and easily one of the fittest women he'd ever seen. And she was even better-looking in person.

'That's Hunter Pierce, isn't it?' Knight said.

Jack nodded in admiration. 'What a great story she is.'

Pierce had lost her husband in a car accident two years before, leaving her with three children under the age of ten. Now an emergency-room doctor in San Diego, she'd once been a twenty-one-year-old diver who'd almost made the Atlanta Olympic team, but had then quit the sport to pursue a career in medicine and raise a family.

Fifteen years later, as a way to deal with her husband's death, she began diving again. At her children's insistence, Pierce started competing again at the age of thirty-six. Eighteen months later, with her children watching, she'd stunned the American diving community by winning the ten-metre platform competition at the US Olympic qualifying meet.

'Absolutely brilliant,' Knight said, watching her waving and smiling as the team from Zimbabwe entered the stadium behind her.

Last to enter was the team from the UK – the host country. Twenty-three-year-old swimmer Audrey Williamson, a two-time gold medallist at Beijing, carried the Union Jack.

Knight pointed out to Jack the various athletes from the British contingent who were said to have a chance to win medals, including marathon runner Mary Duckworth, eighteen-year-old sprint sensation Mimi Marshall, boxer Oliver Price, and the nation's five-man heavyweight crew team.

Soon after, 'God Save the Queen' was sung. So was the Olympic Hymn. The athletes recited the Olympic creed, and a keen anticipation descended over the crowd, many of whom were looking towards the tunnel entry below Knight and Jack.

'I wonder who the cauldron lighter will be,' Jack said.

'You and everyone else in England,' Knight replied.

Indeed, speculation about who would receive the honour of lighting the Olympic cauldron had only intensified since the flame had come to Britain from Greece earlier in the year and been taken to Much Wenlock in Shropshire, where Pierre de Coubertin, the father of the modern Olympics, had been guest of honour at a special festival in 1890.

Since then, the torch had wound its way through England, Wales and Scotland. At every stop, curiosity and rumour had grown.

'The odds-makers favour Sir Cedric Dudley, the UK's five-times gold medallist in rowing,' Knight told Jack. 'But others are saying that the one to light the cauldron should be Sir Seymour Peterson-Allen, the first man to run a mile in under four minutes.'

But then a roar went up from the crowd as the theme from the movie *Chariots of Fire* was played and two men ran into the stadium directly below Knight and Jack, carrying the torch between them.

It was Cedric Dudley running beside . . .

'My God, that's Lancer!' Knight cried.

It *was* Mike Lancer, smiling and waving joyously to the crowd as he and Dudley ran along the track towards the spiral staircase that climbed the replica of the Tower of London at the bottom of which stood a waiting figure in white.

Chapter 41

AT THAT VERY moment, Karen Pope was in the *Sun*'s newsroom on the eighth floor of a modern office building on Thomas More Square near St Katharine Docks on the Thames's north bank. She wanted to go home to get some sleep, but could not break away from the coverage of the opening ceremonies.

Up on the screen, Lancer and Dudley ran towards that figure in white standing at the bottom of a steep staircase that led up onto the tower. Seeing the joy on the faces all over the stadium, Pope's normal cynicism faded and she started to feel weepy.

What an amazing, amazing moment for London, for all of Britain.

Pope looked over at Finch, her editor. The crusty sports veteran's eyes were glassy with emotion. He glanced at her and said, 'You know who that is, don't you? The final torch-bearer?'

'No idea, boss,' Pope replied.

'That's goddamn—'

'You Karen Pope?' a male voice behind her said, cutting Finch off.

Pope turned to see – and smell – a scruffy bicycle messenger who looked at her with a bored expression on her face.

'Yes,' she said. 'I'm Pope.'

The messenger held out an envelope with her name on it, spelled out in odd block letters of many different fonts and colours. Pope felt her stomach yawn open like an abysmal pit.

Chapter 42

AS THE FINAL torch-bearer climbed the Tower of London replica, the entire crowd were cheering and whistling and stamping their feet.

Knight frowned and glanced up at the roof of the Orbit and the guardsmen flanking the cauldron. How the hell were they going to get the flame from the top of the Tower of London replica to the top of the Orbit?

The final torch-bearer raised the flame high overhead as the applause turned thunderous and then cut to a collective gasp.

Holding his bow, an arrow strung, Robin Hood leaped into the air off the scaffolding above the south stage and flew out over the stadium on guy wires, heading for the raised Olympic torch.

As the archer whizzed past, he dipped the tip of his arrow into the flame, igniting it. Then he soared on, higher and higher, drawing back his bowstring as he went.

When he was almost level with the top of the Orbit, Robin Hood twisted and released the fiery arrow, which arced over the roof of the stadium, split the night sky, and passed between the Queen's guardsmen, inches over the cauldron.

A great billowing flame exploded inside the cauldron, turning the stadium crowd thunderous once more. The voice of Jacques Rogge, the chairman of the International Olympic Committee rang out over the public address system:

'I declare the 2012 London Games open!'

Fireworks erupted off the top of the Orbit and exploded high over East London while church bells all over the city began to ring. Down on the stadium floor, the athletes were all hugging each other, trading badges, and taking pictures and videos of this magical moment when each and every dream of Olympic gold seemed possible.

Looking at the athletes, and then up at the Olympic flame while chrysanthemum rockets burst in the sky, Knight got teary-eyed. He had not expected to feel such overwhelming pride for his city and for his country.

Then his mobile rang.

Karen Pope was near-hysterical: 'Cronus just sent me another letter. He takes credit for the death of Paul Teeter, the American shot-putter!'

Knight grimaced in confusion. 'No, I just saw him – he's . . .'

Then Knight understood. 'Where's Teeter?' he shouted at Jack and started running. 'Cronus is trying to kill him!'

Chapter 43

KNIGHT AND JACK fought their way down through the crowd. Jack was barking into his mobile, informing the stadium's security commander of the situation. They both showed their Private badges to get onto the stadium floor.

Knight spotted Teeter holding the US flag and talking to Filatri Mundaho, the Cameroonian sprinter. He took off across the infield just as the American flag began to topple. The flag-bearer went with it and collapsed to the ground, convulsing, bloody foam on his lips.

By the time Knight reached the US contingent, people were screaming for a doctor. Dr Hunter Pierce broke through the crowd and went to the shot-putter's side while Mundaho watched in horror.

'He just falls,' the ex-boy soldier said to Knight.

Jack looked as stunned as Knight felt. It had all happened so fast. Three minutes' warning. That's all they'd been given. What more could they have done to save the American?

Suddenly, the public address system crackled and Cronus's weird flute music began playing.

Panic surged through Knight. He remembered Selena Farrell turning crazed in her office, and then realised that many of the athletes around him were pointing up at the huge video screens around the Olympic venue, all displaying the same three red words:

OLYMPIC SHAME EXPOSED

Part Three

THE FASTEST MAN ON EARTH

Chapter 44

KNIGHT WAS INFURIATED. Cronus was acting with impunity, not only managing to poison Teeter but somehow hacking into the Olympic Park's computer system and taking over the scoreboard.

Could Professor Farrell do such a thing? Was she capable?

Mike Lancer ran up to Knight and Jack, looking as if he had aged ten years in the past few moments. He pointed at the screens. 'What the hell does that mean? What's that infernal music?'

'It's Cronus, Mike,' Knight said. 'He's taking credit for the attack.'

'What?' Lancer cried, looking distraught. Then he spotted Dr Pierce and the paramedics gathered around the US shot-putter. 'Is he dead?'

'I saw him before Dr Pierce got to him,' Knight said. 'He had bloody foam around his mouth. He was convulsing and choking.'

Shaken, bewildered, Lancer said, 'Poison?'

'We'll have to wait for a blood test.'

'Or an autopsy,' Jack said as paramedics put an unconscious Teeter on a gurney and rushed towards the ambulance with Dr Pierce in tow.

Some in the remaining crowd at the Olympic stadium were softly clapping for the stricken American. But more were heading for the exits, holding their hands to their ears to block out the baleful flute music, and shooting worried glances at Cronus's message still glowing up there on the screens.

OLYMPIC SHAME EXPOSED

Jack's voice shook as the ambulance pulled away: 'I don't care what claim Cronus might have. Paul Teeter was one of the good guys, a gentle giant. I went to see one of his clinics in LA. The kids adored him. Absolutely adored him. What kind of sick bastard would do such a thing on a night like this to such a good person as him?'

Knight recalled Professor Farrell fleeing her office the day before. Where was she? Did Pottersfield have her in custody? Was she Cronus? Or one of the Furies? And how did they poison Teeter?

Knight went to Mundaho, introduced himself, and asked him what had happened. The Cameroonian sprinter said in broken English that

Teeter was sweating hard and had looked flushed in the minutes before he collapsed.

Then Knight grabbed other American athletes and asked whether they'd seen Teeter drink anything before the start of the opening ceremony. A high-jumper said he had seen the shot-putter drinking from one of the thousands of plastic water bottles that London Olympic volunteers, or Game Masters, were handing out to athletes as they lined up for the parade of nations.

Knight told Jack and Lancer who went ballistic and barked into his radio, ordering all Game Masters held inside the Olympic Park until further notice.

The security commander, who had arrived on the scene a few minutes earlier, glared up at the glowing screens and bellowed into his radio, 'Shut down the PA system and end that goddamn flute music! Get that message off the scoreboards, too. And I want to know how in the bloody hell someone cracked our network. Now!'

Chapter 45

Saturday, 28 July 2012

PAUL TEETER, LEADING field athlete and tireless advocate for disadvantaged youth, died en route to hospital shortly after midnight. He was twenty-six.

Hours later, Knight suffered a nightmare that featured the flute music, the severed head of Denton Marshall, the blood blooming on Richard Guilder's chest, Joe Mascolo crashing through the cocktail table at the Lobby Bar, and the bloody foam on the shot-putter's lips.

He awoke with a start, and for several heart-racing moments the Private investigator had no idea where he was.

Then he heard Luke sucking his thumb in the darkness and knew. He began to calm down and pulled the sheets up around his shoulders, thinking of Gary Boss's face when Knight had arrived home at three in the morning.

The place had been a shambles and his mother's personal assistant vowed to never, ever babysit Knight's insane children again. Even if Amanda quintupled his salary he would not do it.

His mother was upset with Knight as well. Not only had he cut out on her the night before, he hadn't responded to her calls after Teeter's death had been announced. But he'd been swamped.

Knight tried to doze again, but his mind lurched between worry about finding a new nanny for his kids, his mother, and the contents of Cronus's second letter. He, Jack and Hooligan had examined the letter in the clean room at Private London shortly after Pope brought them the package at around one a.m.

'What honour can there be in a victory that is not earned?' Cronus had written at the start of the letter. 'What glory in defeating your opponent through deceit?'

Cronus claimed that Teeter was a fraud 'emblematic of the legions of corrupt Olympic athletes willing to use any illegal drug at their disposal to enhance their performance.'

The letter had gone on to claim that Teeter and other unnamed athletes at the London Games were using an extract of deer and elk antler 'velvet' to increase their strength, speed, and recovery time. Antler is the fastest growing substance in the world because the nutrient-rich sheathing, or velvet, that surrounds it during development is saturated with IGF-1, a super-potent growth hormone banned under Olympic rules. Under careful administration, however, and delivered by mouth spray rather than direct injection, the use of antler velvet was almost impossible to detect.

'The illicit benefits of IGF-1 are enormous,' Cronus wrote. 'Especially to a strength athlete like Teeter because it gives him the ability to build muscle faster, and recover faster from workouts.'

The letter had gone on to accuse two herbalists – one in Los Angeles and another in London – of being involved in Teeter's elaborate deception.

Documents that accompanied the letter seemed to shore up Cronus's claims. Four were receipts from the herbalists showing sales and delivery of red-deer velvet from New Zealand to the post-office box of an LA construction company that belonged to Teeter's brother-in-law Philip. Other documents purported to show the results of independent cutting-edge tests on blood taken from Teeter.

'They clearly note the presence of IGF-1 in Teeter's system within the last four months,' Cronus wrote before concluding. 'And so this wilful cheat, Paul Teeter, had to be sacrificed to cleanse the Games and make them pure again.'

On the couch in the twins' nursery, several hours

after reading those words, Knight stared at the dim forms of his children, thinking, is this how you make the Olympics pure again? By murdering people? What kind of insane person thinks that way? And why?

Chapter 46

I ROAM THE city for hours after Teeter's collapse on the global stage, secretly gloating over the vengeance we've taken, revelling in the proof of our superiority over the feeble efforts of Scotland Yard, MI5 and Private. They'll never come close to finding my sisters or me.

Everywhere I go, even at this late hour, I see Londoners in shock and newspapers featuring a photo of the Jumbotron in the stadium and our message: *Olympic Shame Exposed!*

And the headlines: *Death Stalks the Games!*

Well, what did they think? That we'd simply let them continue to make a mockery of the ancient rites of sport? That we'd simply let them defile the precepts of fair competition, earned superiority, and immortal greatness?

Hardly.

And now Cronus and the Furies are on the lips of billions upon billions of people around the globe, uncatchable, able to kill at will, bent on exposing and eliminating the dark side of the world's greatest sporting event.

Some fools are comparing us to the Palestinians who kidnapped and murdered Israelis during the 1972 summer Games in Munich. They keep describing us as terrorists with unknown political motives.

Those idiots aside, I feel as though the world is beginning to understand me and my sisters now. A thrill goes through me when I realise that people everywhere are sensing our greatness. They are questioning how it could be that such beings walk among them, holding the power of death over deceit and corruption, and making sacrifices in the name of all that is good and honourable.

In my mind I see the monsters that stoned me, the dead eyes of the Furies the night I slaughtered the Bosnians, and the shock on the faces of the broadcasters explaining Teeter's death.

At last, I think, I'm making the monsters pay for what they did to me.

I'm thinking the same thing as dawn breaks and bathes the thin clouds over London in a deep red hue that makes them look like raised welts.

I knock on the side entrance of the house where the Furies live, and enter. Marta is the only one of the sisters still awake. Her dark agate eyes are shiny with tears and she hugs me joyfully, her happiness as burning as my own.

'Like clockwork,' she says, closing the door behind me. 'Everything went off perfectly. Teagan got the bottle to the American, and then changed and slipped out before the chaos began, as if it were all fated.'

'Didn't you say the same thing when London got the Olympics?' I ask. 'Didn't you say that when we found the corruption and the cheating, just like I said we would?'

'It's all true,' Marta replies, her expression as fanatical as any martyr's. 'We are fated. We are superior.'

'Yes, but make no mistake: they will hunt us now,' I reply, sobering. 'You said we were fine on all counts?'

'All counts,' Marta confirms, all business now.

'The factory?'

'Teagan made sure it's sealed tight. No possibility of discovery.'

'Your part?' I ask.

'Went off flawlessly.'

I nod. 'Then it's time we stay in the shadows. Let Scotland Yard, MI5 and Private operate on high alert long enough for them to tire, to imagine that we're done, and allow themselves to let their guard down.'

'According to plan,' Marta says. Then she

hesitates. 'This Peter Knight – is he still a threat to us?'

I consider the question, and then say, 'If there is one, it's him.'

'We found something, then. Knight has a weakness. A large one.'

Chapter 47

KNIGHT JERKED AWAKE in the twins' nursery. His mobile was ringing. Sun flooded the room and blinded him. He groped for the phone and answered.

'Farrell's gone,' Inspector Elaine Pottersfield said. 'Not at her office. Not at her home.'

Knight sat up, still squinting, and said, 'Did you search both of them?'

'I can't get a warrant until my lab corroborates the match that Hooligan got.'

'Hooligan found something more last night in Cronus's second letter.'

'What?' Pottersfield shouted. 'What second letter?'

'It's already at your lab,' Knight said. 'But Hooligan picked up some skin cells in the envelope. He gave you half the sample.'

'Goddamn it, Peter,' Pottersfield cried. 'Private must not analyse anything to do with this case without—'

'That's not my call, Elaine,' Knight shot back. 'It's the *Sun*'s call. The paper is Private's client!'

'I don't care who the—'

'What about your end?' Peter demanded. 'I always seem to be giving you information.'

There was a pause before she said, 'The big focus is on how Cronus managed to hack into the . . .'

Knight noticed that the twins weren't in their cots and stopped listening. His attention shot to the clock. Ten a.m.! He hadn't slept this late since before the twins were born.

'Gotta go, Elaine! Kids,' he said and hung up.

Every worrying thought that a parent could have sliced through him, and he lurched through the nursery door and out onto the landing above the staircase. What if they've fallen? What if they've mucked around with . . .?

He heard the television spewing coverage of the 400-metre freestyle relay swimming heats, and felt as if every muscle in his body had changed to rubber. He had to hold tight to the railings to get down to the first floor.

Luke and Isabel had pulled the cushions off the sofa and piled them on the floor. They were sitting on them like little Buddhas beside empty cereal and juice boxes. Knight thought he'd never seen anything so beautiful in his life.

He fed, changed and dressed them while tracking

the broadcast coverage of Teeter's murder. Scotland Yard and MI5 weren't talking. Neither was F7, the company hired by LOCOG to run security and scanning at the Games.

But Mike Lancer was all over the news, assuring reporters that the Olympics were safe, defending his actions but taking full responsibility for the breaches in security. Shaken and yet resolved, Lancer vowed that Cronus would be stopped, captured, and brought to justice.

Knight, meanwhile, continued to struggle with the fact that he had no nanny and would not be actively working the Cronus case until he could find one. He'd called his mother several times, but she hadn't answered. Then he called another of the agencies, explained his situation, and begged for a temp. The manager told him she might be able to recruit someone by Tuesday.

'Tuesday?' he shouted.

'It's the best I can do – the Games have taken everyone available,' the woman said and hung up.

The twins wanted to go to the playground around noon. Figuring it would help them to nap, he agreed. He put them in their buggy, bought a copy of the *Sun*, and walked to a playground inside the Royal Hospital Gardens about ten minutes from his house. The temperature had fallen and there wasn't a cloud in the sky. London at its finest.

But as Knight sat on a bench and watched Luke playing on the big-boy slide and Isabel digging in the sandbox, his thoughts weren't on his children or on the exceptional weather for the first full day of Olympic competition. He kept thinking about Cronus and wondering if and when he'd strike again?

A text came in from Hooligan: 'Skin cells in second letter are male, no match yet. Off to Coventry for England-Algeria football match.'

Male? Knight thought. Cronus? So Farrell was one of the Furies?

In frustration, Knight picked up the newspaper. Pope's story dominated the front page under the headline: *Death Stalks The Olympics*.

The sports reporter led with Teeter's collapse and death in a terse, factual account of the events as they had unfolded at the opening ceremony. Near the end of the piece, she'd included a rebuttal of Cronus's charges from Teeter's brother-in-law who was in London for the Games. He claimed that the lab results Cronus had provided were phoney, and that he, in fact, was the person who had bought deer-antler velvet. Working on construction sites all day long as he did, he said it gave him relief from chronic back spasms.

'Hello? Sir?' a woman said.

The sunlight was so brilliant at first that Knight could only see the outline of a female figure standing in front of him holding out a flyer. He was about to say he wasn't interested, but then he put his hand to his brow to block the sun's glare from his eyes. The woman had a rather plain face, short dark hair, dark eyes, and a stocky athletic build.

'Yes?' he said, taking the flyer.

'I am so sorry,' she said with a humble smile, and he heard the soft East European accent for the first time. 'Please, I see you have children and I was wondering do you know someone who needs or do you yourself need a babysitter?'

Knight blinked several times in astonishment and then looked down at her flyer, which read: 'Experienced babysitter/nanny with excellent references available. Undergraduate degree in early-childhood development. Accepted into graduate programme in speech-language pathology.'

It went on, but Knight stopped reading and looked up at her. 'What's your name?'

She sat down beside him, with an eager smile.

'Marta,' she said. 'Marta Brezenova.'

Chapter 48

'YOU'RE AN UNEXPECTED answer to my prayers, Marta Brezenova, and your timing could not have been better,' Knight announced, feeling pleased at his good fortune. 'My name is Peter Knight, and I am actually in desperate need of a nanny at the moment.'

Marta looked incredulous and then happy. Her fingers went to her lips as she said, 'But you are the first person I've handed my flier to! It's like fate!'

'Maybe,' Knight said, enjoying her infectious enthusiasm.

'No, it is!' she protested. 'Can I apply?'

He looked again at her flier. 'Do you have a C.V.? References?'

'Both,' she said without hesitation, then dug in her bag and brought out a professional-looking C.V. and an Estonian passport. 'Now you know who I am.'

Knight glanced at the C.V. and the passport before saying: 'Tell you what. Those are my kids over there. Luke's on the slide and Isabel is in the sandbox. Go and introduce yourself. I'll look this over and give your references a call.'

Knight wanted to see how his kids interacted with Marta as a total stranger. He'd seen them revolt against so many nannies that he did not want to bother calling this woman's references if she and the twins did not click. No matter how badly he needed a nanny it wouldn't be worth the effort if they did not get along.

But to his surprise Marta went to Isabel, the more reserved of his children, and won her over almost immediately, helping her build a sandcastle and generating such enthusiasm that Luke soon left the slide to help. In three minutes, she had Lukey Knight – the big, bad, biting terror of Chelsea – laughing and filling buckets.

Seeing his children fall so easily under Marta's sway, Knight read the C.V. closely. She was an Estonian citizen, mid-thirties, but had done her undergraduate studies at the American University in Paris.

During her last two years at the university, and for six years after graduating, she had worked as a nanny for two different families in Paris. The mothers' names and phone numbers were included.

Marta's C.V. also indicated that she spoke English, French, Estonian and German, and had been accepted into the graduate programme in speech-language pathology at London's City University. She was due to join the course in 2014. In many ways, Knight thought, she was typical of the many educated women streaming into London these days: willing to take jobs beneath their qualifications in order to live and survive in the greatest city in the world.

My luck, Knight thought. He got out his mobile and started calling the references, thinking: Please let this be real. Please let someone answer the—

Petra DeMaurier came on the line almost immediately, speaking French. Knight identified himself and asked if she spoke English. In a guarded tone, she said that she did. When he told her that he was thinking of hiring Marta Brezenova as a nanny for his young twins, she turned effusive, praising Marta as the best nanny her four children had ever had, patient, loving, yet strong-willed if necessary.

'Why did she leave your employ?' Knight asked.

'My husband was transferred to Vietnam for two years,' she said. 'Marta did not wish to accompany us, but we parted on very good terms. You are a lucky man to have her.'

The second reference, Teagan Lesa, was no less positive, saying, 'When Marta was accepted for graduate studies in London, I almost cried. My three children *did* cry, even Stephan who is normally my brave little man. If I were you, I'd hire her before someone else does. Better yet, tell her to come back to Paris. We wait for her with open arms.'

Knight thought for several moments after hanging up, knowing he should check with the universities here and in Paris, something he couldn't do until Monday at the earliest. Then he had an idea. He hesitated, but then called Pottersfield back.

'You hung up on me,' she snapped.

'I had to,' Knight said. 'I need you to check an Estonian passport for me,'

'I most certainly will not,' Pottersfield shot back.

'It's for the twins, Elaine,' Knight said in a pleading tone. 'I've got an opportunity to hire them a new nanny who looks great on paper. I just want to make sure, and it's the weekend and I have no other way to do it.'

There was a long silence before Pottersfield said, 'Give me the name and passport number if you've got it.'

Knight heard the Scotland Yard inspector typing after he read her the number. He watched Marta get onto the slide, holding Isabel. His daughter on the slide? That was a first. They slid to the bottom with only a trace of terror surfacing on Isabel's face before she started clapping.

'Marta Brezenova,' said Pottersfield. 'Kind of a plain Jane, isn't she?'

'You were expecting a supermodel moonlighting as a nanny?'

'I suppose not,' Pottersfield allowed. 'She arrived in the UK on a flight from Paris ten days ago. She's here on an educational visa to attend City University.'

'Graduate programme in speech-language pathology,' Knight said. 'Thanks, Elaine. I owe you.'

Hearing Luke shriek with laughter, he hung up and spotted his son and his sister running through the jungle gym with Marta in hot pursuit, playing the happy monster, laughing maniacally.

You're not much to look at, Knight thought. But thank God for you, anyway. You're hired.

Chapter 49

Monday, 30 July 2012

EARLY THAT AFTERNOON, Metropolitan Police Inspector Billy Casper eyed Knight suspiciously, and said, 'Can't say I think it's proper for you to have access. But Pottersfield wanted you to see for yourself. So go on up. Second floor. Flat on the right.'

Knight mounted the stairs, fully focused on the investigation now that Marta Brezenova had come into the picture. The woman was a marvel. In less than two days she'd put his children under a spell. They were cleaner, better behaved, and happier. He'd even checked with City University. No doubt. Marta Brezenova had been accepted on their speech-language pathology programme. He hadn't bothered to call the American University in Paris. That aspect of his life felt settled at last. He'd even called up the agency that had offered him part-time help and had cancelled his request.

Now Inspector Elaine Pottersfield was waiting for Knight at the door to Selena Farrell's apartment.

'Anything?' he asked.

'A lot, actually,' she said. After he'd put on gloves and slip-ons she led him inside. A full crime-scene unit from Scotland Yard and specialists from MI5 were tearing the place apart.

They went into the professor's bedroom, which was dominated by an oversized dressing table that featured three mirrors and several drawers open to reveal all manner of beauty items: twenty different kinds of lipstick, an equal number of nail-polish bottles, and jars of make-up.

Dr Farrell? It didn't fit with the professor whom Knight and Pope had met in the office. Then he looked around and spotted the open closets, which were stuffed with what looked like high-end expensive women's clothing.

Was she a secret fashionista or something?

Before Knight could express his confusion, Pottersfield gestured past a crime tech examining a laptop on the dressing table towards a filing cabinet in the corner. 'We found all sorts of written diatribes against the destruction the Games caused in East London, including several poisonous letters to Denton—'

'Inspector?' the crime tech interrupted excitedly. 'I think I've got it!'

Pottersfield frowned. 'What?'

The tech struck the keyboard and from the computer flute music began to play, the same haunting melody that had echoed inside the Olympic Stadium on the night Paul Teeter was poisoned, the same brutal tune that had accompanied Cronus's letter accusing him of using an illicit performance-enhancing substance.

'That's on the computer?' Knight asked.

'Part of a simple *.exe* file designed to play the music and to display this.'

The tech turned the screen to show three words centred horizontally:

OLYMPIC SHAME EXPOSED

Chapter 50

Tuesday, 31 July 2012

WEARING A SURGICAL hair-cap and mask, a long rubber apron and the sort of high-sleeved rubber gloves that butchers use to disembowel cattle, I carefully load the third letter into an envelope addressed to Karen Pope.

More than sixty hours have passed since we slew the monster Teeter, and the initial frenzy that we caused in the global media has subsided considerably because the London Games have gone on, and gold medals have been won.

On Saturday we dominated virtually every broadcast and every written account of the opening ceremonies. On Sunday, the stories about the threat we posed were shorter and focused on law-enforcement efforts to figure out how the Olympic computer system was hacked, as well as insignificant coverage of the impromptu memorial service that the US athletes held for the corrupt swine Teeter.

Yesterday we were merely context for news features that trumpeted the fact that, apart from Teeter's murder, the 2012 Summer Olympics were going off flawlessly. This morning we didn't even make page one, which was dominated by the search of Serena Farrell's home and office where conclusive evidence had been found linking her to the Cronus murders; and by reports that Scotland Yard and MI5 had launched a nationwide manhunt for the classics professor.

This is troubling news at some level, but not unexpected. Nor is the fact that it will take more than a death or two to destroy the modern Olympic movement. I've known that ever since the night when London won the right to host the Games. My sisters and I have had seven years since to work out our intricate plan for vengeance, seven years to penetrate the system and use it to our advantage, seven years to create enough false leads to keep the police distracted and uncertain, unable to anticipate our final purpose until it's much too late.

Still wearing the apron and gloves, I slip the envelope into a plastic Ziploc bag and hand it to Petra, who stands with Teagan, both sisters clad in disguises that render them fat and unrecognisable to anyone but me or their older sister.

'Remember the tides,' I say.

Petra says nothing and looks away from me, as if she is having an internal argument of some sort. The act creates unease in me.

'We will, Cronus,' Teagan says, sliding on dark sunglasses below the official Olympic Volunteer cap she wears.

I go to Petra and say, 'Are you all right, sister?'

Her expression is conflicted, but she nods.

I kiss her on both cheeks, and then turn to Teagan.

'The factory?' I ask.

'This morning,' she replies. 'Food and medicine enough for four days.'

I embrace her and whisper in her ear: 'Watch your sister. She's impulsive.'

When we part, Teagan's face is expressionless. My cold warrior.

Removing the apron and gloves, I watch the sisters leave, and my hand travels to that crablike scar on the back of my head. Scratching it, the hatred ignites almost instantly, and I deeply wish that I could be one of those two women tonight. But, in consolation, I remind myself that the ultimate revenge will be mine and mine alone. The disposable mobile in my pocket rings. It's Marta.

'I managed to put a bug in Knight's mobile before he left for work,' she informs me. 'I'll tap the home computer when the children sleep.'

'Did he give you the evening off?'

'I didn't ask for it,' Marta says.

If the stupid bitch were in front of me right now, I swear I'd wring her pretty little neck. 'What do you mean, you didn't ask?' I demand in a tight voice.

'Relax,' she says. 'I'll be right where I'm needed when I'm needed. The children will be asleep. They'll never even know I was gone. And neither will Knight. He told me not to expect him until almost midnight.'

'How can you be sure the brats will be sleeping?'

'How else would I do it? I'm going to drug them.'

Chapter 51

SEVERAL HOURS LATER, inside the Aquatics Centre in the grounds of the Olympic Park, US diver Hunter Pierce flipped backwards off the ten-metre platform. She spun through the chlorine-tainted air, corkscrewing twice before slicing the water with a cutting sound, leaving a shallow whirlpool on the surface and little else.

Knight joined the packed house, cheering, clapping and whistling. But no one in the crowd celebrated more than the American diver's three children – one boy and two girls – in the front row, stamping their feet and waving their hands at their mother as she surfaced, grinning wildly.

That was Pierce's fourth attempt, and her best in Knight's estimation. After three dives she had been in third place behind athletes from South Korea and Panama. The Chinese were a surprisingly distant fourth and fifth.

She's in the zone, Knight thought. She feels it.

As he'd been for much of the past two hours, Knight was standing in the exit gangway opposite the ten-metre platform, watching the crowd and the competition. Nearly four days had passed since Teeter's death, four days without subsequent attack, and one day since the discovery of the software program in Selena Farrell's computer designed to breach and take over the Olympic Stadium's electronic scoreboard system.

Everyone was saying it was over. Capturing the mad professor was only a matter of time. The investigation was simply a manhunt now.

But Knight was nevertheless concerned that another killing might be coming. He'd taken to studying the Olympic schedule at all hours of the night, trying to anticipate where Cronus might strike again. It would be somewhere high-profile, he figured, with intense media coverage, as there was here in the Aquatics Centre as Pierce tried to become the oldest woman ever to win the platform competition.

The American diver hoisted herself from the pool, grabbed a towel, ran over, and slapped the outstretched hands of her children before heading towards the jacuzzi to keep her muscles supple. Before she got there, a roar went up at the scores that flashed on the board: all high eights and nines. Pierce had just moved herself into the silver medal position.

Knight clapped again with even more enthusiasm. The London Games needed a feel-good story to counteract the pall that Cronus had cast over the Games, and this was it. Pierce was defying her age, the odds, and the murders. Indeed, she'd become something of a spokesman for the US Team, decrying Cronus in the wake of Teeter's death. And now here she was, within striking distance of gold.

I am damn lucky to be here, Knight thought. Despite everything, I'm lucky in many ways, especially to have found that Marta.

The woman felt like a gift from on high. His kids were different creatures around her, as if she were the Pied Piper or something. Luke was even talking about using the 'big-boy loo'. And she was incredibly professional. His house had never looked so organised and clean. All in all, it was as if a great weight had been lifted from Knight's shoulders, freeing him to hunt for the madman stalking the Olympics.

At the same time, however, his mother had begun to retreat into her old pre-Denton Marshall ways. She'd opted to hold a memorial for Marshall after the Olympics, and had then disappeared into her work. And there was a bitterness that crept into her voice every time Knight talked to her.

'Do you ever answer your mobile, Knight?' Karen Pope complained.

Startled, Knight looked round, surprised to see the reporter standing next to him in the entryway. 'I've been having problems with it, actually,' he said.

That was true. For the past day, there'd been an odd static audible during Knight's cellular connections, but he had not had time to have the phone looked at.

'Get a new phone, then,' Pope snapped. 'I'm under a lot of pressure to produce and I need your help.'

'Looks to me like you're doing just fine on your own,' Knight said.

Indeed, in addition to the story about the things found on Farrell's home computer, Pope had published an article detailing the results of Teeter's autopsy: the shot-putter had been given a cocktail not of poisons but of drugs designed to radically raise his blood pressure and heart rate, which had resulted in a haemorrhage of his pulmonary artery, hence the bloody foam that Knight had seen on his lips.

In the same story, Pope had got an inside scoop from Mike Lancer explaining how Farrell must have isolated a flaw in the Olympics' IT system, which had allowed her a gateway into the Games' server and the scoreboard set-up.

Lancer said the flaw had been isolated and fixed and all volunteers were being doubly scrutinised. Lancer also revealed that security cameras had caught a woman wearing a Games Master uniform handing Teeter a bottle of water shortly before the Parade of Athletes but she'd been wearing one of the hats given to volunteers, which had hidden her face.

'Please, Knight,' Pope pleaded. 'I need something here.'

'You know more than me,' he replied, watching as the Panamanian in third place made an over-rotation on her last dive, costing her critical points.

Then the South Korean athlete in first place faltered. Her jump lacked snap and it affected the entire trajectory of her dive, resulting in a mediocre score.

The door was wide open for Pierce now, Knight thought, growing excited. He could not take his gaze off the American doctor as she began to climb to the top of the diving tower for her fifth and final dive.

Pope poked him in the arm and said, 'Someone told me Inspector Pottersfield is your sister-in-law. You have to know things that I don't.'

'Elaine does not talk to me unless she absolutely has to,' Knight said, lowering his binoculars.

'Why's that?' Pope asked, sceptically.

'Because she thinks I'm responsible for my wife's death.'

Chapter 52

KNIGHT WATCHED PIERCE reach the three-storey-high platform, and then he glanced over at Pope to find that the reporter was looking shocked.

'Were you? Responsible?' she asked.

Knight sighed. 'Kate had problems during the pregnancy, but wanted the delivery to be natural and at home. I knew the risks – we both knew the risks – but I deferred to her. If she'd been in hospital, she would have lived. I'll wrestle with that for the rest of my life because, apart from my own feelings of loss and remorse, Elaine Pottersfield won't let me forget it.'

Knight's admission confused and saddened Pope. 'Anyone ever tell you that you're a complicated guy?'

He did not reply. He was focused on Pierce, praying that she'd pull it off. He'd never been a huge sports fan, but this felt . . . well, monumental for some reason. Here she was, thirty-eight, a widow and a mother of three about to make her fifth and final dive, the most difficult in her repertoire.

At stake: Olympic gold.

But Pierce looked cool as she settled and then took two quick strides to the edge of the platform. She leaped out and up into the pike position. She flipped back towards the platform in a gainer, twisted, and then somersaulted twice more before knifing into the water.

The crowd exploded. Pierce's son and daughters began dancing and hugging each other.

'She did it!' Knight cried and felt tears in his eyes and then confusion: why was he getting so emotional about this?

He couldn't answer the question, but he had goose bumps when Pierce ran to her children amid applause that turned deafening when the scores went up, confirming her gold-medal win.

'OK, so she won,' Pope said snippily. 'Please, Knight. Help a girl out.'

Knight had an angry look about him as he yanked out his phone. 'I've got a copy of the complete inventory of items they found at Farrell's flat and her office.'

Pope's eyes grew wide. Then she said, 'Thanks, Knight. I owe you.'

'Don't mention it.'

'It is over, then, really?' Pope said, with more than a little sadness in her voice. 'Just a manhunt from here on out. With all the beefed-up security, it would be impossible for Farrell to strike again. I mean, right?'

Knight nodded as he watched Pierce holding her children, smiling through her tears, and felt thoroughly satisfied. Some kind of balance had been achieved with the American diver's performance.

Of course, other athletes had already shown remarkable fortitude in the last four days of competition. A swimmer from Australia had come back from a shattered right leg last year to win swimming gold in the men's 400-metre freestyle race. A flyweight boxer from Niger, raised in abject poverty and subjected to long periods of malnourishment, had somehow developed a lion's heart that had allowed him to win his first two boxing matches with first-round knockouts.

But Pierce's story and her vocal defiance of Cronus seemed to echo and magnify what continued to be right with the modern Olympic Games. The doctor had shown grace under incredible pressure. She'd shaken off Teeter's death and had won. As a result the Games no longer felt as tainted. At least to Knight.

Then his mobile rang. It was Hooligan.

'What do you know that I don't, mate?' Knight asked in an upbeat voice, provoking a sneer from Pope.

'Those skin cells we found in the second letter?' Hooligan said, sounding shaken. 'For three days, I get no match. But then, through an old friend from MI5, I access a NATO database in Brussels. And I get a hit – a mind-boggling hit.'

Knight's happiness over Pierce's win subsided, and he turned away from Pope, saying, 'Tell me.'

'The DNA matches a hair sample taken in the mid-1990s as part of a drug-screening test given to people applying to be consultants to the NATO peacekeeping contingent that went to the Balkans to enforce the ceasefire.'

Knight was confused. Farrell had been in the Balkans at some point in the 1990s. But Hooligan had said his initial examination indicated that the skin cells in the second letter from Cronus belonged to a male.

'Whose DNA is it?' Knight demanded.

'Indiana Jones,' Hooligan said, sounding very disappointed. 'Indiana Fuckin' Jones.'

Chapter 53

FIVE MILES AWAY, and several hundred yards south of the Thames in Greenwich, Petra and Teagan walked under leaden skies towards the security gate of the O2 Arena, an ultramodern white-domed structure perforated by and trussed to yellow towers that held the roof in place. The O2 Arena sat at the north end of a peninsula and normally played host to concerts and larger theatrical productions. But for the Olympics it had been transformed into the gymnastics venue.

Petra and Teagan were dressed in official Games Master uniforms, and carried official credentials that identified them as recruited and vetted volunteers for that evening's Olympic highlight event: the women's team gymnastics final.

Teagan looked grim, focused, and determined as they walked towards the line of volunteers and concessionaires waiting to clear security. But Petra appeared uncertain, and she was walking with a hesitant gait.

'I said I was sorry,' Petra said.

Teagan said icily: 'Hardly the actions of a superior being.'

'My mind was elsewhere,' her sister replied.

'Where else could you possibly be? This is the moment we've waited for!'

Petra hesitated before complaining in a whisper: 'This isn't like the other tasks that Cronus has given us. It feels like a suicide mission. The end of two Furies.'

Teagan halted and glared at her sister. 'First the letter and now doubts?'

Petra's attitude hardened. 'What if we get caught?'

'We won't.'

'But—'

Teagan cut her off, asking archly, 'Do you honestly want me to call Cronus and say that now, at the last minute, you are leaving this to me? Do you really want to provoke him like that?'

Petra blinked and then her expression twisted towards alarm. 'No. No, I never said anything like that. Please. I'll . . . I'll do it.' She straightened and brushed her jacket with her fingers. 'A moment of doubt,' she added. 'That's all. Nothing more than that. Even superior beings entertain doubt, sister.'

'No, they don't,' said Teagan, thinking 'impetuous'

and 'lacking in attention to detail' – wasn't that how Cronus had described her younger sister?

Some of that was definitely true. Petra had just now proved it, hadn't she?

As they'd waited on a pavement near King's College, their only stop on the way to the gymnastics venue, the youngest of the Furies had forgotten to keep her gloves on when getting out the latest letter to Pope. Teagan had gone over the package with a disposable wipe, and had then held it with the wipe until she could pass the envelope to a bicycle messenger who gave them a sharp but cursory glance in their fat-women disguises.

As if in reaction to the same memory, Petra raised her chin towards Teagan. 'I know who I am, sister. I know what fate holds for me. I'm clear about that now.'

Teagan hesitated, but then gestured to Petra to lead on. Despite her sister's doubts, Teagan felt nothing but waves of certainty and pleasure. Drugging a man to death was one thing, but there was no substitute for looking the person you were about to kill in the eye, showing them your power.

It had been years since that had happened – since Bosnia, in fact. What she had done back then should have been fuel for nightmares, but it was not so for Teagan.

She often dreamed of the men and boys she'd

executed in the wake of her parents' death and the gang rape. Those bloody dreams were Teagan's favourites, true fantasies that she enjoyed reliving again and again.

Teagan smiled, thinking that the acts she would commit tonight would ensure that she'd have a new dream for years to come, something to celebrate in the dark, something to cling to when times got rough.

At last they reached the X-ray screeners. Stone-faced Gurkhas armed with automatic weapons flanked the checkpoint, and for a moment Teagan feared that Petra might baulk and retreat at the show of force.

But her sister acted like a pro and handed her identification to the guard, who ran her badge through a reader and checked her face against computer records that identified her as 'Caroline Thorson'. Those same records indicated that she was a diabetic and therefore cleared to bring an insulin kit into the venue.

The guard pointed to a grey plastic tub. 'Insulin kit and anything metal in there. Jewellery, too,' he said, pointing at the pitted silver ring she wore.

Petra smiled, tugged the ring off and set it beside the insulin kit in the tray. She walked through the metal-detectors without incident.

Teagan took off a ring identical to her sister's and

put it in the tray after her credentials checked out. 'Same ring?' the guard said.

Teagan smiled and gestured towards Petra. 'We're cousins. The rings were presents from our grandma who loved the Olympics. The poor dear passed on last year. We're wearing them in her honour to every event we work.'

'That's nice,' the guard said, and waved her through.

Chapter 54

THE ORBIT'S OBSERVATION deck revolved slowly clockwise, offering a panoramic view of the interior of the Olympic Stadium where several athletes and coaches were inspecting the track, and of the Aquatics Centre that Knight had only just left.

Standing at the deck's railing in a cooling east wind that sent clouds scudding across a leaden sky, Mike Lancer squinted at Knight and said: 'You mean the television guy?'

'And Greek antiquities curator at the British Museum.'

Jack Morgan said, 'Does Scotland Yard know about this yet?'

Knight had called Jack Morgan and had been told that he and Lancer were up on the Orbit, inspecting security on the Olympic flame. Knight had rushed over. He nodded to Jack's question and said, 'I just spoke with Elaine Pottersfield. She has squads en route to the museum and to his house.'

For several moments there was silence, and all Knight was really aware of was the smell of carbon in the air, coming from the Olympic cauldron burning on the roof above them.

'How do we know for sure that Daring has gone missing?' Jack asked.

Knight replied, 'I called his secretary before I called Elaine, and she told me that the last time anyone saw Daring was last Thursday night around ten o'clock when he left the reception for his exhibit. That was probably six hours after Selena Farrell was last seen as well.'

Lancer shook his head. 'Did you see that coming, Peter? That they could have been in on it together?'

'I didn't even consider the possibility,' Knight admitted. 'But they both served with NATO in the Balkans during the mid-1990s, they both had issues with the modern Olympic Games, and there's no denying the DNA results.'

Lancer said, 'Now that we know who they are, it's only a matter of time until they're caught.'

'Unless they manage to strike again before they're caught,' Jack said.

The LOCOG security adviser blanched, puffed out his lips, and exhaled with worry. 'Where? That's the question I keep asking myself.'

'Somewhere big,' Knight said. 'They killed during the opening ceremony because it gave them a world audience.'

Jack said, 'Okay, so what's the biggest event left?'

Lancer shrugged. 'The sprints have drawn the most interest. Millions of people applied for seats in the stadium this coming Sunday evening – the final of the men's 100-metre sprint – because of the possibility of a showdown between Zeke Shaw and Filatri Mundaho.'

'What about today or tomorrow? What's the ticket everyone wants?' Knight asked.

'Has to be the women's gymnastics, I'd think,' Jack said. 'Carries the biggest television audience in the States, anyway.'

Lancer glanced at his watch and reacted as though his stomach had just soured. 'The women's team final starts in less than an hour.'

Anxiety coiled through Knight as he said, 'If I were Cronus, and wanted to make a big statement, women's gymnastics *is* where I'd attack next.'

Lancer grimaced and started heading for the lift, saying, 'I hate to say it, but I think you may be right, Peter.'

'What's the fastest way to the gymnastics venue?' Jack demanded, hustling after the LOCOG member.

'Blackwall Tunnel,' Knight said.

'No,' Lancer said. 'Scotland Yard's got it closed during the competitions to prevent a possible car bombing. We'll go by river bus.'

Chapter 55

AFTER CHECKING IN with Petra's immediate supervisors, the sisters scouted out the seats for which she would act as usher. They were low and at the north end of the O2 Arena, just off the vault floor. Teagan left her sister at that point, and found the hospitality suite to which she'd been assigned as a waitress. She told her team leader there that she would return after a quick trip to the loo.

Petra was waiting. They took stalls next to each other.

Teagan opened the seat-cover dispenser in her stall and retrieved two slender, green CO_2 canisters and two sets of plastic tweezers that had been taped there.

She kept one and passed the other under the partition that separated the stalls. In return, Petra handed Teagan two tiny darts, scarcely as long as a bee's sting, with miniature plastic vanes glued to tiny insulin needles and stuck to a small strip of duct tape.

Next came a six-inch length of thin clear plastic tubing with miniature pipe-fitting hardware at either end. Teagan took off her ring and then screwed the male fitting into one of the silver pits on the back of the ring.

Satisfied with the connection, she unscrewed it and coiled the line back to where she'd attached the CO_2 cartridge. She taped the cartridge and coiled gas line to her forearm, and then slid on the ring.

She'd no sooner finished than Petra pushed the vial from the insulin kit under the partition. Teagan used her tweezers to grab one of the darts. She stuck the tip of its needle through the rubber gasket into the vial and the liquid it contained, drew it out, and inserted it vane first into a tiny hole on her ring opposite the gas connection.

After dipping the second tiny dart, she blew on it until the liquid dried, and then stuck it ever so carefully into the lapel of her uniform in case she needed a second shot. With utmost care, she drew down her blouse sleeve before flushing the loo and leaving the stall.

Petra appeared as Teagan washed her hands. She smiled uncertainly at her older sister, but then whispered, 'Aim twice.'

'Shoot once,' Teagan said, thinking that this felt like part of a dream already. 'Do you have your bees?'

'I do.'

Chapter 56

UNDER A SPITTING rain an unseasonal fog crept west up the Thames to meet the river bus as it sped past the Isle of Dogs, heading towards the North Greenwich peninsula and the Queen Elizabeth II Pier. The boat was packed with latecomers holding tickets to the team gymnastics finals, which were just a few minutes from starting.

Knight's attention, however, was not on the other passengers; it roved off the bow of the ferry, looking towards the brilliantly lit O2 Arena dome coming closer, feeling strongly that it could be the scene of Farrell and Daring's next strike.

Beside him, Lancer was talking insistently on his phone, explaining that he was on the way with reinforcements for the security detail, which he ordered to be on highest alert. He had already called Scotland Yard's Marine Unit and had been told that a patrol boat was anchored off the back of the arena.

'There it is,' Jack said, pointing through the mist at a large rigid inflatable craft with dual outboard engines bobbing in the water south of them as they rounded the head of the peninsula.

Five officers in black raincoats and carrying automatic weapons stood in the boat, watching them. A single officer, a woman in a dry suit, rode an ultra-quiet black jet ski that trailed the river bus into the dock.

'Those are primo counter-terror vessels, especially that sled,' Jack said in admiration. 'No chance of entry or escape by water with those suckers around.'

Security around the actual arena was just as tight. There were ten-foot-high fences around the venue with armed Gurkhas every fifty yards. The screening process was tough. There was still a long line waiting to get in. Without Lancer it would have taken them at least half an hour to clear the scanners. But he'd got them inside in less than five minutes.

'What are we looking for?' Knight asked as they heard applause from the entryway in front of them, and a woman's voice on the public address system announcing the first rotation of the women's team finals.

'Anything out of the ordinary,' Lancer said. 'Absolutely anything.'

'When was the last time dogs swept the building?' Jack asked.

'Three hours ago,' Lancer said.

'I'd bring them back,' Jack said as they emerged into the arena itself. 'Are you monitoring mobile traffic?'

'We jammed it,' Lancer said. 'We figured it was easier.'

While LOCOG's security chief gave orders over his radio to recall the canine-sniffer bomb squad, Knight and Jack scanned the arena floor, seeing teams lining up near individual pieces of gymnastics apparatus.

The Chinese were at the south end of the venue, preparing to compete on the uneven parallel bars. Beyond, the Russians were doing stretching exercises beside the balance beam. The UK contingent, which had performed remarkably well in the qualifying rounds thanks to gutsy performances by star gymnast Nessa Kemp, was arranging gear near the floor-exercise mat. At the far end of the arena, the Americans were preparing to vault. Guards, many of them Gurkhas as well, stood at their posts around the floor, facing away from the competitors so they could scan the crowd for threat with zero distraction.

Knight concluded that an attack on one of the athletes down on the floor was virtually impossible.

But what about their safety back in the locker rooms? Or on the way to and from the Olympic Village?

Would the next target even be an athlete?

Chapter 57

AT SIX-FIFTEEN that Tuesday evening, the last of the Chinese gymnasts stuck her dismount off the balance beam, landing on her feet with nary a bobble.

The crowd inside the Chinese Gymnastics Federation's luxury box high in the arena roared with delight. With one round to go, their team was winning handsomely. The Brits were a surprising second, and the Americans sat solidly in third place. The Russians had unexpectedly imploded and were trailing a distant fourth.

Amid the celebration, Teagan set her drinks tray on the bar and then dropped a pen on purpose. She squatted and in seconds had the thin gas line running beneath her wrist, up across her palm, past her little finger and attached to the back of the ring.

She stood to smile at the bartender. 'I'm going to clear glasses for a bit.'

He nodded and returned to pouring wine. As the Chinese team moved to the vaulting pit, Teagan's senses were on fire. She slipped through the crowded luxury box towards a stocky woman in a grey suit who was watching at the window.

Her name was Win Bo Lee. She was chairman of the national committee of the Chinese Gymnastics Association, or CGA. She was also, in her own way, as corrupt as Paul Teeter and Sir Denton Marshall had been. Cronus was right, Teagan thought. People like Win Bo Lee deserved exposure and death.

As she neared the woman, Teagan held her right arm low and by her waist while her left hand slipped into the pocket of her uniform coat and felt something small and bristly. When the distance between her and Win Bo Lee was less than two feet, she snapped her hand sharply upward and squeezed the right side of the ring with her little finger.

With a soft spitting noise rendered inaudible by the joyous conversations in the hospitality suite, the tiny dart flew and stuck in the back of Win Bo Lee's neck. The CGA's chairman jerked, and then cursed. She tried to reach around the back of her neck. But before she could, Teagan slapped her there, dislodging the dart, which fell to the floor. She crushed it with her shoe.

Win Bo Lee twisted around angrily and glared at Teagan, who looked deeply into her victim's eyes, savouring them, imprinting them in her memory, and then said, 'I got it.'

She crouched down before the Chinese woman could reply and acted as if she were picking something up with her left hand. She stood and showed Win Bo Lee a dead bee.

'It's summer,' Teagan said. 'Somehow they get in here.'

Win Bo Lee stared at the bee and then up at Teagan, her temper cooling, and said, 'You are quick, but not quicker than that bee. It stung me hard!'

'A thousand pardons,' Teagan said. 'Would you like some ice?'

The CGA chairman nodded as she reached around to massage her neck.

'I'll get you some,' Teagan said.

She cleared the table in front of the CGA chairman, took one last look into Win Bo Lee's eyes, and then left the glasses at the bar. Heading towards the exit with no intention of returning, Teagan was already replaying every moment of her quiet attack as if it were a slow-motion highlight on a sports reel.

Chapter 58

I AM SUPERIOR, Petra told herself as she moved parallel to the vault pit along the railing and towards the Gurkha with the thin black moustache. I am not like them. I am a weapon of vengeance, a weapon of cleansing.

She carried a stack of towels that hid her right hand when she smiled at the Gurkha with the moustache, and said, 'For the vault station.'

He nodded. It was the third time the fat woman had brought towels to the pit, so he didn't bother to go through them.

I am superior, Petra said over and over in her mind. And then, as it had as a young girl, during the rape and the killings, everything seemed to go strangely silent and slow-motion for her. In that altered state, she spotted her quarry: a slight man in a red sweat-jacket and white trousers, who was starting to pace as the first Chinese woman adjusted the springboard and prepared to vault.

Gao Ping was head coach of the Chinese women's gymnastics team and a known pacer in big competitions. Petra had seen the behaviour in several films of Ping that she'd studied. He was a demonstrative, high-energy man who liked to goad his athletes to big performances. He was also a coach who had committed repeated crimes against the Olympic ideals, thereby sealing his fate.

The assistant coach, a woman named An Wu, and no less a criminal herself, had taken a seat, her face as emotionless as Ping's was expressive. An Wu was an easier target than the ever-moving head coach. But Cronus had ordered Petra to take Ping first, and the assistant coach only if the opportunity followed.

Petra slowed in order to match her movement to Ping's pacing. She handed the towels over the rail to another Game Master, and moved at an angle to the Chinese coach, who was bent over, exhorting his tiny athlete to greatness.

The first Chinese girl took off down the runway.

Ping took two skipping steps after her, and then stopped right in front of Petra, no more than eight feet away.

She rested her hand on the rail, intent on the head coach's neck. When the Chinese girl hit the springboard, Petra fired.

Private Games

I am a superior being, she thought as the dart hit Ping.

Superior in every way.

Chapter 59

THE CHINESE COACH slapped at the back of his neck just before his athlete nailed her landing and a roar went up from the crowd. Ping winced and looked around, bewildered by what had happened. Then he shook the sting off and ran clapping towards his vaulter, who beamed and shook her clasped hands above her head.

'That little girl crushed that,' Jack said.

'Did she?' Knight said, lowering his binoculars. 'I was watching Ping.'

'The Joe Cocker of gymnastics?' Jack remarked.

Knight laughed, but then saw the Chinese coach rubbing at his neck before starting his histrionic ritual all over again as his next athlete got set to vault.

'I think Joe Cocker got stung,' Knight said, raising his binoculars again.

'By what, a bee? How can you see that from here?'

'I can't see any bee,' Knight said. 'But I saw his reaction.'

Behind them, Knight heard Lancer talking in a strained voice into his radio to the arena's internal and external security forces, fine-tuning how they were going to handle the medal ceremony.

Knight felt uneasy. He raised his binoculars and watched the Chinese coach cheer three more women through their vaults. As his last athlete took off down the runway, Ping danced like a voodoo man. Even his taciturn assistant, An Wu, got caught up in the moment. She was on her feet, hand across her mouth as the last girl twisted and somersaulted off the horse.

An Wu suddenly slapped at her neck as if she'd been stung.

Her athlete stuck her landing perfectly.

The audience erupted. The Chinese had won gold, and the UK silver, the best finish ever for a British gymnastics team. The coaches and athletes from both nations were celebrating. So were the Americans, who'd taken bronze.

Knight was aware of it all while using his binoculars to scan the raucous crowd cheering and aiming cameras above the vaulting pit. With Ping doing a high-step dance and his girls celebrating with him, the attention of virtually everyone at that end of the arena was on the victorious Chinese team.

Except for a heavyset platinum-blonde Game Master. She had her back turned to the celebration and was hurrying with an odd gait up the stairs away from the arena floor. She disappeared along the walkway, heading for the outer halls.

Knight felt suddenly short of breath. He dropped his binoculars and said to Jack and Lancer, 'There's something wrong.'

'What?' Lancer demanded.

'The Chinese coaches. I saw them both slap at their necks, as if they'd been stung. Ping and then Wu. Right after the assistant coach slapped her neck, I saw a chunky platinum-blonde female Game Master hurrying out when everyone else was focused on the Chinese, cheering that last vault.'

Jack closed one eye, as if aiming at some distant target.

Lancer pursed his lips, 'Two slaps, and an overweight usher moving to her post? Nothing more than that?'

'No. It just seemed out of synch with . . . out of synch, that's all.'

Jack asked, 'Where did the volunteer go?'

Knight pointed across the arena. 'Out the upper exit between sections 115 and 116. Fifteen seconds ago. She was moving kind of funny, too.'

Lancer picked up his radio and barked into it. 'Central, do you have a Game Master, female, platinum-blonde hair, heavyset, on camera up there in the hallways off 115?'

Several tense moments passed as Olympic workers moved the medals podium out onto the arena floor.

At last Lancer's radio squawked: 'That's a negative.'

Knight frowned. 'No, she has to be there somewhere. She just left.'

Lancer looked at him again before saying into his radio: 'Tell officers if they see a Game Master in that area, chubby female with platinum-blonde hair, she is to be detained for questioning.'

'We might want to get a medic to look at the coaches,' Knight said.

Lancer replied, 'Athletes frown on being treated by strangers, but I'll alert the Chinese medical teams at the very least. Does that cover it?'

Knight almost nodded before saying, 'Where are those security cameras being monitored?'

Lancer gestured up towards a mirror-faced box in the balcony above them.

'I'm going up there,' Knight said. 'Get me in?'

Chapter 60

PETRA FOUGHT NOT to hyperventilate as she closed the door to the middle stall in the ladies' loo just west of the high north entry to the arena. She took a deep breath and felt like screaming with the sense of power surging through her, a power that she'd long forgotten.

See? I am a superior being. I have slain monsters. I have meted vengeance. I am a Fury. And monsters don't catch Furies. Read the myths!

Shaking with adrenalin, Petra ripped off her platinum-blonde wig, revealing her ginger hair pinned against her scalp. She dug the plastic barrettes out and let her short locks fall free.

Petra reached up and grabbed hold of the outer metal edges of the seat-cover dispenser. She tugged and the entire unit came free of the wall. She set it on the seat, then reached deep into the dark cavity she'd exposed and came up with a knapsack made of dark blue rubber, a dry bag that contained a change of clothes.

She set the bag on top of the dispenser, stripped off her volunteer's uniform, and hung it on a peg on the stall door. Then she peeled off the rubber prostheses that she'd glued to her hips, belly and legs to make herself look chubby. She looked at the dry bag, thinking how much more heavy and cumbersome it would be, given their anticipated escape route, and then dropped the rubber prostheses inside the hollow wall along with the wig.

Four minutes later, the seat-cover dispenser back in place and her uniform concealed in the dry bag, Petra left the loo stall.

She washed her hands and took stock of her outfit: low blue canvas sneakers, snug white jeans, a sleeveless white cotton sweater, a simple gold necklace, and a blue linen blazer. She added a pair of designer spectacles with clear lenses and smiled. She could have been any old posh now.

The stall to Petra's immediate right opened.

'Ready?' Petra asked without looking.

'Waiting on you, sister,' Teagan said, coming to the mirror beside Petra. Her dark wig had gone, revealing her sandy hair. She was dressed in casual attire and carried a similar knapsack-style dry bag. 'Success?'

'Two,' Petra said.

Teagan tilted her head in reappraisal. 'They'll write myths about you.'

'Yes, they will,' said Petra, grinning, and together the two Furies headed for the lavatory door.

Over loudspeakers out in the hall, they heard the arena announcer say, 'Mesdames et Messieurs, Ladies and Gentlemen, take your seats. The medal ceremonies are about to begin.'

Chapter 61

KNIGHT'S ATTENTION ROAMED over various split images on the security monitors in front of him, all showing camera views of the upper hallway off the O2 building's sections 115 and 116, where fans were hurrying back into the arena.

Two women, one slender with stylish sandy hair and the other equally svelte with short ginger hair, came out of the women's lavatory and merged with pedestrian traffic returning to the inner arena. Knight considered them only briefly, still searching for a brassy, beefy blonde in a Games Master uniform.

But something about the way the redhead had walked when she left the toilet nagged at Knight, and he looked back to the feed on which he'd seen them. They were gone. Had she been limping? It had looked that way, but she was slender, not fat, and a redhead, not a blonde.

The medal ceremony began with the awarding of

the bronze medals. Knight trained his binoculars north from the security station, looking for the redhead and her companion among the fans still hurrying back to their seats.

Knight's efforts were hampered by the announcement of the silver-medal award to Great Britain. That sent the host-country crowd up on its feet, clapping, whistling and catcalling. Several lads at the north end of the arena unfurled large Union Jack flags and waved them about wildly, further obscuring Knight's view.

The flags were still waving when the Chinese team was called to the high spot on the podium. Knight temporarily abandoned the search and looked for the Chinese coaches.

Ping and Wu stood off to the side of the floor-exercise mat beside a short, stocky Chinese woman in her fifties.

'Who is she?' Knight asked one of the men manning the video station.

He looked and replied, 'Win Bo Lee. Chairman of the Chinese Gymnastics Association. Bigwig.'

Knight kept his binoculars on Ping and Wu as the Chinese national anthem began and the country's red flag started to rise. He was expecting an emotional outpouring from the Chinese head coach.

To his surprise, however, he thought Ping looked oddly sombre for a man whose team had just won its

Olympic event. Ping was looking at the ground and rubbing the back of his neck, not up at the Chinese flag as it reached the arena rafters.

Knight was about to turn his binoculars north again to look for the two women when Win Bo Lee suddenly wobbled on her feet as if she were dizzy. The assistant coach, Wu, caught the CGA chairman by the elbow and steadied her.

The older woman wiped at her nose and looked at her finger. She appeared alarmed and said something to An Wu.

But then Knight's attention caught jerky movement beside the older woman. As the last few bars of the Chinese national anthem played, Ping lurched up onto the floor-exercise mat. The victorious head coach staggered across the spring-loaded floor toward the podium, his left hand clutching his throat, and his right reaching out to his triumphant team as if they were rope and he was drowning.

The anthem ended. The Chinese girls looked down from the flag, tears flowing down their cheeks, only to see their agonised coach trip and sprawl onto the mat in front of them.

Several girls started to scream.

Even from halfway across the arena, Knight could see the blood dribbling from Ping's mouth and nose.

Chapter 62

BEFORE PARAMEDICS COULD reach the fallen coach, Win Bo Lee complained hysterically of sudden blindness before collapsing with blood seeping from her mouth, eyes, nose, and ears.

The fans began to grasp what was happening and shouts and cries of disbelief and fear pierced the arena. Many started grabbing their things and heading towards the exits.

Up in the arena's security pod, Knight knew that An Wu, the assistant coach, was in mortal danger, but he forced his attention away from the drama developing on the arena floor to watch the camera feeds showing the walkway where the two women had entered the arena. The men manning the security station were inundated with radio traffic.

One of them suddenly roared, 'We've got an explosion immediately south-east of the venue on the riverbank! River Police responding!'

Thank God no one heard the bomb inside the

arena, because more fans were now moving towards the exits and would have caused a stampede. An Wu dropped to the floor suddenly, bleeding also and adding to the building terror.

And then, right there on the nearest screen on the security console, Knight spotted the sandy blonde and the redhead leaving the north arena along with a steady flow of jittery sports fans.

Though he could not make out their faces, the redhead was definitely limping. 'It's her!' Knight shouted.

The men monitoring the security station barely glanced at him as they frantically tried to respond to questions flying at them over radios from all over the arena. Realising they were being overcome by the rapid pace of developments, Knight bolted for the door to the security pod, wrenched it open and started pushing though the shocked crowds, hoping to intercept the women.

But which way had they gone? East or west?

Knight decided they'd head for the exit closest to transportation, and therefore ran down the west hallway, searching among the stream of people coming at him until he heard Jack Morgan shout, 'Knight!'

He glanced to his right and saw Private's owner hustling out of the inner arena.

'I've got them!' Knight cried. 'Two women, a

sandy blonde and a redhead. She's limping! Call Lancer. Have him seal the perimeter.'

Jack ran with him, trying to use his phone while weaving through the crowd that was trying to leave.

'Damn it!' Jack grunted. 'They're jamming mobile traffic!'

'Then it's up to us,' Knight said and ran faster, determined that the two women would not get away.

In moments they reached the section of the north hallway he'd watched on camera. There was no way they could have got past him, Knight thought, cursing himself for not taking the east passage. But then, suddenly, he caught a glimpse of them several hundred feet ahead: two women going out through a fire-exit door.

'Got them!' Knight roared, holding his badge up and yanking out his Beretta. He shot twice into the ceiling, and bellowed, 'Everyone down!'

It was as if Moses had parted the Red Sea. Olympic fans began diving to the cement floor and trying to shield themselves from Knight and Jack who sprinted towards the fire-escape door. And that was when Knight understood.

'They're going for the river!' he cried. 'They set off a bomb as a diversion to pull the River Police away from the arena!'

Then the lights flickered and died, throwing the entire gymnastics venue into pitch darkness.

Chapter 63

KNIGHT SKIDDED TO a halt in the blackness, feeling as if he was tottering at the edge of a cliff and struck with vertigo. People were screaming everywhere around him as he dug out a penlight on the key chain he always carried. He snapped it on just as battery-powered red emergency lights started to glow.

He and Jack sprinted the last seventy feet to the fire-escape door and tried to shoulder it open. Locked. Knight shot out the lock, provoking new chaos among the terrified fans, but the door flew open when they kicked it.

They hurtled down the fire-escape stairs and found themselves above the arena's back area, which was clogged with media production trucks and other support vehicles for the venue. Red lights had gone on here as well, but Knight could not spot the pair of escaping women at first because there were so many people moving around below them, shouting, demanding to know what had happened.

Then he saw them, disappearing through an open door at the north-east end of the arena. Knight barrelled down the staircase, dodged past irate broadcast personnel, and spotted a security guard standing at the exit.

He showed his badge and gasped, 'Two women. Where did they go?'

The guard looked at him in confusion. 'What women? I was—'

Knight pushed past him and ran outside. Every light at the north end of the peninsula was dead, but thunder boomed and lightning cracked all around, giving them flashes of flickering vision.

The unseasonal fog swirled. Rain was pelting down. Knight had to throw up a forearm to shield his eyes. When the next flashes of lightning came, he peered along the nine-foot chain-link fence that separated the arena from a path along the Thames that led east and south to the river-bus pier.

The sandy-blonde Fury was crouched on the ground on the other side of the fence. The redhead had cleared the top and was climbing down.

Knight raised his gun, but it all went dark again and his penlight was no match for the night and the storm.

'I saw them,' Jack grunted.

'I did too,' Knight said.

But rather than go straight after the two women, Knight ran to the barrier where it was closest, pocketing the light and stuffing the gun into the back of his jeans. He clambered up the fence and jumped off the top.

It had been four days since he'd been run over, but Knight's sore ribs still made him hiss with pain when he landed on the paved path. To his left, still well out on the water, he spotted the next ferry coming.

Jack landed beside Knight and together they raced towards the pier, which was lit by several dim red emergency lights. They slowed less than twenty yards from the ramp that led down onto the pier itself. Two Gurkhas lay dead on the ground, their throats slit from ear to ear.

Rain drummed on the surface of the dock. The river bus's engines growled louder as it approached. But then Knight heard another engine start up.

Jack heard it too. 'They've got a boat!'

Knight vaulted the chain that was strung across the entrance to the ramp and ran down onto the dock, sweeping his gun and penlight from side to side, looking for movement.

A Metropolitan Police officer, the woman who'd been riding the jet sled, lay dead on the pier, eyes bulging, her neck at an unnatural angle. Knight ran past her to the edge of the dock, hearing an outboard motor starting to accelerate in the fog and rain.

He noticed the officer's jet sled tied to the pier, ran to it, saw the key in the ignition, jumped on, and started it while Jack grabbed the officer's radio and got on behind Knight, calling, 'This is Jack Morgan with Private. Metropolitan River Police officer dead on Queen Elizabeth II Pier. We are in pursuit of killers on the river. Repeat, we are in pursuit of killers on the river.'

Knight twisted the throttle. The sled leaped away from the pier, making almost no noise, and in seconds they were deep into the fog.

The mist was thick, reducing visibility to less than ten metres, and the water was choppy with a strong current drawn east by the ebbing tide. Radio traffic crackled on Jack's radio in response to his call.

But he did not answer and turned down the volume so they could better hear the outboard coughing somewhere ahead of them. Knight noticed a digital compass on the dashboard of the sled.

The outboard was heading north by north-east in the middle of the Thames at a slow speed, probably because of the poor visibility. Feeling confident that he could catch them now, Knight hit the throttle hard and prayed they did not hit anything. Were there buoys out here? There had to be. Across the river, he could just make out the blinking light at Trinity Buoy Wharf.

'They're heading towards the River Lea,' Knight yelled over his shoulder. 'It goes back through the Olympic Park.'

'Killers heading towards Lea river mouth,' Jack barked into the radio.

They heard sirens wailing from both banks of the Thames now, and then the outboard motor went full throttle. The fog cleared a bit and no more than one hundred metres ahead of them on the river Knight spotted the racing shadow of a bow rider with its lights extinguished, and heard its engine screaming.

Knight mashed his throttle to close the gap at the same moment he realised that the escape boat wasn't heading towards the mouth of the Lea at all; it was off by several degrees, speeding straight at the high cement retaining wall on the east side of the confluence.

'They're going to hit!' Jack yelled.

Knight let go the throttle of the jet sled a split second before the speedboat struck the wall dead on and exploded in a series of blasts that mushroomed into fireballs and flares that licked and seared through the rain and the fog.

Debris and shrapnel rained down, forcing Knight

and Jack to retreat. They never heard the quiet
sounds of three swimmers moving eastward with
the ebbing tide.

Chapter 64

Wednesday, 1 August 2012

THE STORM HAD passed and it was four in the morning by the time Knight climbed into a taxi and gave the driver his address in Chelsea.

Dazed, damp, and running on fumes, his mind nevertheless spun wildly with all that had happened since the Furies had run their boat into the river wall.

There were divers in the water within half an hour of the crash, searching for bodies, though the tidal currents were hampering their efforts.

Elaine Pottersfield had been pulled off the search of James Daring's office and apartment, and had come to the O2 Arena as part of a huge Scotland Yard team that had arrived in the wake of the triple murder.

She'd debriefed Knight, Jack and Lancer, who'd been rushing to the arena floor when the lights went out and the venue erupted in chaos. The former decathlon champion had had the presence of mind to order the perimeter of the arena sealed after he'd heard Knight's shots in the hallway, but his action had not come in time to prevent the Furies' escape.

When Lancer ordered electricians to get the lights back on they found that a simple timer-and-breaker system had been attached to the venue's main power line, and that the relay that triggered the backup generators had been disabled. Power was restored within thirty minutes, however, which enabled Knight and Pottersfield to study the security video closely while Lancer and Jack went to help screen the literally thousands of witnesses to the triple slaying.

To their dismay the video of the two Furies showed little of their faces. The women seemed to know exactly when to turn one way or another, depending on the camera angles. Knight remembered spotting them leaving the lavatory after the chubby Game Master disappeared and before the medal ceremony began, and said, 'They had to have switched disguises in there.'

He and Pottersfield went to search the loo. On the way, Knight's sister-in-law said she'd found flute music on Daring's home computer as well as essays – tirades, really – that damned the commercial and corporate aspects of the modern

Olympics. In at least two instances, the television star and museum curator had remarked that the kind of corruption and cheating that went on in the modern Olympics would have been dealt with swiftly during the old Games.

'He said the gods on Olympus would have struck them down one by one,' Pottersfield said as they entered the lavatory. 'He said their deaths would have been a "just sacrifice".'

Just sacrifice? Knight thought bitterly. Three people dead. For what?

As he and Pottersfield searched the lavatory, he wondered why Pope had not called him. She must have received another letter by now.

Twenty minutes into the search, Knight found the loose seat-cover dispensary and tugged it out of the wall. A minute later he fished out a platinum-blonde wig from inside, handed it to Pottersfield, and said, 'That's a big mistake there. There has to be DNA evidence on that.'

The inspector grudgingly slipped the wig into an evidence bag. 'Well done, Peter, but I'd rather that no one else should know about this – at least, not until I can have it analysed. And most certainly not your client, Karen Pope.'

'Not a soul,' he promised.

Indeed, around three that morning, shortly before Knight left the O2 Arena, he'd found Jack again and not mentioned the wig. Private's owner informed him, however, that a guard at the gate where all Game Master volunteers cleared security distinctly remembered the two chunky cousins who came through the scanners early, one with diabetes, both wearing identical rings.

The computer system remembered them as 'Caroline and Anita Thorson', cousins who lived north of Liverpool Street. Police officers sent to the flat found two women called Caroline and Anita Thorson, but both of them were sleeping. They claimed not to have been anywhere near the O2 Arena much less being accredited Game Masters for the Olympics. They were being brought to New Scotland Yard for further questioning, though Knight did not hold much hope for a breakthrough there. The Thorson women had been used, their identities stolen.

The taxi pulled up in front of Knight's house just before dawn with him figuring that Cronus or one of his Furies was a very sophisticated hacker and that they had to have had access at some point to the arena's electrical infrastructure.

Right?

He was so damn tired that he couldn't even answer his own question. He paid the driver and told him to wait. Knight trudged to his front door, went in, and turned on the hallway light. He heard a creaking noise and looked in the playroom. Marta yawned on the couch, dropping the blanket from her shoulders.

'I'm so sorry,' Knight said softly. 'I was at the gymnastics venue and they were jamming mobile traffic. I couldn't get through.'

Marta's hand went to her mouth. 'I saw it on the television. You were there? Did they catch them?'

'No,' he said despairingly. 'We don't even know if they're alive or not. But they've made a big mistake. If they're alive, they'll be caught.'

She yawned again, wider this time, and said, 'What mistake?'

'I can't go into it,' Knight replied. 'There's a taxi waiting for you out front. I've already paid your fare.'

Marta smiled drowsily. 'You're very kind, Mr Knight.'

'Call me Peter. When can you be back?'

'One?'

Knight nodded. Nine hours. He'd be lucky to be able to sleep for four of them before the twins awoke, but it was better than nothing.

As if she were reading his mind, Marta headed towards the door, saying, 'Isabel and Luke were both very, very tired tonight. I think they'll sleep in for you.'

Chapter 65

SHORTLY AFTER DAWN that morning, racked with a headache that felt like my skull was being axed in two, I thundered at Marta: 'What mistake?'

Her eyes exuded the same dead quality I'd first seen the night I rescued her in Bosnia. 'I don't know, Cronus,' she said. 'He wouldn't tell me.'

I looked around wildly at the other two sisters. 'What mistake?'

Teagan shook her head. 'There was no mistake. Everything went exactly according to plan. Petra even got off the second shot on Wu.'

'I did,' Petra said, looking at me with an expression that bordered on delirium. 'I was superior, Cronus. A champion. No one could have executed the task better. And on the river, we jumped off the boat well before it hit the wall and we timed the tides right on the money. We were a perfect ten all round.'

Marta nodded. 'I was back at Knight's home

almost two hours before he came in. We've won, Cronus. They'll shut down the Olympics now, for sure.'

I shook my head. 'Not even close. The corporate sponsors and the broadcasters won't let them stop until it's too late.'

But what mistake could we have made?

I look at Teagan. 'What about the factory?'

'I left it sealed tight.'

'Go and check,' I say. 'Make sure.' Then I go to a chair by the window, wondering again what error we could have made. My mind rips through dozens of possibilities, but the truth is that my information is incomplete. I can't devise countermeasures if I do not know the nature of this supposed error.

Finally I glare at Marta. 'Find out. I don't care what you have to do. Find out what the mistake is.'

Chapter 66

AT TWENTY TO noon that same Wednesday, Knight pushed Isabel in the swing at the playground inside the gardens of the Royal Hospital. Luke had figured out the swing on his own, and was pumping wildly with his feet and hands, trying to get higher and higher. Knight kept slowing him down gently.

'Daddy!' Luke yelled in frustration. 'Lukey goes up!'

'Not so up,' Knight said. 'You'll fall out and crack your head.'

'No, Daddy,' Luke grumbled.

Isabel laughed. 'Lukey already has a cracked head!'

That did not go over well. Knight had to take them off the swings and separate them, Isabel in the sandbox and Luke on the jungle gym. When they'd finally become absorbed in their play, he yawned, checked his watch – another hour and a quarter until Marta was scheduled to return – and went to the bench and his iPad, which he'd been using to track the news coverage.

The country, and indeed the entire world, was in an uproar over the slayings of Gao Ping, An Wu and Win Bo Lee. Heads of state around the globe were condemning Cronus, the Furies, and their brutal tactics. So were the athletes.

Knight clicked on a hyperlink that led him to a BBC news video. It led with reaction to the killings of the Chinese coaches, and featured parents of athletes from Spain, Russia, and the Ukraine who fretted about security and wondered whether to dash their children's dreams and insist that they leave. The Chinese had protested vigorously to the International Olympic Committee, and issued a release stating their frustration that the host nation seemed unable to provide as safe a venue for the Games as Beijing had four years before in Beijing.

But the BBC story then tried to lay blame for the security breaches. There were plenty of targets, including F7, the corporate-security firm hired to run the surveillance equipment at the venues. An F7 spokesman vigorously defended their operation, calling it 'state of the art' and run by 'the most qualified people in the business'. The BBC piece also noted that the computer-security system had been designed by representatives of Scotland Yard and MI5 and had been touted as 'impenetrable' and 'unbeatable' before the start of the Games. But neither law-enforcement organisation was responding to questions about what were obviously serious breaches.

That left the focus on 'an embattled Mike Lancer' who'd faced the cameras after several members of Parliament had called for him to step down or be fired.

'I'm not one to dodge blame when it's warranted,' Lancer said, sounding alternately angry and grief-stricken. 'These terrorists have managed to find cracks in our system that we could not see. Let me assure the public that we are doing everything in our power to plug these cracks, and I know that Scotland Yard, MI5, F7 and Private are doing everything they can to find these murderers and stop them before any other tragedy can befall what should rightly be a global celebration of youth and renewal.'

In response to the calls for Lancer's head, LOCOG chairman Marcus Morris was playing the stiff-upper-lip Brit, adamantly opposed to giving ground to Cronus and positive that Lancer and the web of UK security forces in place would prevent further attacks, find the killers, and bring them to justice.

Despite the overall gloomy tone of the piece, the video closed on something of a positive note. The scene was the Olympic Village, where shortly after dawn hundreds of athletes poured out onto the lawns and pavements. They burned candles in memory of the slain. American diver Hunter Pierce, Cameroonian sprinter Filatri Mundaho, and the girls of the Chinese gymnastics team had spoken, denouncing the murders as an 'insane, unwarranted, and direct assault on the fabric of the games'.

The piece closed with the reporter noting that police divers were continuing to probe the murky depths of the Thames near its confluence with the River Lea. They had found evidence that the speed-boat that had slammed into the river wall had contained explosives. No bodies had turned up.

'These facts do not bode well for an already shaken London Olympics,' he'd intoned, ending the story.

'Knight?'

Sun reporter Karen Pope was coming through the gate into the playground, looking anxious and depressed.

Knight frowned. 'How did you find me here?'

'Hooligan told me you like to come here with your kids,' she replied and her unease deepened. 'I tried your house first, then came here.'

'What's wrong?' Knight asked. 'Are you all right?'

'No, I'm not, actually,' the reporter said in a shaky voice as she sat down on the bench with him. Tears welled in her eyes. 'I feel like I'm being used.'

'Cronus?'

'And the Furies,' she said, wiping angrily at her tears. 'I didn't ask for it, but I have become part of their insanity, their terror. At first, you know, I admit it: I welcomed the story. Bloody brilliant for the career and all that, but now . . .'

Pope choked up and looked away.

'He's written to you again?'

She nodded and in a lost voice said: 'I feel like I've sold my soul, Knight.'

At that he saw the reporter in an entirely new light. Yes, she was abrasive and insensitive at times. But deep down she was human. She had a soul and principles; and this case tore at both. His estimation of Pope rose immeasurably.

'Don't think that way,' Knight said. 'You don't support Cronus, do you?'

'Of course not,' she sniffed.

'Then you're just doing your job: a difficult thing, but necessary. Do you have the letter with you?'

Pope shook her head. 'I dropped it off with Hooligan this morning.' She paused. 'A messenger brought it to me last night at my flat. He said two fat women met him in front of King's College and gave him the letter to deliver. They were wearing official Olympic volunteer uniforms.'

'It fits,' Knight said. 'What reason did Cronus give for killing the Chinese?'

'He claims that they were guilty of state-sponsored child enslavement.'

Cronus claimed that China routinely ignored Olympic age rules, doctoring birth certificates in order to force children into what was effectively athletic servitude. These practices were also fraud. Ping and Wu knew that sixty per cent of the Chinese women's gymnastics team was underage. So did Win Bo Lee, who Cronus claimed was the architect of the entire scheme.

'There are plenty of supporting documents,' Pope said. 'Cronus makes the case quite well. The letter says the Chinese "enslaved underage children for state glory", and that the punishment was death.'

She looked at Knight, crying again. 'I could have published it all last night. I could have called my editor and made the deadline for today's paper. But I couldn't, Knight. I just . . . They know where I live.'

'Lukey wants milk, Daddy,' Luke said.

Knight turned from the distraught reporter to find his son staring at him expectantly. Then Isabel appeared. 'I want milk too!'

'Bollocks,' Knight muttered, and then said apologetically, 'I forgot the milk, but I'll go and get some right now. This is Karen. She works for the newspaper. She's a friend of mine. She'll sit with you until I get back.'

Pope frowned. 'I don't think . . .'

'Ten minutes,' Knight said. 'Fifteen, tops.'

The reporter looked at Luke and Isabel who studied her, and said reluctantly, 'Okay.'

'I'll be right back,' Knight promised.

He ran across the playground and out through the Royal Hospital grounds towards his home in Chelsea. The one-way trip took six minutes exactly and he arrived sweating and breathing hard.

Knight put his key in the lock and was upset to find the door unlocked. Had he forgotten to secure it? It was completely unlike him, but he was operating on limited, broken sleep, wasn't he?

He stepped inside the front hallway. A floorboard creaked somewhere above him. And then a door clicked shut.

Chapter 67

KNIGHT TOOK FOUR quiet steps to the front hall closet and reached up high on a shelf for his spare Beretta.

He heard a noise like furniture moving and slid off his shoes, thinking: My room or the kids'?

Knight climbed the stairs as stealthily as a cat, looking all around. He heard another noise ahead of him. It was coming from his room. He crept down the hallway, gun up, and peered inside, seeing the desk on top of which his laptop lay shut.

He paused, listening intently. For several moments he heard nothing more.

Then the loo flushed. Thieves commonly relieve themselves in the homes of their victims. Knight had known that for years and figured he was dealing with a burglar. Stepping over the threshold into his bedroom, he aimed the pistol at the closed door. The handle twisted. Knight flipped off the safety.

The door swung open.

Marta stepped out and spotted Knight. And the gun.

Gasping, her hand flew to her chest and she screamed, 'Don't shoot!'

Knight's brows knitted, but he lowered his pistol several inches. 'Marta?'

The nanny was gasping. 'You scared me, Mr Knight! My God, my heart feels like the fireworks.'

'I'm sorry,' he said, dropping the pistol to his side. 'What are you doing here? I'm not supposed to see you for another hour.'

'I came early so you can go to work early,' Marta replied breathlessly. 'You left me the key. I came in, saw the buggy gone, and thought you'd gone to the park, so I started to clean the kitchen and then came up to do the nursery.'

'But you're up here in my bedroom,' Knight said.

'I'm sorry,' Marta replied plaintively, and then, in an embarrassed tone, she added: 'I had to pee. Badly.'

After a moment's pause in which he saw no guile on the nanny's part, he pocketed the gun. 'I apologise, Marta. I'm under stress. I overreacted.'

'It's both our faults, then,' Marta said, just before Knight's phone rang.

He snatched it up and immediately heard Isabel and Luke crying hysterically.

'Pope?' he said.

'Where are you?' the reporter demanded in a harried voice. 'You said you'd be right back, and your kids are throwing a world-class shit fit.'

'Two minutes,' he promised and hung up. He looked at Marta, who appeared worried. 'My friend,' he said. 'She's not very good with kids.'

Marta smiled. 'Then it is a very good thing I came early, yes?'

'A very good thing,' Knight said. 'But we're going to have to run.'

He sprang down the stairs and into the kitchen, seeing that the breakfast dishes had been cleaned and put away. He got milk and put it, some biscuits, and two plastic cups in a bag.

He locked the front door and together they hurried back to the park, where Luke was sitting off by himself in the grass, whacking the ground with his shovel, while Isabel knelt in the sandbox, crying and imitating an ostrich.

Pope was just standing there, out of her league, baffled about what to do.

Marta swooped in and gathered up Luke. She tickled his belly, which caused him to giggle and then to cry, 'Marta!'

Isabel heard that, stopped crying, and pulled her hair out of the sand. She spotted Knight coming towards her and broke into a grin. 'Daddy!'

Knight scooped up his daughter, brushed the

sand from her hair, and kissed her. 'Daddy's here. So is Marta.'

'I want milk!' Isabel said, pouting.

'Don't forget the biscuits,' Knight said, handing his daughter and the sack containing the milk to the concerned nanny, who brought the kids over to a picnic table and began to feed them.

'What caused the meltdown?' Knight asked Pope.

Flustered, the reporter said, 'I don't know, actually. It was just like there was a time bomb ticking that I couldn't hear until it went off.'

'That happens a lot,' Knight remarked with a laugh.

Pope studied Marta. 'The nanny been with you long?'

'Not a week yet,' Knight replied. 'But she's bloody fantastic. Best I've—'

Pope's mobile rang. She answered and listened. After several moments she cried, 'No fucking way! We'll be there in twenty minutes!'

The reporter clicked off her phone, and spoke with quiet urgency, 'That was Hooligan. He pulled a fingerprint off the package that Cronus sent me last night. He's run it and wants us at Private London ASAP.'

Chapter 68

SURROUNDED BY A four-day growth of orange beard, the grin on Hooligan's face put Knight in mind of a mad leprechaun. It didn't hurt the image when Private London's chief scientist did a jig out from behind his lab desk, and said, 'We've got a third name and, as Jack might say, it's a whopper that set off alarms. I've had two calls from The Hague in the past hour.'

'The Hague?' Knight said, confused.

'Special prosecutor for Balkan War Crimes Tribunal,' Hooligan said as Jack rushed in, looking pale and drawn. 'The print belongs to a woman wanted for genocide.'

It was all coming at Knight so fast that his mind was awhirl with disjointed thoughts. Daring and Farrell had both worked with NATO in some capacity at the end of the Balkan war, right? But war crimes? Genocide?

'Let's hear it,' Jack said.

Hooligan went to a laptop computer and gave it several commands. On a large screen at one end of the lab, a grainy black and white photograph of a young teenage girl appeared. Her hair was chopped short in a bowl cut and she wore a white, collared shirt. Knight could not tell much more about her because the photograph was so blurry.

'Her name is Andjela Brazlic,' Hooligan said. 'This picture was taken approximately seventeen years ago, according to the war-crimes prosecutor, which puts her in her late twenties now.'

'What did she do?' Knight asked, trying to match the girl's blurry face with the charge of genocide.

Hooligan gave his computer another command and the screen jumped to an overexposed snapshot of three girls wearing white shirts and dark skirts, standing with a man and a woman whose heads were out of frame. Knight recognised the bowl-cut hairdo on one and realised he'd been looking at a blow-up of this picture. Glaring sunlight obliterated the faces of the other two girls, who had longer hair and were taller. He guessed them to be fourteen and fifteen.

Hooligan cleared his throat and said, 'Andjela and her two sisters there – Senka, the oldest, and Nada, the middle girl – were indicted on charges that they participated in genocidal acts in and around the city of Srebrenica in late 1994 and early 1995, near the end of the civil war that exploded on the break-up of the former Yugoslavia. Allegedly the sisters were part of the kill squads Ratko Mladic oversaw that executed eight thousand Bosnian Muslim men and boys.'

'Jesus,' Pope said. 'What makes three young girls join a kill squad?'

'Gang rape and murder,' Hooligan replied. 'According to the special prosecutor, not long after this photograph was taken in April 1994 Andjela and her sisters were raped repeatedly over the course of three days by members of a Bosnian militia that also tortured and murdered their parents in front of them.'

'That would do it,' Jack said.

Hooligan nodded grimly. 'The sisters are alleged to have executed more than one hundred Bosnian Muslims in retaliation. Some were shot. But most were struck through the skull, and post-mortem through the genitals, with a pickaxe – the same sort of weapon that was ultimately used to kill their mother and father.

'It gets worse,' Private London's chief scientist pressed on. 'The war-crimes prosecutor told me that eyewitnesses testified that the sisters took sadistic delight in killing the Bosnian boys and desecrating their bodies, so much so that the terrified mothers of Srebrenica came up with an apt nickname for them.'

'What was that?' Knight asked.

'The Furies.'

'Jesus,' Jack said. 'It's them.'

A moment of silence passed before Jack said to the reporter, 'Karen, would you excuse us for a moment? We have to discuss something that has nothing to do with this case.'

Pope hesitated, and then nodded awkwardly, saying, 'Oh, of course.'

When she'd gone, Jack looked back at Knight and Hooligan. 'I have something to tell you that's going to be tough to hear.'

'We've been fired from the Olympic security team?' Knight asked.

Jack shook his head. He looked pale. 'Far from it. No, I just left a meeting with investigators from the Air Accident Investigative Branch, the ones looking into the plane crash.'

'And?' Hooligan said.

Jack swallowed hard. 'They've found evidence of a bomb aboard the jet. There was no mechanical malfunction. Dan, Kirsty, Wendy and Suzy were all murdered.'

Chapter 69

'THIS BETTER BE good, Peter,' Elaine Pottersfield grumbled. 'I'm under insane pressure, and I'm not in much of a mood for a fine-dining experience.'

'We're both under insane pressure,' Knight shot back. 'But I have to talk to you. And I need to eat. And you need to eat. I figured why not meet here and kill three birds with one stone.'

'Here' was a restaurant near Tottenham Court Road called Hakkasan. It had been Kate's favourite Chinese restaurant in London. It was also the inspector's favourite Chinese restaurant in London.

'But this place is packed,' Pottersfield said, taking a seat with some reluctance. 'It will probably take an hour to . . .'

'I've already ordered,' Knight said. 'The dish Kate liked best.'

His sister-in-law looked down at the table. At that angle she looked every bit Kate's older sister. 'Okay,' she said at last. 'Why am I here, Peter?'

Knight gave her the rundown on the Brazlic sisters – the Furies – and their alleged war crimes. As he was finishing his summary, their dinner, a double order of Szechuan Mugyu beef, arrived.

Pottersfield waited until the waiter left before asking, 'And when were these sisters last heard of?'

'July 1995, not long after the NATO-supervised ceasefire expired,' Knight replied. 'They were supposedly apprehended by Bosnian police officers after the mother of two of their victims recognised the Furies when they tried to buy food in a local produce market. According to that same mother, the girls were taken at night to a police station in a small village south-west of Srebrenica where they were to be turned over to NATO forces who were investigating the atrocities.'

Pottersfield said, 'And what? They escaped?'

Knight nodded. 'Villagers heard automatic-weapon fire coming from inside the police station in the dead of night. They were too frightened to investigate until the following morning when the bodies of seven Bosnians, including the two police officers, were found massacred. The Brazlics have been hunted ever since, but none of them surfaced until today.'

'How did they get out of the police station?' Pottersfield asked. 'I'm assuming they'd been placed in restraints.'

'You would think so,' Knight agreed. 'But here's the other strange thing. Mladic's kill squads used, for the most part, Soviet-era full-copper-jacket ammunition. So did the Bosnian police. It was Red Army surplus and found in all their unfired weapons. But the seven Bosnian men in the station were killed by 5.56-millimetre rounds throwing a very different kind of bullet – the kind given to NATO peacekeepers, in fact.'

Pottersfield picked at her meal with chopsticks, thinking. After several bites, she said, 'So maybe one of the men who were killed that night had a NATO weapon and the sisters got hold of it and fought their way out.'

'That's one plausible scenario. Or a third party helped them, someone who was part of the NATO operation. I'm leaning towards that explanation.'

'Evidence?' she asked.

'The bullets, primarily,' Knight said. 'But also because James Daring and Selena Farrell were in the Balkans in the mid-1990s attached to that NATO mission. Daring was assigned to protect antiquities from looters. But apart from that photo I saw of Farrell holding an automatic weapon in front of a NATO field truck, her role in the operation remains a mystery to me.'

'Not for long,' Pottersfield said. 'I'll petition NATO for her files.'

'The war-crimes prosecutor is already on it,' Knight said.

The Scotland Yard inspector nodded, but her focus was far away. 'So what's your theory: that this third entity in the escape – Daring or Farrell or both – could be Cronus?'

'Perhaps,' Knight said. 'It follows, anyway.'

'In some manner,' she allowed while still managing to sound sceptical.

They ate in silence for several minutes before Pottersfield said: 'There's only one thing that bothers me about this theory of yours, Peter.'

'What's that?' Knight asked.

His sister-in-law squinted and waved her chopsticks at him. 'Let's say you're right and Cronus was the person or persons who helped the sisters escape, and let's say that Cronus managed to turn these war criminals into anarchists, Olympics haters, whatever you want to call them.

'The evidence to date reveals people who are not only brutal, but brutally effective. They managed to penetrate some of the toughest security in the world twice, kill, and escape twice.'

Knight saw where she was going: 'You're saying they're detail-orientated, they've planned to the last factor, and yet they make mistakes with these letters.'

Pottersfield nodded. 'Hair, skin, and now a fingerprint.'

'Don't forget the wig,' Knight said. 'Anything on that?'

'Not yet, though this war-crimes angle should help us if DNA samples were ever taken from the sisters.'

Knight ate a couple more bites, and then said, 'There's also a question as to whether Farrell, Daring or both of them had the wherewithal, the financial means to concoct a deadly assault on the Olympics. It has to cost money, and lots of it.'

'I thought of that too,' Pottersfield replied. 'This morning we took a look at James Daring's bank accounts and credit-card statements. That television show has made him wealthy. And his accounts show several major cash withdrawals lately. Professor Farrell, on the other hand, lives more modestly. Except for hefty purchases at expensive fashion boutiques here and in Paris, and getting her hair done at trendy salons once a month, she leads a fairly austere life.'

Knight recalled the dressing table and the high-end clothes in the professor's bedroom and tried again to make it fit with the dowdy woman he'd met at King's College. He couldn't. Was she dressing up to meet Daring? Was there something between them that Knight and his colleagues weren't aware of?

He glanced at his watch. 'I'll pay and take my leave, then. The new nanny is working overtime.'

Pottersfield looked away as he put his napkin on the table and raised his hand for the bill. 'How are they?' she asked. 'The twins?'

'They're fine,' Knight said, and then gazed sincerely at his sister-in-law. 'I know they would love to meet their Aunt Elaine. Don't you think they deserve to have a relationship with their mother's sister?'

It was as if invisible armour instantly enclosed the Scotland Yard inspector. Her posture went tight and she said, 'I'm simply not there yet. I don't know if I could bear it.'

'Their birthday's a week from Saturday.'

'Do you honestly think I could ever forget that day?' Pottersfield asked, getting up from the table.

'No, Elaine,' Knight replied. 'And neither will I. Ever. But I have hope that at some point I'll be able to forgive that day. I hope you will, too.'

Pottersfield said, 'You'll settle the bill?'

Knight nodded. She turned to leave. He called after her, 'Elaine, I'll probably be having a birthday party for them at some point. I'd like it if you came.'

Pottersfield looked over her shoulder at him, her voice raspy when she replied. 'Like I said, Peter, I don't know if I'm there yet.'

Chapter 70

IN THE TAXI on the way home to Chelsea, Knight wondered if his sister-in-law would ever forgive him. Did it matter? It did. It depressed him to think that his kids might never get to know their mother's last living relative.

Rather than sink into a mood, however, he forced his mind to other thoughts.

Selena Farrell was a *fashionista*?

It bothered him so much that he called Pope. She answered, sounding as if she was in a bad temper. They'd had an argument in Hooligan's lab earlier in the day about when and how she should deal with the war-crimes information. She'd wanted to publish immediately, but Knight and Jack had argued that she should wait to get independent corroboration from The Hague and from Scotland Yard. Neither man wanted the information attributed to Private.

Pope said, 'So did your sister-in-law corroborate the fingerprint match?'

'I think that will probably be tomorrow at the earliest,' Knight said.

'Brilliant,' the reporter said sarcastically. 'And the prosecutor at The Hague is not returning my calls. So I've got nothing for tomorrow.'

'There's something else you could be looking into,' Knight offered as the taxi pulled up in front of his home. He paid the driver and stood out on the pavement, describing the dressing table and clothes at Selena Farrell's home.

'High fashion?' Pope asked, incredulous. 'Her?'

'Exactly my reaction,' Knight said. 'Which means a lot of things, it seems to me. She had to have had sources of money outside academia. Which means she had a secret life. Find it, and you just might find her.'

'All well and good for you to say,' Pope began.

God, she irritated him. 'It's what I've got,' he snapped. 'Look, Pope, I have to tuck my kids in. I'll talk to you tomorrow.'

He hung up, feeling as though the case had consumed him the way the mythical Cronus had consumed his own children. That thought left him supremely frustrated. If it wasn't for the Olympics he'd be working full-time to find out who had killed his colleagues at Private and why. When this was over he told himself he would not stop until he solved that crime.

Knight went inside and climbed the stairs, hearing a door slide over carpet, followed by footsteps. Marta was leaving the nursery. She saw Knight, and held her index finger to her lips.

'Can I say goodnight?' he whispered.

'They're already asleep,' Marta said.

Knight glanced at his watch. It was just eight. 'How do you do that? I can never get them down before ten.'

'An old Estonian technique.'

'You'll have to teach it to me sometime,' Knight said. 'Eight a.m.?'

She nodded. 'I will be here.' Then she hesitated before moving past him and going down the stairs. Knight followed her, thinking he'd have a beer and then get to sleep early.

Marta put on her jacket and started to open the front door before looking back at him, 'Have you caught the bad people?'

'No,' Knight said. 'But I feel like we're getting awfully close.'

'That's good,' she said. 'Very, very good.'

Chapter 71

SITTING AT HER desk in the *Sun*'s newsroom later that evening, half-watching the highlights of England's remarkable victory over Ghana in the final round of group-stage football, Pope fumed yet again over the fact that she could not reveal the link between Cronus and the Furies and war crimes in the Balkans.

Even her editor, Finch, had told her that, amazing as it was, she did not have enough to publish the story; and might not have for two, maybe even three days, at least until the prosecutor in The Hague agreed to talk to her on the record.

Three days! she moaned to herself. That's Saturday. They'll never publish that kind of story on a Saturday. That means they'll wait for Sunday. Four days!

Every hard-news journalist in London was working the Cronus case now, all of them chasing Pope, trying to match or better her stories. Until today she'd been way out ahead of the curve. Now, however, she feared that the war-crime angle might leak before she could lay full claim to it in print.

And what was she to do in the meantime? Sit here? Wait for the war-crimes prosecutor to call? Wait for Scotland Yard to run the print against their database and confirm it to the world?

The situation was driving her batty. She should go home. Get some rest. But she was unnerved by the fact that Cronus knew where she lived: she felt afraid to go home. Instead, she started poring over every angle of the story, trying to figure out where she could best push it forward.

At last her thoughts turned grudgingly to Knight's advice that she should look more closely into Selena Farrell. But it had been four days since the professor's DNA had been matched to the hair found in the first letter from Cronus, and three days since MI5 and Scotland Yard had launched the manhunt for her, and there'd been nothing. She'd vanished.

Who am I to look if *they* can't find her? Pope thought before her pugnacious side asserted itself: Well, why *not* me?

The reporter chewed on her lip, thinking about Knight's revelation that Farrell was a fashion connoisseur, and then remembered the full list of evidence taken from the professor's house and office that he had sent her the day before at the Aquatics Centre. She'd looked through the list, of course, searching for the evidence of anti-Olympics sentiment, checking the essays denouncing the Games, and the recording of the flute music.

But she hadn't been looking for clothes, now had she?

Pope called up the evidence list and began scrolling. It didn't take her long to find references to cocktail dresses from Liberty of London and skirts and blouses from Alice by Temperley. Big-money frocks. Hundreds of pounds, easy.

Knight said she'd had a secret life. Maybe he was right.

Excited now, Pope began scouring her notebook, looking for a phone number for the professor's research assistant, Nina Langor. Pope had talked to the assistant several times during the past four days, but Langor had consistently claimed that she was baffled by her boss's sudden disappearance and had no idea why Farrell's DNA would have surfaced in the Cronus investigation.

The research assistant answered her phone guardedly, and sounded shocked when Pope told her about Farrell's haute-couture lifestyle.

'What?' Langor said. 'No. That's impossible. She used to make fun of fashion and hairdos. Then again, she used to wear a lot of scarves.'

'Did she have any boyfriends?' Pope asked. 'Someone to dress up for?'

Langor got defensive. 'The police asked the same thing. I'll tell you what I told them. I believe she's gay, but I don't know for sure. She's a private person.'

The assistant said she had to go, leaving Pope at eleven o'clock that Wednesday evening feeling as if she'd run multiple marathons in the past six days and was suddenly exhausted. But she forced herself to return to the evidence list and continued on, finding nothing until the very end, when she saw reference to a torn pink matchbook with the letters *CAN* on it.

She tried to imagine a pink matchbook bearing the letters *CAN*. Cancer institute? Breast cancer awareness? Wasn't pink the colour of that movement? Something else?

Stymied by her inability to make the evidence talk, Pope made a last-ditch effort around midnight, using a technique that she'd discovered quite by accident a few years before when she'd been presented with disparate facts that made no sense.

She started typing strings of words into Google to see what came up.

'PINK CAN LONDON' yielded nothing of interest. 'PINK CAN LONDON OLYMPICS' got her no further.

Then she typed: 'LONDON PINK CAN GAY
FASHION DESIGN LIBERTY ALICE'.

Google gnawed at that search query and then spat
out the results.

'Oh,' Pope said, smiling. 'So you are a lipstick
lesbian, professor.'

Chapter 72

Thursday, 2 August 2012

AT TEN THE following evening Pope turned along Carlisle Street in Soho.

It had been an insanely aggravating and fruitless day. The reporter had called the war-crimes prosecutor ten times and had been assured each time by a saccharine, infuriatingly polite secretary that he would be returning her call soon.

Worse, she'd had to follow a story in the *Mirror* that described the intense global manhunt for Selena Farrell and James Daring. Worse still, she'd had to follow a story in *The Times* about initial autopsy and toxicology reports on the dead Chinese gymnastics coaches. Holes the size of bee stings had been found in both their necks. But they had not died of anaphylactic shock. They'd succumbed to a deadly neurotoxin called *calciseptine* derived and synthesised from the venom of a black mamba snake.

A black mamba? Pope thought for the hundredth time that day. Every paper in the world was going loony over that angle, and she'd missed it.

It only made her more determined when she went through the doors of the Candy Club, submitted to a security search of her bag by a very large Maori woman, and then entered the ground-floor bar. The club was surprisingly crowded for a Thursday night, and the reporter instantly felt uncomfortable when she noticed several glamorous women watching her, evaluating her.

But Pope walked right up to them, introduced herself, and showed them a photograph of Selena Farrell. The bar staff hadn't seen her, nor had the next six women the reporter asked.

She went back to the bar then, spotting a pink matchbook that looked like the one described in the evidence list. One of the bartenders came over to her, and Pope asked what she'd recommend for a cocktail.

'Candy Nipple?' the bartender said. 'Butterscotch schnapps and Baileys?'

The reporter wrinkled her nose. 'Too sweet.'

'Pimm's, then,' said a woman on the barstool next to Pope. Petite, blonde, late thirties, and extremely attractive, she held up a highball glass with a mint sprig sticking out from the top. 'Always refreshing on a hot summer's night.'

'Perfect,' Pope replied, smiling weakly at the woman.

Pope had meant to show the picture of Farrell to the bartender, but she'd already walked away to prepare her Pimm's. Pope set the photo on the bar and turned to the woman who'd recommended the drink. She was studying the reporter in mild amusement.

'First time at the Candy Club?' the woman asked.

Pope flushed. 'Is it that obvious?'

'To the trained eye,' the woman said, a hint of lechery crossing her face as she held out a well-manicured hand. 'I'm Nell.'

'Karen Pope,' she said. 'I write for the *Sun*.'

Nell's eyebrows rose. 'I do so enjoy Page 3.'

Pope laughed nervously. 'Unfortunately, I don't.'

'Pity,' Nell said, her face falling. 'Not even a wee bit?'

'A pity, but no,' Pope replied, and then showed Nell the photograph.

Nell sighed and leaned closer to Pope to study the picture of Farrell with no make-up, and wearing a matching peasant skirt and scarf.

'No,' Nell said, with a dismissive gesture. 'I know I've never seen *her* here. She isn't exactly the type. But *you*, I must say, most definitely fit in here.'

Pope laughed again before gesturing at the picture and saying, 'Think of her in a tight cocktail dress from Liberty of London or Alice by Temperley, and her hair done by Hair by Fairy, and, well, you can't see it from this angle, but she has this tiny mole on her jaw.'

'A mole?' Nell sniffed. 'You mean with little hairs sticking out of it?'

'More like a beauty spot. Like Elizabeth Taylor used to have?'

Nell looked confused, and then she studied the photograph again.

A moment later, she gasped, 'My God – it's Syren!'

Chapter 73

Friday, 3 August 2012

KNIGHT HEARD FEET padding around at seven-thirty that morning. He opened his eyes and saw Isabel holding her Pooh Bear blanket.

'Daddy,' she said in high seriousness. 'When am I three?'

'August the eleventh,' Knight grumbled, and glanced at that picture of Kate on the moor in Scotland. 'A week from tomorrow, honey.'

'What's today?'

'Friday.'

Isabel thought about that. 'So one more Saturday and one more Friday, and then the next one?'

Knight smiled. His daughter always fascinated him with the out-of-the box way her mind worked. 'Yes,' he replied. 'Give me a kiss.'

Isabel kissed him. Then her eyes widened. 'We get presents?'

'Of course, Bella,' Knight replied. 'It will be your birthday.'

She got wildly excited, clapping her hands and dancing in a tight circle before stopping dead in her tracks. 'What presents?'

'What presents?' Luke asked from the doorway. He was yawning as he came into the room.

'I can't tell you that,' Knight said. 'It won't be a surprise.'

'Oh,' Isabel said, disappointed.

'Lukey three?' his son asked.

'Next week,' Knight assured him, and then heard the front door open. Marta. Early again. The world's first perfect nanny.

Knight put on a tracksuit bottom and a T-shirt, and carried the twins down the stairs. Marta smiled at them. 'Hungry?'

'It's my birthday two Fridays and a Saturday from now,' Isabel announced.

'And Lukey,' her brother said. 'I'm three.'

'You *will* be three,' Knight corrected.

'We'll have to plan a party then,' Marta said, as Knight set the kids down.

'A party!' Isabel cried and clapped.

Luke hooted with delight, spun in circles, and cried, 'Party! Party!'

The twins had never had a birthday party, or at least not on the exact date of their birth. That day had been so bitter-sweet that Knight had moved cake and ice-cream celebrations to a day or two later, and had kept the celebration deliberately low-key. He was torn now over how he should reply to Marta's suggestion.

Luke stopped spinning and said, 'Balloons?'

'Mr Knight?' Marta said. 'What do you think? Balloons?'

Before Knight could answer, the doorbell rang, and then rang again, and again, and again, followed by someone pounding the knocker so hard that it sounded like a mason chipping stone.

'Who the hell is that?' Knight groaned, heading towards the door. 'Can you get them breakfast, Marta?'

'Of course,' she said.

The pounding on the door knocker started again before he looked through the security peephole to see an exasperated Karen Pope on his front step.

'Karen,' he called out to her. 'I don't have time to—'

'Make time,' she barked. 'I've made a break in the case.'

Knight ran his fingers back through his sleep-ravaged hair, and then opened the door. Looking like she'd been up all night herself, Pope barged in while Marta went towards the kitchen with Luke and Isabel.

'Lukey want sausages,' Luke said.

'Sausages it is,' Marta replied as they disappeared.

'What's the break?' Knight asked Pope, heading into the living area and clearing enough toys off the couch for them to sit down.

'You were right,' the reporter said. 'Selena Farrell had a secret life.'

She told Knight that the professor had an alter ego called Syren St James, a name that she would adopt when she went to the Candy Club to pick up women. As Syren, Farrell was everything the professor was not: flamboyant, funny, promiscuous, a party girl of the highest order.

'Selena Farrell?' Knight said, shaking his head.

'Think of that part of her as Syren St James,' Pope replied. 'It helps.'

'And you know all this how?' he asked, smelling sausages frying off in the kitchen.

'From a woman named Nell who frequents the Candy Club and has had several one-night stands with Syren over the past few years. She identified her by that mole at her jawline.'

Knight remembered how he'd thought the professor would have been attractive under the right circumstances. He should have listened to his instincts.

'When was the last time she saw, uh, Syren?' he asked.

'Last Friday, late in the afternoon before the Games opened,' Pope replied. 'She came into the Candy Club dressed to kill, but blew Nell out, saying she already had a date. Later, Nell saw Syren leave with a stranger, a woman wearing a pill hat with a black lace veil that covered the upper part of her face. I'm thinking that woman could be one of the Brazlic sisters, aren't you?'

In Knight's kitchen, something fragile crashed and shattered.

Chapter 74

THE OLYMPIC VILLAGE is well past its first stirring now. Swimmers from Australia are already heading to the Aquatics Centre where the men's 1,500-metre heats will unfold. Cyclists from Spain are going to the Velodrome for a quick ride before the men's team pursuit competition later in the day. A Moldovan handball team just passed me. So did that American basketball player – that one with the name I always forget.

It's irrelevant. What matters is that we're at the end of week one and every athlete in the village is trying not to think of me and my sisters, trying not to ask themselves whether they'll be next. And yet they can't help but think of us, now can they?

As I predicted, the media has gone berserk over our story. For every weepy television tale of an athlete overcoming cancer or the death of a loved one to win a gold medal, there have been three more about the effect we are having on the games.

Tumours, they've called us. Scourges. Black stains on the Olympics.

Ha! The only tumours and black stains are those generated by the Games. I'm just exposing them for what they are.

Indeed, out walking among the Olympians like this – anonymous, earnest, and in disguise, another me – I'm feeling that, except for a few minor glitches, everything has gone remarkably according to plan. Petra and Teagan took vengeance on the Chinese and executed their escape perfectly. Marta has ingratiated herself into Knight's life and monitors his virtual world, giving me an inside view of whatever investigations have been launched and why. And earlier this morning, I retrieved the second bag of magnesium shavings, the one I hid in the Velodrome during its construction almost two years ago. Right where I left it.

The only thing that bothers me is—

My disposable mobile rings. I grimace. Petra and Teagan were given precise orders before they left on their latest assignment at midday yesterday, and those orders forbade them from calling me at all. Marta, then.

I answer and snap at her before she can speak, 'No names, and toss that phone when we're finished talking. Do you know the mistake?'

'Not exactly,' Marta says, with a note of alarm in

her voice that is quite rare and therefore instantly troubling.

'What's wrong?' I demand.

'They know,' she whispers. In the background I hear a little monster crying.

The crying and Marta's whisper hit me like stones and car bombs, setting off a raging storm in my skull that destroys my balance, and I go down on one knee for fear that I'll keel over. The light all around me seems ultraviolet except for a diesel-green halo that pulses in time with the ripping sensations in my skull.

'You all right?' a man's voice asks.

I can hear the crying on the phone, which now hangs in my hand at my side. I look up through the green halo and see a grounds worker standing a few feet from me.

'Fine,' I manage, fighting for control against a rage building in me, making me want to cut the grounds worker's head off for spite. 'I'm just a little dizzy.'

'You want me to call someone?'

'No,' I say, struggling to my feet. Though the green halo is still pulsing and the ripping goes on in my skull, the air around me is shimmering a bit less.

Walking away from the groundsman, I growl into the phone: 'Shut that goddamn kid up.'

'Believe me, if I could, I would,' Marta retorts. 'Here, I'll go outside.'

I hear a door shut and the beeping of a car horn. 'Better?'

Only a little. My stomach churns when I ask, 'What do they know?'

In a halting voice, Marta tells me that they know about the Brazlic sisters, and it all starts again: the ripping, the diesel-green halo, and the ultraviolent rage that so completely permeates me now that I feel like a cornered animal, a monster myself, ready to rip out the throat of anyone who might approach me.

There's a bench ahead on the path and I sit on it. 'How?'

'I don't know,' Marta replies, and then explains how she overheard Pope mention 'Andjela and the other Brazlic sisters', which had so shocked her that she'd dropped a glass bowl, which had shattered on the kitchen floor.

Wanting to throttle her, I say, 'Does Knight suspect?'

'Me? No,' Marta says. 'I acted embarrassed and apologetic when I told him the glass was wet. He told me not to worry about it, and to make extra sure the floor was free of glass before letting his little brats walk around.'

'Where are they now, Knight and Pope? What else do they know?'

'He left with her ten minutes ago, and said he

would not be back until late,' Marta replies. 'I don't know any more than what I've told you. But if they know about the sisters, then they know what the sisters did in Bosnia, and the war-crimes prosecutors know we are in London.'

'They probably do,' I agree at last. 'But nothing more. If they had more, they'd be tracking you by one of your current names. They'd be at our doors.'

After a moment's silence, Marta asks, 'So what do I do?'

Feeling increasingly sure that the gap between who the Furies were and who they have become is wide enough to prevent a connection, I reply, 'Stay close to those children. We may need them in the coming days.'

Chapter 75

Sunday, 5 August 2012

BY SEVEN P.M. THE intensity inside the Olympic Stadium was beyond electric, Knight thought from his position in the stands on the west side of the venue, high above the track's finish line. The Private London investigator could sense the anticipation rippling through the ninety thousand souls lucky enough to have won a ticket to see who would be the fastest man on Earth. He could also see and hear fear competing with anticipation. People were wondering whether Cronus would attack here.

The event was certainly high-profile enough. The sprint competition so far had gone down as expected. Both Shaw and Mundaho had been brilliant in the 100-metre qualifying heats the day before, each of them dominating and winning easily. But while the Jamaican was able to rest between races, the Cameroonian had been forced to run in the classifications for the 400-metres.

Mundaho had performed almost superhumanly, turning in a time of 43.22 seconds, four one-hundredths of a second off Henry Ivey's world-record performance of 43.18 at the 1996 Atlanta Games.

Two hours ago, Mundaho and Shaw had won their 100-metre semi-final heats, with the Cameroonian just two one-hundredths off Shaw's world record of 9.58 seconds. The men were getting ready to face each other in the 100-metre dash final. After that, Shaw would rest and Mundaho would have to run in the 400-metre semi-finals.

Gruelling, Knight thought as he scanned the crowd through his binoculars. Could Mundaho do it? Win the 100, 200 and 400 at a single Olympic Games?

In the end, did it matter? Would people really care after all that had happened to London 2012? Aside from the joy that Londoners had expressed earlier in the day when Mary Duckworth won the women's marathon, the past forty-eight hours had seen a dramatic ratcheting-up of the anxiety surrounding the Games. On Saturday, the *Sun* had finally published Pope's story describing the link between the killings and the wanted war-crime suspects, the Serbian Brazlic sisters. She had also detailed how both James Daring and Selena Farrell had served in the Balkans at about the same time as the Brazlics were actively executing innocent men and boys in and around the city of Srebrenica.

Farrell, it turned out, had been a volunteer UN observer assigned to NATO in the war-torn area. There were still not many details of the professor's exact duties on the mission, but Pope had discovered that Farrell had been badly hurt in some kind of vehicular accident in the summer of 1995 and had been sent home. After a short convalescence, she'd resumed her doctoral studies and gone on with her life.

The story had caused an uproar that grew when, late on Saturday evening, the body of Emanuel Flores, a Brazilian judo referee, was discovered near a rubbish skip in Docklands, several miles from the ExCel Arena where he'd been working and not on Olympic grounds. An expert in hand-to-hand combat, Flores had nevertheless been garrotted with a length of cable.

In a letter to Pope completely devoid of forensic evidence, Cronus claimed that Flores had accepted bribes to favour certain athletes in the judo competition. The documentation supported the allegations in some ways, and not others.

In reaction, broadcasters and journalists around the world were expressing uniform outrage that Cronus and his Furies seemed to be acting at will.

The media were demanding action from the British government. This morning, Uruguay, North Korea, Tanzania and New Zealand had decided to pull their teams from the final week of competition. Members of Parliament and the Greater London Authority had reacted by stridently renewing calls for Mike Lancer to resign or be fired, and for the manhunt for Daring and Farrell to be intensified.

For his part a visibly shaken Lancer had been in front of cameras all day, defending his efforts. Around noon, he had announced that he was relieving F7 of its command over the entrances to the Olympic Park, and bringing in Jack Morgan of Private to oversee the effort. Together with Scotland Yard and MI5, they decided to institute draconian measures at the venues, including secondary screenings, more identification checks, and pat-downs.

It had not been enough to calm the Games. Ten countries, including Russia, floated the idea that the Olympics should be halted until security was assured.

But in an immediate and aggressive response, a staggering number of athletes had signed a digital petition drafted and distributed by the American diver Hunter Pierce that not only condemned the murders, but also defiantly and forcefully demanded that the IOC and LOCOG not give in to the idea of suspending the games.

To their credit, Marcus Morris, London's Mayor and the Prime Minister were listening to the athletes and dismissing calls to halt the Olympics, saying that England had never bent to terrorism and wasn't about to start now.

Despite the dramatic increase in security measures, some fans had stayed away from what was supposed to be the biggest event of the games. Knight could see scattered empty seats, something that would have been considered impossible before the start of the Olympics. But then again almost everything that had happened so far would have been considered impossible before the Games.

'Bloody bastards have ruined it, Knight,' Lancer said bitterly. The security chief had come up alongside Knight as he was scanning the crowd. Like Knight, Lancer wore a radio nub in his ear tuned to the stadium's security frequency. 'No matter what happens from now on, 2012 will always be the tainted—'

The crowd around them leaped to their feet and started cheering wildly. The final competitors in the men's 100-metre dash were coming out onto the track. Shaw, the reigning Olympic champion, entered first, making little 'stutter' sprints and moving his hands like chopping tools.

Mundaho came out onto the track last and jogged in an almost sleepy lope before crouching and then hopping like a kangaroo down the track with such explosive energy that many in the crowd gasped, and Knight thought: Is that possible? Has anyone ever done that before?

'That man's a freak,' Lancer remarked. 'An absolute freak of nature.'

Chapter 76

THE OLYMPIC FLAME atop the Orbit burned without disturbance or deflection and the flags around the stadium hung flat; the wind had died to nothing – perfect conditions for a sprint race.

The radio nub in Knight's ear crackled with calls and responses between Jack, the security crew, and Lancer, who'd moved off to get a different view. Knight looked around. High atop the stadium, SAS snipers lay prone behind their rifles. A helicopter passed overhead. The war birds had been circling the park all day, and the number of armed guards around the track doubled.

Nothing bad is going to happen in here tonight, Knight told himself. An attack would be suicidal.

The sprinters went to starting blocks that relied on a state-of-the art fully automated timing – FAT – system. Each block was built around ultra-sensitive pressure plates linked to computers to catch any false starts. At the finish line and linked to those same computers was an invisible matrix of criss-crossing lasers calibrated to a thousandth of a second.

The crowd was on its feet now, straining for better views as the announcer called the sprinters to their marks. Shaw was running in lane three, and Mundaho in lane five. The Jamaican glanced at the Cameroonian pivoting in front of his blocks. Setting their running shoes into the pressure sensors, the speedsters splayed their fingertips on the track, heads bowed.

Ten seconds, Knight thought. These guys spend their whole lives preparing for ten seconds. He couldn't imagine it: the pressure, the expectations, the will and the hardship involved in becoming an Olympic champion.

'Set,' the judge called, and the sprinters raised their hips.

The gun cracked, the crowd roared, and Mundaho and Shaw were like twin panthers springing after prey. The Jamaican was stronger in the first twenty metres, uncoiling his long legs and arms sooner than the Cameroonian. But in the next forty metres, the ex-boy soldier ran as if he really did have bullets chasing him.

Mundaho caught Shaw at eighty metres, but could not pass the Jamaican.

And Shaw could not lose the Cameroonian.

Together they streaked down the track, chasing history as if the other men in the race weren't even there, and appeared to lean and blow through the finish simultaneously with a time of 9.38, two-tenths of a second better than Shaw's incredible performance at Beijing.

New Olympic Record!

New World Record!

Chapter 77

THE STADIUM ROCKED with cheers for Mundaho and Shaw.

But who had won?

Up on the big screens, the unofficial results had Shaw in first place and Mundaho in second, and yet their times were identical. Through his binoculars, Knight could see both men gasping for air, hands on their hips, looking not at each other but up at the screens replaying the race in slow motion while judges examined data from the lasers at the finish line.

Knight heard the announcer say that while there had been ties in judged Olympic events like gymnastics in the past, and a tie between two American swimmers at the Sydney 2000 Games, there had never been a tie in any track event at any modern Olympics. The announcer said that the referees would examine photos as well as take the time down to the thousandth of a second.

Knight watched referees huddling by the track, and saw the tallest of them shake his head. A moment later, the screens flashed 'Official Results' and posted Shaw and Mundaho in a dead tie, with a time of 9:382.

'I decline to run another heat,' the referee was heard saying. 'I consider that to have been the greatest foot race of all time and the timing stands. Both men share the world record. Both men win gold.'

The stadium rocked again with cheers, whistles and yells.

Through his binoculars, Knight saw Shaw gazing up at the results and then over at the referee with scepticism and irritation. But then the Jamaican's expression melted into a grin that spread wide across his face. He jogged to Mundaho, who was smiling back at him. They spoke. Then they clasped hands, raised them, and jogged towards their cheering fans, holding the flags of Jamaica and Cameroon above their heads in their free hands.

The men took their long victory lap around the stadium together, and to Knight it was as if a pleasant summer shower had come along to wash foul smoke from the air. Cronus and the Furies now seemed not as powerful a force at the London Olympics as they had been just a few minutes ago.

The sprinters running together in a grand display of sportsmanship was their way of telling the world that the modern Games were still a force to be reckoned with, still a force for good, a force that could demonstrate shared humanity in the face of Cronus's cruel assault.

Shaw said as much when he and Mundaho returned to the finish line and were interviewed by reporters. Knight saw it all up on the big screens.

'When I saw the tie, I could not believe it,' the Jamaican admitted. 'And to tell you the truth, my first response was that I felt angry. I had beaten my own record, but I had not bested everyone as I did in Beijing. But then, after all that has happened at these Games, I saw that the tie was a beautiful thing: good for sprinting, good for athletics, and good for the Olympics.'

Mundaho agreed, saying, 'I am humbled to have run with the great Zeke Shaw. It is the honour of my life to have my name mentioned in the same breath as his.'

The reporter then asked who would win the 200-metre final on Wednesday night. Neither man needed an interpreter. Both tapped their chests and said, 'Me.'

Then each of them laughed and slapped the other on the back.

Knight breathed a sigh of relief when both men

left the stadium. At least Cronus had not targeted those two.

For the next hour, as the men's 1,500-metre semi-finals and the 3,000-metre steeplechase final were run, Knight's mind wandered to his mother. Amanda had promised that she would not turn bitter and retreat into herself as she had after his father's death.

But Knight's past two conversations with Gary Boss indicated that was exactly what she was doing. She would not take his calls. She would not take anyone's calls, even those who wanted to help arrange a memorial for Denton Marshall. According to her assistant, Amanda was spending every waking hour at her table sketching designs, hundreds of them.

He'd wanted to go to see her yesterday and this morning, but Boss had urged him against coming. Boss felt this was something that Amanda needed to go through alone, at least for a few more days.

Knight's heart ached for his mother. He knew at a gut level what she was going through. He'd thought that his own grief for Kate would never end. And in a sense it never would. But through his children he'd found a way to keep going. He prayed his mother would find her own way apart from through work.

Then he thought of the twins. He was about to

call home to say goodnight when the announcer called for competitors in the men's 400-metre semi-finals.

People were on their feet again as Mundaho appeared in the tunnel from the warm-up track. The Cameroonian jogged out, as confident as he had been before the 100-metre event, moving in his characteristic loose-jointed way.

But instead of taking those explosive kangaroo hops, the Cameroonian began to skip and then to bound, his feet coming way up off the track surface and swinging forward as if he were a deer or a gazelle.

What other man can do that? Knight thought in awe. Where did the idea that he could even do that come from? The bullets flying at his back?

The Cameroonian slowed near his blocks on lane one, at the inside rear of the staggered start. Could Mundaho do it? Run a distance four times longer than what he'd just sprinted in world record time?

Evidently Zeke Shaw wanted to know as well because the Jamaican sprinter reappeared in the entry linking the practice track to the stadium and stood with three of the Gurkhas, all looking north towards the runners about to compete.

'Mark,' the official called.

Mundaho set his race shoes with their tiny metal

stubs against the blocks. He crouched and tensed when the official called: 'Set.'

The gun went off in the near-silent stadium.

The Cameroonian leaped off the blocks.

A thousandth of a second later a blinding silver-white light blasted from the blocks as they exploded and disintegrated, throwing out a low-angle wave of fire and hot jagged bits of metal that smashed into Mundaho's lower body from behind, hurling the Cameroonian off his feet and onto the track where he lay crumpled and screaming.

Part Four

MARATHON

Chapter 78

KNIGHT WAS SO shocked that he was unable to move for several seconds. Like many in the stadium he watched and listened in gut-clenched horror as Mundaho writhed on the track, sobbing and groaning in agony as he reached down to his charred and bleeding legs.

The other sprinters had stopped, looking back in shocked disbelief at the carnage in lane one. The intense metallic flame died, leaving the track where the blocks had been scorched and throwing off a burned chemical odour that reminded Knight of signal flares and tyres burning.

Paramedics raced towards the Cameroonian sprinter and several race officials who'd also been hit by the burning shrapnel.

'I want everyone involved with those starting blocks held for questioning,' Lancer bellowed over the radio, barely in control. 'Find the timing judges, referees, everyone. Hold them! All of them!'

Around Knight, fans were coming out of their initial shock, some crying, some cursing Cronus. Many began to move towards the exits while volunteers and security personnel were trying to maintain calm.

'Can you get me on the field, Jack? Mike?' Knight asked.

'That's a negative,' Jack said.

'Double that negative,' Lancer said. 'Scotland Yard has already ordered it sealed for their bomb-forensics unit.'

Knight was suddenly furious that this had happened to Mundaho and to the Olympics – the Games had been caught up in the festering recesses of a twisted mind and made to suffer for it. He did not care what Cronus was going to claim the sprinter had done. Whatever he had or had not done, Mundaho did not deserve to be lying burned on the track. He should have been blowing the rest of the sprinters away in his quest for athletic immortality. Instead, he was being lifted onto a stretcher.

The stadium around Knight began to applaud as paramedics started to wheel the Cameroonian sprinter towards a waiting ambulance. They had IVs in his arm, and had obviously given him drugs, though Knight could still see through his binoculars that the boy soldier was racked with hideous pain.

Knight heard people saying that London would have to end the Games now, and felt furious that Cronus might have won, that it all might be finished now. But then he heard a cynic in the crowd say that there was no chance the Games would be cancelled. He'd read a story in the *Financial Times* that indicated that while London 2012's corporate sponsors and the official broadcasters were publicly aghast at Cronus's actions, they were privately astounded at the twenty-four-hour coverage the Games were receiving, and the public's seemingly inexhaustible appetite for the various facets of the story.

'The ratings for these Olympics are the highest in history,' the cynic said. 'I predict: no chance they'll be cancelled.'

Knight had no time to think about any of it because Shaw, carrying the Cameroonian flag, suddenly came running out of the stadium's entryway, along with the dozen or so competitors who were still in the 400-metre competition. They ran to the rear of the ambulance, exhorting the crowd to chant 'Mundaho! Mundaho!'

The people remaining in the stadium went crazy with emotion, weeping, cheering – and screaming denouncements of Cronus and the Furies.

Despite the medical personnel around him, despite the agony ripping through his body, and

315

despite the drugs, Mundaho heard and saw what his fellow athletes and the fans were doing for him. Before the paramedics slid him into the ambulance, the Cameroonian sprinter raised his right arm and formed a fist.

Knight and everyone else in the stadium cheered the gesture. Mundaho was injured but not broken, burned but still a battle-hardened soldier. He might never run again, but his spirit and the Olympic spirit were still going strong.

Chapter 79

FEELING AS THOUGH she wanted to puke, Karen Pope swallowed antacid pills and stared uncomprehendingly at the television in the *Sun* newsroom as the medics loaded the stout-hearted Cameroonian sprinter into the back of the ambulance. She and her editor, Finch, were waiting for Cronus's latest letter to arrive. So were the Metropolitan Police detectives who'd staked out the lobby, waiting for the messenger and hoping to trace rapidly where the letter had been collected.

Pope did not want to see what Cronus had to say about Mundaho. She did not care. She went to her editor and said, 'I quit, Finchy.'

'You can't quit,' Finch shot back. 'What are you talking about? This is the story of a lifetime you're on here. Ride it, Pope. You've been bloody brilliant.'

She burst into tears. 'I don't want to ride it. I don't want to be part of killing and maiming people. This isn't why I became a journalist.'

'You aren't killing or maiming anyone,' Finch said.

'But I'm helping to!' she shouted. 'We're like the people who published the manifesto of the Unabomber over in the States when I was a kid! We're abetting murder, Finch! I'm abetting murder, and I just won't. I can't.'

'You're not abetting murder,' Finch said, softening his voice. 'And neither am I. We are chronicling the murders, the same way journalists before us chronicled the atrocities of Jack the Ripper. You're not helping Cronus, you're exposing him. That's our obligation, Pope. That's *your* obligation.'

She stared at him, feeling small and insignificant. 'Why me, Finch?'

'I dunno. Maybe we'll find out someday. I dunno.'

Pope could not argue any more. She just turned, went to her desk, sat in her seat and put her head down. Then her BlackBerry beeped, alerting her to an incoming message.

Pope exhaled, picked up the mobile and saw that the message was an e-mail with an attachment from 'Cronus'. She wanted to bash her phone into shards, but she kept hearing her editor telling her it was her duty to expose these insane people for what they were.

'Here it is, Finch,' she called tremulously across the room. 'Somebody better tell the police that there's no messenger coming.'

Finch nodded and said, 'I'll do it. You've got an hour to deadline.'

Pope hesitated. Then she got angry and opened the attachment.

Cronus had expected Mundaho to die on the track.

His letter justified the 'killing' as 'just retribution for the crime of hubris', the greatest of all the sins in the era of myth. Arrogance, vanity, in all things prideful and a challenger to the gods, these were the accusations that Cronus threw at Mundaho.

He attached copies of e-mails, texts and Facebook messages between Mundaho and his Los Angeles-based sports agent, Matthew Hitchens. According to Cronus, the discussions between the men were not about competing for greatness for the sake of greatness and for the approval of the gods, as was the case during the ancient Olympics.

Instead, Cronus depicted the correspondence as grossly focused on money and material gain, with lengthy discussions over how winning the sprint jackpot at the London Olympics could increase Mundaho's global value by several hundred million dollars over a twenty-year endorsement career.

'Mundaho put up for sale the gift that the gods gave him,' Cronus concluded. 'He saw no glory in the simple idea of being the fastest man. He saw only gain, and therefore his arrogance towards the gods shone ever more brilliantly. In effect, Mundaho thought of himself as a god, entitled to great riches and to immortality. For the crime of hubris, retribution must always be swift and certain.'

But Mundaho's not dead, Pope thought with satisfaction.

She yelled to Finch: 'Do we have a number for Mundaho's sports agent?'

Her editor thought a moment and then nodded. 'It's here in a master list we compiled for the Games.'

He gave the number to Pope, who texted a message to the sports agent: KNOW U R WITH MUNDAHO. CRONUS MAKES CLAIMS AGAINST HIM AND U. CALL ME.

Pope sent the text, put the phone down and started framing the story on her computer, all the while telling herself that she wasn't helping Cronus. She was fighting him by exposing him.

To her surprise her phone rang within five minutes. It was an audibly distraught Matthew Hitchens en route to the hospital where they'd taken Mundaho. She expressed her condolences and then hit the sports agent with Cronus's charges.

'Cronus isn't giving you the whole story,' Hitchens complained bitterly when she'd finished. 'He doesn't say why Filatri wanted that kind of money.'

'Tell me,' Pope said.

'His plan was to use the money to help children who've survived war zones, especially those who've been kidnapped and forced to fight and die as soldiers in conflicts they don't understand or believe in. We've already set up the Mundaho Foundation for Orphaned Children of War, which was supposed to help Filatri achieve his dream beyond the Olympics. I can show you the formation documents. He signed them long before Berlin, long before there was any talk of him winning three gold medals.'

Hearing that, Pope saw how she could fight back. 'So you're saying that, in addition to ruining the dreams and life of one ex-boy soldier, Cronus's acts may have destroyed the hopes and chances of war-scarred children all over the world?'

Hitchens got choked up, saying: 'I think that just about sums up this tragedy.'

Pope thought of Mundaho, squeezed her free hand into a fist, and said, 'Then that is what my story will say, Mr Hitchens.'

Chapter 80

Monday, 6 August 2012

A FORCE FIVE typhoon rampages through my brain, throwing daggers of lightning brighter than burning magnesium, and everything around me seems saturated with electric blues and reds that don't shimmer or sparkle so much as sear and bleed.

That stupid bitch. She betrayed us. And Mundaho escaped a just vengeance. I feel like annihilating every monster in London.

But I'll settle for one.

I'm more than aware that this move could upset a careful balance I've struck for more than fifteen years. If I handle this wrong, it could come back to haunt me.

The storm in my skull, however, won't let me consider these ramifications for very long. Instead, like watching a flickering old movie, I see myself stick a knife in my mother's thigh, again and again;

322

and I remember in a cascade of raw emotion how good, how right it felt to have been wronged, and then avenged.

Petra is waiting for me when I reach my home at around four in the morning. Her eyes are sunken, fearful, and red. We are alone. The other sisters have gone on to new tasks.

'Please, Cronus,' she begins. 'The fingerprint was a mistake.'

The typhoon spins furiously again in my mind, and it's as though I'm looking at her down this whirling crackling funnel.

'A mistake?' I say in a soft voice. 'Do you realise what you've done? You've called the dogs in around us. They can smell you, Andjela. They can smell your sisters. They can smell *me*. They've got a cage and gallows waiting.'

Petra's face twists up in an anger equal to my own. 'I believe in you, Cronus. I've given you my life. I killed both Chinese coaches for you. But yes, I made a mistake. One mistake!'

'Not one,' I reply in that same soft voice. 'You left your wig in the wall at the lavatory at the gymnastics venue. They've got your DNA now too. It was impetuous. You did not follow the plan.'

Petra begins to shake and to cry. 'What do you want me to do, Cronus? What can I do to make it right?'

For several moments I don't reply, but then I sigh and walk towards her with open arms. 'Nothing, sister,' I say. 'There's nothing you can do. We fight on.'

Petra hesitates. Then she comes into my arms and hugs me so fiercely that for a moment I'm unsure what to do.

But then my mind seizes on the image of an IV line stuck in my arm and connected to a plastic bag of liquids, and for a fleeting instant I consider what that image has meant to me, how it has consumed me, driven me, made me.

I am much taller than Petra. So when I return her hug, my arms fall naturally around the back of her neck and press her cheek tightly to my chest.

'Cronus,' she begins, before she feels the pressure building.

She begins to choke.

'No!' she manages in a hoarse whisper and then thrashes violently in my arms, trying to punch and kick me.

But I know all too well how dangerous Petra is, how viciously she can fight if she is given a chance; and my grip on her neck is relentless and grows tighter and stronger before I take a swift step back, and then twist my hips sharply.

The action yanks Petra off her feet and swings her through the air with such force that when I whipsaw my weight back the other way, I hear the vertebrae in her neck crack and splinter as if struck by lightning.

Chapter 81

Wednesday, 8 August 2012

SHORTLY AFTER TEN that morning, Marcus Morris shifted uncomfortably on the pavement outside the Houses of Parliament. But then he looked out forcefully at the cameras and microphones and the mob of reporters gathered around him. 'Though he remains our respected colleague, someone who worked for more than ten years to see these Games realised, Michael Lancer has been relieved of his duties for the duration of the Olympics.'

'About bloody time!' someone shouted, and then the entire mob around *Sun* reporter Karen Pope exploded, roaring questions at the chairman of the London Organising Committee like losing traders in a stock-market commodity pit.

Most of the questions were ones that Pope wanted answered as well. Would the Games go on? Or would they be suspended? If they went on, who would replace Lancer as the committee's chief of security? What about the growing number of countries withdrawing their teams from competition? Should they be listening to the athletes who steadfastly argued against stopping or interrupting the Games?

'We *are* listening to the athletes,' Morris insisted in a strong voice. 'The Olympics will go on. The Olympic ideals and spirit will survive. We will not buckle under to this pressure. Four top specialists from Scotland Yard, MI5, the SAS, and Private will oversee security for us in the final four days of the Games. I am personally heartbroken that some countries have chosen to leave. It is a tragedy for the Games and a tragedy for the athletes. For the rest, the Games go on.'

Morris followed a phalanx of Metropolitan Police officers who opened a hole in the mob and moved towards a waiting car. The vast majority of the media surged as one after the LOCOG leader, bellowing all manner of questions.

Pope did not follow them. She leaned against the wrought-iron fence that surrounded the Parliament buildings and reviewed her notes from the morning and evening before.

In a journalistic coup, she'd tracked down Elaine Pottersfield and learned that, as well as radically intensifying the manhunt for Selena Farrell and

James Daring, law-enforcement efforts were also focusing on the starting blocks that had exploded, maiming Filatri Mundaho.

Mundaho remained in a critical condition in Tower Bridge Hospital, but was said to be exhibiting a 'tremendous fighting spirit' in the wake of two emergency operations to remove the shrapnel and treat his burns.

The starting blocks were another story. Made by Stackhouse Newton and based on the company's famed 'TI008 International Best' system, the starting blocks that had exploded had been used ten times by ten different athletes in the previous days of qualifying.

The blocks had been conducted to and from the track by IOC officials, and had been set up by a crew of timing specialists who claimed to have observed no issue with the blocks before the explosion. Several of those timing specialists had actually been injured at the same time as Mundaho.

Between competitions, the blocks had been locked away in a special room below ground at the stadium. The Olympic track-and-field official who had locked the blocks away on the Saturday evening before the explosion was the same official who had unlocked the storage room late on Sunday afternoon. His name was Javier Cruz, a Panamanian, and he had been the most grievously injured of the race officials, losing an eye to the flying metal.

Scotland Yard bomb experts said the device was a block of metal machined to replicate exactly Stackhouse Newton standards. Only this block had been hollowed enough for shaved magnesium to be inserted along with a triggering device. Magnesium, an incredibly combustible material, explodes and burns with acetylene intensity.

Pottersfield said, 'The device would have killed a normal man. But Mundaho's superhuman reaction time saved his life if not his limbs.'

Pope flipped her notebook closed and reckoned she had enough material for her piece now. She thought of calling Peter Knight to find out if he could add anything to what she knew, but then she spotted a tall figure leaving the visitors' gate at the side of the Houses of Parliament, shoulders hunched forward as he hurried south on St Margaret Street in the direction opposite to that being taken by the now dissipating mob of reporters.

She glanced back at them, realised that none of them had spotted Michael Lancer, and ran after him. She caught up with Lancer as he entered Victoria Tower Gardens.

'Mr Lancer?' she said, slowing beside him. 'Karen Pope – I'm with the *Sun*.'

The former Olympics security chief sighed and looked at her with such despair that she almost didn't have the heart to question him. But she could hear Finch's voice shouting at her.

'Your firing,' she said. 'Do you think it's fair?'

Lancer hesitated, struggling inside, but then he hung his head. 'I do. I wanted the London Games to be the greatest in history and the safest in history. I know that we tried to think of every possible scenario in our preparations over the years. But the truth is that we simply did not foresee someone like Cronus, a fanatic with a small group of followers. In short, I failed. I'll be held responsible for what happened. It's my burden to bear and no one else's. And now, if you'll excuse me, I have to begin to live with that for the rest of my life.'

Chapter 82

Friday, 10 August 2012

LAST TIME I'LL have to visit this hellhole, Teagan thought five days later as she pushed a knapsack through a hole that had been clipped in a chain-link fence surrounding a condemned and contaminated factory building several miles from the Olympic Park.

She wriggled through after the knapsack, then picked it up and glanced at the inky sky. Somewhere a foghorn brayed. Dawn was not far off and she had much to do before she could leave this wretched place for ever.

The dew raised the scent of weeds as she hurried towards the dark shadow of the abandoned building, thinking how her sister Petra must be settling into her new life on Crete. Teagan had read the story about the fingerprint and had feared that Cronus would be insanely angry with her sister. Instead, his

331

reaction had been practical rather than vengeful: her sister was being sent to Greece early to prepare the house where they would live when all this was over.

Entering the building through a window she'd kicked out months before, Teagan imagined the house where Petra was: on a cliff above the Aegean, whitewashed walls dazzling against a cobalt sky, filled with all they could ever want or need.

She turned on a slim red-lensed torch, clipped it to the cap she wore, and used the soft glow to navigate through what had once been the production floor of a textile mill. Wary of loose debris, she made her way to a staircase that descended into a musty basement.

A stronger odour came to her soon enough, so eye-wateringly foul that she stopped breathing through her nose and put the knapsack up on a bench that had only three legs. Bracing her weight against the bench to stop it from rocking, she took out eight IV bags.

Teagan arranged them in their proper order, and then used a hypodermic needle to draw liquid from a vial before shooting equal amounts into four of the bags. Finished, she took the key that hung on a chain around her neck and picked up the eight IV bags, four in each hand.

When she reached the door where the stench was worse, she set the bags on the floor and slid the key into the padlock. The hasp freed with a click. She pocketed the lock and pushed the door open, knowing that if she were to breathe in through her nose now she'd surely retch.

A moan became a groan echoing up out of the darkness.

'Dinner time,' Teagan said, and closed the door behind her.

Fifteen minutes later, she left the storage room feeling confident in the steps she had taken, the work she had done. Four days from now the—

She heard a crash from above her on the old production floor. Voices laughed and jeered before another crash echoed through the abandoned factory. She froze, thinking.

Teagan had been in the factory a dozen times in the last year, and she'd never once encountered another human being inside and did not expect to. The building was contaminated with solvents, heavy metals and other carcinogens, and the exterior fence carried multiple hazardous-waste warning signs to that effect.

Her initial reaction was to go on the attack. But Cronus had been explicit. There were to be no confrontations if they could be avoided.

She switched off her torch, spun around, felt for the door of the storeroom and shut it. She groped in her pocket for the padlock, found it finally, and set the hasp through the iron rings on the door and the jamb. A bottle bounced down the staircase behind her and shattered on the basement floor. She heard footsteps coming and drunken male voices.

Teagan reached up in the darkness to snap the lock shut and felt the hasp catch before she ran a few steps and then paused, unsure. Had it locked?

A torch beam began to play back towards the staircase. She took off without hesitation this time, up on her toes the way sprinters run. She had long ago committed the layout of the factory to memory and dodged into a hall that she knew would take her to a stone stairway and a bulkhead door.

Two minutes later, she was outside. Dawn threw its first rosy fingers of light across the London sky. She heard more crashing and hooting inside the factory and decided it was probably a mob of drunken yobs bent on vandalism. She told herself that once they got a whiff of that basement they wouldn't be doing any further exploring. But as she crawled back through the hole in the fence, all Teagan could think about was the padlock, and whether it had clicked shut after all.

Chapter 83

MID-AFTERNOON THAT second Friday of the Games, the third from last day of competition, Peter Knight entered the lab at Private London and hurried gingerly to Hooligan, holding out a box wrapped in brown paper and parcel tape.

'Is this a bomb?' Knight asked, dead serious.

Private London's chief scientist tore his attention away from one of the *Sun*'s sports pages, which featured a piece on England's chances in the Olympic football final against Brazil. He looked uneasily at the package. 'What makes you think it's a bomb?'

Knight tapped a finger on the return address.

Hooligan squinted. 'Can't read that.'

'Because it's ancient Greek,' Knight said. 'It says, "Cronus".'

'Fuck.'

'Exactly,' Knight said, placing the box on the table

beside the scientist. 'Just picked it up at the front desk.'

'Hear anything inside?' Hooligan asked.

'No ticking.'

'Could be rigged digitally. Or remote-controlled.'

Knight looked queasy. 'Should we clear out? Call in the bomb squad?'

The scientist scratched at his scruffy red beard. 'That's Jack's call.'

Two minutes later, Jack was standing inside the lab, looking at the box. The American appeared exhausted. This was one of the few breaks he'd had from running security at the Olympic Park since taking over on Monday. There had been no further attacks after the Mundaho incident; and that was, in Knight's estimation, largely due to Jack's herculean efforts.

'Can you X-ray the box without blowing us up?' Jack asked.

'Can always try, right?' Hooligan said, picking up the box as if it had teeth.

The scientist took the box to a work table at the far end of the lab. He started up a portable scanner similar to those being used at the Olympic venues, set the box outside the scanner, and waited for it to warm up.

Knight watched the box as if it could seal his fate. Then he swallowed hard – suddenly wanting to leave the lab in case there actually was a bomb in it. He had two children who would be three years old tomorrow. Somehow, he felt, he still had his mother. So could he risk being in a closed room with a potentially explosive device? To get his mind off the danger, he glanced at the screen showing the news highlights and image after image of gold medal-winning athletes from all over the world taking their victory laps, waving the flags of their nations and that of Cameroon.

It had all been spontaneous, the athletes showing their respect to Mundaho and defiance of Cronus. Scores of them had taken up the Cameroonian flag, including the English football team after it won its semi-final against Germany two evenings before. The media was eating it up, selling the gesture as a universal protest against the lunatic stalking the Games.

The American diver Hunter Pierce remained at the forefront of the protest against Cronus. She had been interviewed almost every day since Mundaho's tragedy, and each time she had spoken resolutely of the athletes' solidarity in their refusal to allow the Games to be halted or interrupted.

Mundaho's condition had been upgraded to 'serious': he had third-degree burns and wounds over much of his lower body. But he was said to be alert, well aware of the protests, and taking heart from the global outpouring of support.

As encouraging as that all was, Knight still tore his attention away from the screen in Private London's lab, believing that the assault would not stop simply because of the athletes' protests. Cronus would try to attack again before the end of the Games.

Knight was sure of it. But where would he strike? And when? The relay races tomorrow afternoon? The football final between England and Brazil at Wembley Stadium on Saturday evening? The men's marathon on Sunday? Or the closing ceremony that night?

'Here we go,' Hooligan said, pushing the box received from Cronus onto a small conveyor belt that carried it through the scanner. He twisted the scanner's screen so that they all could see.

The box came into view and so did its contents.

Knight flinched.

'Jesus Christ,' Jack said. 'Are those real?'

Chapter 84

THE WOMAN'S DEATHLY-PALE hands had been severed at the wrists with a blade and a saw that had left the flesh smooth and the bones ragged and chipped.

Hooligan asked, 'Should I fingerprint her?'

'Let's leave that to Scotland Yard,' Jack said.

'No matter,' Knight said, 'I'm betting those hands belong to a war criminal.'

'Andjela Brazlic?' Jack asked.

Hooligan nodded. 'The odds are definitely there, eh?'

'Why send them to you?' Jack asked Knight.

'I don't know.'

The question continued to haunt Knight on his way home later that evening. Why him? He supposed that Cronus was sending a message with the hands. But about what? The fingerprint she'd left on the box? Was this Cronus's way of displaying his ruthlessness?

Knight called Elaine Pottersfield and told her that Hooligan was bringing the hands to Scotland Yard. He laid out his suspicions about their identity.

'If they are Andjela Brazlic's, it shows dissension in Cronus's ranks,' the inspector said.

'Or Cronus is simply saying that it's fruitless to track this particular war criminal. She made a mistake. And now she's dead.'

'That all?' Pottersfield asked.

'We're going to Kate's forest in the morning,' Knight said. 'And the party is at five-thirty.'

The silence was brief. 'I'm sorry, Peter,' she said, and hung up.

Knight reached home around ten, wondering if his sister-in-law would ever come to terms with him – or with Kate's death. It wasn't until he was standing at his front door that he allowed himself to realise that three years before, right about this time, his late wife had gone into labour.

He remembered Kate's face after her waters had broken – no fear, just sheer joy at the impending miracle. Then he recalled the ambulance taking her away. Knight opened the door of his home and went inside, as deeply confused and heartbroken as he'd been thirty-six months before.

The house smelled of chocolate, and two brightly wrapped presents sat on the table in the hallway. He grimaced, realising that he hadn't yet had the chance to go shopping for the kids. Work had been all-consuming. Or had he just let it be all-consuming so that he would not have to think about their birthday and the anniversary of their mother's death?

With no good answer to any of it, Knight examined the presents and was surprised to see that they were from his mother, the gift tags signed: 'With love, Amanda'.

He smiled and tears brimmed in his eyes; if his mother had taken the time from her isolation, grief, and bitterness to buy her grandchildren presents, then maybe she was not allowing herself to retreat as completely as she had after his father's death.

'I'll go home, then, Mr Knight,' Marta said, coming out of the kitchen. 'They are asleep. Kitchen is clean. Fudge made. Luke made an unsuccessful attempt at the big-boy loo. I bought party bags, and ordered a cake too. I can be here all day tomorrow through the party. But I will need Sunday off.'

Sunday. The men's marathon. The closing ceremony. Knight had to be available. Perhaps he could talk his mother or Boss into coming one more time.

'Sunday off, and you really don't need to be here before noon tomorrow,' Knight said. 'I usually take them to Epping Forest and High Beach Church on the morning of their birthday.'

'What's there?' Marta asked.

'My late wife and I were married at the church. Her ashes are scattered in the woods out there. She was from Waltham Abbey and the forest was one of her favourite places.'

'Oh, I'm sorry,' Marta said uncomfortably, and moved towards the door. 'Noon, then.'

'Noon sounds good,' Knight said and shut the door behind her.

He shut off the lights, checked on the kids, and went to his bedroom.

Knight sat on the edge of his bed, gazing at Kate looking out from the photo at him, and remembering in vivid detail how she'd died.

He broke down, sobbing.

Chapter 85

Saturday, 11 August 2012

'I'M THREE!' ISABEL yelled in her father's ear.

Knight jerked awake from a nightmare that featured Kate held hostage by Cronus – not the madman stalking the Olympics, but that ancient Greek figure carrying a long scythe and hungering to eat his children.

Dripping in sweat, his face contorted with dread, Knight looked in bewilderment at his daughter who now appeared upset and was stepping back from her father, holding her blanket tight against her cheek.

His senses came back to him, and he thought: She's fine! Luke's fine! It was just a horrible, horrible dream.

Knight breathed out, smiled, and said, 'Look at how big you are!'

'Three,' Isabel said, her grin returning.

'Lukey three, too!' his son announced from the doorway.

'You don't say,' Knight said as Luke bounced up onto the bed and into his arms. Isabel climbed up after him and cuddled him.

His children's smells surrounded him and calmed him and made him realise again what a lucky, lucky person he was to have them in his life, part of Kate that would live on and grow and become themselves.

'Presents?' Luke asked.

'They're not here yet,' Knight said, too quickly. 'Not until the party.'

'No, Daddy,' Isabel protested. 'That funny man bring presents yesterday. They're downstairs.'

'Mr Boss brought them?' he asked.

His son nodded grimly. 'Boss no like Lukey.'

'His loss,' Knight said. 'Go and get the presents. You can open them up here.'

That set off a stampede as both children scrambled off the bed. Twenty seconds later they were running back into the room, gasping and grinning like little fools.

'Go ahead,' Knight said.

Giggling, they tore into the wrapping and soon had the presents from Amanda open. Isabel's gift was a beautiful silver locket on a chain. They opened the locket to find a picture of Kate.

'That mummy?' Isabel asked.

Knight was genuinely touched at his mother's thoughtfulness. 'Yes – so you can take her with you everywhere,' he said in a hoarse voice.

'What this, Daddy?' Luke asked, eyeing his present suspiciously.

Knight took it, examined it, and said, 'It's a very special watch, for a very big boy. You see – it has Harry Potter, the famous wizard, on the dial, and there's your name engraved on the back.'

'Big-boy watch?' Luke asked.

'Yes,' Knight said, and then teased: 'We'll put it away until you're bigger.'

Outraged, his son shoved out his wrist. 'No! Lukey big boy! Lukey three!'

'I completely forgot,' Knight said, and put the watch on his son's wrist, pleasantly surprised that the strap was a near-perfect fit.

While Luke paraded around admiring his watch, Knight hung the locket around Isabel's neck, closed the chain clasp and oohed and aahed when she looked at herself in the mirror, the spitting image of Kate as a little girl.

He changed Luke's nappy, then bathed and fed them both before getting Isabel into a dress and his son into blue shorts and a white collared shirt. With admonitions not to get their clothes dirty, Knight set himself a record time showering, shaving and dressing. They left the house at nine, went to the garage nearby, and retrieved a Range Rover that they rarely used.

Knight drove north through the streets with Isabel and Luke in their car seats behind him, listening to the news on the radio. It was the last full day of Olympic competition with many relay-race finals to be decided that afternoon.

The announcers talked of the heavy criticism being heaped on Scotland Yard and MI5 over their inability to make any kind of a major breakthrough in the Cronus investigations. No mention was made of the war-criminal's hands though. Pottersfield had asked that it should be kept quiet for the time being.

Many athletes who were finished with the competition were already leaving. Most others, like Hunter Pierce, had vowed to remain at the Olympic Park until the end, no matter what Cronus and his Furies might try.

Knight drove to Enfield, then east and south of Waltham Abbey towards High Beach and Epping Forest.

'Lots of trees,' Isabel said when they'd entered the forest proper.

'Your mummy liked lots of trees.'

The dappled sunlight shone through the foliage that surrounded High Beach Church, which sat in a clearing not far into the woods. There were several cars parked, but Epping Forest was a popular place to walk, and Knight did not expect anyone else to be here specifically for Kate. His mother was lost in her own grief, and Kate's parents had both died young.

They went into the empty church where Knight got the children each to light a candle in their mother's memory. He lit one for Kate, and then lit five more for his colleagues who had died in the plane crash. Holding Isabel and Luke's hands, he led them from the church and out along a path that led into the woods.

A light breeze rustled the leaves. Six or seven minutes later, the vegetation thinned and they passed through a tumbledown stone wall into a sparse grove of ancient oaks growing in long untamed grass that sighed in the summer wind.

Knight stood a while looking at the scene, hugging his children to him, and struggling to control his emotions for their sake.

'Your mummy used to go to that church as a little girl, but she liked to come out here,' he told them softly. 'She said the trees were so old that this was a blessed place where she could talk to God. That's why I spread her . . .'

He choked up.

'It was a perfect choice, Peter,' a woman's emotion-drenched voice said behind them. 'This was Kate's favourite place.'

347

Knight turned, wiping tears from his eyes with his sleeve.

Holding tight to his trouser leg, Isabel asked, 'Who's that lady, Daddy?'

Knight smiled. 'That's your Aunt Elaine, darling. Mummy's older sister.'

Chapter 86

'I KNEW I couldn't make the party,' Knight's sister-in-law explained quietly on the ride back into London while the children slept in the back of the car. 'And, anyway, I thought meeting them there would make me feel better.'

They were nearing the garage where Knight kept the Range Rover.

'Did it?' Knight asked.

Pottersfield nodded and her eyes got glassy. 'It seemed right, as if I could feel her there.' She hesitated and then said, 'I'm sorry. The way I treated you. I know it was all Kate's decision to have the twins at home. I just . . .'

'No more talk of that,' Knight said, parking. 'We're beyond all that. My children are lucky to have you in their lives. *I'm* lucky to have you in my life.'

She sighed, and smiled sadly. 'Okay. Need any help?'

Knight looked over his shoulder at his sleeping

children. 'Yes. They're getting too big to carry that far by myself.'

Pottersfield took Isabel and Knight hoisted Luke, and they walked the short distance to his house. He heard the television playing inside.

'The new nanny,' he said, fishing for his keys. 'She always arrives early.'

'You don't hear that much any more.'

'It's brilliant, actually,' Knight admitted. 'She's a miracle, the only one ever to tame them. She's got them helping to clean up their room and going to sleep at a snap of her fingers.'

He opened the door and Marta appeared almost instantly. She frowned to see Luke fast asleep on her father's shoulder. 'Too much excitement, I think,' she said, took him from Knight and looked curiously at Pottersfield.

'Marta, this is Elaine,' Knight said. 'My sister-in-law.'

'Oh, hello,' Pottersfield said, studying Marta. 'Peter speaks highly of you.'

Marta laughed nervously, and bobbed her head, saying, 'Mr Knight is too kind.' She paused and asked, 'Did I see you on the television?'

'Maybe. I work at Scotland Yard.'

Marta looked ready to reply when Isabel woke up grumpily, looked at her aunt, and whined, 'I want my daddy.'

Knight took her from Pottersfield, saying, 'Daddy has to go to work for a few hours, but he'll be back in time for the party.'

Marta said, 'We'll go and get cake soon. And balloons.'

Isabel brightened and Luke woke up. Pottersfield's mobile rang.

The inspector listened closely, began nodding, and then said, 'Where are they taking her?'

She listened while Marta came and took Isabel from Knight and shepherded the children down the hall towards the kitchen, saying, 'Who wants apple juice?'

Pottersfield snapped shut her phone, looked at Knight and said, 'A constable just picked up Serena Farrell wandering incoherent, filthy, and covered in her own excrement somewhere inside the ruins of the old Beckton Gas Works. They're bringing her to St Thomas's Hospital.'

Knight glanced back over his shoulder at Marta, who held Isabel and Luke's hands tightly.

'I'll be back by five to help you put up decorations,' he promised.

'Everything will be under control by then,' she replied confidently. 'Leave everything to me, Mr Knight.'

351

Chapter 87

'ARE YOU SURE?' I demand, doing everything in my power not to scream into my mobile.

'Positive,' Marta hisses back at me. 'She was found wandering around the Beckton Gas Works, not far from the factory. Who was there last?'

First Petra and now you, Teagan, I think murderously as I glance at Marta's sister next to me behind the wheel of her car. My thoughts are boiling again. But I reply cryptically to Marta: 'Does it matter?'

'I'd go and clean that factory out if I were you,' Marta says. 'They're right behind us.'

It's true. Over the homicidal buzz I've got going in my ears, I can almost hear the baying of dogs.

What a blunder! What a colossal blunder! Farrell wasn't supposed to be freed until tomorrow morning, a diversion that would draw all police attention to her while I completed my revenge. I should have just killed Farrell when I had the chance. But no, I had to be clever. I had to pile deception upon deception upon deception. But this one has backfired on me.

My fingers go to that scar on the back of my head and the hatred ignites.

My hand has been forced. My only hope is ruthlessness.

'Take the children,' I say. 'Now. You know what to do.'

'I do,' Marta replies. 'The little darlings are already fast asleep.'

Chapter 88

THE SIGHTS, SOUNDS, and smells of St Thomas's Hospital unnerved Knight in a way he did not expect. He hadn't been back in a medical facility of any sort since Kate's body had been taken to one and it made him feel disorientated by the time he and Pottersfield reached the intensive-care unit.

'This is what she looked like when they found her,' the Metropolitan Police officer guarding the room said, showing them a picture.

Farrell was dressed as Syren St James, filthy in the extreme, and looking as dazed as a lobotomy patient. An IV line hung from one hand.

'She talking?' Pottersfield asked.

'Babbled about a body with no hands,' the officer said.

'No hands?' Knight said, glancing at Pottersfield.

'Not much of what she said made sense. But you might have a better chance now that they've given her an anti-narcotic.'

'She was on narcotics?' Pottersfield asked. 'We know that for certain?'

'Powerful doses, mixed with sedatives,' he replied.

They entered the intensive-care unit. Professor Selena Farrell lay asleep in a bed surrounded by monitoring equipment, her skin a deathly grey. Pottersfield went to her side and said, 'Professor Farrell?'

The professor's face screwed up in anger. 'Go away. Head. Hurts. Bad.' Her words were slurred and trailed off at the end.

'Professor Farrell,' Pottersfield said firmly. 'I'm Inspector Elaine Pottersfield of the Metropolitan Police. I have to speak with you. Open your eyes, please.'

Farrell's eyes blinked open and she cringed. 'Turn off lights. Migraine.'

A nurse closed the unit's curtains. Farrell opened her eyes again. She gazed around the room, saw Knight, and looked puzzled. 'What happened to me?'

'We were hoping *you* could tell *us*, professor,' Knight said.

'I don't know.'

Pottersfield said, 'Can you explain why your DNA – from your hair, to be exact – was found in one of the letters from Cronus to Karen Pope?'

The information was slow to penetrate Farrell's

Knight. 'My DNA? No, I don't remember.'

'What *do* you remember?' Knight demanded.

Farrell blinked and groaned, and then said: 'Dark
room. I'm on a bed, alone. Tied down. Can't get up.
My head is splitting open, and they won't give me
anything to stop it.'

'Who are "they"?' Knight demanded.

'Women. Different women.'

Pottersfield was beginning to look irritated. She
said, 'Selena, do you understand that your DNA
links you to seven murders in the last two weeks?'

That shocked the professor and she became more
alert. 'What? Seven . . .? I haven't killed anyone. I
never . . . What, what day is it?'

'Saturday, 11 August 2012,' Knight replied.

The professor moaned, 'No. It felt like I was only
there overnight.'

'In the dark room with women?' Pottersfield
asked.

'You don't believe me?'

'No,' Pottersfield said.

Knight said, 'Why did you fake getting sick and
flee your office when Karen Pope played the flute
music to you?'

Farrell's eyes widened. 'It made me sick, because
. . . I'd heard it before.'

James Patterson

Chapter 89

I TERMINATE THE call to Marta and look over at Teagan, feeling as if I'd like to rip her head off right now. But she's behind the wheel and an accident is out of the question at this late stage of the game.

'Turn around,' I say, struggling for calm. 'We've got to go to the factory.'

'The factory?' Teagan replies nervously. 'It's broad daylight.'

'Farrell escaped. She was picked up inside the gasworks. Knight and the Scotland Yard inspector Pottersfield is with her at the hospital right now.'

Teagan loses colour.

'How could that have happened?' I demand softly. 'She wasn't supposed to be freed until tomorrow morning. It was your responsibility to see to that, sister.'

Panic-stricken, she says, 'I should have told you, but I knew how much pressure you were under. There were drunken lads inside the factory when I

357

was there yesterday morning. I figured the smell would keep them from the room. They must have broken the lock and let her go or something. I don't know.'

'We've got to clean the place,' I say. 'Get us there. Now.'

We don't talk during the rest of the drive, or during our entry into the toxic factory grounds, or as we sneak inside the basement. I have only been here once before, so Teagan leads. We both carry rubbish bags.

The smell coming from the open storage room door is obscenely foul. But Teagan goes inside without hesitation. I glance at the iron rings on the door and the frame, unbroken, and then let my gaze travel across the floor.

The lock's in the corner, its hasp open but not busted.

I crouch, pick it up, and loop the hasp around my middle finger like a brass knuckle, hiding the lock inside my palm. Inside, Teagan is already gloved and stuffing used IV equipment into the rubbish bag.

'Let's get this done,' I say, and move towards her before squatting down to pick up a used syringe with my left hand.

Rising, feeling the urge to vengeance enfolding me like an old lover, I move the needle towards the rubbish bag as a feint before letting go with an uppercut, with the hasp leading.

Teagan never has a chance. She never sees the blow coming.

The impact crushes her larynx.

She staggers backward, choking, purple-faced, her eyes bulging right out of her head, staring at me in disbelief. The second blow breaks her nose, hurls her against the wall, and makes her understand that I am an infinitely superior being. My third strike connects with her temple and she crumples in the grime.

Chapter 90

'OF COURSE YOU'D heard that music before,' Pottersfield shot back. 'It was all over your computer. So was a program used to take control of the Olympic Stadium's electronic billboard on the night of the opening ceremony.'

'What?' the professor cried, struggling to sit upright and wincing in pain. 'No, no! Someone began sending me that music about a year ago on my phone machine and in attachments to e-mails from blind accounts. It was like I was being stalked. After a while, any time I heard it I got sick.'

'Convenient nonsense,' Pottersfield snapped. 'What about the program on your computer?'

'I don't know what program you're talking about. Someone must have put it on there – maybe whoever was sending me the music.'

Knight was incredulous. 'Did you report this cyber-stalking to anyone?'

The classics professor nodded firmly. 'Twice, as a matter of fact, at Wapping police station. But the detectives said flute music was not a crime, and I had no other proof that someone was stalking me. I said I had suspicions about who was behind the music, but they didn't want to hear any of it. They advised me to change my phone number and my e-mail address, which I did. It stopped. And the headaches stopped, too – until you played the music again in my office.'

Knight squinted, trying to make sense of this explanation. Was it possible that Farrell had been set up as a diversion of some sort? Why hadn't she just been killed?

Pottersfield must have been thinking along the same lines because she asked, 'Who did you think was behind the music?'

Farrell gave a little shrug. 'Well, I've only known one person in my life who plays a Pan flute.'

Knight and Pottersfield said nothing.

'Jim Daring,' the professor said. 'You know, the guy at the British Museum? The one who has the television show?'

That changed things, Knight thought, remembering how Daring had spoken highly of Farrell and repeatedly told him and Pope to go and see her. Was it all part of an attempt to frame her?

Pottersfield still sounded sharply sceptical. 'How

do you know he played a Pan flute and why ever would he use the music to harass you?'

'He had a Pan flute in the Balkans in the 1990s. He used to play it for me.'

'And?' Knight said.

Farrell looked uncomfortable. 'He, Daring, was interested in me romantically. I told him I wasn't interested, and he got angry and then obsessed. He stalked me back then. I reported him, too. In the end it didn't matter. I was injured in a truck accident and airlifted out of Sarajevo. I haven't seen him personally since.'

'Not once in how many years?' Knight asked. 'Sixteen? Seventeen?'

'And yet you suspected him?' Pottersfield said.

The professor's expression turned stony. 'I had no one else to suspect.'

'I imagine not,' the police inspector said. 'Because he's missing, too. Daring, I mean.'

The confusion returned to Farrell's face. 'What?'

Knight said, 'You claim you were held in a dark room and tended by women. How did you get out?'

The question threw Farrell for several moments, before she said, 'Boys, but I'm not . . . No, I definitely remember I heard boys' voices, and then I passed out again. When I woke up I could move my arms and legs. So I got up and found a door and . . .' She hesitated and looked off into the distance. 'I think I was in some kind of old factory. There were brick walls.'

Pottersfield said, 'You told the officer about a dead body without hands.'

There was fear on the professor's face as she looked back and forth between Knight and Pottersfield. 'There were flies on her. Hundreds.'

'Where?'

'I don't know,' Farrell said, grimacing and rubbing at her head. 'Somewhere in that factory, I think. I was dizzy. I fell a lot. I couldn't think straight at all.'

After a long pause, Pottersfield seemed to come to some sort of conclusion. She pulled out her mobile, got up, and took several steps away from Farrell's hospital bed. A moment later she said, 'It's Pottersfield. You're looking for an abandoned factory of some sort near the Beckton gasworks. Brick walls. There could be a body in there with no hands. Maybe more.'

In the meantime, Knight thought of the reporting that Karen Pope had done on Farrell, and asked, 'How did you get into that room in the factory?'

The professor shook her head. 'I don't remember.'

'What's the last thing you *do* remember?' Pottersfield said, shutting her phone.

Farrell blinked, then tensed up and replied, 'I can't say.'

Knight said, 'Would Syren St James know?'

The name clearly confused the professor, who asked softly, 'Who?'

'Your alter ego among the elite lesbians of London,' Pottersfield said.

'I don't know what you're—'

'—Everyone in London knows about Syren St James,' Knight said, cutting her off. 'She's been in all the papers.'

The professor looked crushed. 'What? How?'

'Karen Pope,' Knight replied. 'She found out about your secret life and wrote about it.'

Farrell cried weakly, 'Why would she do that?'

'Because the DNA linked you to the killings,' Pottersfield said. 'It still does. The DNA says that you're involved somehow with Cronus and his Furies.'

Farrell went hysterical, shouting: 'I am not Cronus! I am not a Fury! I've had another life, but that's no one's business but my own. I've never had anything to do with any killings!'

The attending nurse burst into the room and ordered Knight and Pottersfield out.

'One more minute,' Pottersfield insisted. 'You were in the Candy Club the last time you were seen, two weeks ago last night, on Friday, 27 July.'

That seemed to puzzle the professor.

'Your friend Nell said she saw you there,' Knight said. 'She told Pope you were with a woman wearing a pill-box hat with a veil that hid her face.'

Farrell grasped at the memory, and then nodded slowly. 'Yes, I went with her to her car. She had wine in the car and poured me some and . . .' She gazed at Pottersfield. 'She drugged me.'

'Who is *she*?' Pottersfield demanded.

Farrell, embarrassed, said, 'Her real name? I couldn't tell you. I assume she was like me, operating under an alias. But she told me to call her Marta. She said she was from Estonia.'

Chapter 91

VIOLENT THUNDERSTORMS STRUCK London late that Saturday afternoon.

Lightning brought rain that pelted off the windscreen as Pottersfield's unmarked police car sped towards Chelsea, its siren wailing. The inspector kept glancing furiously at Knight who looked as if he was fighting a ghost as he punched in Marta's mobile number yet again.

'Answer,' he kept saying. 'Answer, you bitch.'

Pottersfield shouted: 'How could you not have checked her out, Peter?'

'I *did* check her out, Elaine!' Knight shouted back. 'You did, too! She was just so perfect for what I needed.'

They screeched to a halt in front of Knight's place where several other police cars were already parked, their lights flashing. Despite the rain, a crowd was gathering. Uniformed officers were already starting to put up barriers.

Knight leaped from Pottersfield's vehicle, feeling as if he were tottering on the edge of a dark and unfathomable abyss.

Bella? Little Lukey? It was their birthday.

Inspector Billy Casper met Knight at the door, his expression sombre. 'I'm sorry, Peter. We got here too late.'

'No,' he cried, rushing inside. 'No.'

Everywhere Knight looked he saw the things that surrounded his children: toys, baby powder, and packages of balloons, streamers and candles. He walked numbly past it all and into the kitchen. Luke's cereal bowl from breakfast still had milk in it. Isabel's blanket lay on the floor beside her high chair.

Knight picked it up, thinking that Bella must be lost without it. The enormity of his predicament suddenly threatened to crush him. But he refused to collapse, and fought back in the only way he knew how: he kept moving.

He found Pottersfield and said, 'Check her flat. Her address is on her C.V. And her prints have to be everywhere in here. Can you track her mobile number?'

'If she's got it turned on,' Pottersfield said. 'In the meantime, call your friend Pope, and I'll get to the media people I know. We'll get the twins' faces everywhere, Peter. Someone will have seen them.'

Knight began to nod, but then said, 'What if that's what they want?'

'What?' Pottersfield asked. 'Why?'

'A sideshow,' he said. 'A diversion. Think about it. If you put their faces everywhere and tell the public that they've been kidnapped by a woman believed to be an associate of Cronus, law-enforcement manpower and media attention go to Isabel and Luke, leaving the Olympics open to a final attack.'

'We've got to do something, Peter.'

Knight couldn't believe he was saying it, but he replied, 'We can wait them out for a few hours at least, Elaine. See if they get nervous. See if they call. If they don't by, say, eight, then by all means, put their faces everywhere.'

Before Pottersfield could reply, Knight pulled out his mobile and punched in Hooligan's number.

Knight heard cheering in the background and Hooligan crowed: 'Did you catch that, Peter? It's 1-1. We're tied!'

'Come to my house,' Knight said. 'Now.'

'Now?' Hooligan cried, sounding a little drunk. 'Have you gone crazy? This is for the bloody gold medal and I've got midfield seats.'

'Cronus has my kids,' Knight said.

Silence, then: 'No! Fuck. I'll be right there, Peter. Right there.'

Knight hung up. Elaine held out her hand for his mobile. 'I'll need it for a few minutes while we put on a trace.'

He handed her the phone and went upstairs. He got Kate's picture and brought it with him into the nursery as thunder shook the house. He sat on the couch, looked at the empty cots and the wallpaper that Kate had picked out and wondered if he had been destined for tragedy and loss.

Then he noticed the bottle of children's liquid antihistamine on the changing table. He set Kate's picture down and went over, noticing that the bottle was almost empty. At that he felt duped and enraged. Marta had been drugging his kids right under his nose.

Pottersfield came in. She glanced at the photograph of Kate on the couch, and then handed Knight his phone. 'You're now linked to our system. Any call coming in to your number we should be able to trace. And I just got an alert. We found two bodies in a condemned factory contaminated with hazardous waste not far from the gasworks. Both women in their thirties. One was beaten to death within the last few hours – no ID. The other died earlier this week and was handless. We're assuming it's Andjela Brazlic and her older sister, Nada.'

'Two Furies gone. It's just Marta and Cronus now,' Knight said dully, putting down the children's cold-medicine bottle. 'Do you think Daring could be Cronus? After what Farrell told us. The stalking in the Balkans? The flute?'

'I don't know.'

Knight suddenly felt gripped by doubt, intense and claustrophobic. 'Does it matter where I am when a call comes in?'

'It shouldn't,' Pottersfield replied.

He set Kate's photograph down on the changing table and said, 'I can't just sit here, Elaine. I feel like I have to move. I'm going to take a walk. Is that okay?'

'Just keep your mobile on.'

'Tell Hooligan to call me when he gets here. And Jack Morgan should be notified. They're at the stadium for the relays.'

She nodded and said, 'We'll find them.'

'I know,' he said with wavering conviction.

Knight put on his raincoat and left by the rear door in case the media were already camped outside. He walked down the alley, trying to decide whether to wander aimlessly or to get the car and drive back to High Beach Church to pray. But then he understood that he really had just one place to go, and only one person he wanted to see.

Knight altered direction and trudged through the rainy city, passing pubs and hearing cheering coming from inside. It sounded as though England was winning football gold while he was losing everything that ever mattered to him.

His hair and his trouser legs were soaking wet when he reached the door on Milner Street and rang the bell and pounded the knocker while looking up at the security camera.

The door opened, revealing Boss. 'She can't be seen,' he said sharply.

'Get out of my way, little man,' Knight said in a tone so threatening that his mother's assistant stood aside without further protest.

Knight opened the door of his mother's studio without knocking. Amanda was hunched over her design table, cutting fabric. A dozen or more original new creations hung on mannequins around the room.

His mother looked up icily. 'Haven't I made it abundantly clear that I wish to be left alone, Peter?'

Walking towards her, Knight said, 'Mother—'

But she cut him off: 'Leave me alone, Peter. What in God's name are you doing here? It's your children's birthday. You should be with them.'

It was the final straw. Knight felt dizzy and then blacked out.

Chapter 92

KAREN POPE HURRIED through the drizzling rain and the dimming light towards Knight's house in Chelsea. She'd been tipped off by the *Sun*'s police reporter that something big was going on at the Private investigator's home, and she'd gone there immediately, dialling Knight's number constantly on the way.

But Pope kept getting an odd beeping noise and then a voice saying that his number was 'experiencing network difficulties'. She could see the police barrier ahead and . . .

'Oi, Peter call you in too, then?' Hooligan asked, trotting up beside her. His eyes were red and his breath smelled of cigarettes, garlic and beer. 'I came from the bloody gold-medal game. I missed the winning goal!'

'Missed it for what?' she demanded. 'Why are the police here?'

He told her and Pope felt like crying. 'Why? Why his kids?'

It was the same thing she asked Pottersfield when they got inside.

'Peter believes that it's a diversionary tactic,' the inspector said.

Hooligan could not hide the slight slur in his voice, saying, 'Maybe. I mean this Marta was here for the past fortnight, right?'

'Give or take, I think,' Pope said.

'Right, so I'm asking myself why?' Hooligan replied. 'And I'm thinking Cronus sends her in as a spy. He can't get someone inside Scotland Yard, but he can get this Marta inside Private, right?'

'So?' Pottersfield said, squinting.

'Where are Peter's computers? His phones?'

'He's got his mobile with him,' Pottersfield said. 'House phone is in the kitchen. I saw the computer upstairs in his room.'

Twenty minutes later, Hooligan found Pottersfield and Pope talking with Billy Casper. 'Thought you'd want to see this, inspector,' he said, holding up two small evidence bags. 'Picked up the bug on the phone and the keystroke recorders on the DSL cable. I'm betting his mobile's bugged as well. Maybe more.'

'Call him,' Pottersfield said.

'I tried,' Hooligan said. 'And texted him. I'm getting no answer, other than something about network difficulties.'

Chapter 93

DARKNESS WAS FALLING outside Amanda's studio. Knight's mobile lay on the coffee table. He sat on the couch, looking at the phone, his brain feeling scalded and his stomach emptier than it had ever been.

Why hadn't they called?

His mother sat beside him, saying, 'It's more than anyone as good as you should have to bear, but you can't give up hope, Peter.'

'Absolutely not,' Boss said emphatically. 'Those two barbarians of yours are fighters. You have to be as well.'

But Knight felt as beaten as he had while holding his newborns and watching his wife's body rushed to the ambulance. 'It's their birthday,' he said softly. 'They were expecting what any three-year-old expects. Cake and ice cream and . . .'

Amanda reached out and stroked her son's hair. It was such a rare and unexpected gesture that Knight looked at her with a feeble smile on his face. 'I know how horrid life's been for you lately, Mother, but I wanted to thank you for caring about them. The only presents they got to open were from you.'

She looked surprised. 'Is that so? I didn't think they'd get there so soon.'

'I took them over,' Boss said. 'I thought they should be there.'

Knight said, 'Thank you, Boss. They loved them. And I must say, Amanda, that putting the pictures of Kate in the locket was one of the kindest and most thoughtful things you've ever done.'

His mother, normally stoic, got tears in her eyes. 'Boss and I worried because they weren't toys.'

'No, no, they loved them,' Knight insisted. 'Luke was wearing that watch as if it was a gold medal. And the necklace fits Isabel perfectly. I don't think she'll ever take it off.'

Amanda blinked several times, and then glanced at Boss before asking, 'You think they're wearing them now, Peter? The watch and the necklace?'

'I would assume so,' Knight replied. 'I didn't see them in the house.'

Amanda looked at Boss who was grinning. 'Did you activate them?'

Boss replied: 'Even before I registered the warranties!'

'What are you two talking about?' Knight said.

'Didn't you look at the boxes they came in, Peter?' Amanda cried. 'The necklace and watch were manufactured by Trace Angels, a company I've invested in. There are tiny GPS transmitters embedded in the jewellery so that parents can track their children!'

Chapter 94

KNIGHT BOLTED OUT the door of his mother's house, watching two tiny heart-shaped icons pulsing and moving slowly on a map on the screen of his iPhone.

According to the map, Luke and Isabel were less than two miles away! That realisation had caused Knight to run from his mother's without a moment's hesitation, going out into the street to find a cab and to see why his phone was having trouble connecting inside.

Knight punched in Elaine Pottersfield's number again, and got nothing but a message about network problems. He was about to turn and rush back into Amanda's home when he saw a taxi coming.

He hailed it, and jumped inside. 'Lancaster Gate Tube station,' he said.

'Yah, mon,' the driver said. 'Hey, it's you!'

Knight did a double take, realising it was the same driver who'd chased the taxi that had tried to run him and Lancer down.

'Cronus has my kids.'

'De crazy guy who blew up Mundaho?' the Jamaican cried.

'Go like hell, man,' Knight said.

They roared north-west towards Brompton Road while Knight tried Pottersfield's number again. It did not go through, but he'd no sooner ended the attempt than the iPhone buzzed, alerting him to a text.

It was from Hooligan and read: 'AT YOUR HOUSE. YOUR COMPUTER AND PHONE BUGGED. ASSUME YOUR MOBILE BUGGED 2. MAYBE TRACEABLE. CALL.'

Traceable? Knight thought. They've been tracking *me*?

'Pull over,' he yelled.

'But your kids, mon!' the taxi driver said.

'Pull over,' Knight said, forcing himself to calm down. He glanced at the beating hearts on his screen. They'd gone into an address on Porchester Terrace.

'Do you have a mobile?'

'My old lady's phone died this morning,' the driver said, stopping at the kerb. 'I gave her mine to use while hers be fixed.'

'Son of a . . .' Knight said. He looked at the screen one last time and memorised the address where the twins were being held.

Then he handed the phone to the driver along with two fifty-pound notes. 'Listen carefully, mate. I'm going to leave this phone with you, and you're going to drive it out to Heathrow.'

'What?'

'Don't argue,' Knight said, now scribbling on a business card. 'Drive it to Heathrow and then circle back to this address in Chelsea. You'll see police there. Ask for Inspector Pottersfield or Hooligan Crawford – he's with Private. Give them the phone. There'll be a reward in it for you.'

'What about your kids, mon?'

But Knight was already gone, running across Brompton Road towards Montpelier Street, heading north towards Hyde Park, thinking that the last thing he wanted was to have police arrive in force, surround the place, and force Marta's hand – or Cronus's hand, for that matter. It could cost Luke and Isabel their lives and Knight could not survive that. He'd scout the place out, and then find a phone to alert Elaine, Jack, Hooligan, Pope, and everyone else in London.

Knight was gasping for air by the time he reached the trail that paralleled the west shore of The Serpentine. His lungs were on fire when he left the park ten minutes later and crossed Bayswater Road, across from Lancaster Gate Tube station.

He went west along Bayswater Road, passed a

crowd of revellers at the Swan Pub still celebrating England's' come-from-behind victory over Brazil, and finally took a right onto Porchester Terrace. The address he sought was on the west side of the street towards Fulton Mews.

Knight stayed on the east pavement, moving methodically north until he'd got as close to the address as he dared in case the street was being monitored. He desperately wished he'd had his binoculars with him, but could see that the white apartment building had balconies on every floor and iron bars on the ground-floor windows.

There were identical apartment buildings on either side of the building Knight was targeting. Every window in the building was dark except for a light that glowed from French doors leading to the balcony of a flat on the north-east corner of the third floor. Was this where Marta was holding his children?

Rain began to fall again, hard enough for Knight to decide he would not look out of place if he put up the hood on his raincoat and walked past the building on the east side of the street.

Were Isabel and Luke inside? Cronus? Was this their hideout? Knight walked past, taking what he hoped would look like casual glances at the doorway, wondering if he should risk crossing to the other side for a closer look before he went to one of the hotels over on Inverness Terrace to call Elaine.

Then he noticed how close that balcony was to the balcony immediately to the north, which was attached to a wholly separate building. It appeared to Knight that anyone would almost certainly be able to see from that balcony on the adjacent building into the apartment where he thought Luke and Isabel might be being held.

Hell, you could probably jump from one balcony to the other.

Knight slowed and studied the facades of the apartment buildings, trying to figure out how to climb up there. But then lights went on behind the French windows of the adjacent balcony. Someone was home there.

Instantly a plan hatched in Knight's mind. He'd ring their bell, explain what was going on, and ask to use their phone to call Pottersfield and to access the balcony for surveillance purposes. But then he thought to go to the rear of the two buildings to see if any other lights were on. It took him three minutes. No other lights. He returned to Porchester Terrace just as a woman came out through the front door of the apartment building he wished to enter.

Knight bolted past her, smiled at her as if they were old friends, bounded up the steps, and caught the security door before it could shut. Even better.

He'd go straight up and knock at the door of the flat on the south-east corner of the third floor. When they saw his Private badge they were sure to let him in.

He ran up the two flights of stairs and came out into a centre hallway that smelled of frying sausages. The third floor was divided into four separate flats. Knight went to the south-east-facing flat, number 3B, heard a television inside, and knocked sharply before holding up his Private badge and ID to the peephole.

He heard footsteps approach and then a pause before locks were thrown and the apartment door opened to reveal a puzzled Michael Lancer who said, 'Knight? What are you doing here?'

Chapter 95

LANCER WORE A tracksuit and looked as though he had not shaved in days. And his eyes were sunken and hollow as if he'd slept little since being fired from his position with the London Organising Committee.

'*You* live here, Mike?' Knight asked incredulously.

'Past ten years,' Lancer replied. 'What's going on?'

Puzzled now, Knight said. 'Can I come in?'

'Uh, sure,' Lancer said, standing aside. 'Place is a mess, but . . . why are you here?'

Knight walked down a hallway into a well-appointed living area. Beer bottles and old Chinese takeaway containers littered the coffee table. The southern wall was exposed brick. Pressed against it was an open armoire that held a television tuned to the BBC's wrap-up of the last full day of Olympic competition. Beside it was a desk and on top of it a glowing laptop computer. A blue cable came out from the side of the computer and was plugged into a wall socket.

Seeing that cable, it all suddenly seemed to make some sense to Knight.

'What do you know about your neighbours on the other side of that wall?' he asked, spotting the French window that led out onto the balcony.

'You mean in the other building?' Lancer asked, puzzled.

'Exactly,' Knight said.

The LOCOG member shook his head. 'Nothing. It's been empty for almost a year, I believe. I mean, I haven't seen anyone on the balcony for almost that long.'

'Someone's in there now,' Knight said, and then gestured at the blue cable. 'Is that a CAT 5e line linked to the Internet?'

Lancer seemed to be struggling to understand where Knight was going with all these questions. 'Yes, of course.'

'No Wi-Fi?' Knight asked.

'The CAT has much higher security. Why are you so interested in the flat in the building next door?'

'Because I believe that Cronus or one of his Furies has rented it so they could tap into your computer line.'

Lancer's jaw dropped. 'What?'

'That's how they were able to crack the Olympic

security system,' Knight went on. 'They tapped into your line, stole your passwords, and in they went.'

The former decathlon athlete looked at his computer, blinking. 'How do you know all this? How do you know they're next door?'

'Because my children are in there.'

'Your children?' Lancer said, shocked.

Knight nodded, his hands balled into fists. 'A woman named Marta Brezenova, a nanny I hired recently, kidnapped them on Cronus's behalf. She doesn't know that the twins are wearing pieces of jewellery fitted with a GPS transmitter. Their signals are coming from that flat.'

'Jesus,' Lancer said, dumbstruck. 'They were right next to me the whole . . . we've got to call Scotland Yard, MI5. Get a special-weapons unit in here.'

'You do that,' Knight said. 'I'm going to see if I can look into that flat from your balcony. And tell them to come in quiet. No sirens. I don't want my kids getting killed on a knee-jerk reaction.'

Lancer nodded emphatically, pulled out his mobile, and began punching in numbers as Knight slipped out through the French window onto the rain-soaked balcony. He moved past wet patio furniture and tried to see into the other flat.

The other balcony was less than six feet away, featured an iron balustrade, and was empty, apart from some old wet leaves. The French window had gauzy white curtains hanging over it that let light out, but gave Knight no clear idea of the interior layout. To his right, Knight could hear Lancer talking on his phone, explaining what was going on.

A wind came up. The French window on the far balcony blew open several inches, revealing a stark white carpet and a white country-style table on which several computers stood glowing, all connected to blue CAT 5e lines.

Knight was about go back into Lancer's apartment to tell him what he'd seen when he heard his son whine from somewhere in the adjacent flat: 'No, Marta! Lukey want to go home for birthday party!'

'Shut up, you spoiled little bastard,' Marta hissed before Knight heard a loud slap and Luke went hysterical. 'And learn to use the loo!'

Chapter 96

THE PRIMAL INSTINCT of a father wanting to protect his child seized Knight so completely that without considering the consequences he climbed up on Lancer's railing thirty feet above the ground, crouched, and dived forward.

As Knight pushed off from the wet rail his shoes slipped ever so slightly, and he knew in an instant that he wasn't going to make it onto the floor of the balcony next door. He wasn't even going to reach the railing, and he thought for sure that he was going to plunge and break every bone in his body.

But somehow his fingers snagged the bottom of the iron balustrade where it met the balcony floor and he grabbed at it for dear life, dangling and wondering how long he could hold on.

'Shut up!' Marta snapped inside, and slapped Luke again.

The little boy's sobs turned bitter, and that was enough to trigger a massive surge of adrenalin in

Knight. He swung his body left and right like a pendulum, feeling the iron biting into his hands, but not caring because on the third swing he was able to catch the edge of the balcony floor with the toe of his right shoe.

Seconds later he was over the railing and onto the balcony itself, his muscles trembling and a chemical taste in his mouth. Luke's crying had become muffled and nasal, as if Marta had gagged Knight's son.

Ignoring the stinging in his hands, Knight gripped his Beretta and eased up to the half-open French window. He peeked inside and saw that the living area was similar in layout to Lancer's place. The furnishings were wildly different, however, with a much colder touch. Everything in the room, except a gold and red tapestry that hung on the right-hand wall, was the same stark white as the carpet. Luke's muffled cries were coming from a hallway by the kitchen.

Knight pushed open the French window and stepped inside. He kicked off his shoes and stalked quickly to the hallway. He had no illusions about what he was doing now. Marta was a part of the death of Denton Marshall. She'd helped destroy his mother's happiness. She had tried to destroy the Olympics, and she'd taken his children. He would not hesitate to kill her to save them.

Luke's cries softened enough for Knight to be able to hear Isabel weeping too, and then a deeper groaning. All of it was coming from a room on the left, its door open and lights on. Knight hugged the wall and reached the doorway. He looked down the hallway beyond and saw two doors, both open, lights off.

It was all going down in the room right next to him. He thumbed the Beretta's safety.

Gun held out in front of him, Knight stepped into the doorway, sweeping his weapon around the room. He spotted Isabel lying on her side on a bare mattress on the floor to his right, tied up, tape across her mouth, looking towards Marta.

The nanny was about fifteen feet from Knight, her back turned to the door, and she was changing Luke's nappy on a table against the wall. She had no idea that he was standing in the doorway behind her, searching for a clear shot.

But James Daring did.

The museum curator and television star was staring at Knight, who understood much of the situation in a heartbeat. Knight stepped forward, aiming the pistol, and said, 'Get away from my son, you war-criminal bitch, or I will head-shoot you and enjoy doing it.'

The nanny pivoted in disbelief towards Knight, her attention darting to a black assault rifle standing in the corner several feet away.

'Don't even think about it,' Knight said, taking another step towards her. 'Get down on your belly, hands up behind your head, or I will kill you. Right now.'

Marta's eyes went dead and vacant, but she started to comply slowly, lowering her centre, watching Knight the way a cornered lioness might.

Knight took another step forward, gripping the Beretta two-handed, seeing her framed in his pistol sights. 'I said get down!' he yelled.

Marta went flat, and put her hands up behind her head.

Glancing at Daring, Knight said, 'Cronus?'

The television personality's eyes glazed before Knight heard a nearby thudding noise and something viciously hard hit his head.

It was like storms he'd seen come up over dry lowlands in Portugal: thunder boomed so loud that it deafened Knight even as heat lightning crackled, sending electric tentacles through his brain, so brilliant that they blinded him into darkness.

Chapter 97

THE SOUNDS OF hydraulic doors opening and shoes slapping on tile stirred Karen Pope from an edge-of-consciousness sleep.

The *Sun* reporter lay on a sofa in Private London's lab, feeling wrecked by a fatigue that was compounded with worry. No one had heard from Knight since he'd walked out the rear door of his house. Not Pottersfield, not Hooligan, not Pope, not Morgan, nor anyone else at Scotland Yard or Private.

They'd waited for him at his home until shortly after dawn when Pottersfield had left to examine the bodies of the two dead women found in the abandoned factory. Pope and Hooligan returned to Private to run the fingerprints that Hooligan had taken at Knight's house through the Balkan War Crimes database.

They'd got a hit almost immediately: Senka, the oldest of the Brazlic siblings, had been all over the place. When Hooligan informed Pottersfield, the inspector told them that preliminary fingerprint work on the more recently slain woman positively identified her as Nada, the middle Brazlic sister.

At that point, around eight a.m. that Sunday, Pope had hit a wall of exhaustion and had lain down on the couch, using one of Hooligan's lab coats for a blanket. How long had she slept?

'Hooligan, wake up,' she heard Jack say. 'There's a beat-up Rasta at the front desk looking for you. He says he's got something that he was supposed to hand-deliver to you for Knight. And he refuses to give it to me.'

At that Pope opened an eye to see the American standing at Hooligan's desk and Private London's chief scientist rousing from a nap. Above him, the clock read 10:20.

Two hours and twenty minutes? Pope sat up groggily, then got to her feet and stumbled after Hooligan and Jack out of the lab to the reception area, where a Jamaican sat painfully in a chair by the lift. A large bandage covered his grossly swollen cheek. His arm was in a cast and secured by a sling.

'I'm Hooligan,' the scientist said.

The Rasta struggled up and held out his good hand, saying, 'Ketu Oladuwa. I drive de cab.'

Hooligan gestured at the cast and bandage. 'Crash?'

Oladuwa nodded. 'Big time, mon. On my way to Heathrow. Broadsided by a panel van. I been in hospital all night.'

Pope said, 'What about Knight?'

'Ya, mon,' the Rasta said, digging in his pocket and coming up with a smashed iPhone. 'He gimme dis one here last night and tell me to drive it to Heathrow and then back to his home to find you or some inspector with da police. I went to Knight's home when I got out of hospital dis morning, and police told me you gone, so I came here.'

'To give us a smashed phone?' Jack asked.

'Wasn't smashed before da accident,' the Rasta said indignantly. 'He said something on dat phone help you find his kids.'

'Fuck,' Hooligan grunted. He snatched the remains of Knight's phone from Oladuwa, spun around and took off for the lab with Pope and Jack close on his heels.

'Hey!' Oladuwa yelled after them. 'Him say I get reward!'

Chapter 98

KNIGHT SURFACED FROM oblivion slowly, starting deep in the reptilian part of his brain with a sense of the smell of meat frying. At first he had no notion of who he was, or where he was, just that odour of meat frying.

Then he understood that he was lying prone on something hard. His hearing returned next, like pounding surf that cleared to static and then to voices, television voices. Knight knew who he was then, and dimly recalled being in the bedroom with his children, Marta, and Daring before it had all gone blank. He tried to move. He couldn't. His wrists and hands were bound.

The flute began, airy and trilling, and Knight forced his eyes open, seeing blurrily that he was not in that bedroom in the white flat any more. The floor below him was hardwood, not carpeted. And the walls around him were dark-panelled and heaved to and fro like the sea churning.

Knight felt nauseated and shut his eyes, still hearing the flute music, and the broadcast announcers arguing before he moved his head and felt a terrible throbbing at the back of his skull. After several seconds he opened his eyes a second time, finding that his focus was now better. He spotted Isabel and Luke unconscious on the floor not far away, still bound and gagged.

Then he twisted his head, trying to locate the source of the music, seeing the side of a four-poster bed at the centre of the room and, on it, James Daring.

Dazed as he was, Knight understood Daring's predicament at a glance. It was the same predicament in which he'd seen the museum curator before it had all gone to blackness: the television star lay spread-eagle on the mattress, lashed to the bedposts and wearing a hospital gown. His mouth was taped shut. An IV line ran into his wrist from a bag hanging on a rack by the bed.

The flute music stopped and Knight saw someone backlit by brilliant sunlight coming towards him across the room.

Mike Lancer carried a black combat shotgun loosely in his left hand, and a glass of orange juice in his right. He set the juice down on a table and squatted down near Knight, gazed at him in amusement, and said, 'Awake at last. Feel like things got rearranged upstairs, did you?' He laughed and displayed the weapon. 'Brilliant, these old riot guns. Even air-driven, the beanbags really pack a wallop, especially if delivered to the head at close range.'

'Cronus?' Knight said, still hazy. He could smell alcohol on Lancer's breath.

Lancer said, 'You know, I had a feeling about you right from the beginning, Knight, or at least since Dan Carter's untimely death: a premonition that you would come closest to figuring me out. But I took the necessary precautions, and here we are.'

Deeply confused, Knight said: 'The Olympics were your life. Why?'

Lancer rested the riot gun against the inside of his knee and reached back to scratch the side of his head. As he did, Knight saw his face flush with anger. He stood up, grabbed the juice glass, and drank from it before saying, 'The modern Games have been corrupt since the beginning. Bribed judges. Genetic freaks. Drug-fuelled monsters. It needed to be cleaned up, and I was the one to . . .'

Even in Knight's blurry state, it didn't sound right, and he said, 'Bullshit. I don't believe you.'

Lancer glared at him before whipping the glass at Knight. It missed and shattered against the wall behind him. 'Who are you to question my motives?' Lancer roared.

Concussion or not, threat or not, things were

becoming clearer to Knight, who said, 'You didn't do this just to expose the Games. You sacrificed them in front of a world audience. There has to be a warped sense of rage behind that.'

Lancer got angrier. 'I am an emanation of the Lord of Time.' He looked over at the twins. 'Cronus. Devourer of children.'

The implied threat terrified Knight. How far gone was the man?

'No,' Knight said, following his foggy instincts. 'Something happened to you. Something that filled you with hatred and made you want to do all this.'

Lancer's voice rose. 'The Olympics are supposed to be a religious festival, one where honourable men and women compete in the eyes of heaven. The modern Games are its exact opposite. The gods were offended by the arrogance of men, the hubris of mankind.'

Knight's vision blurred slightly, and he felt sickened again, but his brain was working better with each passing second. He shook his head. 'The gods weren't offended. *You* were offended. Who were they? The arrogant men?'

'The ones that have died in the last two weeks,' Lancer retorted hotly. Then he smiled. 'Including Dan Carter and your other dear colleagues.'

Knight stared at him, unable to comprehend the depths of the man's depravity. 'You bombed that plane?'

'Carter was getting a little too close,' Lancer replied. 'The others were collateral damage.'

'Collateral damage!' Knight shouted, feeling like he wanted to kill the man standing before him, ripping him limb from limb. But then his head began to throb again and he lay there panting, looking at Lancer.

After several moments he said, 'Who offended you?'

Lancer's expression went hard as he stared off into the past.

'Who?' Knight demanded again.

The former decathlon champion glared at Knight in utter fury, and said, 'Doctors.'

Chapter 99

IN BROAD, BITTER strokes, I tell Knight a story that no one except the Brazlic sisters has ever heard in its entirety, starting with the hatred I was born with, right through stabbing my mother and killing the monsters who stoned me after I went to live with Minister Bob in Brixton, the roughest neighbourhood in all of London.

I tell Knight that after the stoning, in the spring of my fifteenth year, Minister Bob had me enter for a track meet because he thought I was stronger and faster than most boys. He had no idea what I was capable of. Neither did I.

During that first meet I won six events: the 100, 200, javelin, triple jump, long jump and discus. I did it again in a regional competition, and a third time at a junior national meet in Sheffield.

'A man named Lionel Higgins approached me after Sheffield,' I tell Knight. 'Higgins was a private decathlon coach. He told me I had the talent to be the greatest all-around athlete in the world and to win the Olympic gold medal. He offered to help me figure out a way to train full-time, and filled my head with false dreams of glory and a life lived according to Olympic ideals, of competing fairly, may the best man win, and all that nonsense.'

Snorting scornfully, I say: 'The monster slayer in me bought the phoney spiel hook, line and sinker.'

I go on to tell Knight how I lived the Olympic ideals for the next fifteen years of my life. Despite the headaches that would lay me low at least once a month, Higgins arranged for me to join the Coldstream Guards, where in return for a decade of service I'd be allowed to train. I did so, furiously, single-mindedly, some say maniacally for a shot at athletic immortality that finally came for me at the Games in Barcelona in 1992.

'We expected the oppressive heat and humidity,' I say to Knight. 'Higgins sent me to India to train for it, figuring that Bombay would be worse than Spain. He was right. I *was* the best prepared, and I was mentally ready to suffer more than anyone else.'

Wrapped in the darkest of my memories, I shake my head like a terrier breaking a rat's spine, and say, 'None of it mattered.'

I describe how I led the Barcelona decathlon after the first day, through the 110-metre hurdles, high jump, discus, pole vault, and the 400. Temperatures were in the upper nineties and the oppressive, saturated air took its toll on me: I cramped up and collapsed after placing second in the 400.

'They rushed me to a medical tent,' I tell Knight. 'But I wasn't concerned. Higgins and I figured I would need a legal electrolytic boost after day one. I kept calling for my coach, but the medical personnel wouldn't let him in. I could see they were going to put me on an IV. I told them I wanted my own coach to replenish the fluids and minerals I lost with a mixture we'd fine-tuned to my metabolism. But I was in no condition to fight them when they put the needle in my arm and connected it to a bag of God only knows what.'

Looking at Knight, feeling livid, I'm reliving the aftermath all over again. 'I was a ghost of myself the next day. The javelin and the long jump were my best events, and I cratered in both. I didn't finish in the top ten and I was the reigning world champion.'

The anger in me is almost overwhelming when I say, 'No dream realised, Knight. No Olympic glory. No proof of my superiority. Sabotaged by what the modern Games have become.'

Knight stares at me with the same distrustful and fearful expression that Marta gave me when I offered to save her and her sisters in that police station in Bosnia.

'But you were world champion,' Knight says. 'Twice.'

'The immortals win Olympic gold. The superior wins gold. I was robbed of my chance by monsters. It was premeditated sabotage.'

Knight gazes at me in disbelief now, 'And so you started plotting your revenge right then – eighteen years ago?'

'The scope of my revenge grew over time,' I admit. 'It began with the Spanish doctors who doped me. They died of supposedly natural causes in September '93. The referees who oversaw the event were killed in separate car crashes in '94 and early '95.'

'And the Furies?' Knight asks.

I sit on a stool a few feet from him. 'Hardly anyone knows that after my regiment ended its service in the Queen's Guard, we were sent into Sarajevo for a rotation with the NATO peacekeeping mission. I lasted less than five weeks due to a roadside bomb that cracked my head for the second time in my life.'

Knight's words were less slurred now, and his eyes less glassy when he said 'Was that before or after you helped the Brazlic sisters escape from that police station near Srebrenica?'

I smile bitterly. 'After. With new passports and new identities, I brought the Furies to London and set them up in a flat next door. We even cut a secret door behind my armoire and their tapestry so we could appear to live separate lives.'

'Dedicated to destroying the Olympics?' Knight asks acidly.

'Yes, that's right. As I said, the gods were behind this, behind me. It was fate. How else do you explain that very early on in the process I was asked to be a member of the organising committee and, lo and behold, London won the bid. Fate allowed me to be on the inside from the start, hiding things where I needed them, altering them if they suited my purpose, given full access to every inch of every venue. And now with everyone hunting you and your children, fate will allow me to finish what I've begun.'

Knight's face contorts. 'You're insane.'

'No, Knight,' I reply. 'Just superior in ways you can't understand.'

I stand up and start to walk away. He calls after me, 'So are you going to wipe out all the Furies before your big finale? Kill Marta and then escape?'

'Not at all,' I chuckle. 'Marta's out putting your daughter's necklace and your son's watch on trains to Scotland and France respectively. When she's done, she'll return here, release Mr Daring and then kill your children. And then you.'

Chapter 100

KNIGHT'S POUNDING HEAD felt battered, as if it had been struck again. His attention lurched to his sleeping children. The necklace and wristwatch *were* gone. There was no way to trace them now. And what about the taxi driver? Why hadn't he given the phone to Hooligan or Pottersfield? Why hadn't they come for him? Were they tracking Marta to the trains?

Knight looked back to Lancer, who was gathering up a bag and some papers.

'My kids have done nothing,' Knight said. 'They're just three years old. Innocent.'

'Little monsters,' Lancer said flatly, turning for the door. 'Goodbye, Knight. It was nice competing with you, but the better man has won.'

'No, you haven't!' Knight shouted after him. 'Mundaho proved it. You haven't won. The Olympic spirit lives on whatever you do.'

That hit a nerve because Lancer turned and

marched back towards Knight – only to flinch and stop at the sound of a gunshot.

It came from the television and caused Lancer to relax, a smirk on his face.

'The men's marathon has started,' he said. 'The final game has begun. And you know what, Knight? Because I'm the superior man, I'm going to let you live to see the ending. Before Marta kills you, she's going to let you witness exactly how I snuff out that Olympic spirit once and for all.'

Chapter 101

A HALF-HOUR LATER, approaching noon, Pope glanced nervously from coverage of the men's marathon to Hooligan, who was still hunched over the shards of the iPhone, trying to coax Knight's whereabouts from them.

'Anything?' the reporter asked, feeling completely stymied.

'Sim card's pretty fuckin' hammered, eh?' Private London's chief scientist replied without looking up. 'But I think I'm getting close.'

Jack had left to oversee security at the finish line of the men's marathon. Elaine Pottersfield was in the lab, however. The police inspector had arrived only a few moments before, agitated and exhausted by the pressures of the preceding twenty-four hours.

'Where did this cabbie say he picked up Peter?' she asked impatiently.

Pope said, 'Somewhere in Knightsbridge, I think.

If Oladuwa had a mobile we could call him, but he said his wife's got it.'

Pottersfield thought a moment. 'Milner Street in Kensington, perhaps?'

'That was it,' Hooligan grunted.

'Knight was at his mother's, then,' the inspector said. 'Amanda must know something.' She yanked out her phone and started scrolling for her number.

'Here we are,' Hooligan said, raising his head from two sensors clipped to a surviving piece of Knight's sim card to look at the screen, which was covered with the gibberish of code.

He leaned over to a keyboard and began typing even as Pope heard Pottersfield say hello, identify herself as both a police detective and the sister of Knight's dead wife, and ask to speak with Amanda Knight. Then the inspector left the lab.

Two minutes later, Hooligan's screen mutated from electronic hieroglyphics to a blurry screen shot of a website. Pope said, 'What is that?'

'Looks like a map of some sort,' Hooligan replied as the inspector burst back into the lab. 'Can't read the URL, though.'

'Trace Angels!' Pottersfield shouted. 'It says Trace Angels!'

Chapter 102

THE CROWD ALONG the south side of Birdcage Walk, facing St James's Park, is bigger and deeper than I had anticipated. But then again, the men's marathon is one of the final competitions of the Games.

It's beastly hot, half-past eleven, and the leaders are coming around to start the second of four long laps that constitute the racetrack. I hear the crowd's roar, and spot the runners heading west towards the Victoria Memorial and Buckingham Palace.

Carrying a small shoulder sack, I push to the front of the crowd, holding aloft my Olympic security pass, which was never taken from me. It's critical that I be seen now, here, at this moment. I'd planned to find any policeman I could. But when I look down the side of the course, I see someone familiar. I duck the tape and walk towards him, holding up the pass.

'Inspector Casper?' I say. 'Mike Lancer.'

The inspector nodded. 'Seems to me you got a raw deal.'

'Thank you,' I say, then add, 'I'm no longer official, of course, but I was wondering if I could cut across the street when there's a gap in the runners. I wanted to watch from the north side if I could.'

Casper considered the request, then shrugged and said, 'Sure, why not?'

Thirty seconds later, I'm across the street, pushing back through the crowd and into the park. Inside, I move east, glancing at my watch and thinking that Marta will release Daring in ninety minutes or so, right around the end of the marathon, a move that should attract heavy police attention and give me enough of an edge to ensure that I can't possibly be beaten.

I won't be defeated today, I think. Not today. And never again.

Chapter 103

FOR THE LAST thirty minutes, his mouth taped shut, his head pounding and painful, Knight had alternated between trying to break free of his bonds, gasping in frustration, and looking longingly at his comatose children, dully aware of the marathon coverage blaring from the television in Lancer's spare bedroom.

It was 11:55. In mile eleven – kilometre nineteen – just shy of an hour into the race, runners from the UK, Ethiopia, Kenya and Mexico had broken away from the main pack along the Victoria Embankment. They were using each other to chew up ground as they headed past the London Eye towards Parliament at sub-Olympic-record pace despite the blistering heat.

Knight wondered grimly what atrocity Lancer had waiting somewhere along the marathon route. But he refused to contemplate what Marta might have in store for him and the twins in the aftermath of the last race of the Games.

He closed his eyes and began to pray to God and to Kate, pleading with them to help him save their children. He told them he'd be fine about dying if that meant he'd be with Kate again. But the children, they deserved to . . .

Marta walked into the room, carrying the black assault weapon that Knight had seen the night before as well as a plastic bag containing three litre-sized Coke bottles. Her dark locks had been chopped and dyed, leaving her hair a violent blonde tipped with silver highlights that somehow matched the black leather skirt, tank top and calf-length boots she wore. Her heavy make-up changed her appearance still further. If Knight hadn't spent so much time around her in the last two weeks he might never have recognised her as the plain nanny who'd first approached him at the playground.

Marta paid Knight no mind, as if he and everyone else in the room were afterthoughts. She set the Coke bottles on a dresser, then cradled the gun and went to Daring's side. She set the gun down, picked up a hypodermic needle and shot it into the IV line that had been inserted into the museum curator's arm.

'Time to wake up,' she said, and gathered up the gun again.

She fished an apple from her pocket and bit into

it. Her attention shifted lazily to the marathon coverage.

Luke stirred and opened his eyes, looking right at his father. His eyes went wide. Then his brows knitted, his face grew beet-red and he began making whining noises, not of fear but as if he desperately wanted to tell his father something. Knight recognised that red-faced expression and understood the meaning behind the stifled cries immediately.

At the noise, Marta looked over with such a cold expression on her face that Knight's pounding brain screamed at him to make her look at him and not at his son.

Knight began to moan behind his tape. Marta glanced over, chewing her apple, and said, 'Shut up. I don't want to hear you cry like your little boy.'

Instead of complying, Knight moaned louder and smashed his feet against the floor, trying not only to alert someone below but to bother Marta. He wanted to get her talking. He knew enough about hostage negotiation to understand how crucial it was to get a captor talking.

Isabel woke up and started to cry.

Marta took up the gun, stomped over to Knight, and laughed. 'We own the flat below, too. So go ahead, make noise. No one hears you.'

With that she kicked him in the stomach. Knight doubled up and rolled over on his back, gasping and feeling glass from the shattered fruit-juice tumbler crunch beneath him. Luke began to wail. Marta glared at the children. Knight was sure that she was going to kick them. But then she squatted down and ripped the tape off Knight's mouth. 'Tell them to shut up or you're all dead right now.'

'Luke wants to use the loo,' Knight said. 'Take the tape off. Ask him.'

Marta shot him a foul look, then scuttled across to his son and peeled off the tape over his mouth. 'What?'

Knight's son shrank away from Marta, but looked at his father and said, 'Lukey need go poop. Big-boy loo.'

'Crap in your pants for all I care.'

'Big-boy loo, Marta,' the boy insisted. 'Lukey go big-boy. No nappy.'

'Give him a chance,' Knight said. 'He's just three.'

Marta's expression turned into a disgusted sneer. But she got out a knife and cut free Luke's ankles. Gun in one hand, she hauled Knight's son to his feet and snarled, 'If this is another false alarm, I'll kill you first.'

They moved past Daring and disappeared through the door into the hallway. Knight glanced all around, rolled back slightly, and heard glass crunch again, felt tiny shards of it pricking his arms and back.

The pain jolted his brain into realising his opportunity, and he began frantically arching his back and moving around, fingers groping desperately beneath him. Please, Kate. Please.

The index finger of his right hand felt the keen edge of a larger shard of glass, perhaps two inches long, and tried to coax it into his hand. But he fumbled and dropped it. Cursing under his breath, Knight groped again. But he hadn't found it when he heard Luke cry, 'See, Marta? Big boy!'

A second later, he heard a toilet flush. Knight's fingers searched in a frenzy. Nothing. He heard footsteps, arched his hips one more time and pushed himself back closer to where the glass had shattered. Then Luke walked in, wrists still taped in front of him, beaming at his father.

'Lukey big boy now, Daddy,' he said. 'Lukey three. No nappies.'

Chapter 104

'GOOD JOB, LAD,' Knight said, lying back, smiling at his son, glancing at Marta – who was still cradling the gun – and feeling a thick chunk from the bottom of the juice glass lying on the floor just below the small of his back.

The fingers of his right hand closed round it just as Marta said to Luke, 'Go and sit down next to your sister – and don't move.' She turned to inspect Daring, who was now shifting on the bed.

'Wake up,' she said again. 'We have to go soon.'

Daring moaned as Knight twisted the chunk of glass into the duct tape around his wrists and began to saw at it. Luke came dutifully towards his father, smiling and saying, 'Lukey big boy.'

His attention jumping back to Marta, Knight said, 'Brilliant. Now sit down like Marta told you too.'

But his son didn't budge. 'We go home, Daddy?' Luke said, and Bella began to whine in agreement behind her gag. 'We go and have party?'

'Soon,' Knight said, feeling the tape begin to part. 'Very soon.'

But then Marta snatched up the gun and a roll of duct tape and started towards Luke. His son took one look at the tape and cried, 'No, Marta!'

Luke ducked and started to run. Marta became infuriated. Pointing the gun at Knight's son, she barked, 'Sit down. Now. Or you die.'

But Knight's son was too young to understand fully the implications of having a loaded weapon aimed at him. 'No!' Luke said impudently, and jumped onto the mattress beside Isabel, his eyes darting around, looking for escape.

'I'll teach you, then,' Marta said, stalking towards Luke, her stare fully on the boy and not on Knight who felt his wrists come free.

As she passed him, looking to corner his son, Knight lashed out with his bound feet.

They connected hard with Marta's Achilles tendons. She cried out as her legs buckled and she fell sideways to the floor. The gun clattered away.

Knight twisted around, clutching that chunk of glass, and tried to slash her with it. But her reaction time was stunningly fast and practical. She threw up her forearm, taking the cut there before kneeing Knight hard in the chest.

The wind knocked out of him, Knight let go of the glass shard.

Insane with fury, Marta jumped to her feet and snatched up the gun. She marched over to one of the Coke bottles, opened it, and stuffed the muzzle inside and down into the liquid before saying, 'I don't care what Cronus wants. I have had enough of you, and your bastard children.'

Marta deftly wrapped duct tape around her bleeding arm, and then around the gun barrel and the mouth of the bottle before swinging around the crudely silenced weapon. Her eyes had gone dark and dead, and Knight had a glimpse of what all those Bosnian boys must have seen when the Brazlic sisters had come calling. With grim intent, Marta marched towards Luke who still sat beside his sister. She said to Knight, 'The boy goes first. I want you to see how it's done.'

'Lancer is going to kill you!' Knight shouted at her. 'Just like he killed your sisters!'

That stopped her progress. She turned to him and said, 'My sisters are very much alive. They have already escaped from London.'

'No,' Knight said. 'Lancer killed them both. He broke Andjela's neck, and then cut off her hands and sent them to me. Nada's throat was cut from ear to ear.'

'That's a lie!' Marta snarled as she came at him, raising the gun.

'They were found in the same abandoned factory

near the gasworks where you kept Selena Farrell.'

That information made Marta pause briefly. 'How come it hasn't been on the news?'

'They probably haven't alerted the media,' Knight said, fumbling for an answer. 'They do that, you know – hide things.'

'You're lying,' she said. Then she shrugged. 'And even if it is true, so much the better for me. I am sick of them. I think of killing them myself from time to time.'

Marta clicked off the rifle's safety catch.

Chapter 105

SUDDENLY SIRENS WAILED nearby, coming closer, and Knight's spirits surged with renewed hope.

'They're coming for you now,' he said, grinning insanely at Marta and the bottom of the Coke bottle. 'You're going to the gallows, no matter what you do to me and my children.'

'No.' She laughed caustically. 'If they go anywhere, they go next door, not here. In the meantime, I kill you and then use the tunnel to escape.'

She tried to press the Coke bottle against Knight's head. But he batted at it with his hand and jerked around as the sirens came closer and louder. He thought: Buy time. At least the twins will be saved.

But then Marta stepped on the side of Knight's neck with her boot, choking him as she lowered the silenced gun.

He looked up at her cross-eyed and grabbed at her

ankles, trying to upset her balance. But she just ground her boot deeper and harder into his neck until his strength was gone.

Marta peered down at him. 'Goodbye, Mr Knight. Too bad I don't have a pickaxe.'

Chapter 106

KNIGHT THOUGHT OF Kate in the instant before Marta's eyes snapped wide open. She screamed in agony, yanked the Coke bottle away from his head and her boot off his neck, and fired the rifle. With a weird wet thud, the silenced gun blew a hole in the wall just above Knight's head. Coke and plastic fragments showered down on him as Marta screamed in agony once more. Frenzied, she spun away from Knight, groping wildly behind her.

Luke had bitten into Marta's hamstring, and was holding on like a little bulldog while his nanny furiously pounded against him, screaming again and again. Knight kicked her hard in the shin and she dropped the gun before ramming her elbow hard into Luke's side.

The boy slammed against the wall and lay still.

Knight crawled after the gun while Marta glared at Luke and felt down her leg for the gaping wound he'd left. She didn't notice his father until he was inches from the rifle.

She cursed and lunged towards Knight as his finger found the trigger and he tried to swing the gun to point it at her. She swept her other arm round and struck the side of the barrel, deflecting his aim even as the now unsilenced rifle went off again, this time with a deafening boom that disorientated Knight for a second. He looked around, dizzy, praying that he'd managed to shoot Marta somehow.

But then the oldest Fury kicked him in the ribs and ripped the gun from his hands. Gasping – and grinning in triumph – she aimed the muzzle at Knight's unconscious son.

'Watch him die,' she snarled.

The shot this time sounded distant and otherworldly to Knight, but it was aimed perfectly at his breaking heart. He fully expected Luke's small body to jump at the bullet's impact.

Instead, Marta's throat exploded in a slurry of blood before the war-criminal nanny crumpled and sprawled dead between Knight and his son.

Dumbfounded and slack-jawed, Knight twisted his head around and saw Kate's older sister rising from a shooting crouch.

Part Five

THE FINISH LINE

Chapter 107

TWENTY-FIVE MINUTES AFTER Pottersfield had shot and killed the wanted war criminal Senka Brazlic, the police inspector and Knight were in her car, sirens and lights on, racing through the streets of Chelsea and heading towards The Mall where the top runners were well into their fourth and final lap of the marathon route.

Ordinarily, the men's marathon, the final event of the summer Games, would end in the host city's Olympic stadium. But the London organisers – largely at Lancer's urging, it turned out – had decided that sending the runners through the scruffy East End was not the best way to sell the city's stunning attributes to the world.

Instead, the organisers opted to have the marathon contestants run four 6.5-mile laps, each of them featuring some of London's most notable landmarks as telegenic backdrops for the race: from Tower Hill to the Houses of Parliament along the

Thames, past the London Eye and Cleopatra's
Needle. The start and finish would take place on
The Mall, well in sight of Buckingham Palace.

'I want his picture in everyone's mobile, iPhone,
BlackBerry,' Pottersfield shouted into her radio.
'Find him! Having the marathon here was his idea!'

Knight was thinking about how bloody brilliant
she was at her job. She'd called up the Trace Angels
site, seen that the children had been put on trains,
but then thought to look at their whereabouts earlier
and saw the address on Porchester Terrace.

After contacting the trains and getting word from
conductors that there was no one matching the
Knight children's description aboard, she'd led the
police contingent to the building near Lancaster
Gate. They'd been in the Furies' flat when the
crudely silenced gun had gone off next door and
they'd heard it. They'd discovered the entrance to
Lancer's place behind that tapestry on the wall, and
had then thrown a stun grenade a moment after
Knight had fired the weapon.

Setting down her radio, Pottersfield said shakily,
'We'll get him. Everybody's hunting him now.'

Knight grunted, staring out the window into the
glaring sunlight, still feeling dizzy and sore from the
blows he'd taken. 'You okay, Elaine? Having to
shoot?'

'Me? You shouldn't even be here, Peter,'

Pottersfield scolded. 'You should be back there in that ambulance with your kids, going to hospital. You need to be looked at yourself.'

'Amanda and Boss are on their way to meet Luke and Bella. I'll get examined when Lancer's stopped.'

Pottersfield changed down and shot out onto Buckingham Palace Road. 'You're sure Lancer said the attack was on the marathon?'

Knight struggled to remember before replying: 'Before he left, I told him that no matter what he might do, the Olympic spirit would never die. I told him that Mundaho had proved it, and Shaw, and Dr Pierce. That got him insanely angry, and I was certain he would kill me. But then the starting gun for the marathon went off. And he said something like: "The men's marathon. The final game has begun. And because I'm the superior man, I'm going to let you live to see the ending. Before Marta kills you, she's going to let you witness exactly how I snuff out that Olympic spirit once and for all."'

Pottersfield skidded the car to a stop in front of the police barrier opposite St James's Park and got out, holding up her badge to the officers guarding it. 'He's with Private and with me. Where's Inspector Casper?'

The policeman who looked miserable in the stifling heat, pointed north towards the roundabout in front of Buckingham Palace, and said, 'You want me to call him?'

Knight's sister-in-law shook her head before vaulting the barrier and battling her way through the crowd onto Birdcage Walk with Knight following somewhat woozily right behind her. Runners who were well behind the leaders were heading painfully towards the Queen Victoria Memorial at the centre of the roundabout.

Billy Casper was already hustling towards Knight and Pottersfield. 'Sweet Jesus, Elaine,' he said. 'I had the bastard right in front of me not an hour ago. He went into St James's Park.'

'Did you get Lancer's picture?'

'Everyone in the force got it ten seconds ago,' Casper replied, and then looked grim. 'The route is more than ten kilometres long. There's half a million people – maybe more – lining the route. How the hell are we going to find him?'

'At the finish, or somewhere near it,' Knight said. 'It fits his flair for the dramatic. Have you seen Jack Morgan?'

'He's way ahead of you, Peter,' Casper said. 'As soon as he heard Cronus was Lancer and that he was still on the loose, he went straight to the finish arena. Smart guy for a Yank.'

But twenty-six minutes later, as roars went up from back along the marathon route south of St

James's Park, Lancer had still not been sighted, and every aspect of the timing system had been re-examined for possible booby traps.

Standing high atop stands erected along The Mall, Knight and Jack – who had shown up minutes after Knight had asked after him – were using binoculars to look up into the trees to see if Lancer had climbed one and taken up position as a sniper. Casper and Pottersfield were doing much the same on the other side of the street. But their views were hampered by scores of large Union Jack and Olympic flags fluttering on poles running westward towards Buckingham Palace.

'I checked him out myself,' Jack said sombrely, lowering his binoculars. 'Lancer, I mean. When he did some work for us a few years back in Hong Kong. He was squeaky clean, nothing but raves from everyone who'd ever known him. And I don't remember ever seeing that he'd served in the Balkans. I'm sure I would have remembered that.'

'He was there for less than five weeks,' Knight said.

'Long enough to recruit bloodthirsty bitches as mad as he is,' Jack said.

'Probably why he left the deployment off his C.V.,' Knight said.

Before Jack could reply, the roar of the crowd came closer and people in the stands around the

Queen Victoria Memorial leaped to their feet as two policemen on motorcycles appeared about a hundred yards in front of the same four runners who'd broken free of the main pack back at mile twelve.

'The motorcyclists,' Knight said, and threw up his binoculars, trying to see the faces of the officers. But he could tell quickly that neither man was Lancer.

Behind the motorcycles, the top four runners appeared – the Kenyan, the Ethiopian, the barefoot Mexican, and that lad from Brighton – each of them carrying Olympic and Cameroonian hand flags.

After twenty-six miles, three hundred and eighty-five yards, after forty-two thousand, one hundred and ninety-five metres, the Kenyan and the Brit were leading, sprinting side by side. But at the two-hundred-yard mark and hard behind the leaders, the Ethiopian and the Mexican split and sprinted to the leaders' flanks.

The crowd went wild as the whippet-thin runners churned down the final straight towards gold and glory, four abreast and none of them giving ground.

Then, twenty yards from the finish, the lad from Brighton surged forward, and it looked as if the UK was going to have its first men's-marathon gold to go with the historic win by Mary Duckworth in the women's race the previous Sunday.

Astonishingly, however, mere feet from the finish

line, the Brighton lad slowed, the runners raised their flags, and the foursome went through the tape together.

For a second, the crowd was stunned and Knight could hear broadcasters braying about the unprecedented act and what it was supposed to mean. And then everyone on The Mall saw it for what it was and started lustily to cheer the gesture, Peter Knight included.

He thought: You see that, Lancer? Cronus? You can't snuff out the Olympic spirit because it doesn't exist in any one place; it's carried in the hearts of every athlete who's ever striven for greatness, and it always will be.

'No attack,' Jack said when the cheering died down. 'Maybe the show of force along the route scared Lancer off.'

'Maybe,' Knight allowed. 'Or maybe he wasn't talking about the end of the marathon at all.'

Chapter 108

THE NAUSEATING ENDING to the men's marathon keeps replaying on the screens around the security stations as I wait patiently in the sweltering heat in the line at the north entrance to the Olympic Park off Ruckholt Road.

My head is shaven and, along with every bit of exposed skin, has been stained with henna to a deep russet tone ten times as dark as my normal colour. The white turban is perfect. So is the black beard, the metal bracelet on my right wrist and the Indian passport, and the sepia-brown contact lenses, the glasses and the loose white Kurta pyjamas and tunic that together with a dab of patchouli oil complete my disguise as Jat Singh Rajpal, a tall Sikh textile trader from Punjab lucky enough to hold a ticket to the closing ceremony.

I'm two feet from the screeners when my face, my normal face, appears on one of the television screens that had been showing the finish of the marathon.

At first I feel panicky. But then I quickly compose myself and take several discreet glances at the screen, hoping it's just some kind of recap of the events of the Olympics including my dismissal from the organising committee. But then I see the banner scrolling beneath my image and the news that I'm wanted in connection with the Cronus murders.

How is it possible! Many voices thunder in my head, triggering one of those insanely blinding headaches. It's everything I can do to stay composed when I step towards an F7 guard, a burly woman, and a young police constable who are inspecting tickets and identification.

'You're a long way from home, Mr Rajpal,' the constable says, looking at me expressionlessly.

'One is willing to make the journey for an event as wonderful as this,' I say in a practised accent that comes through flawlessly despite the pounding in my skull. I have to fight not to reach up under my turban to touch that scar throbbing at the back of my head.

The F7 guard glances at a laptop computer screen. 'Have you been to any other events during the games, Mr Rajpal?' she asks.

'Two,' I say. 'Athletics this past Thursday evening, and field hockey earlier in the week. Monday afternoon. The India-Australia game. We lost.'

She scans the screen and nods. 'We'll need to put

your bag and any other metal objects through the screener.'

'Without hesitation,' I say, putting the bag on the conveyor belt and depositing coins, my bracelet, and my mobile in a plastic tray that follows it.

'No kirpan?' the constable asks.

I smile. Clever lad. 'No, I left the ceremonial dagger at home.'

The constable nods. 'Appreciate that. We've had a few of your blokes try to come in with them. You can go on through now.'

Moments later my headache recedes. I've retrieved my bag, which contains only a camera and a large tube of what appears to be sunscreen. Moving quickly past Eton Manor I cross an elevated pedestrian bridge that leads me onto the north-east concourse. Skirting the Velodrome, the basketball arena and the athletes' village, I make my way continuously south past the sponsors' hospitality area. I pause to look at them, realising that I've overlooked many possible violators of the Olympic ideals.

No matter, I decide. My final act will more than compensate for the oversight. At that thought, my breath quickens. So does my heart, which is hammering when I smile at the guards at the bottom of the loose spiral staircase that climbs between the legs of the Orbit. 'The restaurant?' I say. 'Still open?'

'Until half-past three, sir,' one of them replies. 'You've got two hours.'

'And if I wish for food after that?' I ask.

'The other vendors down here will all be open,' he says. 'Only the restaurant is closing.'

I nod and start the long climb, barely giving heed to the nameless monsters descending the staircase, all of them oblivious to the threat I represent. Twelve minutes later, I reach the level of the slowly turning restaurant, and go up to the maître d'.

'Rajpal,' I say. 'Table for one.'

She frowns. 'Would you be willing to share?'

'It would be a great pleasure,' I reply.

She nods. 'It will still be ten or fifteen minutes.'

'Might I use the gents' while I wait?' I ask.

'Of course,' she says and stands aside.

Other prospective patrons press in behind me, leaving the woman so busy that I'm sure she's already begun to forget about me. When she calls my name, she'll figure I got tired of waiting and left. Even if she has someone check the toilet, they won't find me. Rajpal is already gone.

I go to the gents', and take the stall I need, which is luckily vacant. Five minutes go by before the rest of the facility empties. Then, as quickly as I can, I pull myself up to a sitting position on the stall dividers and push up one of the ceiling tiles to reveal a reinforced crawl-way built so that maintenance workers can easily get at the electrical and cooling systems.

A few moments of struggle and I'm laying up there in the crawl-way, the ceiling tile back in place. Now all I have to do is calm myself, prepare myself, and trust in fate.

Chapter 109

KNIGHT AND JACK were inside the Olympic Park by four that afternoon. The sunlight was still glaring and the heat shimmered off the track. According to Scotland Yard and MI5, which had together seized control of security under orders from the Prime Minister, Mike Lancer had made no effort to get inside the park with his security pass, which someone had smartly flagged immediately after the warning about him had been issued.

Around four-thirty, Knight's head was still aching as he followed Jack into the empty stadium where teams with sniffer dogs were patrolling. At the moment, his thoughts were less about finding Lancer than they were about his children. Were they all right in hospital? Was Amanda by their side?

Knight was about to make a call to his mother when Jack said, 'Maybe he did get spooked at the marathon. Maybe that was his last chance: he saw it wasn't going to work, and he's making his escape.'

'No,' Knight said. 'He's going to try something here. Something big.'

'He'll have to be Houdini,' Jack observed. 'You heard them, they've gone to war-zone security levels. They're putting double teams of SAS snipers up high and every available cop in the halls and stairways.'

'I'm hearing you, Jack,' Knight said. 'But given what the insane bastard has done so far, we can't be sure that *any* security level is going to work. Think about it. Lancer oversaw a billion and a half dollars in security spending for the Olympics. He knows every contingency that Scotland Yard and MI5 provided for in their plans. And for much of the past seven years that lunatic has had access to every inch of every venue as it was built. Every goddamn inch.'

Chapter 110

AT THREE-THIRTY THAT afternoon, echoing through the fourteen-inch gap between the restaurant ceiling and the roof of the Orbit, I hear hydraulic gears being braked and halted, and feel the slow rotation of the observation deck stop. Closing my eyes and calming my breathing, I prepare for what lies ahead. My fate. My destiny. My just and final due.

At ten minutes to four I squeeze the tube of special skin cream onto the turban cloth and use it to turn my skin near-black. A maintenance crew enters and cleans the room below me. I can hear their mops sluicing the floor for several minutes, followed by half an hour of silence that is interrupted only by the soft sounds of the movement it takes to stain my head, neck and hands.

At twelve minutes past four, the first sniffer dog team enters the gents', and I have the sudden terrible thought that the monsters might have been clever enough to bring an article of my clothing to prime their beasts. But the patrol is in and out in under a minute, fooled no doubt by the smell of the patchouli oil.

They return at five and again at six. When they leave after the third time, I know that my hour is at hand. Cautiously, I grope around under a strip of insulation, finding a loaded ammunition clip put there seven months ago. Pocketing the clip, I lower myself into the stall and then strip off my remaining clothes, leaving me two-tone, black and white, and a terror to behold in the mirror.

Naked now except for my wristwatch, I rip a length of the turban fabric and wrap the two ends around my hands, leaving an eighteen-inch section dangling slack. Taking a position tight to the wall next to the gents' door, I settle down to wait.

At six forty-five, I hear footsteps and men's voices. The door opens and comes right up against my face before it swings back the other way to reveal the back of a tall, athletic black monster in a tracksuit and carrying a large duffel bag.

He is big. I assume he's skilled. But he is no match for a superior being.

The slack turban fabric flicks over his head and settles below his chin. Before he can even react, I've got my knee in his back and I'm throttling the life out of him. Seconds later, still feeling the quivering and soft nasal whining of his death, I drag the monster's body to the farthest stall, and then move to his duffel bag, glancing at my watch. Thirty minutes until showtime.

It takes me less than half that to don the parade uniform of the Queen's guardsman and set the black bearskin hat on my head, feeling its familiar weight settle above my eyebrows and tight to my ears. After a minor adjustment, I've got the leather chinstrap taut and snug against my jaw. Last, I pick up his automatic rifle, knowing very well that it's empty. I don't care. The ammo clip is full.

Then I return to the middle stall and wait. At a quarter past seven, I hear the door open and a voice growl, 'Supple, we're up.'

'On it in two,' I reply, disguising my voice with a cough. 'Go to the hatch.'

'See you topside,' he says.

I hope not, I think before I hear the door close behind him.

Out of the stall now, I go to the door, tracking the sweep second hand of my watch. At exactly ninety seconds, I take a deep breath and step out through the door and into the hallway, carrying the duffel bag.

At a quick pace, eyes gazing straight ahead, my face expressionless, I walk through the restaurant to the glass doors on the right-hand side of the dining room. Two SAS men are already unlocking the doors. As they swing them open, exposing me to the heat, I set my dufflel bag to one side next to another identical one, and charge past them onto the observation platform and towards a narrow doorway that is open and guarded by yet another SAS man.

I've timed it perfectly. The guard hisses, 'Cutting it bloody close, mate.'

'Shaving it close is what the Queen's Guard do, mate,' I say, ducking past him and into a tight stairwell with a narrow steel staircase that rises to a retracting hatch door and open air.

I can see the early-evening sky and clouds racing above me. Hearing distant trumpets calling, I climb towards my fate, so close now that I can feel it like a muscle burn and taste it like sweet sweat on my lips.

Chapter 111

THE TRUMPETERS STOOD to either side of the stage down on the floor of the Olympic Stadium, blowing a plaintive melody that Knight did not recognise.

He stood high in the stands at the north end of the venue, using binoculars to scan the crowd. He was tired, his head aching, and was feeling overly irritated by the lingering heat and the sound of the trumpets launching the closing ceremony. As it stopped, the screens around the stadium jumped to a feed showing a medium-range view of the Olympic cauldron high atop the Orbit and flanked as it had been since the opening ceremony by the ramrod-straight Queen's guardsmen.

The guardsmen on the raised platform above the roof shouldered their guns, pivoted through forty-five degrees and marched stiff-legged, their free arms pumping, in opposite directions towards two new guardsmen who climbed up onto the roof from hatches on either side of the observation deck and moved towards the platform and cauldron. The guards passed each other exactly halfway between the cauldron and the stairwell. The guards who were being relieved of duty disappeared from the roof and the new pair climbed the platform from either side to stand rigidly at attention beside the Olympic flame.

Knight roamed the crowd for the next hour and a half. As the summer sky began to darken and breezes began to stir, he was buoyed by the fact that despite the threat Lancer still posed, an incredible number of athletes, coaches, judges, referees and fans had decided to attend the closing ceremony when they could just as easily have gone home to more certain safety.

The affair had originally been planned as a celebration as joyous as the opening ceremony had been before the death of the American shot-putter. But the organisers had tweaked the ceremony in light of the murders, and had made it more sombre and meaningful by enlisting the London Symphony Orchestra to back Eric Clapton who delivered a heart-wrenching version of his song 'Tears in Heaven'.

In that same vein, as Knight moved south inside the stadium, Marcus Morris was now giving a speech that was part elegy to the dead and part celebration of all the great and wonderful things that had happened at the London Games in spite of Cronus and his Furies.

Knight glanced at the programme and thought: We've got a few more speeches, a spectacle or two, the turning over of the Olympic flag to Brazil; and then a few words by the mayor of Rio and . . .

'Anything, Peter?' Jack asked over the radio. They'd changed security frequencies in case Lancer was trying to monitor their broadcasts.

'Nothing,' he replied. 'But it still doesn't feel right.'

That thought was paramount in Knight's mind until the organisers broke from the scheduled programme to introduce some 'special guests'.

Dr Hunter Pierce appeared on the stage along with Zeke Shaw and the four runners who'd won marathon gold. They pushed Filatri Mundaho in a wheelchair before them, a sheet over his legs. Medical personnel followed.

Mundaho had suffered third-degree burns over much of his lower body, and had endured several excruciating abrasion procedures during the past week. The co-world-record holder in the 100 metres should have been in agony, unable to rise from his hospital bed. But you'd never have known it.

The orphaned ex-boy soldier's head was up, proud and erect. He was waving to the crowd, which leaped to its collective feet and began cheering for him. Knight's eyes watered. Mundaho was showing

James Patterson

incredible, incredible courage, along with an iron will and a depth of humanity that Lancer could not even begin to fathom.

They gave the sprinter his gold-medal ceremony, and during the playing of the Cameroonian national anthem Knight was hard pressed to find someone in the stadium who wasn't teary-eyed.

Then Hunter Pierce began to talk about the legacy of the London Games, arguing that it would ultimately signify a rekindling of and rededication to Pierre de Coubertin's original Olympic dreams and ideals. At first Knight was held enraptured by the American diver's speech.

But then he forced himself to tune her out, to try to think like Lancer and like Lancer's alter ego Cronus. He thought about the last few things that the madman had said to him. He tried to see Lancer's words as if they were printed on blocks that he could pick up and examine in detail: AT THE END, JUST BEFORE YOU DIE, KNIGHT, I'M GOING TO MAKE SURE THAT YOU AND YOUR CHILDREN WITNESS HOW I INGENIOUSLY MANAGE TO SNUFF OUT THE OLYMPIC SPIRIT FOR EVER.

Knight considered each and every word, exploring their meaning in every sense. And that's when it hit him, the seventh to last word in the sentence.

He triggered his radio microphone, and said, 'You

don't snuff out a spirit, Jack.'

'Come back with that, Peter?' Jack said.

Knight was already running towards the exit, saying, 'Lancer told me he was going to "snuff out the Olympic spirit forever".'

'And?'

'You don't snuff out a spirit, Jack. You snuff out a flame.'

Chapter 112

LOOK AT ME now, hiding in plain sight of a hundred thousand people and cameras linked to billions more.

Fated. Chosen. Gifted by the gods. I am clearly a being superior in every way, certainly superior to pathetic Mundaho and Shaw and that conniving bitch Hunter Pierce, and the other athletes down there on the stage inside the stadium, all of them condemning me as a . . .

The wind is picking up. I shift my attention into the wind: north-west, far beyond the stadium, far beyond London. Out there on the horizon dark clouds are boiling up into thunderheads. What could be more fitting as a backdrop?

Fated, I think, before I hear a roar go up in the stadium.

What's this? Sir Elton John and Sir Paul McCartney are coming onto the stage and taking seats at opposite white pianos. Who's that with them? Marianne Faithfull? Oh, for pity's sake, they're singing 'Let it Be' to Mundaho.

At their monstrous screeching, you can't begin to understand how much I want to abandon my stance of attention, rub my scar and end this hypocritical pap right now. But, with my eyes locked dead ahead into the approaching storm, I tell myself to stay calm and follow the plan to its natural and fated ending.

To keep the infernal singing from getting to me, I focus on the fact that, just a few minutes from now, I *will* reveal myself. And when I do I'll be able to rejoice in their shared horror: McCartney, John, and Faithfull too. I'll watch them all trampling over Mundaho as they run for the exits and I joyously make one final sacrifice in the name of every true Olympian who ever lived.

Chapter 113

HEARING THE CROWD in the stadium singing 'Let it Be', Knight raced towards the base of the Orbit, seeing Jack already there ahead of him, interrogating the Gurkhas guarding the staircase that wound its way up the tower's DNA-like superstructure towards the circular observation deck.

When Knight arrived, legs cramping and head splitting, he gasped, 'Was Lancer up there?'

'They say the only people who went up after three-thirty were some SAS snipers, a dog team, and the two Queen's guardsmen protecting the—'

'Can we alert them, the men on the roof?' Knight said, cutting Jack off.

'I don't know,' Jack said. 'I mean, I don't think so.'

'I think Lancer plans to blow up the cauldron, maybe this entire structure. Where's the propane tank and feeder line that keep the flame alight?'

'It's over this way,' called the strained voice of a man hurrying them.

Stuart Meeks was head of facilities at the Olympic Park. A short man in his fifties who sported a pencil-thin moustache and slicked-back hair, he carried an iPad and sweated profusely as he used an electronic code to open a door set flush in the concrete floor. The steps beneath the door led down into a massive utility basement that ran beneath the western legs of the Orbit and out under the river and the plaza towards the stadium.

'How big is the tank down there?' Knight asked as Meeks lifted the door.

'Huge – five hundred thousand litres,' Meeks said, holding out the iPad, which showed a schematic of the gas system. 'But as you can see here it serves all the propane needs in the park, not just the cauldron. The gas is drawn from the main reservoir here into smaller holding tanks at each of the venues – and in the athletes' village, of course. It was designed, like the electrical station, to be self-sufficient.'

Knight gaped at him. 'Are you saying if it blows, everything blows?'

'No, I don't . . .' Meeks stopped. He turned pale. 'I honestly don't know.'

Jack said, 'Peter and I were with Lancer ten days ago up on the observation deck shortly after he'd finished inspecting security on the cauldron. Did Lancer go down into this basement during that inspection, Stu?'

Meeks nodded. 'Mike insisted on looking at everything one last time. From the tank and up the line, all the way to the coupling that connects the piping to the cauldron. It took us more than an hour.'

'We don't have an hour,' Knight said.

Jack was already on the steep ladder, preparing to climb down to inspect the giant propane tank. 'Call in the dogs again, Stu. Send them down as soon as they get here. Peter, trace the gas line up to the roof.'

Knight nodded before asking Meeks if he had any tools with him. The facilities director unsnapped a Leatherman from a pouch on his hip and told Knight he'd send the schematic of the gas-line system to his phone. No more than twenty yards up the spiral staircase that climbed the Orbit, Knight felt his phone buzz, alerting him to the arrival of the schematic.

He was about to open the link when he thought of something that made the diagram seem irrelevant at this point. He keyed his microphone and said, 'Stuart, how is the gas line to the cauldron controlled? By that I mean is there a manual valve up there that controls the gas flow that will have to be moved for the flame in the cauldron to go out, or will it be done electronically?'

'Electronically,' Meeks replied. 'Before it connects to the cauldron the line runs through a crawl space that's part of the ductwork in the ceiling above the restaurant and below the roof.'

Despite the pounding in his skull and his general sense of irritability, Knight was picking up the pace as he climbed. The wind was strong now. In the distance he thought he heard the rumble of thunder.

'Any way to get on the roof?' he asked.

'There are two hatches with retractable doors and staircases on opposite sides of the roof,' Meeks said. 'That's how the guardsmen have been climbing up and down for their shifts. There's also an exhaust grate in the ductwork several feet from that valve you asked about.'

Before Knight could think about that, he heard Jack say, 'Main tank appears clear. Stuart, we know the max volume and what it's holding?'

There was long pause before the Olympic Park's facility supervisor said in a hoarse voice, 'It was filled again at dawn, day before yesterday, Jack.'

Two hundred feet above the Olympic Park, Knight now understood that underground between the Orbit and the stadium was a mega-explosive device certainly capable of toppling the tower, but also of causing tremendous damage to the south end of the stadium and everyone seated there. Not to mention what might happen if a central explosion set off other detonations around the venue.

'Evacuate, Jack,' Knight said. 'Tell security to stop

the ceremony and get everyone out of the stadium, and out of the park.'

'But what if he's watching?' Jack said. 'What if he can trigger it remotely?'

'I don't know,' Knight said, feeling torn. His personal inclination was to turn around and get the hell out of there. He was a father. He'd already almost died once today. Could he dare tempt fate twice?

Still climbing, Knight toggled on the schematic on his phone, looking for the digitally controlled cauldron valve that was somewhere between the roof and the restaurant ceiling. At a glance, he felt almost sure that that control valve was the most likely place for Lancer to attach a triggering device to the main gas line.

If he could reach it, he could defuse it. If he couldn't . . .

Chapter 114

LIGHTNING FLASHED IN the near distance and the wind began to gust as Knight reached the entrance to the observation deck of the Orbit. Samba music blared from inside the Olympic stadium as part of Brazil's tribute to the 2016 games.

Though they'd been warned that he was coming, the Gurkhas at the entry insisted on checking Knight's ID before allowing him to enter. Inside he was met by the senior SAS man, a guy named Creston, who said that he and his team and the skeleton television camera crew had been on the deck since roughly five o'clock when the restaurant had been closed to everyone but the Queen's guardsmen who were using the gents' inside to change in and out of uniform.

Queen's Guard, Knight thought. Lancer's regiment served in the Guard. Hadn't he said that?

'Get me in that restaurant,' Knight said. 'There

might be a triggering device tied into the gas line above the kitchen.'

In seconds, Knight was running through the restaurant towards the kitchen with the SAS man in tow. Knight looked over his shoulder at him. 'Are the roof hatches open?'

'No,' Creston said. 'Not until the end of the ceremony. They're timed.'

'No way to talk to the guardsmen up there?'

He shook his head. 'They aren't even armed. It's a ceremonial bit.'

Knight pressed his microphone. 'Stuart, where do I go up through the ceiling?'

'In the kitchen, left of the oven hood,' Meeks replied. 'The kitchen is past the toilets and through the double doors.'

As Knight went into the hallway towards the kitchen, he saw the gents', remembered that the guardsmen got changed there, and had a sudden strange intuition. 'When did the relieved guards leave?' he asked the SAS man.

Creston shrugged. 'Right after their shift. They had seats inside the stadium.'

'They changed and left?'

He nodded.

Still, rather than barge on into the kitchen, Knight stopped and pushed on the door of the ladies' toilet.

'What are you doing?' Creston asked.

'Not sure,' Knight said, seeing it empty and then squatting to peer under the stalls. All empty.

He quickly crossed to the gents' and did the same, finding a black man's naked body stuffed into the farthest stall.

'We have a dead guardsman in the men's loo up here,' Knight barked into his radio as he headed towards the kitchen. 'I believe Lancer has taken his uniform and is now on the roof.'

He looked at the SAS man. 'Figure out how to get those hatch doors open.'

Creston nodded and took off, with Knight going in the opposite direction, bursting into the kitchen and quickly spotting the trapdoor in the ceiling left of the restaurant's oven hood and vent. Dragging a stainless steel food-preparation table over beneath the trapdoor, he triggered his mike and said, 'Can we get a visual on the guards to confirm that one of them is Lancer?'

Listening to Jack relay the request to snipers high atop the stadium, Knight noticed the padlock on the trapdoor for the first time. 'I need a combination, Stuart,' he said into his radio.

Meeks gave it to him, and with shaking hands Knight spun the dial and felt the lock give. He used a broom to push the trapdoor open, then looked around the kitchen one last time to see if there was anything he might be able to use or might need to

Knight tossed the torch up into the crawl space,
and then swung his arms twice to loosen them
before jumping up and grabbing the sides of the
trapdoor frame. He hung there a second, took a deep
breath, and raised his legs in front of him before
driving them backward with enough force for him to
be able to lurch his way up into the cavity between
the restaurant ceiling and the roof of the Orbit.

Knight pulled out a slim torch, flipped it on and,
pushing the blowtorch in front of him, wriggled
towards a piece of copper pipe that bisected the
ductwork about six feet away. Knight didn't have to
get much closer to see the bumpy black electrical
tape wrapped around it, securing a mobile phone
and something else to the gas line.

'I've got the trigger. It's a small magnesium bomb
taped to the gas line,' he said. 'It's not on a timer.
He's going to blow it remotely. Shut down the entire
gas system. Put out the Olympic flame. Now.'

Chapter 115

BLOW, WINDS, BLOW.

Lightning flashes and thunder blasts north-west towards Crouch End and Stroud Green, not far at all from where my drug-addled parents gave birth to me. It is fitting. It is fated.

Indeed, as the jackass who runs the International Olympic Committee prepares to have the flags lowered, declare the Games over, and order the flame extinguished, I fully embrace my destiny. Breaking from my stance of rigid attention, I gaze into the black wall of the oncoming storm, thinking how remarkable it is that my life has been like a track oval, starting and finishing in much the same place.

Pulling out a mobile phone from my pocket, I hit a number on speed dial and hear it connect. Pocketing the phone, I take up my rifle, take two strides forward and pivot to my right. Towards the cauldron.

Chapter 116

A FEW MINUTES earlier, Karen Pope trudged out into the west stands of the Olympic Stadium just as IOC President Jacques Rogge, looking haggard and grave, walked to the lectern on the stage. The reporter had just filed her latest update to the *Sun*'s website, describing the escape of Knight and his children, the death of Marta and her sisters, and the global manhunt for Mike Lancer.

As Rogge spoke over the noise of a rising wind and against the building rumour of thunder, Pope was thinking that these cursed Games were finally almost over. Goodbye and good riddance as far as she was concerned. She never wanted to write about the Olympics again, though she knew that was an impossible dream. She felt depressed and lethargic, and wondered if what she was feeling was as much battle fatigue as the desperate need to sleep. And Knight wasn't answering his phone. Neither was Jack Morgan, or Inspector Pottersfield.

What was going on that she didn't know about?

As Rogge droned on, preparing to declare the Games at an end, Pope happened to look up at the cauldron atop the Orbit, seeing the flame billow in the wind. She admitted that she looked forward to seeing it extinguished while feeling somewhat guilty about the—

The Queen's guardsman to the cauldron's left suddenly lifted his gun, threw off his bearskin hat, walked out in front of the Olympic flame, pivoted and opened fire. The other guard jerked, staggered, and fell to his side and off the platform. His body hit the roof, slid and slipped off the Orbit, plunging and then gone.

Pope's gasp of horror was obliterated by the screams of the multitude in the stadium rising into one trembling cry before a booming voice coming over the public address system drowned it out: 'You sorry inferior creatures. You didn't think an instrument of the gods would let you off that easily, did you?'

Chapter 117

I CLUTCH THE mobile phone in my left hand, speaking into it, and hearing the power in my voice echo back to me. 'All you SAS snipers out there in the park, don't be stupid. I'm holding a triggering device. If you shoot me, this entire tower, much of the stadium, and tens of thousands of lives will be lost.'

Below me, the crowd erupts and turns as frenzied as rats fleeing a sinking ship. Seeing them scurry and claw, I smile with utter satisfaction.

'Tonight marks the end of the modern Olympics,' I thunder. 'Tonight we snuff out the flame that has burned so corruptly since that traitor de Coubertin came up with this mockery of the true Games more than a century ago!'

Chapter 118

KNIGHT HEARD THE gunshots and Lancer's booming threat through an exhaust grate in the ceiling of the ductwork several feet beyond the gas line and the triggering device.

He didn't have time to try and defuse the trigger, and for all he knew Lancer had booby-trapped it to go off if it was tampered with.

'How about cutting off the tanks?' he asked over his radio.

'It's a disaster, Peter,' Jack shot back. 'He's welded the valves open.'

Above him, Lancer launched into a longer tirade, beginning with the doctors in Barcelona who had drugged him to prevent him from winning gold in the decathlon, from being named the greatest all-around athlete in the world. And in the background, Knight could hear the petrified crowd trying to escape the stadium. He understood he had only one chance.

He pushed the blowtorch forward and crawled after it, past the gas line and the triggering device, until he lay beneath the exhaust grate.

Through the slats he saw flashes of approaching lightning and the billowing glow of the Olympic flame still burning.

Four bolts held the grate in place. All of them looked sealed in some kind of chemical resin. Maybe he could melt it.

Knight grabbed the blowtorch and ignited it. As fast as he could, he heated the resin until it melted. Then he grabbed the nearest bolt head with the pliers on the Leatherman tool that Meeks had given him and wrenched at it. He felt thrilled when it gave.

Chapter 119

LIGHTNING INSCRIBES THE sky and thunder booms like close cannon fire as I bellow at the crazed crowd trying to escape the stadium, 'For these reasons and a thousand others, the modern Games must end. Surely you understand!'

But instead of screams of terror, or even calls of agreement, I'm hearing something I did not expect in return. The monsters are booing me. They're catcalling, and casting filthy slurs on my genius, my superiority.

These are the final indignities of a martyr for a just cause – stabbing, hurtful. But nothing like a roadside bomb, or even a rock, nothing that can stop me from seeing my fate fulfilled.

Still, this rejection is enough to raise a wave of hatred in me like no other, a tsunami of loathing for all the monsters in the stadium before me.

Looking up into the thundering dark sky that is now spitting lightning and hurling rain, I cry, 'For you, Gods of Olympus. I do this all for you!'

Chapter 120

KNIGHT WAS ALREADY well beyond the exhaust vent, up on the raised platform surrounding the cauldron, and now charging at full tilt through the pouring rain.

Before the madman's thumb could hit the mobile's send button, Knight hit Lancer low, hard, and from the side, a stunning blow that caused the crazed Olympian to lurch and fall to the floor of the platform. His automatic weapon skittered away.

Knight landed on top of Lancer, who was still clutching the mobile phone. The former decathlon champion was some ten years older than Knight. But he quickly proved bigger, stronger, and more skilled as a fighter.

Lancer backhanded Knight so hard that the Private London agent was thrown off, and almost slammed his face against the searing wall of the cauldron. The infernal heat and the drenching rain revived him almost instantly.

He twisted, seeing that Lancer was trying to regain his feet. But Knight kicked viciously at the madman's ankle and connected. Lancer howled, stumbled to one knee and was rising again when Knight got his right forearm around the man's bull neck from behind, trying to get a choke hold on him and seize the mobile before the gas bomb could be triggered.

He squeezed Lancer's throat and grabbed at his thumb, trying to pry loose his grip on the phone. But then Lancer jammed his chin down on Knight's forearm, twisted his torso, and threw elbow punches that struck Knight hard on ribs still bruised from the Fury's attempt to run him down.

The Private London agent grunted in dire pain but held on, thinking of Luke and Isabel before taking a cue from his son. He bit brutally at the back of the insane man's head, feeling a chunk of thick scar tissue tear away from Lancer's scalp. Lancer screamed in agony and rage.

Knight bit again, this time lower, his teeth sinking into neck muscles as a lion might try to cripple a buffalo.

Lancer went berserk.

He swung and bucked, bellowing in blind primal fury and throwing meaty fists over his shoulder, hitting Knight in the head before pummelling his torso with elbow blows again, left and right, blows so hard that several of the Private agent's ribs cracked and broke.

It was too much for him.

Knight's breath was knocked out of him and the pain in his side erupted with such force that he grunted, releasing both his bite and the chokehold that he'd had on Lancer's neck. He fell to the platform in the rain, groaning and fighting for air and a relief from the agony that now consumed him.

Blood dripping from his bite wounds, Lancer turned and glared down at Knight in triumph and in loathing.

'You had no chance, Knight,' he gloated, backing away and raising the mobile phone towards the sky again. 'You were up against an infinitely superior being. You had no—'

Knight flung the Leatherman at Lancer.

It flew end over end before the narrow prongs of the pliers struck Lancer and pierced deep into his right eye.

Staggering backwards, still clutching the mobile, reaching futilely for the tool that had sealed his fate, Lancer let out a series of blood-curdling screams worthy of some mythical creature of doom, like Cronus after Zeus threw him deep into the darkest and deepest pit in Tartarus.

For a second, Knight feared Lancer would find his balance and manage to trigger the bomb.

But then thunder exploded directly over the Orbit, throwing a single white-hot jagged bolt that ignored the lightning rods fixed high above the observation deck and struck the butt end of the Leatherman tool protruding from Lancer's eye, electrocuting the self-described instrument of the gods and hurling him back and over into the cauldron where he was engulfed and consumed by the roaring Olympic flame.

Epilogue

Monday, 13 August 2012

ON THE THIRD floor of St Thomas's Hospital, sitting in a wheelchair, Knight smiled stiffly at the people gathered around the beds that held Luke and Isabel. While the effects of what turned out to be a concussion had mellowed to a dull thumping in his head, his broken and bruised ribs were killing him, making each breath feel like saws working in his chest.

But he was alive. His kids were alive. The Olympics had been saved and avenged by forces far beyond Knight's understanding. And Inspector Elaine Pottersfield had just entered the room carrying two small chocolate cakes, each adorned with three lit birthday candles.

Never one to miss the chance to sing, Hooligan broke into 'Happy Birthday' and was joined by the twins' nurses and doctors, and by Jack Morgan,

Karen Pope, and Knight's mother. Even Gary Boss, who'd arrived early to decorate the hospital room with bright balloons and bunting, joined in.

'Close your eyes and make a wish,' the twins' aunt said.

'Dream big!' their grandmother cried.

Isabel and Luke closed their eyes for a second, and then opened them, took deep breaths and blew out every one of the candles. Everyone cheered and clapped. Pottersfield cut the cakes.

Ever the journalist, Pope asked, 'What did you wish for?'

Knight's son got annoyed. 'Lukey not telling you. It's secret.'

But Isabel looked at Pope matter-of-factly and said, 'I wished we could have a new mummy.'

Her brother's face clouded. 'No fair. That's what Lukey wished for.'

There were soothing sounds of sympathy all around and Knight felt his heart break once again.

His daughter was staring at him. 'No more nannies, Daddy.'

'No more nannies,' he promised, glancing at his mother. 'Right, Amanda?'

'Only if they are under my direct and constant supervision,' she said.

'Or mine,' Boss said.

Cake and ice cream were served. After several

bites, Pope said, 'You know what threw me about Lancer, kept me from ever considering him as a suspect?'

'What's that?' Hooligan asked.

'He had one of his Furies try to run him down on day one,' she said. 'Right?'

'Definitely,' Knight said. 'I'll bet he had that planned from the beginning. I just happened to be there.'

'There was another clue if you think about it,' Hooligan said. 'Cronus never sent you a letter detailing the reasons why Lancer should die.'

'I never thought of that,' Knight said.

'Neither did I,' Jack said, getting up from his chair and dumping his paper plate into the wastebasket.

After they had finished eating and had unwrapped the presents that everyone seemed to have brought, Knight's children were soon drowsy. When Isabel's eyes closed, and Luke started to rock and suck his thumb, Amanda and Boss left with whispered promises to return in the morning to help see home Knight and the twins.

His sister-in-law was next to depart, saying, 'Hiring a war criminal as your nanny was not your finest hour, Peter, but ultimately you were brilliant. Absolutely brilliant. Kate would have been so proud of how hard your fought for your children, for the Olympics, for London, for everyone.'

Knight's heart broke yet again. 'I'd hug you, Elaine, but—'

She blew him a kiss, said she was going to check up on Selena Farrell and James Daring, and walked out the door.

'I've got a present for you before I leave, Peter,' Jack said. 'I want you to have an obscene raise, and I want you to take your kids to somewhere tropical for a few weeks. It's on Private. We'll work out the details after I get back to LA. Speaking of which, I've got a jet to catch.'

After Private's owner had gone, Pope and Hooligan got up to leave as well. 'We are off to the pub, then,' Hooligan said. 'Highlights of the entire Olympic football tournament to watch.'

'We?' Knight said, arching his eyebrow at Pope.

The reporter slipped her arm around Hooligan's waist and smiled. 'Turns out we share a lot in common, Knight. My brothers are all football-mad lads as well.'

Knight smiled. 'There's a certain symmetry there.'

Hooligan grinned and threw his arm around Pope's shoulder. 'Think you're right about that, Peter.'

'Bloody right,' Pope said and they departed, laughing.

The nurses followed and Knight was left alone in the hospital room with his children. He looked up at the television for a moment and saw a shot of the Olympic flame still burning over London. After Lancer's death, Jacques Rogge had asked that the flame should burn on a while longer, and the government had immediately agreed.

It was, Knight decided, a good thing.

Then he let his attention dwell on Luke and Isabel, thinking how beautiful they were, and thanking the gods for saving them from a cruel ending.

He sighed, thinking of how his heart had fallen apart when Isabel and Luke had both wished for a new mother, and again when Elaine had told him how proud Kate would have been of him.

Kate. He missed her still and thought morosely that maybe she had been his singular mate, the one and only love that fate had in store for him. Maybe it was his destiny to go on alone. To raise the children and . . .

A knock came at the door and an American woman's cheery voice called softly from out in the hall, 'Mr Knight? Are you in there?'

Knight looked towards the door. 'Yes?'

A very beautiful and athletic woman slipped in. He knew her immediately and tried to get to his feet, whispering, 'You're Hunter Pierce.'

'I am,' the diver said, smiling brightly now and studying him closely. 'Don't get up. I heard you were injured.'

'Only a bit,' he said. 'I was lucky. We were all lucky.'

Pierce nodded, and Knight could not help but think that she was dazzling up close and in person.

He said, 'I was there at the Aquatics Centre. When you won gold.'

'Were you?' she said, pressing her fingers to the small of her neck.

Knight's eyes were watering and he did not know why. 'I reckon it was the finest example of grace under pressure that I've ever had the honour of witnessing. And the way you spoke out against Cronus, forcefully, consistently. It was . . . well, simply remarkable, and I hope people have told you that.'

The diving champion smiled. 'Thank you. But all of us – Shaw, Mundaho, all of the athletes – they sent me here to tell you that we thought *your* performance last night outshone us all.'

'No, I . . .'

'No, really,' Pierce said emphatically. 'I was there in the stadium. So were my children. We saw you fight him. You risked your life to save ours, and the Olympics, and we, I . . . I wanted to thank you in person from the bottom of my heart.'

Knight felt emotion welling up in his throat. 'I . . . don't know what to say.'

The American diver looked over at his children.

'And these are the brave twins we read about in the *Sun* this morning?'

'Luke and Isabel,' Knight says. 'The lights of my life.'

'They're beautiful. I'd say you're a blessed man, Mr Knight.'

'Call me Peter,' he said. 'And, honestly, you can't know how grateful I am to be here and to have them here. What a blessing it all is. And, well, to have you here too.'

There was a long moment when they were both looking at each other as if they'd just recognised something both familiar and long forgotten.

Pierce cocked her head, and said, 'I'd only meant to pop in for a bit, Peter, but I just had a better thought.'

'What's that?' he asked.

The American diver smiled again, and then affected a corny British accent, saying: 'Would you fancy me wheeling you out of here down to the café? We can have a spot of tea and catch up while your little lovelies are off sailing in the Land of Nod?'

Knight felt flooded with happiness.

'Yes,' he said. 'Yes, I believe I'd like that very much.'

AVAILABLE IN PAPERBACK FROM JANUARY 2013

Private: No. 1 Suspect

James Patterson
& Maxine Paetro

Jack Morgan is accused of a horrific murder – and not even his own world-class investigators can prove he didn't do it.

Since former US Marine Jack Morgan started Private, it has become the world's most effective investigation firm – sought out by the famous and the powerful to discreetly handle their most intimate problems. Private's investigators are the smartest, the fastest, and the most technologically advanced in the world – and they always uncover the truth.

When his former lover is found murdered in Jack's bed, he is instantly the number one suspect. While Jack is under police investigation and fighting to clear his name, the mob strong-arms him into recovering $30 million in stolen pharmaceuticals for them. And the beautiful owner of a chain of luxury hotels persuades him to quietly investigate a string of murders at her high-class establishments.

With Jack and his team stretched to breaking point, one of his most trusted colleagues threatens to leave Private, and Jack realises he is facing his biggest challenge yet.

arrow books

Turn the page for an extract of

CHAPTER 1

THE CAR WAS waiting for me at LAX. Aldo was out at the curb, holding a sign reading, 'Welcome Home Mr. Morgan.'

I shook Aldo's hand, threw my bags into the trunk, and slid onto the cushy leather seat in the back. I'd done six cities in three days, the return leg from Stockholm turning into a twenty-five-hour journey through airline hell to home.

I was wiped out. And that was an understatement.

'Your packet, Jack,' Aldo said, handing a folder over the divider. The cover was marked 'Private,' the name of my private investigation firm. Our main office was in LA, and we had branches in six countries with clients all over the map who demanded and paid well for services not available through public means.

I had worried lately that we were growing too big too fast, that if big was the enemy of good, *great* didn't stand a chance. And most of all, I wanted Private to be great.

I tucked the folder from Accounting into my briefcase and as the car surfed into the fast lane, I took out my BlackBerry. Unread messages ran into triple digits, so I chose selectively as I thumbed through the list.

The first e-mail was from Viviana, the stunner who'd sat next to me from London to New York. She sold 3-D teleconferencing equipment, not exactly must-have technology, but it was definitely interesting.

There was a text from Paolo, my security chief in Rome, saying, 'Our deadbeat client is now just dead. Details to follow.' I mentally kissed a two-hundred-thousand-euro fee good-bye and moved to texts from the home team.

Justine Smith, my confidante and number two at Private, wrote, 'We've got some catching up to do, bud. I've left the porch light on.' I smiled, thinking that as much as I wanted to see her, I wanted to shower and hit the rack even more.

I sent Justine a reply, then opened a text from Rick Del Rio. 'Noccia wants to see you pronto, that prick.'

The text was like a gut punch.

Carmine Noccia was the scion of the major Mob family by that name, capo of the Las Vegas branch, and my accidental buddy because of a deal I'd had to make with him six months before.

If I never saw Carmine Noccia again, it would be way too soon.

I typed a four-letter reply, sent it to Del Rio, and put my phone back into my pocket as the car turned into my driveway. I collected my bags and watched Aldo back out, making sure he didn't get T-boned on Pacific Coast Highway.

I swiped my electronic key fob across the reader and went through the gate, pressed my finger to the biometric pad, and entered my home sweet home.

For a half second, I thought I smelled roses, but I chalked it up to the delight of standing again in my own house.

I started stripping in the living room and by the time I'd reached the bathroom, I was down to my boxers, which I kicked off outside the shower stall.

I stood under water as hot as I could stand it, then went into my bedroom and hit the wall switch that turned on the lights on either side of the bed.

For a long moment, I stood frozen in the doorway. I couldn't understand what I saw – because it made no sense. How could Colleen be in my bed? Her sweater was soaked with blood.

What the hell was this?

A tasteless prank?

I shouted her name, and then I was on my knees beside the bed, my hand pressing the side of her neck. Her skin was as warm as life – but she had no pulse.

Colleen was wearing a knee-length skirt and a blue cardigan, clothes I'd seen her wear before. Her rose-scented hair was fanned out around her shoulders and her violet-blue eyes were closed. I gripped her shoulders and gently shook her, but her head just lolled.

Oh, Jesus. No.

Colleen was dead.

How in God's name had this happened?

CHAPTER 2

I'D SEEN COUNTLESS dead while serving in Afghanistan. I've worked murders as part of my job for years, and I've even witnessed the deaths of friends.

None of that protected me from the horror of seeing Colleen's bloody and lifeless form. Her blood spattered the bedspread, soaking through. Her sweater was so bloody I couldn't see her wounds. Had she been stabbed? Shot? I couldn't tell.

The covers were pulled tight and I saw no sign of a struggle. Everything in the room was exactly as I had left it four days ago – everything but Colleen's dead body, right here.

I thought about Colleen's attempted suicide after we'd broken up six months ago – the scars were visible: silver lines on her wrists. But this was no suicide.

There was no weapon on or near the bed.

It looked as if Colleen had come into my bedroom,

put her head on the pillow, and then been killed while she slept.

And that made no sense.

Just then, my lagging survival instinct kicked in. Whoever had killed Colleen could still be in the house. I went for the window seat where I kept my gun.

My hands shook as I lifted the hinged top of the window seat and grabbed the metal gun box. It was light. Empty.

I opened the closet doors, looked under the bed, saw no one, no shells, no nothing. I stepped into jeans, pulled on a T-shirt, then walked from window to window to door, checking locks, staring up at skylights looking for broken panes.

And I backtracked through my mind.

I was certain the front door had been locked when I came home. And now I was sure that every other entry point was secure.

That could only mean that someone had entered my house with an electronic gate key and biometric access – someone who knew me. Colleen had been my assistant and my lover for a year before we'd broken up. I hadn't deleted her codes.

Colleen wasn't the only one with access to my house, but maybe I wouldn't have to guess who had killed her.

My house was watched by the best surveillance

system ever made. There were cameras posted on all sides, over the doorways, sweeping the highway, and taking in 180 degrees of beachfront beyond my deck.

I opened the cabinet doors on the entertainment unit in the living room and flipped the switch turning on the six video monitors stacked in two columns of three. All six screens lit up – and all six screens were blank. I stabbed the buttons on the remote control again and again before I realized the hard drive was gone. Only a detached cord remained.

I grabbed the phone by the sofa and called Justine's direct line at the office. It was almost seven. Would she still be there?

She answered on the first ring.

'Jack, you hungry after all?'

'Justine. Something bad has happened.'

My voice cracked as I forced myself to say it.

'It's Colleen. She's dead. Some *bastard* killed her.'

CHAPTER 3

I OPENED THE front door and Justine swept in like a soft breeze. She was a first-class psychologist, a profiler, smart – hell, brilliant. Thank God she was here.

She put her hand on my cheek, searched my eyes, said, 'Jack. Where is she?'

I pointed to the bedroom. Justine went in and I followed her, standing numb in the doorway as she walked to the bed. She moaned, 'Oh, no,' and clasped her hands under her chin.

Even as I stood witness to this heartbreaking tableau, Colleen was still alive in my mind.

I pictured her in the little house she had rented in Los Feliz, a love nest you could almost hold in cupped hands. I thought about her twitching her hips in skimpy lingerie, big fuzzy slippers on her feet, sprinkling her thick brogue with her granny's auld Irish sayings: 'There'll be caps on the green and no one to fetch 'em.'

'What does that mean, Molloy?' I'd asked her.

'Trouble.'

And now here she was on my bed. Well beyond trouble.

Justine was pale when she came back to me. She put her arms around me and held me. 'I'm so sorry, Jack. So very sorry.'

I held her tight – and then, abruptly, Justine jerked away. She pinned me with her dark eyes and said, 'Why is your hair wet?'

'My hair?'

'Did you take a shower?'

'Yes, I did. When I came home, I went straight to the bathroom. I was trying to wake myself up.'

'Well, this is no dream, Jack. This is as real as real can be. When you showered, had you seen Colleen?'

'I had no idea she was here.'

'You hadn't told her to come over?'

'No, Justine, I didn't. *No.*'

The doorbell rang again.

CHAPTER 4

THE ARRIVAL OF Dr. Sci and Mo-bot improved the odds of figuring out what had happened in my house by 200 percent.

Dr. Sci, real name Seymour Kloppenberg, was Private's chief forensic scientist. He had a long string of degrees behind his name, starting with a PhD in physics from MIT when he was nineteen – and that was only ten years ago.

Mo-bot was Maureen Roth, a fifty-something computer geek and jack-of-all-tech. She specialized in computer crime and was also Private's resident mom.

Mo had brought her camera and her wisdom. Sci had his scene kit packed with evidence-collection equipment of the cutting-edge kind.

We went to my room and the four of us stood around Colleen's dead body as night turned the windows black.

We had all loved Colleen. Every one of us.

'We don't have much time,' Justine said, breaking the silence, at work now as an investigator on a homicide. 'Jack, I have to ask you, did you have anything to do with this? Because if you did, we can make it all disappear.'

'I found Colleen like this when I got home,' I said.

'Okay. Just the same,' said Justine, 'every passing minute makes you more and more the guy who did it. You've got to call it in, Jack. So let's go over everything, fast and carefully. Start from the beginning and don't leave anything out.'

As Mo and Sci snapped on latex gloves, Justine turned on a digital recorder and motioned to me to start talking. I told her that after I got off the plane, Aldo had met me at British Airways arrivals, 5:30 sharp.

I told her about showering, then finding Colleen's body. I said that my gun was missing as well as the hard drive from my security system.

I said again that I had no idea why Colleen was here or why she'd been killed. 'I didn't do it, Justine.'

'I know that, Jack.'

We both knew that when the cops got here, I would be suspect number one, and although I had cop friends, I couldn't rely on any of them to find Colleen's killer when I was so darned handy.

I had been intimately involved with the deceased.

There was no forced entry into my house.

The victim was on my bed.

It was what law enforcement liked to call an open-and-shut case. Open and shut on me.

CHAPTER 5

IF YOU'RE NOT the cops on official business, processing an active crime scene is a felony. It's not just contaminating evidence and destroying the prosecution's ability to bring the accused to trial, it's accessory to the crime.

If we were caught working the scene, I would lose my license, and all four of us could go to jail.

That said, if there was ever a time to break the law, this was it.

Mo said, 'Jack, please get out of the frame.'

I stepped into the hallway and Mo's Nikon flashed.

She took shots from every angle, wide, close-up, extreme close-ups of the wounds in Colleen's chest.

Sci took Colleen's and my fingerprints with an electronic reader while Mo-bot ran a latent-print reader over hard surfaces in the room. No finger-print powder required.

Justine asked, 'When did you last see Colleen alive?'

I told her that I'd had lunch with her last Wednesday, before I left for the airport.

'Just lunch?'

'Yes. We just had lunch.'

A shadow crossed Justine's eyes, like clouds rolling in before a thunderstorm. She didn't believe me. And I didn't have the energy to persuade her. I was overtired, scared, heartsick, and nauseated. I wanted to wake up. Find myself still on the plane.

Sci was talking to Mo. He took scrapings from under Colleen's nails, and Mo sealed the bags. When Sci lifted Colleen's skirt, swab in hand, I turned away.

I talked to Justine, told her where Colleen and I had eaten lunch on Wednesday, that Colleen had been in good spirits.

'She said she had a boyfriend in Dublin. She said she was falling in love.'

I had a new thought. I spun around and shouted, 'Anyone see her purse?'

'No purse, Jack.'

'She was brought here,' I said to Justine. 'Someone had her gate key.'

Justine said, 'Good thought. Any reason or anyone you can think of who could have done this?'

'Someone hated her. Or hated me. Or hated us both.' Justine nodded. 'Sci? Mo? We have to get out of here. Will you be all right, Jack?'

'I'm not sure,' I said.

'You're in shock. We all are. Just tell the cops what you know,' she said as Sci and Mo packed up their kits.

'Say you took a very long shower,' Sci said, putting his hand on my shoulder. 'Make that a long bath and then a shower. That should soak up some of the timeline.'

'Okay.'

'The only prints I found were yours,' said Mo-bot.

'It's *my* house.'

'I know that, Jack. There were no prints other than yours. Check the entry card reader,' she said. 'I would do it, but we should leave.'

'Okay. Thanks, Mo.'

Justine squeezed my hand, said she'd call me later, and then, as if I had dreamed them up, they were gone and I was alone with Colleen.

JAMES
PATTERSON

**To find out more about James Patterson
and his bestselling books, go to
www.jamespatterson.co.uk**

Also by James Patterson

ALEX CROSS NOVELS

Along Came a Spider • Kiss the Girls • Jack and Jill •
Cat and Mouse • Pop Goes the Weasel • Roses are Red •
Violets are Blue • Four Blind Mice • The Big Bad Wolf •
London Bridges • Mary, Mary • Cross • Double Cross •
Cross Country • Alex Cross's Trial (*with Richard DiLallo*) •
I, Alex Cross • Cross Fire • Kill Alex Cross

THE WOMEN'S MURDER CLUB SERIES

1st to Die • 2nd Chance (*with Andrew Gross*) •
3rd Degree (*with Andrew Gross*) • 4th of July
(*with Maxine Paetro*) • The 5th Horseman (*with Maxine Paetro*)
• The 6th Target (*with Maxine Paetro*) • 7th Heaven (*with
Maxine Paetro*) • 8th Confession (*with Maxine Paetro*) •
9th Judgement (*with Maxine Paetro*) • 10th Anniversary
(*with Maxine Paetro*) • 11th Hour (*with Maxine Paetro*)

DETECTIVE MICHAEL BENNETT SERIES

Step on a Crack (*with Michael Ledwidge*) • Run for Your Life
(*with Michael Ledwidge*) • Worst Case (*with Michael Ledwidge*) •
Tick Tock (*with Michael Ledwidge*) • I, Michael Bennett
(*with Michael Ledwidge*)

STAND-ALONE THRILLERS

Sail (*with Howard Roughan*) • Swimsuit (*with Maxine Paetro*) •
Don't Blink (*with Howard Roughan*) • Postcard Killers
(*with Liza Marklund*) • Toys (*with Neil McMahon*) •
Now You See Her (*with Michael Ledwidge*) • Kill Me If You Can
(*with Marshall Karp*) • Guilty Wives (*with David Ellis*)

NON-FICTION

Torn Apart (*with Hal and Cory Friedman*) •
The Murder of King Tut (*with Martin Dugard*)

ROMANCE

Sundays at Tiffany's (*with Gabrielle Charbonnet*) •
The Christmas Wedding (*with Richard DiLallo*)

FAMILY OF PAGE-TURNERS

MAXIMUM RIDE SERIES

The Angel Experiment • School's Out Forever •
Saving the World and Other Extreme Sports •
The Final Warning • Max • Fang • Angel • Nevermore
(*to be published August 2012*)

DANIEL X SERIES

The Dangerous Days of Daniel X (*with Michael Ledwidge*) •
Daniel X: Watch the Skies (*with Ned Rust*) • Daniel X: Demons
and Druids (*with Adam Sadler*) • Daniel X: Game Over
(*with Ned Rust*)

WITCH & WIZARD SERIES

Witch & Wizard (*with Gabrielle Charbonnet*) •
Witch & Wizard: The Gift (*with Ned Rust*) •
Witch & Wizard: The Fire (*with Jill Dembowski*)

MIDDLE SCHOOL SERIES

Middle School: The Worst Years of My Life
(*with Chris Tebbetts and Laura Park*) • Middle School: Get Me
Out of Here! (*with Chris Tebbetts and Laura Park*)

GRAPHIC NOVELS

Daniel X: Alien Hunter (*with Leopoldo Gout*) • Maximum Ride:
Manga Vol. 1 (*with NaRae Lee*) • Maximum Ride: Manga Vol. 2
(*with NaRae Lee*) • Maximum Ride: Manga Vol. 3 (*with NaRae
Lee*) • Maximum Ride: Manga Vol. 4 (*with NaRae Lee*) •
Maximum Ride: Manga Vol. 5 (*with NaRae Lee*)

For more information about James Patterson's novels, visit
www.jamespatterson.co.uk

Or become a fan on Facebook

We support

I'm proud to support the National Literacy Trust, an independent charity that changes lives through literacy.

Did you know that millions of people in the UK struggle to read and write? This means children are less likely to succeed at school and less likely to develop into confident and happy teenagers. Literacy difficulties will limit their opportunities throughout adult life.

The National Literacy Trust passionately believes that everyone has a right to the reading, writing, speaking and listening skills they need to fulfil their own and, ultimately, the nation's potential.

My own son didn't use to enjoy reading, which was why I started writing children's books – reading for pleasure is an essential way to encourage children to pick up a book. The National Literacy Trust is dedicated to delivering exciting initiatives to encourage people to read and to help raise literacy levels. To find out more about the great work that they do, visit their website at www.literacytrust.org.uk.

James Patterson

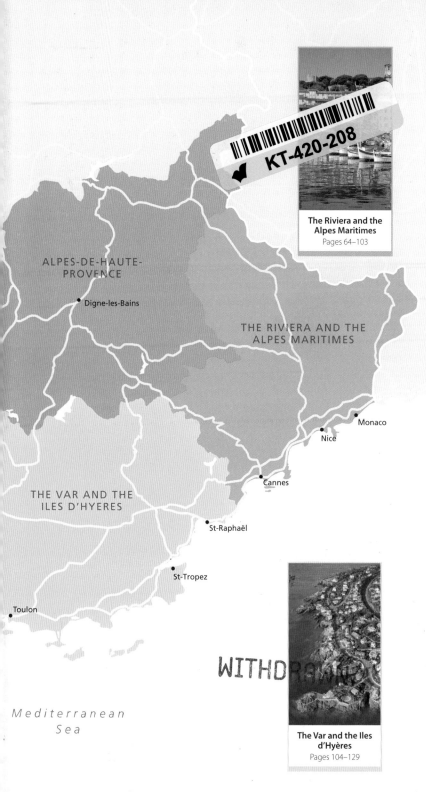

KT-420-208

The Riviera and the Alpes Maritimes
Pages 64–103

ALPES-DE-HAUTE-
PROVENCE

Digne-les-Bains

THE RIVIERA AND THE
ALPES MARITIMES

Monaco

Nice

THE VAR AND THE
ILES D'HYERES

Cannes

St-Raphaël

St-Tropez

Toulon

WITHD

**The Var and the Iles
d'Hyères**
Pages 104–129

Mediterranean
Sea

Provence
& the Côte d'Azur

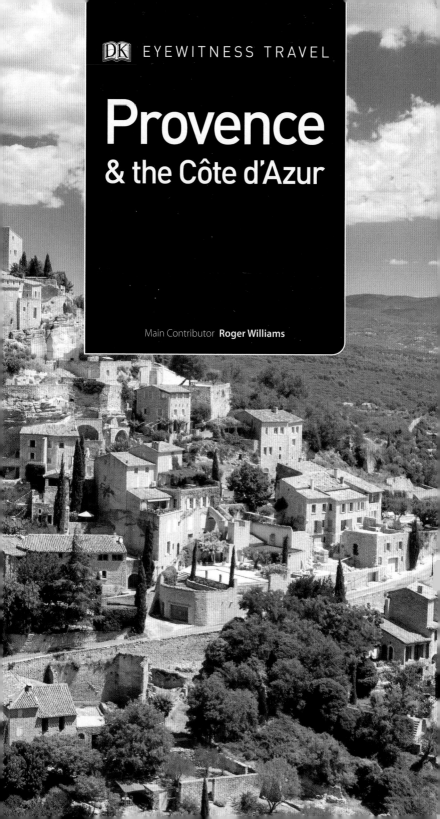

DK EYEWITNESS TRAVEL

Provence
& the Côte d'Azur

Main Contributor **Roger Williams**

Penguin
Random
House

Project Editor Jane Simmonds
Art Editor Jane Ewart
Senior Editor Fay Franklin
Editors Tom Fraser, Elaine Harries, Fiona Morgan
Designers Claire Edwards, Pippa Hurst, Malcolm Parchment

Contributors
John Flower, Jim Keeble, Martin Walters

Photographers
Max Alexander, John Heseltine, Kim Sayer, Alan Williams

Illustrators
Stephen Conlin, Richard Draper, Steve Gyapay, Chris D Orr Illustration, John Woodcock

Printed and bound in China

First published in the UK in 1995
by Dorling Kindersley Limited
80 Strand, London WC2R 0RL

17 18 19 20 10 9 8 7 6 5 4 3 2 1

Reprinted with revisions
1995, 1996, 1997, 1999, 2000, 2001, 2002, 2003, 2004, 2006, 2008, 2010, 2012, 2014, 2016, 2018

Copyright 1995, 2018
© Dorling Kindersley Limited, London
A Penguin Random House Company

A CIP catalogue record is available from the British Library.

ISBN 978-0-2413-0596-6

Floors are referred to throughout in accordance with French usage; ie the "first floor" is the floor above ground level.

MIX
Paper from
responsible sources
FSC™ C018179

Boats lined up at the Port of Nice, located in the old town in Nice *(see pp84–9)*

Introducing Provence

Lavender fields surrounding the Abbaye de Sénanque *(see pp168–9)*

The information in this
DK Eyewitness Travel Guide is checked regularly.
Every effort has been made to ensure that this book is as up-to-date as possible at the time of going to press. Some details, however, such as telephone numbers, opening hours, prices, gallery hanging arrangements and travel information, are liable to change. The publishers cannot accept responsibility for any consequences arising from the use of this book, nor for any material on third party websites, and cannot guarantee that any website address in this book will be a suitable source of travel information. We value the views and suggestions of our readers very highly. Please write to: Publisher, DK Eyewitness Travel Guides, Dorling Kindersley, 80 Strand, London, WC2R 0RL, UK, or email: travelguides@dk.com.

◀ **Title page** Hilltop village of Gordes, Vaucluse   **Front cover main image** Blooming lavender field and Borie stone shed, Provence
Back cover image The beautiful old town of Gordes, Provence

Contents

A souvenir store in the picturesque Les Baux-de-Provence *(see pp146–7)*

Palais des Papes in Avignon *(see pp48–9)*

HOW TO USE THIS GUIDE

This guide will help you get the most from your stay in Provence. It provides both expert recommendations and detailed practical information. *Introducing Provence* maps the region and sets it in its historical and cultural context. *Provence Area by Area* describes the important sights, with maps, photographs and detailed illustrations. Suggestions for food, drink, accommodation, shopping and entertainment are in *Travellers' Needs*, and the *Survival Guide* has tips on everything from the French telephone system to getting to Provence and travelling around the region.

Provence Area by Area

In this guide, Provence has been divided into five separate regions, each of which has its own chapter. A map of these regions can be found inside the front cover of the book. The most interesting places to visit in each region have been numbered and plotted on a *Regional Map*.

Each area of Provence can be quickly identified by its colour coding.

1 Introduction
The landscape, history and character of each region is described here, showing how the area has developed over the centuries and what it has to offer the visitor today.

A locator map shows the region in relation to the whole of Provence.

Exploring the Riviera and the Alpes Maritimes

Getting Around

Sights at a Glance

2 Regional Map
This gives an illustrated overview of the whole region. All the sights are numbered and there are also useful tips on getting around by car and public transport.

Features and story boxes highlight special or unique aspects of a particular sight.

3 Detailed information on each sight
All the important towns and other places to visit are described individually. They are listed in order, following the numbering on the Regional Map. Within each town or city, there is detailed information on important buildings and other major sights.

● Juan-les-Pins

● Antibes

● Vallauris

Pablo Picasso (1881–1973)
Picasso, the giant of 20th-century art, spent most of his later life in Provence, inspired by its luminous light and brilliant colours. He came first to Juan-les-Pins in 1920, and returned to Antibes in 1946 with François Gilot. He was given a studio in the medieval Grimaldi palace, where, after wartime Paris, his work became infused with Mediterranean light and joyful images. No other artist has succeeded with so many art forms, and the Antibes collection is a testimony to his versatility. He died at Mougins, aged 92.

4 Major Towns
An introduction covers the history, character and geography of the town. The main sights are described individually and plotted on a Town Map.

A Visitors' Checklist gives contact points for tourist and transport information, plus details of market days and local festival dates.

The town map shows all main through roads as well as minor streets of interest to visitors. All the sights are plotted, along with the bus and train stations, parking, tourist offices and churches.

5 Street-by-Street Map
Towns or districts of special interest to visitors are shown in detailed 3-D, with photographs of the most important sights. This gives a bird's-eye view of towns or districts of special interest.

A suggested route for a walk covers the most interesting streets in the area.

For all the top sights, a Visitors' Checklist provides the practical information you will need to plan your visit.

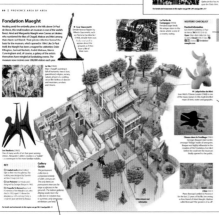

Fondation Maeght

6 The Top Sights
These are given two or more pages. Important buildings are dissected to reveal their interiors; museums have colour-coded floorplans to help you locate the most interesting exhibits.

The gallery guide explains the layout of the museum and gives details on the arrangement and display of the collection.

INTRODUCING
PROVENCE

DISCOVERING PROVENCE

The following tours have been designed to include as many of Provence's highlights as possible, with a minimum amount of travelling. First come a pair of two-day tours of the region's most popular cities, Nice and Avignon; either can be followed individually or as part of a week-long tour. These are followed by three seven-day tours of the region. The first covers the Côte d'Azur, with its beaches, dramatic scenery and exceptional art museums. The second takes in the major

sites along the banks of the River Rhône from Orange to the Camargue, including some of France's best-preserved Roman and medieval monuments. The third, designed specifically for drivers, covers many of the most iconic landscapes and villages of Provence. All have extra suggestions for extending trips to 10 days. Pick one or mix and match, but before setting out, be sure to check the listing of events (pp36–9) and perhaps adjust a tour so as not to miss any of the fun.

Nice
Stylish umbrellas and sun loungers lined up along the shore at the promenade des Anglais Beach Club.

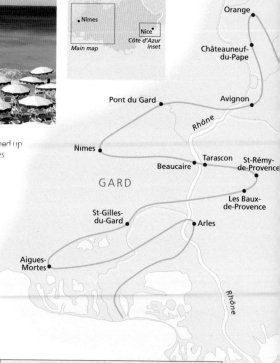

A Week on the Côte d'Azur

- Wander through the morning market in **Nice**, and visit the delightful Musée Matisse.

- Tour the spectacular Villa Ephrussi de Rothchild at **St-Jean-Cap-Ferrat**, and watch the sun set over the Riviera from **Eze**.

- Marvel at the sea life in **Monaco's** Musée Océanographique; see the Roman "trophy" at **La Turbie**.

- Delve into contemporary art at **St-Paul de Vence**, and visit Renoir's home in **Cagnes-sur-Mer**.

- Discover the joyful Picassos in **Antibes**, and relax on the beach at fashionable **Juan-les-Pins.**

- Take in the glamour of **Cannes** and the tranquillity of the **Iles de Lérins**.

◄ *Entrance to the port of Marseille, 1754, by Joseph Vernet*

Vaison-la-Romaine
Sitting on the river Ouvèze, this attractive stone-and-red-roof town has fascinating Roman remains including a theatre still used for the town's summer festival, a hilltop Haute Ville and some of Provence's most chic pavement cafés for relaxing in after a day of sightseeing.

A Week Along the Rhône

- Enjoy **Marseille's** iconic *bouillabaisse* in the scenic Vieux Port.

- Test the acoustics in **Orange's** ancient theatre, and the wines at **Châteauneuf-du-Pape**.

- Tour the medieval Palais des Papes in **Avignon**.

- Marvel at the **Pont du Gard**, and the Roman monuments in **Nîmes**

- Visit the places Van Gogh painted in **St-Rémy**; enjoy breathtaking views from the citadel of **Les Baux-de-Provence**.

- Explore the walled city of **Aigues-Mortes** on the edge of the **Camargue**.

- Discover the ancient and medieval masterpieces of **Arles**, France's "Little Rome".

A Week in Classic Provence

- Take in the arty charms of **Aix**, the former capital of Provence and birthplace of Paul Cézanne.

- Tour through the beautiful Provençal villages and landscapes of the **Petit Luberon**.

- Shop for antiques in **L'Isle-sur-la-Sorgue**, and wonder at the mysterious **Fontaine-de-Vaucluse**.

- Discover the vine-clad landscapes and wines grown under the **Dentelles de Montmirail**; seek out the Roman relics of chic **Vaison-la-Romaine**.

- Visit the striking *village perché* of **Gordes**; inhale the lavender at the 12th-century **Abbaye de Sénanque**; and stroll through **Roussillon's** dramatic ochre quarries.

Key

═══ A Week Along the Rhône

═══ A Week in Classic Provence

═══ A Week on the Côte d'Azur

2 Days in Nice

Nice has a fascinating historic centre, a wealth of museums and a stunning waterfront.

- **Arriving** Nice Airport is 7 km (4.5 miles) from the city. Buses link it with the centre.
- **Moving on** The journey from Nice to Avignon on a TGV train is just under 3 hours.

See pp84–9 for information on sights in Nice.

Day 1
Morning Start with a stroll through Nice's bustling Italianate Old Town: don't miss the **Cathédrale Ste-Réparate** with its glazed tile dome and the art-filled **Chapelle du la Miséricorde**. Take in the heady colours and fragrances of the market in the **cours Saleya**, then make your way up to the summit of the **Colline du Château** gardens for the best view over the Baie des Anges.

Afternoon Visit the elegant district of Cimiez to discover the life and work of one-time Nice resident Henri Matisse at the **Musée Matisse**. Stop by the serene **Monastery of Notre-Dame**, where the artist is buried, then see the **Musée Chagall**, filled with colourful paintings of biblical themes.

Day 2
Morning Explore two different aspects of Nice: start in the 17th century (when the city was part of Italy) at the ornate Baroque **Palais Lascaris**, with its prize collection of antique musical instruments. Then leap ahead four centuries at the striking **Musée d'Art Moderne et d'Art Contemporain**, set amid an outdoor sculpture garden.

Afternoon Stroll along the famous **promenade des Anglais** and consider lunch and a swim at one of the seaside bathing establishments. Or pay a visit to Nice's history museum, the **Villa Masséna** next door

Blue lounge chairs lined up along the promenade in Nice

to the famed **Hotel Négresco**. In the evening, enjoy a drink or dinner in the lively **cours Saleya**.

To extend your trip…
Take a scenic day trip on the **Train des Pignes** *(p185)* and visit **Entrevaux** *(p191).*

2 Days in Avignon

A lively city on the Rhône river, Avignon is home to the Palais des Papes and excellent museums.

- **Arriving** The Avignon and Nîmes airports are only operational in summer. For the rest of the year, Marseille has the nearest international airport (88 km/54 miles); direct TGV trains run from the airport to Avignon in only 54 minutes.

See pp170–72 for information on sights in Avignon.

Day 1
Morning Plunge straight into Avignon's glory days on a tour of the **Palais des Papes**, the biggest medieval palace in the world. Afterwards, visit the nearby **Cathédrale Notre-Dame-des-Doms**, with the tombs of two popes and the hilltop gardens of the **Rocher des Doms**.

Afternoon Discover the rich Gothic art patronized by the papal court at the **Musée du Petit Palais**, then walk along the famous **Pont St-Bénézet** bridge. Afterwards stroll the atmospheric medieval lanes of rue du Roi-René and rue des Teinturiers.

Day 2
Morning Visit the city's two outstanding art museums, the **Musée Calvet** and **Musée Anglandon**, then relax at a café in bustling **place de l'Horloge**.

Afternoon Take the bus over the Rhône to **Villeneuve-lès-Avignon** *(p134)*. Climb one of its towers (**Fort St-André** or the **Tour de Philippe le Bel**) for wonderful views over Avignon. See the masterpiece of the Avignon School of painting, Enguerrand Quarton's *Coronation of the Virgin*, in the **Musée Pierre de Luxembourg**, then visit the monastery it was painted for: the vast **Chartreuse du Val-de-Bénédiction**.

To extend your trip…
Make a day trip to **Nîmes** *(pp136–7)* and the majestic **Pont du Gard** *(p135).*

Dining alfresco on rue des Teinturiers alongside the river Sorgue, Avignon

The Jardin Botanique Exotique at 19th-century Villa Val Rahmeh, Menton

A Week on the Côte d'Azur

- **Duration** 7 days – with suggestions for extending it to a 10-day tour.
- **Airport** Arrive and depart from Nice Côte d'Azur airport.
- **Transport** Lignes d'Azur buses go everywhere; trains serve coastal towns. Hire a car in Cannes to head inland.

Day 1: Nice
Pick a day from the city itinerary on p12.

Day 2: St-Jean-Cap-Ferrat, Villefranche-sur-Mer, Eze
Take the tour of the Villa Ephrussi de Rothschild and its spectacular gardens *(p90)* at **St-Jean-Cap-Ferrat** *(p89)*, then follow the beautiful path that starts just east of the port of St-Jean-Cap-Ferrat. Relax on the free beach at **Villefranche-sur-Mer** *(p92)*; wander through the town's skein of medieval lanes and sit in one of its buzzing waterfront cafés. Then head up to **Eze** *(p92)*, a stunning *village perché* to watch the sun set over the Riviera.

Day 3: Monaco, La Turbie and Menton
Discover the astonishing sea creatures in the Musée Océanographique in **Monaco** *(pp94–8)*, and visit its Palais Princier, for a peek into the lives of the Grimaldis, Europe's oldest ruling family. Head up the slopes above Monaco to **La Turbie** *(p93)*, famous for its ancient Trophée d'Auguste, erected in honour of Augustus. Descend to **Menton** *(pp102–3)* for a walk through its tropical gardens and a look at the Musée Jean Cocteau. In the evening, head back to Monaco and stop for a drink in **Monte-Carlo's** *(pp96–7)* glamorous Café de Paris and perhaps try your luck in Europe's most famous casino.

Day 4: St-Paul de Vence and Cagnes-sur-Mer
Contemporary art reigns at charming **St-Paul de Vence** *(p79)*, in the exquisite **Fondation Maeght** *(pp80–81)*, in the town's many galleries and the Colombe d'Or *auberge*. Next, aim for **Cagnes-sur-Mer** *(p82)*, for the eclectic Château Musée Grimaldi and the moving Musée Renoir, the Impressionist's last home.

Day 5: Antibes and Juan-les-Pins
Wander through the streets of old **Antibes** *(p76)*, ogle the billionaires' yachts in the marina and take in the excellent Musée Picasso housed in a waterfront castle. Stroll past the glamorous villas of Cap d'Antibes, and spend a lazy afternoon on the beach in **Juan-les-Pins** *(p76)*.

Day 6: Cannes and the Iles de Lérins
Discover the two sides of **Cannes** *(pp72–3)*: the swanky Croisette, with its world-famous hotels and the Palais des Festivals, and the old town, with its bustling Marché Forville. The market is a great place to pick up a picnic for a trip to one of the **Iles de Lérins** *(pp74–8)*: choose between peaceful, monastic St-Honorat or larger Ste-Marguerite, with its links to the Man in the Iron Mask.

> **To extend your trip…**
> Visit the Roman ruins of **Fréjus** *(p129)* 36 km (22 miles) west of Cannes and the chic resort of **St-Tropez** *(pp122–6)*; the following day head to **Hyères** *(p119)* 51 km (32 miles) from Cannes to sail to the car-free island of **Porquerolles** *(p118)*.

Roman statuary at the Musée d'Art Classique de Mougins

Day 7: Mougins, Grasse, Gorges du Loup, Gourdon, Vence
Start in **Mougins** *(p70)*, famed for its great restaurants. Admire the works of former resident Picasso in the Musée de la Photographie and visit the captivating Musée d'Art Classique. Discover how perfume is made in **Grasse** *(p70)* at the Musée International de la Parfumerie, then drive the dramatic **Gorges du Loup** *(p69)*, stopping off at the breathtaking village of **Gourdon** *(p69)* and the delightful town of **Vence** *(p78)* before returning to Nice.

> **To extend your trip…**
> Go north from Grasse 64 km (40 miles) to **Castellane** *(p190)* to explore the even more spectacular **Gorges du Verdon** *(pp188–9)*.

A Week Along the Rhône

- **Duration** 7 days – with additional suggestions to extend it to 10 days.
- **Airports** Arrive at and depart from Marseille Provence Airport.
- **Transport** This tour can be made using a combination of trains and buses, although hiring a car would allow more flexibility.

Day 1: Marseille

A day is just enough to scratch the surface of **Marseille** (pp154–6). Start in the picturesque Vieux Port, with its morning fish market and the Abbaye de St-Victor. Enjoy the spectacular views from Notre-Dame-de-la-Garde, and visit the Palais Longchamp, with its fine arts collection. Stroll the Canebière before tucking into *bouillabaisse* for dinner.

Diners enjoying *bouillabaisse* at the Miramar Restaurant, Marseille's Vieux Port

> **To extend your trip…**
> Take a boat trip and swim in Marseille's dramatic **Les Calanques** (p157). Visit the wine town of **Cassis** (p157).

Day 2: Orange and Châteauneuf-du-Pape

Take the train to **Orange** (pp165–7) to visit its incomparable Roman Théâtre Antique, scene of summer theatre and dance festivals, and the well-preserved Arc de Triomphe. In the afternoon, head south to **Châteauneuf-du-Pape** (p168) for a tasting of the famous wines before dinner.

Day 3: Avignon

Pick a day from the city itinerary on p12.

> **To extend your trip…**
> Hire a car and take a day trip to **Fontaine-de-Vaucluse** (p169) 33 km (20 miles) east of Avignon; the hill town of **Gordes** (p173), **Abbaye de Sénanque** (p168) and **Roussillon** (p173) are nearby.

Day 4: Pont du Gard, Nîmes, Beaucaire and Tarascon

Cross the Rhône to visit antiquity's most beautiful aqueduct – the majestic **Pont du Gard** (p135), before moving on to the city it served, **Nîmes** (pp136–7). Don't miss the amphitheatre, Les Arènes, the Maison Carrée – a well-preserved Roman temple – and the Castellum, where the aqueduct's water was distributed. Head back to the Rhône, where the medieval castles of **Beaucaire** (p143) (famous for its bullfights) and **Tarascon** (p144) (known for its Tarasque and Souleïado fabrics) face each other across the river.

Day 5: St-Rémy-de-Provence and Les Baux-de-Provence

St-Rémy-de-Provence (p144) is one of Provence's most attractive towns, and was frequently painted by Van Gogh. Take a walk out to the Clinique St-Paul to see some views painted by Van Gogh, and the nearby ruins of Greco-Roman Glanum. Next, head into the mini-mountain chain of **Les Alpilles** (p145) and the citadel of **Les Baux-de-Provence** (p146), once the medieval setting of the troubadour Court of Love; the views are wonderful.

Day 6: St-Gilles-du-Gard and Aigues Mortes

Along with its iconic white horses, black bulls and pink flamingoes, the **Camargue** (pp140–43) has several fascinating historic sites. Begin at **St-Gilles-du-Gard** (p143) and the magnificent Romanesque façade of the Abbaye de St-Gilles, then head south to explore the unique 13th-century walled crusader town of **Aigues-Mortes** (pp138–9).

Day 7: Arles

France's "Little Rome", **Arles** (pp148–9) boasts both an ancient theatre and amphitheatre, the Thermes de Constantin and the intriguing Musée de l'Arles Antique. Also visit the cloisters of the church of St-Trophime, Les Alychamps cemetery and the Espace Van Gogh, with exhibits relating to the painter's sojourn in Arles.

> **To extend your trip…**
> Uncover the history of the Carmargue in the **Musée de la Camargue** (p143); spot birds at the **Parc Ornithologique du Pont-de-Gau** (p142) and visit the Romany pilgrimage church at lively **Saintes-Maries-de-la-Mer** (p142).

Roman sarcophagus or tombs showing boar hunters, Musée de l'Arles Antique, Arles

For practical information on travelling around Provence, see pp244–53

A Week in Classic Provence

- **Duration** 7 days – or 10 with the additional trips.
- **Airports** Arrive and depart from Marseille Provence Airport.
- **Transport** Hiring a car is the best option. Although much of this itinerary is technically possible by bus, infrequent connections will make getting around difficult.

Brantes and Mont Ventoux, north Luberon Mountains

Day 1: Aix-en-Provence
Today a cosmopolitan university city and venue of a famous music festival, **Aix** (pp152–3) was once the capital of Provence. Stroll through the historic centre, with its elegant 17th- and 18th-century hôtels and fountains. Don't miss the Cathédrale St-Sauveur, with its triptych of *The Burning Bush*, the adjacent Musée du Palais de l'Archevêché, with a unique collection of secular Beauvais tapestries, and the luxurious 17th-century villa, the Pavillon de Vendôme.

Day 2: More Aix and the Montagne Ste-Victoire
Aix is also synonymous with Paul Cézanne: see his paintings in the Musée Granet, and visit his evocative studio, which has been left unchanged. Take a scenic drive around Cézanne's beloved Montagne Ste-Victoire, which he painted many times, and have a drink at his favourite Café des Deux Garçons.

Day 3: Abbaye de Silvacane, Petit Luberon, Cavaillon
Some of Provence's most beautiful landscapes and villages are in the Petit Luberon, north of Aix. Stop at the 12th-century Cistercian **Abbaye de Silvacane** (p151), then take the driving tour (pp174–5), starting in **Lourmarin** and continuing through the delightful villages of **Bonnieux, Lacoste, Ménerbes and Oppède-le-Vieux**. End up in **Cavaillon** (p174), famous for melons; stay overnight to visit its exceptional morning market.

Day 4: L'Isle-sur-la-Sorgue, Fontaine-de-Vaucluse and Carpentras
Wander through pretty **L'Isle-sur-la-Sorgue** (p169), with its canals and weekend antiques market. Just upriver, visit the source of the Sorgue at the **Fontaine-de-Vaucluse** (p169), along with its paper mill and Musée d'Histoire 1939–45. Continue on to **Carpentras** (p168), which has a 14th-century synagogue and a cathedral.

Day 5: The Dentelles de Montmirail and Vaison-la-Romaine
The Dentelles de Montmirail mountains are among Provence's most beautiful landscapes. Take the scenic drive (p163), starting in **Beaumes-de-Venise**, famous for its dessert wine, and carrying on to **Vacqueyras** and **Gigondas**, home to a famous

A weekend antiques fair in L'Isle-sur-la-Sorgue, the "Venice of Provence"

red wine. In chic **Vaison-la-Romaine** (p162), visit the boutiques of the Haute Ville.

> **To extend your trip…**
> Spend a day exploring **Mont Ventoux** (p164), 32 km (20 miles) from Vaison – by car, bicycle or on foot.

Day 6: Gordes, Abbaye de Sénanque and Roussillon
Head back south through the **Dentelles** (p163), pausing in the old Huguenot village of **Malaucène**, and Le Barroux, for the views from its château. Next comes the striking **Gordes** (p173), a *village perché*. Visit the nearby 12th-century **Abbaye de Sénanque** (pp168–9) and finish in **Roussillon** (p173), taking a stroll through its ochre quarries.

Day 7: Apt, La Tour d'Aigues and Pertuis
Charming **Apt** (p176) has a fascinating cathedral; learn about Apt's famous crystallized fruits at the Musée de l'Aventure Industrielle. Go through the Parc Naturel Régional du Luberon; stop at **La Tour d'Aigues** (p177) for the Renaissance château and ceramics museum, then at **Pertuis** (p177) to see its Gothic Eglise St-Nicolas before heading back to Marseille.

> **To extend your trip…**
> Head 42 km (26 miles) east from Apt to **Forcalquier** (p186). Spend two days in the Alpes-de-Haute Provence.

Putting Provence on the Map

Provence is situated in the sun-blessed southeast corner of France, edged to the south by the Mediterranean. Its most illustrious stretch of coastline, roughly from Menton to Bandol, is also known as the Côte d'Azur, although the nearer to Italy it gets the more likely it is to be referred to as the Riviera. To the east are Italy and the Alps, to the west, the Rhône river. The region covers an area of over 30,000 sq km (18,650 sq miles) with a population of about 4.9 million.

Spain ←

English Channel

UNITED KINGDOM

Harwic

Reading London

M4

M3

M20

Dov

Portsmouth

Poole

Newhaven

Cherbourg

Dieppe

Le Havre

Rouen

N13

A13

Caen

Plymouth, Ireland ↑

Plymouth, Weymouth ↑

Roscoff

N12

Brest

St-Malo

Alençon

Chartre

N165

N12

Rennes

A28

A81

A11

Le Mans

Lorient

St-Nazaire

Nantes

Angers

Tours

A11

A85

Loire

Gijón ↙

A83

A10

Les Sables-d'Olonne

N137

Poitiers

La Rochelle

A2

N10

A10

Limoges

Bordeaux

A89

Brive-la-Gaillarde

Arcachon

Dordogne

A2

Garonne

Europe

NORWAY

SWEDEN

NORTH SEA

DENMARK

UNITED KINGDOM

REP. OF IRELAND

NETHERLANDS

POLAND

BELGIUM

GERMANY

CZECH REPUBLIC

SLOVAKIA

ATLANTIC OCEAN

FRANCE

SWITZ

AUSTRIA

HUNGARY

SLOV.

CROATIA

BOSNIA HERZ.

SERBIA

ITALY

MONTEN.

KOS

MAC

PORTUGAL

SPAIN

ALBANIA

GREECE

St Nazaire ↗   Plymouth, Portsmouth ↑   Portsmouth ↑

Bay of Biscay

A63

A65

A62

Gijón

Santander

Biarritz

Toulouse

Bilbao

Pau

A64

Tarbes

Key

Area covered by this guide

Ferry service

Airport

Motorway

Major road

Railway line

AP68

A8

A1

A15

Vitoria Gasteiz

Pamplona

AP1

Andorra

ANDORRA

Burgos

AP15

Huesca

A22

SPAIN

0 kilometres   100

0 miles   100

Soria

AP68

Ebro

Zaragoza

A2

AP2

Lleida

For additional map symbols *see back flap*

A PORTRAIT OF PROVENCE

In a comparatively short time, Provence has changed its face. A few generations ago it was, to the French, a place of indolent southern bumpkins. To foreigners, it was an idyllic spot, but one reserved, it seemed to many, for the rich or artistic. Now Provence, more than any other region, is where the French would choose to live and work, and its holiday routes buzz with both local and international traffic all year round.

The high-tech industry based here can attract top-flight staff, not just from France but from all over the world.

Still, Provence remains an essentially rural region. At its edges, it has a lively Latin beat: almost Spanish among the *gardians* of the Camargue in the west, Italian in Nice to the east. The rest of the region is mostly traditional and conservative. Only in games of *pétanque* or discussions about European bureaucracy does the talk become animated. But, once engaged in conversation, Provençals are the most generous and warmest of hosts. There is an all-pervading Frenchness, of course, which means that people are polite and punctilious.

Shopkeepers always greet you as you enter, but open and close on the dot. Lunch, in Provence, is sacrosanct.

Traditions are important to the people of Provence. Local crafts are not quaint revivals, but respected, time-honoured occupations. Festivals, such as La Bravade in St-Tropez, have been taking place for the last 450 years. Artists who came here for the light and the scenery found other inspirations, too. Picasso himself learned the potter's art at the wheel of a Provençal craftsman. Homes will have hand-turned local chestnut or oak furniture, *terre rouge* clay pots, Moustiers *faïence*, Biot glassware and furnishings using the traditional *indiennes* patterns of Arles and Nîmes.

Locals enjoying a leisurely game of *pétanque* at Châteauneuf-du-Pape

◀ Basilique de Notre-Dame-de-la-Garde in Marseille

A traditional bakery in Ville-sur-Auzon, in Vaucluse

Islam, as well as by pagan gods. Religious beliefs are so well mixed that it is often difficult to separate them. Carnival and Corpus Christi extend Easter, which has more importance here than in many other parts of Europe. Christmas, too, is an elaborate affair. The rituals begin as early as 4 December, St Barb's day, with the planting of grains of wheat, a pagan symbol of renewal and rebirth.

Superstitions linger in the countryside. An egg, salt, bread and matches, humble representations of elemental concepts, may be given to a newborn baby, while carline thistles may be seen nailed to front doors for good luck.

The home is run as it has been for generations. Provençal kitchens, at the heart of family life, are famous. Combining simplicity with bounty, they mix the aroma of herbs with the generosity of wine. In the envious and admiring eyes of visitors, they are the epitome of taste.

A colourful fruit and vegetable market

Tradition and Customs

Good taste is inbred. In rural communities, the familiarity of the weather, the seasons and the harvests are sources of constant discussion. Gardens, full of fruit trees, vegetables and flowers, are a matter of pride. Even city-dwellers know how the best produce should be grown, and may well have access to a country relation's plot. Market stalls are beautifully laid out and carefully scrutinized and, no matter how abundant the fruit, the vegetables or the wine, they are all grist for debate.

There are still heated discussions fuelled by the latest developments imposed by the European Union, whose legislation, farmers say, has in the past had a detrimental effect on productive Provençal land, when for example ancient vineyards were grubbed up and landowners' wealth sent into rapid decline.

The harvest cycle is close to the gods, whose benificence can affect the crops as surely as any EU bureaucrat. As Catholic as the rest of France, the people of Provence are also touched with a mystic sense that has been influenced by Mithraism and

Landscape and People

Provence has a typically Mediterranean landscape: the mountains drop down to the sea; communities perch on crags or cling to remote hillsides. It is little wonder that traditions live on here. For centuries, too, it was a place for outlaws from France, who could assume new identities here and carry on with their lives. Perhaps as a result, strangers

Harvesting linden blossoms to make *tilleul* infusion

The dramatic, isolated crags of Les Pénitents des Mées, in Alpes-de-Haute-Provence

were not to be trusted, and remained outsiders forever. A seemingly trivial slight might spark a feud which could last for generations. There are still villages today where one family does not speak to another, even though each has long forgotten why. This attitude, and its tragic implications, was finely portrayed by Yves Montand, with Gérard Depardieu as the shunned outsider, in Claud Berri's films of Marcel Pagnol's *Jean de Florette* and *Manon des Sources*. The more cosmopolitan coast is the territory of *film noir*. Here, the tradition of silence and family ties has not always been beneficial. Jean-Paul Belmondo and Alain Delon romanticized it in *Borsalino;* Gene Hackman revealed its dark underside in *The French Connection.*

In 1982, the Antibes-based English novelist Graham Greene published an exposé of corruption in Nice. In 1994, Yann Piat, anti-drugs campaigner and member of parliament, was assassinated in Hyères.

Peillon, a perched village in Provence

The fact that Piat was a woman made no difference to her enemies, ironic in a region where women have not been treated as equals. Alphonse Daudet noted the Provençal male's "incurable contempt" for women, however, the Queen of Arles is elected for her virtues as an upholder of the traditional Provençal values. It was also this region that nurtured the 20th century's icon of French womanhood, Brigitte Bardot. Furthermore, the town of Aix-en-Provence has had a female mayor since 2001.

There are great rewards for the visitor who can appreciate the many facets of Provence – its traditions as well as its beauty and glamour. But, the more often you return, the more you will realize, as have some of the world's greatest artists and writers, that part of the endless allure of Provence lies within the very secrets that it refuses to surrender.

The Natural History of Provence

A fascinating array of insects, birds, animals and flowers flourish in the varied habitats available in Provence, from the Mediterranean to coastal wetlands, rocky gorges and the remote peaks of the Alpes Maritimes. The area has the mildest climate in France: hot, mainly dry summers, and warm, mild winters near the coast. In early spring the myriad flowers are at their best, while numbers of unusual birds are at their highest in late spring. Many of the wilder areas have been made into reserves, often with routes marked out for exploration.

Mont Ventoux's lower slopes are flower-covered in the spring *(see p164).*

The Luberon *(see pp174–6)* is a huge limestone range, rich in orchids, such as this military orchid. It is also a hunting ground for birds of prey.

Les Alpilles' limestone ridge *(see p145)* attracts birds of prey, including Bonelli's eagles, Egyptian vultures and eagle owls, as well as this more mild-mannered bee-eater.

• Orange

Carpentras •

• Avignon

Vaucluse

Rhône

• Arles

Bouches-du-Rhône and Nîmes

The Camargue, at the delta of the river Rhône, is one of Europe's most important wetlands *(see pp140–41).* Water birds that thrive here include purple herons and the greater flamingo. Lizards, such as this ocellated lizard, can also be seen.

• Marseille

The Côte Bleue is rich in marine life, such as octopuses, in the deeper waters.

The Montagne Ste-Victoire is a limestone range that attracts walkers and climbers. It was one of Cézanne's favourite subjects.

The Plaine de la Crau is 50,000 ha (193 sq miles) of stony plains and steppe-like grasslands southeast of Arles, home to birds like this hoopoe, and the rare pin-tailed sandgrouse.

Les Calanques *(see p157)* are narrow inlets bounded by cliffs. The rocky slopes are home to woodland birds such as owls.

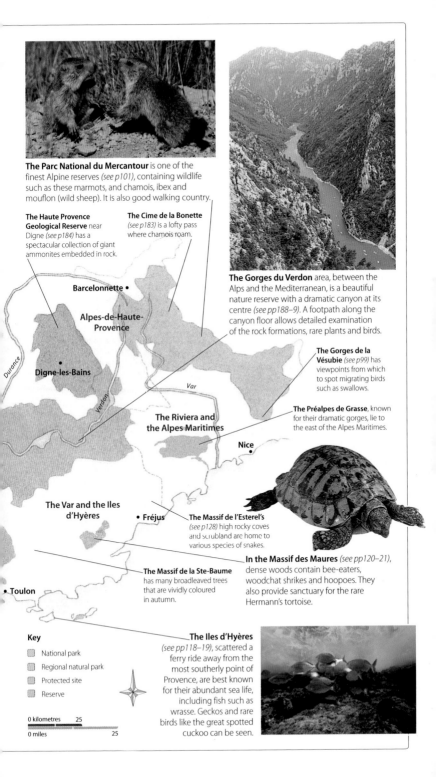

The Parc National du Mercantour is one of the finest Alpine reserves *(see p101)*, containing wildlife such as these marmots, and chamois, ibex and mouflon (wild sheep). It is also good walking country.

The Haute Provence Geological Reserve near Digne *(see p184)* has a spectacular collection of giant ammonites embedded in rock.

The Cime de la Bonette *(see p183)* is a lofty pass where chamois roam.

The Gorges du Verdon area, between the Alps and the Mediterranean, is a beautiful nature reserve with a dramatic canyon at its centre *(see pp188–9)*. A footpath along the canyon floor allows detailed examination of the rock formations, rare plants and birds.

Barcelonnette •

Alpes-de-Haute-Provence

Durance

• Digne-les-Bains

Verdon

Var

The Gorges de la Vésubie *(see p99)* has viewpoints from which to spot migrating birds such as swallows.

The Préalpes de Grasse, known for their dramatic gorges, lie to the east of the Alpes Maritimes.

The Riviera and the Alpes Maritimes

Nice
•

The Var and the Iles d'Hyères

• Fréjus

The Massif de l'Esterel's *(see p128)* high rocky coves and scrubland are home to various species of snakes.

In the Massif des Maures *(see pp120–21)*, dense woods contain bee-eaters, woodchat shrikes and hoopoes. They also provide sanctuary for the rare Hermann's tortoise.

The Massif de la Ste-Baume has many broadleaved trees that are vividly coloured in autumn.

• Toulon

The Iles d'Hyères *(see pp118–19)*, scattered a ferry ride away from the most southerly point of Provence, are best known for their abundant sea life, including fish such as wrasse. Geckos and rare birds like the great spotted cuckoo can be seen.

Key

- ▦ National park
- ▦ Regional natural park
- ▦ Protected site
- ▦ Reserve

0 kilometres   25

0 miles   25

Perched Villages

Some of the most attractive architectural features of Provence are the *villages perchés*, or perched villages. They rise like jagged summits on the hilltops where they were built for safety in the political turmoil of the Middle Ages. From their lofty heights they kept vigil over the hinterland as well as the coast. They were built around castle keeps and wrapped in thick ramparts, a huddle of cobbled streets, steps, alleys and archways. Few were able to sustain their peasant communities beyond the 19th-century agrarian reforms, and a century of poverty and depopulation followed. Today many of the villages have been restored by a new generation of artists, craftworkers and holiday-makers.

The mountainous site of Peillon *(see p99)* is typical of the way perched villages blend organically with the landscape.

St-Paul de Vence

Many of the key features of this typical village perché have been preserved. The medieval ramparts were completely reinforced by Francis I in the 16th century. Today it is again besieged – as one of France's most popular tourist sights (see p79).

PLACE CHARLES DE GAULLE

RUE DE LA POURTOUNE

RUE DES DORIERS

RUE DES BAUQUES

MONTÉE DE L'ÉGLISE

RUE DE L

RUE GRANDE

COURTINE ST PAUL

BASTION ST REMY

REMPARTS

Complicated entrances confused invaders and provided extra security against attack.

The church was always the focal point of the village.

Side entrances were never obtrusive or elaborate, but were usually small and, as in Eze *(see p92)*, opened onto narrow, winding lanes. Sometimes there were more gates or abrupt turns within the walls to confuse attacking soldiers, making the town easier to defend.

Castles and keeps *(donjons)*, and sometimes fortified churches, were always sited with the best viewpoint in the village, and provided sanctuary in times of crisis. Many, like the castle at Eze *(see p92)*, were often attacked and are now in ruins.

The church sustained the religious life of the community. As in Les Baux *(see p146)*, it was usually built near the keep of the castle, part of a central core of communal buildings, and was often fortified. The bell would be rung to warn of impending attack.

Fountains were essential to the village, often being the sole source of water. Many, like this one in Vence *(see p78)*, were elaborately embellished.

The arcades lent support to the buildings in the narrow, winding streets, as here in Roquebrune *(see p102)*. They also gave shelter from sun and rain.

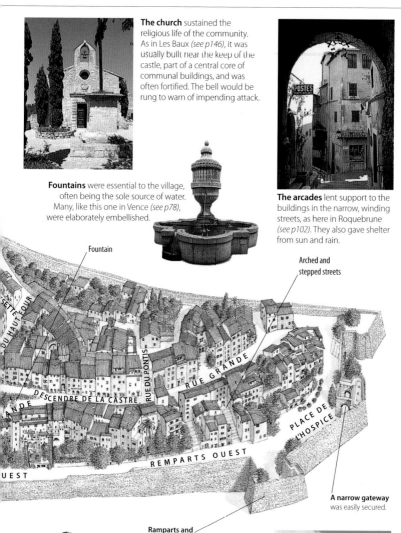

Fountain

Arched and stepped streets

RUE DU PONTIS

RUE GRANDE

DESCENDRE DE LA CASTRE

SETTE DU HAUT-FOUR

PLACE DE L'HOSPICE

REMPARTS OUEST

A narrow gateway was easily secured.

Ramparts and bastions provided solid defences.

The ramparts surrounded the entire village with thick stone walls, often with houses built into them. The defences, like those of St-Paul de Vence *(see p79)*, were strengthened in the 16th century under Francis I and by Vauban, Louis XIV's military architect. Today they offer superb views.

Main gates were always narrow so they could be closed off and defended in times of attack. Some gates had the additional protection of portcullises. Peille *(see p99)* in the Alpes Maritimes is a typical Medieval village, full of narrow, cobbled streets, which also helped defend the village.

Rural Architecture in Provence

Traditional architectural features are reminders of how influential the weather is on living conditions in rural Provence. Great efforts are made to ease the biting gusts of the Mistral and the relentless heat of the summer sun. Thick stone walls, small windows and reinforced doors are all recognizable characteristics. Traditional farmhouses were built entirely from wood, clay, stone and soil, all locally found materials. Rows of hardy cypress trees were planted to act as a windbreak on the north side; plane and lotus trees provided shade to the south.

Bories (see p173) are drystone huts built using techniques dating back to 2,000 BC.

The Provençal Mas

Found across rural Provence, the mas *is a low, squat stone farmhouse. Protection and strength are vital to its construction – walls are made of compact stone blocks and the wooden doors and shutters are thick and reinforced. Outbuildings often included a cellar, stables, a bread oven and dovecote.*

Chimneys are stone-built, low and squat, and lie close to the roof.

Canal roof tiling, or *tuiles romaines*, is typical of the south.

Dovecot

Roughly cut stone bricks are used to make the walls.

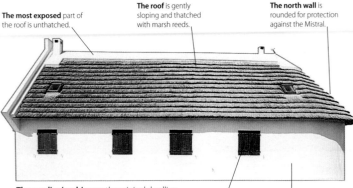

The most exposed part of the roof is unthatched.

The roof is gently sloping and thatched with marsh reeds.

The north wall is rounded for protection against the Mistral.

The *gardian's* cabin was the original dwelling place of the bull herdsman or *gardian* of the Camargue. It is a small, narrow structure, consisting of a dining room and bedroom, divided by a reed screen and furnished simply.

The windows are small and reinforced.

Walls are made of compressed clay and straw, known as cob.

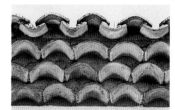

The tiled roofs are gently sloping and are influenced by Roman design, with a decorative frieze (génoise) under the eaves. The tiles are made of thick, red terracotta and curved in shape – a double or triple layer of tiles are set in mortar and protrude beyond the wall.

Windows are built on three sides of the mas but none on the north to avoid the Mistral's full blast. They are kept small to prevent the winter winds coming in, but large enough to let light in.

Interlocking clay tiles form canals, allowing rainwater to run down and drain off the roof.

The Mistral winds blow so fiercely that the mas was often built facing the southeast to minimize the wind's impact. Roofs are built low to the ground, covering the living quarters and annexes. The gentle slope prevents the tiles blowing and sliding off.

The walls are rendered smooth with plaster.

Stone ice houses were built near the mas and used for storage during the winter months. Blocks of ice were cut and put in the huts, insulated with hay.

Ironwork Bell Towers

Wrought-iron bell towers have been a speciality in Provence since the 16th century. Their light, open framework allows strong winds to blow through and the sound of the bells to carry for miles. The design and complexity depends on the size and purpose of the building. These examples illustrate the skills of local craftsmen across the region.

Highly ornate bell tower in Aix

The bell tower of St-Jérôme in Digne-les-Bains

The Hôtel de Ville bell tower in Orange

Notre-Dame's bell tower in Sisteron

Architectural Styles in Provence

From the imperial grandeur of Roman constructions to the modern domestic designs of Le Corbusier, Provence has a magnificent array of architectural styles. The Middle Ages saw a flourishing of great Romanesque abbeys and churches and from the 16th to the 18th centuries, as prosperity increased, châteaux and town houses were built. With the expansion of towns in the 19th century came an increase in apartment blocks and public buildings to accommodate the fast-growing population. Today, successful restoration has taken place, but often in haste. The demands of tourism have taken their toll, particularly on the coast, resulting in some ugly developments.

An 18th-century fountain in Pernes-les-Fontaines

Roman Architecture (20 BC–AD 400)

The quality of Roman architecture is illustrated by the many extant amphitheatres, triumphal arches and thermal baths found across the region, all built with large blocks of local limestone.

Ornate high-relief

The triumphal arch of Glanum *(see pp144–5)* is the original entrance to the oldest Roman city in Provence. Carvings on the outer arch show Caesar's victory over the Gauls and Greeks.

Doric columns on second storey

Both storeys have 60 arcades

Nîmes Arènes, built in the 1st century AD *(see p136)*

Nîmes' well-preserved Maison Carrée *(see p136)*

Roman Architecture (11th–12th Centuries)

The high point of Provençal architecture came after the Dark Ages. It was a combination of Classical order and perfection, inspired by Roman design and new styles from northern and southern Europe. This style is characterized especially in religious buildings by elegant symmetry and simplicity.

Multiple arches

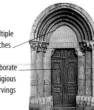

Elaborate religious carvings

This church entrance in Seyne *(see p182)* is an example of 13th-century Romanesque architecture. The slight point of the multiple arches hints at a move away from strict Romanesque purity.

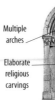

Clustered pillar

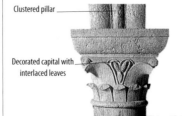

Decorated capital with interlaced leaves

Capital from the Abbaye du Thoronet *(see p112)*

The Abbaye de Sénanque, founded in 1148 *(see pp168–9)*

Late Middle Ages
(13th–16th Centuries)

Feuding and religious wars led
to people withdrawing to towns,
protected by fortified walls and gates.
Communication between houses
was often by underground passages.
Streets were roughly paved and water
and sewage were carried away by
a central gutter.

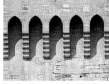

Tour de la Campana in the Palais des
Papes (see pp48–9)

Street in St-Martin-Vésubie (see p99)
showing central gutter

Aigues-Mortes (see pp138–9)
was built by Louis IX in the
13th century, according to
a strict grid pattern. This
strategically placed fort
overlooks both sea and land.

Crenellation or
battlements

Portcullis used
against invaders

Classical Architecture
(17th–18th Centuries)

The severity and order of the
Classical style was relieved by
elaborate carvings on doorways
and windows. Gardens became
more formal and symmetrical.

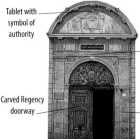

Tablet with
symbol of
authority

Refined
stone

Carved Regency
doorway

Neo-Classical
pillar

The 17th-century Barbentane château,
fronted by formal gardens (see p134)

**The Musée du Palais de
l'Archevêché** in Aix (see
p152) has elaborately carved
wooden entrance doors.

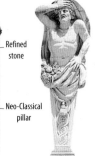

Pavillon de Vendôme detail,
Aix-en-Provence (see p153)

Modern Architecture
(1890–Present Day)

The magnificent hotels and villas
of the belle époque have given
way to more utilitarian housing
and public buildings. But the
numerous modern art galleries
represent the highest standards
of 20th-century architecture.

Le Corbusier's Cité Radieuse (see p156)

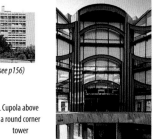

Rounded
pavilion

Cupola above
a round corner
tower

The palatial Négresco hotel in Nice (see p88)

**The Musée d'Art
Moderne et d'Art
Contemporain in Nice**
(see p89) is made up of
square towers, linked by
glass passageways.

Artists of Provence

Provence inspired many of the most original 19th- and 20th-century painters. They were attracted by the luminescent quality of the light here, and the consequent brilliance of the colours. Cézanne, who was a native, and Van Gogh, a convert, were both fired by the vibrant shades of the landscape. The Impressionists Monet and Renoir came early, and followers included Bonnard, Signac and Dufy. The two giants of 20th-century painting, Matisse and Picasso, both settled here. The artistic tradition is kept alive by small galleries in almost every town, as well as major museums throughout the region.

Jean Cocteau (1889–1963) spent many years on the coast and created his museum in Menton *(see p103)*. *Noce imaginaire* (1957) is one of his murals from the Salle des Mariages.

Victor Vasarely (1906–97) restored the château in Gordes. His Kinetic and Op Art can be seen in Aix-en-Provence *(see p153)*.

Regions of Provence

Orange
Sisteron
Digne-les-Bains
Avignon
Gordes
Nîmes
Area of main map
Menton
Arles
Aix-en-Provence
Martigues
Marseille
St-Raphaël
St-Tropez
Toulon

Vincent Van Gogh (1853–90) painted Van Gogh's Chair (1888) in Arles *(see pp148–50)*. His two years here and in St-Rémy *(see pp144–5)* were his most prolific.

Paul Cézanne (1839–1906), in his desire to scour the "depth of reality", often painted his native Aix *(see pp152–3)*.

Mougins

Valla

Paul Signac (1863–1935) came to St-Tropez in 1892, painting it in his palette of rainbow dots *(see pp122–6)*.

Le Cannet
Golfe-Jua

Cannes

Pointe Croisette

Félix Ziem (1821–1911), born in Burgundy, was a great traveller. He adored Venice, and found the same romantic inspiration by the canals of Martigues *(see p151)*, where he painted *La Camargue, Coucher de Soleil.*

0 kilometres 5
0 miles 5

Pablo Picasso (1881–1973) created this goat-like jug, Cabri (1947), while in Vallauris, where he learned the potter's craft. It is now in the Musée Picasso, Antibes *(see p77)*.

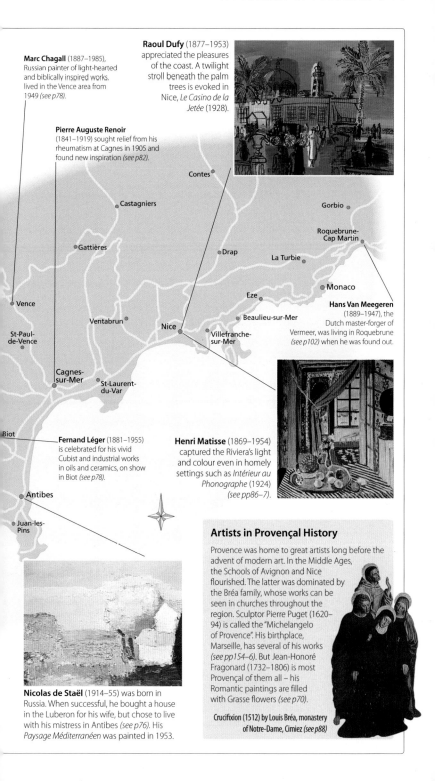

Marc Chagall (1887–1985), Russian painter of light-hearted and biblically inspired works, lived in the Vence area from 1949 *(see p78)*.

Raoul Dufy (1877–1953) appreciated the pleasures of the coast. A twilight stroll beneath the palm trees is evoked in Nice, *Le Casino de la Jetée* (1928).

Pierre Auguste Renoir (1841–1919) sought relief from his rheumatism at Cagnes in 1905 and found new inspiration *(see p82)*.

Contes

Castagniers

Gorbio

Roquebrune-Cap Martin

Gattières

Drap

La Turbie

Monaco

Vence

Eze

Ventabrun

Nice

Beaulieu-sur-Mer

Hans Van Meegeren (1889–1947), the Dutch master-forger of Vermeer, was living in Roquebrune *(see p102)* when he was found out.

St-Paul-de-Vence

Villefranche-sur-Mer

Cagnes-sur-Mer

St-Laurent-du-Var

Biot

Fernand Léger (1881–1955) is celebrated for his vivid Cubist and industrial works in oils and ceramics, on show in Biot *(see p78)*.

Henri Matisse (1869–1954) captured the Riviera's light and colour even in homely settings such as *Intérieur au Phonographe* (1924) *(see pp86–7)*.

Antibes

Juan-les-Pins

Artists in Provençal History

Provence was home to great artists long before the advent of modern art. In the Middle Ages, the Schools of Avignon and Nice flourished. The latter was dominated by the Bréa family, whose works can be seen in churches throughout the region. Sculptor Pierre Puget (1620–94) is called the "Michelangelo of Provence". His birthplace, Marseille, has several of his works *(see pp154–6)*. But Jean-Honoré Fragonard (1732–1806) is most Provençal of them all – his Romantic paintings are filled with Grasse flowers *(see p70)*.

Nicolas de Staël (1914–55) was born in Russia. When successful, he bought a house in the Luberon for his wife, but chose to live with his mistress in Antibes *(see p76)*. His *Paysage Méditerranéen* was painted in 1953.

Crucifixion (1512) by Louis Bréa, monastery of Notre-Dame, Cimiez *(see p88)*

Writers in Provence

The Nobel Laureate Frédéric Mistral (1830–1914) was the champion of the Provençal language, but better known are the local writers who have captured the Provençal character: Alphonse Daudet, Jean Giono, Emile Zola and Marcel Pagnol. French writers such as Dumas and Hugo used Provençal backdrops for their fiction; foreign writers also found inspiration in the region.

1920 Consumptive New Zealand short story writer Katherine Mansfield recuperates in Menton *(see pp102–3)* and writes *Miss Bull* and *Passion* among other pieces.

1895 Jean Giono is born in Manosque *(see p186)*. Work like *The Man who Planted Trees* evokes the region.

Alphonse Daudet

1892 The last part of *Thus Spake Zarathustra* by German Friedrich Nietzsche is published. He devised it after traversing the path in Eze *(see p92)* which was later named after him.

Frédéric Mistral

An early edition of *The Count of Monte Cristo*

1869 Alphonse Daudet publishes *Collected Letters from my Windmill*, set in a windmill at Fontvieille *(see p147)*.

1904 Poet Frédéric Mistral declared joint winner of the Nobel Prize.

1844 Alexander Dumas publishes *The Count of Monte Cristo*, set in the Château d'If, Marseille *(see p156)*.

1870 Death in Cannes of Prosper Mérimée, author of *Carmen*, Bizet's opera.

1840	1855	1870	1885	1900	1915
1840	1855	1870	1885	1900	1915

1862 *Les Misérables* by Victor Hugo is published. The early chapters are set in Digne-les-Bains *(see p184)*.

1887 Journalist Stéphen Liégeard introduces the term, *Côte d'Azur*.

1907 Provençal poet, René Char, is born in L'Isle-sur-la-Sorgue.

1868 Edmond Rostand, author of *Cyrano de Bergerac* (1897) is born in Marseille *(see pp154–6)*.

1919 Edith Wharton, American author of *The Age of Innocence*, visits Hyères *(see p119)*. A street is named after her.

Edith Wharton

Early Writers

For centuries, troubadour ballads and religious poems, or *Noels*, formed the core of literature in Provence. While certain unique individuals stand out, it was not until 1854, with Mistral's help, that Provençal writers found their own "voice".

1327 Petrarch *(see p49)* falls in unrequited love with Laura de Noves in Avignon, inspiring his *Canzonière* poems.

1555 Nostradamus, from St-Rémy, publishes *The Prophecies*, which are outlawed by the Vatican.

1764 Tobias Smollett "discovers" Nice. (He published his book, *Travels through France and Italy*, in 1766.)

1791 Marquis de Sade, the original sadist, publishes *Justine*, written while imprisoned in the Bastille.

Petrarch's Laura de Noves

Somerset Maugham

1926 British author W Somerset Maugham buys the Villa Mauresque, Cap Ferrat, and writes *Cakes and Ale* (1930).

Emile Zola

1885 *Germinal* published by Emile Zola, boyhood friend of Cézanne, as part of his 20-novel cycle, *The Rougon-Macquarts* (1871–93), set partly round Aix.

1931 Briton Aldous Huxley writes *Brave New World* in Sanary-sur-Mer (*see p116*), the setting for *Eyeless in Gaza* (1936).

1933 Thomas Mann, who wrote *Death in Venice* (1913), flees Germany for Sanary (*see p116*) with his two sons and his brother Heinrich.

St-Exupéry's poignant fable, Le Petit Prince

1944 Antoine de St-Exupéry, aviator and author of *Vol de Nuit* (1931) and *Le Petit Prince* (1943), goes missing. His last flight passed his sister's house at Agay.

Marcel Pagnol

1974 Death of film director and writer Marcel Pagnol, whose *Marseille Trilogy* explored his Provençal childhood.

1980 British actor Dirk Bogarde, having moved to Provence in the early 1970s, publishes his first novel, *A Gentle Occupation*.

Lawrence Durrell

1985 The last volume of Briton Lawrence Durrell's *Avignon Quintet* is published.

1989 Briton Peter Mayle's book *A Year in Provence* generates interest in the Luberon.

| 30 | 1945 | 1960 | 1975 | 1990 | 2005 |

| 30 | 1945 | 1960 | 1975 | 1990 | 2005 |

1978 Marseille-born Sébastien Japrisot publishes the award-winning *L'Eté Meurtrier*, set in a Provençal village.

1954 Françoise Sagan, aged 18, writes *Bonjour Tristesse* (1954) about the Esterel coast.

Albert Camus

1957 Albert Camus buys a house in Lourmarin (*see p175*), where he writes an autobiographical novel, not published until 1994.

The Fitzgeralds

1934 American author F Scott Fitzgerald's South of France-based *Tender is the Night* is published. Scott and his wife Zelda stay in a villa at Juan-Les-Pins in 1926.

Le Clézio

1994 Jean-Marie Gustave Le Clézio (born 1940 in Nice) is voted Best Living French Writer by the readers of *Lire* magazine.

1993 Briton Anthony Burgess, the author of *A Clockwork Orange* (1962), writes his final work, *Dead Man in Deptford*, in Monaco.

1985 Patrick Süskind's novel *Perfume*, in which much of the action takes place in Grasse, is published.

Graham Greene

1982 Britain's Graham Greene writes *J'Accuse – The Dark Side of Nice*.

The Beaches of Provence

From the untamed expanses of the Rhône delta to the hot spots of the Riviera, via the cliffs and coves of the Var, the coastline of Provence is extremely varied. Resort beaches around the towns of the Riviera, such as Menton, Nice and Monte-Carlo, are crowded and noisy in the height of summer. They often charge a fee, but are usually well-kept and offer good watersports facilities. It is, however, possible to seek out quieter corners away from the crowds if you know where to look.

The Côte d'Azur beaches offer warmth and sunshine all year long, making towns such as Villefranche-sur-Mer *(see p92)* very popular with tourists.

The Camargue beaches *(see pp140–42)* at the mouth of the Rhône delta, are often deserted. The long, flat sands are ideal for horse riding, but there is a shortage of amenities.

The Côte Bleue is dotted with fishing ports and elegant summer residences. Pine trees line the beaches.

Arles

Salon de Provence

BOUCHES-DU-RHONE AND NIMES

Aix-en-Provence

Saintes-Maries-de-la-Mer

Camargue

① Martigues

Carry-le-Rouet

Marseille

Aubagne

Côte Bleue

Les Calanques ②

Bandol

Sanary-sur-Mer

Cap Sicié

Les Calanques
(see p157) are beautiful and dramatic fjord-like inlets situated east of Marseille. The sheer white cliffs, some 400 m (1,312 ft) high, drop vertically into the tempting, blue water.

Cap Sicié is a small peninsula that juts out from the Var mainland. It is famed for its strong winds and waves, ideal for experienced windsurfers.

Provence's Ten Best Beaches

① **Best sandy beach**
Plage de Piémanson, east of the Camargue, is remote enough for nudist bathing.

② **Best deep-sea diving**
The deep Calanques waters are ideal for exploring.

③ **Best sea fishing**
Bandol and Sanary-sur-Mer are charming resorts, where the tuna boats make their daily catch.

④ **Best small resort beach**
Le Lavandou offers all amenities on a small scale.

⑤ **Best trendy beach**
Tahiti-Plage in St-Tropez is the coast's showcase for fun, sun, fashion and glamour.

⑥ **Best family beaches**
Fréjus-Plage and the beach of St-Raphaël are clean, safe and have excellent facilities for families.

⑦ **Best star-spotter's beach**
Cannes' beautiful setting, with its scenic harbour, casino and stylish beaches, attracts the rich and famous.

⑧ **Best teen and twenties beach**
The all-night bars, cafés and nightclubs of Juan-les-Pins make this a lively resort.

⑨ **Best activity beach**
Watersports fanatics gather at the Ruhl-Plage in Nice for the jet-skiing and parasailing.

⑩ **Best winter beach**
Menton is the warmest resort on the Riviera and the sun shines all year round, ideal for relaxing winter holidays.

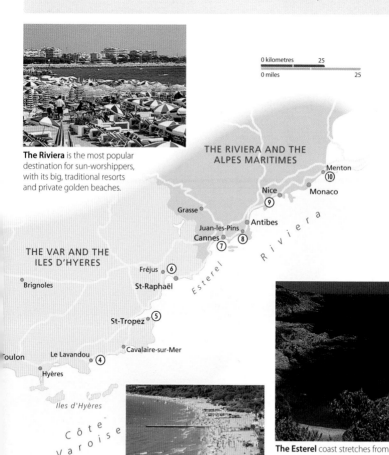

The Riviera is the most popular destination for sun-worshippers, with its big, traditional resorts and private golden beaches.

THE RIVIERA AND THE ALPES MARITIMES

0 kilometres   25

0 miles   25

THE VAR AND THE ILES D'HYERES

Grasse

Juan-les-Pins
Cannes ⑦ ⑧

Nice ⑨

Menton ⑩

Monaco

Antibes

Brignoles

Fréjus ⑥

St-Raphaël

St-Tropez ⑤

Toulon

Le Lavandou ④

Hyères

Cavalaire-sur-Mer

Iles d'Hyères

Côte Varoise

Esterel

Riviera

The Côte Varoise has a beach to suit all tastes, offering popular family resorts, small fishing ports and excellent snorkelling.

The Esterel coast stretches from Cannes to St-Raphaël. Its most striking features are the red cliffs and rocks, deep ravines and secluded coves.

PROVENCE THROUGH THE YEAR

Provence is at its prettiest in spring, when flowers bring livelihoods to perfume-makers and pleasure to passers-by. It can also be surprisingly cold as this is when the Mistral blows its strongest.

Summer fruit and vegetables are both abundant and beautiful, filling the local markets. The midsummer heat is added to by the fires of St Jean and the Valensole plains are striped with lavender, the indelible colour of

the region. To entertain the thousands of holidaymakers, July and August are filled with music festivals. Come autumn, vineyards turn to copper and the grapes are harvested. Snows blanket the mountains from December and skiers take to the slopes. Throughout the year, every town and village celebrates with a *fête*, often with traditional costume and lively activities. For information, contact the local tourist office *(see p237)*.

Women in traditional costume at the Feria de Paqûes in Arles

Spring

By the time March begins, lemons have already been harvested and the almond blossom has faded. Pear, plum and apricot blossom brightens the landscape and the first vegetables of spring are ready for the markets: asparagus, beans and green artichokes known as *mourre de gats*. By May, fruit markets are coloured with the first ripe cherries and strawberries of the year.

Southern mountain slopes warm to the sunshine and come alive with alpine flowers but the northern slopes remain wintery. Broom turns hillsides deep yellow and bees start to make honey from the sweet-smelling rosemary flowers. Flocks of sheep begin the journey of transhumance up to the summer pastures, and on the vast plains maize, wheat and rape push their way up through the softening earth.

March
Festin des Courgourdons *(last Sun)*, Nice *(see pp88–9)*. Folklore and sculpted gourd *fête*.

April
Procession aux Limaces *(Good Friday)*, Roquebrune-Cap-Martin *(see p102)*. The streets are lit with shell lamps and a parade of locals dressed as disciples and legionnaires recreate the entombment of Christ.
Printemps de Châteauneuf-du-Pape – Salon des Vins *(early April)*, Châteauneuf-du-Pape *(see p168)*. Spring wine festival displaying products of local wine growers.
Fête de la St-Marc *(end April)*, Châteauneuf-du-Pape *(see p168)*. Wine contest. (The year's vintage is blessed on the 1st weekend in August.)
Feria de Paqûes *(Easter)*, Arles *(see pp148–50)*. Arletans turn out in their traditional costume for a *feria*. The *farandole* is danced to the accompaniment of the *tambourin* drum and *galoubet* flute to mark the beginning of the famous bullfighting season.

May
Fête des Gardians *(1 May)*, Arles *(see pp148–50)*. The town is taken over by the *gardians* or cowboys who look after the Camargue cattle herds.
Pèlerinage des Gitans avec Procession à la Mer de Sainte Sarah *(24–25 May)*, Stes-Maries-de-la-Mer *(see pp228–9)*.
Festival International du Film *(two weeks in May)*, Cannes *(see pp72–3)*. The most prestigious annual film festival.
La Bravade *(16–18 May)*, St-Tropez *(see p228)*.
Fête de la Transhumance *(late May–early June)*, St-Rémy *(see p144)*. Celebrates the ancient custom of moving sheep to higher ground for the summer.
Grand Prix Automobile de Formule 1 *(weekend after Ascension)*, Monaco *(see p98)*. The only Grand Prix raced on public roads laps up an impressive 3,145 km (1,954 miles).
Feria *(Pentecost)*, Nîmes *(see pp136–7)*. The first major bullfighting event of the year takes place at Les Arènes.

Thousands of sheep parade through St-Rémy during the Fête de la Transhumance

Average Daily Hours of Sunshine

Hours
12
9
6
3
0

Jan Feb Mar Apr May Jun Jul Aug Sep Oct Nov Dec

Sunshine Chart
The summer months are guaranteed to be hot, with the intensity climaxing in July. Even in the winter, coastal towns can have up to 150 hours of sunshine a month, but be warned: it is often the icy Mistral that blows the clouds away in early spring.

Summer

The Côte d'Azur is essentially a playground in summer, particularly in August when the French take their holidays. Rafters take to the rivers and scuba divers explore the varied sealife. For laid-on entertainment, there are music festivals throughout the region.

Three national celebrations are also manifest: fireworks and bonfires brighten the skies on the **Fête de St-Jean** (June 24). **Bastille Day** (July 14) is celebrated with fireworks while **Assumption Day** (August 15) is a time for great feasting.

June
Fête de la Tarasque (last w/e), Tarascon (see p144). According to local legend, the Tarasque monster once terrorized the region. An effigy of the monster is paraded through the town.
Festival International d'Art Lyrique (June & July), Aix-en-Provence (see pp152–3). Extensive programme of classical music concerts and opera is staged in the courtyard theatre of the Archbishop's Palace.

July
Festival de la Sorgue (weekends in July), Fontaine-de-Vaucluse & l'Isle-sur-la-Sorgue (see p169). Concerts, boat races and floating markets on the river Sorgue.
Festival d'Avignon (mid- to late July), Avignon (see p229).
Chorégies d'Orange (all month), Orange. This long-established

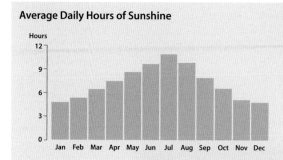

Celebrating the Fête de St-Jean with fireworks over Marseille harbour

The legendary Tarasque

opera season is held in the acoustically perfect Roman theatre (see pp166–7).
Jazz à Juan (mid- to late July), Juan-les-Pins (see p76). One of the area's top jazz festivals.
Jazz à Toulon (mid-July–early Aug), Toulon (see p116–17). Free concerts in different squares every day throughout the town.
Recontres Internationales de la Photographie (Jul–Sep), Arles (see pp148–50). The National School of Photography was set up in 1982 as a result of this festival, and each year the town is transformed into a photographic arena.

August
Corso de la Lavande (first weekend), Digne-les-Bains (see p229).
Véraison Festival – A Medieval Celebration (early Aug), Châteauneuf-du-Pape (see p168). A medieval market comes alive with 200 actors, music,

dancing, jousting and wine wagons open for tasting.
Fête du Jasmin (first week-end), Grasse (see pp70–71). Floats, music and dancing in the town.
Procession de la Passion (5 Aug), Roquebrune-Cap-Martin (see p102). Over 500 locals take part in staging Christ's passion, enacted since the Virgin saved the town from plague in 1467.
Le Festival de Musique (all month), Menton (see pp102–3). Chamber music in the square.

Holiday-makers on the crowded beaches of the Côte d'Azur

Average Monthly Rainfall

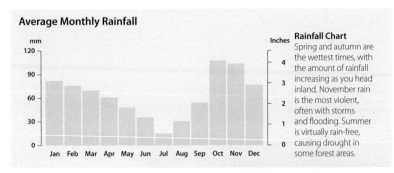

Rainfall Chart
Spring and autumn are the wettest times, with the amount of rainfall increasing as you head inland. November rain is the most violent, often with storms and flooding. Summer is virtually rain-free, causing drought in some forest areas.

Autumn

When summer is over, it is time for the *vendange*, the grape harvest. In the Camargue, rice is ready to be brought in. Walnuts are picked and, in the Maures, sweet chestnuts are collected. The woods also yield rewards for mushroom hunters, while in Vaucluse and the Var truffles are harvested from oak woods and sold on the market stalls, notably at Richerenches.

The hunting season begins in November. Small birds, such as thrushes, and ducks fall from flight into the pot and wild boar are bagged, their feet kept as talismans. Sheep are brought down to their winter pastures.

A grape picker at work during the autumn harvest

On the hunt for truffles in the woods of Haute Provence

September

Fête des Prémices du Riz
(early Sep), Arles *(see pp148–50)*.
This festival of the rice harvest coincides with the last Spanish-style bullfights of the year.

Féria des Vendanges *(second week)*, Nîmes *(see pp136–7)*.
An enjoyable combination of wine, dancing and bullfights.
Festival de la Navigation de Plaisance *(mid-Sep)*, Cannes *(see pp72–3)*. Yachts from around the world meet in the harbour. **Fête du Vent** *(mid-Sep)*, Marseille *(see pp154–6)*. Kites from all over the world decorate the sky for two days on the Plages du Prado.

October

Fête de Sainte Marie Salomé
(Sunday nearest 22 Oct), Stes-Maries-de-la-Mer. A similar festival to the Gypsy Pilgrimage held in May *(see pp228–9)* with a procession through the town's streets to the beach and the ritual blessing of the sea.
Foire Internationale de Marseille *(end of Sep–early Oct)*, Marseille *(see pp154–6)*. Thousands of visitors pour into the city to enjoy the annual fair. Various activities and sports are organized with crafts, music and folklore entertainment from over 40 different countries.

November

Fête du Prince (Fete Nationale)
(19 Nov), Monaco *(see pp94–8)*.
The second smallest independent state in Europe celebrates its national day with a firework display over the harbour.
Festival International de la Danse *(biennial, late-Nov or early Dec)*, Cannes *(see pp72–3)*. A festival of contemporary dance and ballet with an impressive programme of international performances.

Performers at the Festival International de la Danse in Cannes

Average Monthly Temperature

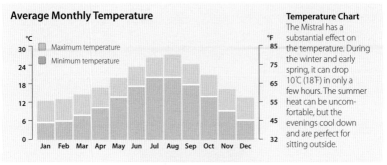

Maximum temperature
Minimum temperature

Jan Feb Mar Apr May Jun Jul Aug Sep Oct Nov Dec

Temperature Chart
The Mistral has a substantial effect on the temperature. During the winter and early spring, it can drop 10˚C (18˚F) in only a few hours. The summer heat can be uncomfortable, but the evenings cool down and are perfect for sitting outside.

Winter

There is an old saying in Provence used to describe winter: "*l'hiver a ges d'ouro,*" "winter has no hours". It is a time to open the jams of the summer, to make the geese and duck *confits* and to turn the olive harvest into oil.

Snow soon cuts off mountain passes and, at weekends, locals and visitors take to the many ski resorts, warmed by juniper or wild strawberry liqueurs.

Christmas is heralded by the sale of *santons*, the figurines used to decorate Provence's distinctive cribs. Epiphany is another important festival, when the Three Kings are fêted with crown-shaped pastries.

December

Foire aux Santons *(all month)*, Marseille *(see pp154–6)*. The largest fair honouring the symbolic clay figures that are an integral part of Christmas.
Fête du Millesime – Vin de Bandol *(early December)*, Bandol *(see p116)*. Every wine-grower in the town has their own stand and there is free wine-tasting. A different theme is chosen every year with activities and much merriment.
Noël and midnight mass *(24 Dec)*, Les Baux-de-Provence *(see pp146–7)*. A traditional festive feast of the shepherds before mass.

January

Rallye de Monte-Carlo *(late Jan, pp96–7)*. A major event in the motor sporting calendar.
Festival du Cirque *(end of month)*, Monaco *(see p98)*. Circus shows from around the globe.

Relaxing in the winter sun in the Alpes-de-Haute-Provence

February

Fête du Citron, *(late Feb–early Mar)*, Menton *(see pp102–3)*. Floats and music fill the town during the lemon festival.
Fête du Mimosa *(third Sunday)*, Bormes-les-Mimosas *(see pp120–21)*.

The annual festival in celebration of the medieval perched village's favourite flower.
Carnaval de Nice, *(all month)*, Nice. France's largest pre-Lent festival *(see p228)*.

Public Holidays

New Year's Day (1 Jan)
Easter Sunday and Monday
Ascension (sixth Thursday after Easter)
Whit Monday (second Monday after Ascension)
Labour Day (1 May)
VE Day (8 May)
Bastille Day (14 Jul)
Assumption Day (15 Aug)
All Saints' Day (1 Nov)
Remembrance Day (11 Nov)
Christmas Day (25 Dec)

A colourful creation at the Fête du Citron in Menton

THE HISTORY OF PROVENCE

Few regions of France have experienced such a varied and turbulent history as Provence. There is evidence, in the form of carvings, tools and weapons, of nomadic tribes and human settlements from 300,000 BC. The introduction of the vine, so important today, can be credited to the Phoenicians and Greeks who traded along the coast. Perhaps more crucially, Provence was the Romans'"Province" and few regions of their vast empire have retained such dramatic buildings; the theatre at Orange, the arenas of Arles and Nîmes, the Pont du Gard and the imposing trophy of La Turbie are all testimony to past Roman power.

The Middle Ages proved a stormy period of feuding warlords and invasions; the many fortified hilltop villages that characterize the region were a desperate attempt at defence. The papacy dominated the 14th century, and the magnificent palace the popes built in Avignon remains today. The arts flourished too, especially under King René in his capital of Aix. After his death in 1480, Provence lost its independence and its history became enmeshed with that of France. Religious war took its toll and the Great Plague of Marseille killed tens of thousands in 1720.

A beguiling climate and improved transport in the 19th century began to attract artists and foreign nobility. Tiny fishing villages grew into glamorous Riviera resorts. The allure remains for millions of tourists, while economic investment means it is also a boom area for the technology industry.

A 16th-century map of Marseille and its harbour

◀ Detail of an illuminated 13th-century manuscript showing a troubadour playing to a royal audience

Ancient Provence

Rock carvings, fragments of paintings and remains from primitive settlements suggest that Provence was first inhabited a million years ago. Carvings in the Grotte de l'Observatoire in Monaco and the decorated Grotte Cosquer near Marseille are among the oldest of their kind in the world. Nomadic tribes roamed the land for centuries, notably the Celts from the north and the Ligurians from the east. Not until the arrival of the Phoenicians and the Greeks did trade flourish in a more structured way and Provençal society become more stable.

"Double Head" Carving
This stone figure (3rd century BC) probably decorated a Celtic sanctuary.

The _bories_ at Gordes date back to 3,500 BC.

Celtic Doorway
(3rd century BC) The niches in the pillars held the embalmed heads of Celtic heroes.

The Grotte des Fées at Mont de Cordes contain prehistoric carvings often associated with modern astrological symbols.

The Foundation of Marseille

When Greek traders arrived in 600 BC, their captain, Protis, attended a feast in honour of the local chief's daughter, Gyptis. She chose Protis as her husband. The chief's dowry to Protis and Gyptis was the strip of land on which Marseille grew.

St-Blaise, once a heavily fortified Greek trading centre, has only minimal remains.

The Grotte Cosquer, with paintings dating to 30,000 BC, is accessible only from the sea.

Wine jars, bound for Greece from 1,000 BC onwards, were found in Les Calanques near Marseille.

1,000,000 BC Earliest human presence in Provence at Grotte de l'Observatoire in Monaco; use of bone as a tool

400,000 BC Fire first used in Nice

60,000 BC Neanderthal hunters on the Riviera

1,000,000 BC		5000	4500	4000	3500

30,000 BC Appearance of _Homo sapiens_ (modern man); cave painting at Grotte Cosquer

3,500 BC First _borie_ villages

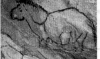

Cave painting from Grotte Cosquer

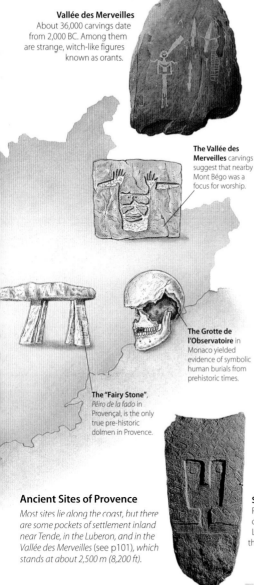

Vallée des Merveilles
About 36,000 carvings date from 2,000 BC. Among them are strange, witch-like figures known as orants.

The Vallée des Merveilles carvings suggest that nearby Mont Bégo was a focus for worship.

The Grotte de l'Observatoire in Monaco yielded evidence of symbolic human burials from prehistoric times.

The "Fairy Stone", *Peiro de la fado* in Provençal, is the only true pre-historic dolmen in Provence.

Ancient Sites of Provence

Most sites lie along the coast, but there are some pockets of settlement inland near Tende, in the Luberon, and in the Vallée des Merveilles (see p101), which stands at about 2,500 m (8,200 ft).

Standing Stone
Prehistoric stelae, like this carved stone from the Luberon, are scattered throughout Provence.

Where to See Ancient Provence

Many museums, such as the Musée Archéologique, Nîmes *(see p136)*, have excellent collections of ancient artifacts. The well-preserved *bories* in the Luberon *(see p173)* illustrate early village communities; the Grotte de l'Observatoire in Monaco *(see p98)* is an example of an even more primitive settlement.

Borie Village at Gordes
These dry-stone dwellings *(see p173)* have for centuries been used by nomadic shepherds.

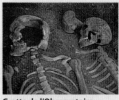

Grotte de l'Observatoire
Skeletons uncovered here have characteristics linking them with southern African tribes.

2,500–2,000 BC Carvings at Vallée des Merveilles

Hannibal crossing the Alps

380 BC Celtic invasions of Provence

3000	2500	2000	1500	1000	500 BC

2,000 BC Tombs carved at Cordes

600 BC Greek traders settle at St-Blaise. Founding of Marseille

218 BC Hannibal passes through region to reach Italy

Gallo-Roman Provence

The Romans extended their empire into Provence towards the end of the 2nd century BC. They enjoyed good relations with the local people and within 100 years created a wealthy province. Nîmes and Arles became two of the most significant Roman towns outside Italy; colonies at the Site Archéologique de Glanum and Vaison-la-Romaine flourished. Many fine monuments remain and museums, for instance at Vaison-la-Romaine, display smaller Roman treasures.

Christ's followers are reputed to have brought Christianity to the region when they landed at Les-Saintes-Maries-de-la-Mer in AD 40.

Pont Julien (3 BC)
This magnificently preserved triple-arched bridge stands 8 km (5 miles) west of Apt.

Marble Sarcophagus (4th century)
The Alyscamps in Arles (*see p150*), once a vast Roman necropolis, contains many carved marble and stone coffins.

Two temples, dedicated to the emperor Augustus and his adopted sons, Caius and Lucius, date from 20 BC.

Triumphal Arch at Orange
Built in about 20 BC this is, in spite of much crude restoration, one of the best preserved Roman triumphal arches. Carvings depict the conquest of Gaul and sea battle scenes.

The fortified gate is thought to have been built by Greeks, who occupied Glanum from the 4th century BC.

Roman Glanum

The impressive ruined site at Glanum reveals much earlier Roman and Greek settlements. This reconstruction shows it after it was rebuilt in AD 49 (see p145).

118 BC Provincia founded – first Gallo-Roman Province

125 BC Roman legions defend Marseille against Celto-Ligurian invaders

Consul Marius

49 BC Emperor Julius Caesar lays siege to Marseille for supporting his rival, Pompey. Romans rebuild Glanum

40 BC Vaison-la-Romaine ranks among Roman Gaul's wealthiest towns

2nd-century BC Venus d'Arles

100 BC	AD 1	100

123 BC Romans make Entremont first Provençal settlement

102 BC Consul Marius defeats invading German tribes; over 200,000 killed

3 BC Pont Julien built

AD 40 "Boat of Bethany" lands at Les-Saintes-Maries-de-la-Mer

14 BC Emperor Augustus defeats Ligurians in Alpes Maritimes. Trophy at La Turbie erected (*see p93*)

121 BC Foundation of Aquae Sextiae, later to become Aix-en-Provence

Les-Stes-Maries-de-la-Mer
Mary Magdalene, Mary Salome and Mary Jacobe reputedly sailed here in AD 40. The town where they landed is named in their honour and continues to attract pilgrims *(see p142).*

Where to See Gallo-Roman Provence

Arles *(see pp148–50)* and Nîmes *(see pp136–7),* with their amphitheatres and religious and secular buildings, offer the most complete examples of Roman civilization. Orange *(see p165)* and Vaison-la-Romaine *(see p162)* contain important monuments, and the Pont du Gard *(see p135)* and Le Trophée d'Auguste *(see p93)* are unique.

Théâtre Antique d'Orange
Built into a hill, this Roman theatre would have held up to 7,000 spectators *(see pp166–7).*

Cryptoportico
The foundations of Arles' forum, these horseshoe-shaped underground galleries were probably used as grain stores *(see p150).*

The baths occupied three rooms, each used for bathing at a different temperature.

The Forum, the commercial centre of the Roman town, was surrounded by a covered gallery.

Jewellery from Vaison-la-Romaine
1st-century AD jewellery was found in excavations of the Roman necropolis.

Roman Flask
Well-preserved ancient Roman glassware and everyday items have been found in many areas of Provence.

413 Visigoths seize Languedoc

476 Western Roman Empire collapses

| 0 | 300 | 400 | 500 |

300 Arles reaches height of its prestige as a Roman town

Abbaye St-Victor, founded in AD 416, in Marseille

Medieval Provence

With the fall of the Roman Empire, stability and relative prosperity began to disappear. Although Provence became part of the Holy Roman Empire, the local counts retained considerable autonomy and the towns became fiercely independent. People withdrew to hilltops to protect themselves from attack by a series of invaders, and *villages perchés (see pp24–5)* began to develop. Provence became a major base for Christian Crusaders, intent on conquering Muslim territories in Africa and Asia.

The Great Walls, finally completed in 1300, 30 years after Louis IX's death, were over 1.6 km (1 mile) long and formed an almost perfect rectangle.

St-Trophime Carving
The monumental 12th-century portal at St-Trophime in Arles *(see p148)* is adorned with intricate carvings of saints and scenes from the Last Judgment.

Louis IX's army consisted of 35,000 men plus horses and military equipment.

Louis IX

St Martha and the Tarasque
This 9th-century legend proved the strength of Christianity. The saint is said to have lured the Tarasque dragon to its death, using hymns and holy water *(see p144).*

The Seventh Crusade
Hoping to drive the Muslims out of the Holy Land, Louis IX (St Louis) of France set sail from his new port, Aigues-Mortes (see pp138–9), in 1248. It was a spectacular occasion, with banners waving and his army singing hymns.

536 Provence ceded to the Franks

737–9 Anti-Frankish rebellions in Avignon, Marseille and Arles brutally suppressed by Charles Martel

855 Kingdom of Provence created for Charles the Bald, grandson of Charlemagne

949 Provence divided into four counties

600 | **700** | **800** | **900**

Battle between the Crusaders and the Saracens

800 First wave of Saracen invasions

924 Hungarians sack Nîmes

Charles the Bald

Troubadour Ivory (c. 1300)
The poetry of Provençal troubadours tells how knights wooed virtuous women through patience, courtesy and skill.

Notre-Dame-de-Beauvoir Chapel At the top of a path from Moustiers (see p190), the chapel has a fine Romanesque porch and nave.

1500 ships set sail for the Holy Land on 28 August 1248.

St Christopher Fresco The Tour Ferrande in Pernes-les-Fontaines (see p168) contains religious frescoes from 1285. They are among the oldest in France.

Where to See Medieval Provence

The highlights are undoubtedly the Romanesque abbeys and churches, especially the "three sisters": Silvacane (see p151), Le Thoronet (see p112) and Sénanque (see p168). Fortified villages perchés, such as Gordes (see p173) and the spectacular 11th-century citadel at Les Baux-de-Provence (see p146), testify to the unrest and horrific violence that scarred this period of Provence's history.

Les Pénitents des Mées
These are said to be 6th-century monks turned to stone for gazing at Saracen women (see p185).

Silvacane Abbey (1175–1230)
This beautiful, austere Cistercian abbey was Provence's last great Romanesque abbey.

974 Saracens defeated at La Garde-Freinet

Seal of Simon de Montfort

1213 Battle of Muret: de Montfort defeats count of Toulouse and King of Aragon

1209 French military leader Simon de Montfort marches on Provence

1246 Charles of Anjou marries Béatrice, heiress of Provence, to become Count of Provence

1248 Louis IX embarks on Seventh Crusade from Aigues-Mortes

1000	1100	1200	1300

1032 Provence becomes part of Holy Roman Empire

1096–1099 First Crusade

1112 Raymond-Bérenger III, Count of Barcelona, marries the Duchess of Provence

1186 Counts of Provence declare Aix their capital

1125 Provence shared between Barcelona and Toulouse

1187 Remains of St Martha discovered at Tarascon

1274 Papacy acquires Comtat Venaissin

1295 Death of Guiraut Riquier, the "Last Troubadour"

1280 Relics of Mary Magdalene found at St-Maximin-la-Ste-Baume

Papal Avignon

When the papacy temporarily abandoned war-torn Italy, Avignon became the centre of the Roman Catholic world. From 1309 until 1377 seven French popes ruled unchallenged. When a new Italian pope, Urban VI, was elected, the French cardinals rebelled. In 1378 they chose a rival pope, Clement VII, thus causing a major schism that lasted until 1403. During the 14th century the papal court in Avignon became a wealthy centre for both learning and the arts, extending its influence across the region.

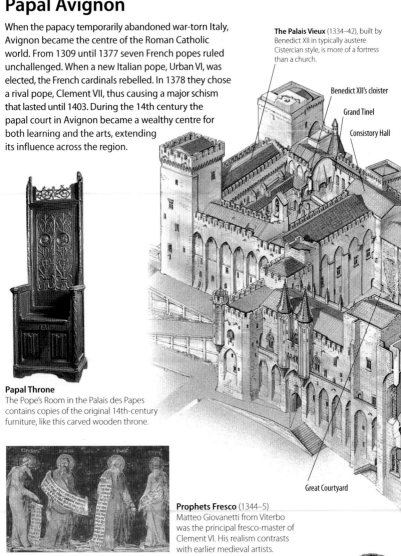

The Palais Vieux (1334–42), built by Benedict XII in typically austere Cistercian style, is more of a fortress than a church.

Benedict XII's cloister

Grand Tinel

Consistory Hall

Great Courtyard

Papal Throne
The Pope's Room in the Palais des Papes contains copies of the original 14th-century furniture, like this carved wooden throne.

Prophets Fresco (1344–5)
Matteo Giovanetti from Viterbo was the principal fresco-master of Clement VI. His realism contrasts with earlier medieval artists.

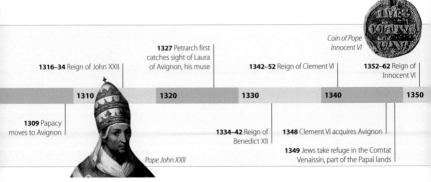

1316–34 Reign of John XXII

1327 Petrarch first catches sight of Laura of Avignon, his muse

1342–52 Reign of Clement VI

Coin of Pope Innocent VI

1352–62 Reign of Innocent VI

1310   **1320**   **1330**   **1340**   **1350**

1309 Papacy moves to Avignon

1334–42 Reign of Benedict XII

1348 Clement VI acquires Avignon

1349 Jews take refuge in the Comtat Venaissin, part of the Papal lands

Pope John XXII

Death of Clement VI
Clement VI came to Avignon to "forget he was pope". In 1348 he bought the town for 80,000 florins and built the splendid Palais Neuf.

Where to see Papal Provence

Avignon is surrounded by evidence of religious and aristocratic splendour. With the presence of the wealthy papacy – a kind of miniature Vatican – abbeys, churches and chapels flourished. The Musée du Petit Palais (see p172) in Avignon contains examples of work by the artists who were encouraged to work at the papal court.

Villeneuve Charterhouse
Innocent VI established this, the oldest charterhouse in France, in the 1350s (see p134).

Châteauneuf-du-Pape
John XXII's early 14th-century castle became the popes' second residence. The keep and walls still stand today (see p168).

Pope's Room

Stag Room Frescoes
The hunting scenes are a reminder that monastic life was not only about learning and prayer.

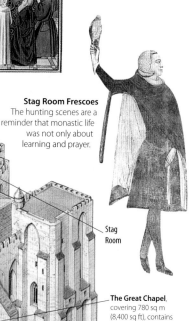

Stag Room

The Great Chapel, covering 780 sq m (8,400 sq ft), contains the restored papal altar.

The Palais Neuf was built by Clement VI in 1342–52.

Great Audience Hall

Palais Des Papes
The maze of corridors and rooms in the Palais des Papes (see p172), built over 18 years (1334–52), were richly decorated by skilled artists and craftsmen introduced from Italy. The building's scale is overwhelming.

Petrarch (1304–74)
The great Renaissance poet Petrarch considered papal Avignon to be a "sewer" and a place of corruption.

1362–70 Reign of Urban V

1378–94 Reign of anti-pope Clement VII

1370–78 Reign of Gregory XI

1394–1409 Reign of anti-pope Benedict XIII

1360	1370	1380	1390	1400

363 Grimaldis recapture Monaco

1377 Papacy returns to Rome

Effigy of Urban V

Anti-Pope Benedict XIII

1403 Benedict XIII flees Avignon

René and the Wars of Religion

The end of the 15th century saw the golden age of Aix-en-Provence *(see pp152–3)*, then Provence's capital. Under the patronage of King René, art and culture flourished and the Flemish-influenced Avignon School was formed. After René's death, Provence was annexed by the French king, Louis XI. Loss of independence and subsequent involvement with French politics led to brutal invasions by Charles V. The 16th-century Wars of Religion between "heretic" Protestants and Catholics resulted in a wave of massacres, and the wholesale destruction of churches and their contents.

Detail of the Triptych
René's favourite château at Tarascon *(see p144)* on the Rhône is realistically painted.

King René, himself a poet, painter and musician, was a great influence on Provençal culture.

Nostradamus
Born in St-Rémy *(see pp144–5)*, the physician and astrologer is best known for his predictions, *The Prophecies* (1555).

Massacres of Protestants and Catholics
The religious wars were brutal. Thousands of Protestants were massacred in 1545, and 200 Catholics died in Nîmes in 1567.

Burning Bush Triptych
Nicolas Froment's painting (1476) was commissioned by King René. The star of the Cathédrale de St-Sauveur, Aix, it depicts a vision of the Virgin and Child surrounded by the eternal Burning Bush of Moses.

1434–80 Reign of Good King René

Retable from Avignon

1501 Parliament de Provence created

1486 Union of Provence with France

| 1425 | 1450 | 1475 | 1500 |

1481 Charles du Maine, Count of Provence and René's nephew, gives Provence to King of France

1496 Military port built at Toulon

King René

The Annunciation

The Master of Aix, one of René's artistic circle, painted this Annunciation. Dark symbolism, including the owl's wings of the angel Gabriel, undercuts this usually joyful subject.

The Bush, burning but unconsumed, was a pagan and Christian symbol of eternal life.

Where to See 15th- and 16th-century Provence

Architecture from this period can be seen today in the fine town houses and elegant streets of Aix (see pp152–3) and Avignon (see pp170–2). The Musée Granet, also in Aix, contains several interesting examples of religious paintings. A collection of period furniture is exhibited in the Musée Grobet-Labadié in Marseille (see p155).

Château at Tarascon
This 13th-century château (see p144) was partly rebuilt by Louis II of Anjou and then completed by King René, his son.

Holy Roman Emperor, Charles V, by Titian

Between 1524 and 1536, Charles V (Charles I of Spain) attacked Provence frequently as part of his war against France.

The saints John the Evangelist, Catherine of Alexandria and Nicolas of Myra are behind Queen Jeanne.

Rhinoceros Woodcut by Albrecht Dürer

In 1516, Marseille's Château d'If (see p156) was briefly home to the first rhinoceros to set foot in Europe. It was in transit as a gift for the Pope, but died later in the journey.

Moses is seen receiving the word of God from an angel.

Queen Jeanne, René's second wife, is shown kneeling in adoration.

1525 Jews in Comtat Venaissin forced to wear yellow hats

1545 Massacre of Protestants in Luberon villages

1577 First soap factory in Marseille

1598 Edict of Nantes signals end of Wars of Religion

| 1525 | 1550 | 1575 | 1600 |

1524 Invasion of Charles V

1562 Wars of Religion commence

Protestant martyrdom

Classical Provence

Provence in the 17th and 18th centuries saw a decrease in regional allegiance and growth of national awareness. Towns grew and majestic monuments, town houses *(hôtels)* and châteaux proliferated. But despite economic development in the textile industry and the growth of the ports of Toulon and Marseille, the period was bleak for many, culminating in the devastating plague of 1720. The storming of the Bastille in Paris in 1789 sparked popular uprisings and revolutionary marches on Paris.

Pavillon de Vendôme
Jean-Claude Rambot made the Atlantes for this building (1667) in Aix *(see pp152–3)*.

The death toll
was over 100,000 in the last plague in Europe.

Boat-building in Toulon
Toulon, a strategic port, was famous for its boat-building. Galley slaves, chained to their oars, were a great tourist attraction in the 17th century.

Corpses were hauled in carts to mass graves.

Santon Crib Scene
The *santon* ("little saints" in Provençal) cribs were first made after the Revolution, when the churches were shut. They soon became a very popular local craft.

The Great Plague
Vue du Cours pendant la Peste by Michel Serre depicts the 1720 plague in Marseille, brought by a cargo boat from Syria. Over half of Marseille's population died. All contact with the city was banned and huge walls were built to halt the epidemic, but it still spread as far as Aix, Arles and Toulon.

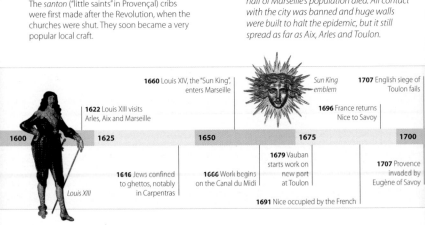

1660 Louis XIV, the "Sun King", enters Marseille

Sun King emblem

1707 English siege of Toulon fails

1622 Louis XIII visits Arles, Aix and Marseille

1696 France returns Nice to Savoy

1600	1625	1650	1675	1700

1616 Jews confined to ghettos, notably in Carpentras

Louis XIII

1666 Work begins on the Canal du Midi

1679 Vauban starts work on new port at Toulon

1691 Nice occupied by the French

1707 Provence invaded by Eugène of Savoy

Napoleon Seizes Toulon
Junior officer Napoleon Bonaparte first made his name when he took Toulon from occupying English troops in 1793.

Cours Belsunce, built in 1670 in the Italian style, was lined with trees and Baroque palaces.

Monks, led by the devout Jean Belsunce, the Bishop of Marseille, gave succour to the dying.

Where to See Classical Provence

Avignon (see pp170–72) and Aix (see pp152–3) have period town houses with fine doorways and staircases. Jewish synagogues and remains of Jewish enclaves can be found in Cavaillon (see p174), Forcalquier (see p186) and Carpentras (see p168). The 18th-century Jardin de la Fontaine in Nîmes (see pp136–7) can still be visited.

Pharmacy at Carpentras
The 18th-century Hôtel-Dieu (hospital) houses a chapel and a pharmacy containing faïence apothecary jars.

Fontaine du Cormoran
The best known of the 36 fountains in Pernes-les-Fontaines is the 18th-century carved Cormoran fountain.

Marshal Sébastien Vauban
Louis XIV's brilliant military architect, Vauban, fortified towns and ports including Toulon and Antibes.

Moustiers Faïence
Brought to France from Italy in the 17th century, traditional faïence features pastoral scenes in delicate colours.

1713 Treaty of Utrecht cedes Orange to France

1718 Nice becomes part of new Kingdom of Sardinia

1791 Avignon and Comtat Venaissin annexed to France

1779 Roman mausoleum at Aix demolished

1793 Breaking of siege of Toulon catapults Napoleon Bonaparte to fame

1725	1750	1775	1800

1720 Great Plague strikes Marseille and spreads throughout Provence

1771 Aix parliament suppressed

1787 Provençal silk harvest fails

The Great Plague, Marseille

1789 Storming of the Bastille, Paris; Provençal peasants pillage local châteaux and monasteries

1792 Republicans adopt Rouget de Lisle's army song: *La Marseillaise*

The Belle Époque

From the start of the 19th century, the beguiling climate, particularly the mild winters, of coastal Provence attracted foreign visitors, from invalids and artists to distinguished royalty and courtesans. Railways, grand hotels, exotic gardens, opulent villas and the chic promenade des Anglais in Nice were built to meet their needs. Queen Victoria, the Aga Khan, King Leopold of Belgium and Empress Eugénie – Napoleon III's wife and doyenne of Riviera royalty – all held court. Artists and writers came in droves to revel in the light and freedom.

Homage à Mistral
Frédéric Mistral created the Félibrige group in 1854 to preserve Provençal culture.

Printing in Marseille
Cheap labour, ample paper supplies and good communications fostered the development of printing.

Belle époque **decor**
featured gilt, ornate chandeliers and marble.

High society included famous courtesans as well as their rich and royal lovers.

Grasse Perfume
More modern methods of cultivation and distillation played an important role in the expanding 19th-century perfume-making industry.

Monte-Carlo Casino Interior
From being the poorest European state in 1850, Monaco boomed with the opening of the first Monte-Carlo casino in 1856, as seen in Christian Bokelmann's painting. The fashionable flocked to enjoy the luxury and glamour, while fortunes were won and lost (see pp96–8).

1815 Napoleon lands at Golfe-Juan

1830 Beginnings of tourism around Nice

1861 Monaco sells Roquebrune and Menton to France

1860 Nice votes for union with France

1859 Mistral publishes his epic poem, *Mirèio*

| 1800 | 1820 | 1840 | 1860 |

Paul Cézanne

1839 Marseille-Sète railroad begun. Birth of Cézanne

1854 Founding of Félibrige, the Provençal cultural school

1869 Opening of Suez Canal brings trade to Marseille; railway extended to Nice

Vineyard blight
Ravaged by phylloxera, vines in Provence and across France were replaced by resistant American root stocks.

Tourism
By the late 19th century, sun and sea air were considered beneficial to health.

Where to See Belle Époque Provence

Although many have been destroyed, villas and hotels built in the extravagant *belle époque* style still survive on the Côte d'Azur. The Négresco in Nice *(see pp88–9)* is especially fine. Other period pieces include the Cathédrale Orthodoxe Russe, also in Nice, and, on St-Jean-Cap-Ferrat, the Ephrussi de Rothschild Villa and Gardens *(see pp90–91)*. In Beaulieu the Villa Grecque Kérylos, Rotunda and gardens are typical of the era *(see p92)*.

InterContinental Carlton, Cannes
Built in 1911, this ostentatious Riviera landmark is still an exclusive hotel *(see p73)*.

Monte-Carlo Opéra
Charles Garnier designed this opera house *(see pp96–7)*, as well as the Casino.

Van Gogh's Provence
Van Gogh produced turbulent works in the Clinique St-Paul in St-Rémy *(see pp144–5)*.

Casino tables were sometimes draped in black mourning when a gambler succeeded in breaking the bank with a major win.

1879 Monte-Carlo Opéra opens

Casino at Monte-Carlo

1909 Earthquake centred on Rognes in the Bouches-du-Rhône causes widespread damage.

1880

1900

1920

1888–90 Van Gogh works in Provence

1904 Mistral wins Nobel prize for Literature for *Mirèio*

Provence at War

After the economic drain caused by World War I, Provence enjoyed increasing prosperity as the tourist industry boomed. While much of the interior remained remote and rural, the vogue for sea-bathing drew crowds to resorts such as Cannes and Nice from the 1920s onwards. Provence continued to build on its image as a playground for the rich and famous, attracting visitors from Noël Coward to Wallis Simpson. The 1942–44 German occupation brought an end to the glamorous social life for many, and some towns, including St-Tropez and Marseille, were badly damaged by Germans and Allies.

Tourism
As swimming in the sea and sun-bathing became fashionable pursuits, resorts along the Riviera attracted many new visitors. In the 1930s a nudist colony opened on the Ile du Levant.

Monaco Grand Prix
This race around the principality's streets was started on the initiative of Prince Louis II in 1929. It is still one of the most colourful and dangerous Formula 1 races.

Precious ammunition and arms were dropped from Allied planes or captured from the Nazis.

Antoine de Saint-Exupéry
France's legendary writer-pilot disappeared on 31 July 1944 while on a reconnaissance flight (see p33).

La Résistance
After 1942 the Résistance (or maquis after the scrubland that made a good hiding place) was active in Provence. The fighters were successful in Marseille and in preparing the coastal areas for the 1944 Allied invasion.

1925 Coco Chanel arrives on the Riviera

1930 Novelist D H Lawrence dies in Vence

Coco Chanel

1920	1925	1930

F Scott Fitzgerald

1924 Scott and Zelda Fitzgerald spend a year on the Riviera

1928 Camargue National Park created

1930 Pagnol begins filming *Marius*, *Fanny* and *César* trilogy in Marseille

Marcel Pagnol (1905–74)
Pagnol immortalized Provence and its inhabitants in his plays, novels and films, depicting a simple, rural life *(see p33)*.

Many who joined the Résistance had scarcely left school. Training was often only by experience.

Allied Landings
On 14 August 1944, Allied troops bombarded the coast between Toulon and Marseille and soon gained ground.

Marseille Exhibition
The 1922 exhibition was an invitation to enjoy the cosmopolitan delights of Marseille.

Where to See 1920s to 1940s Provence

The now slightly seedy suburbs of Hyères *(see p119)* retain evidence of graceful living after World War I. Toulon harbour's bristling warships *(see pp116–17)* are a reminder of the French navy's former power. The activities of the Résistance are well documented in the Musée d'Histoire 1939–45 in Fontaine-de-Vaucluse *(see p169)*.

Les Deux Garçons, Aix
This still chic café was frequented by Winston Churchill and Jean Cocteau among others *(see pp152–3)*.

La Citadelle, Sisteron
Rebuilt after the Allied bombing in 1944, the impressive citadel has displays on its turbulent history *(see p182)*.

1942 Nazis invade southern France; French fleet scuttled in Toulon harbour

1943 *Maquis* resistance cells formed

1940 Italians occupy Menton

1935

1940

1939 Cannes Film Festival inaugurated, but first festival delayed by war

Liberation of Marseille

1944 American and French troops land near St-Tropez; liberation of Marseille

Post-War Provence

Paid holidays, post-war optimism, and the
St-Tropez sun cult all made the Riviera the magnet
it has remained for holiday-makers. The region still
offers a rich variety of produce – olive oil, wine, fruit,
flowers and perfume – though industry, especially
in the high-tech sector, grows apace. The environment
has suffered from over-development, pollution and
forest fires. The 1960s saw massive North African
immigration, and today unemployment creates
racial and political tension.

Port-Grimaud
The successful "Provençal Venice",
a car-free leisure port, was built by
François Spoerry in 1966 in regional
village style (see p127).

Bus Stop by Philippe Starck
The modern architecture of
Nîmes typifies many bold
projects in the region.

Beach at Nice
Though many are pebbly, the
Riviera beaches still attract
dedicated sun-worshippers.

Fires
The devastating forest
fires that ravage the
region are fought by
planes that scoop up
sea water.

Picasso

1946 Picasso
starts painting
in the Grimaldi
Castle, Antibes

1956 Grace Kelly marries
Monaco's Prince Rainier III

1952 Le
Corbusier's Cité
Radieuse built

1961 Art
festival of new
Ecole de Nice

1962 Lower Durance engineered to
develop hydro-electric power

1970 Sophia-Antipolis
technology park
opens near Antibes

1977 First section of
Marseille underground
railway opened

1940	1950	1960	1970	1980

1954 Matisse dies

1956 Roger Vadim films *And God Created
Woman*, starring Brigitte Bardot, in St-Tropez

1959 Floods in Fréjus

1970 Autoroute du
Soleil completed

1962 Algerian Independence – French
North Africans (*pieds-noirs*) settle in Provence

1973 Picasso dies at Mougins

1971 The "French Connection"
drug ring is exposed

1982 Princess Grace is
killed in car accident

Winter Sports
Skiing has become increasingly popular *(see p100)*. Isola 2000, near Nice, a purpose-built, futuristic resort, was built in 1971.

Colombe d'Or café
Once an artists' haunt, this is now one of St-Paul de Vence's chic celebrity venues *(see p79)*.

Cannes Film Festival
Brigitte Bardot   Kim Novak

First held in 1946, the festival (see p72) *has become the world's annual film event, a glamorous jamboree of directors, stars and aspiring starlets.* And God Created Woman, *starring Brigitte Bardot, became a* succès de scandale *in 1956.*

Where to See Modern Provence

Some of the most striking modern architecture includes Le Corbusier's Cité Radieuse in Marseille *(see p156)*, the Musée d'Art Moderne et d'Art Contemporain in Nice *(see p89)* and the Norman Foster-designed Carré d'Art in Nîmes *(see p136)*. Large-scale rebuilding programmes in towns such as Marseille *(see pp154–6)*, St-Tropez *(see pp122–6)* and Ste-Maxime *(see p127)* have concentrated on new buildings that blend well with the existing ones.

St-Tropez
Successful post-war restoration means it is often difficult to tell new buildings from old.

Fondation Maeght
The building reflects the modern use of traditional Provençal style and materials *(see pp80–81)*.

1998 Jacques Médecin dies in Uruguay, self-exiled after a year in jail in France

2001 TGV Méditerranée link with Paris launched

Prince Albert II

2005 Prince Rainier III dies and is succeeded by his only son, Prince Albert II

2013 EU designates Marseille as European Capital of Culture

1992 Floods in son-la-Romaine

1990	2000	2010	2020

2002 Euro replaces Franc as legal tender

TGV train

2016 Terrorist attack in Nice on Bastille Day claims 86 lives

1990 Jacques Médecin, Mayor of Nice, flees to Uruguay to avoid trial for corruption and tax arrears

2011 Prince Albert II marries Charlene Wittstock

2009 J M G Le Clézio wins the Nobel Prize for Literature

PROVENCE AREA BY AREA

Provence at a Glance

From natural wonders and historic architecture to the
cream of modern art, Provence is a region with something
for everyone. Even the most ardent sun-worshipper will be
tempted into the cool shade of its treasure-filled museums
and churches. Visitors who come in the footsteps of the
world's greatest artists will be equally dazzled by the
wild beauty of the Gorges du Verdon and the Camargue.
In a region packed with delights, those shown here
are among the very best.

Papal Avignon's medieval architectural
splendour *(see pp170–71)*

The beautifully preserved Roman theatre
at Orange *(see pp166–7)*

Orange

Carpentras

VAUCLUSE

Avignon

Cavaillon

Manosque

Arles

Salon de
Provence

Pertuis

**BOUCHES-DU-RHONE
AND NIMES**

Aix-en-Provence

Martigues

Marseille

Aubagne

Wildlife in its natural habitat in the
Camargue *(see pp140–41)*

```
0 kilometres      25
0 miles           25
```

The massive basilica of St-Maximin-la-Ste-Baume, housing relics of
St Mary Magdalene *(see pp114–15)*

◀ The stunning town of Moustiers-Ste-Marie, Alpes-de-Haute-Provence

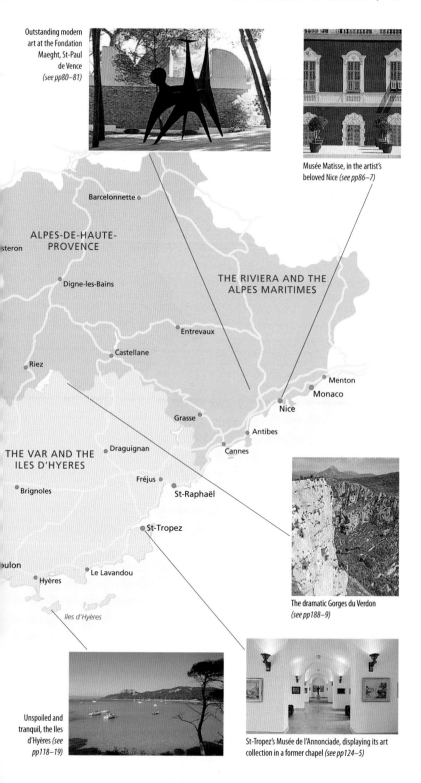

Outstanding modern art at the Fondation Maeght, St-Paul de Vence *(see pp80–81)*

Musée Matisse, in the artist's beloved Nice *(see pp86–7)*

ALPES-DE-HAUTE-PROVENCE

Barcelonnette

steron

Digne-les-Bains

THE RIVIERA AND THE ALPES MARITIMES

Entrevaux

Castellane

Riez

Menton

Monaco

Nice

Grasse

Antibes

Draguignan

Cannes

THE VAR AND THE ILES D'HYERES

Brignoles

Fréjus

St-Raphaël

St-Tropez

oulon

Le Lavandou

Hyères

Iles d'Hyères

The dramatic Gorges du Verdon *(see pp188–9)*

Unspoiled and tranquil, the Iles d'Hyères *(see pp118–19)*

St-Tropez's Musée de l'Annonciade, displaying its art collection in a former chapel *(see pp124–5)*

THE RIVIERA AND THE ALPES MARITIMES

The French Riviera is, without doubt, the most celebrated seaside in Europe. Just about everybody who has been anybody for the past 100 years has succumbed to its glittering allure. This is the holiday playground of kings and courtesans, movie stars and millionaires, where the seriously rich never stand out in the crowd.

There is a continual complaint that the Riviera is not what it used to be, that the Cannes Film Festival is mere hype, that grand old Monte-Carlo has lost all sense of taste and that Nice isn't worth the trouble of finding a parking space. But look at the boats in Antibes harbour, glimpse a villa or two on Cap Martin, or observe the baubles on the guests at the Hôtel de Paris in Monte-Carlo; money and class still rule.

The Riviera is not just a millionaire's watering hole: a diversity of talent has visited, seeking patrons and taking advantage of the luminous Mediterranean light. This coast is irrevocably linked with the life and works of Matisse and Picasso, Chagall, Cocteau and Renoir. It lent them the scenery of its shores and the rich environment of hill villages like St-Paul de Vence. This village has echoed to the voices of such luminaries as Bonnard and Modigliani, F Scott Fitzgerald and Greta Garbo. Today, its galleries still spill canvases on to its medieval lanes.

The Alpes Maritimes, which incorporates the principality of Monaco, is renowned for its temperate winter climate. The abundance of flowers here attracted the perfume industry and the English – who created some of the finest gardens on the coast. Inland, the mountainous areas of Provence offer a range of skiing activities in superb mountain scenery, and a chance to try traditional Alpine food.

Relaxing on the promenade des Anglais, Nice

◀ Cannes Old Town, known locally as Le Suquet, overlooking the harbour

Exploring the Riviera and the Alpes Maritimes

The rocky heights of the pre-Alps lie in tiers, running east to west and tumbling down to the Riviera's dramatic, Corniche-hemmed coast. On bluffs and pinnacles, towns and villages keep a watchful eye on the distant blue sea. Towards the Italian border, the Alpine ridges run from north to south, cut by torrents and gorges which provide snowy winter slopes for skiers. Much of the higher ground is occupied by the Parc National du Mercantour *(see p101)*, home of the ibex and the chamoix. Its jewel is the prehistoric Vallée des Merveilles, less than two hours from the contrasting bustle of the Riviera.

Getting Around

The A8 from Italy runs inland, parallel to the coast. Between this highway and the sea, from Nice to Menton, are three corniches. The Grande Corniche follows the Roman road, Julia Augusta, via La Turbie. The Moyenne Corniche passes through Eze, and the Corniche Inférieure visits all coastal resorts. The inland roads are narrow and winding, so allow more time for your journey. Grasse and Cannes are linked by a regular bus service, and bikes can be hired at some railway stations. Other bus links are also good. The largest airport in the region and second busiest in France, is at Nice, west of the city.

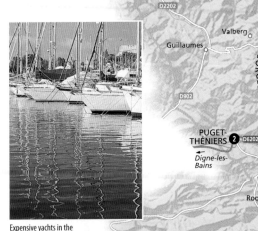

Expensive yachts in the colourful harbour at Antibes

Sights at a Glance

For additional map symbols *see back flap*

View from Roquebrune towards Nice

Isola

Isola 2000

D2205

29

TIONAL DU MERCANTOUR

Saint-Sauveur-sur-Tinée

Saint-Martin-Vésubie

Roquebillière

Vallée des Merveilles

D6204

Réffet

Pointe de Trois-Communes

30 TENDE

St-Dalmas

Roya

l'Authion

28 FORÊT DE TURINI

Lantosque

31 SAORGE

Breil-sur-Roya

Villars-sur-Var

D2205

VALLÉE DE LA VÉSUBIE

St-Jean-la-Rivière

Peïra-Cava

D2204

D6204

Ventimiglia

Tinée

D6202

27

D2566

LUCÉRAM **26**

32 SOSPEL

Plan-du-Var

D2565

Escarène

Esteron

Var

PEILLE **25**

Ste-Agnes

San Remo

A8

GORBIO **33**

35 MENTON

PEILLON **24**

34

ROQUEBRUNE-CAP-MARTIN

LA TURBIE **22**

D2

BEAULIEU-SUR-MER

D6098

23 MONACO

14 VENCE

D6202

20 **21** EZE

ST-PAUL DE VENCE

15

A8

NICE **17**

19 VILLEFRANCHE-SUR-MER

NEUVE-LOUBET

13

CAGNES-SUR-MER

16

18 ST-JEAN-CAP-FERRAT

BIOT **12**

Cros-de-Cagnes

D6098

10 ANTIBES

Key

VALLAURIS

Golfe-Juan

9 JUAN-LES-PINS

Cap d'Antibes

ILES DE LÉRINS

The sunshine and relaxing atmosphere of a café in Nice

Impressive upstream view of the upper
Gorges du Cians

❶ Gorges du Cians

Road map E3. ✈ Nice. 🚌 Nice,
Touët-sur-Var, Valberg. 🚌 Pl Charles
Ginésy, Valberg (04 93 23 24 25).

Among the finest natural sights
in the region, these gorges are
a startling combination of deep
red slate and vivid mountain
greenery. They follow the course
of the river Cians, which drops
1,600 m (5,250 ft) in 25 km
(15 miles) from Beuil to Touët-
sur-Var. At Touët, through a grille
in the floor of the church nave,
you can see the torrent below.

Approaching from the lower
gorges, olives give way to
scrubland. It is not until Pra
d'Astier that the gorges become
steep and narrow: at their
narrowest, the rock walls entirely
obliterate the sky. Higher still
up the gorge, you may spot
saffron lilies in June.

At the upper end of the
gorges, overlooking the Vallée
du Cians, is the 1,430-m (4,770-ft)
eyrie of Beuil. Now a military
sports centre, it was first fortified
by the counts of Beuil, members
of the aristocratic Grimaldi
family (see pp82–3). They lived
here until 1621, despite staff
revolt: one count had his throat
cut by his barber and another
was stabbed by his valet. The
last, Hannibal Grimaldi, was
tied to a chair and strangled by
two Muslim slaves. Stones from
their château were used to build
the Renaissance chapel of the
White Penitents in the 1687
Eglise St-Jean-Baptiste.

❷ Puget-Théniers

Road map E3. 🏔 1,920. 🚌 🚌 RD
6202 (04 93 05 05 05). **Closed** Oct–
Mar. 🌐 provence-val-dazur.com

This attractive village lies at the
foot of a rocky peak, nestling at
the confluence of the Roudoule
and the Var beneath the ruins of
a château that belonged to the
Grimaldi family (see pp82–3). The
old town has some fine medieval
houses with overhanging roofs,
but the chief attraction is the
13th-century parish church
Notre-Dame de l'Assomption.
The delightful altarpiece, *Notre-
Dame de Bon Secours* (1525),
is by Antoine Ronzen.
Inside the entrance, the
altarpiece of the Passion
(1520–25) – the
masterpiece of the
church – is by Flemish
craftsmen, working with
the architect and sculptor
Matthieu d'Anvers.

Beside the main road,
the statue of a woman
with her hands tied
is called *L'Action
Enchaînée*, by Aristide
Maillol (1861–1944).
It commemorates
the local revolution-
ary, Louis-Auguste
Blanqui. He was born in the
town hall in 1805 and became
one of the socialist heroes of the

L'Action Enchaînée, in
Puget-Théniers square

Paris Commune in 1871. A year
later he was imprisoned for life
and served seven years, having
already spent 30 years in jail.

❸ St-Cézaire-
sur-Siagne

Road map E3. 🏔 3,850.
🚌 3 rue de la République
(04 93 60 84 30). 🗓 Tue & Sat.
🌐 saintcezairesursiagne.fr

Dominating the steep-sided
Siagne valley, St-Cézaire has
been inhabited since pre-Roman
times. The walls and gates of
the village are reminders
of its feudal past. At its heart
is the 13th-century Eglise
Paroissiale Notre-Dame
de Sardaigne, which houses
a Gallo-Roman tomb dis-
covered nearby – a fine
example of Provençal
Romanesque design.
From the medieval part
of the village, there is a
magnificent viewpoint.
To the northeast of the
village are the **Grottes
de St-Cézaire-sur-
Siagne** – iron-rich
caves filled with
beautiful rock
crystallization.
Dramatic stalactites and
stalagmites have formed on
the cave ceilings and floors,

Antoine Ronzen's altarpiece *Notre-Dame de Bon Secours* (1525), Puget-Théniers

creating enchanting shapes, reminiscent of flowers, animals and toadstools. If touched, the stalactites become remarkably resonant, but leave this to the guide. Red oxide in the limestone gives a rich colour to the caves' chambers: the Fairies' Alcove, Great Hall, Hall of Draperies and Organ Chamber, all connected by narrow underground passages, one of which ends abruptly, 40 m (130 ft) below ground, at the edge of an abyss.

Grottes de St-Cézaire-sur-Siagne
1481 route des Grottes. **Tel** 04 93 60 22 35. **Open** Feb–mid-Nov: daily. obligatory. **grotte-saintcezaire.com**

Inside the remarkable Grottes de St-Cézaire-sur-Siagne

The village of Gourdon, on the edge of a rocky cliff

❹ Gourdon

Road map E3. 421.
1 pl Victoria (08 11 81 10 67).
gourdon06.fr

For centuries, villages were built on hilltops, surrounded by ramparts. Gourdon is a typical *village perché (see pp24–5)*, its shops filled with regional produce, perfume and local art. From the square at its precipitous edge, there is a spectacular view of the Loup valley and the sea with Antibes and Cap Roux in the distance.

There are good views, too, from the gardens of the **Château de Gourdon**, built in the 12th century by the seigneurs du Bar, overlords of Gourdon, on the foundations of what was once a Saracen fortress. Its vaulted rooms are remnants of Saracen occupation. The terrace gardens were laid out by André Le Nôtre when the château was restored in the 17th century. There are three distinct gardens – the Jardin à l'Italienne, the Jardin de Rocaille (or Provençal Gardens) and the Jardin de l'Apothicaire with its own centrally located sundial. Although the château is still privately owned and not open to the public, visitors can take a guided tour of the gardens in groups during the summer months.

Château de Gourdon
Tel 04 93 09 68 02. **Open** by reservation for groups of 10 or more. May–Aug: call ahead to check for times. **chateau-gourdon.com**

Journey in the Gorges du Loup

The village of Gourdon is on the edge of the Gorges du Loup, the most accessible of many dramatic gorges running down to the coast. The route up to the Gorges du Loup begins at Pré-du-Loup, just east of Grasse, and leads to Gourdon. From Gourdon, the D3 goes up into the gorge and offers the best views, turning back down the D6 after 6.5 km (4 miles).

Descending on the left bank, the road passes the great pothole of Saut du Loup and the Cascades des Demoiselles, where the river's lime carbonate content has partly solidified the vegetation. Just beyond is the 40-m (130-ft) Cascade de Courmes, which has a treacherously slippery stairway under it.

The D2210 continues to Vence, passing via Tourrettes-sur-Loup, an art and craft centre on a high plateau. The 15th-century church has a triptych by the Bréa School and a 1st-century altar dedicated to the Roman god Mercury.

The 40-m (130-ft) Cascade de Courmes

❺ Grasse

Road map E3. 🚐 52,000. 🚌 🛈 Pl de la Buanderie (04 93 36 66 66). 🚌 Sat. 🌐 **grassetourisme.fr**

Once known for its leather tanning industry, Grasse became a perfume centre in the 16th century. The tanneries have vanished, but three major perfume houses are still here. Today, perfume is mainly made from imported flowers, but each year, Grasse holds a Jasmine festival (see p37). The best place to discover the history of perfume is the **Musée International de la Parfumerie**, which has a garden of fragrant plants. It also displays *bergamotes*, decorated scented *papier-mâché* boxes. At **Molinard** there is also a museum and visitors can create their own perfume.

Grasse became fashionable after 1807–8 when Princess Pauline Bonaparte recuperated here. Queen Victoria often wintered at the Grand Hotel.

Artist Jean-Honoré Fragonard (1732–1806) was born here and the walls of the **Villa-Musée Fragonard** are covered with his son's murals. The artist's *Washing of the Feet* hangs in the 12th-century **Ancienne Cathédrale Notre-Dame-du-Puy**, in the old town. The cathedral also houses three works by Rubens. The **Musée d'Art et d'Histoire de Provence** has Moustiers ware. 18th–19th century Provençal costumes and jewellery can be seen at the **Musée Provençal du Costume et du Bijou**.

🏛 **Musée International de la Parfumerie**
2 blvd du Jeu de Ballon. **Tel** 04 97 05 58 11. **Open** daily. **Closed** public hols. 🚼 ♿ 📷 🌐 **museesdegrasse.com**

🏛 **Molinard**
60 blvd Victor Hugo. **Tel** 04 93 36 01 62. **Open** daily. **Closed** 1 Jan, 25 Dec. 🚼 🌐 **molinard.com**

🏛 **Villa-Musée Fragonard**
23 blvd Fragonard. **Tel** 04 97 05 58 00. **Open** daily. **Closed** 1 Jan, 1 May, 25 Dec. 🚼 📷 by appt. 📷

🏛 **Musée d'Art et d'Histoire de Provence**
2 rue Mirabeau. **Tel** 04 97 05 58 00. **Open** daily. **Closed** 1 Jan, 1 May, 25 Dec. 🚼 📷 by appt. 📷

Exterior of the Musée International de la Parfumerie in Grasse

❻ Mougins

Road map E3. 🚐 18,200. 🚌 🛈 39 place des Patriotes (04 92 92 14 00). 🌐 **mougins-tourisme.com**

This old hilltop town (see pp24–5), huddled inside the remains of 15th-century ramparts and fortified Saracen Gate, is one of the finest in the region. Mougins is a smart address: it has been used by royalty and film stars, while Picasso spent his final years living with his wife in a house opposite the Chapelle de Notre-Dame-de-Vie. This priory house, sitting at the end of an alley of cypresses, is now privately owned and closed to the public.

Mougins is also one of the smartest places in France to eat. Among its many high-class restaurants, is stylish gastronomic restaurant **La Place de Mougins** (see p209).

The **Musée de la Photographie** has a fine permanent collection of Picasso's photographs. The eclectic collection at the **Musée d'Art Classique de Mougins** includes Roman, Greek and Egyptian art alongside pieces by Picasso, Cézanne, Andy Warhol and Damien Hirst. There are also interesting displays of jewellery and Greek war helmets and armour.

🏛 **Musée de la Photographie**
Porte Sarrazine. **Tel** 04 93 75 85 67. **Open** daily. **Closed** Jan, 25 Dec.

🏛 **Musée d'Art Classique de Mougins**
32 rue Commandeur. **Tel** 04 93 75 18 65. **Open** daily. **Closed** 25 Dec. 🚼 🌐 **mouginsmusee.com**

Jacques-Henri and Florette Lartigue, Musée de la Photographie, Mougins

The Perfumes of Provence

For the past 400 years, the town of Grasse has been the centre of the perfume industry. Before that it was a tannery town, but in the 16th century, Italian immigrant glove-makers began to use the scents of local flowers to perfume soft leather gloves, a fashion made popular by the Queen, Catherine de' Médici. Enormous acres of lavender, roses, jonquils, jasmine and aromatic herbs were cultivated. Today, cheaper imports of flowers and high land prices mean that Grasse focuses on the creation of scent. The power of perfume is evoked in Patrick Süskind's disturbing novel, *Perfume*, set partly in Grasse, in which the murderous perfumer exploits his knowledge of perfume extraction to grisly effect.

Picking early morning jasmine

Jasmine being processed

Creating a Perfume

Essences are extracted by various methods, including distillation by steam or volatile solvents, which separate the essential oils. *Enfleurage* is a costly and lengthy method for delicate flowers such as jasmine and violet. The blossoms are layered with lard which becomes impregnated with scent.

Steam distillation is one of the oldest extraction processes originally developed by the Arabs. It is now used mainly for flowers such as orange blossom. Flowers and water are boiled together in a still and the essential oils are extracted by steam in an *essencier*, or oil decanter.

Vast quantities of blossoms are required to create the essence or "absolut" perfume concentrate. For example, almost a ton of jasmine flowers are needed to obtain just one litre of jasmine essence.

The best perfumes are created by a perfumer known as a "nose" who possesses an exceptional sense of smell. The nose harmonizes fragrances rather like a musician, blending as many as 300 essences for a perfume. Today, scents can be synthesized by using "head-space analysis" which analyzes the components of the air above a flower.

❼ Cannes

Lord Brougham, British Lord Chancellor, put Cannes on the map in 1834 when he stopped there on his way to Nice. He was so entranced by the climate of what was then a tiny fishing village that he built a villa and started a trend for upper-class English visitors. Today, Cannes may not attract blue blood but it has become a town of festivals, the resort of the rich and famous. It is busy all year round, its image reinforced by the Film Festival *(see p36)*. With its casinos, fairs, beach, boat and street life, there is plenty to do, even though Cannes lacks the great museums and monuments of less glamorous resorts.

Relaxing deck chairs on the seafront, Hôtel Martinez

Exploring Cannes

The heart of the city is built around the Bay of Cannes and the palm-fringed seafront boulevard de la Croisette. Here there are luxury boutiques and hotels and fine views of La Napoule Bay and the Esterel heights. The eastern end of the bay curves out to Pointe de la Croisette, where the medieval Fort de la Croix once stood. The town's two gaming houses, **Casino Les Princes** and **Casino Croisette**, are both open all year.

Brougham persuaded King Louis-Philippe to donate two million francs to build the Cannes harbour wall. Between La Pantiero and rue Félix Faure are the *allées* de la Liberté. Shaded by plane trees and surveyed by a statue of Lord Brougham, this open space is ideal both for *boules* and the colourful morning flower market. It provides a fine view of the harbour, which is filled with pleasure craft and fishing boats. Behind the *allées* is the rue Meynadier, where you can buy delicious pasta, bread

and cheese. This leads you to the **Marché Forville**. Fresh regional produce turns up here every day except Monday. The small streets meander up from the *marché* to the old Roman town of Canoïs Castrum. This area was named after the reeds that grew by the seashore, and is now known as Le Suquet. The Provençal Gothic church in the centre of the old town, **Notre-Dame de l'Espérance**, was completed in 1648.

The Cannes Film Festival has been held here every May since 1946. The main venue is the **Palais des Festivals**, but there are cinemas all over town, some of which are open to the public, and film screening starts as early as 8:30am. The beach has been a focus for paparazzi since 1953, when Brigitte Bardot's beautiful pout put her on the world's front pages.

The city's connection to cinema is also highlighted by the **Murs peints de Cannes**,

Famous handprint of Faye Dunaway

15 giant murals inspired by the Seventh Art, which can be found at various locations across town.

The main hotels in Cannes have their own beaches with bars and restaurants, where prices match their standing. Celebrities are most likely to be seen at the Carlton, Majestic and Martinez. There is a cover charge to enter most beaches in Cannes, where imported sand covers the natural pebbles, and sun-loungers cost extra. Just next to the festival building there is also a free public beach.

🎦 Palais des Festivals et des Congrès

1 blvd de la Croisette. **Tel** 04 92 99 84 00. 📠 04 92 99 84 22. 🌐 **palaisdesfestivals.com**

Built in 1982, this unmistakably modern building stands beside the Vieux Port at the west end of the promenade. It is the chief venue for the *Palmes d'Or* and other internationally recognised awards sufficiently prestigious for the film business to take them seriously, and much business goes on, so that the festival is not all hype and publicity. Some 78,000 official tickets are distributed to professionals only. Apart from its use for the great Film Festival, the building also houses a casino and a nightclub, and is a regular conference venue. In the nearby *allée* des Stars, handprints of such famous celebrities as American actress Faye Dunaway are immortalized in pavement cement.

Cannes Old Town, known locally as Le Suquet, overlooking the harbour

InterContinental Carlton, the height of luxury at Cannes

🏛 Musée de la Castre

Château de la Castre, Le Suquet.
Tel 04 93 38 55 26. **Open** Tue–Sun
(Jul–Aug: daily). **Closed** 1 Jan, 1 May,
1 & 11 Nov, 25 Dec. 🗓 🗓 by appt.

🏨 InterContinental Carlton

58 la Croisette. **Tel** 04 93 06 40 06.
w carlton-cannes.com *See Where
to Stay p198.*

This ultimate symbol of comfort
and grace contains 343 rooms and
39 suites, and has its own private
sandy beach. It was designed and
built in 1911 by the architect,
Charles Dalmas. The huge
Rococo-style dining room, where
the colonnades rise to an ornate
ceiling with finely wrought
cornices, is unchanged. The
hotel's wedding-cake exterior
is studded with tiny balconies,
and the window frames,
cornices and attic pediments
are decorated with stucco. The
hotel's twin black cupolas are
said to be modelled on the
breasts of the notorious Belle
Otéro, a Spanish courtesan and
dancer who captivated Dalmas.
The Carlton was so revered
that in World War II, a *New
York Times* journalist asked
a commanding officer to
protect what he considered
to be the world's finest hotel.

The old Cannes castle, erected
by the Lérins monks in the
11th and 12th centuries,
houses this museum. Set
up in 1877, it contains some
fine archaeological and
ethnographical collections
from all over the world,
ranging from South Sea Island
costumes to Asian art and
African masks. Also housed in
the Cistercian St-Anne chapel
is a collection of superb
musical instruments. The
11th-century **Tour de la Castre**
is worth climbing for the view.

Cannes

① Palais des Festivals et
   des Congrès
② InterContinental Carlton
③ Musée de la Castre

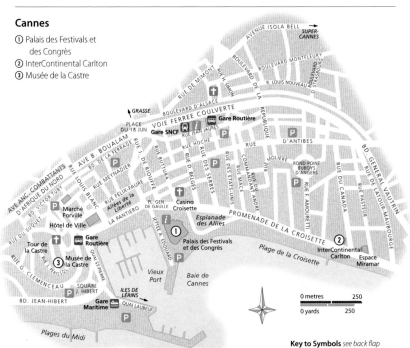

0 metres   250
0 yards   250

Key to Symbols *see back flap*

❽ Iles de Lérins

Although only a 15-minute boat ride from the glitter of Cannes, the Iles de Lérins reflect a contrasting lifestyle, with their forests of eucalyptus and umbrella pine and their tiny chapels. The two islands, separated only by a narrow strait, were once the most powerful religious centres in the south of France. St-Honorat is named after the Gallo-Roman, Honoratus, who visited the smaller island at the end of the 4th century and founded a monastery. Some believe that Ste-Marguerite was named after his sister, who set up a nunnery there. Its fort is well known as the prison of the mysterious 17th-century Man in the Iron Mask, who spent 11 years here.

★ **Fort Ste-Marguerite**
Built under Richelieu and strengthened by Vauban in 1712, its ground floor has a maritime museum.

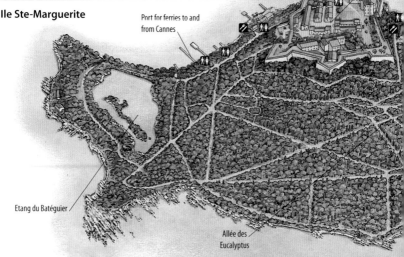

Ile Ste-Marguerite

Port for ferries to and from Cannes

Etang du Batéguier

Allée des Eucalyptus

Chapelle St-Michel

Ile St-Honorat

Chapelle St-Sauveur

St Honorat et les Saints de Lérins
This icon of St Honorat can be found in the Abbaye de Lérins.

Chapelle St-Caprais
St Honorat was the disciple of St Caprais during his first visit to Provence.

The Man in the Iron Mask
The mystery man was imprisoned in Fort Royal from 1687 to 1698, then moved to the Bastille, where he died in 1703.

Remains on Ste-Marguerite
Excavations on the coast near the fort have revealed houses, mosaics, wall paintings and ceramics which date back to around the 3rd century BC.

VISITORS' CHECKLIST

Practical Information
Road map E4. Fort Ste-Marguerite/ Musée de la Mer: **Tel** 04 93 38 55 26. **Open** daily (Oct–May: Tue– Sun). **Closed** 1 Jan, 1 May, 1 & 11 Nov, 25 Dec. 🚹 Monastère Fortifié & Abbaye de Lérins: **Tel** 04 92 99 54 00. **Open** daily.
W abbayedelerins.com

Transport
🚢 Cannes: quai Laubeuf for Ste-Marguerite (04 92 98 71 36, 04 92 98 71 30 & 04 92 98 71 31); for St-Honorat (04 92 98 71 38).

Allée du Grand Jardin

Route de la Convention
Both the islands have many paths leading through the densely wooded interior as well as round the coast.

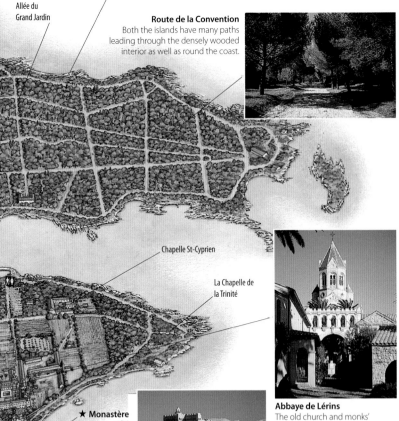

Chapelle St-Cyprien

La Chapelle de la Trinité

Abbaye de Lérins
The old church and monks' quarters were incorporated in the 19th-century building.

★ Monastère Fortifié
Built in 1073 by Abbot Aldebert, to protect the monks from Saracen pirates, this "keep" gives views as far as Esterel. Some rooms may be closed due to restoration work, check before visiting.

0 metres 1000
0 yards 1000

❾ Juan-les-Pins

Road map E4. 🚗 76,770. 🚌 🚈
ℹ️ Palais des Congres, 60 chemin
des Sables (04 22 10 60 01).
🌐 antibesjuanlespins.com

To the east of Cannes is the
hammerhead peninsula of Cap
d'Antibes, a promontory of pines
and coves where millionaires'
mansions grow. Just next door
is one of the finest beaches in
the area tucked in the west side
of the cape in Golfe-Juan, where
Napoleon came ashore from Elba
in 1815. This is a 20th-century
resort, promoted by American
railroad heir Frank Jay Gould,
who attracted high society
in the 1920s and 1930s when
writers F Scott Fitzgerald and
Ernest Hemingway stayed here.

Today, in the high season, it is
filled with a young crowd. The
area at the junctions of boulevards Baudoin and Wilson is
filled with bars. Action centres
round the 1988 casino, the
Palais des Congrés, and Penedé
Gould pine grove, which gives
shelter to the International Jazz
à Juan Festival (see p37) in July.

A glimpse of nightlife in one of the vibrant
streets of Juan-les-Pins

❿ Antibes

Road map E3. 🚗 76,770 (Commune
of Antibes). 🚌 🚈 ℹ️ 42 ave
Robert Soleau (04 22 10 60 10).
🌐 Mon–Sun (daily Jul & Aug).
🌐 antibesjuanlespins.com

Originally the ancient Greek
trading post of Antipolis, Antibes
became heavily fortified over the
centuries, notably by Vauban in
the 17th century, who built the
main port and Fort Carré, where
Napoleon was allegedly
temporarily imprisoned.

The old town is pleasant, with
a picturesque market place in

Spectacular pleasure yachts in Antibes harbour

cours Masséna. The town's high
points include the 12th-century
towers of the church and Grimaldi
castle on the site of Antipolis. The
Cathédrale Notre-Dame, which
took over the town's watchtower
as a belfry, has a wooden crucifix
from 1447, a 16th-century Christ
and a fine Louis Bréa altarpiece
depicting the Virgin Mary.

The Château Grimaldi nearby
houses the **Musée Picasso**,
which displays over 50 drawings,
paintings, and ceramics created
by the artist when he used the
museum as a studio during 1946.

The exceptional modern art
collection includes works by
Ernst, Modigliani, Léger, Miró
and Nicolas de Staël in the last
two years of his life.

Further south, the **Musée
d'Histoire et d'Archéologie** in the
fortified Bastion St-André houses
Greek and Etruscan finds, including
a 3rd-century BC inscription to the
spirit of Septentrion, a boy who
danced at the Antipolis theatre.

Marineland leisure park, north
of Antibes, includes a shark-filled
aquarium and other attractions
such as polar bears and whales.

🎣 **Marineland**
306 ave Mozart. **Tel** 0892 426 226.
Open Feb–Dec: daily. 🌿 ♿ 🏠 🚻
🌐 marineland.fr

🏛️ **Musée Picasso**
Château Grimaldi, Place Mariejol.
Tel 04 93 95 85 98. **Open** Tue–Sun.
Closed 1 Jan, 1 May, 1 Nov, 25 Dec.
🌿 ♿ 🚻 ✉️ 🏠

🏛️ **Musée d'Histoire et
d'Archéologie**
Bastion St-André. **Tel** 04 93 95 85 98.
Open Feb–Oct: Tue–Sun; Nov–Jan:
Tue–Sat. **Closed** 1 Jan, 1 May,
1 Nov, 25 Dec. 🌿 ♿ 🏠

⓫ Vallauris

Road map E3. 🚗 31,000. 🚌 ℹ️ 67
ave George Clemenceau (04 93 63 82 58)
& Golfe-Juan Vieux Port (04 93 63 73 12).
🚗 Mon–Sat. 🌐 vallauris-golfe-juan.fr

In summer, the wares of potters
spill on to the avenue of
this pottery capital. Picasso
revitalized this industry, the
history of which is traced in
the **Musée de la Ceramique**,
together with a collection of
contemporary pieces. In the
square is Picasso's sculpture
L'Homme au Mouton (1943).
La Guerre et la Paix (1952) is in the
Musée National Picasso, housed
in the Romanesque chapel
of the Château de Vallauris.

🏛️ **Musée de la Ceramique**
Pl de la Libération. **Tel** 04 93 64 71 83.
Open Wed–Mon (Jul–Aug: daily).
Closed 1 Jan, 1 May, 1 & 11 Nov,
25 Dec. 🌿

🏛️ **Musée National Picasso**
Pl de la Libération. **Tel** 04 93 64 71 83.
Open Wed–Mon (Jul–Aug: daily).
Closed 1 Jan, 1 May, 1 & 11 Nov,
25 Dec. 🌿 🏠

Tourists inspect merchandise in Vallauris,
the pottery capital of Provence

Pablo Picasso (1881–1973)

Picasso, the giant of 20th-century art, spent most of his later life in Provence, inspired by its luminous light and brilliant colours. He came first to Juan-les-Pins in 1920, and returned to Antibes in 1946 with Françoise Gilot. He was given a studio in the seafront Grimaldi palace, where, after wartime Paris, his work became infused with Mediterranean light and joyful images. No other artist has succeeded with so many art forms, and the Antibes collection is a taste of his versatility. He died at Mougins, aged 92.

Violin and Sheet of Music (1912), now in Paris, is a Cubist collage from the period when Picasso experimented with different forms.

Les Demoiselles d'Avignon (1907), now in New York, was the first Cubist painting. Its bold style shocked the art world of the day.

La Joie de Vivre (1946), is one of Picasso's main works from the Antibes period, using favourite mythological themes. He is the bearded centaur playing the flute, and Françoise Gilot is the Maenad who dances while two fauns leap about and a satyr plays a panpipe.

The Goat (1946), also in Antibes, is one of his best-known images. In 1950 he made his famous goat sculpture using a wicker basket as the ribcage.

L'Homme au Mouton (1943) was sculpted in an afternoon. It stands in the main square of Vallauris, also home of *La Guerre et la Paix* (1952).

⓬ Biot

Road map E3. 🚋 10,300. 🚌 🚍
ℹ️ 4 Chemin neuf (04 93 65 78 00).
🗓️ Tue. 🌐 **biot-tourisme.com**

The picturesque village of Biot, which has 12 themed walks (available at the tourist office), was the main pottery town in the region until Pablo Picasso revived the industry in Vallauris after World War II. Today, Biot is renowned for its bubble-flecked glassware, with eight glassworks, including **La Verrerie de Biot** where visitors can marvel at master craftsmen at work.

Biot was once the domain of the Knights Templar *(see p127)*, and some fortifications remain, such as the 1566 Porte des Migraniers (grenadiers). The church has two fine 16th-century works: *L'Ecce Homo*, attributed to Canavesio, and *La Vierge au Rosaire*, attributed to Louis Bréa.

The **Musée National Fernand Léger** contains many of the artist's vibrant works.

🏛️ **Musée National Fernand Léger**
316 chemin du Val-de-Pome. **Tel** 04 92 91 50 20. **Open** Wed–Mon. **Closed** 1 Jan, 1 May, 25 Dec. 🅿️ ♿ 📷 📽️ 🏠
🌐 musees-nationaux-alpesmaritimes.fr/fleger

🏛️ **La Verrerie de Biot**
Chemin des Combes. **Tel** 04 93 65 03 00. **Open** daily. **Closed** 1 & 15–27 Jan, 1 May, 25 Dec. ♿ 📽️ 🏠
🌐 verreriebiot.com

Detail of Léger mosaic from the eastern façade of the museum, Biot

⓭ Villeneuve-Loubet

Road map E3. 🚋 15,000. 🚌 ℹ️ 16 ave de la Mer (04 92 02 66 16). 🗓️ Wed & Sat. 🌐 **villeneuve-tourisme.com**

This old village is dominated by a restored medieval castle built by Romée de Villeneuve. It is also where the celebrated chef, Auguste Escoffier, (1846–1935) was born. The man who invented the *bombe Néro* and *pêche Melba* was *chef de cuisine* at the Grand Hotel, Monte-Carlo before he was persuaded to become head chef at the Savoy in London. The **Musée Escoffier de l'Art Culinaire**, in the house of his birth, contains many showpieces

Chef Auguste Escoffier, born in Villeneuve-Loubet

in almond paste and icing sugar, and over 1,800 menus, dating back to 1820. Each summer, the town celebrates Escoffier with a gastronomic festival.

🏛️ **Musée Escoffier de l'Art Culinaire**
3 de la rue Escoffier. **Tel** 04 93 20 80 51. **Open** daily (Feb–May & Oct: pm only). **Closed** Nov–Jan, public hols. 📷 🏠 🌐 fondation-escoffier.org

⓮ Vence

Road map E3. 🚋 19,500. 🚌 ℹ️ 8 place du Grand-Jardin (04 93 58 06 38). 🗓️ Tue & Fri. 🌐 **vence-tourisme.fr**

A delightful old cathedral town on a rocky ridge, Vence has long attracted artists. The English writer D H Lawrence died here in 1930.

The old town is entered by the Porte de Peyra (1441), beside the place du Frêne, named after its giant ash tree planted to commemorate the visits of King François I and Pope Paul III. The 16th-century castle of the lords of Villeneuve, seigneurs of Vence, houses the museum and the **Fondation Emile Hugues**, named after an illustrious former mayor.

The cathedral, one of the smallest in France, stands by the site of the forum of the Roman city of Vintium. Vence was a bishopric from the 4th to the 19th centuries. Its notable prelates included Saint Véran (d AD 492), and Bishop Godeau (1605–72). The 51 oak and pear choir

The Creation of Biot Glassware

Biot is the capital of glass-blowing on the coast. Local soils provide sand for glass-making, and typical Biot glass is sturdy, with tiny air bubbles (known as *verre à bulles*). The opening of Léger's museum led to an increased interest in all local crafts, and to the arrival of the Verrerie de Biot workshop in 1956. This revived old methods of making oil lamps, carafes and narrow-spouted *porrons*, from which a jet of liquid can be poured straight into the mouth.

stalls are carved with satirical figures. Marc Chagall designed the mosaic of *Moses in the Bulrushes* in the chapel (1979).

Henri Matisse *(see pp86–7)* decorated the **Chapelle du Rosaire** between 1947 and 1951 to thank the Dominican nuns who nursed him through an illness. An exhibition is dedicated to Matisse's preparatory drawings for the chapel.

Fondation Emile Hugues
Château de Villeneuve. **Tel** 04 93 24 24 23. **Open** Tue–Sun. **Closed** 1 Jan, 1 May, 25 Dec.

Chapelle du Rosaire
Ave Henri Matisse. **Tel** 04 93 58 03 26. **Open** Tue & Thu: am; Mon–Wed & Sat: pm **Closed** mid-Nov–mid-Dec, public hols.

⑮ St-Paul de Vence

Road map E3. 3,500. Vence and Nice. 2 rue Grande (04 93 32 86 95). **W** saint-pauldevence.com

This classic medieval *village perché (see pp24–5)* was built behind the coast to avoid Saracen attack. Between 1543 and 1547, it was re-ramparted, under François I, to stand up to Savoy, Austria and Piedmont. A celebrity village, it was first "discovered" by Bonnard, Modigliani and other artists of the 1920s. Since that time, many of the rich and famous literati and glitterati have flocked to St-Paul de Vence. Most famously, these personalities slept, dined, and, in the case of Yves Montand and Simone Signoret, had their wedding reception at the

Simone Signoret and Yves Montand in St-Paul de Vence

Colombe d'Or *auberge (see p210)*. Today the *auberge* has one of the finest 20th-century private art collections, built up over the years thanks to the owner's friendship with artists and sometimes in lieu of payment of bills. The priceless dining-room décor includes paintings by such world-famous artists as Miró, Picasso and Braque. In the Romanesque and Baroque church, there is a painting, *Catherine of Alexandria*, attributed to Claudio Coello. There are also

gold reliquaries and a fine local 13th-century enamel Virgin. The **Musée d'Histoire Locale** nearby features waxwork costumed characters and a tableaux of scenes from the town's rich past, and the old castle keep adjacent is now used as the town hall. Just in front of the museum, the 17th-century White Penitents chapel was decorated by Belgian artist Jean-Michel Folon.

The main street runs from the 14th-century entrance gate of Porte Royale and past the Grande Fontaine to Porte Sud. This gives on to the cemetery, a resting place for Chagall, the Maeghts and many locals. It also offers wonderful views.

Just outside St-Paul de Vence, on La Gardette Hill, is Josep Lluis Sert's striking concrete and rose **Fondation Maeght** *(see pp80–81)*, one of Europe's finest modern art museums.

Musée d'Histoire Locale and Chapelle Folon
Pl de la Mairie. **Tel** 04 93 32 41 13. **Open** daily. **Closed** 1 Jan, Nov, 25 Dec.

Entrance to Chapelle du Rosaire in Vence, decorated by Henri Matisse

Fondation Maeght

Nestling amid the umbrella pines in the hills above St-Paul de Vence, this small modern art museum is one of the world's finest. Aimé and Marguerite Maeght were Cannes art dealers who numbered the likes of Chagall, Matisse and Miró among their clients and friends. Their private collection formed the basis for the museum, which opened in 1964. Like St-Paul itself, the Maeght has been a magnet for celebrities: Duke Ellington, Samuel Beckett, André Malraux, Merce Cunningham and, of course, a galaxy of the artists themselves have mingled at fundraising events. The museum now receives over 200,000 visitors each year.

★ **Cour Giacometti**
Slender bronze figures by Alberto Giacometti, such as *L'Homme Qui Marche I* (1960), inhabit their own shady courtyard or appear about the grounds as if they have a life of their own.

La Vie (1964)
Marc Chagall's painting is full of humanity: here is love, parenthood, religion, society, nature; all part of a swirling, circus-like tableau of dancers and musicians, acrobats and clowns.

Les Renforts (1963)
One of many works of art that greet arriving visitors, Alexander Calder's creation is a "stabile" – a counterpart to his more familiar mobiles.

KEY

① **Cowled roofs** allow indirect light to filter into the galleries. The building was designed by Spanish architect Josep Lluis Sert.

② **Les Poissons** is a mosaic pool designed by Georges Braque in 1963.

③ **Chapelle St-Bernard** was built in memory of the Maeghts' son, who died in 1953, aged 11. Above the altarpiece, a 12th-century Christ, is a stained-glass window by Braque.

Gallery Guide

The permanent collection is comprised entirely of 20th-century art. The only items on permanent view are the large sculptures in the grounds. The indoor galleries display works from the collection in rotation but, in summer, only temporary exhibitions are held.

La Partie de Campagne (1954) Fernand Léger lends his unique vision to the classic artistic scene of a country outing.

VISITORS' CHECKLIST

Practical Information
623 chemin Gardettes, St-Paul-de-Vence. **Tel** 04 93 32 81 63.
Open 10am–6pm daily (Jul–Sep: to 7pm). **Closed** 24 & 31 Dec. 🚫
🖼 🖼 Library. 🌐 **fondation-maeght.com**

★ Labyrinthe de Miró
Joan Miró's *l'Oiseau Lunaire* (1968) is one of the many statues in this multi-levelled maze of trees, water and gargoyles.

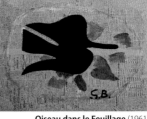

Oiseau dans le Feuillage (1961) Georges Braque's bird nestles amongst "foliage" made of newsprint. Braque was highly influential in the creation of the Fondation, but died before he could see the museum finally opened to the public.

③

L'Eté (1917)
Pierre Bonnard settled in Provence for the last 22 years of his life, becoming a close friend of Aimé Maeght. Matisse called Bonnard "the greatest of us all".

Main entrance and information

Pierre-Auguste Renoir's studio at Les Collettes

⑯ Cagnes-sur-Mer

Road map E3. ⓜ 47,/156. 🚗 🚌
ℹ️ 6 blvd Maréchal Juin (04 93 20 61 64). 📅 Tue–Sun. 🌐 cagnes-tourisme.com

There are three parts to Cagnes-sur-Mer: Cros-de-Cagnes, the fishing village and beach; Cagnes-Ville, the commercial centre; and Haut-de-Cagnes, the upper town.

Haut-de-Cagnes is the place to head for. This hill-top town is riven with lanes, steps and vaulted passages. It is dominated by the **Château-Musée Grimaldi** but also has some fine Renaissance houses and the church of St-Pierre, where the Grimaldis are entombed.

East of Cagnes-Ville is Les Collettes, built in 1907 among ancient olive trees by Pierre-Auguste Renoir (1841–1919). He came here, hoping that the climate would relieve his rheumatism and stayed for the rest of his life. A picture of Renoir in his last year shows him still at work, a brush tied to his crippled hand.

Now the **Musée Renoir** at Les Collettes is almost exactly as it was when the artist died. In the house are 14 of Renoir's paintings, as well as works by his friends Bonnard and Dufy. Renoir's beloved olive groves are the setting for the bronze *Venus Victrix* (1915–16).

🏛️ **Musée Renoir**
Chemin des Collettes.
Tel 04 93 20 61 07. **Open** Wed–Mon.
Closed 1 Jan, 1 May, 25 Dec.
📷♿🎦

Château-Musée Grimaldi

In the Middle Ages the Grimaldi family held sway over many of the Mediterranean coastal towns. The castle that towers over Haut-de-Cagnes was built by Rainier in 1309 as a fortress-prison; in 1620 his descendant, Jean-Henri, transformed it into the handsome palace which shelters behind its dramatic battlements. Mercifully, the château survived the worst ravages of the Revolution and later occupation by Piedmontese troops in 1815. It now houses an eclectic mixture of museums, from olives to modern art.

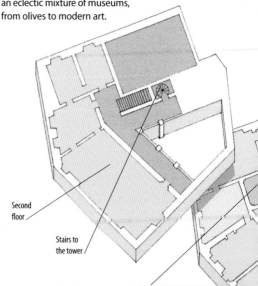

Second floor

Stairs to the tower

The chapel contains a wealth of religious ornamentation, both ancient and modern.

★ **Donation Suzy Solidor**
This 1930s chanteuse was painted by 244 artists during her lifetime. The 40 works on display include portraits by Jean Cocteau (*above*) and Kisling (*above right*).

Gallery Guide

The olive tree museum is on the ground floor, along with exhibits about life in the medieval castle. The Suzy Solidor collection is displayed in a former boudoir on the first floor. Selections from the permanent collection of modern Mediterranean art, as well as temporary exhibitions, are on the first and second floors.

Renaissance Courtyard
Filled with lush greenery and dappled sunlight, this central space rises past two levels of marble-columned galleries to the open sky.

VISITORS' CHECKLIST

Practical Information
Place du Château, Cagnes-sur-Mer.
Tel 04 92 02 47 30. **Open** 10am–noon, 2–6pm Wed–Mon (Nov–Apr: to 5pm). **Closed** 1 Jan, 25 Dec.

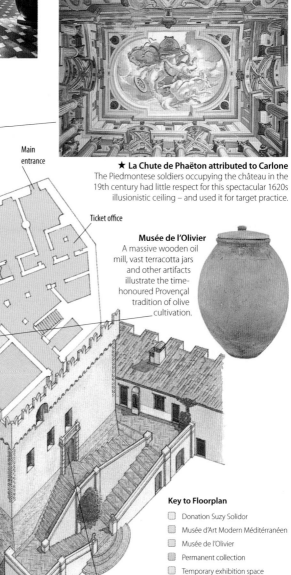

First floor

Ground floor

Main entrance

★ **La Chute de Phaëton attributed to Carlone**
The Piedmontese soldiers occupying the château in the 19th century had little respect for this spectacular 1620s illusionistic ceiling – and used it for target practice.

Ticket office

Musée de l'Olivier
A massive wooden oil mill, vast terracotta jars and other artifacts illustrate the time-honoured Provençal tradition of olive cultivation.

To place du Château

Exit

Key to Floorplan

☐ Donation Suzy Solidor
☐ Musée d'Art Modern Méditérranéen
☐ Musée de l'Olivier
☐ Permanent collection
☐ Temporary exhibition space
☐ Non-exhibition space

⑰ Street-by-Street: Nice

A dense network of pedestrian alleys, narrow buildings and pastel, Italianate façades make up Vieux Nice or the Old Town. Its streets contain many fine 17th-century Italianate churches, among them St-François-de-Paule, behind the Opéra, and l'Eglise du Jésus in the rue Droite. Most of the seafront, at quai des Etats-Unis, is taken up by the Ponchettes, a double row of low houses with flat roofs, a fashionable walk before the promenade des Anglais was built. To the east of this lies the Colline du Château, occupied in the 4th century by Greeks who kept fishing nets on the quay.

★ Cathédrale Ste-Réparate
Built in 1650 by the Nice architect J-A Guiberto in Baroque style, this has a fine dome of glazed tiles and an 18th-century tower.

Palais de Justice
This awesome building was inaugurated on 17 October 1892, replacing the smaller quarters used before Nice became part of France. On the same site was a 13th-century church and convent.

★ Cours Saleya
The site of an enticing vegetable and flower market, it is also a lively area at night.

Opera House
Built in 1855, the ornate and sumptuous *Opéra de Nice* has its entrance just off the quai des Etats-Unis.

RUE DE LA BOUCHERI
RUE DU MARCHE
RUE F GALL
RUE COLONNA D'ISTRIA
RUE DE LA PREFECT
PLACE DU PALAIS
PLAC PIER GAUT
RUE RAOUL
RUE ALEXANDRE MARI
BOSIO
RUE L GASSIN
RUE ST-F DE PAULE
COU

Chapelle de la Miséricorde
Designed in 1740 by Guarino Guarinone, this Baroque masterpiece has a fine Rococo interior. The Nice altarpieces are by Louis Bréa and Jean Miralhet.

VISITORS' CHECKLIST

Practical Information
Road map F3. 347,800.
i 5 promenade des Anglais
(04 92 70 74 07). Tue–Sun.
Carnival (Feb), Nice Jazz Festival
(July). w nicetourisme.com

Transport
7 km (4.5 miles) SW.
Ave Thiers. Quai du
Commerce.

★ Palais Lascaris
18th-century statues of Mars and Venus flank the staircase. The *trompe l'oeil* ceiling is by Genoese artists.

Tourist Train
It passes the market, old town and castle gardens.

Les Ponchettes
One of Nice's most unusual architectural features is the row of low white buildings along the seafront once used by fishermen, now a mix of galleries and ethnic restaurants.

0 metres 100
0 yards 100

Key
— Suggested route

Nice: Musée Matisse

Henri Matisse (1869–1954) first came to Nice in 1916, and lived at several addresses in the city before settling in Cimiez for the rest of his life. His devotion to the city and its "clear, crystalline, precise, limpid" light culminated, just before his death in 1954, with a bequest of works. Nine years later they formed the museum's core collection, sharing space with archaeological relics in the Villa des Arènes, next to the Cimiez cemetery, which holds the artist's simple memorial. Since 1993 the entire villa, complete with its new extension, has been devoted to celebrating his life, work and influence.

★ Nu Bleu IV (1952)
The celebrated "cut-outs" were made in later life when Matisse was bedridden.

First floor

Matisse in his Studio (1948)
The museum's photographic collection offers a unique insight into the man and his work. Robert Capa's picture shows him drafting the murals for the Chapelle du Rosaire at Vence *(see pp78–9)*.

Ground floor

★ Fauteuil Rocaille
A gilded Rococo armchair, painted by Matisse in 1946, is among many of his personal belongings that are on display in the museum.

Main entrance

Gallery Guide
The ground and first floors display works from the museum's permanent collection, from which items are sometimes loaned out to other museums. The subterranean wing is used for exhibitions devoted to Matisse and his contemporaries.

Key to Floorplan
☐ Permanent collection
▨ Temporary exhibition space

Liseuse à la Table Jaune (1944)
The tranquillity of this work belies the troubles that beset Matisse in World War II, including a major operation and the arrest of his wife for Resistance work.

VISITORS' CHECKLIST

Practical Information
164 ave des Arènes de Cimiez, Nice. **Tel** 04 93 81 08 08. **Open** 10am–6pm Wed–Mon. **Closed** 1 Jan, Easter Sunday, 1 May, 25 Dec. 🚫 ♿ 🎧 📷 📱
W **musee-matisse-nice.org**

Torse Debout
This bronze of 1909 was given to the museum in 1978 by the artist's son, Jean.

Mezzanine

Children's workshop

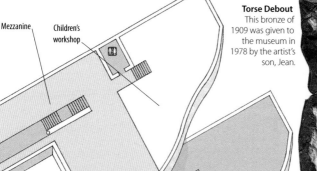

Lower ground floor

Exit

The upper floors of the villa hold a library and resource centre for students and researchers.

Trompe l'Oeil Façade
The decorative stonework that adorns the 17th-century Villa des Arènes is, in fact, a masterful disguise of plain walls, only visible close up.

★ **Nature Morte aux Grenades** (1947)
Ripe pomegranates feature in a favourite setting: an interior with a window to "skies… as brilliantly blue as Matisse's eyes", as the poet Aragon put it.

Exploring Nice

Nice is France's largest tourist resort and fifth biggest city. It has the second busiest airport in France and more banks, galleries and museums than anywhere else outside the capital. Each year, Nice hosts a lavish pre-Lent carnival, ending with a fireworks display and the Battle of the Flowers *(see p228)*. The city has its own dialect and its own cuisine of *socca*, chickpea pancakes, but the ubiquitous pizza ovens lend a rich Italian flavour.

Beach and promenade des Anglais, one of the major attractions of Nice

A glimpse of the city

Nice lies at the foot of a hill known as the Château, after the castle that once stood there. The flower and vegetable market (Tue–Sun) in the Cours Saleya is a shoppers' paradise. The fashionable quarter is the Cimiez district, on the hills overlooking the town, where the old monastery of **Notre-Dame** is worth a visit. Lower down, next to the **Musée Matisse** *(see pp86–7)*, are the remains of a Roman amphitheatre and baths. Artifacts are on show at the nearby archaeological museum.

The city's most remarkable feature is the 19th-century promenade des Anglais, which runs right along the seafront. Built in the 1820s, it is today a pleasant 5-km (3-mile) highway. Until World War II, Nice was popular with aristocrats. Queen Victoria stayed here in 1895, and in 1912, Tsar Nicholas II built the onion-domed **Cathédrale Orthodoxe Russe** (Ave Nicolas II, Du Tzarévitch; 00 81 09 53 45;

open daily) in St-Philippe. At the heart of the city, the promenade du Paillon is a strip of parkland with a central waterway that runs from the old town, through the centre to the promenade des Anglais. It also hosts arts projects, sports events and includes a children's park.

🏨 Hotel Négresco

37 promenade des Anglais. **Tel** 04 93 16 64 00. *See Where to Stay (see p198).*

This palatial hotel was built in 1912 for Henri Négresco, once a gypsy-violin serenader, who went bankrupt eight years later. In the *salon royale* hangs a Baccarat chandelier made from 16,000

Ornate statue at the fountain in place Masséna

Nice

1. Hotel Négresco
2. Villa Masséna
3. Musée Chagall
4. Cathédrale Ste-Réparate
5. Palais Lascaris
6. Musée d'Art Moderne et d'Art Contemporain (MAMAC)

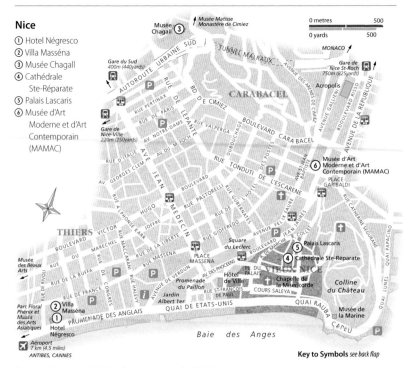

For hotels and restaurants in this region see pp198–9 and pp208–11

stones. The infamous American dancer Isadora Duncan spent her last months here in 1927. She died tragically outside the hotel when her trailing scarf caught in the wheel of her Bugatti and broke her neck.

Villa Masséna

65 rue de France. **Tel** 04 93 91 19 10. **Open** Wed–Mon. **Closed** 1 Jan, Easter, 1 May, 25 Dec.

This 19th-century Italianate villa belonged to the great-grandson of Napoleon's Nice-born Marshal. Its Empire-style main hall has a bust of the Marshal by Canova. Among its exhibits are religious works, paintings by Niçois primitives, white-glazed faïence pottery (see p190) and Josephine's gold cloak.

Musée Chagall

36 ave Dr Ménard. **Tel** 04 93 53 87 20. **Open** Wed–Mon. **Closed** 1 Jan, 1 May, 25 Dec. in summer. **W** musee-chagall.fr

This museum houses the largest collection of Marc Chagall's work. There are 17 canvases from his Biblical Message series, including five versions of *The Song of Songs*.

Russian Orthodox cathedral in St-Philippe

Three stained-glass windows depict the *Creation of the World*, and the large mosaic reflected in the pool is of the prophet Elijah.

Cathédrale Ste-Réparate

3, place Rossetti. **Tel** 08 92 70 74 07 for guided tours. **Open** daily.

This 17th-century Baroque building has a handsome tiled dome. The interior is lavishly decorated with plasterwork, marble and original panelling.

Palais Lascaris

15 rue Droite. **Tel** 04 93 62 72 40. **Open** Wed–Mon. **Closed** 1 Jan, Easter Sunday, 1 May, 25 Dec.

This salon of this stuccoed 17th-century palace has a *trompe l'oeil* ceiling, said to be by Carlone. The palace now houses a museum of musical instruments.

Musée des Arts Asiatiques

405 promenade des Anglais. **Tel** 04 92 29 37 00. **Open** Wed–Mon. **Closed** 1 Jan, 1 May, 25 Dec.

This museum has outstanding examples of ancient and 20th-century art from across Asia in Kenzo Tange's uncluttered white marble and glass setting.

Musée des Beaux-Arts

33 ave des Baumettes. **Tel** 04 92 15 28 28. **Open** Tue–Sun. **Closed** 1 Jan, Easter, 1 May, 25 Dec. **W** musee-beaux-arts-nice.org

Once home to a Ukranian princess, this 1878 villa houses a collection begun with a donation by Napoleon III. Three centuries of art cover work by Jules Chéret, Carle Van Loo, Van Dongen, and Impressionists and Post-Impressionists such as Bonnard, Dufy and Vuillard.

Musée d'Art Moderne et d'Art Contemporain (MAMAC)

Place Yves Klein. **Tel** 04 97 13 42 01. **Open** Tue–Sun. **Closed** 1 Jan, Easter, 1 May, 25 Dec.

Housed in a strikingly original building with marble-faced towers and glass passageways, the collection reflects the history of the *avant-garde*, including Pop Art by Andy Warhol and work by Ecole de Nice artists such as Yves Klein.

Amazing hillside view over St-Jean-Cap-Ferrat

⑱ St-Jean-Cap-Ferrat

Road map F3. 1,913. Nice. Beaulieu-sur-Mer. St-Jean-Cap-Ferrat. 5/59 ave Denis Séméria (04 93 76 08 90). **W** saintjeancapferrat-tourisme.fr

The Cap Ferrat peninsula is a playground for the rich, with exclusive villas, luxury gardens and fabulous yachts in the St-Jean marina.

King Léopold II of Belgium started the trend in the 19th century, when he built his Les Cèdres estate on the west side of the cape, overlooking Villefranche. Later residents have included the Duke and Duchess of Windsor, David Niven and Edith Piaf. High hedges and gates protect these villas, but one of the finest, housing the **Musée Ephrussi de Rothschild** (see pp90–91), is open to the public.

There is a superb view from the little garden of the 1837 lighthouse at the end of the cape. A pretty walk leads around the Pointe St-Hospice, east of the port at **St-Jean-Cap-Ferrat**, a former fishing village with old houses fronting the harbour.

For a fee, you can enjoy one of the town's two private beaches: **Plage de Passable** or **Plage de Paloma**. Both offer sun loungers, water sports and boat excursions.

Plage de Passable

Chemin de Passable. **Tel** 04 93 76 06 17. **Open** daily (Easter–Sep).

Plage de Paloma

1 route de Saint Hospice. **Tel** 04 93 01 64 71. **Open** daily (Easter–Sep).

Yves Klein's *Anthropométrie* (1960) in the Musée d'Art Moderne et d'Art Contemporain

St-Jean-Cap-Ferrat: Ephrussi de Rothschild Villa and Gardens

Béatrice Ephrussi de Rothschild (1864–1934) could have led a life of indolent luxury, but her passions for travel and fine art, combined with an iron will, led to the creation of the most perfect "dream villa" of the Riviera, Villa Ile-de-France. Despite interest shown by King Léopold II of Belgium for the land, she succeeded in purchasing it and later supervised every aspect of the villa's creation. It was completed in 1912 and, although she never used it as a primary residence, Béatrice hosted garden parties and soirées here until 1934. The villa remains a monument to a woman of spirit and vision.

★ **Fragonard Room**
The fine collection of working drawings by Jean-Honoré Fragonard (1732–1806) includes this sketch, wryly named *If he were as faithful to me.*

Béatrice, Aged 19
Her meek appearance belies a woman who, a contemporary once observed, "commands flowers to grow during the Mistral".

Béatrice's Boudoir
Béatrice's writing desk is a beautiful piece of 18th-century furniture by cabinetmaker Jean-Henri Riesener (1734–1806).

KEY

① **The State Room** looks out on to the French garden, combining the pleasures of a sea breeze with the comfort of elegant surroundings.

② **First-floor apartments**

Villa Ile-de-France
Béatrice christened her villa following a pattern established by another villa she owned named "Rose de France". Its stucco walls are coloured in a lovely shade of rose pink.

Covered Patio
Combining Moorish and Italian elements, this airy space rises the full height of the villa. The marble columns, mosaic flooring and diffused light complement the Renaissance religious works on the walls.

Entrance to villa and assembly point for guided tours

To ticket office and car park

Cabinet des Singes
Béatrice's love of animals is epitomized by this tiny room. Its wooden panels are painted with monkeys dancing to the music of the diminutive 18th-century Meissen monkey orchestra.

★ Gardens
The main garden is modelled on a ship's deck – Béatrice employed extra staff to wander around in sailors' uniforms. There are nine themed gardens, including Japanese and Florentine gardens.

★ State Room
Like every room in the villa, the decor here is lavish, with wood ornamentation from the Crillon in Paris, Savonnerie carpets, and chairs upholstered in 18th-century Savonnerie tapestries.

⓲ Villefranche-sur-Mer

Road map F3. 🚇 5,795. 🚉 🚌
ℹ️ Jardin François Binon (04 93
01 73 68). 🗓️ Wed, Sat, Sun.
🌐 villefranche-sur-mer.com

This unspoilt town overlooks
a beautiful natural harbour,
deep enough to be a naval
port, with a lively waterfront
lined by bars and cafés.

Chapelle St-Pierre on the
quay, once used for storing
fishing nets, was renovated
in 1957, when Jean Cocteau
added lavish frescoes. Steep
lanes climb up from the
harbour, turning into tunnels
beneath the tightly packed
buildings. The vaulted rue
Obscure has provided shelter
from bombardment as recently
as World War II. The Baroque
Eglise St-Michel contains a
16th-century carving of St Rock
and his dog and a 1790 organ.

Within the 16th-century Citadelle de St-Elme are the chapel,
open-air theatre and museums.

🏛️ **Chapelle St-Pierre**
4 quai Amiral Courbet. **Tel** 04 93 76
90 70. **Open** Wed–Mon. **Closed** mid-
Nov–mid-Dec, 25 Dec. 🈺

⓳ Beaulieu-sur-Mer

Road map F3. 🚇 3,800. 🚉 🚌
ℹ️ Pl Clemenceau (04 93 01 02 21).
🗓️ daily. 🌐 beaulieusurmer.fr

Hemmed in and protected by
a rock face, this is one of the
Riviera's warmest resorts in
winter, with two beaches: the
Baie des Fourmis and, by the
port, Petite Afrique. The casino,

Fishing in the natural harbour at Villefranch-sur-Mer

formal gardens and the Belle
Epoque Rotunda, now
a conference centre and
museum, add to Beaulieu's
old-fashioned air. Among its
hotels is La Réserve, founded by
Gordon Bennett, the owner of
the *New York Herald*. As a stunt,
in 1871, he sent journalist
H M Stanley to rescue the
Scottish missionary and explorer
Dr Livingstone, who was looking
for the source of the Nile.

Beaulieu-sur-Mer is the site
of the **Villa Grecque Kérylos**.
Built by archeologist Théodore
Reinach, it resembles an ancient
Greek villa. Authentic techniques
and precious materials were

used to create lavish mosaics,
frescoes and inlaid furniture.
There are also numerous
original Greek ornaments, and
an antique sculpture gallery.

🏛️ **Villa Grecque Kérylos**
Impasse Gustave Eiffel. **Tel** 04 93
01 01 44. **Open** daily. 🈺 🏛️
🌐 villakerylos.fr

⓴ Eze

Road map F3. 🚇 2,574. 🚉 🚌
ℹ️ Pl Général de Gaulle (04 93 41
26 00). 🗓️ Sun. 🌐 eze-tourisme.com

Eze, a dramatic *village perché*
(see pp24–5) is a cluster of
ancient buildings some 429 m
(1,407 ft) above the sea. The
Jardin Exotique, built around
the ruins of a 14th-century
castle, offers stunning views
as far as Corsica.

Flower-decked, car-free
streets lead to an 18th-century
church. Its bust of Christ is
made from olive wood that
survived the terrible fires that
raged close by in 1986.

🏛️ **Jardin Exotique**
Rue du Château. **Tel** 04 93 41 10 30.
Open daily. **Closed** Christmas week. 🈺

Steps of the elegant Belle Epoque Rotunda (1886), Beaulieu-sur-Mer

For hotels and restaurants in this region see pp198–9 and pp208–11

❷ La Turbie

Road map F3. 🚶 3,200. 🚌 *i* 2 pl Detras (04 93 41 21 15). 🛒 Thu. W ville-la-turbie.fr

High above Monte-Carlo is one of the finest views on the Riviera, reached by a stretch of the Grande Corniche that crosses ravines and tunnels through mountains. The village of La Turbie, scented with bougain-villea, has two medieval gate-ways. Its oldest houses, dating from the 11th–13th centuries, are on the Roman Via Julia.

View of Trophée d'Auguste from the village of La Turbie

🏛 Musée du Trophée d'Auguste

18 cours Albert 1er. **Tel** 04 93 41 20 84. **Open** Tue–Sun. **Closed** 1 Jan, 1 May, 1 & 11 Nov, 25 Dec. 🚼 🚻 📷 by appt. 📷 W la-turbie.monuments-nationaux.fr

The most spectacular feature of La Turbie is the Trophée d'Auguste, a huge Roman monument, built out of white local stone, which marked the division between Italy and Gaul. Its construction was ordered in 6 BC by the Roman Senate to

Monument detail, Trophée d'Auguste

honour Augustus's victory in 13 BC over 44 fractious Ligurian tribes. The original trophy was 50-m (164-ft) tall and had niches with statues of each of the campaign's victors. There were stairs leading to all parts of the structure.

When the Romans left, the trophy was gradually dismantled. In the 4th century, St Honorat chipped away at the monu-ment because it had become the object of pagan worship. Later it served both as a fort and as a stone quarry. It was partly

destroyed on the orders of Louis XIV, who feared it would fall into enemy hands during the invasion of Provence by Savoy in 1707. Restoration was first begun in 1905, and continued in 1923 by an American, Edward Tuck. Today, the triumphal inscription of Roman victory has been restored to its original position.

A small museum on the site documents the history of the trophy, with fragments of the monument, pieces of sculpture, inscriptions, drawings and a small-scale model.

The spectacular panorama from the terraces of the trophy takes in Cap Ferrat and Eze. Monaco, at 480 m (1,575 ft) below, seems breathtakingly close, like an urban stage set seen from a seat in the gods.

Among visitors impressed with La Turbie and its trophy, was the poet Dante (1265–1321), and his comments are inscribed on a plaque in rue Comte-de-Cessole. From the end of this street there is a fine view of the monument.

🏛 Eglise St-Michel-Archange

Open daily. 🚻 The 18th-century Nice Baroque church was built with stones plundered from the trophy. Inside there is an altar of multi-coloured marble and a 17th-century onyx and agate table, which was used for communion. Its religious paintings include two works by the Niçois artist Jean-Baptiste Van Loo, a portrait of St Mark attributed to Veronese, and a Piéta from the Bréa School.

Trophée d'Auguste

This triumphal monument had a square podium, a circular colonnade and a stepped cone which was surmounted by the statue of Augustus.

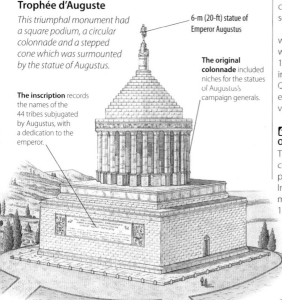

6-m (20-ft) statue of Emperor Augustus

The original colonnade included niches for the statues of Augustus's campaign generals.

The inscription records the names of the 44 tribes subjugated by Augustus, with a dedication to the emperor.

㉓ Monaco

If you come to Monaco by car, you may well travel in on the Moyenne Corniche, one of the world's most beautiful coastal highways. Arriving amid the sky-scrapers of present-day Monaco, it is hard to imagine its turbulent history, much of it centred on Monaco-Ville. The palace, cathedral and museums are all in this old part of town, set on the Rock, a sheer-sided, flat-topped finger of land extending 792 m (2,600 ft) into the sea. First a Greek and later a Roman colony, it was bought from the Genoese in 1309 by François Grimaldi. In spite of family feuds and at least one political assassination, the Grimaldis, whose crest shows two sword-waving monks, remain the world's oldest ruling monarchy.

Modern Monaco
Lack of space has led to vertical building, and a striking skyline of skyscrapers and apartment blocks.

Palais Princier
The Grimaldis have ruled from here since the 14th century. The palace dates from the 16th–17th centuries but its towers are Genoese of 1215. The constitution insists it is guarded by French *carabiniers*. (See p98).

KEY

① **Museum of Vieux Monaco**

② **Monaco Top Cars Collection**, is an automobile museum displaying Prince Rainier III's private collection of more than one hundred antique cars.

Cathédrale
This Neo-Romanesque construction in cream-coloured stone sits on a rocky spur. Among its treasures are two early 16th-century screens by Bréa, *La Pietà* and *St-Nicolas*. (See p98).

Musée Océanographique
Erected on a sheer cliff, high above the Mediterranean, Monaco has one of the best aquaria in Europe. It is also used as a scientific research institute. *(See p98).*

VISITORS' CHECKLIST

Practical Information
Road map F3. 🚗 35,000. 🛈 2a blvd des Moulins (00 377 92 16 61 16). 🚇 daily. 🎪 Festival du Cirque (Jan); Grand Prix (May); Fête Nationale (19 Nov).
🌐 visitmonaco.com

Transport
✈ 15 km (9 miles) SW Nice.
🚉 Pl Ste Dévote (08 36 35 35 35)

Théâtre du Fort Antoine
This ancient fort has been converted into a theatre which shows a wide range of productions in summer.

Typical Old Town Villa
Hidden in a labyrinth of passages are fountains, tiny squares and elegant façades.

The Royal Family

Monaco was ruled from 1949 by the businesslike Prince Rainier Louis Henri Maxence Bertrand de Grimaldi. He was the 26th ruling prince, a descendant of the Grimaldi who, disguised as a monk, entered the Monaco fortress in 1297. At that time the territory extended to Antibes and Menton. Prince Rainier's wife, former film star Grace Kelly, whom he married in 1956, died tragically in 1982. Their son, Albert, inherited the $200 million throne on Rainier's death in 2005. In July 2011, Albert married former Olympic swimmer and model Charlene Wittstock in a civil ceremony, held in the Palais Princier. In 2014, Albert and Charlene became parents to twins, Jacques and Gabriella.

Prince Rainier III and Grace Kelly at their engagement party in 1956

Monaco: Monte-Carlo

The dramatic heights of Monte-Carlo are the best-known area of Monaco. People flock to the annual car rally in January and many of the world's greatest singers perform here in the opera season. Monte-Carlo is named after Charles III, who opened the first casino in 1856, to save himself from bankruptcy. Such was his success that in 1883 he abolished taxation. Although Queen Victoria thought Monte-Carlo a den of iniquity, her view was not shared by other aristocrats, including Edward VII, who were regular visitors. The stunning Casino and Opera House were built by Charles Garnier, architect of the Paris Opéra. Between Monaco-Ville and Monte-Carlo lies La Condamine, a shopping and commercial centre surrounding the luxury yachts.

View of Monte-Carlo
It is worth pausing at La Turbie *(see p93)* to admire the panorama.

Jardin Exotique
Plants normally grown in balmy climates flourish here, and its grottoes housed prehistoric animals and humans 200,000 years ago *(see p98)*.

La Condamine
The quays are pleasant yacht-watching promenades laid out by Albert I. The current prince added a water sports pool, and it is also a popular setting for funfairs.

KEY

① Palais Princier

② La Turbie

③ Eglise Ste-Dévote

④ Hôtel Hermitage

⑤ Centre de Congrès

VISITORS' CHECKLIST

Practical Information
Road map F3. 🅸 2a blvd des
Moulins (00 377 99 99 20 00).
Grimaldi Forum (cultural
centre): **Tel** 00 377 99 99 3000.
Open daily. 🎏 Monte-Carlo
Rally (Jan); Festival International
de Feux d'Artifice (fireworks)
(Jul–Aug). 🎭 daily.

Transport
🚋 Pl Ste Dévote.

Le Brasserie du Café de Paris
Ladies' man Edward VII was a
regular visitor to this renovated
belle époque triumph. The dessert
crêpe suzette was named after
one companion.

Salle Garnier
Designed by Charles Garnier
in 1878, this was where ballet
innovators such as Diaghilev
and Nijinksy congregated.

Casino
In a 3-day gambling spree
in 1891, Charles Deville
Wells turned £4,000
into a million francs,
inspiring the song, *The
Man Who Broke the Bank
at Monte-Carlo (see p98).*

Exploring Monaco

After the Vatican, Monaco is the world's smallest sovereign state. It covers 1.95 sq km (0.75 sq miles), about half the size of New York City's Central Park. Its inhabitants, 20 per cent Monégasque citizens, pay no taxes and enjoy the world's highest per capita income. Monégasque, a Ligurian language derived from Provençal French and Genoese Italian, is reflected in street names, such as *piaca* for place, *carrigiu* for rue, but the official language is French. The euro is used here and most of France's laws apply. Monaco's road network is complex, so drivers should plan routes with care.

Renowned French marine explorer Jacques Cousteau

Monaco Grand Prix, one of the major attractions of Monte-Carlo

🏰 Palais Princier
Pl du Palais. **Tel** 00 377 93 25 18 31. **Open** Apr–Oct: daily.

Monaco's seat of government, this castle-palace is protected by cannons donated by Louis XIV, and sentries who change daily at 11:55am. The interior features priceless furniture and frescoes.

🏛 Museum of Vieux Monaco
2 rue Emile de Loth. **Tel** 00 377 93 50 57 28. **Open** Jun–Sep: Wed–Fri.

The museum houses a range of exhibits such as paintings, ceramics, furniture and costumes, demonstrating the heritage of Monaco. An initiative taken by the representatives of the old Monégasque families to preserve their national identity, the place allows visitors to catch a glimpse of daily life in the old days.

🎰 Casino
Pl du Casino. **Tel** 00 377 98 06 21 75. **Open** from 2pm daily.
W casino-montecarlo.com

Renovated in 1878 by Charles Garnier *(see p55)*, the casino sits on a terrace with superb views of Monaco. Its interior is still decorated in *belle époque* style. Roulette is played in the opulent Salle Médecin, blackjack in the Salons Privés and American games in the Salle des Amériques.

🏛 Nouveau Musée National de Monaco
Villa Sauber, 17 ave Princesse Grace. **Tel** 00 377 98 98 91 26. Villa Paloma, 56 blvd du Jardin-Exotique. **Tel** 00 377 98 98 48 60. **Open** for exhibitions only, check website for details. **Closed** 1 Jan, Grand Prix, 19 Nov, 25 Dec.
W nmnm.mc

Two spectacular villas house this museum charting the cultural, historical and artistic heritage of the Principality. The Villa Sauber, a fine example of *belle époque* architecture, hosts entertainment exhibits. Villa Paloma, with its beautiful Italian garden, shows modern and contemporary art, architecture and design.

🏛 Cathédrale
Ave St-Martin. **Tel** 00 377 93 30 87 70. **Open** daily.

The 12th-century church of St-Nicolas was replaced by this 19th-century Neo-Romanesque building in La Turbie stone. Its old altarpiece, by Louis Bréa, is by the ambulatory, with its tombs of princes and bishops. The much-mourned Princess Grace is buried here.

🏛 Musée Océanographique
Ave St-Martin. **Tel** 00 377 93 15 36 00. **Open** daily. **Closed** 1 Jan, Grand Prix, 25 Dec. Cinema.
W oceano.mc

Founded by Prince Albert I in 1910, this clifftop museum has an aquarium filled with rare marine plants and animals, a collection of shells, coral and pearls, and a life-sized model of a giant squid. Marine explorer Jacques Cousteau was director here for 30 years until 1988. The roof terrace offers superb views.

🌿 Jardin Exotique
62 blvd du Jardin Exotique. **Tel** 00 377 93 15 29 80. **Open** daily. **Closed** 19 Nov, 25 Dec. restricted.
W jardin-exotique.mc

A vast array of magnificent tropical and sub-tropical plants grow here. The adjoining **Grotte de l'Observatoire**, is where prehistoric animals lived 200,000 years ago. The **Musée d'Anthropologie Préhistorique**, accessible via the gardens, displays prehistoric tools, figurines and bones.

The casino's magnificent Salle Médecin

㉔ Peillon

Road map F3. ᠕ 1,449. ℹ 4 carriera
Centrale (06 24 97 42 25)
🌐 tourismepaca.tr

At a level of 373 m (1,225 ft), this
pretty *village perché* is said by
locals to mark the extremity of the
inhabited world. Its streets are
stepped and narrow, with houses
that have scarcely changed since
the Middle Ages. There is an attractive cobbled square with fine
views, and the 18th-century parish
church has an unusual octagonal
lantern. But most impressive of
all are Giovanni Canavesio's frescoes in the Chapelle des Pénitents
Blancs. Peillon is ideally placed
for woodland walks leading
to both Peille and La Turbie.

The Gorges de la Vésubie in the pine-forested Vallée de la Vésubie

altarpiece by Honoré Bertone.
The Hôtel de Ville is in the domed
18th-century former Chapelle
de St-Sébastien, and there is
a museum in rue de la Turbie.

㉖ Lucéram

Road map F3. ᠕ 1,234. 🚌
ℹ Maison de Pays, Pl Adrien Barralis
(04 93 79 46 50). 🌐 luceram.fr

In the midst of this pretty, Italianate
village is the tiled roof of the 15th-
century Eglise Ste-Marguerite, which
contains art by Nice's Primitive
masters, notably Louis Bréa, the
artist of the 10-panelled altarpiece,
who made Lucéram a centre for
religious painting. Other treasures
include a silver statue of the
Tarascon dragon and Ste Marguerite
(see p144). The church is the setting
for a Christmas service, where
shepherds, accompanied by
flutes and tambourines, bring
lambs and fruit as offerings.

Ancient arch across a narrow street
in Peillon

㉕ Peille

Road map F3. ᠕ 2,343. 🚌 ℹ 15 rue
Centrale (04 93 82 14 40). 🌐 peille.fr

Peille is a charming medieval
village with a view from its war
memorial across the Peillon Valley
and as far as the Baie des Anges.
Behind the village looms the
vast Pic de Baudon, rising to
1,264 m (4,160 ft).
   The town is full of cobbled
alleys and covered passages.
At the end of place A-Laugier,
beyond a Gothic fountain, two
arches beneath a house rest
on a Romanesque pillar.
   The Counts of Provence were
lords of the castle, and the 12th-
century church of Ste-Marie has a
picture of Peille in the Middle Ages.
There is also a fine 16th-century

Italian-style houses in Lucéram, set
between two ravines

㉗ Vallée de la Vésubie

✈ Nice. 🚌 St-Martin-Vésubie.
ℹ Hotel de Ville, St-Martin-Vésubie
(04 93 03 60 10). 🌐 vesubie-
mercantour.com

Some of the most attractive
landscape around Nice can be
uncovered and enjoyed in the
valley of the river Vésubie, with
its dense pine forests, alpine
pastures, peaks and cascades. The
river rises high in the snowy Alps
near the Italian border, courses
past Roquebillière to the west of
the Parc National du Mercantour
(see p101) and dives through
the Gorges de la Vésubie before
entering the river Var, 24 km
(15 miles) north of Nice airport.
   The Vésubie is created from
the Madone de Fenestre and the
Boréon torrents, which meet at
St-Martin-Vésubie. This popular
summer mountaineering centre
is surrounded by waterfalls,
summits and lakes. In its fine
17th-century church is a
12th-century statue of Notre-
Dame-de-Fenestre. Each year
this statue is carried to the
Chapelle de la Madone de
Fenestre, 12 km (8 miles) to
the east, for a three-month stay.
   The Gorges de la Vésubie
begins at St-Jean-la-Rivière, and
there is a spectacular panorama
at la Madonne d'Utelle, above
the fortified village of Utelle.
In places, the dramatic gorge,
etched with coloured rock,
runs up to 244 m (800 ft) deep.
Sadly, the road beside it has
few stopping places from
which to admire the view.

Skiing in the Alpes d'Azur

Provence offers a wide range of skiing activities in the Alpes d'Azur. Around one hour from the coast, in breathtaking mountain scenery, there are more than 20 resorts, with over 250 ski-runs. The *après-ski* includes ice-skating, riding on snowmobiles and a chance to sample traditional Alpine food such as delicious *raclette* melted cheese. In summer, Auron and Isola 2000, resorts in the Parc National du Mercantour, offer swimming, cycling and horse-riding in dramatically contrasting surroundings to the Côte d'Azur.

Snowbound Valberg, a winter resort since 1935

Auron

Altitude 1,600 m (5,250 ft) – 2,100 m (6,890 ft).
Location 97 km (60 miles) from Nice via RN 202 and D 2205.
Ski Runs 43 runs – 9 black, 15 red, 16 blue, 3 green.
Ski Lifts 20 including 8 chair lifts and 2 cable cars.

Isola 2000

Altitude 2,000 m (5,250 ft) – 2,310 m (7,584 ft).
Location 90 km (56 miles) from Nice via RN 202, D 2205 and D 97.
Ski Runs 42 runs – 3 black, 11 red, 21 blue, 7 green.
Ski Lifts 22 including 2 cable cars and 9 chairlifts. Funicular railway.

Valberg

Altitude 1,500 m (4,921 ft) – 2,100 m (6,890 ft).
Location 86 km (51 miles) from Nice via RN 202, CD 28, CD 202 or CD 30.
Ski Runs 56 runs – 6 black, 28 red, 10 blue, 12 green.
Ski Lifts 23 including 6 chair lifts.

Climbing a frozen waterfall, or "frozen fall climbing", in one of the many alpine resorts

Getting ready for a few hours of snow-shoe trekking

Auron	Isola 2000	Valberg	Alpine Activities
•	•	•	Cross-country skiing
•	•	•	Disabled skiing
•	•	•	Horse riding
•	•	•	Horse-driven buggy rides
	•		Ice circuit driving
•	•	•	Ice skating
	•		Kart Cross on ice
	•	•	Mono-skiing
	•	•	Night skiing
	•		Skijoring
	•		Ski jumping
•	•	•	Ski school
•	•	•	Ski touring
•	•	•	Snowboarding
	•		Snow scooter circuits
•	•	•	Snow-shoe trekking
	•		Speed ski school
•	•	•	Aquatic centre/pool, sauna and Jacuzzi

Snowboarding in the alpine resort of Isola 2000

㉘ Forêt de Turini

Road map F3. 🚌 l'Escarène, Sospel. 🚌 Moulinet, Sospel. 🛈 La Bollène (01 93 03 60 54).

Between the warm coast and the chilly Alps, from the Gorges de la Vésubie to the Vallée de la Bévéra, lies this humid, 3,497-sq km (1,350-sq mile) forest. Beech, maple and sweet chestnut thrive here, and pines grow to great heights. At the forest's north-eastern edge is the 1,889-m (6,197-ft) mountain of l'Authion, site of heavy fighting in the German retreat of 1945. Casualties are recorded on a war memorial.

The neighbouring Pointe des Trois-Communes, at 2,082 m (6,830 ft), offers superb views of the pre-Alps of Nice and the peaks of the Mercantour national park.

㉙ Le Parc National du Mercantour

Road map E2 & F2. 🚌 Nice. 🚌 St Etienne de Tinée, Auron. 🛈 Maison du Parc, St Etienne de Tinée (04 93 02 42 27). 🖥 **mercantour.eu**

Scoured by icy glaciers and bristling with rocky summits, this sparsely populated park covers 70,000 ha (270 sq miles). Among its unusual wildlife are the chamois, the ibex and the *mouflon*, a sheep which originated in Corsica. Sometimes visible in the mornings is the marmot, a rodent which is prey to golden eagles, and the exotic lammergeier, a bearded vulture with orange-red feathers and black wings. There are also many brightly coloured butterflies and alpine flowers.

Tower at Tende

㉚ Tende

Road map F2. 🏔 2,200. 🚌 🛈 103 ave 16 Sep 1947 (04 93 04 73 71). 🛒 Wed. 🖥 **tendemerveilles.com**

Sombre Tende once guarded the mountain pass connecting Pied-mont and Provence, now bypas-sed by a tunnel. Its tall, green schist buildings appear piled on top of each other. Only a wall

remains of the castle of Lascaris' feudal lords, near the cemetery above the town. Tende's unusual towers include that of the 15th-century church of **Notre-Dame-de-l'Assomption**. Lions support the pillars around the Renaissance doorway and there are green schist columns inside.

The **Vallée des Merveilles**, the most spectacular part of Mercantour national park, can be visited with a guide. For information, contact the tourist office at Tende or St-Dalmas. The most direct route starts from Lac des Mesches car park. A two-and-a-half-hour walk leads to Lac Long and Le Refuge des Merveilles. The Mont Bégo area has 36,000 engravings, dating from 2,000 BC, carved into the rock face. They reveal a Bronze Age culture of shepherds and farmers. In Tende, the **Musée des Merveilles** is worth a visit. Southeast of Tende, there are fine paintings in the church at La Brigue. Jean Canavesio's 15th-century frescoes of *La Passion du Christ*, and the lurid *Judas pendu* are in the nearby **Chapelle Notre-Dame-des-Fontaines**.

🏛 Musée des Merveilles
Ave du 16 Septembre 1947. **Tel** 04 93 04 32 50. **Open** Wed–Mon. **Closed** public hols, 2 weeks mid-Mar & mid-Nov. ♿ 📷

Walkers above Lake Allos, Parc National du Mercantour

㉛ Saorge

Road map F3. 🏔 450. 🚌 🛈 La Mairie, Avenue Docteur Joseph Davéo (04 93 04 51 23). 🖥 **saorge.fr**

Saorge is the prettiest spot in the Roya Valley. Set in a natural amphitheatre high over the river, its slate-roofed houses are tiered between narrow alleys, in the style of a typical stacked village or *village empilé*.

Olive-wood carvings are traditional, and carved lintels date many houses to the 15th century, when Saorge was a stronghold. It was taken by the French under Masséna in 1794.

Churches range from the dank 15th-century St-Sauveur with an Italian organ to the Baroque church of the Franciscan monas-tery and the octagonal tower and Renaissance frescoes of **La Madone-del-Poggio** (open during European Heritage days only).

View of Saorge from the Franciscan monastery terrace

❷ Sospel

Road map F3. 3,650.
19 ave Jean Medecin (04 93 04 15 80). Thu, Sun. **sospel-tourisme.com**

This charming resort has a 13th-century toll tower, which was restored after bomb damage in World War II, when the town's bravery earned it the Croix de Guerre. Fort St-Roch, built in 1932 as protection against a possible Italian invasion, has a museum with exhibits on the Maginot line. The church of St-Michel contains one of François Bréa's best works, and has a lovely façade, as does the Palais Ricci. The interior of the White Penitent chapel is magnificent.

🏛 Musée Maginot de la Seconde Guerre Mondiale
Fort St-Roch. **Tel** 04 93 04 00 70. **Open** Apr–Jun & Sep: Sat, Sun & public hols pm; Jul & Aug: Tue–Sun pm.

Impressive *trompe l'oeil* façades of houses in Sospel

❸ Gorbio

Road map F3. 1,300. La Mairie, 30 rue Garibaldi (04 92 10 66 50).

More than a thousand species of flowers have been identified in the sunny Gorbio valley, which produces vegetables, as well as fruit, wine and oil. Until the last century the area was entirely supported by its olive production.

Often shrouded in mist in the mornings, Gorbio itself is a *village perché (see pp24–5)*, with sea views. The old Malaussène fountain stands by the entrance to the narrow cobbled lanes, and an elm tree in the square was planted in 1713. The church

Early morning Gorbio, surrounded by olive groves

has a conical belfry, a typical feature of the region. Each June a procession marks the Penitents' ritual, when the village lanes twinkle with the lights from oil lamps made from snail shells.

A good hour's walk from Gorbio is Ste-Agnès, at 671 m (2,200 ft) it is the highest *village perché* on the coast.

❹ Roquebrune-Cap-Martin

Road map F3. 12,800.
218 ave Aristide Briand (04 93 35 62 87). Wed. **rcm-tourisme.com**

Roquebrune is said to have the earliest feudal **château** in France, the sole example of the Carolingian style. Built in the 10th century by Conrad I, Count of Ventimiglia, to ward off Saracen attack, it was later remodelled by the Grimaldis *(see p95)*. Wealthy Englishman Sir William Ingram, one of the first wave of tourist residents,

View of Château Grimaldi de Roquebrune, overlooking Cap Martin

bought the château in 1911 and added a mock medieval *tour anglaise*.

At the turn of the century, Cap Martin was the Côte d'Azur's smartest resort, attracting the era's glitterati. Empératrice Eugénie, wife of Napoléon III, wintered here. Winston Churchill, Coco Chanel and Irish poet W B Yeats also visited. Architect Le Corbusier, who drowned off the cape in 1965, has a coastal path named after him.

A number of important prehistoric remains have been found around Roquebrune, some in caves such as the **Grotte du Vallonet**. Just outside the village, on the Menton road, is the *olivier millénaire*, one of the oldest olive trees in the world, which is believed to be at least 1,000 years old.

Every August since 1467, in gratitude for being spared from the plague, Roquebrune's inhabitants take part in scenes from the Passion *(see p37)*.

🏠 Château Grimaldi de Roquebrune
Pl William Ingram **Tel** 04 93 35 07 22. **Open** daily. **Closed** Fri (Nov–Dec), public hols.

❺ Menton

Road map F3. 29,670.
Palais de l'Europe, 8 ave Boyer (04 92 41 76 76). Tue–Sun. **tourisme-menton.fr**

Just a mile from the border, Menton is the most Italian of the French resorts. Tucked in by mountains, it is a sedate town with a Baroque square and a promenade stretching towards Cap Martin.

Menton has several fine tropical gardens, and citrus fruits thrive in a climate mild enough for the lemon festival in February *(see p39)*. The **Palais de l'Europe** of the *belle époque* (1909), once a casino, now a cultural centre, is beside the **Jardin Biovès**. The **Jardin Botanique Exotique** has tropical plants and is in the grounds of Villa Val Rahmeh. Above the town is the **Jardin des Colombières** designed by artist and writer Ferdinand Bac (1859–1952). This private garden reputedly has France's oldest carob tree and can be visited in the summer by appointment.

The jetties offer good views of the old town, and steps lead to Parvis St-Michel, a fine square paved with the Grimaldi coat of arms, where summer concerts are held. To the left side are the twin towers of the Baroque **Basilica St-Michel**, its main altarpiece by Manchello (1565). Behind the marina is Garavan where New Zealand writer Katherine Mansfield lived, in the Villa Isola Bella, from 1920–22.

🏛 Musée des Beaux-Arts
Palais Carnolès, 3 ave de la Madone. **Tel** 04 93 35 49 71. **Open** Wed–Mon. **Closed** public hols. 📷

The 17th-century palace, now Menton's main art museum, was once the summer residence of the princes of Monaco. It has paintings by Graham Sutherland (1903–80), an honorary citizen, 13th- to 18th-

century Italian, French and Flemish art, and works by Utrillo and Dufy.

🔲 Salle des Mariages
Mairie de Menton, Pl Ardoino. **Tel** 04 92 10 50 00. **Open** Mon–Fri. **Closed** public hols. 📷

Jean Cocteau decorated this room in 1957 with colourful images of a fisherman and his bride, and the less happy story of Orpheus and Eurydice, and Provençal motifs such as using a fish for a fisherman's eye.

🏛 Musée Jean Cocteau – Collection Severin Wundermun
2 quai de Monléon. **Tel** 04 89 81 52 50. **Open** Wed–Mon. **Closed** 1 Jan, 1 May, 1 Nov, 25 Dec. 📷
🌐 **museecocteaumenton.fr**

Cocteau supervised the conversion of this former

17th-century fort into his museum. He designed the mosaic on the ground floor, and donated his first tapestry and other pieces.

🏰 Cimetière du Vieux-Château
Rue du Vieux-Château. **Tel** 04 93 57 95 99.

Each terrace of this former castle site accommodates a separate faith. Webb Ellis, inventor of rugby, is buried here, as is Rasputin's assassin, Prince Youssoupov.

🏛 Musée de Préhistoire Régionale
Rue Loredan Larchey. **Tel** 04 93 35 84 64. **Open** Wed–Mon. **Closed** public hols.

The museum's fine local history and archaeological pieces include the skull of 30,000-year-old "Grimaldi Man".

Jean Cocteau (1889–1963)

Born near Paris in 1889, Cocteau spent much of his very public life around the Côte d'Azur. A man of powerful intellect and great élan, he became a member of the Académie Française in 1955. Among other talents, Cocteau was a dramatist (*La Machine Infernale*, 1934); the writer of *Les Enfants Terribles* (1929), and a surrealist film director. *Orphée* (1950) was partly shot against the barren landscape at Les Baux *(see p146)*. He died before his museum opened in 1967.

Mosaic at the entrance of the Musée Jean Cocteau in Menton

View over Menton from Ferdinand Bac's Jardin des Colombières

THE VAR AND THE ILES D'IIYÈRES

The Var is a region of rolling lands, rocky hills, thick forests and swathes of vineyards. To the north, Provençal villages are thinly scattered by mountain streams, on hilltops and in valleys; to the south, a series of massifs slope down to the coast making this stretch of the Côte d'Azur the most varied and delightful shore in France.

The A8 autoroute runs through the centre of the Var, dividing it roughly into two sections. To the south of this artery the influence of the sea is unmistakable. Toulon, the departmental capital, occupies a fine deep-water harbour that is home to the French Mediterranean fleet. Beyond it are the pleasant resorts of Bandol and Sanary, where Jacques Cousteau first put scuba-diving to the test. To the east are the sandy beaches beneath the great slab of the Massif des Maures. The Var's most famous resort, St-Tropez, facing north in the crook of a bay, lies in a glorious landscape of vineyards. Beyond it, just past Fréjus, the first Roman settlement in Gaul, the land turns blood red in the twinkling inlets and coves below the beautiful Corniche de l'Esterel, which heads east towards the Riviera. The more remote areas to the north of the autoroute have always provided a retreat from the bustling activity of the coast. This is where the Cistercians built their austere Abbaye du Thoronet. Today visitors escape inland from the summer traffic around St-Tropez to the sparsely populated Haut Var, where towns seem to grow from tufa rock.

Highlights include wines from the Côtes de Provence, and fresh tuna from quayside restaurants. Music enthusiasts should spare time to hear both the organ at St-Maximin-la-Ste-Baume, Provence's finest Gothic building, and the string quartets at the festival in the hill towns near Fayence. Visitors can also go walking, sailing and sunbathing, and enjoy a rich collection of museums and architecture.

Sunrise over the boats in St-Tropez harbour

◄ The meandering Corniche de l'Esterel, St-Raphaël

Exploring the Var and the Iles d'Hyères

The Var *département* covers about 6,000 sq km (2,300 sq miles). It combines a stunning coastline sprinkled with red cliffs, delightful bays and the Iles d'Hyères, which spill out from its southernmost point, with dramatic chains of hills, rising up behind the coast and further inland. The slopes of the Massif des Maures and the Haut Var are home to a fascinating array of flora and fauna, as well as to the many producers of Côtes-de-Provence wines.

View of the Abbaye du Thoronet

Sights at a Glance

1. Barjols
2. Haut Var
3. Comps-sur-Artuby
4. Mons
5. Fayence
6. Bargemon
7. Draguignan
8. Les-Arcs-sur-Argens
9. Lorgues
10. Abbaye du Thoronet
12. Brignoles
13. St-Maximin-la-Ste-Baume pp114–15
14. Bandol
15. Sanary-sur-Mer
16. Toulon pp116–17
17. Iles d'Hyères pp118–19
18. Hyères
19. Le Lavandou
20. Bormes-les-Mimosas

22. Ramatuelle
23. St-Tropez pp122–6
24. Port-Grimaud
25. Grimaud
26. Ste-Maxime
27. St-Raphaël
28. Massif de l'Esterel
29. Fréjus

Tours

11. Côtes de Provence
21. Massif des Maures

Key

━━━ Motorway

━━━ Major road

━━━ Secondary road

═══ Minor road

━━━ Scenic route

╍╍╍ Main railway

──── Minor railway

━━━ Regional border

△ Summit

0 kilometres   10

0 miles   10

For additional map symbols *see back flap*

Les Issambres beach, north of Ste-Maxime

Getting Around

The uplands of the Maures and Esterel force the A8 auto route and DN7 road inland, leaving the coast to the more scenic routes: the Corniche d'Or in the Massif de l'Esterel is one of France's loveliest. The combination of stunning views and tight bends means you should allow plenty of time for your journey. The unspoiled Haut Var is easy to get to by car. Alternatively, the railway reaches as far as Les-Arcs-sur-Argens, from where you can explore the region by bus. Comps-sur-Artuby is a good tour base for the Gorges du Verdon (see pp188–9).

Le Logis-du-Pin

Trigance

Bargème

3 COMPS-SUR-ARTUBY

D955

D563

4 MONS

St-Cézaire-sur-Siagne

Grasse

HAUT VAR

Châteaudouble

6 BARGEMON

5 FAYENCE

St-Paul-en-Forêt

Lac de St-Cassien

2

Aups

Tourtour

D955

Callas

D562

A8

Cannes

Villecroze

Pierre de la Fée

DN7

D560

7 DRAGUIGNAN

Mont Vinaigre 620m

Flayosc

D1555

D4

MASSIF DE L'ESTEREL

D6098

9 LORGUES

Le Muy

Puget-sur-Argens

Pic de Cap Roux 452m

Entrecasteaux

8 LES-ARCS-SUR-ARGENS

DN7

28

ABBAYE DU THORONET 10

FRÉJUS 29

SAINT-RAPHAËL 27

Agay

CÔTES DE PROVENCE

11

Vidauban

D25

Fréjus-Plage

D559

Cabasse

A8

DN7

Saint-Aygulf

Le Luc

V A R

A57

Les Issambres

D75

La Garde Freinet

D558

26 SAINTE-MAXIME

Notre-Dame-des-Anges

21

GRIMAUD 25

24 PORT-GRIMAUD

D39

D98

23 SAINT-TROPEZ

MASSIF DES MAURES

D14

Chartreuse de la Verne

Cogolin

Collobrières

Moulins de Paillas 322m

La Môle

D559

Cap Camarat

22

RAMATUELLE

Cavalaire-sur-Mer

BORMES-LES-MIMOSAS 20

LE LAVANDOU

19

Port-de-Miramar

Cap Benat

LES D'HYÈRES

17

Île du Levant

Porquerolles

Île de Porquerolles

Île de Port Cros

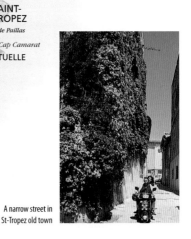

A narrow street in St-Tropez old town

A traditional flute-maker at work in Barjols

❶ Barjols

Road map D4. 3,135. Blvd Grisolle (04 94 77 20 01). Sun. la-provence-verte.net/ot_barjols

Once renowned for its seething tanneries, Barjols lies peacefully among woods and fast-flowing streams. In 1983, after almost 400 years, the leather industry finally folded. The many abandoned factories have become bustling artisans' studios.

Today, it is these local craftsmen who bring manufacturing acclaim to the area. Two traditional Provençal instruments, the three-holed flute (*galoubet*) and the narrow drums (*tambourins*), were still made in Barjols until recently.

These instruments resound each January at the annual *fête* of St-Marcel, the town's patron saint. About every four years the ceremony includes the slaughter and roasting of an ox in the square. This is followed by a colourful "tripe dance" inside and outside the 11th-century church of Notre-Dame-de-l'Assomption, where St-Marcel's relics can be seen. The ceremony commemorates the survival of the town after a siege in 1350. For information about roastings contact the tourist office.

Of the many stone fountains dotted around the town, the most famous is the mossy *Champignon* in place Capitaine Vincens. It stands under what is reputed to be the largest plane tree in Provence. Between the church and the old tanneries are the restored buildings of the old quartier du Réal. Exotic

porticoes, particularly on the Renaissance Hôtel de Pontevès, add spice to some otherwise drab streets.

❷ Haut Var

Road map D3. Toulon-Hyères, Nice. Les Arcs. Aups. Pl Martin Bidouré, Aups (04 94 84 00 69). aups-tourisme.com

The most remote and unspoiled lands of the Var are situated between Barjols and Comps-sur-Artuby, up towards the Gorges du Verdon (see pp188–9). Much of the land near here has been taken over by the military.

Aups, set among undulating hills on the plateau edge, is the region's centre. Epicureans may be drawn by the local honey, olive oil and the truffle market each Thursday morning in winter. It is an attractive town with a grand old square and castle ruins. The 15th-century St-Pancrace church has a Renaissance doorway. Also worth a visit is the **Musée Simon Segal**, which is housed in a former Ursuline convent. The museum contains works by Segal and Paris painters, as well as local scenes.

About 5 km (3 miles) north-west on the D9 is the village of Moissac-Bellevue. Many of its buildings date from the 16th and 17th centuries and its church was mentioned in a papal edict of 1225.

View of Entrecasteaux château near Cotignac, Haut Var

South from Aups is Villecroze. The town is set against a natural backdrop of caves on three levels, which local lords in the 16th century turned into dwellings, known as the **Grottes Troglodytiques**. The arcaded streets and the keep of the feudal castle give the town a medieval flavour. A short drive from Villecroze leads up to the hill village of Tourtour, a smaller, prettier and more popular place. Renowned French expressionist painter Bernard Buffet lived his last days here. Two of his creations – large, metal-built insect sculptures are still displayed in the village.

The valley town of Salernes lies in the opposite direction, 10 km (6 miles) west on the D51. Smoke pumps from the

Troglodyte dwellings in Villecroze

The 110 m (361 ft) Artuby bridge spanning the Canyon du Verdon

kilns of its 15 ceramic factories. Salernes is one of the best-known Provençal tile-making centres, noted for *tomettes* – hexagonal terracotta floor-tiles.

Cotignac, west of Salernes, is an echo of Villecroze, with a cave-pocked cliff behind it. Behind the *mairie*, a river springs from the rocks and beyond is an open-air theatre.

The region's most intriguing château is **Entrecasteaux**, 15 km (8 miles) east of Cotignac. The 17th-century castle is filled with the present owner's 17th- to 18th-century collection of paintings, artifacts, tapestries and furniture. The garden, by Le Nôtre, is publicly owned.

Musée Simon Segal
Rue Albert Premier, Aups. **Tel** 04 94 70 01 95. **Open** Jun–Sep: Wed–Mon.

Grottes Troglodytiques
Villecroze. **Tel** 04 94 70 63 06. **Open** Apr–Jun: Fri–Mon; Jul–Sep: daily.

Château d'Entrecasteaux
83570 Entrecasteaux. **Tel** 04 94 04 43 95. **Open** Easter–mid-Jun: Sun & public hols; mid-Jun–Sep: Sun–Fri. **chateau-entrecasteaux.com**

❸ Comps-sur-Artuby

Road map D3. 338. 2 ave Lazare Carnot, Draguignan (04 98 10 51 05).

The eastern approach to the Gorges du Verdon *(see pp188–9)* passes through Comps-sur-Artuby. The village nestles at the foot of a rock topped by the 13th-century chapel of **St-André**, which has been restored. From the church there are grand views of the Artuby Gorges.

To the east lies Bargème, a village of steep streets and hollyhocks with a population of just 86. At 1,094 m (3,589 ft) it is the highest community in the Var. The village itself is closed to all traffic.

Dominating Bargème is a large, partially ruined but nevertheless remarkably well preserved 14th-century castle. Also worth a visit is the 13th-century Romanesque **Eglise St-Nicolas** which contains a carved, wooden altarpiece depicting Saint Sebastian.

❹ Mons

Road map E3. 885.
Pl St Sébastien (04 94 76 39 54).

Dramatically situated on a rock-spur, Mons, with its tiny lanes and overhanging arches, has an almost magical appeal. The place St-Sébastien looks out across the entire coast, from Italy to Toulon.

Originally a Celtic-Ligurian settlement, its Château-Vieux quarter dates from the 10th century, but it was mainly built by Genoese who repopulated the village after ravages by the plague in the 14th century. The first families came in 1461 from Figounia near Ventimiglia; their legacy is the local dialect, *figoun*, which still survives thanks to the unusually isolated position of the village. Nearby is the *roche taillée*, a Roman aqueduct carved from solid rock. There are also many dolmens in the surrounding area.

One of the quiet streets of the picturesque village of Mons

Truffles

This richly flavoured and treasured fungal delicacy of the Var is traditionally sniffed out by trained pigs. The golfball-sized truffles are collected during the winter, when they are at their most fragrant, from underground near the roots of oak trees. Local markets specialize in truffles when they are in season, though their rarity means that they tend to be very expensive.

A trained pig hunting for truffles

View over Bargemon's terracotta rooftops to the wooded hills beyond

❺ Fayence

Road map E3. 🗺 5,500. 🚌 ℹ️ Pl
Léon Roux (04 94 76 20 08). 🗓 Tue,
Thu, Sat. 🌐 **paysdefayence.com**

The hillside town of Fayence
is the largest between
Draquignan and Grasse and is
an international centre for local
crafts as well as gliding. Dominated by a wrought-iron clock
tower, it still has a few remains
of its 14th-century defences
including a Saracen-style gate.

The **Eglise St-Jean-Baptiste**
was built in the 18th century
with a baroque marble altar
(1757) by a local mason,
Dominique Fossatti. Its terrace
offers a sweeping view over
the town's glider airfield.

On the hillside opposite,
in the community of Tourettes,
there is a striking château.

Part modelled on the Cadet
school in St Petersburg, it was
constructed in 1824 for General
Alexandre Fabre, who once
worked as a military engineer
for Tsar Alexander I of Russia.
He originally intended to make
the building a public museum,
but failed to finish the task
and so it remains private.

There are a number of
attractive villages nearby.
Among the best are Callian
and Montauroux to the east
and Seillans, 5 km (3 miles)
to the west, where the
German-born painter Max
Ernst (1891–1976) chose
to spend his last years. The
prestigious Musique en Pays
de Fayence festival in October
brings string quartets who
perform in some of the
charming local churches.

❻ Bargemon

Road map E3. 🗺 1,550. 🚌 Les Arcs.
🚌 ℹ️ Ave Pasteur (04 94 47 81 73).
🗓 Thu. 🌐 **ot-bargemon.fr**

This medieval village, fortified in
AD 950, has three 12th-century
gates and a tower from the mid-
16th-century. The village is laid out
around a number of squares with
fountains, shaded by plane trees.

The angels' heads on the high
altar of the 15th-century church,
St-Etienne, now the Musée-
Galerie Honoré Camos, are
attributed to the school of Pierre
Puget, like those in the **Chapelle
Notre-Dame-de-Montaigu**
above the town. The chapel also
contains an oak-wood carving
of the Virgin brought here in
1635. The **Fossil and Mineral
Museum** on rue de la Résistance
displays over 3,000 pieces.

❼ Draguignan

Road map D4. 🗺 38,317. 🚌 ℹ️ 2 ave
Lazare Carnot (04 98 10 51 05). 🗓 Wed,
Sat. 🌐 **tourisme-dracenie.com**

During the day, the former
capital of the Var *département* has
the busy air of a small market
town. At night, however, the only
sign of life is groups of young
people in the place des Herbes.
Baron Haussmann, planner
of modern Paris, laid out

Traditional Pottery and Crafts

Cotignac, Aups and Salernes are at the centre of an
exciting revitalization of Provençal crafts, which
includes weaving, pottery, stone and wood carving.
A regional speciality is hand-crafted domestic
pottery made using traditional techniques and
designs, as well as local clays in a wonderful
variety of colours. Examples of all these
crafts can be found in small shops and
studios, or craft fairs and local markets.
There are good buys to be had, but
do shop around to avoid being
unknowingly overcharged.

A Provençal potter at work

Draguignan's 19th-century boulevards. At the end of his plane-tree-lined allées d'Azémar, there is a Rodin bust of the prime minister Georges Clemenceau (1841–1929) who represented Draguignan for 25 years.

The main interest lies in the pedestrianized old town. Its 24-m (79-ft) clockless clock tower, built in 1663, stands on the site of the original keep and there is a good view from its wrought-iron campanile. The **Eglise St-Michel**, in the place de la Paroisse, contains a statue of St Hermentaire, first bishop of Antibes. In the 5th century he slew a local dragon, giving the town its name.

Draguignan has two good local museums. The **Musée des Arts et Traditions Provençales** is concerned with the region's social and economic history. It occupies buildings that date back to the 17th century. Regional country life is illustrated using reconstructed kitchens and barns. Exhibits include beautiful hand-painted wooden horses. The **Musée Municipal d'Art et d'Histoire** shows local and regional archaeology as well as eye-catching collections of both ceramics and furniture. The adjoining library houses a lavishly illuminated 14th-century manuscript of the *Roman de la Rose*, considered to be the most important book of courtly love *(see p146)* in France (by appointment only).

St Hermentaire slaying the dragon

Northwest of the town on the D955 is the enormous prehistoric dolmen Pierre de la Fée, or Fairy Stone *(see p43)*.

🏛 **Musée des Arts et Traditions Provençales**
15 rue Joseph-Roumanille.
Tel 04 94 47 05 72. **Open** Tue–Sat.
Closed 1 May, 25 Dec. 📷 🏠 ♿ ltd.

🏛 **Musée Municipal d'Art et d'Histoire**
9 rue de la République. **Tel** 04 98 10 26 85. **Closed** for restoration until 2020. ♿

Pierre de la Fée, the giant dolmen outside Draguignan

❽ Les-Arcs-sur-Argens

Road map D4. 🚗 7,153. 🚉 🚌
🛈 Place du Général de Gaulle (04 94 73 37 30). 🗓 Thu.
🌐 tourisme-dracenie.com

Wine centre for the Côtes de Provence *(see pp112–3)*, Les Arcs has a medieval quarter, Le Parage, based around the 13th-century Château de Villeneuve. The **Eglise St-Jean-Baptiste** (1850), in the rue de la République, contains a screen by Louis Bréa (1501).

East of Les Arcs on the D91 is the 11th-century Abbaye de Ste-Roseline, which was named after Roseline de Villeneuve, daughter of Arnaud de Villeneuve, Baron of Arcs. Legend has it that when Roseline's father stopped her while taking food to the poor, her provisions turned into roses. She entered the abbey in 1300 and later became its abbess.

The Romanesque **Chapelle Ste-Roseline** contains the well-preserved body of the saint in a glass shrine. There is also a famous Chagall mosaic *(see p31)*.

🔲 **Chapelle Ste-Roseline**
RD 91, Les Arcs-sur-Argens. **Tel** 04 94 73 37 30. **Open** Tue–Sun pm. **Closed** mid-Dec–Jan, public hols. ♿

Mosaic by Marc Chagall (1887–1985) in the Chapelle Ste-Roseline

❾ Lorgues

Road map D4. 🏠 9,341. 🚌
ℹ 12 rue du 8 mai (04 94 73 92 37).
🗓 Tue. 🌐 **lorgues-tourisme.fr**

Nestling on a slope beneath oak and pine woodland, Lorgues is surrounded by vineyards and olive groves. Its old town was fortified in the 12th century. Today, two 14th-century gates and city wall remains can be seen. The town centre's handsome square is shaded by a large plane tree. Lorgues has many 18th-century municipal buildings and monuments and one of France's longest plane-tree avenues.

In the centre of town is the stately **Collégiale St-Martin**, consecrated in 1788. Its organ, dating from 1857, is the finest example of the work of the Augustin Zeiger factory, Lyon. Also on display is a marble Virgin and Child (1694) which came from the Abbaye du Thoronet and is attributed to the school of Pierre Puget.

❿ Abbaye du Thoronet

Road map D4. 83340 Le Thoronet.
Tel 04 94 60 43 90. **Open** daily.
Closed 1 Jan, 1 May, 1 & 11 Nov,
25 Dec. 🅿 ♿ restricted. 🎥 📷

Founded in 1146, Le Thoronet was the first Cistercian building in Provence. Lost in deep woodland, it occupies a typically remote site. Along

Graceful cloisters on the north side of the Abbaye du Thoronet

with the two Romanesque abbeys of Sénanque (see pp168–9) and Silvacane (see p151), it is known as one of the three "Cistercian sisters" of Provence.

The cool geometry of the church, cloister, dormitory and chapter house reflects the austerity of Cistercian principles. Only the bell tower breaks with the order's strict building regulations: instead of wood, it is made of stone, to enable it to withstand the strong Provençal winds.

Dilapidated by the 1400s, the abbey was finally abandoned in 1791. Its restoration, like that of many medieval Provençal buildings, was instigated by Prosper Mérimée, Romantic novelist and Napoleon III's Inspector of Historic Monuments, who visited in 1834.

Just beside the abbey is the modern Monastère de Bethléem, home to Cistercian nuns.

⓫ Côtes de Provence Tour

The Côtes de Provence wine-growing region reaches from the Haut Var to the coast. Dozens of roadside vineyards offer tastings and a chance to buy. This rural route suggests a few accessible and well-regarded producers, starting at the Maison des Vins in Les Arcs. Here you can find out about local wines, plot your own route, buy wine from the producers, and even book to stay at a vineyard. The tour passes a few interesting towns en route. For more information on the region's wines, see pages 206–7.

Tips for Drivers

Tour length: 100 km (62 miles).
Stopping-off points: The Maison des Vins should be your first stopping point – it is open all day. Around the route motorists should have no difficulty in spotting places to stop and sample, though many of the wine producers close between noon and 2pm. The Lac de Carcès makes a good place for a picnic. (See also pp250–51.)

⑥ Entrecasteaux
From Entrecasteaux, dominated by its huge 17th-century château, follow signs for Les Saigues to find Château Mentone, which produces organic wines.

L
Saigu

Château
Mentone

D50

D31

⑥

D562   Argens   D562

⑤

D13

Domaine de
l'Abbaye

D79

④

④ Le Thoronet
The Domaine de l'Abbaye vineyard is named after Le Thoronet's beautiful abbey.

D13

⑤ Carcès
As you head north, the Lac de Carcès is on the left in a steep valley. The town's castle remains and gardens are worth seeing.

Key
▬▬▬ Tour route
═══ Other roads

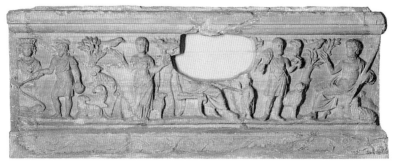

La Gayole sarcophagus, dating from the 2nd or 3rd century, in the Musée du Pays Brignolais

⓬ Brignoles

Road map D4. 🏙 16,881. 🚌
ℹ Carrefour de l'Europe (04 94 72
04 21). 🛍 Sat. 🅦 ot-brignoles.
provenceverte.fr

Bauxite mines have stained the Brignoles countryside red: vital to the region's economy, over a million tonnes of metal are mined here annually. The medieval town remains above it all, quiet and empty for most of the year. An unexpected

delight is the **Musée du Pays Brignolais** in a 12th-century castle that was built as a summer retreat for the Counts of Provence. The eclectic collection includes La Gayole marble sarcophagus, which is carved with images in both the pagan and Christian traditions; a boat made of cement designed by J Lambot (1814–87), who gave the world reinforced concrete; and a collection of votive offerings. St Louis,

bishop of Toulouse and patron of Brignoles, was born in a palace beside the Eglise St-Sauveur in 1274. The church has a 12th-century portico and a side entrance in the rue du Grand Escalier.

🏛 Musée du Pays Brignolais
2 place des Comtes de Provence.
Tel 04 94 69 45 18. **Open** Apr–
Sep: Wed–Sun; Oct–Mar: Wed–Sat.
Closed 1 Jan, Easter, 1 May, 1 Nov,
25 Dec. 🗷 🅦 museebrignolais.com

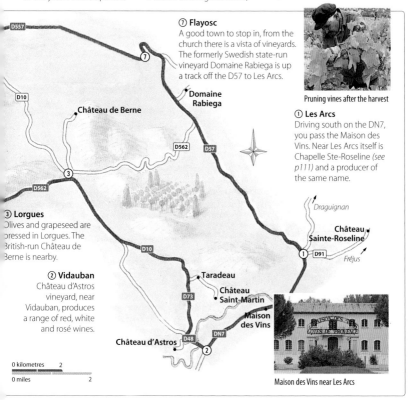

⑦ Flayosc
A good town to stop in, from the church there is a vista of vineyards. The formerly Swedish state-run vineyard Domaine Rabiega is up a track off the D57 to Les Arcs.

Pruning vines after the harvest

① Les Arcs
Driving south on the DN7, you pass the Maison des Vins. Near Les Arcs itself is Chapelle Ste-Roseline (see p111) and a producer of the same name.

③ Lorgues
Olives and grapeseed are pressed in Lorgues. The British-run Château de Berne is nearby.

② Vidauban
Château d'Astros vineyard, near Vidauban, produces a range of red, white and rosé wines.

D557
D10
Château de Berne
Domaine Rabiega
D562
D57
Draguignan
D562
Château Sainte-Roseline
D10
D91
Fréjus
Taradeau
Château Saint-Martin
D73
Maison des Vins
Château d'Astros
D48
DN7

0 kilometres   2
0 miles   2

Maison des Vins near Les Arcs

⓭ St-Maximin-la-Ste-Baume

Surrounded by hills and vineyards, St-Maximin-la- Ste-Baume is dominated by the basilica Ste-Marie-Madeleine and its attached monastery. According to Provençal tradition, the basilica was built on the site of the tombs of St Mary Magdalene and of St Maximin, legendary first bishop of Aix *(see pp152–3)*. The saints' remains, hidden from the Saracens *(see pp46–7)*, were rediscovered in 1279. The building, started 16 years later by Charles II, Count of Provence, is the region's finest example of Gothic architecture.

Sarcophagus of St Cedonius
This is one of four 4th-century saints' sarcophagi in the crypt, which was once the burial vault of a Roman villa.

★ **Relics of St Mary Magdalene**
This bronze gilt reliquary (1860) holds the skull of St Mary Magdalene. Although pilgrim popes and princes took away other parts of her body, the majority of her relics can still be found here.

① ②

★ **Ronzen's Retable** (1517–1520)
Antoine Ronzen's wood retable and surrounding panels include the first picture of the Papal Palace in Avignon *(see pp48–9)*.

KEY

① **The apse** was completed in the early 14th century. The present Baroque-style arrangement was finished in 1697.

② **Stairs to crypt**

③ **Former refectory**

★ **Organ**
One of the finest in France, with 2,962 pipes, the organ was built between 1772 and 1774 by Jean-Esprit Isnard. Napoleon's brother Lucien saved it in the Revolution by having the *Marseillaise* played on it whenever a visiting official arrived to dismantle the organ for its metal.

Basilica Entrance
The western side of the basilica has three matching wooden doors. They feature studied carving that contrasts sharply with the surrounding façade, which appears to have been crudely chopped off. When work stopped on the building in 1532, this part was left unfinished.

VISITORS' CHECKLIST

Practical Information
Road map D4. 🛈 Place de l'Hôtel de Ville. **Tel** 04 94 59 84 59. Basilica and Monastery: **Open** 9am–7:30pm daily (except during services). ✝ 6:30pm Sat, 10:30am Sun; call 04 94 78 00 19 for details of weekday services. 🍴 summer only. 📷 summer only. ♿ basilica only.
🖥 **lesamisdelabasilique.fr**

Hôtel de Ville
The town hall, planned and constructed between 1750 and 1779, was formerly the pilgrims' hostelry.

Milestone
Discovered along the Roman Aurelian Way (see p129), this 1st-century milestone is now on display at the entrance to the cloisters.

Cloisters
The cloisters are at the centre of the Royal Monastery, so called because the French kings were its priors. The Domincan friars left in 1957 and it is now a hotel-restaurant.

Boats in the colourful, palm-fringed harbour at Sanary-sur-Mer

⓮ Bandol

Road map C4. 🚶 7,745. 🚉
🚌 *i* Allée Alfred Vivien
(04 94 29 41 35). 🅿 daily.
Ⓦ **bandoltourisme.fr**

Tucked away in a bay, this cheerful resort has a tree-lined promenade, casino and yachting harbour. The shelter of encircling hills makes for excellent grape-growing conditions. Indeed, Bandol has produced superb wines since 600 BC. There are also plenty of shops and restaurants to interest visitors.

⓯ Sanary-sur-Mer

Road map C4. 🚶 16,200.
🚉 Ollioules-Sanary. 🚌 *i* Maison du Tourisme, 1 quai du Levant (04 94 74 01 04). 🅿 Wed. Ⓦ **sanary-tourisme.com**

In the agreeable, clear blue waters of Sanary-sur-Mer, the diver Jacques Cousteau's experiments to develop the modern aqualung took place. Diving and fishing (mainly for tuna and swordfish) are still popular pursuits in this delightful resort, where rows of pink and white houses line the bay. Its name derives loosely from St-Nazaire; the lovely local 19th-century church took the saint's name in

its entirety. Dating from about 1300, the landmark medieval tower in the town still contains the cannon that saw off an Anglo-Sardinian fleet in 1707. It is now part of a hotel. Sanary-sur-Mer has enticed visitors for many years. Once the home of the British writer Aldous Huxley (1894–1963), it was a haven between the wars for innumerable other authors. Bertolt Brecht (1898–1956) and Thomas Mann (1875–1955) fled here from Nazi Germany.
To the east of Sanary, the coast becomes dramatic and rocky. By the peninsula's extremity at the Cap Sicié is the **Notre-Dame-du-Mai** chapel, which was built in the 17th century A pilgrimage destination full of votive offerings, its stepped approach offers a wonderful panorama over the coast and surrounding hills.

Outside town, the **Parc Animalier & Exotique Sanary-Bandol** has wildlife and tropical plants.

Rosé wine from Bandol

🐾 Parc Animalier & Exotique Sanary-Bandol
131 ave Pont d'Aran, Sanary-sur-Mer.
Tel 04 94 29 40 38. **Open** Apr–Sep: 9:30am–7pm daily; Oct & Mar: 9:30am–6pm daily; Nov–Feb: 9:30am–5:30pm Wed, Sat & Sun. **Closed** public hols am. 🅿 ♿ 📷 Ⓦ **zoaparc.com**

⓰ Toulon

Road map D4. 🚶 167,168. ✈ 🚉
🚌 ⛴ *i* 12 place Louis Blanc
(04 94 18 53 00). 🅿 Tue–Sun.
Ⓦ **toulontourisme.com**

Tucked into a fine natural harbour, Toulon is home to France's Mediterranean fleet. In the old town, or along the quays of the Darse Vieille, the *matelots* and the bars reinforce the maritime connection.

In Roman times, Toulon was renowned for its sea snails *(murex)* which, when boiled, produced an imperial-quality purple dye. During the reign of Louis XIV, Pierre Puget (1620–94) was in charge of the port's decoration. Two of his best-known works now support the town-hall balcony. These are

Ornate Baroque entrance to the Musée de la Marine

Strength and *Tiredness*, his 1657 carved marble figures of Atlantes.

The port was extensively damaged in World War II by the Allies and Nazis. Today, much of the town is under restoration. Toulon has a large opera house and several interesting museums, including the **Musée des Arts Asiatiques** located in the Villa Jules Verne, which has been entirely re-designed to house it.

Musée National de la Marine

Place Monsenergue. **Tel** 04 22 42 02 01. **Open** Wed–Mon (Jul-Aug: daily). **Closed** Jan. musee-marine.fr

Imposing statues of Mars and Bellona decorate the grand entrance, once the gateway to the 17th-century city arsenal that stretched for more than 240 ha (595 acres) behind it.

Inside, the museum boasts two vast model galleons, *La Sultane* (1765) and *Duquesne* (1790), used for training. Some figureheads and ships' prows are on show, as are two wooden figures that were carved by Pierre Puget, and various 18th-century naval instruments.

Musée d'Art de Toulon

113 blvd du Maréchal Leclerc. **Tel** 04 94 36 81 01. **Open** Tue–Sun pm only. **Closed** public hols. limited.

A permanent collection of traditional and contemporary Provençal paintings forms the core of this small but illuminating museum. Works by international artists are often included in the first-floor temporary exhibitions.

Musée d'Histoire de Toulon

10 rue Saint Andrieu. **Tel** 04 94 62 11 07. **Open** Mon–Sat pms. **Closed** public hols.

This quaint museum features the young Napoleon and his endeavours in the defence of Toulon, as well as old weapons and a number of historical sketches by Puget.

Cathédrale Ste-Marie-de-la-Seds

Place de la Cathédrale. **Tel** 04 94 92 28 91. **Open** daily.

Directly inland from the town hall, in the Darse Vieille, is the city's 11th-century cathedral. It was treated to a Classical face-lift and extended in the 1600s.

Inside, there are works by Puget and Jean Baptiste Van Loo (1684–1745), as well as a spectacular Baroque altar.

Place Victor Hugo and the opera house in Toulon

Toulon

① Musée National de la Marine
② Musée d'Art de Toulon
③ Musée d'Histoire de Toulon
④ Cathédrale Ste-Marie-de-la-Seds

⑰ Iles d'Hyères

The Iles d'Hyères, also known as the Golden Isles, are three unspoilt islands, found 10 km (6 miles) off the Var coast – Porquerolles, Le Levant and Port-Cros. Their history has been chequered due to their important strategic position: occupiers have included Greeks, Romans and Saracens, as well as ruthless pirates. Today the French Navy uses much of Le Levant. Porquerolles, the largest island, is partly cultivated with vineyards, but also has expanses of pine forest and *maquis*. Both Porquerolles and Port-Cros are national parks, protected for their woodlands (including holm oak, strawberry tree and myrtle), rare birds and rich underwater habitats.

Locator Map

Port-Cros Marine Life

The wooded slopes of the island shelve down into unpolluted sea, where colourful fish swim among beds of Neptune grass. A ready-planned swimming route makes exploration easy.

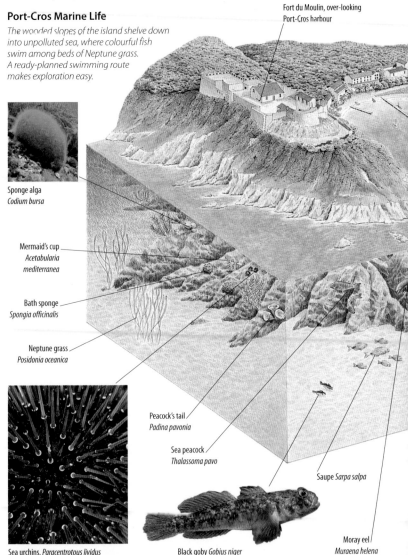

Fort du Moulin, over-looking Port-Cros harbour

Sponge alga
Codium bursa

Mermaid's cup
Acetabularia mediterranea

Bath sponge
Spongia officinalis

Neptune grass
Posidonia oceanica

Peacock's tail
Padina pavonia

Sea peacock
Thalassoma pavo

Saupe *Sarpa salpa*

Moray eel
Muraena helena

Sea urchins, *Paracentrotus lividus*

Black goby *Gobius niger*

Port-Cros Harbour
The tiny, palm-fringed harbour and village of Port-Cros nestle in a sheltered bay to the northwest of the island.

⑱ Hyères

Road map D4. 🏙 57,000. ✈ Toulon-Hyères. 🚉 🚌 🛈 Rotunde du Park Hotel, Ave de Belgique (04 94 01 84 50). 🛒 Tue, Thu & Sat in city centre; Mon, Wed, Fri & Sun in neighbourhoods.
w hyeres-tourisme.com

Hyères is one of the most agreeable towns on the Côte d'Azur, and the oldest of the south of France winter resorts. The town lies at the centre of well-cultivated land that provides fresh fruit and vegetables all year. It has three leisure ports, 25-km (16-miles) of sandy beach and a peninsula facing the Iles d'Hyères.

The new town was called Hyères-les-Palmiers. A palm-growing industry was established here in 1867, soon becoming the largest in Europe. The industry is still important and thousands of palms line the new town boulevards.

Hyères' main church is **St-Louis** in Place de la République. Romanesque and Provençal Gothic, it was completed in 1248. From place Massillon, rue St-Paul leads past the 11th-century **Eglise St-Paul**, full of 17th-century ex-votos. The road continues to the ruined 12th-century Château St-Bernard, which has good views. In the gardens is the Cubist-inspired **Villa de Noailles** (1924), built by Robert Mallet-Stevens for the Vicomte de Noailles. **Jardin Olbius Riquier** has a petting zoo and exotic plants.

🌿 **Jardin Olbius Riquier**
Ave Ambroise Thomas. **Tel** 04 94 00 78 65. **Open** daily. ♿

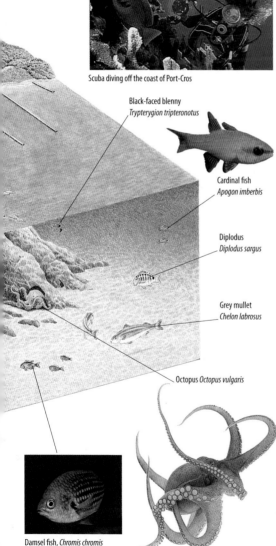

Scuba diving off the coast of Port-Cros

Black-faced blenny
Trypterygion tripteronotus

Cardinal fish
Apogon imberbis

Diplodus
Diplodus sargus

Grey mullet
Chelon labrosus

Octopus *Octopus vulgaris*

Damsel fish, *Chromis chromis*

Façade of a house in Hyères built in Moorish architectural style

Beach at Le Lavandou overlooked by hotels and exclusive villas

⑲ Le Lavandou

Road map D4. ⍩ 5,236. 🚌 🚗
ℹ️ Quai Gabriel Péri (04 94 00 40 50).
📅 Thu. 🇼 ot-lelavandou.fr

An embarkation port for the nearby Iles d'Hyères, Le Lavandou is a fishing village now almost entirely given over to tourism. This is due to its twelve sandy beaches, each with a different coloured sand.

It is a centre for water sports and offers moorings for luxury yachts. Full of bars, nightclubs and restaurants, Le Lavandou is a favourite of younger, less well-heeled visitors.

It takes its name not from the lavender fields in the surrounding hills, but from a *lavoir* (wash-house) depicted in a painting of the town by Charles Ginoux dating from 1736. During the last century, when it was no more than a fishing village, Le Lavandou was popular with artists. The most famous, though not so well known outside France, was Ernest Reyer (1823–99), a composer and music critic after whom the main square is named. From this square there is a view over the Iles du Levant and Port-Cros.

Much of nearby Brégançon is in the hands of the military and the French president has a summer residence there.

⑳ Bormes-les-Mimosas

Road map D4. ⍩ 7,845. 🚌 Hyères.
ℹ️ 1 place Gambetta (04 94 01 38 38).
📅 Wed. 🇼 bormeslesmimosas.com

Bormes is a medieval hill village on the edge of the Dom Forest, bathed in the scent of oleander and eucalyptus and topped with a flower-lined walk around its castle. "Les

Rue Rompi-Cuou, one of the steep, old streets in Bormes-les-Mimosas

㉑ Tour of the Massif des Maures

The ancient mountain range of Maures takes its name from the Provençal *maouro*, meaning dark or gloomy, for the Massif is carpeted in sweet chestnuts, cork trees, oaks and pines with a deeply shaded undergrowth of myrrh and briar, though forest fires have reduced some of it to scrubland. Lying between Hyères and Fréjus, the Massif is nearly 60-km (40-miles) long and 30-km (18-miles) wide. This tour is a simple route that takes you through the wild and often deserted heart of the Massif, through dramatic countryside ranging from flat valley floors covered in cork trees to deep valleys and lofty peaks. A few of the roads are steep and winding.

③ **Village des Tortues**
Keep bearing left on the D75 for the "Tortoise Village", which has saved France's only remaining species of wild tortoise.

④ **Notre-Dame-des-Anges**
Beside this priory and its chapel full of votive offerings, is the highest summit in the Massif at 780 m (2,559 ft).

⑤ **Collobrières**
This riverside village with its hump-backed bridge is famed for its *marrons glacés*. Nearby forests supply bottle corks.

Tips for Drivers

Tour length: 75 km (47 miles)
Stopping-off points: Collobrières is a pleasant lunchtime stop. Allow time to visit Chartreuse de la Verne (04 94 48 08 00 for opening times), which is reached up narrow, steep roads. *(See also pp250–51.)*

Farm workers at Collobrières

Mimosas" was not added to its name until 1968, a century after the plant was first introduced to the south of France from Mexico. A pretty and popular village, Bormes serves a marina of more than 800 berths. Plummeting streets such as Rompi-Cuou lead to lively cafés and coastal views.

A statue of St Francis di Paola stands in front of the attractive 16th-century **Chapelle St-François**, commemorating the saint's timely arrival during a plague outbreak in 1481. The 18th-century church of **St-Trophyme** has restored 18th-century frescoes. The works of local painter Jean-Charles Cazin (1841–1901) are well represented in the **Musée d'Arts et Histoire**.

Musée d'Arts et Histoire
103 rue Carnot. **Tel** 04 94 71 56 60.
Open Tue–Sun (Oct–Apr: Tue–Sat).

Ramatuelle village enclosed by wooded slopes and vineyards

㉒ Ramatuelle

Road map E4. 2,166. Pl de l'Ormeau (04 98 12 64 00). Thu & Sun. ramatuelle-tourisme.com

Surrounded by vineyards, this attractive hilltop village was called "God's Gift" (Rahmatu 'llah) by the Saracens who left behind a gate, now well-restored, in its fortifications, as well as a penchant for figs. It is one of three particularly quaint villages on the St-Tropez peninsula (with Grimaud and Gassin). Gérard Philipe (1922–59), the leading young French actor during the 1950s, is buried here. Theatre and jazz festivals take place here annually.

Nearby, Les Moulins de Paillas (322 m, 940 ft), offers a fine panorama, as does Cap Camarat, with its lighthouse, at the tip of the peninsula, 5 km (3 miles) east of Ramatuelle.

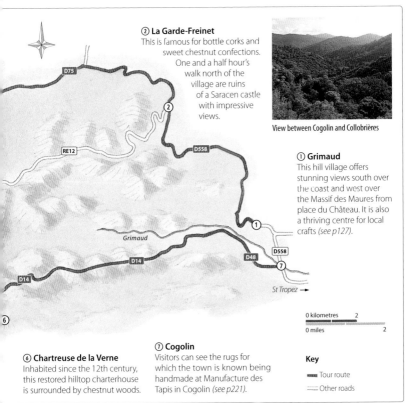

② La Garde-Freinet
This is famous for bottle corks and sweet chestnut confections. One and a half hour's walk north of the village are ruins of a Saracen castle with impressive views.

View between Cogolin and Collobrières

① Grimaud
This hill village offers stunning views south over the coast and west over the Massif des Maures from place du Château. It is also a thriving centre for local crafts (see p127).

Grimaud

St Tropez →

0 kilometres 2
0 miles 2

⑥ Chartreuse de la Verne
Inhabited since the 12th century, this restored hilltop charterhouse is surrounded by chestnut woods.

⑦ Cogolin
Visitors can see the rugs for which the town is known being handmade at Manufacture des Tapis in Cogolin (see p221).

Key
Tour route
Other roads

㉙ Street-by-Street: St-Tropez

Clustered around the old port and nearby beaches, the centre of St-Tropez, partly rebuilt in its original style after World War II (*see p56*), is full of fishermen's houses. In the port itself, traditional fishing boats are still to be seen moored side-by-side with sleek luxury cruisers of all shapes and sizes. Behind the port-side cafés of the quai Jean-Jaurès, the narrow, bustling streets are packed with boutiques and restaurants. The town is overlooked by the church's wrought-iron bell tower in the centre and the citadel just outside.

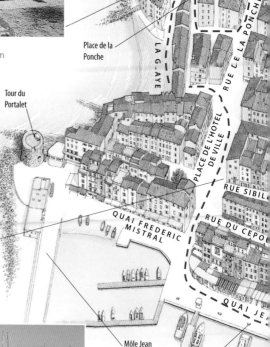

La Fontanette beach leads to a coastal walk with views over Ste-Maxime.

The Ponche quarter is a comparatively quiet and unspoiled area of St-Tropez.

Tour Vieille

Place de la Ponche

Tour du Portalet

The Port de Pêche
The Tour Vieille separates this port from La Glaye beach next door.

St-Tropez Old Town
The ochre-coloured rooftops of the Old Town and azur-blue sea make an arresting view.

Môle Jean Réveille

★ **Quai Jean-Jaurès**
The attractively painted houses and packed cafés lining the quay have enticed visitors and inspired artists for over a century.

View from the Ramparts of the Citadel
The hilltop citadel, situated east of St-Tropez, offers spectacular views over the rooftops of the town and beyond.

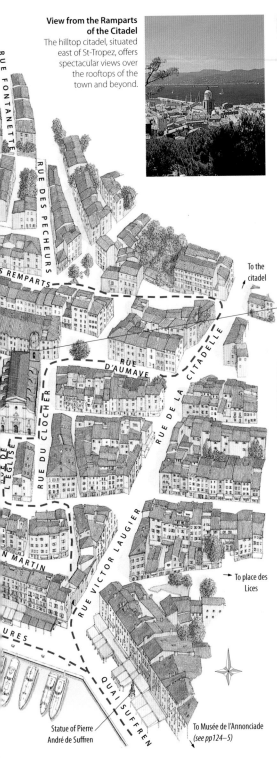

To the citadel

RUE FONTANETTE

RUE DES PECHEURS

S REMPARTS

RÙE D'AUMAVE

RUE DE LA CITADELLE

RUE DU CLOCHER

L'ÉGLISE

N MARTIN

RUE VICTOR LAUGIER

URES

QUAI SUFFREN

To place des Lices

Statue of Pierre André de Suffren

To Musée de l'Annonciade (see pp124–5)

VISITORS' CHECKLIST

Practical Information
Map E4. ⚏ 4,525. ⓘ Quai Jean-Jaurès (08 92 68 48 28). 🛒 Tue & Sat. 🎭 Bravades: 16–18 May, 15 Jun.
ⓦ sainttropeztourisme.com

Transport
🚌 Gare Routière (04 94 56 25 74).

★ **Eglise Notre-Dame de l'Assomption**
Its bust of St Torpès features in the bravade (see p228).

Open Window on the Harbour at St-Tropez (1925–6)
Charles Camoin's painting is now in the Annonciade.

Key

— Suggested route

0 metres   50
0 yards   50

Musée de l'Annonciade

This innovative gallery opened in 1955 in the former Chapelle de l'Annonciade by the old port in St-Tropez. Built in 1568, the building was converted into a museum by architect Louis Süe (1875–1968), funded by art collector Georges Grammont. The collection began with the paintings of Paul Signac and the other artists who followed him to St-Tropez, and now contains many stunning Post-Impressionist works from the late 19th and early 20th centuries. In 1961, 65 valuable works were stolen from the museum, but were recovered and restored a year later.

Le Rameur (1914)
This bold Cubist work is by Roger de la Fresnaye.

★ St-Tropez, la Place des Lices et le Café des Arts
This painting (1925) is one of several that Charles Camoin made of St-Tropez's famous square after he followed Paul Signac and settled in the town.

Temporary exhibition room

★ L'Orage (1895)
Paul Signac's atmospheric work vividly depicts the onset of a storm in St-Tropez harbour.

Gallery Guide

Exhibition space is too limited for all works to be permanently on view, so the display changes frequently. An exhibition room holds temporary displays linked with the permanent collection.

★ Nu Devant la Cheminée (1919)
In this warm, intimate picture, characteristic of the artist, Pierre Bonnard uses delicate tones within a limited colour range to create an effect of light and shade.

Le Temps d'Harmonie
In this study (1893–5) for a larger work, Paul Signac departs from his more usual Pointillist technique, using simple, fluid lines.

Balcony

VISITORS' CHECKLIST

Practical Information
2 rue de l'Annonciade, Place Grammont, St-Tropez. **Tel** 04 94 17 84 10. **Open** Tue–Sun. **Closed** 1 Jan, Ascension, 1 May, 17 May, Nov, 25 Dec.
 ground floor only.

La Nymphe (1930)
This Classically influenced bronze sculpture, one of several excellent works by Aristide Maillol in the Annonciade, is a graceful evocation of ideal beauty.

Deauville, le Champ de Courses
Raoul Dufy's racecourse, painted in 1928, is typical of his interest in glamorous subjects.

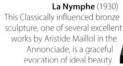

18th-century main entrance

Key to Floorplan
- Ground floor
- Mezzanine
- First floor
- Non-exhibition space

Exploring St-Tropez

This exceptional resort has become a victim of its own charms – the August high season attracts about 80,000 hell-bent hedonists. Following their departure, however, the genuine, peaceful nature of the village is able to shine through. Surrounded by slopes covered with vineyards, looking out over the millpond bay of Golfe St-Tropez and protected by an imposing citadel, its situation remains inviolate. It does, however, face the northerly Mistral which thunders through the town for much of the winter, ensuring it remains a summer haunt.

Baroque-style Eglise Notre-Dame de l'Assomption

Paintings by local artists for sale on the quai Jean-Jaurès

A glimpse of the town

Activity is centred north of the Musée de l'Annonciade, beside the little port. Here, local artists sell their wares and people pass the time of day in the Café de Paris, le Gorille or Senequier (see p219).

The pretty, pastel-painted houses lining the quai Jean-Jaurès can be viewed at their best from the harbour breakwater, the Môle Jean Réveille. These buildings were among the town's sights that inspired Paul Signac (1863–1935) to start painting in St-Tropez. Many other artists followed, all well represented in the Annonciade (see pp124–5).

The old town, just behind the waterfront, is marked by the tower of the Eglise Notre-Dame de l'Assomption. To its north lies the Hôtel de Ville and the Tour Suffren, home of the former local lords. Admiral Pierre André de Suffren (1726–88), "terror of the English", is commemorated by a statue on the quay. Behind the quai Suffren is the place des Lices, a large square crowded with cafés.

Out to the east, beyond the old Ponche quarter and the unspoiled fishing port nearby, lies the 16th-century hexagonal citadel. With fine views from the ramparts, it contains the Musée Naval de St-Tropez. Further east, is La Madrague where Brigitte Bardot used to live. And God Created Woman, the 1959 film shot in St-Tropez starring Bardot, started the celebrity rush to the town.

🏛 Musée de l'Annonciade
See pp124–5.

⛪ Eglise Notre-Dame de l'Assomption
Rue de l'Eglise. **Open** Tue–Sun am.
This 19th-century Baroque church contains several busts

of saints, including one of St Torpès after whom St-Tropez is named. Beheaded for his Christianity, his body was put in a boat with a dog and a cockerel and the boat landed here in AD 68. Every year, his bust is carried through the town in the 16 May bravade.

The impressive hilltop citadel east of St-Tropez

🏛 Musée de la Citadelle
Forteresse. **Tel** 04 94 97 59 43.
Open daily. **Closed** 1 Jan, 1 & 17 May, 11 Nov, 25 Dec. 🈲 ♿
Located in the dungeon of the citadel keep, to the east of the town, this museum houses a collection on the colourful history of St-Tropez and the navy.

🏛 Maison des Papillons
9 rue Etienne Berny. **Tel** 04 94 97 63 45.
Open Apr–Nov: Tue pm & Wed–Sat.
Closed 1 Jan, 1 & 17 May, Ascension, 15 Aug, 1 Nov, 25 Dec. 🈲 ♿ ground floor only.

Hidden in a narrow medieval lane is this amazingly complete collection of butterflies found in France, as well as rare specimens from the Amazon.

Fishing boats and luxury cruisers docked at quai Jean-Jaurès

For hotels and restaurants in this region see pp199–200 and pp211–12

❷❹ Port-Grimaud

Road map E4. 🗺 150. 🚌 *i* Les Terrasses, Rue de l'Amarrage (04 94 55 43 83). ⚓ Thu & Sun. 🅦 **grimaud-provence.com**

This beautiful port village was dreamed up entirely by the renowned Alsace architect François Spoerry (1912–98). In 1962 he bought up the marshy delta lands of the River Giscle west of the Golfe St-Tropez. Four years later, work began on a mini-Venice of 2,500 canal-side houses with moorings covering 90 ha (222 acres). There are now three "zones", a marina and a beach. Its church, **St-François-d'Assise**, in the place d'Eglise, contains some stained glass by Victor Vasarély (1908–97) and offers a sweeping view of the port from the top of its tower.

The whole port is free of traffic and the *coche d'eau* offers a water-taxi service. A major tourist attraction, Port-Grimaud brings in about one million visitors a year.

❷❺ Grimaud

Road map E4. 🗺 2,700. 🚌 *i* 679 route nationale (04 94 55 43 83). ⚓ Thu. 🅦 **grimaud-provence.com**

The medieval, fortified, traffic-free *village perché (see pp24–5)* of Grimaud has a long history dating back to the Gallo-Roman days. During the 11th century, its steep summit allowed Grimaud to dominate the Gulf

View of Port-Grimaud from the Eglise de St-François-d'Assise

of St-Tropez (also known as the Golfe de Grimaud) and control access to the town from the North and Maures mountains. Contrary to popular belief, Grimaud has no connection to the ubiquitous Grimaldi family. Rather it can be associated with the much older Grimaldo family. The castle of Grimaud dates from the 11th century and was reduced to ruins in the Wars of Religion between Catholics and Protestants *(see pp50–51)*.

The view of the coast from its heights made it an ideal vantage point from which to watch for further invasion.

Once called rue Droite, the rue des Templiers is the town's oldest street, lined with arcades designed to be battened down in case of attack. Legend has it that the Knights Templar stayed in Grimaud, but this fact has not been historically attested. In the same street is the pure Romanesque 12th-century church of St-Michel.

One of the popular beaches at Ste-Maxime on a sunny day

❷❻ Ste-Maxime

Road map E4. 🗺 13,900. 🚌 St-Tropez, St-Raphaël. *i* promenade Aymeric Simon-Lorière (08 76 20 83 83). ⚓ daily.

Facing St-Tropez across the neck of the Gulf, Ste-Maxime is protected by hills. Its year-round clientele reaches saturation point in summer. The attractions of this smart resort are its port, prome-nade, sandy beaches, water-sports, nightlife, fairs and casino.

Ste-Maxime was once protected by the monks of Lérins, who named the port after their patron saint and put up the defensive Tour Carrée des Dames which now serves as the **Musée de la Tour Carrée**. The church opposite contains a 17th-century green marble altar that was brought from the former Carthusian monastery of La Verne in the Massif des Maures.

🏛 Musée de la Tour Carrée
Place Mireille de Germond. **Tel** 04 94 96 70 30. **Open** Wed–Sun (Sep–Jun: pm only). **Closed** 1 Jan, 1 May, 25 Dec, Feb. 📷

Grimaud, dominated by the castle ruins

❼ St-Raphaël

Road map E4. 🚗 34,716. 🚌 🚆
ℹ️ Quai Albert Premier (04 94 19 52 52).
🛒 Tue–Sun. 🌐 **saint-raphael.com**

This staid family resort dates to Roman times when rich families came to stay at a spot near the modern seafront casino. Napoleon put the town on the map when he landed here in 1799 on his return from Egypt, and 15 years later when he left St-Raphaël for exile on Elba.

Popularity came when the Parisian satirical novelist Jean-Baptiste Karr (1808–90) publicized the town's delights. In the old part is the 12th-century church of St-Raphaël and the **Musée Archéologique**, which contains Greek amphorae and other underwater finds.

🏛 Musée Archéologique
Place de la Vieille Eglise. **Tel** 04 94 19 25 75. **Open** Mar–Jun: Tue pm–Sat; Jul–Sep: Tue–Sat; Nov–Feb: Tue pm–Sat am. **Closed** public hols.

Tourist poster of St-Raphaël from the 19th century

❽ Massif de l'Esterel

Road map E4. ✈️ Nice. 🚌 🚆 Agay, St-Raphaël. ℹ️ Quai Albert Premier, St-Raphaël (04 94 19 52 52) & 86 ave de Cannes, Mandelieu-La Napoule (04 93 93 64 64).

The Esterel, a mountainous volcanic mass, is a wilderness compared to the popular coast. Although it rises to no more than 620 m (2,050 ft), and a succession of fires has laid waste its forests, its innate ruggedness and the dramatic colours of its porphyry

Château de la Napoule, now an art centre

rocks remain intact. Until the mid-1800s, it was a refuge for highwaymen and escaped prisoners from Toulon. Here, after being fêted on arrival in St Raphaël, Napoleon and his coach were robbed of all their valuables while on their way out of town heading to Paris.

The north side of the massif is bounded by the DN7 which runs through the Esterel Gap, following the Roman Aurelian way from Cannes to Fréjus. To reach Mont Vinaigre, at the Testanier crossroads 11 km (7 miles) from Fréjus, follow the road leading to the Malpey ranger station. Park there and do the final 45 minutes on foot. This is the highest point on the massif, and there is a fine panorama from the Alps to the Massif des Maures.

On the seaward side of the massif the D1089 from St-Raphaël twists along the top of startlingly red cliffs to Agay. This resort has the best anchorage on the coast. It is famous for its red porphyry, from which the Romans cut columns for their Provençal monuments. Be aware that there is only one paved road (mostly one-way) to reach Agay and no access to return to the seafront between Agay and Theoule.

Round the bay is Pointe de Baumette where there is a memorial to French writer and World War II aviator, Antoine de St-Exupéry (*see p33*). The road continues to Anthéor and the Pointe de l'Observatoire. Just before here, a left turn leads to the circuit of the Cap Roux and Pic de l'Ours.

The coast road continues through a series of resorts to the

start of the Riviera, at La Napoule. Here there is a 14th-century château refurbished by American sculptor Henry Clews (1876–1937), who left work scattered about the estate. The château is now an art centre, the **Fondation Henry Clews**. The pedestrian route leading inland to the Col Belle-Barbe from the coast passes on the right a turn to the 452-m (1483-ft) Pic du Cap Roux. An hour's walk to the top is rewarded by a sweeping view of the coast.

Inland from Col Belle-Barbe over the Col du Mistral up to the Col des Trois Termes, the path then twists south to Col Notre-Dame. A 45-minute walk leads to the dramatic 496-m (1,627-ft) Pic de l'Ours. Between here and the coast is the 323-m (1,060-ft) Pic d'Aurelle, which also provides an impressive vista.

🏛 Fondation Henry Clews
1 blvd Henry Clews, Mandelieu-La Napoule. **Tel** 04 93 49 95 05. **Open** daily; Nov–Feb: Mon-Fri pm. **Closed** 25 Dec. 🚫 📷 🎥 ♿ Apr–Sep 📷 🌐 **chateau-lanapoule.com**

Remaining timber on the fire-ravaged Massif de l'Esterel

㉙ Fréjus

Road map E4. 🚶 52,344. 🚉 St Raphaël.
🚌 ℹ 249 rue Jean-Jaurès (04 94 51
83 83). 🕐 Tue, Wed, Fri, Sat & Sun.
🌐 **frejus.fr**

Visibly, though not ostentatiously, wealthy in history, Fréjus is one of the highlights of the coast. The oldest Roman city in Gaul, it was founded by Julius Caesar in 49 BC and greatly expanded by Augustus. Lying on the Aurelian way – a huge road built in the reign of Augustus from Rome to Arles – it covered 40 ha (100 acres), had a population of 30–40,000 and, as a port, was second in importance only to Marseille.

Although substantial sections of the Roman city were decimated by the Saracens in the 10th century, a few parts of their walls remain, including a tower of the western Porte des Gaules. The opposite eastern entrance, the Porte de Rome, marks one end of a 40-km (25-mile) aqueduct, the ruins of which amble alongside the DN7 towards the Siagnole river near Mons.

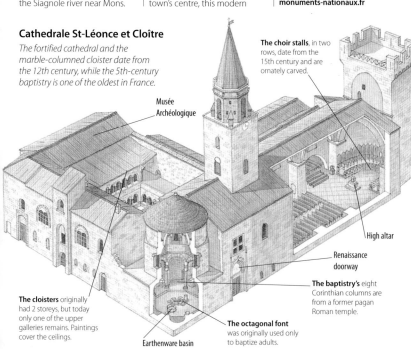

Mosaic in the Musée Archéologique in Fréjus

Just to the north of here the remains of the semicircular, 1st-century theatre can be viewed. In their midst, performances are still held. The praetorium or Plateforme – military headquarters that formed the eastern citadel – lie to the south. North of the Porte des Gaules, on the road to Brignoles, stands the large 1st–2nd-century **Arènes**, built to hold 6,000 spectators, now used for music and dance.

The spectacular **Cathédrale St-Léonce et Cloître** houses a Musée Archéologique with finds from all around Fréjus. The Chapelle Notre-Dame, decorated by Cocteau, and Musée d'Histoire Locale are also well worth a visit. South of the town is the Butte St-Antoine citadel, which once overlooked the harbour. The canal linking the harbour to the sea began silting up in the 10th century; by the 1700s it was entirely filled in, forming Fréjus-Plage. A little over 2 km (1 mile) from the town's centre, this modern

Well in the centre of the Cathedral cloisters at Fréjus

resort stretches along a sandy beach towards St-Raphaël. North of the Arènes is a Buddhist Pagoda commemorating Vietnamese soldiers who died serving in the French army.

🏛 **Arènes de Fréjus**
Rue Vadon. **Tel** 04 94 51 34 31.
Open Apr–Sep: Tue–Sun; Oct–Mar: Tue–Sat. **Closed** public hols. 🐾

⛪ **Cathédrale St-Léonce**
58 rue du Cardinal Fleury. **Tel** 04 94 52 14 01. **Open** daily. Cloisters: daily (Oct–May): Tue–Sun). **Closed** Mon (winter), public hols. 🐾 cloisters.
📷 📷 🌐 **cathedrale-frejus. monuments-nationaux.fr**

Cathedrale St-Léonce et Cloître

The fortified cathedral and the marble-columned cloister date from the 12th century, while the 5th-century baptistry is one of the oldest in France.

The choir stalls, in two rows, date from the 15th century and are ornately carved.

Musée Archéologique

High altar

Renaissance doorway

The baptistry's eight Corinthian columns are from a former pagan Roman temple.

The cloisters originally had 2 storeys, but today only one of the upper galleries remains. Paintings cover the ceilings.

The octagonal font was originally used only to baptize adults.

Earthenware basin

BOUCHES-DU-RHÔNE AND NÎMES

This southwestern corner of Provence has a feel that's unique in the region. It is the land of Van Gogh, brightly patterned materials and beaches of shifting sands. Its wildest point is the Camargue in the Rhône delta, a place of light and colour, lived in for centuries by gypsies and by cowboys who herd the wild horses and bulls.

Many inland towns reflect the region's Greek and Roman past. The Greeks first settled in France circa 600 BC and founded Marseille, now a cosmopolitan cultural centre and the country's second largest city. The Romans, who arrived after them, built the theatre at Arles and the amphi-theatre at Nîmes, and left the remains of Classical houses at the archaeological site of Glanum. The skeleton of a Roman aqueduct runs beween a spring at Uzès to a water tower at Nîmes, a great feat of engineering best seen at Pont du Gard.

"A race of eagles" is how Frédéric Mistral, the Provençal writer *(see p32)* described the Lords of Baux, bloodthirsty warriors who ruled in the Middle Ages from an extraordinary eyrie in Les Baux-de-Provence. This former fief was paradoxically famous as a Court of Love *(see p146)* during the 13th century. Louis IX (Saint Louis) built the fortified city of Aigues-Mortes for the Crusaders. In the 15th century, Good King René *(see pp50–51)*, held his court in the castle of Tarascon and in Aix-en-Provence, the ancient capital of Provence. Aix's university, founded by René's father in 1409, is still the hub of this lively student town.

The area provides great walks and stunning scenery, particularly in the Alpilles and around Marseille. The films and books of Marcel Pagnol *(see 157)* and the stories of Daudet *(see p147)*, which have influenced perceptions of Provençal people and life, are set in this region. The Camargue maintains a unique collection of flora and fauna, providing, in addition to fine vistas, superb horse riding and bird-watching.

Produce on display in the colourful food market, Aix-en-Provence

◀ Hiking in the Sormiou *calanque*, one of the many inlets between Marseille and Cassis

Exploring Bouches-du-Rhône and Nîmes

At the mouth of the Rhône lie the flat, wetland marshes and sand dunes of the Camargue wildlife reserve. Further inland, cities such as Aix-en-Provence, Arles and Nîmes are awash with ancient architecture. Northeast of Arles, the herb-covered chain of the Alpilles rises from the surrounding plains to the heady heights of Les Baux, and there are some stunning walks through the mountains. St-Rémy-de-Provence makes a good base for exploring the Alpilles. Popular coastal towns are Marseille and the scenic port of Cassis. A short car or boat trip away lie Les Calanques, deep, narrow inlets set between pine trees and white cliffs.

Atlantes grace the doorway of the Pavillon de Vendôme in Aix

For additional map symbols *see back flap*

Sights at a Glance

1. Villeneuve-lès-Avignon
2. Barbentane
3. Abbaye de St-Michel-de-Frigolet
4. Pont du Gard
5. *Nîmes pp136–7*
6. *Aigues-Mortes pp138–9*
7. *La Camargue pp140–3*
8. St-Gilles
9. Beaucaire
10. Tarascon
11. St-Rémy-de-Provence
12. Les Alpilles
13. Les Baux-de-Provence
14. Fontvieille
15. Abbaye de Montmajour
16. *Arles pp148–50*
17. Martigues
18. Salon-de-Provence
19. Abbaye de Silvacane
20. *Aix-en-Provence pp152–3*
21. *Marseille pp154–7*
22. Aubagne
23. Les Calanques
24. Cassis

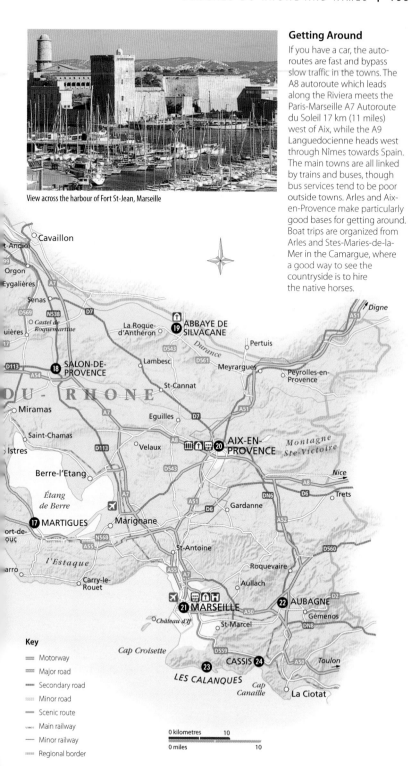

View across the harbour of Fort St-Jean, Marseille

Getting Around

If you have a car, the auto-routes are fast and bypass slow traffic in the towns. The A8 autoroute which leads along the Riviera meets the Paris-Marseille A7 Autoroute du Soleil 17 km (11 miles) west of Aix, while the A9 Languedocienne heads west through Nîmes towards Spain. The main towns are all linked by trains and buses, though bus services tend to be poor outside towns. Arles and Aix-en-Provence make particularly good bases for getting around. Boat trips are organized from Arles and Stes-Maries-de-la-Mer in the Camargue, where a good way to see the countryside is to hire the native horses.

Cavaillon

t-Andiol

Orgon

Eygalières

Senas

Cuières

Castel de
Roquemartue

La Roque-
d'Anthéron

**ABBAYE DE
SILVACANE** 19

Pertuis

Digne

Lambesc

Durance

Meyrargues

Peyrolles-en-
Provence

**SALON-DE-
PROVENCE** 18

St-Cannat

D U - R H O N E

Miramas

Eguilles

**AIX-EN-
PROVENCE** 20

Montagne
Ste-Victoire

Saint-Chamas

Velaux

Nice

Istres

Berre-l'Etang

Trets

Étang
de Berre

Gardanne

MARTIGUES 17

Marignane

ort-de-
ouc

St-Antoine

D560

l'Estaque

arro

Carry-le-
Rouet

Roquevaire

Aullach

MARSEILLE 21

AUBAGNE 22

Château d'If

St-Marcel

Gémenos

Cap Croisette

Toulon

CASSIS 24

23

LES CALANQUES

Cap
Canaille

La Ciotat

Key

- Motorway
- Major road
- Secondary road
- Minor road
- Scenic route
- Main railway
- Minor railway
- Regional border

0 kilometres   10

0 miles   10

Part of the Chartreuse du Val-de-Bénédiction, Villeneuve

❶ Villeneuve-lès-Avignon

Road map B3. 🏛 12,735. 🚉 Avignon. 🚌 🛈 1 pl Charles David (04 90 25 61 33). 🛍 Thu & Sat. 🆆 tourisme-villeneuvelezavignon.fr

This town arose beside the Rhône, opposite Avignon *(see pp170–71)*, and the connecting bridge, Pont St-Bénézet, was guarded by the **Tour de Philippe le Bel**, built in 1307. Its rooftop terrace, 176 steps up, gives a fine panorama of the papal city. Even better is the view from the two giant 40-m (130-ft) round towers at the entrance to the impressive 14th-century **Fort St-André**, which enclosed a small town, monastery and church.

Between these two bastions lies the 14th-century Eglise-Collégiale Notre-Dame. In the **Musée Pierre de Luxembourg** is *The Coronation of the Virgin*

(1453) by Enguerrand Quarton, regarded as the best work of the Avignon School. This work was painted for the abbot of the **Chartreuse du Val-de-Bénédiction**, which was founded by Innocent VI in 1356. There are three cloisters and a chapel dedicated to St John the Baptist decorated with frescoes by Giovanetti da Viterbo. The building is now used as a cultural centre.

🏰 Fort St-André
Tel 04 90 25 45 35. **Open** daily. **Closed** 1 Jan, 1 May, 1 & 11 Nov, 25 Dec. 🅿 🆆 fort-saint-andre.monument-nationaux.fr

🏛 Musée Municipal Pierre de Luxembourg
Rue de la République. **Tel** 04 90 27 49 66. **Open** Tue–Sun. **Closed** Jan, 1 & 11 Nov, 25 Dec. 🅿

🏛 Chartreuse du Val-de-Bénédiction
Rue de la République. **Tel** 04 90 15 24 24. **Open** daily. **Closed** 1 Jan, 1 May, 1 & 11 Nov, 25 Dec. 🅿 🗂 in summer. 🚻 in summer. 🛈 in winter. 🅿 🆆 chartreuse.org

❷ Barbentane

Road map B3. 🏛 4,067. 🚉 Avignon, Tarascon. 🚌 🛈 3 rues des Pénitents (04 90 90 85 86). 🆆 barbentane.fr

Members of Avignon's Papal court liked to build summer houses in Barbentane, beside the Rhône 10 km (6 miles) south of the city. One such, opposite the 13th- to 15th-century Notre-Dame-de-Grace, was the handsome Maison des Chevaliers, which was

owned by the Marquises of Barbentane. Only the 40-m (130-ft) Tour Anglica remains of the town's 14th-century castle. Just outside the medieval quarter is the Château de Barbentane, a finely decorated Italianate mansion, built in 1674 by the Barbentane aristocracy who still own and reside in it.

In the town is the 16th- to 17th-century **Moulin de Mogador**, which was used as an oil mill and now hosts dinners.

Façade of the 17th-century Château de Barbentane

❸ Abbaye de St-Michel de Frigolet

Road map B3. **Tel** 04 90 95 70 07. **Open** 8am–6pm daily. Phone to reserve for groups. 🗂 3pm Sun. 🅿 🆆 frigolet.com

The abbey is situated south of St-Michel de Frigolet, in the La Montagnette countryside. A cloister and small church date from the 12th century, but in 1858 a Premonstratensian abbey was founded and one of the most richly decorated churches of that period was built. The whole interior is colourfully painted, with stars and saints on the pillars and ceiling. After a brief period of exile in Belgium at the beginning of the 20th century, the monks returned to Frigolet. The word *frigolet* is Provençal for thyme.

The ceiling of the abbey church of St-Michel de Frigolet

❹ Pont du Gard

Road map A3. 🚌 Nîmes. ℹ️ Place des Grands Jours, Remoulins (04 66 37 22 34). **Open** daily 🌐 ot-pontdugard.com

Begun around 19 BC, this bridge is part of an aqueduct which transported water from a spring near Uzès to Roman Nîmes *(see pp136–7)*. An underground channel, bridges and tunnels were engineered to carry the 20 million litre (4.4 million gallon) daily water supply 50 km (31 miles). The three-tiered structure of the Pont du Gard spans the Gardon valley and was the tallest aqueduct in the Roman empire.

The Pont du Gard, the tallest of all Roman aqueducts at 48 m (158 ft)

Trademark graffiti left by 18th-century masons on the stones

Its huge limestone blocks, some as heavy as 6 tonnes, were erected without mortar. The water channel, covered by stone slabs, was in the top tier of the three. Skilfully designed cutwaters ensured that the bridge has resisted many violent floods.

It is not known for certain how long the aqueduct remained in use but it may still have been functioning as late as the 9th century AD. The adjacent road bridge was erected in the 1700s. The **Site du Pont du Gard** has a museum (open daily in summer) tracing the aqueduct's history.

Protruding stones for supporting scaffolding during construction

The Remains of the Aqueduct

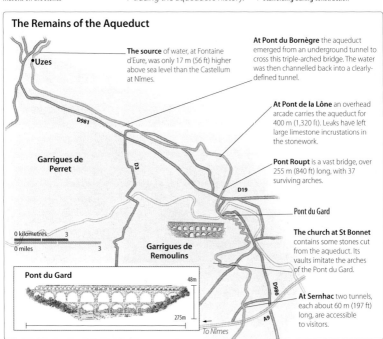

The source of water, at Fontaine d'Eure, was only 17 m (56 ft) higher above sea level than the Castellum at Nîmes.

At Pont du Bornègre the aqueduct emerged from an underground tunnel to cross this triple-arched bridge. The water was then channelled back into a clearly-defined tunnel.

At Pont de la Lône an overhead arcade carries the aqueduct for 400 m (1,320 ft). Leaks have left large limestone incrustations in the stonework.

Pont Roupt is a vast bridge, over 255 m (840 ft) long, with 37 surviving arches.

Pont du Gard

The church at St Bonnet contains some stones cut from the aqueduct. Its vaults imitate the arches of the Pont du Gard.

At Sernhac two tunnels, each about 60 m (197 ft) long, are accessible to visitors.

Uzes

D981

Garrigues de Perret

D3

D19

Garrigues de Remoulins

D986

A9

0 kilometres 3
0 miles 3

Pont du Gard

48m

275m

To Nîmes

❺ Nîmes

A magnificent carved black bull at the end of the avenue Jean-Jaurès highlights Nîmes' passion for bullfighting. Crowds fill Les Arènes, the Roman amphitheatre, for bullfights during the two annual *ferias (see pp36–8)*. Year round, the city's biggest draw is its fine Roman architecture, and it is a great city of the arts. The city's textile industry is famous for creating denim *(de Nîmes)*, worn by the Camargue cowboys. Most shops stock vividly coloured Provençal fabrics, known as *indiennes (see p221)*.

Exploring Nîmes

Roman veterans from Emperor Augustus's 31 BC Egyptian campaign introduced the city's coat of arms: a crocodile chained to a palm tree. Today, the logo is splashed on everything from bollards to road signs.

Nîmes' generous boulevards give it a wide-open feel. A renaissance of modern building, art and design, including the fine Carré d'Art, lends a touch of class. Some of the newer monuments, such as the Fontaine du Crocodile in place du Marché, are becoming as well known as Nîmes' most familiar landmark, the Castellum.

The city's coat of arms: a crocodile and palm tree

❶ Les Arènes (L'Amphithéâtre)

Place des Arènes. **Tel** 04 66 21 82 56. **Open** daily. **Closed** Feria de Pentecôte, Feria des Vendanges & performance days. 🅿 🅰 restricted. 🅲
🆆 arenes-nimes.com

The most dramatic of the city's Roman ruins is the 1st-century amphitheatre. At 130 m (427 ft) by 100 m (328 ft) and with seating for 22,000, it is slightly smaller than Arles' amphitheatre *(see p150)*. It was built as a venue for gladiatorial combat, and you can see a demonstration of their fighting technique. After Rome's collapse in AD 476, it became a fortress and knights' headquarters. Until its 19th-century restoration, it was used as home for 2,000 people in slum conditions. Today it is thought to be one of the best preserved of all Roman amphitheatres.

❶ Porte d'Auguste

Blvd Amiral Courbet.

With a central arch 6 m (20 ft) high and 4 m (13 ft) wide, this gate was built to take horsemen and carriages, since the main road from Rome to Spain, the Domitian Way, passed through the middle of Nîmes.

An ancient inscription tells visitors that the city walls were built in 15 BC.

❶ Musée du Vieux Nîmes

Pl aux Herbes. **Tel** 04 66 76 73 70. **Open** Tue–Sun. **Closed** 1 Jan, 1 May, 1 Nov, 25 Dec. 🅲
The 17th-century Bishop's Palace just east of the cathedral houses this museum. The old-fashioned interior has been beautifully restored: the summer room has Directoire and Empire-style furnishings and Old Town views.

❶ Carré d'Art (Musée d'Art Contemporain)

Pl de la Maison Carrée. **Tel** 04 66 76 35 70. **Open** Tue–Sun. 🅿 🅲 🅰 🅲
🅲 🆆 carreartmusee.com
On the opposite side of the square from the Maison Carrée, this modern, light-flooded art complex opened in 1993 and was designed by Norman Foster.

Modernist façade of Norman Foster's Carré d'Art

❶ Maison Carrée

Pl de la Maison Carrée. **Tel** 04 66 21 82 56. **Open** daily. 🅿 🆆 arenes-nimes.com

The Maison Carrée ("square house") is the world's best-preserved Roman temple. Built by Marcus Agrippa, it is Hellenic with Corinthian columns around the main hall. Louis XIV's chief minister, Colbert, wanted it taken brick by brick to Versailles. A multimedia film – *Nemausus, the birth of Nîmes* – is shown inside the temple.

❶ Musée d'Histoire Naturelle

13 bis blvd Amiral Courbet. **Tel** 04 66 76 73 45. **Open** Tue–Sun. **Closed** 1 Jan, 1 May, 1 Nov, 25 Dec. 🅲
Set around a cloister and 17th-century chapel, this museum, still undergoing renovation, covers three themes: the prehistoric period, ethnography and zoology. Visitors can see collections devoted to mammals and birds, including bears, the Siberian tiger, the Canadian moose and even a prehistoric auroch or bull.

The Roman amphitheatre, today used for bullfights at festival times

There are also rooms on botany, geology, mineralogy, palaeontology and prehistoric archaeology, spread over three floors. The archaeological collection will be moved to the Musée de la Romanité once it opens. The atmospheric chapel in this one-time Jesuits' College is used for temporary displays.

🏛 Musée des Beaux-Arts
Rue Cité Foulc. **Tel** 04 66 28 18 32. **Open** Tue–Sun. **Closed** 1 Jan, 1 May, 1 Nov, 25 Dec. 🐾 ♿

A diverse collection in the Fine Art Museum includes paintings by Boucher, Rubens and Watteau. The ground floor displays a large Roman mosaic, *The Marriage of Admetus*, found in 1883 in Nîmes' former covered market.

🏛 Cathédrale Notre-Dame et St-Castor
Pl aux Herbes. **Tel** 04 66 67 27 72. **Open** daily & for services.

Nîmes' cathedral, in the centre of the Old Town, dates from the 11th century but was extensively rebuilt in the 19th century. The west front has a partly Romanesque frieze with scenes from the Old Testament.

🏛 Castellum
Rue de la Lampèze.

Between the Porte d'Auguste and the Tour Magne, set in the Roman wall, is the Castellum, a tower used for storing the water brought in from Uzès via the aqueduct at Pont du Gard (*see p135*). The water was distributed in the town by means of a canal duct system.

🏛 Les Jardins de la Fontaine
Quai de la Fontaine. **Tel** 04 66 21 82 56 (Tour Magne). **Open** daily.

The city's main park lies at the end of the wide avenue Jean-Jaurès. It was named after an underground spring harnessed in the 18th century. The park's 2nd-century Temple of Diana is today in ruins. Benedictine nuns lived there during the Middle Ages and converted it into a church, which was sacked in the Wars of Religion (*see pp50–51*).

At the summit of the 114-m (374-ft) Mont Cavalier stands the 32-m (105-ft) octagonal Tour Magne. Of all the towers originally set in Nîmes' Roman wall, this is the most remarkable. Dating from 15 BC, it is the earliest surviving Roman

VISITORS' CHECKLIST

Practical Information
Road map A3. 🚉 150,019. 🛈 6 rue Auguste (04 66 58 38 00) & Pavillon de l'Esplanade, Esplanade Charles de Gaulle. 🏠 daily. 🎪 Feria de Pentecôte (May/Jun); Feria des Vendanges (late Sep). 🌐 ot-nimes.fr

Transport
✈ Nîmes-Arles-Camargue. 🚉 Pl de l'ONU.

building in France. There are 140 steps, worth climbing for a fine view of Mont Ventoux.

L'Obéissance Récompensée by Boucher, Musée des Beaux-Arts

Nîmes
① Les Arènes
② Porte d'Auguste
③ Musée du Vieux Nîmes
④ Carré d'Art
⑤ Maison Carrée
⑥ Musée d'Histoire Naturelle
⑦ Musée des Beaux-Arts
⑧ Cathédrale Notre-Dame et St-Castor

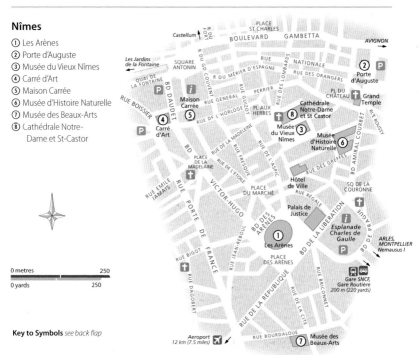

Key to Symbols *see back flap*

❻ Aigues-Mortes

A lone, sturdy sentinel set among the salt marshes of the Camargue, Aigues-Mortes ("dead waters" in Provençal) looks today much as it must have done when it was completed, around 1300. Then, however, the Rhône had not yet deposited the silt which now landlocks the town. Canals transported the vast stone blocks to make its walls from the quarries of Beaucaire, and the town's founder, Louis IX, set sail from under the shadow of Tour de Constance on his crusade of 1248 *(see pp46–7)*. Only the Hundred Years' War saw its ramparts breached: now its gates are always open to the besieging armies of admiring visitors.

Tour de la Poudrière
was the arsenal, where weapons and gun-powder were stored.

Porte de l'Arsenal

RUE DE L'ARSENAL

RUE HOCHE

RUE HOCHE

RUE ROGER

SALENGRO

RUE F.M.

RUE BAUDIN

BOULEVARD GAMBETTA

RUE DE

King Louis IX
Saint Louis, as he was to become, built Aigues-Mortes as his only Mediterranean sea port. People had to be bribed to come and settle in this inhospitable spot.

Porte de la Reine
was named for Anne of Austria, who visited the town in 1622.

Tour de la Mèche or "wick tower" held a constant flame used to light cannon fuses.

Chapelle des Pénitents Blancs

Tour du Sel

★ The Ramparts
The 1,634-m (1-mile) long walls are punctuated by ten gates, six towers, arrow slits and overhanging latrines.

Chapelle des Pénitents Gris
Built around 1607, this chapel is still used by an order founded in 1400. Named for their grey cowls, they walk with their white-cowled former rivals in the Palm Sunday procession.

For hotels and restaurants in this region see pp200–1 and pp212–15

Porte de la Marine
This was the main portside gate. Ships were moored by the Porte des Galions, anchored to a vast metal ring known as an *organeau*.

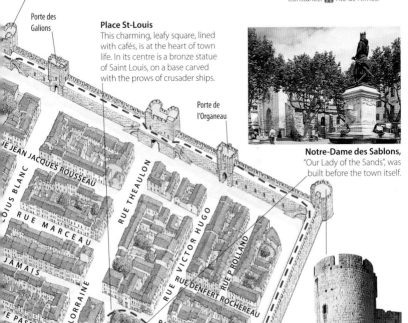

Porte des Galions

Place St-Louis
This charming, leafy square, lined with cafés, is at the heart of town life. In its centre is a bronze statue of Saint Louis, on a base carved with the prows of crusader ships.

Porte de l'Organeau

E JEAN JACQUES ROUSSEAU

OIUS BLANC

RUE MARCEAU

JAMAIS

E PASTEUR

RUE ALSACE LORRAINE

E PUBLIQUE

RUE THEAULON

RUE VICTOR HUGO

RUE DENFERT ROCHEREAU

RUE ROLLAND

ST-LOUIS

RUE SADI-CARNOT

GRAND RUE JEAN JAURES

RUE AMIRAL COURBERT

Porte de la Gardette

Notre-Dame des Sablons,
"Our Lady of the Sands", was built before the town itself.

Tour des Bourguignons
In the massacre of 1421 Gascons took the town from Burgundy. There were too many bodies to bury, so salted bodies were kept here.

Key
— Suggested route

0 metres 100
0 yards 100

★ **Tour de Constance**
This tower often held religious prisoners: first Catholic, then Calvinist, and then Huguenot women such as Marie Durand, freed in 1768 after 38 years.

❼ The Camargue

This flat, scarcely habited land is one of Europe's major wetland regions and natural history sites. Extensive areas of salt marsh, lakes, pastures and sand dunes, covering a vast 140,000 ha (346,000 acres), provide a romantic and haunting environment for the wildlife. Native horses roam the green pastures and are ridden by the traditional cowboys of the region, the *gardians*, (see p26) who herd the black bulls. Numerous sea birds and wildfowl also occupy the region, among them flocks of greater flamingoes. North of the reserve, rice is cultivated in paddy fields. Many of the thousands of visitors confine their exploration to the road between Arles and Saintes-Maries-de-la-Mer, and miss the best of the wild flora and fauna.

Camargue Bulls
Periodically, the herds of black bulls are rounded up by the *gardians* to perform in local bullfights. The larger bulls are sold to Spain.

Camargue Birds

This region is a haven for bird spotters, particularly during the spring when migrant birds visit on their journey north. Resident birds include little egrets and marsh harriers. This is the only French breeding site of the slender-billed gull, and the red-crested pochard, rarely seen in Europe, also breeds here.

Little egret
(*Egretta garzetta*)

Collared pratincole
(*Glareola pratincola*)

Slender-billed gull
(*Larus genei*)

Marsh harrier (*Circus aeruginosus*)

Black-winged stilt
(*Himantopus himantopus*)

Red-crested pochard
(*Netta rufina*)

Méjanes

PLAINE DE LA CAMARGUE

PETITE CAMARGUE

Le Petit Rhône

D572

D570

D570

Ⓟ ①

Stes-Maries-de-la-Mer

KEY

① **Parc Ornithologique du Pont-de-Gau** bird reserve *(see p142)* is where most birds in the Camargue live and where, twice a year, over 350 species of migrating birds stop off on their journey north or south.

② **Musée de la Camargue** *(see p143).*

③ **Information Centre for Nature Reserve**

Camargue Horses
These hardy animals are direct descendants of pre-historic horses. The foal's coat turns white between the ages of four and seven.

European Beavers
European beavers came close to extinction at the start of the 20th century, when they were hunted for their fur. These nocturnal animals were protected in 1905 and began to colonize the region in the 1970s.

Greater Flamingoes
Some 10,000 pairs of these exotic, bright pink birds breed in the Camargue. They are often seen feeding on the marshes of the Etang de Vaccarès, although their main breeding ground is on the saltier lagoons towards the south.

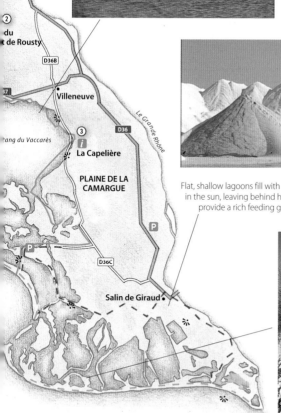

The Salt Industry
Flat, shallow lagoons fill with sea water, which then evaporates in the sun, leaving behind huge salt deposits. These expanses provide a rich feeding ground for waders such as avocets.

Dune Vegetation
The sand dunes form a line between the lagoons and salt marshes and the sea. Among the many wild flowers that grow here is sea chamomile.

Key

— Nature reserve boundary

- - Walking routes

- - Walking and cycling routes

0 kilometres 5
0 miles 5

Exploring the Camargue

The unique character of the Camargue has given rise to unusual traditions. The native white horses and black bulls are ranched by *manadiers* and herded, branded and tended by the region's cowboys, or *gardians*, whose small, low, whitewashed houses dot the landscape. Local bullfights are advertised in Saintes-Maries-de-la-Mer, the main tourist centre of the region and chief place to stay, also renowned for its gypsy population. It has a sandy beach and offers watersports and boat trips. Tourist offices throughout the area provide information on walks, but the best views are from the 7-km (5-mile) footway and cycle path along the Digues-de-la-Mer (sea dyke) from the town. Several sights within the Camargue have been turned into museums and exhibitions of local life and natural history. Several ranches and activity centres organize rides and riding holidays.

A bloodless Camargue bullfight in Méjanes

A place of pilgrimage

The three Marys who gave Saintes-Maries-de-la-Mer its name are Mary Magdalene, Mary Jacobe (the Virgin Mary's sister) and Mary Salome, mother of the apostles James and John. Set adrift after the Crucifixion with, among others, their servant Sara, Saint Martha and her brother Lazarus, they landed here in their boat. They built a shrine to the virgin, and while the others went to spread the word of the gospel, Mary Jacobe, Mary Salome and Sara stayed behind.

In winter, the town is an unpretentious, low-rise resort. It overflows during the May and October festivals, when Mary Salome and Mary Jacobe are celebrated, their statues marched to the sea to be blessed. The larger festival is in May, when gypsies from all over the world come to pay homage to their patron saint, Sara, the black Madonna who lies in the crypt of the 9th-century **Eglise de Notre-Dame-de-la-Mer**. An effigy is also paraded through the streets.

Eglise de Notre-Dame-de-la-Mer, in Saintes-Maries-de-la-Mer

Afterwards there are bullfights, horse races and flamenco dances (see pp228–9). The church is also worth visiting for the view from its rooftop walkway.

Throughout the centre of the town are cheery restaurants with checked tablecloths, and shops selling patterned skirts, shirts and scarves, lucky charms and Romany souvenirs.

Still in the Saintes-Maries area, 4.5 km (3 miles) north of the centre on the banks of the Etang de Ginès, lies the **Parc Ornithologique du Pont-de-Gau**, with a vast range of Camargue birdlife (see p140).

⬛ Eglise de Notre-Dame-de-la-Mer

19 pl Jean XXIII. Church: **Tel** 04 90 97 80 25. **Open** daily. Walkway: **Open** Apr–Nov & school hols: daily; Dec–Mar: Wed, Sat & Sun pm. ⬛ 6pm Tue–Sat, 10:30am Sun. ⬛ for walkway.

The church dates back to the 4th century, but has been destroyed and rebuilt due to excavations of the saints and its early (and valuable) relics. These are all on display here. The population of the village increases dramatically during the summer and the great pilgrimages. Over 200,000 pilgrims and visitors enter the "Door of Faith" every year. Pilgrims are welcomed and offered guided tours.

⬛ Domaine de la Palissade

13129 Salin de Giraud. **Tel** 04 42 86 81 28. **Open** Feb & Nov: Wed–Sun; Mar–Oct: daily. ⬛

This natural reserve boasts rich flora and fauna, which can be explored either on foot, through walks ranging from 30 minutes to 3 and a half hours in duration, or on a Camargue horse.

⬛ Parc Ornithologique du Pont-de-Gau

RD 570, Pont-de-Gau **Tel** 04 90 97 82 62. **Open** daily. **Closed** 25 Dec. ⬛ ⬛ ⬛ ⬛ parcornithologique.com

Most of the birds that live in or migrate through the region are represented in this reserve. Huge aviaries house birds that might otherwise be hard to spot. Try to keep to the signposted paths to avoid damage or disturbance (see p140).

🏛 Musée de la Camargue

Parc Naturel Régional de Camargue,
Mas du Pont de Rousty. (On the D570,
10 km south west of Arles). **Tel** 04 90 97
10 82. **Open** Wed–Mon. **Closed** Jan,
1 May, 25 Dec, Nov–Dec: Sat & Sun. 🦽 📷 **w** museedelacamargue.com

A traditional Provençal *mas* or
farmhouse *(see pp26–7)*, that
only a short time ago was part
of a farm raising cattle and
sheep, has been converted
to accommodate a fascinating
museum of the Camargue.
The main part of the museum
is housed in a huge sheep
barn, built in 1812 and skilfully
restored. Displays, including
video footage and slide shows,
provide an excellent introduction to traditional life in the
Camargue and to the unique
plant and animal life of the
Camargue delta. Among the
many subjects covered are the
lives of the Camargue cowboys,
and the *grand* and *petit* Rhône
rivers which once flowed far to
the east past Nîmes. Many of
the displays are focused on
traditional life at the time of
poet and champion of the
Provençal language, Frédéric
Mistral, *(see p32)*, a local man
who won the Nobel Prize for
literature in 1904.

A signposted 3.5-km (2-mile)
nature trail leads out from the
museum to the Marré de la
Grand Mare and back again by a
pleasant circular route. Examples
of traditional *mas* husbandry
are marked on the way. An
observation tower at the end of
the walk gives great views over
the surrounding countryside.

Honey buzzard enclosure at the
Pont-de-Gau bird sanctuary

The fine Romanesque façade of the abbey church at St-Gilles-du-Gard

❽ St-Gilles-du-Gard

Road map A3. 🔼 13,838. 🚌 Nîmes
ℹ 1 place F Mistral (04 66 87 33 75).
🕑 Thu & Sun. **w** tourisme.saint-
gilles.fr

Called the "Gateway to the
Camargue", St-Gilles is famous
for its **Abbaye de St-Gilles.** In
medieval times the abbey was
vast. The building was damaged
in 1562 during the Wars of
Religion and all that remains are
the west façade, chancel and
crypt. The carved façade is the
most beautiful in all Provence.
It includes the first sculpture
of the Passion in Christendom,
from the late 12th century.

Founded by Raymond VI
of Toulouse, the abbey
church was the Knights of
St John's first priory in Europe.
It soon became one of the key
destinations on the pilgrimage
route to Santiago de Compostela
in Spain and a port of embarkation
for the Crusades *(see pp46–7)*.
The crypt houses the tomb
of Saint Gilles, a hermit who
arrived by raft from Greece.

The belltower of the original
abbey contains *La Vis*, a spiral
staircase which is a masterpiece of stonemasonry.

❾ Beaucaire

Road map B3. 🔼 16,000. 🚆 Tarascon.
🚌 **ℹ** 24 cours Gambetta (04 66 59
26 57). 🕑 Thu & Sun. **w** provence-
camargue-tourisme.com

The bullring in Beaucaire
occupies the site of one of the
largest fairs in Europe. Held

The unique troglodyte Abbaye de
Saint-Roman near Beaucaire

every July for the past seven
centuries, it attracted up to a
quarter of a million people. A
smaller version of the fair takes
place today, with a procession
through the town on 21 July.

It was inaugurated by
Raymond VI in 1217, who
enlarged the **Château de
Beaucaire.** This was later used by
the French kings to look down on
their Provençal neighbours across
the river. It was partly dismantled
on the orders of Cardinal
Richelieu but the triangular keep
and enough of the walls remain
to indicate its impressive scale.
There is a Romanesque chapel
within the walls, and medieval
spectacles, including frequent
displays of falconry.

The **Abbaye de St-Roman**
is situated 5 km (3 miles) to the
northwest of Beaucaire. Dating
from the 5th century, it is the only
troglodyte monastery in Europe.

🏰 Château de Beaucaire

Place Raymond VII. **Tel** 04 66 59 90 07.
Open Wed–Sun (Jul–Aug: daily). 📷

The legendary Tarasque, the terror of Tarascon

⑩ Tarascon

Road map B3. 🏛 13,600. 🚉 🚌
ⓘ Ave de la République (04 90 91
03 52). 🛍 Tue & Fri. 🗼 **tarascon.fr**

The gleaming white vision of
the **Château Royal de Provence**
is one of the landmarks of
the Rhône. Little is left of the
glittering court of Good King
René who finished the building
his father, Louis II of Anjou, began early in the 15th century
(see pp50–51). Following René's
death in 1480, Provence fell to
France, and the castle became a
prison until 1926. A drawbridge
leads to the poultry yard and
garrison quarters. Beside it rises
the impressive main castle,
centred on a courtyard from
where two spiral staircases
lead to royal apartments and
other rooms in its sturdy
towers. Prisoners' graffiti and
some painted ceiling panels
remain, but the only adornment
is a handful of borrowed
17th-century tapestries which
depict the deeds of Roman
general Scipio (237–183 BC).

The **Collégiale Ste-Marthe,**
nearby has a tomb in the crypt
to the monster-taming saint.
According to legend, St Martha
(see p46) rescued the inhabitants from the Tarasque, a
man-eating monster, half lion,
half armadillo, which gave the
town its name. The event is
celebrated each June in the
Fête de la Tarasque (see p37).

In the old town is the 16th-
century Cloître des Cordeliers
where exhibitions are held. On
the arcaded Rue des Halles is
the 17th-century town hall, with
a carved façade and balcony.

The fairy-tale Château de Tarascon,
stronghold of Good King René

The traditional life of the area
and its hand-printed fabrics is
seen in the **Musée Souleïado**.
The ancient textile industry was
revived in 1938, under the name
Souleïado, meaning "the sun
passing through the clouds" in
Provençal. In the museum are
40,000 18th-century woodblocks,
many of them still used for the
company's colourful prints.

The **Musée d'Art et d'Histoire**,
housed in the Couvent des
Cordeliers, covers the history of
the Fête de la Tarasque, and also
holds temporary art exhibitions.

🏠 **Château Royal de Provence**
Blvd du Roi René. **Tel** 04 90 91 01 93.
Open daily. **Closed** 1 Jan, 1 May, 1 &
11 Nov, 25 Dec. 🖼 🕙 📷
🗼 **chateau.tarascon.fr**

🏛 **Musée Souleïado**
39 rue Charles Deméry. **Tel** 04 90 91
08 80. **Open** Mon–Sat. **Closed** 1 Jan,
1 & 11 Nov, 25 Dec. 🖼 📷 Wed.

🏛 **Musée d'Art et d'Histoire**
Pl Frédéric Mistral. **Tel** 04 90 91 38 71.
Open May & Oct–Jan: Mon–Fri; Jun–
Sep: Tue–Fri & Sat pm.

⑪ St-Rémy-de-Provence

Road map B3. 🏛 10,600. 🚌 Avignon.
ⓘ Pl Jean-Jaurès (04 90 92 05 22).
🛍 Wed & Sat. 🗼 **saintremy-de-provence.com**

St-Rémy is ideal for exploring
the Alpilles countryside which
supplies the plants for its traditional herboristeries, or herb shops.
In nearby Graveson, the **Musée
des Arômes et du Parfum**
displays implements of their craft.

St-Rémy's **Eglise St-Martin**
contains an exceptional organ,
which can be heard during the
summer festival "Organa", or on
Saturday recitals.

One of the town's most
attractive 15th–16th-century
mansions is now a museum.
The **Musée des Alpilles** has a fine
ethnographic collection. The well-
known 16th-century physician
and astrologer, Nostradamus,
was born in a house in the outer
wall of the avenue Hoche, in
the old quarter of St-Rémy.

The **Musée Estrine Centre**, in
the 18th-century Hôtel Estrine,
houses modern and contemporary art. Temporary exhibits pay
tribute to Van Gogh's relationship
with St-Rémy. In May 1889, after
he had mutilated his ear, Van
Gogh arrived at the **Cloître et
Cliniques de St-Paul de Mausole**,
which is situated between the
town and Glanum. The grounds
and the 12th-century monastery
house a museum and culture
centre in which an entire wing
is dedicated to the painter's stay.
You can visit a reconstruction
of Van Gogh's room and the
field that he painted 15 times.

Just behind the clinic is Le Mas
de la Pyramide, a farmstead half-
built into the rock, which was
once a Roman quarry. The

Herbs and spices on sale in St-Rémy
market, place de la République

The triumphal arch at the Site Archéologique de Glanum, built in the reign of Augustus, a 15-minute walk from the centre of St-Rémy

remains of the earliest Greek houses in Provence, from the 4th-century BC, are in **Site Archéologique de Glanum** *(see p44)*, a Greco-Roman town at the head of a valley in the Alpilles. Dramatic memorials, known as Les Antiques, still stand along the roadside – a triumphal arch from 10 BC, celebrating Caesar's conquest of the Greeks and Gaul, and a mausoleum dating from about 30 BC.

🏛 Musée des Arômes et du Parfum
Ancien chemin d'Arles, Graveson-en-Provence. **Tel** 04 90 95 81 72. **Open** daily. **Closed** 1 Jan, 1 May, 25 Dec. 🅰 📷 **W** museedesaromes.com

🏛 Musée des Alpilles
Place Favier. **Tel** 04 90 92 68 24. **Open** May–Sep: Tue–Sun; Oct–Apr: Tue–Sat pm only. **Closed** 1 Jan, 1 May, 25 Dec. 📷

🏛 Musée Estrine Centre
8 rue Estrine. **Tel** 04 90 92 34 72. **Open** Tue–Sun (Mar & Nov: pm only). **Closed** Dec–Feb. 📷 🅰 restricted. **W** musee-estrine.fr

🏛 Cloître et Cliniques de St-Paul de Mausole
Chemin St-Paul. **Tel** 04 90 92 77 00. **Open** Mar–Dec: daily. **Closed** public hols. 📷 🅰 **W** saintpauldemausole.fr

🏛 Site Archéologique de Glanum
Rte des Baux. **Tel** 04 90 92 35 07. **Open** Apr–Sep: daily; Oct–Mar: Tue–Sun. **Closed** 1 Jan, 1 May, 1 & 11 Nov, 25 Dec. 📷 🅰 📷 **W** site-glanum.fr

⑫ Les Alpilles

Road map B3. 🚃 Arles, Tarascon, Salon-de-Provence. 🚌 Les Baux-de-Provence, St-Rémy-de-Provence, Eyguières, Eygalières. ℹ️ St-Rémy-de-Provence (04 90 92 05 22).

St-Rémy-de-Provence is on the western side of the limestone massif of Les Alpilles, a 24-km (15-mile) chain between the Rhône and Durance rivers. A high point is **La Caume**, at 387 m (1,270 ft), reached from St-Rémy, just beyond Glanum.

East of St-Rémy, the road to Cavaillon runs along the north side of the massif, with a right turn to Eygalières. The painter Mario Prassinos

(1916–85) lived here. Just beyond the village is the 12th-century Chapelle St-Sixte.

The road continues towards Orgon where there are views across the Durance Valley and the Luberon. Orgon skirts the massif on the eastern side. A right turn leads past the ruins of Castelas de Roquemartine and Eyguières, a pleasant village with a Romanesque church. It is a two-hour walk to Les Opiés, a 493-m (1,617-ft) hill crowned by a tower. This forms part of the GR6 which crosses the chain to Les Baux, one of the best walking routes in Provence. From Castelas de Roquemartine the road heads back west towards Les Baux.

The chalky massif of Les Alpilles, "Little Alps", in the heart of Provence

A late 18th-century fresco showing the Baux warriors in battle against the Saracens in 1266

⑱ Les Baux-de-Provence

Road map B3. 🏛 470. 🚌 🛈 La Maison du Roy (04 90 54 34 39). 🅦 lesbauxdeprovence.com

Les Baux sits on a spur of the Alpilles (*bau* in Provençal means escarpment) and the historic **Château des Baux** has views across to the Camargue (*see pp140–43*). The most dramatic fortress site in Provence, it has nearly two million visitors a year, so avoid midsummer, or go early in the morning. The pedestrianized town has a car park beside the Porte Mage gate.

When the Lords of Baux built their fine citadel here in the 10th century, they claimed one of the three wise men, King Balthazar, as an ancestor and took the star of Bethlehem as their emblem. These fierce warriors originated the troubadour Courts of Love and wooed noble ladies with poetry and songs. This became the medieval convention known as courtly love and paved the way for a literary tradition.

The citadel ruins lie on the heights of the escarpment. Their entrance is via the 14th-century Tour-du-Brau. A plateau extends to the end of the escarpment, where there is a monument to the poet Charloun Rieu (1846–1924). In the town centre, two other museums of local interest are

Monument to poet Charloun Rieu

the **Fondation Louis Jou** and the **Musée des Santons**. Next door to the 12th-century Eglise St-Vincent is the Chapelle des Pénitents Blancs, decorated in 1974 by the local artist Yves Brayer. Just north of Les Baux lies the **Carrières de Lumières**.

🏰 Château des Baux
Tel 04 90 54 55 56. **Open** daily.
🅦 chateau-baux-provence.com
This majestic fortified castle offers breathtaking views of the surrounding region from Aix to Arles.

🏛 Fondation Louis Jou
Hôtel Brion, Grande Rue. **Tel** 04 90 54 34 17. **Open** by appt. 🎟
Medieval books are housed here, along with a collection of prints and drawings by Dürer, Goya and Jou, the local engraver after whom the museum is named.

🏛 Musée des Santons
La Maison du Roy. **Tel** 04 90 54 34 39. **Open** daily.
In the 16th-century old town hall, a Provençal crib scene has been created, representing the nativity at Les Baux. Handmade clay *santons* or figurines (*see p52*), representing saints and local figures, show the evolution of Provençal costume.

🏛 Carrières de Lumières
Route de Maillane. **Tel** 04 90 54 47 37. **Open** daily. **Closed** mid-Jan–Feb. 🎟 🅖 🅦 carrieres-lumieres.com
Located on the D27 road to the north of Les Baux and within walking distance of the main car park in Les Baux is the Val d'Enfer or the Valley of Hell. This jagged gorge, said to be inhabited by witches and spirits, may have inspired some of Dante's poetry. It is also the site where bauxite was discovered in 1822 by the mineralogist Berthier, who named it after the town. It was in this big quarry that the Cathédrale d'Images

View of the citadel and village of Les Baux

or presently, the Carrières de Lumières was established. The imaginative slide show is projected not only onto the white limestone walls of the natural theatre, but also the floor and ceiling, creating a three dimensional effect. The 35-minute show is renewed each year. Accompanied by captivating music, it is an extraordinary audio-visual experience.

Les Baux's Chapelle des Pénitents, next to the Eglise St-Vincent

⑭ Fontvieille

Road map B3. 🗺 3,700. 🚌 🚉
ⓘ Ave des Moulins (04 90 54 67 49).
🗓 Mon & Fri. 🌐 **fontvieille-provence.com**

Fontvieille is an agreeable country town in the flat fruit and vegetable lands of the irrigated Baux Valley. Halfway between Arles and Les Alpilles, the town makes an excellent centre from which to explore. Until the French Revolution in 1789, the town's history was

bound up with the Abbaye de Montmajour. The oratories that stand at the four corners of the small town were erected in 1721 to celebrate the end of the plague *(see pp52–3)*.

To the south on the D33, set on a stony hill is the Moulin de Daudet and further on at Barbegal are the remarkable remains of a Roman aqueduct.

⑮ Abbaye de Montmajour

Road map B3. Route de Fontvieille. **Tel** 04 90 54 64 17. **Open** Apr–Sep: daily; Oct–Mar: Tue–Sun. **Closed** 1 Jan, 1 May, 1 & 11 Nov, 25 Dec. ♿ ♿

Standing out like Noah's ark on Mount Ararat, 5 km (3 miles) northwest of Arles, this Benedictine abbey was built in the 10th century. At the time, the site was an island refuge in marshland. The handful of monks in residence spent all their spare time draining this area of marshland between the Alpilles chain and the Rhône.

The abbey is an imposing place, though all the Baroque buildings were destroyed by fire in 1726 and never restored. The original church is said to have been founded by Saint Trophime as a sanctuary from the Romans. It grew rich in the Middle Ages when thousands of pilgrims arrived at Easter to purchase pardons. After 1791, the abbey was broken up by two successive owners who bought it from the state. The

The cloisters and keep of the Abbaye de Montmajour

abbey was largely restored in the 19th century.

The **Eglise Notre-Dame** is one of the largest Romanesque buildings in Provence. Below, the 12th-century crypt has been built into the sloping hill. The cloister has double pillars ornamented with beasts and lies in the shadows of the 26-m (85-ft) tower, built in the 1360s. It is worth climbing the 124 steps to the tower platform to see the stunning view across to the sea. Also carved into the hillside is the atmospheric **Chapelle de St-Pierre**. It was established at the same time as the abbey and is a primitive place of worship. There are a number of tombs in the abbey grounds, but the principal burial area is the 12th-century **Chapelle Ste-Croix**. It lies not far to the east and is built in the shape of a Greek cross.

Daudet's Windmill

The Moulin de Daudet is one of the most famous literary landmarks in France. Alphonse Daudet was born in Nîmes in 1840 and made his name in Paris. The windmill is the setting of Daudet's *Letters from my Windmill*, stories about Provençal life, first published in 1860 and popular ever since. He observed the local characters and wrote about their lives with irony and pathos. He never actually lived in the mill, but made imaginative use of some of the resident miller's tales. When he stayed in Fontvieille he was a guest in the 19th-century Château de Montauban. He came to find respite from the capital, but returned there in order to write his stories. The mill cannot be visited, but there is a small museum located in the château dedicated to Daudet.

⑯ Street-by-Street: Arles

Many tourist sites in Arles bear the stamp of their Roman past, and all are within comfortable walking distance of the central place de la République. On its north side is the Hôtel de Ville, behind which is the place du Forum. This square is the heart of modern life in Arles. Another place to sit at a café and observe the Arlésiens is the boulevard des Lices, where the lively twice-weekly market is held. Some of the shops here and in nearby rue Jean-Jaurès sell bright Provençal fabrics. For museum-buffs, an inclusive ticket (*Passeport Avantage*) gives access to all the museums (except temporary exhibits) and monuments (except Abbaye de Montmajour).

Les Thermes de Constantin are all that remain of Constantine's Palace, built in the 4th century AD.

Musée Réattu
This museum on the banks of the Rhône houses 18th–19th century and modern art, including this figure of *Le Griffu* (1952) by Germaine Richier.

Hôtel de Ville

Cryptoportico
These three, vaulted subterranean galleries, from the 1st century BC, were built as foundations for the forum. Access is via the Hôtel de Ville.

★ **Eglise St-Trophime**
This fine Romanesque church has a 12th-century portal of the *Last Judgment*, including saints and apostles.

L'Espace Van Gogh, a cultural centre

Roman Obelisk
An ancient obelisk with fountains at its base (one of which is shown here) stands in the place de la République. It came from the Roman circus across the Rhône.

0 metres   100
0 yards   100

★ **Les Arènes**
This is one of the largest,
best-preserved Roman
monuments in Provence.
The top tier provides an
excellent panoramic view
of Arles.

VISITORS' CHECKLIST

Practical Information
Road map B3. 53,500.
Blvd des Lices (04 90 18 41 20).
Wed, Sat. Feria de Pâques
(Easter); Fête des Gardians (1 May);
Fêtes d'Arles (Jul); Feria du Riz (Sep).
arlestourisme.com

Transport
Nîmes-Garons.
Ave P Talabot.

★ **Théâtre Antique**
Once a fortress, its stones
were later used for other
buildings. These last
remaining columns are
called the "two widows".

RUE DE GRILLE
TEMBRE
RUE BARBES
ISSES
RUE ARISTIDE BRIAND
RUE A TARDIEU
OLAI RUE BALECHOU
ROND-POINT DES ARENES
RUE DE LA BASTILLE
RUE DIDEROT
RUE DE LA CALADE
PLACE DE
LA MAJOR
RUE DU GRAND COUVENT
RUE DE LA MADELEINE
RUE DU CLOITRE
RUE PORTE DE LAURE
MONTEE VAUBAN
BOULEVARD DES LICES

**Eglise Notre-Dame-
de-la-Major** is
dedicated to Saint
George, patron saint
of the Camargue
gardians (cowboys).

**Cloister of
St-Trophime**
This sculpted capital
is a fine example
of the Romanesque
beauty of the cloister.

Van Gogh in Arles

Vincent Van Gogh painted
over 300 canvases in the 15
months he lived in Arles, but
the town has none of his work.
In belated appreciation of this
lonely artist, the Hôtel-Dieu
has been turned into L'Espace
Van Gogh, with a library and
exhibition space. Several sites
are evocative of him, however;
the Café Van Gogh in the
place du Forum has been
renovated to look as it did
in his *Café du Soir*.

Courtyard of L'Espace Van Gogh, formerly
known as Hôtel-Dieu

Key

— Suggested route

Exploring Arles

The city of Arles was a Greek site expanded by the Romans into a "little Rome". Here, on the most southerly crossing point on the Rhône, they built shipyards, baths, a racetrack and an arena. Then the capital of the three Gauls – France, Spain and Britain – Arles remains one of the most distinctive towns in Provence with fine relics from its Gallo-Roman past. Cars should be parked outside the narrow lanes of the old town.

Sarcophagi in the historic cemetary of Les Alyscamps

🏛 Les Arènes
Rond-point des Arènes. **Tel** 04 90 49 59 05. **Open** daily. **Closed** 1 Jan, 1 May, 1 Nov, 25 Dec & for bullfights and events. 🐾 🎧 🅦 **arenes-arles.com**

The most impressive of the surviving Roman monuments, the amphitheatre is on the east side of the old town. It was the largest of the Roman buildings in Gaul. Slightly oval, it measures 136 m (446 ft) by 107 m (351 ft) and could seat 20,000. Mosaics decorated the floors of some internal rooms, the better to wash down after bloody affrays. Today Spanish and Provençal bullfights are held regularly in the arena.

Just to the southwest of the amphitheatre is the elegant Roman **Théâtre Antique**, which has 2,000 tiered seats arranged in a hemisphere.

🏛 Musée Départemental de l'Arles Antique
Presqu'île du Cirque Romain. **Tel** 04 13 31 51 03. **Open** Wed–Mon. **Closed** 1 Jan, 1 May, 1 Nov, 25 Dec. 🐾 🅷 📷 🅦 **arles-antique.cg13.fr**

Arles became Christian after Constantine's conversion in AD 312. This museum displays fine examples of Romano-Christian sculpture, while a wing opened in 2013 houses a Roman flat-bottomed barge, rescued from the Rhône riverbed.

🏛 Cryptoportico
Place de la République. **Tel** 04 90 49 38 20. **Open** daily (mid-May–Oct). **Closed** 1 Jan, 1 May, 1 Nov, 25 Dec. 🐾 🅦 **patrimoine.ville-arles.fr**

These huge subterranean galleries (see p45), ventilated by air shafts, were part of the forum's structure.

🏛 Les Alyscamps
Ave des Alyscamps. **Tel** 04 90 49 38 20. **Open** daily. **Closed** 1 Jan, 1 May, 1 Nov, 25 Dec. 🐾 🅷

From Roman to late Medieval times, Les Alyscamps was one of the largest and most famous cemeteries in the Western world. Romans avoided it at night, making it an ideal meeting place for early Christians, led by St Trophime. Christians were often buried by the tomb of Genesius, a Roman servant and beheaded Christian martyr.

🏛 Eglise St-Trophime
Place de la République. **Tel** 04 90 96 07 38. **Open** daily. **Closed** 1 Jan, 1 May, 1 Nov, 25 Dec. 🐾 cloisters. 🎧 🅷 🅦 **patrimoine.ville-arles.fr**

This is one of the most beautiful Romanesque churches in Provence. The portal and cloisters are decorated with biblical scenes. St Trophime, thought to be the first bishop of Arles in the early 3rd century, appears with St Peter and St John on the carved northeast pillar.

🏛 Les Thermes de Constantin
Rue du Grand-Prieuré. **Tel** 04 90 49 38 20. **Open** daily. **Closed** 1 Jan, 1 May, 1 Nov, 25 Dec. 🐾

Built by the Roman emperor Constantine in 306 AD, these once vast public baths fell into ruin, but were partially restored at the end of the 19th century. The three remaining original buildings attest to the ingenuity of Roman engineering.

🏛 Musée Réattu
10 rue du Grand-Prieuré. **Tel** 04 90 49 37 58. **Open** Tue–Sun. **Closed** 1 Jan, 1 May, 1 & 11 Nov, 25 Dec. 🐾 🅦 **museereattu.arles.fr**

The local artist Jacques Réattu (1760–1833) and his contemporaries form the basis of this collection. A Picasso donation and a photographic display are among 20th-century works.

🏛 Fondation Vincent van Gogh Arles
35 rue du Dr Fanton. **Tel** 04 90 93 08 08. **Open** Tue–Sun (Apr–Sep: daily). 🐾 🅷 🅦 **fondation-vincent vangogh-arles.org**

Housed in the 15th-century Hôtel Léautaud de Donines, this museum has a dynamic collection of the artist's paintings as well as contemporary artworks highlighting van Gogh's influence on 20th- and 21st-century artists.

View of Arles from the opposite bank of the Rhône

⑰ Martigues

Road map B4. 📷 48,200. 🚗 🚌
ℹ Rond Point de l'Hôtel de Ville
(04 42 42 31 10). 🛍 Thu & Sun.
🌐 martigues-tourisme.com

The Etang de Berre, situated between Marseille and the Camargue, has the largest petroleum refinery industry in France, which dominates the landscape. However, on the inland side of the Canal de Caronte is the former fishing port and artists' colony of Martigues, which still attracts a holiday crowd.

Martigues lies on both banks of the canal and on the island of Brescon, where the Pont San Sébastien is a popular place for artists to set up their easels. Félix Ziem (1821–1911) was the most ardent admirer of this "little Venice" *(see p30)*; his paintings and works by contemporary artists can be viewed in the **Musée Ziem**.

🏛 Musée Ziem

Blvd du 14 Juillet. **Tel** 04 42 41 39 60.
Open Wed–Sun pm (Jul Aug: Wed Mon). **Closed** public hols.

Canal San Sébastien in Martigues, known as the Birds' Looking-Glass

⑱ Salon-de-Provence

Road map B3. 📷 44,500. 🚗
🚌 ℹ 249 pl Morgan (04 90 56 27 60). 🛍 Wed & Sun.
🌐 visitsalondeprovence.com

Known for its olives (the olive oil industry was established in the 1400s) and soap, Salon-de-Provence is dominated by the castellated **Château de l'Empéri**. Once home of the archbishops

The 12th-century Cistercian Abbaye de Silvacane

of Arles, this now contains the Musée de l'Empéri, which has a large collection of militaria from Louis XIV to World War I.

The military tradition in the town is upheld by the French Air Force officers' college, La Patrouille Aérienne de France.

Near the château is the 13th-century **Eglise de St-Michel** and in the north of the old town is the Gothic **St-Laurent**, where the French physician and astrologer Nostradamus, Salon's most famous citizen, is buried. Here, in his adopted home, he wrote *Les Centuries*, his book of predictions, published in 1555. It was banned by the Vatican, as it foretold the diminishing power of the papacy. But his renown was widespread and in 1560 he was made Charles IX's physician.

Salon hosts a 10-day classical music festival, from late July to August, with concerts in the château, Eglise de St-Michel, Abbaye de Sainte-Croix and the town's theatre.

Nostradamus, astrologer and citizen of Salon

🏰 Château de l'Empéri

Montée du Puech. **Tel** 04 90 44 72 80.
Open Tue–Sun pm. **Closed** 1 Jan, 1 May, 1 Nov, 24–25 Dec, 31 Dec. 🖼

⑲ Abbaye de Silvacane

Road map C3. **Tel** 04 42 50 41 69.
Open Jun–Sep: daily; Oct–May: Tue–Sun. **Closed** 1 Jan, 1 May, 25 Dec. 🖼
🏠 🌐 abbaye-silvacane.com

Like her two Cistercian sisters, Silvacane is a harmonious 12th-century monastery tucked away in the countryside. A bus from Aix-en-Provence runs regularly to Roque-d'Anthéron, the nearest village. The abbey was founded on the site of a Benedictine monastery, in a clearing of a "forest of reeds" *(silva canorum)*. It adheres to the austere Cistercian style, with no decoration. The church, with nave, two aisles and a high, vaulted transept, is solid, bare and echoing. The cloisters, arcaded like a pigeon loft, are 13th century and the refectory 14th century. Shortly after the refectory was built, all the monks left and the church served the parish. After the Revolution, it was sold as state property and became a farm until transformed back into an abbey.

⑳ Aix-en-Provence

Provence's former capital is an international students' town, with one of the region's most cosmopolitan streets of restaurants and bars, rue de la Verrerie. The university was founded by Louis II of Anjou in 1409 and flourished under his son, Good King René (see pp50–51). Another wave of prosperity transformed the city in the 17th century, when ramparts, first raised by the Romans in their town of Aquae Sextiae, were pulled down, and the mansion-lined cours Mirabeau was built. Aix's renowned fountains were added in the 18th century.

The cours Mirabeau, grandest of Aix's boulevards

Exploring Aix

North of the cours Mirabeau, between the **Cathédrale St-Sauveur** and the place d'Albertas, lies the town's old quarter. Sights include the **Musée du Palais de l'Archevêché**, housed in the former Bishop's palace, and the 17th-century Hôtel de Ville. Built around a courtyard by Pierre Pavillon, it stands in a square now used as a flower market. Nearby is the 16th-century clock tower.

Just outside the old town are the ancient Roman baths, the **Thermes Sextius**, and nearby is the 18th-century spa complex.

Aix's finest street, the cours Mirabeau, is named after the orator and revolutionary Comte de Mirabeau. At its western end is the Fontaine de la Rotonde, a cast-iron fountain built in 1860. The north side is lined with shops, pâtisseries and cafés, the most illustrious being the 18th-century Les Deux Garçons (see p219). The south side is lined with elegant mansions: No. 4, Hôtel de Villars (1710); No. 10, the Hôtel d'Isoard de Vauvenargues (1710), former residence of the Marquis of Entrecasteau who murdered his wife here; No. 19, Hôtel d'Arbaud

Jouques (1730); No. 20, Hôtel de Forbin (1656); and Hôtel d'Espagnet at No. 38, once home to the Duchess of Montpensier, known as "La Grande Mademoiselle", niece of Louis XIII. South of the cours Mirabeau is the Quartier Mazarin built during the time of Archbishop Michel Mazarin. Aix's first Gothic church, St-Jean-de-Malte, now houses the **Musée Granet**. The museum has also been expanded into the Chapelle des Pénitents Blancs, a few steps away from the original building.

The splendid 17th-century Hôtel de Ville, with the flower market in front

🏛 Cathédrale St-Sauveur

34 pl des Martyrs de la Résistance. **Tel** 04 42 23 45 65. **Open** daily (timings vary, call ahead). 🚫 for cloisters. 🌐 **cathedrale-aix.net**

The cathedral at the top of the old town creaks with history. The main door has solid walnut panels sculpted by Jean Guiramand (1504). On the right there is a fine 4th–5th-century baptistry, with a Renaissance cupola standing on 2nd-century Corinthian columns. These are from a basilica which stood here beside the Roman forum. The jewel of the church is the triptych of *The Burning Bush* (1476, see pp50–51) by Nicolas Froment. South of the cathedral are tiled Romanesque cloisters.

🏛 Musée du Palais de l'Archevêché

Ancien Palais de l'Archevêché, 28 place des Martyrs de la Résistance. **Tel** 04 42 23 09 91. **Open** Wed–Mon. **Closed** 1 May, 25 Dec. 🚫

Apart from magnificent 17th- and 18th-century Beauvais tapestries, the museum has costumes and stage designs from 1948 onwards, used in the annual Festival International d'Art Lyrique (see p37).

🏛 Musée Estienne de Saint-Jean (Vieil Aix)

17 rue Gaston de Saporta. **Tel** 04 42 91 89 78. **Open** Wed–Mon. 🚫

This eclectic collection includes furniture, a 19th-century crèche parlante and figures from the Corpus Christi parade commissioned by King René.

🏛 Hôtel de Caumont Centre d'Art

3 rue Joseph Cabassol. **Tel** 04 42 20 70 01. **Open** daily. 🚫 ♿ 🔲 🌐 **caumont-centredart.com**

Housed in an 18th-century hotel, the Caumont Art Centre hosts temporary art exhibitions and a programme of concerts and lectures. A film on Paul Cézanne's life in Aix is also screened daily.

🏛 Musée Granet

Pl St-Jean de Malte. **Tel** 04 42 52 88 32. **Open** Tue–Sun. **Closed** 1 Jan, 1 May, 25 Dec. 🚫 🎫 🚫 🌐 **museegranet-aixenprovence.fr**

The city's main museum is in a 17th-century former priory of the

Cézanne's studio, filled with his furniture and personal belongings

VISITORS' CHECKLIST

Practical Information
Road map C4. ᴍ 145,000.
ℹ 300 ave Giuseppe Verdi
(04 42 16 11 61). 🏠 daily.
🎭 Fest d'Art Lyrique (Jun–Jul).
🔲 aixenprovencetourism.com

Transport
🚉 Ave Victor Hugo. 🚌 Ave de
l'Europe

Knights of Malta. François Granet (1775–1849), a local artist, bequeathed his collection of French, Italian and Flemish paintings to Aix, including Ingres' *Portrait of Granet* and *Jupiter and Thetis*. There are also works by Granet and other Provençal painters, eight canvases by Paul Cézanne, plus artifacts from Roman Aix.

🏛 Fondation Vasarely
1 ave Marcel Pagnol. **Tel** 04 42 20 01 09. **Open** daily. **Closed** 1 Jan, 24, 25 & 26 Dec. 🌀 🛗 ground floor. 📷 🎥 🔲
🔲 fondationvasarely.org

This series of innovative black-and-white metal hexagons was designed by the king of Op Art Victor Vasarely in the mid-1970s. Alongside his monumental works, the gallery's exhibitions promote art in the city at a national and international level.

🚇 L'Atelier de Cézanne
9 ave Paul Cézanne. **Tel** 04 42 21 06 53. **Open** Mar–Oct: daily; Nov–Feb: Mon–Sat. **Closed** 1 May, 25 Dec. 🌀 📷 🖥 Mar–Oct. 🔲 cezanne-en-provence.com

Ten minutes' walk uphill from the Cathédrale St-Sauveur is the house of renowned artist Paul Cézanne *(see p30)*, who was unfortunately jeered at during his lifetime in his hometown. The studio is much as he left it when he died in 1906. Not far from here you can see the scenic Montagne Ste-Victoire, a favourite subject of the painter.

🏛 Pavillon de Vendôme (Arts Décoratifs)
13 rue de la Molle or 32 rue Célony. **Tel** 04 42 91 88 75. **Open** Wed–Mon. **Closed** Jan, 1 May, 25 Dec. 🌀

One of Aix-en-Provence's grandest houses, built for Cardinal de Vendôme in 1667 and later enlarged, the main entrance is supported by two figures of Atlantes. The beautiful rooms are filled with Provençal furniture and portraits.

Aix-en-Provence

① Cathédrale St-Sauveur
② Musée du Palais de l'Archevêché
③ Musée Estienne de Saint-Jean (Vieil Aix)
④ Hôtel de Caumont Centre d'Art
⑤ Musée Granet
⑥ Pavillon de Vendôme (Arts Décoratifs)

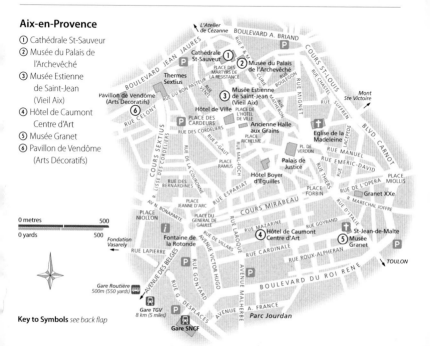

0 metres 500
0 yards 500

Key to Symbols *see back flap*

㉑ Marseille

France's premier port and oldest major city is in a surprisingly attractive setting, centred on the Vieux Port, which fishing boats enter between the guardian forts of St-Jean and St-Nicolas. On the north side are the commercial docks and the old town, rebuilt after World War II. People have lived here for 26 centuries, its mixture of cultures being so varied that Alexandre Dumas called it "the meeting place of the entire world".

Boats moored at Marseille's Vieux Port

Exploring Marseille

Inland, running from the end of the port, is La Canebière – cannabis walk – a big, bustling boulevard which stretches from former hemp fields down to the port where the hemp was made into rope.

At the top of La Canebière is the Neo-Gothic Eglise des Réformés. A left and a right turn lead to boulevard Longchamp, and a walk along its length brings you to the Palais Longchamp. This is not really a palace, but more an impressive folly in the form of a colonnade that fans out around a fountain and ends in two large wings. These wings support a natural history and a fine arts museum.

Behind the palace is the city's zoo. Beyond the grid of shopping streets to the south, the town rises towards the basilica of Notre-Dame-de-la-Garde, which provides an unparalleled view of the city. If you visit the morning fish market on the quai des Belges, you can delight in Marseille's famed *bouillabaisse* (see pp204–5) at one of the many fish restaurants nearby. Just

behind the quai des Belges, at the back of St-Ferréol, is the Jardin des Vestiges, where remains of the Greek settlement, dating from the 4th century BC, have been found.

🏛 La Vieille Charité

2 rue de la Vieille Charité. **Tel** 04 91 14 58 38. **Open** Tue–Sun. **Closed** public hols. 🅿 🏠 💻 🚻 🅆 vieille-charite-marseille.com

The old town's finest building is the Vieille Charité, a large, well-restored hospice designed by Pierre Puget (1620–94), architect

to Louis XIV. Begun in 1671, its original purpose was to house rural migrants. It is centred on a chapel, now used as an exhibition area. The first floor has a rich collection of ancient Egyptian artifacts in the Musée d'Archéologie Méditerranéenne and the second floor displays African and Oceanic art.

🏛 Cathédrale de la Major

Place de la Major. **Tel** 04 91 90 52 87. **Open** Wed–Mon.

The old town descends on the west side to the Cathédrale de la Major, a Neo-Byzantine confection completed in 1893. Its crypt contains the tombs of the bishops of Marseille. Beside it, small and beautiful, is the 11th-century Ancienne Cathédrale de la Major, part of which was sacrificed in the building of the new cathedral. Inside are a reliquary altar of 1073 and a 15th-century altar.

🏛 Musée des Docks Romains

10 place Vivaux. **Tel** 04 91 91 24 62. **Open** Tue–Sun. **Closed** public hols. 🅿 🅆 musee-des-docks-romain. hols.

During post-war rebuilding the Roman docks were uncovered. A small museum, mainly displaying large storage urns once used for wine, grain and oil, occupies the site of the docks, now buried in the foundations of a residential block.

🏛 Musée d'Histoire de Marseille

2 rue Henri Barbusse. **Tel** 04 91 55 36 63. **Open** Tue–Sun. **Closed** public hols. 🅿 🅒 🅆 musee-histoire-marseille-voie-historique.fr

Formerly located at the Centre Bourse, this renovated and

The Palais Longchamps, a 19th-century folly set around a fountain

expanded historical museum now sits on the archaeological site of the Jardin des Vestiges, which has been reclassified as Marseille's ancient sea port. Surrounded by the remains of the port, with its fortifications and docks dating from the 1st century, visitors can follow the paved Roman road leading to the entrance of the museum. The museum retraces the history of the city and its port, from prehistoric times to the present day, around the theme of navigation. There are ten maritime wrecks, including the hull of an important 3rd-century ship and seven ancient Greek and Roman vessels. Other interesting exhibits include medieval ceramics, a relief map of the city as it was in 1848 and sarcophagi unearthed at nearby excavations. A visit to the museum ends with displays on the latest developments in Marseille and predictions about the future of the city.

The Jardin des Vestiges, Greek ruins outside the Musée d'Histoire de Marseille

⊞ Musée Cantini

19 rue Grignan. **Tel** 04 91 54 77 75. **Open** Tue–Sun. **Closed** public hols. 🖼 📷 🔤 culture.marseille.fr

The Musée Cantini is housed in the 17th-century Hôtel de Montgrand. Its collection of 20th-century art, donated along with the building by the sculptor Jules Cantini, includes Fauve, Cubist and Surrealist paintings.

Basilique de Notre-Dame-de-la-Garde in Marseille

⊞ Musée Borély – la Musée des Arts Décoratif, de la Mode et de la Faïence

Château Borély, 134 av Clôt Bey. **Tel** 04 91 55 33 60. **Open** Tue–Sun. **Closed** public hols. 🖼 🔤 🏛 🔤 culture.marseille.fr/patrimoine-culturel/le-château-borély

Château Borély, a masterpiece of 18th-century architecture, now houses an exhibition devoted to decorative arts and furniture, fashion from the 17th century to the present day, and earthenware and ceramics. Outdoor shows and concerts take place in the château's gardens.

⊞ Abbaye de St-Victor

Pl St-Victor. **Tel** 04 96 11 22 60. **Open** daily. 🖼 for crypt. 🔤 saintvictor.net

Marseille's finest piece of religious architecture is St Victor's basilica, between Notre-Dame and the port. This religious fortress belonged to one of the most powerful abbeys in Provence. It was founded in the 5th century by a monk, St Cassian, in honour of St Victor, martyred two centuries earlier. There are crypts containing catacombs, sarcophagi and the cave of St Victor.

On 2 February St-Victor becomes a place of pilgrimage. Boat-shaped cakes are sold to commemorate the legendary arrival in Provence of the Stes-Maries (see p45).

⊞ Basilique de Notre-Dame-de-la-Garde

Rue Fort du Sanctuaire. **Tel** 04 91 13 40 80. **Open** daily. 💻 🔤 notredamedelagarde.com

The basilica of Notre-Dame-de-la-Garde, which dominates the

VISITORS' CHECKLIST

Practical Information
Road map C4. 🗺 960,000. 🚉 11 la Canebière (08 26 50 05 00). 🚌 Mon–Sat. 🎉 Fête de la Chandeleur (2 Feb). 🔤 marseille-tourisme.com

Transport
✈ 25 km (15 miles) NW Marseille. 🚉 🚌 pl Victor Hugo. ⛴ SNCM, 61 bd des Dames; Chateau d'If ferry, Quai des Belges.

south of the town at 155 m (500 ft), is a 19th-century Neo-Byzantine extravaganza. It is presided over by a golden Madonna on a 46-m (150-ft) bell tower. Much of the interior decoration is by the Düsseldorf School. Many come for the incomparable view over the city.

⊞ Musée Grobet-Labadié

140 blvd Longchamp. **Tel** 04 91 62 21 82. **Closed** for renovation (call for details). 🖼 📷 🔤 culture.marseille.fr/les-musees-de-marseille

To the north of the city, at the top of boulevard Longchamp, is the finest house in Marseille, with one of the most unusual interiors in the region. It was built in 1873 for a Marseille merchant, Alexandre Labadié. The house and its collection were given to the city in 1919 by his daughter, Marie-Louise.

The Musée Grobet-Labadié has a fine furniture collection, tapestries, 17th–19th century paintings, and many objects of interest, including unusual musical instruments, among them silk and ivory bagpipes.

Detail of *The Flagellation of Christ*, in the Musée Grobet-Labadié

🏛 Palais Longchamp

Blvd de Montrichet. Musée des Beaux-Arts (left wing): **Tel** 04 91 14 59 30. **Open** Tue–Sun. **Closed** public hols. 🅿 🆆 musee-des-beaux-arts.marseille.fr Museum d'Histoire Naturelle (right wing): **Tel** 04 91 14 59 50. **Open** Tue–Sun. **Closed** public hols. 🅿 🆆 museum-marseille.org

This 19th-century palace is home to the Musée des Beaux-Arts and the Museum d'Histoire Naturelle, with its stuffed animal collection. The renovated Musée des Beaux-Arts contains works by local artists as well as paintings by French, Italian and Flemish old masters.

🏯 Château d'If

Vieux Port. **Tel** 04 91 59 02 30. **Open** daily (Sep–Mar: Tue–Sun). 🅿 🖉 Feb–Nov.

Fact, fiction and legend mingle in this island castle in the bay of Marseille. It was a barren island until 1516, when François I decided to make it a fortress. It was built in 1529, and turned into a prison in 1540 until World War I. Famous inmates have included Alexander Dumas' fictional Count of Monte Cristo, the legendary Man in the Iron

The Château d'If in the bay of Marseille, a prison in reality and fiction

Mask (see p75) and the real Comte de Mirabeau. In 1516, the first rhinoceros to set foot in Europe was brought ashore here, and drawn by Albrecht Dürer (see p51).

🏢 Cité Radieuse

280 blvd Michelet. **Tel** 08 26 50 05 00 (for guided tour information). **Open** Tue–Sat.

A landmark in modern architecture, Radiant City was opened in 1952. This vertical, concrete construction by Le Corbusier includes shops, social clubs, schools and crèches (see p29).

🏛 Musée des civilisations de l'Europe et de la Méditerranée (MuCEM)

7 Promenade Robert Laffont. **Tel** 04 84 35 13 13. **Open** Wed–Mon. **Closed** 1 May, 24 & 25 Dec. 🅿 🅱 🖉 🆆 mucem.org

This museum is split between a striking Post-Modern building on the seafront and the adjacent Fort St-Jean, which are linked together by a roof-level bridge suspended over the sea. It features art from around the Mediterranean, dating back from Neolithic times to the present day.

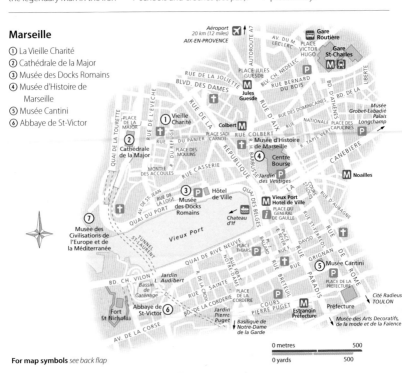

Marseille

① La Vieille Charité
② Cathédrale de la Major
③ Musée des Docks Romains
④ Musée d'Histoire de Marseille
⑤ Musée Cantini
⑥ Abbaye de St-Victor

For hotels and restaurants in this region see pp200–1 and pp212–15

㉒ Aubagne

Road map C4. 45,700. 8 cours Barthelémy (04 42 03 49 98). Tue, Thu, Sat & Sun. **tourisme-paysdaubagne.fr**

Marcel Pagnol's life and work is the main attraction of this simple market town. It has a tradition of making ceramics and *santons (see p52)*. The tableaux can be seen in the Petit Monde de Marcel Pagnol display on the Esplanade de Gaulle about 300 m from the tourist office.

Just outside the town is the headquarters of the French Foreign Legion, moved here from Algeria in 1962. The renovated headquarters has a **Musée de la Légion Etrangère** with memorabilia on display from a variety of campaigns ranging from Mexico to Indo-China and an extensive library.

Musée de la Légion Etrangère
Chemin de la Thuilière. **Tel** 04 42 18 12 41.
Open 10am–12pm & 2–6pm Tue–Sun.
samle.legion-etrangere.com

Poster for Pagnol's film *Marius*

Marcel Pagnol

A plaque at No. 16 cours Barthélemy in Aubagne marks the birthplace of Pagnol, Provençal writer and film-maker. Born in 1895, his holidays were spent in the village of La Treille. His insights into rural Provence enriched tales such as *Jean de Florette* and *Manon des Sources*. The Office de Tourisme has a Circuit Marcel Pagnol, with road routes and walks which take in La Treille and other sites of Pagnol's inspiration.

㉓ Les Calanques

Road map C4. Marseille. Marseille, Cassis. Cassis. Cassis, Marseille. Cassis (08 92 39 01 03).

Between Marseille and Cassis the coast is broken up by *calanques* – enticing fjord-like inlets lying between vertical white cliffs. Continuing deep under the blue waters, they offer safe natural harbours and fascinating aquatic life, with glorious views from the high clifftops *(see also pp34–5)*. Their precipitous faces provide a challenge to climbers. A major attraction is the Parc national des Calanques, the only national park in Europe to inlcude land, marine and semi-urban areas. Opened in 2012, it has around 200 protected animal, plant and marine species.

From Cassis, it is possible to walk to the nearest *calanque*, Port-Miou. Beyond it lies Port-Pin, with occasional pine trees and a shady beach, but the most scenic is En-Vau, which has a sandy beach and needle-like rocks rising from the sea. These walking paths may be closed during peak summer, due to the risk of fire. On the western side, the Sormiou and Morgiou inlets can be approached by road.

In 1991, a cave was found with its entrance 100 m (350 ft) beneath the sea at Sormiou. It is decorated with pictures of prehistoric animals resembling the ancient cave paintings at Lascaux in the Dordogne.

En-Vau, the most beautiful of Les Calanques, along the coast from Cassis

Bear in mind when visiting the area that the main car parks serving Les Calanques beaches are notorious for theft.

㉔ Cassis

Road map C4. 7,600. Quai des Moulins (08 92 39 01 03). Wed & Fri. **ot-cassis.com**

A favourite summer resort of artists such as Derain, Dufy and Matisse, Cassis is a lovely port, tucked into limestone hills. The Romans liked it, too, and built villas here, and when Marseille prospered in the 17th century a number of mansions were erected. It was also a busy fishing centre in the 19th century, and is still known for its seafood. The local delicacy is sea urchins, enjoyed with a glass of Cassis' reputed AOC white wine.

There is **Musée Municipal Méditerranéen**, with items dating back to the Greeks, some rescued from the seabed. It also shows Cassis to have been a substantial trading port up till World War II. There are paintings by Félix Ziem *(see p30)* and by other early 20th-century artists who were equally drawn to Cassis, like Winston Churchill, who learnt to paint here.

There are three good beaches nearby, notably the Plage de la Grande Mer. Between Cassis and La Ciotat are the red cliffs of Cap Canaille, with a 4-hour walk (one-way) along Route des Crêtes.

Musée Municipal Méditerranéen d'Art et Traditions Populaires
Place Baragnon. **Tel** 04 42 18 36 78.
Open Wed–Sat. **Closed** public hols.
restricted.

VAUCLUSE

Vaucluse is a land of vines and lavender, truffles and melons, which many know about through the books of the English expatriate and author Peter Mayle. His works depict village life in the Luberon, an idyllic countryside where Picasso spent his last years. Roussillon, set among ochre quarries, also became the topic of a book, when American sociologist Laurence Wylie experienced village life there in the 1950s.

The jewel of Vaucluse is the fortified riverside city of Avignon, home to the popes during their "Babylonian exile" from 1309–77, and now host to one of the great music and theatre festivals of France. The popes' castle at Châteauneuf-du-Pape is now a ruin, but the village still produces stupendous wines. The Rhône valley wine region is justly renowned, and its vineyards spread as far northeast as the slopes of the towering giant of Provence, Mont Ventoux.

The Roman legacy in Vaucluse is also remarkable. It is glimpsed in the great theatre and triumphal arch in Orange, and in the ruins of Vaison-la-Romaine which were not built over by successive civilizations. Carpentras was also a Roman town, but its claim to fame is its possession of France's oldest synagogue. The story of the Jews, who were given papal protection in Vaucluse, is one of many religious histories which can be traced through the region. Another is the Baron of Oppède's brutal crusade against the Vaudois heretics in 1545, when many villages were destroyed.

Near Oppède, at Lacoste, a path leads to the château of France's notorious libertine Marquis de Sade. Perhaps a more elevated writer was Petrarch, who lived in Fontaine-de-Vaucluse, where the Sorgue river emerges from a mysterious source.

A vine-covered house at Le Bastidon, near the Luberon

◄ Lavender fields in glorious bloom outside the 12th-century Abbaye de Sénanque

Exploring Vaucluse

Vaucluse, which takes its name from the Latin *vallis clausa*
(closed valley), covers 3,540 sq km (2,200 sq miles). It is
bordered by the Rhône in the west, the Durance in the
south, and the foothills of the Alps to the east, and has
a series of highland chains,
dominated by the serene
Mont Ventoux *(see p164)*.
The extraordinary Dentelles
pinnacles are in the west and
to the south is the Vaucluse
Plateau, where the river
Sorgue flows in the beautiful
and dramatic setting of
Fontaine-de-Vaucluse.

Sights at a Glance
1. Bollène
2. Vaison-la-Romaine
4. Mont Ventoux
5. *Orange pp165–7*
6. Caderousse
7. Châteauneuf-du-Pape
8. Carpentras
9. Abbaye de Sénanque
10. Fontaine de Vaucluse
11. L'Isle-sur-la-Sorgue
12. *Avignon pp170–2*
13. Gordes
14. Roussillon
15. Cavaillon
17. Apt
18. Cadenet
19. Ansouis
20. Pertuis
21. La Tour d'Aigues

Tours
3. Dentelles
16. *Petit Luberon pp174–5*

The roofs and terraces of Gordes, crowned by the church and castle

Key

— Motorway
— Major road
— Secondary road
— Minor road
— Scenic route
— Main railway
— Minor railway
— Regional border

For additional map symbols *see back flap*

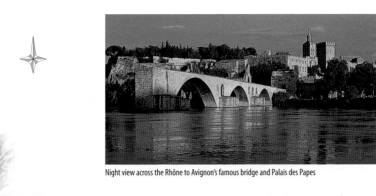

Night view across the Rhône to Avignon's famous bridge and Palais des Papes

Getting Around

The main highways, the A7 Autoroute du Soleil and its accompanying toll-free national road, the D907, travel down the Rhône valley to the west of the region. The main railway line follows these roads, stopping at the principal towns, and the TGV halts at Avignon. The other railway lines across Vaucluse are used for freight, so you may need to take a bus from Avignon to such places as Vaison-la-Romaine, Carpentras and Orange. Boat trips are organized on the Rhône at Avignon.

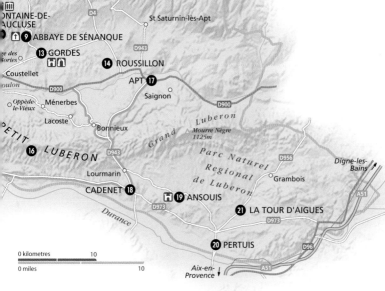

The Belvédère Pasteur garden in Bollène

❶ Bollène

Road map B2. 🏘 14,400. 🚊 🚌
ℹ️ Pl Reynaud de la Gardette
(04 90 40 51 45). 🗓 Mon.
🌐 bollenetourisme.com

Despite being spread along the A7 autoroute, Bollène is pleasant, with airy boulevards and walks beside the river Lez, where there is a camping site. The narrow streets of the old quarter lead to the 11th-century **Collégiale St-Martin**, with its timber saddleback roof and Renaissance doorway. Bollène became famous in 1882, when Louis Pasteur stayed here and developed innoculation against swine fever. The **Belvédère Pasteur** garden above the town has views over the Rhône valley to the Cévennes, the Bollène hydroelectric power station and Tricastin nuclear power plant. The town hosts free open-air concerts from early July to August.

South of Bollène is the clifftop fortress of Mornas, built by the Earl of Toulouse, which was later fought over for its strategic position during the Wars of Religion. The steep climb is rewarded by superb views of the Rhône valley.

❷ Vaison-la-Romaine

Road map B2. 🏘 6,429. 🚌 ℹ️ Pl du Chanoine Sautel (04 90 36 02 11). 🗓 Tue. 🌐 vaison-ventoux-tourisme.com

The pavement cafés in this attractive stone-and-red-roof town on the river Ouvèze are among Provence's most chic.

The modern town sits beside the Roman town, opposite the hilltop Haute-Ville on the other side of the river. Vaison is a smart address for Parisians' second homes and, judging by the opulent remains left by the Romans, it has long been sought after. The Romans lived with the native Celtic Vocontii and the population was around 10,000. Two sites have been excavated, divided by the avenue Général-de-Gaulle. The upper site, known as the Puymin Quarter, has a Roman theatre, still used for Vaison's summer festival in July, centred on dance. Its stage is cut out of rock, and the theatre seats up to 6,000. Many Roman remains come from the villa of a wealthy family, the House of the Messii, and an elegant,

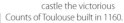

Mosaic in the museum at Vaison-la-Romaine

colonnaded public building, Pompey's Portico. The site is dotted with copies of original statues that are now kept in the **Musée Théo Desplans**, and include a powerful nude of Hadrian and his well-draped empress, Sabina. Many statues were designed to have their heads replaced whenever there was a change of local officials. Other remains include a communal six-seater latrine and a 3rd-century silver bust, which once stood in the hall of a patrician's house in La Villasse, the district on the other side of the avenue Général-de-Gaulle.

The Haute-Ville, which artists and craftspeople helped to re-populate, is reached by means of a Roman bridge, a single 56-ft (17-m) span used for more than 2,000 years until devastating floods necessitated huge repairs. Entrance is via a 14th-century fortified gate. The Romanesque church, built as a **cathedral**, has 7th-century columns in the apse, and a 12th-century cloister. A walk to the summit reveals the ruined castle the victorious Counts of Toulouse built in 1160.

🏛 Roman City
Fouilles de Puymin and Musée Archeologique Théo Desplans, Pl du Chanoine Sautel. **Tel** 04 90 36 50 48.
Open daily. **Closed** Jan. 🅿 📷
♿ restricted. 🎫

Grounds of Roman house with 3rd-century silver bust, Vaison-la-Romaine

❸ A Tour of the Dentelles

Dentelle means "lace", and the Dentelles de Montmirail is the name of the 15-km (9-mile) range of hills that form a lacework of delicate peaks. Not as high or rugged as they initially seem, the Dentelles have good paths and offer some of the most accessible, enjoyable mountain walks in Provence. The paths are bright with broom and flanked by pines, oaks and wild almond trees. When you have had your fill of the stunning scenery, enjoy fine Côtes du Rhône wines and delicious goat's cheese produced in the picturesque villages tucked into the folds of the Dentelles.

Muscat grapes outside Beaumes-de-Venise

① **Vaison-la-Romaine**
A chic town, favoured by wealthy Parisians, Vaison is built on separate Roman and medieval sites. Among its many attractions are the cathedral with its 6th-century sarcophagus of healer St Quenin, and a Romanesque chapel.

Gigondas vineyard

⑥ **Gigondas**
The local red wine is highly regarded and its producers include the master-chef Roux brothers. The Counts of Orange built the 14th-century château.

② **Malaucène**
This former Huguenot stronghold has a clock tower, originally built as a watchtower during the Wars of Religion (see pp50–51).

③ **Le Barroux**
Surrounded by olive and apricot trees, this tiny village is overlooked by a 12th-century château, once a stronghold of the lords of Baux. It has fine views.

⑤ **Vacqueyras**
The home of the famous troubadour, Raimbaud, who died on a Crusade, this village has a church with a 6th-century baptistry.

④ **Beaumes-de-Venise**
This is a town of many restaurants, and the home of Muscat, the town's famous fortified sweet white dessert wine, which can be enjoyed with lunch or dinner.

Tips for Drivers

Tour length: 50 km (30 miles).
Stopping off points: The hilltop village of Crestet; Lafare, a hamlet leading to the 627-m (2057-ft) Rocher du Turc; and Montmirail, a 19th-century spa resort visited by Mistral. (See also pp250–51.)

Key

━━ Tour route
╌╌╌ Other roads

0 kilometres   2
0 miles   2

For additional map symbols see back flap

❹ Mont Ventoux

Road map C2. ✈ Avignon. 🚍 3,000.
🚌 ℹ Ave de la Promenade, Sault-
en-Provence (04 90 64 01 21).
W **ventoux- en-provence.com**

The "Giant of Provence" is the
dominant feature west of the
Alps, a limestone massif which
reaches 1,912m (6,242 ft). It is
easy to reach the car park at the
top, unless there is deep snow,
which can last until April. The
snowline starts at 1,300 m
(4,265 ft), but the limestone
scree of its summit forms
a year-round white cap.

Until 1973 there was a motor
race on the south side of Mont
Ventoux, to the top: speeds
reached up to 145 km/h
(90 mph). A car rally takes place
in Bedoin in June. The roads
have gradually improved and
the worst hairpins are now
ironed out, but the mountain
roads are often included as a
gruelling stage on the Tour de
France. Britain's cyclist Tommy
Simpson suffered a fatal heart
attack here in 1967.

It takes around five hours to
walk to the summit of Mont
Ventoux. Petrarch *(see p49)*
made the first recorded journey
from Malaucène at dawn one
day in May in 1336. As there
were no roads then, it took
him a great deal longer.

Summit of Mont Ventoux during the Mistral season

Engraving of rally motor car ascending
Mont Ventoux (1904)

The mountain is often windy
and its name comes from the
French word *(vent)* for wind.
When the northerly Mistral
blows, it can almost lift you out
of your boots. But the winds dry
the moisture in the sky, painting
it a deep blue colour
and leaving behind
clear vistas.

There are three
starting points for
a walking tour of
the mountain:
Malaucène, on
the north slopes,
Bedoin to the
south and Sault
to the east.
Another direct route for hikers
is from Brantes on the northeast
side, up the Toulourenc valley.
The first two towns both have
tourist offices that organize
guided hikes to see the sun

Monument to cycling hero
Tommy Simpson

rise at the summit. The 21-km
(13-mile) road from Malaucène
passes the 12th-century
Chapelle Notre-Dame-du-
Groseau and the Source
Vauclusienne, a deep pool
tapped for an aqueduct by the
Romans. The ski centre at
Mt Serein is based 5 km
(3 miles) from the
summit. A viewing
table at the peak
helps to discern
the Cévennes,
the Luberon and
Ste-Victoire.
Descending,
the road passes the
Col des Tempêtes,
known for its stormy weather.
The ski centre of Le Chalet-
Reynard is at the junction
to Sault and les Gorges de
la Nesque, and St-Estève has
fine views over the Vaucluse.

Provençal Flowers

Because the temperature on
Mont Ventoux drops between the
foot and the summit by around
11° C (20° F), the vegetation alters
from the lavender and peach
orchards of the plain via the oak,
beech and conifer woodlands to the
arctic flowers towards the summit.
June is the best month for flowers.

Early purple orchid
Orchis mascula

Alpine poppy
Papaver rhaeticum

Trumpet gentian
Gentiana clusii

❺ Orange

Road map B2. 🏔 30,000. 🚊 🚌
ℹ️ 5 cours Aristide Briand (04 90 34 70
88). 🛥 Thu. 🆆 orange-tourisme.fr

This historical town contains
two of the finest Roman
monuments in Europe. The
Théâtre Antique d'Orange is
known for its world-famous
concerts *(see pp166–7)*, while
the Arc de Triomphe celebrates
the honour of Tiberius and the
conquest of Rome after the
Battle of Actium. Orange is also
the centre for the Côtes du
Rhône vineyards and produce
such as olives, honey and
truffles. Around the 17th-
century Hôtel de Ville, streets
open on to peaceful, shady
squares with café terraces.

Side-chapel altar in the Ancienne
Cathédrale Notre-Dame, Orange

Roman Orange

When the first Roman army
attempted to conquer Gaul, it
was defeated near Orange with
a loss of 80,000 men in 105 BC.
When the army came back
three years later and triumphed,
one of the first monuments
built to show supremacy was
the 19-m (63-ft) Arc de Triomphe
on the via Agrippa between
Arles and Lyons, today little used.

The Old Town

Old Orange is centred around
the 17th-century town hall and
**Ancienne Cathédrale Notre-
Dame**, with its crumbling
Romanesque portal, damaged in
the Wars of Religion *(see pp50–51)*.
The theatre's wall dominates the
place des Frères-Mounet. Louis
XIV described it as "the greatest
wall in my kingdom". There is an

excellent view of the theatre, the
city of Orange and the Rhône
plain from **Colline St-Eutrope**.
This is the site of the remains of
the castle of the princes of Orange,
who gave the Dutch royal family
its title, the House of Orange,
through marriage. The family
also lent their name to states
and cities around the world.

🏛 Arc de Triomphe
Ave de l'Arc de Triomphe.
The monument, a UNESCO World
Heritage Site, has excellent
decorations devoted to war and
maritime themes. There is a mod-
ernistic quality, particularly visible
in the trophies above the side
arches. On the east face, Gallic
prisoners, naked and in chains,
broadcast to the world who was
in charge. Anchors and ropes
showed maritime superiority.

When Maurice of Nassau
fortified the town in 1622
by using Roman buildings as
quarries, the arch escaped this
fate by being incorporated into
the defensive walls as a keep.

🏛 Musée d'Art et d'Histoire
d'Orange
1 rue Madeleine Roch. **Tel** 04 90 51
17 60. **Open** daily. 🅿️ 🆆 theatre-
antique.com
The exhibits found in the
courtyard and ground floor reflect
the history of Orange. They include
more than 400 marble fragments
which, when assembled, proved
to be plans of the area, based on

Stone carving of a centaur in the Musée
d'Art et d'Histoire d'Orange

three surveys dating from AD 77.
Also in the museum are portraits
of members of the Royal House
of Orange and paintings by the
British artist, Sir Frank Brangwyn
(1867–1956). One room demons-
trates how printed fabrics were
made in 18th-century Orange.

🏛 L'Harmas de Fabre –
Museum National d'Histoire
Naturelle
Route d'Orange, Serignan du Comtat.
Tel 04 90 70 15 61. **Open** Mon–Fri
(Apr–Oct: also Sat & Sun pm). **Closed**
Wed, 1 May, Christmas hols. 🅿️ 🚗

At Sérignan-du-Cwomtat, 8 km
(5 miles) northeast of Orange is
L'Harmas, the estate of the ento-
mologist and poet Jean-Henri
Fabre (1823–1915). His collection
of insects and fungi, and the
surrounding botanical garden,
attract visitors worldwide.

Arc de Triomphe monument, representing Julius Caesar's conquests

Théâtre Antique et Musée d'Orange

Orange's Roman theatre, a UNESCO World Heritage site, is one of the best preserved in Europe. It was built at the start of the Christian era against the natural height of the Colline-St-Eutrope. Its stage doors were hollow so that actors could stand in front of them and amplify their voices; today other acoustic touches make it ideal for concerts. The *cavea*, or tiered semicircle, held up to 7,000 spectators. From the 16th to 19th centuries, the theatre was filled with squalid housing, traces of which can still be seen. A new roof has been built above the stage, and a multimedia presentation of great moments in the theatre's history takes place in four grottoes behind the tiers of the amphitheatre. Some parts of the theatre may be closed for restoration work, check before visiting.

Awning Supports
Still visible on the exterior walls are corbels which held the huge *velum*-bearing masts.

Main entrance

Roman Theatre
This reconstruction shows the theatre as it would have looked in Roman times. Today it owes its reputation to its exceptional stage wall, the only Roman stage wall to remain intact.

Night Concerts
Cultural events such as *Les Chorégies d'Orange*, a festival of opera, drama and ballet (*see p37*), once frequented by Sarah Bernhardt, have been held here since 1869. The theatre is also a popular rock concert venue.

KEY

① **A canvas awning**, known as a *velum*, protected the theatregoers from sun or rain.

② **The stage curtain** (*aulaeum*) was lowered to reveal the stage, rather than raised. It was operated by machinery concealed beneath the floor of the stage.

③ **Side rooms**, or *parascaenia*, were where actors could rest, and props be stored, when not required on stage.

④ **Each strip** of *velum* awning could be rolled individually to suit the direction of the sunlight.

⑤ **Winched capstans** held and tightened the ropes supporting the *velum*.

The Great Wall
Built of red limestone, this massive construction is 103 m (338 ft) long, 36 m (117ft) high and over 1.8 m (5 ft) thick.

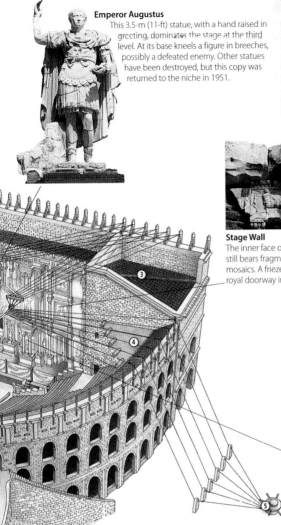

Emperor Augustus
This 3.5-m (11-ft) statue, with a hand raised in greeting, dominates the stage at the third level. At its base kneels a figure in breeches, possibly a defeated enemy. Other statues have been destroyed, but this copy was returned to the niche in 1951.

VISITORS' CHECKLIST

Practical Information
1 rue Madeleine Roch. **Tel** 04 90 51 17 60. **Open** daily. Jan–Feb, Nov–Dec: 9:30am–4:30pm; Mar, Oct: 9:30am–5:30pm; Apr, May, Sep: 9am–6pm; Jun–Aug: 9am–7pm. **Closed** 1 Jan, 25 Dec. (for occasional shows) **W** theatre-antique.com

Stage Wall
The inner face of the stage wall (*Frons Scaenae*) still bears fragments of marble friezes and mosaics. A frieze of centaurs framed the royal doorway in the centre.

Marble Columns
The stage wall had three levels, the two upper levels with 76 marble columns, of which only two remain. The wall's many surfaces broke up sound waves, so that the actors could speak without their voices having an echo.

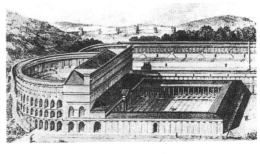

The Great Roman Temple
From 1925–37, excavations took place to the west of the theatre, where 22 houses had been pulled down. They unearthed a vast semicircle and ruins of a temple. Together with the theatre, they would have formed an *Augusteum*, an architectural unit devoted to the worship of Roman emperors.

Exterior of the Romanesque St-Michel church at Caderousse

❻ Caderousse

Road map B2. 🏠 2,700. 🛈 La Mairie, Rue Berbiguier (04 90 51 90 69). 🚌 Tue. 🌐 **caderousse.fr**

This bankside village lies at a point where Hannibal is said to have crossed the river Rhône with his elephants on his way to Rome in 218 BC. For centuries, Caderousse has endured the floods of the Rhône, and plaques on the town hall record the high levels of floodwater. By 1856, the villagers had had enough, and erected a dyke that is still in place. Its four entry points can close if floods should threaten again.

Caderousse has a Romanesque church, St-Michel, to which the Flamboyant Gothic chapel of St-Claude was added during the 16th century.

❼ Châteauneuf-du-Pape

Road map B3. 🏠 2,200. 🚌 🚉 Sorgues, then taxi. 🛈 Place du Portail (04 90 83 71 08). 🌐 **chateauneuf-du-pape-tourisme.fr**

The best-known of the Côtes-du-Rhône wine labels takes its name from an unassuming yellowstone village on a small hill, given over to cellars and restaurants selling the products of the local growers entitled to the *appellation d'origine contrôlée*. The **Musée du Vin** traces the history and current state of the local viniculture.

At the top of the village are the ruins of the **Château des Papes**, mostly burned down in the 16th-century Wars of Religion. From the remaining walls there is a superb view of Avignon and the vineyard-lined clay fields where smooth stones deposited by the Rhône reflect the sun's heat onto 13 varieties

of grapes. The château was built in 1317 by John XXII, an Avignon pope who planted the first vineyards, but it took some 400 years for the wine's reputation to spread. Today, there are 350 Châteauneuf-du-Pape domaines. The nearby town of Pernes-les-Fontaines is known for its 40 fountains, in particular the 18th-century Fontaine du Cormoran. Until 1914, each of the fountains had an individual keeper.

🏛 **Musée du Vin – Maison Brotte**
Ave Pierre de Luxembourg, Châteauneuf-du-Pape. **Tel** 04 90 83 59 44. **Open** daily. **Closed** 1 Jan, 25 Dec. 🚻 restricted. 📷

❽ Carpentras

Road map B3. 🏠 29,500. 🚌 🛈 97 place 25 Août 1944 (04 90 63 00 78). 🚌 Fri. 🌐 **carpentras-ventoux.com**

As the capital of the Comtat Venaissin, this market town is in the centre of the Côtes-du-Ventoux wine region.

Boulevards encircle the old town, but the Porte d'Orange is the only surviving part of the medieval ramparts. In the Middle Ages, the town had a large Jewish community, and their 14th-century **synagogue** is the oldest in France, now used by some 100 families. While not openly persecuted under papal rule, many Jews changed faith and entered the **Cathédrale-St-Siffrein** by its 15th-century south door, the *Porte Juive*. The cathedral is in the centre of the old town, near a smaller version of Orange's Arc de Triomphe. In it are Provençal paintings and statues by local

sculptor Jacques Bernus (1650–1728). The *Hôtel-Dieu* has a fine 18th-century pharmacy, and there are regional costumes in the **Musée Comtadin-Duplessis**.

✡ **Synagogue**
Pl Maurice Charretier. **Tel** 04 90 63 39 97. **Open** Mon–Fri. **Closed** Jewish feast days.

⛪ **Cathédral St-Siffrein**
3 pl Saint-Siffrein. **Tel** 04 90 63 08 33. **Open** Tue–Sat. **Closed** Sun. ♿

🏛 **Musée Comtadin-Duplessis**
234 blvd Albin-Durand. **Tel** 04 90 63 04 92. **Open** Wed–Mon. **Closed** public hols, Oct–Mar. 📷

Pharmacy in the 18th-century *Hôtel-Dieu* at Carpentras

❾ Abbaye de Sénanque

Road map C3. **Tel** 04 90 72 05 86. **Open** late Jan–mid-Nov: Mon–Sat & Sun pm; mid-Nov–early Jan: pms only, by guided tour (in French). 🌐 **senanque.fr**

The beautifully sited Abbaye de Sénanque, surrounded by a tranquil sea of lavender, is best approached from Gordes *(see p173)*. Its monks are often to be seen in the fields.

Like the other abbeys that make up the Cistercian trium-virate in Provence *(see p47)*, Sénanque is harmonious and

Châteauneuf-du-Pape vineyards

unadorned. It was founded in 1148 by an abbott and 12 monks, and the building of the serene north-facing abbey church started 12 years later.

Some roofs of the building are still tiled with limestone slates called *lauzes*, also used for making traditional stone dwellings known as *bories* (*see p173*). The abbey's simply designed interior has stone walls, plain windows and a barrel-vaulted ceiling.

Sénanque reached its zenith in the early 13th century, when the abbey owned several local farms. But new riches brought corruption in the 14th century, and by the 17th century, only two monks remained. In 1854 it was restored and housed Cistercian monks, some of whom remained there from 1926 to 1969. The present monks have been living there since 1988.

Serene Abbaye de Sénanque built in the 12th century

⓾ Fontaine-de-Vaucluse

Road map B3. 🚹 600. 🚌 Avignon. 🛈 Residence Jean Garcin, Ave Robert Garcin (04 90 20 32 22). 🆆 oti-delasorgue.fr

The source of the Sorgue river is one of the natural wonders of Provence. It begins underground, with tributaries that drain the Vaucluse plateau, an area of around 2,000 sq km (800 sq miles). In the closed valley above the town, water erupts from an unfathomable depth to develop into a fully fledged river.

Fontaine-de-Vaucluse, where the Sorgue river begins

Beside the river is the **Moulin à Papier Vallis Clausa**, which produces handmade paper using a 15th-century method. It sells maps, prints and lampshades.

The underground museum, the **Eco-Musée du Gouffre**, features a speleologist's findings over 30 years of exploring Sorgue's dams, caves and waterfalls. The **Musée d'Histoire 1939–1945**, traces the fate of the Resistance during WWII and daily life under Occupation. The **Musée Bibliotheque Pétrarque** was the house where the poet lived for 16 years, and wrote of his love for Laura of Avignon.

🏭 **Moulin à Papier Vallis Clausa**
Chemin du Gouffre. **Tel** 04 90 20 34 14.
Open daily. **Closed** 1–15 Jan, 25 Dec. ♿
📷 🆆 moulin-vallisclausa.com

🏛 **Eco-Musée du Gouffre (Musée de Spéléologie)**
Chemin du Gouffre. **Tel** 04 90 20 34 13.
Open Feb–15 Nov: daily. 📷
♿ restricted. 📷 📷

🏛 **Musée d'Histoire Jean Garcin 1939–45**
Chemin de la Fontaine. **Tel** 04 90 20 24 00. **Open** Apr–Oct: Wed–Mon pm only. **Closed** 1 May, 25 Dec. 📷 ♿

🏛 **Musée Bibliotheque Pétrarque**
Rive gauche de la Sorgue. **Tel** 04 90 20 37 20. **Open** Apr–Oct: Wed–Mon. **Closed** 1 May, Nov–Mar. 📷

⓫ L'Isle-sur-la-Sorgue

Road map B3. 🚹 19,400. 🚗 🚌 🛈 Pl de la Liberté (04 90 38 04 78). 🗓 Mon, Thu, Sat, Sun (antiques). 🆆 oti-delasorgue.fr

A haunt for antique hunters at weekends, this attractive town lies on the river Sorgue, which once powered 70 watermills. Today, 14 idle wheels remain. The ornate 17th-century **Notre-Dame-des-Anges** is a major attraction. The tourist office is in an 18th-century granary, and the Musée du Jouet et de la Poupée Ancienne has displays of antique toys and dolls.

Water wheel near place Gambetta, l'Isle-sur-la-Sorgue

⓬ Street-by-Street: Avignon

Bordered to the north and west by the Rhône, the medieval city of Avignon is the chief city of Vaucluse and gateway to Provence. Its walls cover nearly 4.5 km (3 miles) and are punctuated by 39 towers and seven gates. Within the walls thrives a culturally rich city with its own opera house, university, several foreign language schools and numerous theatre companies. The streets and squares are often filled with buskers, and the Avignon festival in July, which includes theatre, mime and cabaret, has now become a major international event.

Chapelle St-Nicolas, named after the patron saint of bargemen, is a 16th-century building on a 13th-century base. Entrance is via Tour du Châtelet.

Porte du Rhône

★ Pont St-Bénézet
Begun in 1177 by shepherd boy Bénézet, this bridge is the subject of the famous rhyme *Sur le Pont d'Avignon*.

Hôtel des Monnaies
The façade of this former mint, built in 1619, bears the arms of Cardinal Borghese.

RUE DE LIMAS

RUE GRANDE FUSTERIE

RUE DES GROTTES

RUE DE LA BALANCE

RUE ST-ETIENNE

RUE PETITE FUSTERIE

RUE RACINE

PLACE DE L'HORLOGE

Place de l'Horloge
The main square was laid out in the 15th century and is named after the Gothic clock tower above the town hall. Many of today's buildings date from the 19th century.

Key

— Suggested route

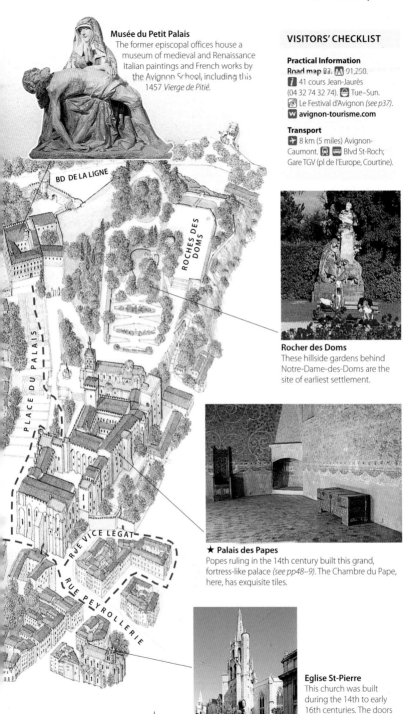

Musée du Petit Palais
The former episcopal offices house a museum of medieval and Renaissance Italian paintings and French works by the Avignon School, including this 1457 *Vierge de Pitié*.

BD DE LA LIGNE

ROCHES DES DOMS

PLACE DU PALAIS

RUE VICE LEGAT

RUE PEYROLLERIE

0 metres 100
0 yards 100

Rocher des Doms
These hillside gardens behind Notre-Dame-des-Doms are the site of earliest settlement.

★ Palais des Papes
Popes ruling in the 14th century built this grand, fortress-like palace *(see pp48–9)*. The Chambre du Pape, here, has exquisite tiles.

Eglise St-Pierre
This church was built during the 14th to early 16th centuries. The doors on its west façade were carved in 1551 by Antoine Valard. Inside is a fine 15th-century pulpit.

Exploring Avignon

Massive ramparts enclose one of the most fascinating towns in southern France. A quick stroll reveals *trompe l'oeil* windows and mansions such as King René's house in the rue du Roi-René. This street leads to the rue des Teinturiers, named after local dyers and textile-makers, where a bridge for pedestrians crosses the river Sorgue to the 16th-century Chapelle des Pénitents Gris.

Palais des Papes in Avignon glimpsed across the river Rhône

🏰 Palais des Papes
Pl du Palais. **Tel** 04 32 74 32 74.
Open daily (times vary). 🚫 🚼 🏛
🖥 📷 W **palais-des-papes.com**

These buildings *(see pp48–9)* give an idea of the grand life under the seven French popes who built a miniature Vatican during their rule here, lasting from 1309–77. They owned their own mint, baked a vast number of loaves every day, and fortified themselves against the French.

Entrance is by means of the Porte des Champeaux, beneath the twin pencil-shaped turrets of the flamboyant Palais Neuf (1342–52), built by Clement VI, which extends south from the solid Palais Vieux (1334–42) of Benoit XII. In the new palace, the main courtyard, La Cour d'Honneur, is the grand central setting for the summer festival *(see p229)*. La Chambre du Pape in the Tour des Anges opposite the entrance has exquisite tiles, and there are fine 14th-century deer-hunting scenes painted by Matteo Giovanetti and others in the adjoining Chambre du Cerf. The larger rooms around the Palais Vieux include the 45-m (148-ft) banqueting hall,

Bird tile in the Chambre du Pape

Le Grand Tinel, and La Salle du Consistoire, where pictures of all the popes are displayed. The chapel beside it has exquisite frescoes painted by Giovanetti between 1346 and 1349.

🏛 Cathédrale Notre-Dame-des-Doms
Pl du Palais. **Tel** 04 90 82 12 21.
Open Mon–Sat & Sun pm.
W **cathedrale-avignon.fr**

This building beside the Palais des Papes was begun in the 12th century. Since then it has been damaged and rebuilt several times. A gilded Madonna was added to the tower in the 19th century, and the original 6th-century altar is now in the Chapelle St-Roch, where two popes are buried.

🏛 Musée du Petit Palais
Pl du Palais. **Tel** 04 90 86 44 58.
Open Wed–Mon. **Closed** 1 Jan, 1 May, 1 Nov, 25 Dec. 🚫 📷
W **petit-palais.org**

Set around an arcaded courtyard, the "little palace", built in 1318, was modified in 1474 to suit Michelangelo's patron, Cardinal Rovere, later Pope Julius II. It became a museum in 1958, and houses Avignon's medieval collection, which

includes works by Simone Martini and Botticelli, as well as works from the Avignon School, and many French and Italian religious paintings.

🏛 Musée Lapidaire
27 rue de la République. **Tel** 04 90 85 75 38. **Open** Tue–Sun. **Closed** 1 Jan, 1 May, 25 Dec. 🚫 W **musee-lapidaire.org**

Once a 17th-century Baroque Jesuit college, the museum has Celtic-Ligurian, Egyptian, Gallic and Roman artifacts, including a 2nd-century Tarasque monster *(see p144)*.

🏛 Musée Calvet
65 rue Joseph Vernet. **Tel** 04 90 86 33 84. **Open** Wed–Mon. **Closed** 1 Jan, 1 May, 25 Dec. 🚫 ♿ restricted.
W **musee-calvet-avignon.com**

This evocative museum was visited by the French writer Stendhal, who left his inscription behind. Renovated in 2003 to permit the display of many of the treasures previously stored in their vaults, the highlight is the 19th–20th-century collection, with works by Soutine, Manet, Dufy, Gleizes and Marie Laurencin.

🏛 Musée Angladon
5 rue Laboureur. **Tel** 04 90 82 29 03.
Open Tue–Sat pm only (call ahead to check). 🚫 📷 W **angladon.com**

This museum cleverly combines modern technology with the intimacy of a private home for displaying this outstanding private collection of 18th–20th-century works of art.

🏛 Collection Lambert
Musée d'Art Contemporain,
5 rue Violette. **Tel** 04 90 16 56 20.
Open Sep–Jun: Tue–Sun; Jul-Aug: daily. **Closed** 1 May. 🚫 📷 ♿ 🏛
📷 W **collectionlambert.com**

Opened in 2000, the Collection Lambert is located in an 18th-century mansion, next to the School of Art. The museum houses an outstanding collection of contemporary art on loan for 20 years from gallery-owner Yvon Lambert. Paintings date from the 1960s, and represents all the major art movements since then.

⓭ Gordes

Road map C3. 🚐 2,000. 🚹 Pl de
Château (04 90 72 02 73). 🏪 Tue.
w luberoncoeurdeprovence.com

Expensive restaurants and hotels
provide a clue to the popularity
of this hilltop village, which
spills down in terraces from a
Renaissance château and the
church of St-Firmin. Its impressive position is the main attraction,
although its vaulted, arcaded
medieval lanes are also alluring.
The village has been popular
with artists since the academic
Cubist painter André Lhote
began visiting in 1938.

The **Château de Gordes** was
built in the 16th century on the
site of a 12th-century fortress.
One of the château's best features is an ornate 16th-century
fireplace in the great hall on the
first floor, decorated with shells,
flowers and pilasters. In the
entrance there is an attractive
Renaissance door. The building
was rented and restored by the
Hungarian-born Op Art painter
Victor Vasarely (1908–97), and
once housed a museum of his
abstract works. The château

Bories

The ancient dwellings known
as *bories* were domed dry-stone
buildings made from *lauzes*
(limestone slabs), with walls
up to 1.5 m (4 ft) thick. They
dated from 2,000 BC and were
regularly rebuilt, using ancient
methods, until the last century
when they were abandoned.
Around 3,000 bories are still
standing, many in fields where
they were used for shelter or
storing implements. Twenty
have been restored in the Village
des Bories, outside Gordes.

now hosts temporary exhibitions during the summer. The
17th-century Caves du Palais
St-Firmin have an impressive
old stone olive press.

Just outside Gordes is the
Village des Bories *(see box)*,
now a museum of rural life.

🏠 **Château de Gordes**
Pl du Chateau. **Tel** 04 90 72 98 64.
Open Apr–Oct: daily. 🖼

🏠 **Village des Bories**
Rte de Cavaillon. **Tel** 04 90 72 03 48.
Open daily. **Closed** 1 Jan, 25 Dec. 🖼

⓮ Roussillon

Road map C3. 🚐 1,350. 🚹 Pl de
la Poste (04 90 05 60 25). 🏪 Thu.
w otroussillon.pagesperso-
orange.fr

The deep ochres used in the
construction of this hilltop
community are stunning. No
other village looks so warm and
rich, so harmonious and inviting.
Its hues come from at least
17 shades of ochre discovered in
and around the village, notably
in the dramatic former quarries
along the Sentier des Ochres.
The entrance to the quarries
is to the east of the village,
a 1-hour and 30-minute trip
from the information office. The
Conservatoire des Ocres et de la
Couleur in the old factory (*open
mid-Feb–Dec: daily*), is worth
visiting. It displays a huge collection of natural pigments, and
runs day courses on the subject.

A superb panorama to the
north can be seen from the
Castrum, the viewing table
beside the church, above the
tables with umbrellas in the
main square.

Before its housing boom,
Roussillon was a typical Provençal
backwater. In the 1950s, American
sociologist Laurence Wylie spent
a year in Roussillon with his family
and wrote a book about village
life, *Un Village du Vaucluse*. He
concluded that Roussillon was
a "hard-working, productive
community", for all its feuds and
tensions. Playwright Samuel
Beckett lived here during WWII,
but his impression was much
less generous.

The hilltop village of Gordes, spilling down in terraces

The 1st-century Roman triumphal arch
behind Cavaillon

⓯ Cavaillon

Road map B3. 🚲 26,000. 🚃 🚌
ℹ️ Pl François Tourel (04 90 71 32 01).
🛒 Mon. 🌐 **luberoncoeurde
provence.com**

The viewing table outside the
Chapelle St-Jacques at the top
of the town renders the Luberon
range in perspective against
Mont Ventoux and the Alpilles
chain. In closer proximity are
the acres of fruit and vegetable
plots, for Cavaillon is France's
largest market garden, synonymous especially with melons. Its
local market competes with the
one in Apt for renown as the
most important in Vaucluse.

Colline St-Jacques was the site
of the pre-Roman settlement
that, under Rome, prospered.
There is a 1st-century Roman arch
in place Duclos nearby. Roman
finds are on display in the **Musée
Archéologique de l'Hotel Dieu**
in the Grand Rue, which leads
north from the church, a former
cathedral dedicated to its 6th-
century bishop, Saint Véran. The
synagogue in rue Hébraïque
dates from 1772, although there
has been one on this site ever
since the 14th century. The
Musée Jouves et Juif Comtadin,
commemorates its history.

🏛 **Musée Archéologique de
l'Hotel Dieu**
Hôtel Dieu, Porte d'Avignon. **Tel** 04 90
72 26 86. **Open** May–Sep: Mon,
Wed–Sat pm only. 📷

🏛 **Musée Jouves et Juif
Comtadin (et de la Synagogue)**
Rue Hébraïque. **Tel** 04 90 71 21 06.
Open Oct–Apr: Mon, Wed–Sat;
May–Sep: Wed–Mon. **Closed** 1 Jan,
1 May, 25 Dec. 📷

⓰ A Tour of the Petit Luberon

The Parc Naturel Régional covers 1,200 sq km (463 sq miles)
of a limestone mountain range running east from Cavaillon
towards Manosque in the Alpes-de-Haute-Provence. It
embraces about 50 communities and a past peppered
with such infamous figures as the Baron of Oppède and the
Marquis de Sade. An unspoiled area, it is ideal for walking.
Its two main centres are Apt and Lourmarin. The D943 in the
Lourmarin Coomb valley divides the park: the Grand Luberon
(see p176) is to the east; and to the west is the Petit Luberon,
a land of limestone cliffs, hidden corries and cedar woods,
with most towns and villages to the north side of the range.

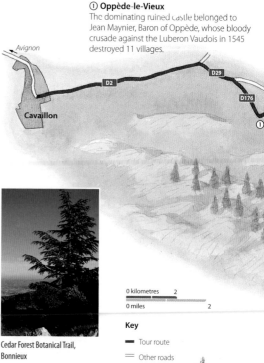

ⓘ **Oppède-le-Vieux**
The dominating ruined castle belonged to
Jean Maynier, Baron of Oppède, whose bloody
crusade against the Luberon Vaudois in 1545
destroyed 11 villages.

Cedar Forest Botanical Trail,
Bonnieux

0 kilometres   2
0 miles   2

Key

━━ Tour route
══ Other roads

Luberon Wildlife

The Parc Naturel Régional is rich
in flora and fauna. The central massif
is wild and exposed on the north
side, sheltered and more cultivated
in the south. A wide range of
habitats exist in a landscape of
white chalk and red ochre cliffs,
cedar forests, moorlands and
river-hewn gorges. Information is
available from La Maison du Parc
in Apt (see p176) which publishes
suggested walks and tours.

Monkey orchid (Orcis
simia) is found on the
sunny, chalky grasslands.

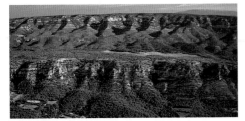
The rugged peaks of the Petit Luberon

Tips for Drivers

Tour length: 40 km (25 miles).
Stopping-off points: Ménerbes has several cafés, Bonnieux is good for lunch and the Cedar Forest has attractive picnic spots. Lourmarin, where Albert Camus lived and was buried, is handy for the Petit and Grand Luberon. All these villages are small, and quickly fill with cars, so you may have to walk some distance, and even climb to castle heights.
w parcduluberon.fr

② Ménerbes
At the foot of this stronghold of 16th-century Calvinists is the Musée du Tire-Bouchon, a fascinating collection of corkscrews, dating from the 17th century.

③ Lacoste
Little remains of the Marquis de Sade's château. Arrested for corrupt practices in 1778, he spent 12 years in prison writing up his experiences.

④ Bonnieux
The Musée de la Boulangerie gives a history of bread making. From here the two-hour Cedar Forest Botanical Trail is a pleasant, scenic walk.

• Abbaye St-Hilaire

Montagne du Luberon

⑤ Lourmarin
The Countess of Agoult, whose family owned the village château, bore the composer Franz Liszt (1811–86) three children: one married Richard Wagner.

↓ *Aix-en-Provence*

Wild boar (*Sus scrofa*, known as *sanglier* in French) is a hunter's prize and a chef's delight.

Eagle owl (*Bubo bubo*, known as *dugas* in Provençal) is judged Europe's largest owl.

Beaver (*Castor fiber*, known as *Castor* in French) builds dams on the Calavon and Durance.

Grand Luberon

This spectacular range of mountains to the east of the Lourmarin Coomb rises as high as 1,125 m (3,690 ft) at Mourre Nègre. The fine view at the summit must be appreciated on foot, and takes several hours from where you leave the car at Auribeau. The area is outstandingly beautiful and ideal to escape from the crowds. The panorama from the top takes in Digne, the Lure mountain and Durance valley, the Apt basin, l'Etang de Berre and Mont Ventoux.

⑰ Apt

Road map C3. 🏔 12,325. 🚌
🚉 Avignon. 🛈 Av Victor Hugo.
🚌 Tue & Sat.

Apt is the northern entry to the Parc Naturel Régional du Luberon (see pp174–5). The **Maison du Parc**, a restored 17th-century mansion, provides information on the area, with details of walks, gîtes d'étapes and flora and fauna.

The busy old town of Apt has a square for playing boules, fountains and plane trees. Surrounded by cherry orchards, it claims to be the world capital of crystallized fruit. The **Musée de l'Aventure Industrielle** explains how the production of crystallized fruits and earthenware pottery combined with the extraction of ochre to bring prosperity to Apt in the 18th and 19th centuries. The town is also famous for truffles and lavender essence. The Saturday market offers Provençal delicacies and entertainment, including jazz, barrel organ music and stand-up comedy. Excursions can be made to the Colorado de Rustrel, the best ochre quarry site by the River Dôa, to the northeast.

The medieval **Cathédrale Ste-Anne** lies at the heart of Apt's old town. Legend has it that the veil of St Anne was brought back from Palestine and hidden in the cathedral by Auspice, who is thought to have been Apt's first bishop. Each July her festival is celebrated with a procession. The Royal Chapel commemorates Anne of Austria. She paid a pilgrimage to Apt to pray for fertility and contributed the funds to finish the chapel, which was finally completed around 1669–70. The treasury inside the sacristy contains the saint's shroud and an 11th-century Arabic standard from the First Crusade (1096–9). In the apse is a 15th–16th-century window that depicts the tree of Jesse.

Nearby is the 17th-century Hôtel d'Albertas.

The items on display in the **Musée d'Histoire et d'Archéologie** consist of prehistoric flints, stone implements, Gallo-Roman carvings, jewellery and mosaics from that period. Just a few miles from Apt, **L'Observatoire Sirene** has an idyllic location and state-of-the-art technology, ideal for star-gazing.

14th-century priest's embroidery

🏛 **Maison du Parc**
60 pl Jean-Jaurès. **Tel** 04 90 04 42 00.
Open Mon–Fri (& Sat Jun–Oct).
🌐 parcduluberon.fr

⛪ **Cathédrale Ste-Anne**
Rue Ste-Anne. **Tel** 04 90 04 85 44.
Open Tue–Sat. 🌐 apt-cathedrale.com

🏛 **Musée de l'Aventure Industrielle**
Pl du Postel. **Tel** 04 90 74 95 30.
Open Sep–Jun: Tue-Sat; Jul–Aug: Mon–Sat. **Closed** Jan, public hols. 🚻 ♿

🏛 **Musée d'Histoire et d'Archéologie**
27 rue de l'Amphithéâtre. **Tel** 04 90 74 95 30. **Open** only on special occasions. 🚻

🏛 **L'Observatoire Sirene**
D34 Lagarde d'Apt. **Tel** 04 90 75 04 17.
Open daily by appt. **Closed** public hols. 🚻 ♿ 🌐 obs-sirene.com

Jam label illustrating traditional produce of Apt

⓲ Cadenet

Road map C3. ⚏ 4,250. ▭ Avignon.
▭ 🛈 11 pl du Tambour d'Arcole,
Château de la Tour d'Aigues (04 90
07 50 29). ▭ Main square: Mon &
Sat (May–Oct behind the church).
W **ot-cadenet.com**

Tucked underneath
the hills in the Durance
valley, Cadenet has 11th-
century castle ruins and
a 14th-century church
with a square bell tower.
Its font is made from a
Roman sarcophagus. In the
main square, which is used
for Cadenet's bi-weekly
market, is a statue
of the town's heroic
drummer boy, André
Estienne, who beat
such a raucous tattoo in the
battle for Arcole Bridge in 1796
that the enemy thought they
could hear gunfire, and retreated.

Drummer boy in Cadenet town square

⓳ Ansouis

Road map C3. ⚏ 1,200. 🛈 Easter–
Sep: Pl de la Vieille Fontaine (09 77
84 33 64). ▭ Sun. W **luberon
cotesud.com**

One of the most remarkable
things about the Renaissance
Château d'Ansouis is that it was
owned by the Sabran family from
1160 until 2008, when it was sold
to a new owner. The Sabrans have
a proven pedigree: in the 13th
century, Gersende de Sabran
and Raymond Bérenger IV's four
daughters became queens of
France, England, Romania and
Naples respectively. In 1298, Elzéar
de Sabran married Delphine de

Puy, a descendant of the Viscount
of Marseille. But she had resolved
to become a nun, so agreed to
the marriage, but not to
its consummation. Both
were canonized in
1369. The castle's
original keep and
two of its four towers
are still visible. Its
gardens include the
Renaissance Garden
of Eden, built on
the former cemetery.
Rousset-Riviere family,
the new owners, has
restored the castle
and expanded its
collection. The **Musée
Extraordinaire de
Georges Mazoyer**,
located south of
the village, displays the artist's
work, Provençal furniture and
a recreated underwater cave,
all in 15th-century cellars.

🏛 **Château d'Ansouis**
Rue du Cartel. **Tel** 04 90 77 23 36.
Open Apr–Oct: Thu–Mon for guided
tours. **Closed** Nov–Mar. ▭
W **chateauansouis.com**

🏛 **Musée Extraordinaire de
Georges Mazoyer**
Rue du Vieux Moulin. **Tel** 04 90 09
82 64. **Open** daily (mid-Sep–mid-Jun:
pm only). ▭ ▭

⓴ Pertuis

Road map C3. ⚏ 19,500. ▭ ▭
🛈 Le Donjon, pl Mirabeau (04 90
79 15 56). ▭ Wed, Fri, Sat.
W **tourismepertuis.fr**

Once the capital of the Pays
d'Aigues, present-day Pertuis

is a quiet town, whose rich and
fertile surrounding area was
gradually taken over by Aix-
en-Provence. Pertuis was the
birthplace of the philandering
Count of Mirabeau's father, and
the 13th-century clock tower
is located in place Mirabeau.

The **Eglise St-Nicolas**, re-built
in Gothic style in the 16th
century, has a 16th-century
triptych and two 17th-century
marble statues. To the south-
west is the battlemented
14th-century **Tour St-Jacques**.

*Triumphal arch entrance to La Tour d'Aigues'
Renaissance château*

㉑ La Tour d'Aigues

Road map C3. ⚏ 4,290. ▭ to
Pertuis. 🛈 Château de la Tour
d'Aigues (04 90 07 50 29). ▭ Tue.
W **luberoncotesud.com**

Nestling beside the grand
limestone mountain ranges
of Luberon, and surrounded by
scenic vineyards and orchards,
this beautiful town takes its name
from a historic 10th-century
tower. The 16th-century castle
completes the triumvirate
of Renaissance châteaux in
the Luberon (the others are
Lourmarin and Ansouis). Built on
the foundations of a medieval
castle by Baron de Central, its
massive portal is based on the
splendid Roman arch at Orange
(see p165). The castle was
damaged in the French
Revolution (1789–94), but
has been partially restored.

🏛 **Château de la Tour d'Aigues**
BP 48. **Tel** 04 90 07 50 29.
Courtyard: **Open** daily. ▭
▭ private tours only (04 90 07 42 10).

Duchess's bedroom in the Château d'Ansouis

ALPES-DE-HAUTE-PROVENCE

In this, the most undiscovered region of Provence, the air is clearer than anywhere else in France, which is why it was the chosen site for France's most important observatory. But the terrain and the weather conditions can be severe. Inaccessibility to areas has restricted development and the traditional, rural way of life is still followed.

Irrigation has helped to improve some corners of this mountainous land. The Valensole plain is now the most important lavender producing area of France. Peaches, apples and pears have been planted in orchards only recently irrigated by the Durance, the region's main river, which has been tamed by dams and a hydro-electric power scheme. These advances have created employment and helped bring prosperity to the region. Another modern development is the Cadarache nuclear research centre, situated just outside Manosque. The town's population has grown rapidly to 20,300 inhabitants, overtaking the region's capital, Digne-les-Bains. Famous for its lavender and healthy living, Digne-les-

Bains is a handsome spa town that has attracted visitors for more than a century and now hopes to enhance its appeal through its devotion to sculpture, which fills the streets.

The region's history and architecture have also been greatly influenced by the terrain and climate. Strategically positioned citadels crown mountain towns such as Sisteron, which was won over by Napoleon in 1815, and the frontier town of Entrevaux. The design of towns and buildings has remained practical, mindful of the harsh winter and strong Mistral winds. Undoubtedly, the beauty of the region is revealed in the high lakes and mountains, the glacial valleys and the colourful fields of Alpine flowers.

Bundles of cut lavender drying in fields near the Gorges du Verdon

◀ Walker at the bottom of the cliff enclosing the Chambre du Roi, one of vast *grés d'Annot* sandstone outcrops in Annot

Exploring Alpes-de-Haute-Provence

This remote and rugged area in the north of Provence covers 6,944 sq km (2,697 sq miles) of mountainous landscape. Its main artery is the Durance river which is dotted with dams, gorges and lakes – a haven for mountaineers and canoeists. One tributary is the Verdon, which runs through the stunning Gorges du Verdon, Europe's answer to the Grand Canyon. The scenery becomes wilder and more rugged in the northeast, with Mont Pelat at the heart of the Parc National du Mercantour. Further south lie the plains of Valensole, which colour the landscape in July when the abundant lavender blossoms.

Fields of lavender on the Valensole plains

Sights at a Glance

1. Sisteron
2. Seyne-les-Alpes
3. Barcelonnette
4. Mont Pelat
5. Colmars
6. Digne-les-Bains
7. Les Pénitents des Mées
8. Lurs
9. Forcalquier
10. Manosque
11. Gréoux-les-Bains
12. Valensole
13. Riez
15. Moustiers-Ste-Marie
16. Castellane
17. St-André-les-Alpes
18. Annot
19. Entrevaux

Tour

14. *Gorges du Verdon pp188–9*

Key

- Motorway
- Major road
- Minor road
- Scenic route
- Minor railway
- International border
- Regional border
- △ Summit

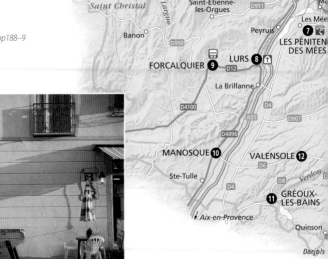

A quiet Provençal-style bar in the mountain town of Castellane, situated in the picturesque old quarter

For additional map symbols *see back flap*

Getting Around

The Durance river provides the point of entry into the region. The A51 autoroute from Aix-en-Provence follows the river to Sisteron and on to La Saulce, just short of Gap. National roads continue to follow the Durance, to Lac de Serre-Ponçon in the north, then east along the Ubaye to Barcelonnette. The region's capital, Digne-les-Bains, is well connected by national roads, but otherwise there are only minor roads. The region's railway line also follows the Durance, connecting Sisteron and Manosque with Aix.

The dramatic Rocher de la Baume, just outside the town of Sisteron

❶ Sisteron

Road map D2. 7,664.
i 1 pl de la République (04 92 61 36 50). Wed & Sat. **W** sisteron-tourisme.fr

Approaching Sisteron from the north or south, it is easy to see its strategic importance. The town calls itself the "gateway to Provence", sitting in a narrow valley on the left bank of the Durance river. It is a lively town, protected by the most impressive fortifications in Provence. However, it has suffered for its ideal military position, most recently in heavy Allied bombardment in 1944.

The **citadelle**, originally built in the 12th century, dominates the town and gives superb views down over the Durance. These defences, though incomplete, are a solid assembly of keep, dungeon, chapel, towers and ramparts, and offer a fine setting for the Nuits de la Citadelle, the summer festival of music, theatre and dance. The cathedral in the main square, **Notre-Dame et St-Thyrse**, is an example of the

A traditional Provençal farmhouse just outside the village of Seyne

Provençal Romanesque school, dating from 1160. At its east end, the 17th-century Chapelle des Visitandines houses the **Musée Terre et Temps**. In the Old Town, small boutiques, cafés and bars line the narrow alleyways called *andrônes*.

Rocher de la Baume on the opposite bank is a popular practice spot for mountaineers.

La Citadelle
Pl de la Citadelle, 04200 Sisteron.
Tel 04 92 61 27 57. **Open** Apr–11 Nov: daily. **W** citadelledesisteron.fr

❷ Seyne-les-Alpes

Road map D2. 1,460. **i** Place d'Armes (04 92 35 11 00). Tue & Fri.
W seynelesalpes.fr

The small mountain village of Seyne dominates the Vallée de la Blanche, sitting 1,260 m (4,134 ft) above sea level. Horses and mules graze in the nearby fields, and there is a celebrated annual horse and mule fair in August. Beside the main road is **Notre-Dame de Nazareth**, a 13th-century Romanesque church with Gothic portals, sundial and large rose window. The path by the church leads up to the **citadelle**, built by Vauban in 1693, which encloses the still-standing 12th-century watchtower. The town is also a centre for winter sports, with facilities nearby at St-Jean, Le Grand Puy and Chabanon.

❸ Barcelonnette

Road map E2. 2,860.
i Pl Frédéric Mistral (04 92 81 04 71). Wed & Sat am only.
W barcelonnette.com

In the remote Ubaye Valley, surrounded by a demi-halo of snowy peaks, lies Provence's northernmost town. It is a flat, open town of cobbled streets, smart cafés and restaurants and quaint gift shops, selling specialities such as raspberry and juniper liqueurs. The town was named in 1231 by its founder Raymond-Bérenger V, Count of Barcelona and Provence, whose great-grandfather of the same name married into the House

Sisteron citadel, strategically positioned high above the Durance valley

Napoleon in Provence

In his bid to regain power after his exile on Elba, Napoleon knew his only chance of success was to win over Sisteron. On 1 March, 1815, he secretly sailed from the island of Elba, landing at Golfe-Juan with 1,026 soldiers.

He hastily started his journey to Paris via Grenoble, making his first stop at Grasse, where the people shut their doors against him. Abandoning carriages, cannon and horses, Napoleon and his troops scrambled along mule-tracks and across difficult terrain, surmounting summits of more than 3,000 ft (1,000 m). At Digne, he lunched at the Hôtel du Petit Paris before spending the night at Malijai Château where he waited for news of the royalist stronghold of Sisteron. He was in luck. The arsenal was empty and he entered the town on 5 March – a plaque on rue du Jeu-de-Paume honours the event. The people were, at last, beginning to warm to him.

The dramatic *Napoleon Crossing the Alps*, painted by Jacques Louis David in 1800

One of the distinctive residential villas in Barcelonnette

of Provence in 1112. The town's Alpine setting gives it a Swiss flavour; it also has Mexican spice. The Arnaud brothers, whose business in Barcelonnette was failing, emigrated to Mexico and made their fortune. Others followed, and on their return in the early 20th century, they built grand villas which encircle the town.

Housed in one of the villas is the **Musée de la Vallée**, where the Mexican connection is explained through illustrations and costumes. There are four other branches of this museum in the Ubaye valley, at St-Paul, Jauziers, Pontis and Le Lauzet.

In summer there is an information point here for the Parc National du Mercantour *(see p101)*. The park stretches along

the Italian border and straddles the Alpes Maritimes region in the south. It is a haven for birds, wildlife and fauna, with two major archaeological sites.

🏛 Musée de la Vallée
10 ave de la Libération. **Tel** 04 92 81 27 15. **Open** Wed–Sat pm (Jul & Aug: daily). **Closed** mid-Nov–mid-Dec, 1 Jan, 1 May, 25 Dec. 🅿 📷 in summer.

❹ Mont Pelat

🚋 Thorame-Verdon. 🚌 Colmars, Allos. 🛈 Pl de la Coopérative, Allos (04 92 83 02 81). 🆆 valdallos.com

This is the loftiest peak in the Provençal Alps, rising to a height of 3,050 m (10,017 ft) and all around are mountains and breathtaking passes, some

of them closed by snow until June. Among them are the Col de Cayolle (2,327 m/7,717 ft) on the D2202 to the east, and the hair-raising Col d'Allos (2,250 m/ 7,380 ft) on the D908 to the west. South of Mont Pelat, in the heart of the Parc National du Mercantour, is the beautiful 50-ha (124-acre) Lac d'Allos. It is the largest natural lake in Europe at this altitude. The setting is idyllic, ringed by snowy mountains, its crystal-clear waters swimming with trout and char. Another record-breaker is Cime de la Bonette, on the D64 northeast of Mont Pelat, at 2,862 m (9,390 ft) the highest pass in Europe. It has what is perhaps the most magnificent view in all this abundant mountain scenery.

Cime de la Bonette, the highest mountain pass in Europe

❺ Colmars

Road map E2. 🚠 400. 🚌
ℹ️ Ancienne Auberge Fleurie (04 92 83
41 92). 🏪 Tue & Fri (Jun–Sep). 🌐 **col
marslesalpes-verdontourisme.com**

Colmars is an unusually complete
fortified town, nestling between
two 17th-century forts. You
can walk along the 12-m (40-ft)
ramparts, which look across
oak-planked roofs. The town is
named after the hill on which
it is built, *collis Martis*, where the
Romans built a temple to the
god Mars. Vauban, the military
engineer, designed its lasting
look. On the north side, an alley
leads to the 17th-century **Fort
de Savoie**, a fine example of
military architecture. From the
Porte de France a path leads
to the Fort de France.

Situated among wooded hills
Colmars is popular in summer,
when time is spent relaxing on
wooden balconies (*soleillades
lit*, sun-traps), or strolling along
alpine paths with beautiful views.
Signposts lead from the town to
the Cascade de la Lance, a waterfall half-an-hour's walk away.

The fortified town of Colmars, flanked by two compact forts

🏰 Fort de Savoie
04370 Colmars. **Tel** 04 92 83 41 92.
Open mid-Jun–mid-Sep: Sat–Mon pm
(Jul–Aug: daily); mid-Sep–mid-Jun: by
appt only. 🅿️ 📷 obligatory.

❻ Digne-les-Bains

Road map D2. 🚠 17,700. 🚉 🚌
ℹ️ Pl du Tampinet (04 92 36 62 62).
🏪 Wed & Sat (Blvd Gassendi).
🌐 **ot-dignelesbains.fr**

The capital of the region
has been a spa town
since Roman times,
primed by seven hot
springs. It still attracts
those seeking various
cures, who visit the
Thermes Digne-les-Bains,
a short drive southeast
of the town. Health
seems to radiate from
Digne's airy streets,
particularly from the
boulevard Gassendi,
named after local mathe
matician and astronomer
Pierre Gassendi (1592–
1655). This is where the

Street sculpture
in Digne

town's four-day lavender
carnival rolls out in August *(see
p229)*, for Digne styles itself the
"capitale de la Lavande". In recent
years, the town has promoted
itself as an important centre
for modern sculpture, which
liberally furnishes the town.

The **Musée Gassendi**, found
in the old town hospice, houses
16th–19th-century French, Italian
and Dutch paintings, a collection
of contemporary art and
19th-century scientific
instruments. Among
portraits of Digne's
famous is Alexandra
David-Néel, one of
Europe's most intrepid
travellers, who died in
1969 aged 101. Her
house, *Samten-Dzong*
(fortress of meditation)
is now the **Maison
Alexandra David-Néel**
and includes a Tibetan
centre and a museum.
At the north end of
boulevard Gassendi is
the 19th-century **Grande
Fontaine** and beyond

lies the oldest part of Digne-les-
Bains. The grand cathedral of
Notre-Dame-du-Bourg, built
between 1200–1330, is the
largest Romanesque church in
Haute Provence. It has its own
archaeological crypt with relics
dating back to the Roman era.

The **Jardin des Cordeliers**,
an enchanting walled garden
in a converted convent, houses
a large collection of medicinal
plants and a sensory garden.

🏛️ Musée Gassendi
64 blvd Gassendi. **Tel** 04 92 31 45 29.
Open Wed–Mon (Oct–mid-May: Sat &
Sun pm only). **Closed** public hols,
25 Dec–2 Jan. 🅿️ ♿ 📷 🔊
🌐 **musee-gassendi.org**

🏛️ Maison Alexandra David-Néel
27 ave Maréchal Juin. **Tel** 04 92 31
32 38. **Open** Apr–Jun & Sep–Mar: Tue–
Sun (Dec–Mar: pm only); Jul–Aug:
daily, by guided tour only. 📷 📷
🌐 **alexandra-david-neel.org**

🌿 Jardin des Cordeliers
Couvent des Cordeliers, Ave Paul
Martin. **Tel** 04 92 31 59 59. **Open** Mar–
Nov: Mon pm–Fri. **Closed** public hols.
♿ 📷

❼ Les Pénitents des Mées

Road map D3. ✈ Marseille 🚉 St-Auban. 🚌 Les Mées. ℹ La Mairie, 18 blvd de la République (04 92 34 36 38).

The curiously-shaped Pénitents des Mées, dominating the area

One of the most spectacular geological features in the region is Les Pénitents des Mées, a serried rank of columnar rocks more than 100 m (300 ft) high and over a mile (2 km) long. The strange rock formation is said to be a cowled procession of banished monks. In local mythology, monks from the mountain of Lure took a fancy to some Moorish beauties, captured by a lord during the time of the Saracen invasion in the 6th century. Saint Donat, a hermit who inhabited a nearby cave, punished their effrontery by turning them into stone.

The small village of Les Mées is tucked away at the north end. Walk up to the chapel of St-Roch for a view of the rocks' strange formation of millions of pebbles and stones.

❽ Lurs

Road map D3. ⛰ 390. 🚌 La Brillanne. ℹ Mairie (04 92 79 95 24).

The Bishops of Sisteron and the Princes of Lurs were given ownership of the fortified town of Lurs in the 9th century, under the command of Charlemagne.

In the early 20th century the small town was virtually abandoned, and was only repopulated after World War II, mainly by printers and graphic artists, who keep their trade in the forefront of events with an annual competition.

The narrow streets of the old town, entered through the Porte d'Horloge, are held in by the medieval ramparts. North of the restored Château of the Bishop-Princes is the beginning of the 300-m (900-ft) **Promenade des Evêques** (Bishops' walk), lined with 15 oratories leading to the chapel of Notre-Dame-de-Vie and stupendous views over the sea of poppy fields and olive groves of the Durance valley.

Head north out of Lurs on the N96, to the 12th-century **Prieuré de Ganagobie**. The church has beautifully restored red-, black- and white-tiled mosaics, inspired by oriental and Byzantine design and imagery. Offices are held several times a day by the monks – visitors may attend.

🏛 Prieuré de Ganagobie
N96, 04310. **Tel** 04 92 68 00 04. **Open** Tue–Sun pms. **Closed** 1 week in mid-Jan. 📷

Floor mosaic of the church of the 12th-century Prieuré de Ganagobie

Le Train des Pignes

An enjoyable day out is to be found on the Chemin de Fer de Provence, a short railway line that runs from Digne-les-Bains to Nice. It is the remaining part of a network that was designed to link the Côte d'Azur with the Alps, built between 1891 and 1911. Today the Train des Pignes, a diesel train, usually with two carriages, runs four times a day throughout the year. It is an active and popular service, used by locals going about their daily business as much as by tourists. It rattles along the single track at a fair pace, rolling by the white waters of the Asse

de Moriez and thundering over 16 viaducts, 15 bridges and through 25 tunnels.

The train journey is a great way of seeing the countryside, although the ride can be bumpy at times. The most scenic parts are in uninhabited countryside, such as between St-André-les-Alps and Annot, where the *grès d'Annot* can be seen (*see p191*). The journey takes about 3 hours each way and can be broken en route. Entrevaux (*see p191*) is a good place to stop. For tickets, call 04 92 03 80 80 (from Nice), 04 92 31 01 58 (from Digne-les-Bains) or visit http://tourisme. trainprovence.com

Scenic view of Forcalquier, the former capital of Alpes-de-Haute-Provence

❾ Forcalquier

Road map C3. 🚗 4,875. 🚌
ℹ️ 13 pl du Bourguet (04 92 75 10 02).
🅿️ Mon, Thu. 🌐 haute-provence-tourisme.com

Crowned by a ruined castle and domed chapel of the 19th-century Notre-Dame-de-Provence, this town – once an independent state and the capital of the region – is now a shadow of its former self. Although the weekly market is a lively affair, drawing local artists and artisans.

There are some fine façades in the old town, but only one remaining gate, the Porte des Cordeliers. The Couvent des Cordeliers (closed to visitors) dates from 1236, and is where the local lords have been entombed.

The **Musée Départemental Ethnologique** in nearby Mane preserves the history of the people and culture of Haute-Provence. The **Observatoire de Haute Provence** to the south of the town was sited here after

a study in the 1930s to find the town with the cleanest air. The Centre d'Astronomie nearby is a must for star-gazers.

🏛️ Musée Départemental Ethnologique
N100, Mane. **Tel** 04 92 75 70 50.
Open Feb–Apr & Oct–mid-Dec: Wed–Mon; May–Sep: daily. **Closed** 24, 25 & 31 Dec. 🅿️ 📷 for groups. 📷

🔭 Observatoire de Haute Provence
St-Michel l'Observatoire. **Tel** 04 92 70 64 00. **Open** Easter–1 Nov: Wed pm.
🅿️ from the Office de tourisme.
📷 only. 🌐 obs-hp.fr

❿ Manosque

Road map C3. 🚗 22,825. 🚌 🚌
ℹ️ Pl du Docteur Joubert (04 92 72 16 00). 🅿️ Sat. 🌐 ville-manosque.fr

France's national nuclear research centre, Cadarache, has brought prosperity to Manosque, a town which has sprawled beyond its original hill site above the

Durance. The centre has 13th- and 14th-century gates, Porte Soubeyran and Porte Saunerie. The perfume shop in rue Grande was once the atelier of writer Jean Giono's mother and the second floor belonged to his father *(see p32)*. The **Centre Jean Giono** tells the story of his life. The town's adoptive son is the painter Jean Carzou, who decorated the interior of the **Couvent de la Présentation** with apocalyptic allegories of modern life.

🎫 Centre Jean Giono
3 blvd E Bourges. **Tel** 04 92 70 54 54.
Open Tue–Sat (Oct–Mar: pm only).
Closed public hols, 25 Dec–2 Jan.
🅿️ 📷 🌐 centrejeangiono.com

🎫 Couvent de la Présentation
9 blvd Elémir Bourges. **Tel** 04 92 87 40 49. **Open** Apr–Oct: 10am–12:30pm & 2–6pm Tue–Sat; Nov–Mar: 2–6pm Wed–Sat. **Closed** Sun, public hols, 23 Dec–2 Jan. 🅿️

⓫ Gréoux-les-Bains

Road map D3. 🚗 2,640. 🚌 ℹ️ 7 pl Hôtel de Ville (04 92 70 01 00). 🅿️ Tue & Thu. 🌐 greouxlesbains.com

The thermal waters of this spa town have been enjoyed since antiquity, when baths were built by the Romans in the 1st century AD. Gréoux flourished in the 19th century, and the waters can still be enjoyed at the Etablissement Thermal, on the east side of the village, on Avenue du Verdon, where bubbling, sulphurous water arrives at the rate of 100,000 litres (22,000 gallons) an hour.

Lavender and Lavendin

The famous flower of Provence colours the Plateau de Valensole every July. Lavender began to be cultivated in the region in the 19th century and provides the world with around 80 per cent of its needs. Harvesting continues until September and is mostly mechanized although, in some areas, it is still collected in cloth sacks slung over the back. After two or three days' drying it is sent to a distillery.

These days the cultivation of a hybrid called lavendin has overtaken traditional lavender. Lavender is now used mainly for perfumes and cosmetics, lavendin for soaps.

Harvesting the abundant lavender in Haute Provence

The sweeping fields of the Plateau de Valensole, one of the largest lavender-growing areas of Provence

A restored castle ruin of the Templars is on a high spot and an open-air theatre is in the grounds. **Le Musée des Miniatures, poupées et jouets du Monde** is a museum with 148 miniatures from 1832 to the present, including dolls, costumes and toy trains.

🎠 **Le Musée des Miniatures, poupées et jouets du Monde**
16 ave des Alpes. **Tel** 06 84 62 71 23. **Open** mid-Apr–Oct: Mon, Wed & Fri pm only. **Closed** public hols. 🅿 🔌 👣 for groups.

Corinthian columns front the Gallo-Roman baths in Gréoux-les-Bains

⑫ Valensole

Road map D3. 🔺 3,330. **𝑖** Pl des Héros de la Résistance (04 92 74 90 02). 🚌 Sat. 🌐 **valensole.fr**

This is the centre of France's most important lavender-growing area. It sits on the edge of the Valensole plains with a sturdy-towered Gothic church at its height. Admiral Villeneuve, the unsuccessful adversary of Admiral Nelson at the Battle of Trafalgar,

was born here in 1763. Signs for locally made lavender honey are everywhere and just outside the town is the **Musée Vivant de l'Abeille**. This is an interactive museum explaining the intriguing life of the honey bee, with informative demonstrations, photographs and videos. In the summer, you can visit the beehives and see the beekeepers at work.

🏛 **Musée Vivant de l'Abeille**
Rte de Manosque. **Tel** 04 92 74 85 28. **Open** Tue–Sat. **Closed** public hols. 🔌 🅿

⑬ Riez

Road map D3. 🔺 1,850. 🚌 **𝑖** Pl de la Mairie (04 92 77 99 09). 🚌 Wed & Sat. 🌐 **ville-riez.fr**

At the edge of the sweeping Valensole plateau is this unspoiled village, filled with small shops selling ceramics and traditional *santons*, honey and lavender. Its grander past is reflected in the Renaissance façades of the houses and mansions in the old town. This is entered through the late-13th-century Porte Aiguyère, which leads on to the peaceful, tree-lined Grand Rue, with fine examples of Renaissance architecture at numbers 27 and 29.

The most unusual site is the remains of the 1st-century AD Roman temple dedicated to Apollo. It stands out of time and place, in the middle of a field by the river Colostre; this

was the original site of the town where the Roman colony, *Reia Apollinaris,* lived. On the other side of the river is a rare example of Merovingian architecture, a small baptistry dating from the 5th century.

The village has a number of fountains: Fontaine Benoîte, opposite Porte Sanson, dates to 1819, although a fountain has existed on this spot since the 15th century; the 17th-century Fontaine de Blanchon is fed by an underground spring – its use was reserved for washing the clothes of the infirm in the days before antibiotics and vaccines; and the soft waters of the spring-fed Fontaine de Saint-Maxime were believed to possess healing qualities for the eyes.

Ruins of the Roman temple in Riez, built in 1st century AD

⓮ Tour of the Gorges du Verdon

The breathtaking chasm of the Gorges du Verdon is one of the most spectacular natural phenomena in France. The Verdon river, a tributary of the Durance, cuts into the rock up to 700 m (2,300 ft) deep. A tour of the gorges takes at least a day and this circular route encompasses its most striking features. At its east and west points are the historic towns of Castellane, the natural entry point to the gorges, and Moustiers-Ste-Marie. Parts of the tour are particularly mountainous, so drivers must be aware of hairpin bends and narrow roads with sheer drops. Weather conditions can also be hazardous and roads can be icy until late spring.

Hikers in one of the deep gorges

⑤ La Palud-sur-Verdon
Organized walking excursions start at the village of La Palud, the so-called capital of the Gorges.

④ Moustiers-Ste-Marie
Set on craggy heights, the town is famed for its faïence *(p190)*.

Flowered-façade in Moustiers

③ Aiguines
The beautifully restored 17th-century château crowns the small village, with fine views down to the Lac de Ste-Croix.

Key

— Tour route
= Other roads
☀ Viewpoint

Tips for Drivers

Tour length: 113 km (72 miles).
Stopping-off points: La Palud-sur-Verdon has several cafés and Moustiers-Ste-Marie is a good place to stop for lunch. For an overnight stop, there are hotels and campsites in the town of Castellane. *(See also pp250–51.)*

The azure-blue waters of the enormous Lac de Ste-Croix

Outdoor Activities

The Verdon gorges have offered fantastic opportunities for the adventurous since Isadore Blanc (1875–1932) made the first complete exploration in 1905. Today's activities include hiking, climbing, canoeing and white-water rafting *(see pp230–31)*. Boating needs to be supervised as the river is not always navigable and the powerful water flow can change dramatically.

White-water rafting down the fast-flowing Verdon river

Gorge explorer Isadore Blanc

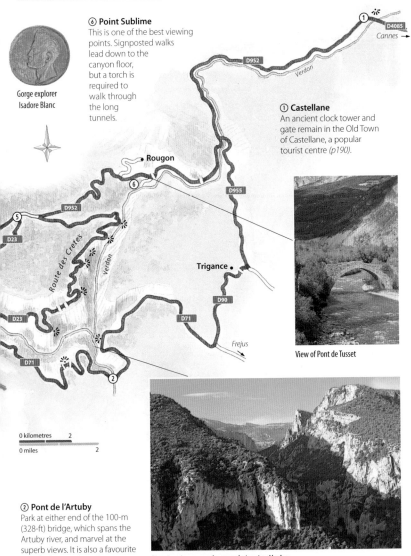

⑥ Point Sublime
This is one of the best viewing points. Signposted walks lead down to the canyon floor, but a torch is required to walk through the long tunnels.

① Castellane
An ancient clock tower and gate remain in the Old Town of Castellane, a popular tourist centre *(p190)*.

View of Pont de Tusset

② Pont de l'Artuby
Park at either end of the 100-m (328-ft) bridge, which spans the Artuby river, and marvel at the superb views. It is also a favourite spot for bungee jumping.

Stunning view across the meandering river Verdon

⑮ Moustiers-Ste-Marie

Road map D3. ⛰ 700. ▦ **i** Pl de l'Eglise (04 92 74 67 84). 🕑 Fri am; craft market (Jul/Aug).
W moustiers.eu

The setting of the town of Moustiers is stunning, high on the edge of a ravine, beneath craggy rocks. Situated in the town centre is the parish church, with a three-storey Romanesque belfry. Above it, a path meanders up to the 12th-century chapel of Notre-Dame-de-Beauvoir. The view across Lac de Ste-Croix is magnificent.

A heavy iron chain, 227 m (745 ft) in length, is suspended above the ravine. Hanging from the centre is a five-pointed, golden star. Although it was renewed in 1957, it is said to date back to the 13th century, when the chevalier Blacas hoisted it up in thanks for his release from captivity during the Seventh Crusade of St Louis *(see p46)*.

Moustiers is a popular tourist town, the streets crowded in summer. This is due to its setting and its ceramics. The original Moustiers ware is housed in the **Musée de la Faïence**. Modern reproductions can be bought in the town. The new **Musée de la Préhistoire** in Quinson, 40 km (25 miles) south, is a must.

▦ Musée de la Faïence
Le Village, Rue du Seigneur de la Clue, Moustiers-Ste-Marie. **Tel** 04 92 74 61 64.
Open Apr–Oct: Wed–Mon; Nov, Dec, Feb & Mar: Sat–Sun. 🅿 🚻 🛒 🔊 📷

Notre-Dame-du-Roc chapel, perched high above the town of Castellane

⑯ Castellane

Road map D3. ⛰ 1,600. ▦ **i** Rue Nationale (04 92 83 61 14). 🕑 Wed & Sat.
W castellane-verdontourisme.com

This is one of the main centres for the Gorges du Verdon, surrounded by campsites and caravans. Tourists squeeze into the town centre in summer and, in the evenings, fill the cafés after a day's hiking, climbing, canoeing and white-water rafting. It is a well-sited town, beneath an impressive 180-m (600-ft) slab of grey rock. On top of this, dominating the skyline, is the chapel of **Notre-Dame-du-Roc**, built in 1703. A strenuous, 30-minute walk from behind the parish church to the top is rewarded with superb views. Castellane was once a sturdy fortress and repelled invasion several times. The lifting of the siege by the Huguenots in 1586 is commemorated every year with firecrackers at the Fête des Pétardiers (last Sun in Jan).

The town's fortifications were completely rebuilt in the 14th century after most of the town, dating from Roman times, crumbled and slipped into the Verdon valley. Most social activity takes place in the main square, place Marcel-Sauvaire, which is lined with small hotels that have catered for generations of visitors.

All that remains of the ram-parts is the Tour Pentagonal and a small section of the old wall, which lie just beyond the 12th-century St-Victor church, on the way up to the chapel.

Moustiers Ware

The most important period of Moustiers faïence was from its inception in 1679 until the late 18th century, when a dozen factories were producing this highly glazed ware. Decline followed and production came to a standstill in 1874, until it was revived in 1925 by Marcel Provence. He chose to follow traditional methods, and output continues.

The distinctive glaze of Moustiers faïence was first established in the late 17th century by Antoine Clérissy, a local potter who was given the secret of faïence by an Italian monk. The first pieces to be fired had a luminous blue glaze and were decorated with figurative scenes, often copied from engravings of hunting or mythological subjects. In 1738, Spanish glazes were introduced and brightly coloured floral and fauna designs were used.

A number of potters continue the tradition, with varying degrees of quality, and can be seen at work in their *ateliers*.

A tureen in Moustiers' highly glazed faïence ware

The narrow streets of Moustiers

⓱ St-André-les-Alpes

Road map D3. 📍 920. 🚉 🚌 **i** Place Marcel Pastorelli (04 92 89 02 39). 🛒 Wed & Sat. **W** saintandrelesalpes-verdontourisme.com

Lying at the north end of the Lac de Castillon, where the river Isolde meets the river Verdon, is St-André. It is a popular summer holiday and leisure centre, scattered around the sandy flats on the lakeside. The lake is man-made, formed by damming the river by the 90-m (295-ft) Barrage de Castillon and is a haven for rafting, canoeing and kayaking as well as swimming and fishing.

Inland, lavender fields and orchards make for picturesque walks and hang-gliding is so popular here that one of the local producers advertises its wine as "the wine of eagles".

⓲ Annot

Road map E3. 📍 1,120. 🚉 **i** Place du Germe (04 92 83 23 03). 🛒 Tue. **W** annot-tourisme.com

The town of Annot, on the Train des Pignes railway line (see p185), has a distinct Alpine feel. Annot lies in the Vaïre valley, crisscrossed by icy waters streaming down from the mountains. The surrounding scenery however, is a more unfamiliar pattern of jagged rocks and deep caves.

Vast sandstone boulders, known as the *grès d'Annot*, are strewn around the town, and

The steep path of zigzag ramps leading to the citadel of Entrevaux

local builders have constructed houses against these haphazard rocks, using their sheer faces as outside walls. The *vieille ville* lies behind the main road, where there is a Romanesque church. The tall buildings that line the narrow streets have retained some of their original 15th- to 18th-century carved stone lintels.

Most Sundays (May–Oct) in summer, a 1909 *belle époque* steam train chugs its way from Puget-Théniers to Annot, a pleasant way for visitors to enjoy the unspoiled countryside.

⓳ Entrevaux

Road map E3. 📍 950. 🚉 🚌 **i** Porte Royale du Pont Levis (04 93 05 46 73). **W** tourisme-entrevaux.fr

It is clear why Entrevaux is called a "fairy-tale town", as you cross the drawbridge and enter through the Porte Royale. The dramatic entrance is flanked by twin towers and from here you enter the Ville Forte.

Fortified in 1690 by the military engineer Vauban (1633–1707), Entrevaux became one of the strongest military sites on the Franco-Savoy border. Even the 17th-century cathedral was skilfully incorporated into the turreted ramparts.

Unlike most military strongholds, the citadel was not built on top of a hill, but strategically placed on a rocky outcrop. It was last used during World War I as a prison for German officers. A steep, zigzag track leads to the citadel, 156 m (511 ft) above the village. The 20-minute climb to the top, past basking lizards, should not be made in the midday heat.

Houses in the town of Annot built against huge sandstone rocks

TRAVELLERS' NEEDS

WHERE TO STAY

The diversity of Provence is reflected in the wide range of hotels it has to offer. Accommodation varies from luxurious palaces like the InterContinental Carlton in Cannes to simple country inns where a warm welcome, peaceful setting and often excellent cuisine are more customary than mod cons. Self-catering holidays are a popular and inexpensive option and on pages 196–7 information is given on renting a rural home or *gîte*, and on camping, as well as how to find B&Bs and youth hostels in the area.

Where to Look

There is no shortage of hotels in Provence and the Côte d'Azur. Ever since the crusades of the Middle Ages, the region has been hosting travellers in a variety of hotels across all price levels. Some of the best value coastal accommodation, especially for families, is found along the shores of the Var between Toulon and St-Tropez. The glamour and glitz come further east – the coast from Fréjus to Menton is predictably extravagant, but you can find accommodation to suit all budgets, from the exclusive Hotel du Cap-Eden-Roc, popular with film stars at Cap d'Antibes, to the 15th-century inn of the Hôtel des Arcades in Biot.

Inland, the major towns of Provence offer a good variety of hotels, from the luxurious mansions of Aix-en-Provence, Avignon and Arles to the more simple hostelries of the Luberon and the Var. Boutique hotels and deluxe *chambres d'hôtes* (B&Bs) have become very fashionable, making the picturesque fantasy of a converted farmhouse or medieval priory set in lavender fields a reality.

Palm trees shading the garden pool, Pastis Hotel St-Tropez *(see p199)*

Travellers seeking tranquillity can travel north to the wilds of Haute Provence where several historic châteaux, *auberges* (country inns) and *relais de poste* (post-houses) provide excellent accommodation and regional cuisine in rustic surroundings.

Those looking for a country idyll should head to the hills and valleys of the Central Var, the Luberon National Park or the foothills of Mont Ventoux. For an exciting, cosmopolitan base, Marseille is a great choice, with excellent hotels and restaurants on offer.

Hotel Types

Hotels in Provence can be divided into several categories. The region's famous luxury establishments include some of the most spectacular hotels in France. Many of these are located near the Mediterranean Sea, or in beautiful inland or hilltop settings. They come with a wide array of sports and spa facilities, private beaches, and usually a gastronomic restaurant.

Known for its art, Provence and the French Riviera also have some of the country's most chic and contemporary boutique hotels and B&Bs, many featuring minimalist or exotic interiors by hip designers. These tend to be located in the cities and resorts, and come equipped with all the modern conveniences, from iPod docks to rain showers. Many of them have spas or beauty and wellness centres.

Provence and the Cote d'Azur also boasts beautiful historic hotels and charming B&Bs. Located in castles, farmhouses, convents, medieval inns or mills, these establishments offer guests a chance to immerse themselves in the region's rich past. Rooms here are generally furnished with antiques, and

Stylish guest room at the luxurious InterContinental Carlton, Cannes *(see p198)*

◀ Antique shop, L'Isle-sur-la-Sorgue

many are set in century-old parks and gardens.

For those travelling with children, family hotels are the ideal option. While the romantic boutique hotels or upmarket B&Bs with antique furnishings may refuse guests under a certain age, most of the family hotels are quite welcoming, and may offer interconnecting rooms. Numerous country hotels now have annexes with bungalow apartments specifically designed for families. These may be only a few steps away from the swimming pool.

Classic hotels are generally purpose-built hotels and inns, many of which are still family-run. These establishments are found in virtually every village and the atmosphere is often extremely informal. The hotel is likely to be the focal point of the village, with the dining room and bar open to non-residents. The annual *Logis de France Fédération* guide, which can be ordered online at www.logis hotels.com, lists these one- and two-star restaurants-with-rooms (*auberges*), often specializing in regional cuisine. Many are basic roadside inns, with a few listed in the main towns and cities, but off the beaten track you can find charming farmhouses and inexpensive seaside hotels.

The classic category also includes some chain hotels, such as the **Campanile** and **Ibis** chains, which offer inexpensive yet comfortable accommodation on the outskirts of towns. They are a reliable option and can be booked directly online or over the phone by credit card.

Other modern chains are geared to the business traveller and are found in most major towns. **Sofitel**, **Novotel** and **Mercure** all have hotels in Aix, Nice and Marseille.

Hotel Prices

In many hotels, the price of each room depends on the view, size, decor or plumbing. Single occupancy rates are usually the same as two sharing – prices are normally per room, not per person. Tax and service

La Bastide de Voulonne, Cabrières d'Avignon-Gordes *(p201)*

are included in the price, with the exception of *pension* (full board) and *demi-pension* (half board), and rates posted are exclusive of breakfast. In more remote areas, half board may be obligatory and is often necessary in places where the hotel has the only restaurant. For stays of just one night, many hotels offer a fixed-price, good value package including the room, dinner and breakfast *(soirée étape)*. In high season, popular coastal hotels may give preference to visitors who want half board.

Prices drop considerably in Provence in low season (Oct–Mar). Many hotels close for five months of the year, reopening for Easter. During festivals *(see pp36–9 and pp228–9)*, prices can rival high-season tariffs. In low season, discount packages are common along the coast. It is worth checking the Internet and the hotel website, as many of the biggest and most famous hotels offer fabulous deals during this period – even the palaces of the Riviera need to fill their rooms in winter.

Hotel Gradings

French hotels are classified by the tourist authorities into five categories: one to five stars, with the best of the five-star hotels called 'palaces'. A few very basic places are unclassified. These ratings give you an indication of the level of facilities you can expect but offer little idea of cleanliness, ambience or

friendliness of the owners. Some of the most charming hotels are blessed with few stars, while the higher ratings sometimes turn out to be impersonal business hotels.

Bed and Breakfast

As old-fashioned family hotels in Provence have been closed down by EU regulations, *chambres d'hôtes* (B&Bs) have risen to take their place. They come in all shapes and sizes, including some very stylish ones as pricey as four-star hotels. Many provide *table d'hôte* dinners on request. They are listed separately in tourist office brochures, and many are inspected and registered by the **Gîtes de France** organization.

Stays on working farms are also an excellent option for families. Listings and useful information pertaining to these can be found on the **Accueil en Provence Paysanne** and **Bienvenue à la Ferme** websites.

Impressive staircase and glass lift at the exclusive Hotel du Cap-Eden-Roc *(see p198)*

Antique-furnished guest room at the romantic Jardins Secrets, Nîmes *(see p200)*

Facilities and Meals

Facilities will vary greatly depending on the location and rating of each hotel. In more remote areas, most hotels have adjoining restaurants and nearly all feature a breakfast room or terrace. Many three-star hotels have swimming pools, which can be a godsend in the summer. Parking is readily available at country hotels. Some city hotels have underground or guarded parking – in larger cities like Marseille and Nice this is becoming a necessity as car crime is a serious problem.

Many Provençal hotels are converted buildings and, while this adds a definite charm, it can mean eccentric plumbing and disturbing creaks and bumps in the night. Some hotels are near a main road or a town square – choosing a room at the back is usually all that is required for a peaceful night. Most hotels and *chambres d'hôtes* now offer free Wi-Fi, at least in the public areas, if not in the rooms.

Traditional French breakfasts are common in Provence and in summer are often enjoyed outside. Evening meals are served daily until about 9pm. Dining rooms are often closed on Sunday – check before you arrive. Check-out time is usually late morning; if you stay any longer you will have to pay for an extra day.

Booking

In high season, it is imperative to book well in advance, especially for any popular coastal hotel. During peak season (Jun–Sep), proprietors may ask for a deposit. Outside peak season you may be able to turn up on the day, but it is always wise to phone ahead to make sure the establishment is open. Check hotel websites, many of which allow you to book online and offer some good deals for Internet bookings.

Self-Catering

Provence is a popular self-catering destination, and many companies specialize in renting anything from rural farm cottages to beach apartments. One of the best organizations is **Gîtes de France**, with its headquarters in Paris, which provides detailed lists of accommodation to rent by the week in each *département*.

The *gîte* owners are obliged to live nearby and are always welcoming, but rarely speak much English. Do not expect luxury from your *gîte* (holiday cottage) as facilities are basic, but it is a great way to get a better insight into real Provençal life. The websites of **Clévacances**, **AirBNB**, **Homelidays** and **Owners Direct** list affordable *gîte* and apartment rentals.

Hostels

For the independent traveller, this is the cheapest, and often the most convivial accommodation option. There are nine youth hostels in Provence, all of which are under the umbrella of **Hostelling International**. A membership card from your national **Youth Hostel Association** (www.yha.org.uk) is required, or an *Ajiste* card, which you can obtain from French hostels. In each university town, the **Centre Régional Information Jeunesse (CRIJ)** can provide a great deal of information about student life and a list of inexpensive accommodation options.

Camping

A popular pastime in Provence, camping remains an inexpensive and atmospheric way of seeing the area. Facilities range from a basic one-star farm or vineyard site to the camping metropolises of the Riviera, complete with water fun parks and satellite TV. **Eurocamp** specializes in family holidays. Luxury tents are pre-assembled at the campsite of your choice,

Camping in Provence, a popular accommodation alternative

and everything is ready on arrival. 'Glamping' – glamorous camping – has become increasingly popular in France, and offers unusual outdoor accommodation. Some campsites require visitors to have a special *camping carnet*, available from clubs such as the **Fédération Française de Camping et de Caravaning**.

Disabled Travellers

Due to the venerable design of most Provençal hotels, few are able to offer unrestricted wheelchair access. Larger hotels have lifts, and hotel staff will go out of their way to aid disabled guests. Most resort hotels and many B&Bs have at least one or two accessible rooms. The **Association des Paralysés de France (APF)** has useful information on their website.

Other useful sources of information are **Mobility International** and **Tourism for All**, who publish a guide to France listing specialized tour operators for disabled travellers.

Recommended Hotels

The hotels and B&Bs listed in this guide have been carefully chosen and are among the best in Provence in their categories: Boutique, Classic, Family, Luxury and Historic. The establishments have been chosen from all over Provence for the quality of accommodation they offer and in some cases, for offering good value for money. The hotel listings on pages 198–201 are arranged by *département* and town according to price.

Among the listings, hotels and B&Bs have been designated as "DK Choice" for one or more of their outstanding features. This could be for the beauty of the location or the views, for the exceptional facilities on offer or the historic charm of the places, or any other feature that sets them apart from the rest of the entries here.

Olive groves surround the pool at serene La Bonne Etape, Château-Arnoux *(see p201)*

DIRECTORY

Hotel Types

Campanile
W campanile.com

French Government Tourist Office
UK: Lincoln House, 300 High Holborn, London WC1V 7JH.
Tel (00 44) 20 70 61 66 00.
W uk.france.fr
US: 29th Floor, 825 Third Ave, New York, NY 10022.
Tel (212) 838 7800.
W us.france.fr

Ibis, Novotel, Sofitel, Mercure
Tel (087) 1663 0624 (UK).
Tel 08 25 88 00 00 (France).
W accorhotels.com

Bed and Breakfast

Accueil en Provence Paysanne
W accueil-paysan-paca.com

Bienvenue à la Ferme
W bienvenue-a-la-ferme.com

Self-Catering

AirBNB
W airbnb.fr

Clévacances
W clevacances.com

Gîtes de France
40 avenue de Flandre, 75019 Paris.
Tel 01 49 70 75 75.
W gites-de-france.com

Homelidays
W homelidays.com

Owners Direct
W ownersdirect.co.uk

Hostels

American Youth Hostel Association
Tel (240) 650 2100 (US).
W hiusa.org

CRIJ Provence Alpes
96 la Canebière, 13001 Marseille.
Tel 04 91 24 33 50.
W crijpa.fr

CRIJ Cote D'Azur
19 rue Gioffredo, 06000 Nice.
Tel 04 93 80 93 93.
W ijca.fr

Hostelling International
UK. **Tel** (01707) 324170.
W hihostels.com

Camping

Eurocamp UK
UK. **Tel** (016) 1694 9014.
W eurocamp.co.uk

Fédération Française de Camping et de Caravaning
78 rue de Rivoli, 75004 Paris.
Tel 01 42 72 84 08.
W ffcc.fr

Disabled Travellers

APF
13 pl Rungis, 75013 Paris.
Tel 01 53 80 15 56.
W apf.asso.fr

Mobility International USA
132 E Broadway, Eugene, Oregon 97401.
Tel (541) 343 1284.
W miusa.org

Tourism for All
7A Pixel Mill, 44 Appleby Road, Kendall, Cumbria LA9 6ES.
Tel (0845) 124 9971.
W tourismforall.org.uk

Where to Stay

The Riviera and the Alpes Maritimes

ANTIBES: Mas Djoliba €€
Family   Map E3
29 av Provence, 06600
Tel *04 93 34 02 48*
Ⓦ hotel-djoliba.com
Charming, old-fashioned farmhouse with palm trees around its pool and terrace.

BEAULIEU-SUR-MER: La Réserve de Beaulieu €€
Luxury   Map F3
5 blvd du Maréchal Leclerc, 06310
Tel *04 93 01 00 01*
Ⓦ reservebeaulieu.com
Elegant hotel with a magnificent seaside pool and spa. Michelin-starred restaurant.

BIOT: Hôtel des Arcades €
Historic   Map E3
14/16 pl des Arcades, 06410
Tel *04 93 65 01 04*
Ⓦ hotel-restaurant-les-arcades.com
Small but comfortable rooms in a 15th-century inn with a quiet, homely atmosphere.

CANNES: L'Hotel Carolina €
Classic   Map E4
35 rue Hoche, 06400
Tel *04 93 38 33 67*
Ⓦ carolina-hotel.com
An affordable option near the Croisette, offering spacious rooms with minibars and flatscreen TVs.

CANNES: InterContinental Carlton €€€
Luxury   Map E4
58 la Croisette, 06400
Tel *04 93 06 40 06*
Ⓦ intercontinental-carlton-cannes.com
Glamorous Art Deco landmark with breathtaking suites and a fabulous private beach.

CAP D'ANTIBES: La Gardiole et La Garoupe €€
Family   Map E3
60–74 chemin de la Garoupe, 06160
Tel *04 92 93 33 33*
Ⓦ hotel-lagaroupe-gardiole.com
Quiet, simple rooms in a 1920s building surrounded by trees. Friendly, helpful staff.

CAP D'ANTIBES: Hotel du Cap-Eden-Roc €€€
Luxury   Map E3
Blvd Kennedy, 06601
Tel *04 93 61 39 01*
Ⓦ hotel-du-cap-eden-roc.com
A Riviera hideaway for the rich and famous; features luxury suites, apartments, seaside cabanas and five clay tennis courts.

EZE: Hermitage du Col d'Eze €
Classic   Map F3
1951 av des Diables Bleus, 06360
Tel *04 93 41 00 68*
Ⓦ ezehermitage.com
This shabby-chic hotel is a good budget option with spectacular mountain views. Free Wi-Fi.

EZE: La Chèvre d'Or €€€
Luxury   Map F3
Rue du Barri, 06360
Tel *04 92 10 66 66*
Ⓦ chevredor.com
A plush hotel with breathtaking views and romantic, individually decorated rooms.

JUAN-LES-PINS: Hotel des Mimosas €€
Classic   Map E4
Rue Pauline, 06160
Tel *04 93 61 04 16*
Ⓦ hotelmimosas.com
Just a short walk from the station, this gracious hotel is surrounded by beautiful tropical gardens.

MENTON: Hotel Napoléon €€
Classic   Map F3
29 porte de France, 06500
Tel *04 93 35 89 50*
Ⓦ napoleon-menton.com
Bright, modern rooms decorated with Jean Cocteau-style prints that offer lovely views of the bay.

MONACO: Novotel Monte Carlo €€
Family   Map F3
16 blvd Princesse Charlotte, 98000
Tel *00 377 99 99 83 00*
Ⓦ novotel.com
Avant-garde style hotel equipped with all modern facilities, located on the historic former site of Radio Monte Carlo.

MONACO: Hôtel Hermitage €€€
Luxury   Map F3
Square Beaumarchais, 98000
Tel *00 377 98 06 40 00*
Ⓦ hotelhermitagemontecarlo.com
Opulent *belle époque* landmark with a spectacular, glass-domed Winter Garden foyer. Private beach and golf course.

NICE: Hotel Windsor €€
Boutique   Map F3
11 rue Dalpozzo, 06000
Tel *04 93 88 59 35*
Ⓦ hotelwindsornice.com
Hotel Windsor offers a vibrant and artistic ambience. Relax in the pool in the exotic garden. Free Wi-Fi.

NICE: Le Négresco €€€
Luxury   Map F3
37 promenade des Anglais, 06000
Tel *04 93 16 64 00*
Ⓦ hotel-negresco-nice.com
A landmark since it opened in 1913, this palatial hotel is popular with the well-heeled who want to soak up the vintage atmosphere.

ST-JEAN-CAP-FERRAT: Hotel Brise Marine €€
Family   Map F3
58 Jean Mermoz, 06230
Tel *04 93 76 04 36*
Ⓦ hotel-brisemarine.com
Located merely steps away from the beach, this family-run hotel offers good views of the harbour. Welcoming staff.

Elegantly laid out breakfast table in a "sea-view" room at Le Négresco, Nice

DK Choice

**ST-JEAN-CAP-FERRAT:
Royal Riviera**
Luxury   €€€
Map F3
3 av Jean Monnet, 06230
Tel *04 93 76 31 00*
W royal-riviera.com
Built in 1904 at a superb location
overlooking "Billionaire's Bay",
Royal Riviera features luminous
and elegantly decorated rooms.
This ultra-stylish hotel has warm,
friendly staff and offers an
impeccable service.

**ST-PAUL DE VENCE:
Le Saint Paul**   €€€
Luxury   Map E3
86 rue Grande, 06570
Tel *04 93 32 65 25*
W lesaintpaul.com
Peaceful and artistic place with
lavishly furnished rooms. Exquisite
walled-in restaurant terrace with
a 17th-century fountain.

**VENCE: Hotel Villa
Roseraie**   €€
Boutique   Map E3
128 av Henri Giraud, 06140
Tel *04 93 58 02 20*
W villaroseraie.com
Belle époque town house with
a colourful, rustic chic decor
and delightful pool and garden.

**VILLEFRANCHE-SUR-MER:
Hôtel Versailles**   €€
Family   Map F3
7 av Princesse Grace, 06230
Tel *04 93 76 52 52*
W hotelversailles.com
Sleek, modern hotel with
magnificent views and a fine
Mediterranean restaurant.

The Var and the Iles
d'Hyères

**BORMES-LES-MIMOSAS:
Domaine du Mirage**   €€
Family   Map D4
38 rue de la Vue des Iles, 83230
Tel *04 94 05 32 60*
W domainedumirage.com
Victorian-style hotel with bright
rooms, each with a terrace or
balcony offering sea views. Good
restaurant and attentive staff.

**COLLOBRIÈRES: Hôtel
des Maures**   €
Classic   Map D4
19 blvd Lazare-Carnot, 83610
Tel *04 94 48 07 10*
W hoteldesmaures.fr
Family-run hotel offering
pleasant, budget-friendly rooms.
Superb traditional restaurant.

**FAYENCE: Moulin de la
Camandoule**   €
Historic   Map E3
*159 chemin de Notre Dame des
Cyprès, 83440*
Tel *04 94 76 00 84*
W camandoule.com
Provençal-style rooms in a
converted 15th-century olive
mill. Excellent on-site restaurant.

**FOX-AMPHOUX: Auberge du
Vieux Fox**   €
Historic   Map D3
Pl de l'Eglise, 83670
Tel *04 94 80 71 69*
Set in a 12th-century priory, this
hotel is a perfect stopover when
visiting the Gorges du Verdon.
Small and cosy rooms.

FRÉJUS: Hôtel L'Arena €€
Classic   Map E4
139–145 rue Gén de Gaulle, 83600
Tel *04 94 17 09 40*
W hotel-frejus-arena.com
Elegant hotel with a warm
Mediterranean decor, exotic
landscaped garden and outdoor
swimming pool. Located in the
heart of the town's historic centre.

GRIMAUD: Les Aurochs   €
Classic   Map E4
Quartier Embaude, 83310
Tel *04 94 81 31 90*
W lesaurochs.com
Housed in a converted sheep
farm near the Grimaud castle.
Choose between tranquil cottages
and rooms with private terraces.

**ÎLE DE PORQUEROLLES: Hôtel
Résidence Les Medes**   €€
Family   Map D5
Rue de la Douane, 83400
Tel *04 94 12 41 24*
W hotel-les-medes.fr
Located near the Courtade
beach, this hotel is set in a pretty
garden with a waterfall and a sun
terrace. Smartly furnished rooms.

**ÎLE DE PORT-CROS:
Le Manoir**   €€€
Historic   Map D5
Île de Port-Cros, 83400
Tel *04 94 05 90 52*
W hotel-lemanoirportcros.com
Simple and romantic century-
old mansion offering a warm
welcome, and delicious food.

**LA CADIÈRE D'AZUR: Hostellerie
Bérard & Spa**   €€
Historic   Map C4
6 rue Gabriel-Péri, 83740
Tel *04 94 90 11 43*
W hotel-berard.com
Converted 11th-century convent
with bright, spacious rooms that
offer magnificent views over the
Bandol vineyards.

Cosy and well-furnished room at the Pastis
Hotel, St-Tropez

**LA CELLE: L'Hostellerie de
l'Abbaye de la Celle**   €€€
Luxury   Map D4
10 pl du Général de Gaulle, 83170
Tel *04 98 05 14 14*
W abbaye-celle.com
Sublimely relaxing 12th-century
abbey hotel with stunning rooms
and a fabulous restaurant.

**PORT-GRIMAUD: Hôtel
le Suffren**   €€
Family   Map E4
16 pl du Marché, 83310
Tel *04 94 55 15 05*
W hotel-suffren.com
Pleasant waterfront hotel featuring
bright, airy rooms with balconies
overlooking the marina.

ST-TROPEZ: Lou Cagnard €€
Classic   Map E4
18 av Paul Roussel, 83990
Tel *04 94 97 04 24*
W hotel-lou-cagnard.com
Charming, wisteria-draped town
house with pretty rooms and a
lush garden.

DK Choice

**ST-TROPEZ: Pastis Hotel
St-Tropez**   €€€
Boutique   Map E4
75 av du Général Leclerc, 83990
Tel *04 98 12 56 50*
W pastis-st-tropez.com
An intimate hideaway furnished
with an eclectic mix of modern
and antique art. The private
garden with centuries-old palm
trees and a pool is the perfect
spot for breakfast or a nightcap.

**SEILLANS-VAR: Hôtel des
Deux Rocs**   €
Historic   Map E3
1 pl Font d'Amont, 83440
Tel *04 94 76 87 32*
W hoteldeuxrocs.com
This lovely 18th-century mansion
is good for families. Fantastic
Mediterranean restaurant.

For more information on types of hotels *see pages 194–5*

TOULON: Ibis Styles Toulon Centre Congrès €
Family   Map D4
Pl Besagne, 83000
Tel *04 98 00 81 00*
Ⓦ ibis.com
Centrally located chain hotel decorated in bright colours. Babysitting available.

TOURTOUR: L'Auberge St-Pierre €
Family   Map D3
Route d'Ampus, 83690
Tel *04 94 50 00 50*
Ⓦ aubergesaintpierre.com
Rural tranquillity in a 16th-century farmhouse with stunning views. Upscale facilities on site include a pool, spa, Jacuzzi and fitness room.

Bouches-du-Rhône and Nîmes

AIX-EN-PROVENCE: Hôtel Cézanne €€
Boutique   Map C4
40 av Victor Hugo, 13100
Tel *04 42 91 11 11*
Ⓦ hotelaix.com
Classy place with colourful designer rooms and an arty decor. Excellent breakfast-brunch buffet includes a glass of champagne.

AIX-EN-PROVENCE: Hôtel Saint Christophe €€
Family   Map C4
2 av Victor-Hugo, 13100
Tel *04 42 26 01 24*
Ⓦ hotel-saintchristophe.com
Superb, well-equipped hotel with Art Deco flair, and a bustling old-fashioned brasserie.

ARLES: Hôtel de l'Amphithéâtre €
Family   Map B3
5–7 rue Diderot, 13200
Tel *04 90 96 10 30*
Ⓦ hotelamphitheatre.fr
Characterful hotel set in a 17th-century building with charming Provençal decor and friendly staff.

DK Choice

ARLES: L'Hôtel Particulier €€€
Historic   Map B3
4 rue de la Monnaie, 13200
Tel *04 90 52 51 40*
Ⓦ hotel-particulier.com
A beautiful mansion with an aristocratic feel, featuring a walled garden, a swimming pool and an exquisite spa and hammam. The guest rooms are elegantly decorated with antiques. Impeccable service.

The colourful interior of Hôtel Cézanne, Aix-en-Provence

CASSIS: Le Clos des Arômes €
Classic   Map C4
10 rue Abbé Paul Mouton, 13260
Tel *04 42 01 71 84*
Ⓦ leclosdesaromes.fr
Old-fashioned but charming, this peaceful Provençal hotel has a lovely garden.

FONTVIEILLE: Villa Régalido €€
Boutique   Map B3
118 av Frédéric Mistral, 13990
Tel *04 90 54 60 22*
Ⓦ laregalido.com
Housed in a converted olive oil mill; offers luxurious rooms. Opt for a bedroom with a terrace overlooking the village.

LES BAUX-DE-PROVENCE: L'Hostellerie de la Reine Jeanne €
Classic   Map B3
Grande Rue, 13520
Tel *04 90 54 32 06*
Ⓦ la-reinejeanne.com
Historical setting for this hotel-restaurant with solidly comfortable rooms. Enjoy panoramic views over Les Baux and dine on the restaurant terrace in summer.

LES BAUX-DE-PROVENCE: Baumanière €€€
Luxury   Map B3
Chemin Departmental 27 Carita, 13520
Tel *04 90 54 33 07*
Ⓦ lacabrodor.com
Beautiful country house set in an idyllic location, offering Provençal-chic bedrooms furnished with antiques. Superb restaurant.

MARSEILLE: Hôtel Saint-Ferreol €
Classic   Map C4
19 rue Pisançon, 13000
Tel *04 91 33 12 21*
Ⓦ hotel-stferreol.com
Centrally located off the main shopping street, this modern, cheery hotel has small but thoughtfully designed rooms.

MARSEILLE: Hotel La Résidence du Vieux Port €€
Boutique   Map C4
18 quai du Port, 13002
Tel *04 91 91 91 22*
Ⓦ hotel-residence-marseille.com
Stylish waterfront hotel designed in the 1950s and inspired by Le Corbusier. Its simple, airy bedrooms with splashes of colour have picture-perfect views.

MARSEILLE: Sofitel Marseille Vieux Port €€
Classic   Map C4
36 blvd Charles Livon, 13007
Tel *04 91 15 59 00*
Ⓦ sofitel.com
Luxury hotel with minimalist style, dark wood and streamlined furniture. Enjoy spectacular views from the top-floor restaurant.

NÎMES: Hôtel des Tuileries €
Classic   Map A3
22 rue Roussy, 30000
Tel *04 66 21 31 15*
Ⓦ hoteldestuileries.com
Excellent centrally located budget hotel with old-fashioned bedrooms. Charming owners.

NÎMES: Jardins Secrets €€€
Boutique   Map A3
3 rue Gaston Maruejols, 30000
Tel *04 66 04 02 04*
Ⓦ jardinssecrets.net
Stylish, romantic hotel furnished with antiques. Superb breakfast spread. Garden oasis with a pool.

ST-RÉMY-DE-PROVENCE: Hôtel L'Amandiere €
Classic   Map B3
Av Théodore-Aubanel, 13210
Tel *04 90 92 41 00*
Ⓦ hotel-amandiere.com
A peaceful retreat with a rustic feel. All rooms offer garden views, but only some have air-conditioning.

SAINTES-MARIES-DE-LA-MER: Mas de la Fouque €€
Boutique   Map A4
Route du Petit Rhône, Departmental 38, 13460
Tel *04 90 97 81 02*
Ⓦ masdelafouque.com
Luxurious hotel and spa offering boudoir-style gypsy trailers and ultra-chic rooms with a private terrace. Great views of Camargue Nature Park.

SALON-DE-PROVENCE: Abbaye de Sainte-Croix €€
Historic   Map B3
Route de Val de Cuech, 13300
Tel *04 90 56 24 55*
Ⓦ abbaye-de-saintecroix.fr
Rustic style former monks' cells in a 12th-century abbey, with fine views from the pool terrace.

VILLENEUVE-LÈS-AVIGNON:
La Magnaneraie €€
Historic Map B3
37 rue Camp de Bataille, 30400
Tel *09 70 38 34 95*
W magnaneraie.najeti.fr
Refined hotel with lovely gardens
and a frescoed restaurant in a
15th-century silkworm nursery.

Vaucluse

AVIGNON: Bristol Hotel €
Classic Map B3
44 cours Jean Jaurès, 84000
Tel *04 90 16 48 48*
W bristol-avignon.com
Pleasant hotel at a convenient
location in the city centre. Family
rooms and garage available.

AVIGNON: Hotel d'Europe €€€
Historic Map B3
12 pl Crillon, 84000
Tel *04 90 14 76 76*
W heurope.com
A 16th-century hotel elegantly
decorated with period furniture.
Beautiful fountain in the garden.

AVIGNON: La Mirande €€€
Luxury Map B3
4 pl de l'Amirande, 84000
Tel *04 90 14 20 20*
W la-mirande.fr
A cardinal's mansion renovated
in 18th-century style. Situated
near the Palais de Papes.

DK Choice
CABRIÈRES D'AVIGNON-
GORDES: La Bastide de
Voulonne €€
Family Map B3
Cabrières d'Avignon, Route des
Beaumettes, Dept 148, 84220
Tel *04 90 76 77 55*
W bastide-voulonne.com
Set in a traditional 18th-century
farm and surrounded by acres
of beautiful grounds, La Bastide
de Voulonne is the ideal spot
for a family break. The heated
pool and terrace offer fantastic
views over the Luberon. The
guesthouse has three family
suites and the friendly owner
offers superb *table d'hôte*
meals. Choose from a variety
of exciting theme-based stays.

GORDES: Le Mas des Romarins €€
Historic Map C3
Route de Sénanque, 84220
Tel *04 90 72 12 13*
W masromarins.com
Charming 18th-century country
house with traditional Provençal
features such as stone fireplaces.

LOURMARIN: Villa Saint Louis €
Historic Map C3
35 rue Henri Savournin, 84160
Tel *04 90 68 39 18*
W villasaintlouis.com
Set in an 18th-century villa
that once served as a coaching
inn, this handsome B&B oozes
faded charm.

PERNES-LES-FONTAINES:
Mas de la Bonoty €
Historic Map B3
355 chemin de la Bonoty, 84210
Tel *04 90 61 61 09*
W bonoty.com
Renovated 17th-century farmhouse
surrounded by fragrant lavender
fields and olive groves.

SEGURET: Domaine de Cabasse €€
Classic Map B2
Route de Sablet, 84110
Tel *04 90 46 91 12*
W cabasse.fr
Comfortable rooms in a working
vineyard with wine tastings for
guests. Excellent restaurant.

VAISON-LA-ROMAINE: Les
Tilleuls d'Elisée €
Historic Map B2
Chemin du Bon Ange, 1 av Jules
Mazen, 84110
Tel *04 90 35 63 04*
W vaisonchambres.info
Centrally located charming B&B
in a traditional farmhouse. Wine
tastings are held in the cellars.

Alpes-de-Haute-Provence

CASTELLANE: Nouvel Hôtel du
Commerce €
Family Map D3
Pl Marcel Sauvaire, 04120
Tel *04 92 83 61 00*
W hotel-du-commerce-verdon.com
Excellent hotel with clean, pretty
rooms and fine garden-restaurant.
The owners are warm and friendly.

DK Choice
CHÂTEAU-ARNOUX:
La Bonne Etape €€
Classic Map D2
Chemin du Lac, 04160
Tel *04 92 64 00 09*
W bonneetape.com
This 18th-century post
house, owned by master chef
Jany Gleize, makes a serene
retreat. Rooms are stunningly
decorated with antiques and
there is a charming heated
pool in the olive groves. Explore
the vast organic gardens that
provide the produce served
in the excellent restaurant
and bistro.

FORCALQUIER: Charembeau €
Historic Map C3
Route de Niozelles, 04300
Tel *04 92 70 91 70*
W charembeau.com
Relax and de-stress in an
18th-century eco-friendly
farmhouse amid rolling hills.
Delicious breakfasts.

MOUSTIERS-STE-MARIE:
La Bastide de Moustiers €€€
Boutique Map D3
Chemin de Quinson, 04360
Tel *04 92 70 47 47*
W bastide-moustiers.com
Rustically chic 17th-century
inn with attractive gardens
and splendid mountain
views. Superb restaurant.

REILLANNE: Auberge de
Reillanne €
Historic Map C3
D214 Le Pigonnier, 04110
Tel *04 92 76 45 95*
W auberge-de-reillanne.com
Surrounded by a beautiful
garden, this serene country
house offers spacious, well-
furnished rooms, each with
a terracotta-tiled bathroom.
Large dining area.

Outdoor swimming pool surrounded by trees at Domaine de Cabasse, Seguret

For more information on types of hotels *see pages 194–5*

WHERE TO EAT AND DRINK

One of the joys of this sunny region is the abundance of fresh, enticing food on offer. The coast of Provence is famous for its seafood restaurants – the best are in the coastal towns of Marseille and Nice, though generally they do not come cheap. For traditional Provençal fare, head inland to the villages of the Var and northern Vaucluse. In the valleys of Haute Provence, the cuisine is simpler, but still delicious, often featuring local game and produce, and the much-loved truffle. Life in the south revolves around mealtimes and villages and towns come to a standstill during the midday meal and at dinner. Lunch is served from noon until 2pm with dinner from 7:30pm until about 10pm, while cafés and bars in towns tend to stay open later, especially in high season (see pp218–19).

Types of Restaurant

The restaurants on pages 208–17 have been selected for their excellent food, decor and ambience. Within each area, entries are listed alphabetically within each price category, from the least to the most expensive. At the expensive end are the gastronomic palaces, where famous chefs showcase French *haute cuisine*. These are usually honoured with one or more Michelin stars. In some restaurants, chefs creatively combine fresh local ingredients. Provençal restaurants specialize in the region's traditional recipes. At classic restaurants you'll find French favourites such as steak and *moules-frites*, or *escargots* and *tournedos Rossini* at more upmarket places. Bistros and brasseries – pub-restaurants serving beer and alcoholic drinks are less formal, and often stay open throughout the day and night. You will also find many places serving foreign cuisine, especially Italian restaurants and pizzerias.

How Much to Pay

Prices in Provence, notably along the fashionable Côte d'Azur, are relatively high. Most restaurants offer fixed-price menus that are better value than à la carte. Lunch is always a good deal – you can enjoy a large repast with wine for around €15–20. Inland, you can dine well for under €40 a head, while on the coast, a good restaurant will generally charge more in the evening. In the deluxe dining rooms of the Côte d'Azur, expect to spend at least €90 a head, although the food will usually be outstanding.

Restaurants are obliged by law to post menu prices outside. These generally include service, but a tip is often expected for good service – up to five per cent of the bill. Tips are usually given in cash. The most widely accepted credit cards are Visa and MasterCard. American Express and Diners Club are also accepted in some restaurants.

Making Reservations

No matter where you are dining, it is always advisable to book, especially for dinner. Most up-market restaurants only have one sitting and are often packed, particularly during high season.

Dining al fresco at Les Deux Garçons brasserie in Aix (see p219)

Reading the Menu

Menus usually comprise three or four courses, with cheese eaten before dessert, while some country restaurants serve six-course extravaganzas, which can take several hours to eat. These days even fixed-price menus tend to offer several choices of *entrée* (starter), main course and dessert. Gastronomic restaurants may serve numerous small, immaculate courses, on a choice of *dégustation* (tasting) menus.

The *entrée* usually includes salads, pâté, Provençal soups and often shellfish. Main dishes are predominantly a choice of lamb, chicken or fish – game is widely available in season.

Coffee is always served after, not with, dessert – you should specify how you like your coffee.

Choice of Wine

Wine is so much a part of everyday life in Provence that you will find a good range at even the smallest establishments (see pp206–7). The price may be off-putting as all restaurants put a large mark-up on wine (up to

L'Olivier, Île de Porquerolles (see p211)

Ferdinand Léger's tiled mural still graces the terrace at La Colombe d'Or, St-Paul de Vence *(see pp210–11)*

300 per cent). Most wine is locally produced and usually served in carafes. If in doubt, choosing the house wine (*la réserve* or *vin de la maison*) is a safe bet. Ordering a *demi* (50 cl) or *quart* (25 cl) is an inexpensive way of sampling the wine before ordering more. French law divides the country's wines into three classes, in ascending order of quality: the lowest level is Vin de France, the intermediate category is Indication géographique protégée (IGP) and the highest category is Appellation d'origine protégée (AOP).

Vegetarian Food

Uniquely vegetarian restaurants are hard to find, as this concept largely has yet to filter down to the carnivorous south, although *bio* (organic) restaurants are increasingly springing up. Most establishments will offer salads, omelettes or soup, or dishes from the *entrée* menu. Pasta and pizza are popular vegetarian standbys.

Children

Meals in Provence are very much a family affair and children are welcome in most places. However, special facilities like high chairs or baby seats are rarely provided. Many establishments have a children's menu and most will be happy to provide smaller dishes at reduced rates.

Service

As eating is a leisurely pastime in France, service can be slow. In small restaurants do not expect rapid attention: there may be only one waiter and dishes are cooked to order.

Wheelchair Access

Wheelchair access to many restaurants is restricted. In summer, this will be less of a problem at establishments with outside terraces. Even so, when booking ahead, ask for a conveniently situated table.

Smoking

Smoking is banned in all public places in France, with restaurant and bar owners facing heavy fines if they do not adhere to

Château Eza in the *village perché* of Eze *(see p209)*

the rules. Outdoors, there may be a special section of the terrace set aside for smokers.

Picnics

Picnicking is the best way to enjoy the wonderful fresh produce, bread, cheeses and *charcuterie* from Provence's enticing markets and shops. Picnic areas along major roads are well marked and furnished with tables and chairs; those along country lanes are better still.

Recommended Restaurants

The restaurants recommended on pages 208–17 include some of the best in Provence. They have been chosen for their reliably good food and service, with the aim of presenting a wide range of cuisine and price ranges in the region's most visited cities, towns, villages and countryside. Many rural restaurants are attached to hotels but serve a predominantly non-residential clientele. These often offer good value for money and are mostly the focus of local social activity.

Among the listings are entries marked as "DK Choice". These are restaurants that have been selected for one or more exceptional features, whether it is the superb quality of the cuisine, the fine atmosphere, a beautiful setting or spectacular views.

The Flavours of Provence

The cooking of Provence is known as *cuisine du soleil* ("the cuisine of the sun") with good reason. Famous for its abundance of glorious, sun-ripe fruit and vegetables, it is also healthy with plenty of fresh fish and seafood and fine-quality, lean meat from mountain pastures. Cheeses tend to be made with goats' milk. Good produce is enhanced by key ingredients: olive oil, garlic and aromatic herbs. Local markets are a colourful feast of seasonal produce: tomatoes, aubergines (eggplants), peppers and courgettes (zucchini), and freshly picked cherries, melons, lemons and figs. Most of all, though, Provence is the land of olives and of rich green olive oil.

Olives and olive oil

Scented, sun-ripened Cavaillon melons in a Provençal market

Vegetables

In Provençal cooking, vegetables play a leading role. They may be served raw as crudités with *aïoli* (garlic mayonnaise) or *tapenade* (puréed anchovies, olives and capers). Tomatoes and courgettes (zucchini) are often stuffed in the Niçois style, with minced meat, rice and herbs. Small violet artichokes come with a sauce of lemon and butter, or sautéed with bacon. A favourite soup is the robust *soupe au pistou*, beans and vegetables laced with a sauce of basil, pine nuts and garlic. *Ratatouille* is a fragrant stew of vegetables cooked with olive oil, garlic and herbs. Popular salads include *salade niçoise* and *mesclun*, a regional mixture of leaves, including rocket, lamb's lettuce, dandelion leaves and chervil.

Mediterranean Fish

The fish of the Mediterranean is highly prized, culminating in the famous *bouillabaisse*. A wide range of fish is caught, including rockfish, *rascasse* (scorpion fish), red mullet, sea bream, John Dory, monkfish and squid. Around Nice, the main catch is sardines and anchovies. Most are best enjoyed simply grilled with herbs, like the classic *loup* (sea

Mussels | Lobster | Prawns (shrimp) | Sea bass | Monkfish | Squid | Clams

Selection of Mediterranean seafood available in Provence

Provençal Dishes and Specialities

Provence has produced several renowned dishes, of which *bouillabaisse* is the most famous. The ingredients of this fish stew vary from place to place, though Marseille claims the original recipe. A variety of local seafood (always including *rascasse*, or scorpion fish) is cooked in stock with tomatoes and saffron. The fish liquor is traditionally served first, with croûtons spread with *rouille*, a spicy mayonnaise, and the fish served afterwards. Once a fishermen's supper, it is now a luxury item you may need to order 24 hours in advance. A simpler version is *bourride*, a garlicky fish soup. Rich red wine stews, known as *daubes*, are another speciality, usually made with beef, but sometimes tuna or calamari. Other classics include *ratatouille* and *salade niçoise*.

Fresh figs

Bouillabaisse Fish often found in this Provençal classic includes monkfish, snapper and conger eel.

Dried spices and herbs on sale at the market in Nice

bass) with fennel. Seafood includes mussels *(moules)*, tiny crabs, giant prawns *(gambas)* and sea urchins *(oursins)*. Look out for trout from the Alpine streams north of Nice and freshwater eels in the Camargue. Popular fish dishes include *soupe de poissons* (fish soup), octopus cooked Provençal style with white wine, tomatoes and herbs, and the famous *brandade de morue*, a speciality of Nîmes, a purée of salt cod, cream, potatoes and olive oil.

Meat and Game

Lamb is one of the popular meats, especially that of Sisteron, where it is grazed on high mountain pastures, resulting in delicately herb-flavoured flesh. Beef is most often served as a *daube*, named after the pot-bellied terracotta dish *(daubière)* in which it is gently cooked for hours. Another speciality is *boeuf gardien*, the bull's-meat stew of the Camargue, served with nutty local red rice. Game from the mountains and woods includes wild rabbit, hare and wild boar. Regional *charcuterie* features *caillettes* (cakes of chopped pork and

Display of the famous and delicious *saussicons d'Arles*

liver with spinach and juniper berries) and the *saucisson* of Arles, once made from donkey but now usually pork.

Fruit and Honey

Elaborate desserts are rare, since there is so much sweet ripe fruit for the picking. Cavaillon melons are among the best in France, and the famous lemons of Menton are celebrated in an annual festival. Candied fruit has been produced in Apt since the Middle Ages. Local honeys are scented with chestnut, lavender or rosemary.

ON THE MENU

Beignets des fleurs de courgette Courgette (zucchini) flower fritters.

Fougasse Flat olive oil bread often studded with olives.

Ratatouille Stew of aubergine (eggplant), tomatoes, courgettes (zucchini) and peppers.

Salade Niçoise Lettuce with hard-boiled egg, olives, green beans, tomatoes and anchovies.

Socca Chickpea (garbanzo) pancakes, a speciality of Nice.

Tarte Tropezienne St-Tropez's indulgent sponge cake stuffed with *crème patissière*.

Tourte des blettes Pie of chard, raisins and pine kernels.

Artichauts à la barigoule Small violet artichokes are stuffed with bacon and vegetables, cooked in wine.

Loup au fenouil A sea bass is stuffed with fennel twigs and baked with white wine or grilled over more twigs.

Boeuf en daube Beef is marinated in red wine, onions and garlic, then stewed with orange peel and tomato.

What to Drink in Provence

The region covered by this book could not encompass a more varied and enticing range of wines. To the north, the stony, heat-baked soil of the southern Rhône nurtures intense, spicy red wines, the best of which is Châteauneuf-du-Pape. In the south, the Mediterranean coast produces a range of lighter, fresh and fruity whites and rosés, as well as some delicious red wines. Especially good are the dry white wines of seaside Cassis and reds or rosés from the tiny fine wine pocket of Bandol. In the past, some Provençal wines had a reputation for not "travelling" well, but the introduction of modern wine-making techniques and more suitable grape varieties are fast improving quality. Here, we suggest a selection of wines to look out for on local menus.

Two bottle styles distinctive of the region's wines

White Wines

Grenache blanc grapes are often blended with other grape varieties to give a rich, bright flavour and crisp acidity to Provençal white wine. Those listed below are perfect with the region's delicious seafood.

Recommended Whites

Clos Ste-Magdeleine
Cassis

Château Val Joanis
Côtes du Luberon

Domaine St-André-de-Figuière
Côtes de Provence

Domaines Gavoty
Côtes de Provence

A fine white Châteauneuf-du-Pape

White Mas de Rey

Rosé Wines

Provençal rosé is no longer just a sweetish aperitif wine in a skittle-shaped bottle. Grape varieties like Syrah give a full flavour and more body. Tavel is a typical example – dry and weighty enough to accompany Provençal flavourings such as garlic and herbs. Bandol's *vin gris* is also highly regarded.

Wine Areas of Provence

Wine-producing areas are concentrated in the southwest of the region, where vineyards cluster on the rocky hillsides (côtes). Les Arcs is a good base for a Côtes de Provence wine tour (see pp112–13).

Recommended Rosés

Château Romassan
Bandol

Commanderie de Bargemone
Côtes de Provence

Commanderie de Peyrassol
Côtes de Provence

Domaine Maby
Tavel

Domaines Gavoty
Côtes de Provence

Domaine Loou rosé *(gris)* wine

Terraced vineyards on the coast above Cassis

Red Wines

At its best, Châteauneuf-du-Pape produces heady, intense wines to accompany the most robust meat dishes. Bandol also makes superb, long-lived red wines. For a lighter alternative, choose a Provençal or Côtes du Rhône red. Wines from one of the named Rhône villages should be of superior quality – or seek out reds from reliable producers in, for example, Les Baux-de-Provence, or the Côtes du Luberon.

A spicy Château-neuf-du-Pape

A Château de Beaucastel red

Fine wine from Château Val Joanis

Recommended Reds

Château de Beaucastel
Châteauneuf-du-Pape

Château du Trignon
Sablet, Côtes du Rhône

Château Val Joanis
Côtes du Luberon

Château de Pibarnon
Bandol

Domaine des Alysses
Coteaux Varois

Domaine Font de Michelle
Châteauneuf-du-Pape

Domaine Tempier
Bandol

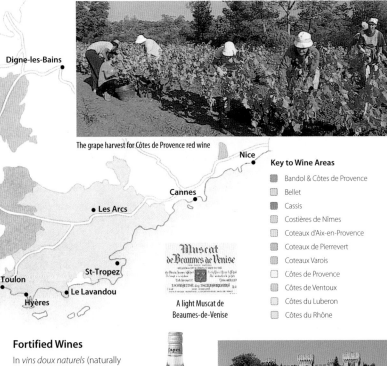

Digne-les-Bains

The grape harvest for Côtes de Provence red wine

Nice

Cannes

Les Arcs

St-Tropez

Toulon · Le Lavandou

Hyères

A light Muscat de Beaumes-de-Venise

Key to Wine Areas

- Bandol & Côtes de Provence
- Bellet
- Cassis
- Costières de Nîmes
- Coteaux d'Aix-en-Provence
- Coteaux de Pierrevert
- Coteaux Varois
- Côtes de Provence
- Côtes de Ventoux
- Côtes du Luberon
- Côtes du Rhône

Fortified Wines

In *vins doux naturels* (naturally sweet wines) fermentation is stopped before all the sugar has turned to alcohol, and the wine is then lightly fortified with spirit. Delicious as a chilled apéritif, with desserts or instead of a liqueur, most are based on the exotically scented Muscat grape and range from cloyingly sweet to lusciously fragrant. Others are based on the red Grenache grape.

Typical Muscat bottle shape

The stony, sun-reflecting soil of the Rhône valley

Where to Eat and Drink

The Riviera and the Alpes Maritimes

ANTIBES: Aubergine €
Provençal **Map** E3
7 rue Sade, 06600
Tel *04 93 34 55 93* **Closed** *Tue*
Lots of aubergines (eggplants), as the name implies, but also many other excellent Provençal dishes. Good home-made desserts.

ANTIBES: Chez Helen €
Bistro **Map** E3
35 rue des Revennes, 06600
Tel *04 92 93 88 52* **Closed** *Sun*
Everything in this organic and vegetarian restaurant – a rare sight in Provence – is made from local produce. Inventive main dishes and *salades composées*.

ANTIBES: Le Nacional €€
Contemporary **Map** E3
61 Pl Nacional, 06600
Tel *04 93 61 77 30* **Closed** *Sun, Mon lunch (Sep–Jun)*
Stylish place serving a wide choice of beef cuts such as Black Angus American and beef tartare cut. Impressive list of French wines.

ANTIBES: Le Vauban €€
Provençal **Map** E3
7 bis rue Thuret, 06600
Tel *04 93 34 33 05* **Closed** *Tue*
Excellent good-value cooking in this simple-looking restaurant. Try the venison with cranberry sauce or Rossini-style beef fillet steak.

**BAR-SUR-LOUP:
L'Ecole des Filles** €€
Bistro **Map** E3
380 ave Amiral de Grasse, 06620
Tel *04 93 09 40 20* **Closed** *Mon, Thu lunch & Sun dinner*
Located in a former village girls' school; offers inventive cooking with an emphasis on seafood.

**BEAULIEU-SUR-MER:
Le Petit Darkoum** €
Moroccan **Map** F3
18 blvd General Leclerc, 06310
Tel *04 93 01 48 59* **Closed** *Mon & Tue*
Refined cuisine from Morocco's south with dishes such as kebabs, tagines and couscous royale served amidst a delightful decor.

BIOT: Les Terraillers €€€
Haute Cuisine **Map** E3
11 route chemin Neuf, 06410
Tel *04 93 65 01 59* **Closed** *Wed & Thu; mid-Oct–Nov*
Enjoy culinary delights such as lobster bisque, truffles and *foie gras* with excellent Provençal wines at this sumptuous restaurant.

BREIL-SUR-ROYA: Le Flavie €
Provençal **Map** F3
17 blvd Jean-Jaurès, 06540
Tel *04 93 54 65 74* **Closed** *Thu; Fri lunch; Nov–mid-Dec*
Cosy and cheerful café that serves delectable stews, roasts and grills, as well as fresh salads and desserts.

**CAGNES-SUR-MER:
Fleur de Sel** €€
Bistro **Map** E3
85 montée de la Bourgade, 06800
Tel *04 93 20 33 33* **Closed** *Apr–Sep: Wed; Oct–Mar: Wed or Thu*
Lofty Haut-de-Cagnes is the lovely setting for this restaurant serving exceptionally refined cooking. Great value set menus.

**CAGNES-SUR-MER:
Château Le Cagnard** €€€
Haute Cuisine **Map** E3
54 rue Sous Barri, 06800
Tel *04 93 20 73 21* **Closed** *Mid-Mar–Apr: Mon & Tue; Oct–mid-Mar: Sun–Wed*
Boasts a scrumptious menu with roast pigeon, langoustines and more. The terrace offers splendid views of the Mediterranean Sea.

Price Guide
Prices are based on a three-course meal for one with half a bottle of house wine, and include tax and service charges.
€ up to €40
€€ €40 to €60
€€€ over €60

CANNES: L'Assiette Provençale €
Provençal **Map** E4
9 quai Saint-Pierre, 06400
Tel *04 93 38 52 14* **Closed** *Mon*
Popular restaurant in the port with a good-value menu that includes oyster platters and dishes such as courgette (zucchini) blossoms, duck and snails.

CANNES: Angolo Italiano €€
Italian **Map** E4
18 rue du Commandent Andre, 06400
Tel *04 93 39 82 57* **Closed** *Mon*
Near the Croisette. Neapolitan-run place with Italian *charcuterie* and cheeses, a range of pasta dishes, grilled meats and seafood on the menu.

CANNES: Le Pastis €€
Bistro **Map** E4
28 rue du Commandant André, 06400
Tel *04 92 98 95 40* **Closed** *Sun*
Good for both casual lunches and dinners. Pastas, salads, sandwiches and omelettes are served over a counter or in booths like an American diner.

CANNES: La Cave €€€
Provençal **Map** E4
9 blvd de la République, 06400
Tel *04 93 99 79 87* **Closed** *Mon lunch, Sat lunch & Sun*
A favourite with both locals and visitors for its upmarket versions of Provençal dishes such as *aïoli aux legumes*, stuffed vegetables and sardines. Excellent wine list.

CANNES: La Palme d'Or €€€
Haute Cuisine **Map** E4
73 la Croisette, 06400
Tel *04 92 98 74 14* **Closed** *Sun–Tue; Jan & Feb*
Exquisitely fashionable restaurant of the famous Hôtel Martinez. A favourite with celebrities. Boasts two Michelin stars. Superb food and an exquisite wine list.

CANNES: Plage L'Ondine €€€
Seafood **Map** E4
64 la Croisette, 06400
Tel *04 93 94 23 15* **Closed** *Wed (off season); mid-Nov–mid-Dec*
Right on the beach, Plage L'Ondine offers the perfect setting to enjoy specialities such as grilled fish and lobster at outdoor tables. Excellent wine list.

Tables on the charming terrace of Les Terraillers, Biot

Fine cured meats displayed in the *salumeria* at La Trattoria, Monaco

COURMES: Auberge de Courmes €
Provençal **Map** E3
3 rue des Platanes, 06620
Tel *04 93 77 64 70* **Closed** Mon
This gracious village inn over-looking the Gorges du Loup offers succulent meat dishes and home-made *clafoutis* for dessert.

EZE: La Gascogne Café €
Bistro **Map** F3
151 ave de Verdun, 06360
Tel *04 93 41 18 50*
Friendly restaurant in the Hôtel du Golf offering innovative dishes with an Italian-Provençal twist.

EZE: Château Eza €€€
Haute Cuisine **Map** F3
Rue de la Pise, 06360
Tel *04 93 41 12 24* **Closed** Mon & Tue
(Jan–Mar)
Delicate and imaginative dishes, garnished with flowers, are served in this Michelin-starred restaurant with splendid Riviera views.

GRASSE:
La Bastide St Antoine €€€
Haute Cuisine **Map** E3
48 ave Henri-Dunant, 06130
Tel *04 93 70 94 94*
Enjoy a feast of unique colours and aromas worthy of the perfume capital in an attractive, flower-filled courtyard.

JUAN-LES-PINS: Ti Toques €
Bistro **Map** E4
9 ave Louis Gallet, 06160
Tel *04 92 90 25 12* **Closed** Sun & Mon
Hidden on a back street, Ti Toques serves delicious meat dishes with plenty of options for vegetarians. Great range of Belgian beers.

LA TURBIE: Café de la Fontaine €
Brasserie **Map** F3
4 ave Général de Gaulle, 06320
Tel *04 93 28 52 79*
The bistro at the Hostellerie Jérôme offers the exceptional cooking of chef Bruno Cirino for bargain prices. The menu features traditional Provençal dishes.

LA TURBIE:
Hostellerie Jérôme €€€
Haute Cuisine **Map** F3
20 rue Comte de Cessole, 06320
Tel *04 92 41 51 51* **Closed** Mon &
Tue *(Sep–Jun); Dec–Mar*
Renowned chef Bruno Cirino presides over this Michelin-starred establishment. The daily menu depends on what is available in the local markets.

MANDELIEU-LA-NAPOULE:
Côté Place €
Provençal **Map** E4
21 pl de la Fontaine, 06210
Tel *04 93 47 59 27* **Closed** Sun
Unpretentious and popular, Côté Place serves dishes from around the Mediterranean: Moroccan tagines, Spanish seafood and Italian *saltimbocca*. All satisfying and fabulously done.

MANDELIEU-LA-NAPOULE:
La Brocherie €€
Seafood **Map** E4
11 ave Henri Clews, 06210
Tel *04 93 49 80 73*
A memorable menu with five seafood starters and all the fish you need: oysters, shellfish platters and mixed grills. Situated right on the quay.

MENTON: Coté Sud €
Italian **Map** F3
15 quai Bonaparte, 06500
Tel *04 93 41 03 69*
Elegant restaurant with a stylish white decor and exquisitely presented dishes. Serves delicious pizzas, seafood and pasta dishes. Warm, friendly welcome.

MENTON: Le Martina €€
Italian **Map** F3
11 pl du Cap, 06500
Tel *04 93 57 80 22* **Closed** Wed; Jan
Le Martina offers a wide choice of antipasti, risotto and pasta dishes, as well as excellent seafood. Good children's menu.

DK Choice

MENTON: Le Mirazur €€€
Haute Cuisine **Map** F3
30 ave Aristide Briand, 06500
Tel *04 92 41 86 86* **Closed** Mon &
Tue; mid-Dec–mid-Feb
A visual and culinary delight, Le Mirazur offers some of the most aesthetically flamboyant dishes ever seen. Chef Mauro prepares colourful combinations of meat and seafood made with herbs and vegetables freshly picked from the restaurant's garden. Savour the meals with superb wine and magnificent views of Menton and the sea.

MONACO: Maya Bay €€
Asian **Map** F3
24 ave Princesse Grace, 98000
Tel *00 377 97 70 74 67* **Closed** Sun
& Mon
Thai cooking with a French touch at this stylish eatery. Plenty of *nems* and dumplings. A separate Japanese restaurant serves *teppan-yaki* and sushi.

MONACO: Le Louis XV €€€
Haute Cuisine **Map** F3
Hôtel de Paris, pl du Casino, Monte-Carlo, 98000
Tel *00 377 98 06 88 64* **Closed** lunch;
Tue & Wed; Dec, mid-Feb–Mar
Capital of Alain Ducasse's culinary empire for more than 25 years, this splendid restaurant in the Hôtel de Paris serves haute cuisine.

MONACO: La Trattoria €€€
Italian **Map** F3
Sporting Monte Carlo, ave Princesse Grace, Monte-Carlo, 98000
Tel *00 377 98 06 71 71* **Closed** Oct–mid-May
Choose from a selection of Italian favourites, including elaborate antipasti, mini pizzas and prosciutto. Spectacular sea views.

MOUGINS: Resto des Arts €
Provençal **Map** E3
Rue du Maréchal-Foch, 06250
Tel *04 93 75 60 03* **Closed** Sun &
Mon *(off season)*
Trendy and artistic place that serves simple, good cooking. Best for grilled meats and stews.

MOUGINS:
La Place de Mougins €€€
Haute Cuisine **Map** E3
Pl du Commandant Lamy, 06250
Tel *04 93 90 15 78* **Closed** Mon & Tue
Stylish restaurant on the village square offering ultra-refined cuisine with unusual combinations of ingredients. Good-value lunch menus.

Splendid dining room at Le Louis XV in the Hôtel de Paris, Monaco

For more information on types of restaurants *see page 202*

NICE: L'Acchiardo €
Provençal **Map** F3
38 rue Droite, 06300
Tel *04 93 85 51 16* **Closed** *Sat &*
Sun; Aug
Set in the heart of Nice's Old
Town. Delicious food in a great
atmosphere and Provençal wine
directly from the barrel.

NICE: Les Amoureux €
Italian **Map** F3
46 blvd Stalingrad, 06300
Tel *04 93 07 59 73* **Closed** *Sun & Mon*
This pizzeria boasts the best
Neapolitan pizza on the Riviera,
with the perfect crust. The menu
also offers other Italian specialities.
Reservations recommended.

NICE: Chez Palmyre €
Provençal **Map** F3
5 rue Droite, 06300
Tel *04 93 85 72 32* **Closed** *Sun*
An institution since the 1920s.
There are only six tables in a tiny
retro dining room that serves
real Niçois home cooking. Always
packed so be sure to book ahead.

NICE: Au Moulin Enchanté €€
Bistro **Map** F3
1 rue Barbéris, 06300
Tel *04 93 55 33 14* **Closed** *Sun & Mon*
A local haunt outside the tourist
zone. Delicious fare with a wide
choice of meat and fish mains.
Good value lunch menu.

NICE: Le Bistrot d'Antoine €€
Bistro **Map** F3
27 rue de la Préfecture, 06300
Tel *04 93 85 29 57* **Closed** *Sun & Mon*
An ancient favourite in the
Vieille Ville, revived by a young
couple. Perfect traditional
cooking; impeccable service.
Reservations recommended.

NICE: La Merenda €€
Provençal **Map** F3
4 rue Raoul Bosio, 06300
Closed *Sat & Sun*
Michelin star chef Dominique Le
Stanc prepares authentic regional
classics. The place doesn't have
any telephone. Friendly service.

NICE: Le Chantecler €€€
Haute Cuisine **Map** F3
37 promenade des Anglais, 06000
Tel *04 93 16 64 00* **Closed** *Sun &*
Mon; Jan
Located in the Hotel Négresco.
Opulent 19th-century dining
room; offers a menu lavishly
punctuated with truffles and
caviar. Famous wine cellar.

NICE: Flaveur €€€
Classic French **Map** F3
25 rue Gubernatis, 06000
Tel *04 93 62 53 95* **Closed** *Sat lunch,*
Sun & Mon
Run by a dynamic trio, this bistro-
style restaurant offers classic dishes
marked by a distinct yet judicious
touch of exotic spices and herbs.

PEILLON: L'Authentique €€€
Provençal **Map** F3
2 pl Auguste Arnulf, 06440
Tel *04 93 79 91 17* **Closed** *Wed*
Elegant Niçois cooking served on
a shaded terrace with fine views.
Locally sourced ingredients and
many vegetarian options.

ROQUEBRUNE-CAP-MARTIN:
Au Grand Inquisiteur €€
Classic French **Map** F3
15 & 18 rue du Château, 06190
Tel *04 93 35 05 37* **Closed** *Mon*
An intimate, family-run place at
the heart of the village. The menu
features traditional dishes made
with quail, *escargots* and venison.

ST-JEAN-CAP-FERRAT:
Le Pirate €€
Seafood **Map** F3
Nouveau Port, 06230
Tel *04 93 76 12 97* **Closed** *Nov–*
Mar dinner
Perfect setting on the picturesque
port and an appetizing menu.
Choose from a variety of grilled
fish and seafood risottos.

ST-MARTIN-VESUBIE:
L'Ô à la Bouche €
Classic French **Map** F2
Le Boréon, 06450
Tel *04 93 02 98 42* **Closed** *mid-Nov–*
mid-Dec
Quality cooking in the mountains
with a chance to catch your own
trout. Also a brasserie offering
burgers, fondues and raclette.

ST-PAUL DE VENCE:
La Colombe d'Or €€
Provençal **Map** E3
Pl du Général de Gaulle, 06570
Tel *04 93 32 80 02* **Closed** *Nov–Dec*
Legendary artists' retreat packed
with original pieces of art. Simple
but excellent Provençal cooking
that still attracts the rich and
famous. Superb wine list.

STE-AGNÈS: Le Righi €
Provençal **Map** F3
1 pl du Fort, 06500
Tel *04 92 10 90 88* **Closed** *Wed*
Enjoy good solid home cooking
and amazing views at Le Righi.
Try the ravioli, gnocchi, stewed
boar and lamb cooked in hay.

SOSPEL: La Cabraia €
Provençal **Map** F3
1 pl de la Cabraia, 06380
Tel *04 93 04 00 54* **Closed** *Thu*
Located in the town centre, this
cheery restaurant serves fresh fish,

Luxurious Regency-style decor at Le Chantecler in Le Négresco, Nice

Fresh vegetables from the chef's garden at Hostellerie Bérard, La Cadière d'Azur

home-made gnocchi and pasta dishes and gourmet desserts. Sit on the terrace to enjoy the sun.

THÉOULE-SUR-MER: Jilali B €€
Seafood **Map** E4
16 rue Trayas, 06590
Tel 04 93 75 19 03 **Closed** Mon–Wed lunch; mid-Nov–Jan
Innovative seafood dishes with a touch of the exotic – spices, saffron and coconut. Splurge on the excellent *bouillabaisse*. Terrace with splendid sea views.

TOUET-SUR-VAR: Chez Paul €
Classic French **Map** E3
4260 ave Général de Gaulle, 06710
Tel 04 93 05 71 03 **Closed** Wed; Sun–Tue dinner
A simple village inn offering tasty home-made fare: steaks, rabbit and game dishes. Pizzas and a good kids' menu too.

VALBONNE: Lou Cigalon €€€
Haute Cuisine **Map** E3
6 blvd Carnot, 06560
Tel 04 93 12 01 61 **Closed** Sun, Mon & Thu
An elegant emerging restaurant, north of Cannes, with a hearty menu based around game dishes, duck and wild mushrooms.

VENCE: La Litote €€
Bistro **Map** E3
5 rue de l'Evêché, 06140
Tel 04 93 24 27 82 **Closed** Mon
Relaxing and full of charm with tables under shaded lime trees, La Litote offers the perfect setting to enjoy inventive cooking from a rising young chef.

VILLEFRANCHE-SUR-MER:
La Mère Germaine €€
Seafood **Map** F3
9 quai Courbet, 06230
Tel 04 93 01 71 39 **Closed** mid-Nov–Christmas
A favourite on the port since 1938. The cuisine at La Mère Germaine revolves around dishes made from fish and shellfish. They take their *bouillabaisse* seriously.

VILLEFRANCHE-SUR-MER:
L'Oursin Bleu €€
Seafood **Map** F3
11 quai de l'amiral Courbet, 06230
Tel 04 93 01 90 12 **Closed** Jan
Combines traditional seafood recipes with new interpretations to create stylish dishes, rich in colour. There's a big aquarium in the foyer to enjoy while waiting.

The Var and the Iles d'Hyères

COGOLIN: Grain de Sel €
Bistro **Map** E4
6 rue du 11 Novembre, 83310
Tel 04 94 54 46 86 **Closed** Sun & Mon; late Nov–early Dec
Bright and cheerful bistro with an open kitchen. Deceptively simple Provençal dishes are packed with flavour. Outside tables in summer.

COLLOBRIÈRES: La Petite
Fontaine €
Provençal **Map** D4
1 pl de la République, 83610
Tel 04 94 48 00 12 **Closed** Mon; Feb, two weeks in Sep
Provençal home cooking with large portions and wonderful flavours. Try the *tarte à la provençale*. Superb wines.

DK Choice

FAYENCE: L'Escourtin €€
Provençal **Map** E3
159 Chemin de Notre Dame des Cyprès, 83440
Tel 04 94 76 00 84
Closed Wed, Thu lunch
Set in an idyllic location within an ancient olive mill, L'Escourtin is part of the Hôtel Moulin de la Camandoule. The interiors are furnished with antiques and flowers. Authentic cuisine with game dishes, *foie gras* and fish in subtle sauces flavoured with fresh herbs and produce from the delightful garden.

FAYENCE: Le Castellaras €€€
Provençal **Map** E3
461 chemin de Peymeyan, 83440
Tel 04 94 76 13 80 **Closed** Mon & Tue; Jan–mid-Feb
A beautiful farmhouse where the chef combines lamb, veal and crayfish with local produce to create wonderful dishes. A flowery terrace with spectacular views. Côtes de Provence wines.

FRÉJUS: Faubourg de Saigon €
Vietnamese **Map** E4
126 rue St-François de Paule, 83600
Tel 04 94 53 65 80 **Closed** Sun & Mon
Enjoy hearty portions of authentic, spicy Vitenamese dishes at this small, unassuming restaurant. Try spring rolls, the house speciality.

HYÈRES: Grand Baie €
Seafood **Map** D4
5 pl du Belvédère, Giens, 83400
Tel 04 94 58 28 16
A terrace with a wonderful view over the bay and simple, first-rate seafood. There is also a good choice of grilled meats.

HYÈRES: Ola Le Rêve €
Seafood **Map** D4
4 port la Gavine, 83400
Tel 04 94 38 59 34 **Closed** Mon & Tue
Located on the marina, this friendly place specializes in sea-food cooked on the spot, such as squid or king prawns *à la plancha*.

ÎLE DE PORQUEROLLES:
L'Olivier €€€
Seafood **Map** D5
Île de Porquerolles Ouest, 83400
Tel 04 94 58 34 83 **Closed** Mon (except Jul & Aug); Oct–Apr
Located in the Hotel Le Mas du Langoustier, an island retreat, L'Olivier offers a unique culinary experience. The menu features mostly seafood, including lobster, langoustines and shellfish.

LA CADIÈRE D'AZUR:
Hostellerie Bérard €€€
Classic French **Map** C4
6 rue Gabriel-Péri, 83740
Tel 04 94 90 11 43 **Closed** Mon & Tue
Michelin-starred restaurant using produce from the chef's garden. French *haute cuisine*, cooked with sincerity. Also an informal bistro with an excellent seasonal menu.

LE LAVANDOU:
La Farigoulette €€
Seafood **Map** D4
1 ave du Capitaine Thorel, La Fossette 83980
Tel 04 94 71 06 85
La Farigoulette offers inventive and colourful dishes. Especially good for seafood: *bouillabaisse*, grilled fish and lobster pasta.

For more information on types of restaurants *see page 202*

Stylish dining terrace overlooking the Mediterranean at La Vague d'Or, St-Tropez

ST-RAPHAËL: L'Etoile €
Provençal **Map** E4
2170 route de la Corniche, 83700
Tel *04 94 83 10 44* **Closed** *Wed; mid-Nov–mid-Feb*
Welcoming, laid-back place with the perfect setting on the little Port de Boulouris. Good risottos and Provençal seafood.

ST-RAPHAËL: Le Bouchon
Provençal €€
Contemporary **Map** E4
45 rue de la République, 83700
Tel *04 94 53 89 18* **Closed** *Sun & Mon*
Charming restaurant with tables under plane trees. A good place for *aïoli façon pastorel* (an assortment of seafood and vegetables with garlic mayonnaise).

ST-TROPEZ: Le Bistrot St-Tropez €€
Bistro **Map** E4
3 pl des Lices, 83990
Tel *04 94 97 11 33*
Trendy brasserie with low lighting and elegant interiors. The eclectic menu has something for everyone – grilled fish, steak tartare, sushi and spring rolls.

ST-TROPEZ: Le Sporting €€
Bistro **Map** E4
42 pl des Lices, 83990
Tel *04 94 97 00 65*
Escape the excess of St-Tropez without leaving town in this local's refuge that serves good main dishes, as well as burgers, salads and omelettes.

ST-TROPEZ: Au Caprice des Deux €€€
Provençal **Map** E4
40 rue du Portail Neuf, 83990
Tel *04 94 97 76 78* **Closed** *Tue (except Jul & Aug); Sun–Wed winter; Nov–mid-Feb*
Cheerful ambience with candles and mirrors in an old Provençal house. Refined cuisine with dishes such as *foie gras* terrine with onion jam. Do not miss the piña colada sorbet.

ST-TROPEZ: La Vague d'Or €€€
Haute Cuisine **Map** E4
Plage de la Bouillabaisse, 83990
Tel *04 94 55 91 00* **Closed** *early Oct–late April*
Luxurious Michelin-starred restaurant in Hotel Résidence de la Pinède. Chef Arnaud Donckele creates elegant dishes using exotic ingredients such as Barolo vinegar and chestnut honey.

TOULON: Le Chantilly €
Brasserie **Map** D4
15 pl Pierre Puget, 83000
Tel *04 94 09 32 92* **Closed** *Sun*
Running since 1907, this retro-style bistro opens its doors early and offers classic dishes as well as more cutting-edge options with organic salmon and chicken. Good vegetarian menu, too.

TOULON: La Lampa €
Brasserie **Map** D4
117 quai de la Sinse, 83000
Tel *04 94 03 06 09*
Set on the quay with outside tables offering fine views. Good for a light lunch of salads and *moules-frites*, as well as something more ambitious such as grilled fish and meat dishes.

Bouches-du-Rhône and Nîmes

AIGUES-MORTES: Le Bistrot Paiou €
Bistro **Map** A4
1 rue du 4 Septembre, 30220
Tel *04 66 71 44 95*
The chef's specials at this small bistro change daily, depending on fresh produce from the market. The modest but well-chosen wine list features local winemakers.

Tranquil park setting at Le Mas d'Entremont, Aix-en-Provence

AIGUES-MORTES: Le Dit-Vin €
Bistro **Map** A4
6 rue du 4 Septembre, 30220
Tel *04 66 53 52 76*
Chic restaurant and tapas bar, and a wine cellar visible through the floor. Don't miss the delicious *bouillabaisse*. Pretty garden setting and attentive staff.

AIX-EN-PROVENCE: Brasserie Leopold €
Brasserie **Map** C4
2 ave Victor-Hugo, 13100
Tel *04 42 26 01 24*
This Art Deco classic is great for a full-scale meal, snack or just a drink. The menu features regional cuisine and traditional brasserie fare including *sauerkraut*.

AIX-EN-PROVENCE: Le Formal €€
Gastronomic **Map** C4
32 rue Espariat, 13100
Tel *04 42 27 08 31* **Closed** *Sun & Mon; late Aug–early Sep*
Refined culinary works of art, with plenty of truffles, served in a contemporary designed vaulted cellar. Good value lunch menus.

AIX-EN-PROVENCE: Le Mas d'Entremont €€
Provençal **Map** C4
315 route d'Avignon, 13090
Tel *04 42 17 42 42* **Closed** *Nov–mid-Mar*
Enjoy fine dishes such as roasted wild prawns with citrus fruits and fillet of Montbéliard beef at this hotel-restaurant in the middle of a park. Excellent Provençal wines.

AIX-EN-PROVENCE: L'Esprit de la Violette €€€
Contemporary **Map** C4
10 ave de la Violette, 13100
Tel *04 42 23 02 50* **Closed** *Sun & Mon*
Chef Marc de Passorio creates interesting flavour combinations with local produce. Set in a mansion-style house with lovely gardens outside of town.

ARLES: La Grignotte €
Provençal **Map** B3
6 rue Favorin, 13200
Tel *04 90 93 10 43* **Closed** *Sun*
Cheerful and unpretentious place. Try the fish soup and bull stew with Camargue rice and a carafe of house wine.

ARLES: La Gueule du Loup €€
Provençal **Map** B3
39 rue des Arènes, 13200
Tel *04 90 96 96 69* **Closed** *Sun, Mon lunch, mid Jan–mid Feb*
Charming restaurant with a handful of tables in a former family home. Serves exquisite Provençal fare. Superb desserts.

ARLES: L'Atelier de Jean-Luc Rabanel
€€€
Gastronomic   **Map** B3
7 rue des Carmes, 13200
Tel *04 90 91 07 69* **Closed** *Mon & Tue*
Michelin star chef Jean-Luc Rabanel creates exquisite artistic masterpieces based on organic produce from his garden. Book well in advance.

ARLES: La Chassagnette
€€€
Organic   **Map** B3
Le Sambuc, 13200
Tel *04 90 97 26 96* **Closed** *Tue, Wed; Feb, Nov & Christmas week*
Chef Armand Arnal runs France's most famous organic restaurant surrounded by lush gardens near the Camargue. There is a special vegetarian menu as well.

ARLES: Chez Bob
€€€
Provençal   **Map** B3
Route du Sambuc, Villeneuve Gageron 13200
Tel *04 90 97 00 29* **Closed** *Mon & Tue*
Relish regional specialities while sitting in the eclectically decorated dining room or the pleasant terrace. Reserve at least a week in advance.

ARLES: Lou Marques
€€€
Gastronomic   **Map** B3
9 blvd Lices, 13200
Tel *04 90 52 52 52*
Elegant restaurant located in the characterful Hôtel Jules César, with a garden terrace and classic Provençal dishes. Excellent value lunch menus.

CASSIS: Le Grand Bleu
€€
Seafood   **Map** C4
12 quai les Baux, 13260
Tel *04 42 01 23 23* **Closed** *Wed*
Informal portside restaurant specializing in simply prepared fresh seafood at affordable prices. The service is warm and friendly.

CASSIS: La Villa Madie
€€€
Gastronomic   **Map** C4
Ave Revestel, Anse de Corton, 13260
Tel *04 96 18 00 00* **Closed** *Mon & Tue; Jan–mid-Feb*
Enjoy idyllic views over the Mediterranean along with spectacular seafood at this Michelin-starred restaurant. Alternatively, try its less expensive La Petite Cuisine bistro.

LES BAUX-DE-PROVENCE: Le Café des Baux
€€
Provençal   **Map** B3
Rue du Trencat, 13520
Tel *04 90 54 52 69* **Closed** *Nov–Mar*
Hip restaurant run by award-winning pastry chef Pierre Walter. The savoury dishes are a culinary delight as well.

A view of the excellent wine cellar at Le Julien, Marseille

LES BAUX-DE-PROVENCE: L'Oustau de Baumanière
€€€
Gastronomic   **Map** B3
Chemin Départementale 27, Le Val d'Enfer, 13520
Tel *04 91 91 55 40* **Closed** *Jan–Mar*
Popular with celebrities, this superb restaurant in a gorgeous setting boasts two Michelin stars and a private heliport. Inventive cuisine using exquisite ingredients.

MARSEILLE: Beach Café
€
Classic French   **Map** C4
214 quai du Port, 13002
Tel *04 91 91 55 40* **Closed** *Mon; two weeks at Christmas*
Informal outdoor terrace and a menu comprising tasty salads, meats, fish, snacks and lots of ice cream choices. Perfect for kids.

MARSEILLE: Le Boucher
€
Steakhouse   **Map** C4
10 rue de Village, 13006
Tel *04 91 48 79 65* **Closed** *Sun & Mon; Aug, Easter*
Secret restaurant for meat lovers hidden behind the façade of a butcher shop. Traditional recipes and succulent *entrecôtes* for two. Delicious home-made fries.

MARSEILLE: Toinou
€
Seafood   **Map** C4
3 cours Saint-Louis, 13001
Tel *04 91 33 14 94*
The place for seafood platters; features the freshest of oysters, mussels and prawns served with crusty bread and white wine.

MARSEILLE: Le Julien
€€
Classic French   **Map** C4
114 rue Paradis,13006
Tel *04 91 37 06 22* **Closed** *Sat lunch, Sun, Mon dinner*
Friendly place specializing in French classics such as veal sweetbreads with morels and *baba au rhum*. Wide-ranging menu; great desserts.

MARSEILLE: La Table du Fort
€€
Bistro   **Map** C4
8 rue Fort Notre Dame, 13007
Tel *04 91 33 97 65* **Closed** *Sat lunch, Sun–Mon lunch; Jul*
Charming restaurant run by a young couple. Serves beautifully prepared seafood, poultry and meat dishes, plus scrumptious desserts. Reservations essential.

MARSEILLE: Vinonéo
€€
Classic French   **Map** C4
6 pl Daviel, 13002
Tel *04 91 90 40 26* **Closed** *Sun; Mon–Wed dinner*
Cool, contemporary cuisine by a winemaker. Features hot dishes, cold meats and cheese platters. Great wine pairings by the glass.

> ### DK Choice
>
> **MARSEILLE: L'Epuisette** €€€
> Seafood   **Map** C4
> *158 rue du Vallon des Auffes, 13007*
> **Tel** *04 91 52 17 82* **Closed** *Sun & Mon; one week in Mar*
> A glass dining room overlooking the turquoise sea is L'Epuisette's unbeatable setting. This elegant restaurant has been in business for decades and from the calm and relaxing atmosphere to the charming staff, everything is perfect. The cuisine includes heavenly *bouillabaisse*, lobster tagine and other seafood delicacies. Extensive wine list and gorgeous desserts.

MARSEILLE: Le Petit Nice – Passédat
€€€
Seafood   **Map** C4
Anse de Maldormé, Corniche du Président J F Kennedy, 13007
Tel *04 91 59 25 92* **Closed** *Sun & Mon*
This hotel-restaurant boasts three Michelin stars. Relish chef Gerard Passédat's sublime *bouillabaisse*, seafood and wonderful desserts.

MARTIGUES: Le Cabanon de Maguy
Provençal   €   **Map** B4
2 quai des Anglais,13500
Tel 04 42 49 32 51   **Closed** *Sun & Mon; three weeks in Jan*
Feast on delicious duck breast in honey and rosemary, aubergine caviar and fish soup in a relaxed atmosphere. Delightful terrace.

MAUSSANE-LES-ALPILLES: La Fleur de Thym
Provençal   €   **Map** B3
15 ave de la Vallée des Baux, 13520
Tel 04 90 54 54 00   **Closed** *Sat lunch, Sun dinner (Sep–Jun); Mon; Dec*
One of the best bargains around Les Baux. Limited but excellent menu. Charming atmosphere and friendly service.

MAUSSANE-LES-ALPILLES: Le Clos St-Roch
Mediterranean   €€   **Map** B3
87 ave de la Vallée des Baux, 13520
Tel 04 90 98 77 15   **Closed** *Wed & Thu*
Head for the patio in the walled courtyard in the summer or for the indoor fireplace in the winter, and enjoy the modern Mediterranean-inspired cuisine.

NÎMES: Au Flan Coco
Classic French   €   **Map** A3
21 rue du Grand Couvent, 30900
Tel 04 66 21 84 81   **Closed** *Sun & Mon*
Set in a medieval convent; offers huge salads, classic mains and tasty *pat'à coco* (potato pie). The takeaway menu is ideal for picnics.

NÎMES: Au Plaisirs des Halles
Provençal   €   **Map** A3
4 rue Littré, 30000
Tel 04 66 36 01 02   **Closed** *Sun & Mon*
Sleek, contemporary ambience to match the cuisine. Try the shrimp and scallop tempura or the local speciality, *brandade*. Exceptional regional wine list.

NÎMES: Le Vintage
Bistro   €   **Map** A3
7 rue de Bernis, 30000
Tel 04 66 21 04 45   **Closed** *Sun, Mon (except Jul & Aug)*
Cosy restaurant and wine bar with a menu that features *foie gras*, duck and steaks. Shaded outdoor tables.

NÎMES: Alexandre
Gastronomic   €€€   **Map** A3
2 rue Xavier Tronc, Garons, 30128
Tel 04 66 70 08 99   **Closed** *Sep–Jun: Sun dinner, Mon & Tue; Jul–Aug: Sun & Mon; mid-Feb–mid-Mar; 2 weeks in summer.*
An unforgettable dining experience in a lovely garden setting. Sublime food and enchanting desserts from the Michelin-star chef Michel Kayser.

Shaded outdoor terrace overlooking the garden at Alexandre, Nîmes

NÎMES: Vincent Croizard
Gastronomic   €€€   **Map** A3
17 rue des Chassaintes, 30900
Tel 04 66 67 04 99   **Closed** *Sun dinner–Tue lunch; Sun & Mon (Jul–Sep)*
Ring a doorbell to enter this chic restaurant hidden on a narrow street. Chef Vincent Croizard prepares an exquisite parade of little dishes.

ST-RÉMY-DE-PROVENCE: La Cantina
Italian   €   **Map** B3
18 blvd Victor Hugo, 13210
Tel 04 90 90 90 60   **Closed** *Mon & Tue; mid-Feb–mid-Mar, mid-Nov–early Dec*
Informal and relaxed trattoria specializing in thin crust pizzas and pasta dishes. Good selection of Italian wines. Perfect for kids.

ST-RÉMY-DE-PROVENCE: La Medina
Moroccan   €   **Map** B3
34 blvd Mirabeau, 13210
Tel 04 32 62 86 74   **Closed** *Wed*
A nice change of pace, this quiet restaurant offers excellent tagines, couscous and a variety of French dishes. Pleasant summer terrace and garden.

ST-RÉMY-DE-PROVENCE: Comptoir 36
Bistro   €€   **Map** B3
36 ave Marechal Juin, 13210
Tel 04 90 94 41 12   **Closed** *Sun; three weeks in Jan*
Young chefs Lisa and Rudy prepare delectable food from fresh, locally sourced produce at this modern bistro and wine bar. Regular live music.

SAINTES-MARIES-DE-LA-MER: El Campo
Spanish   €   **Map** A4
13 rue Victor Hugo, 13460
Tel 04 90 97 84 11   **Closed** *Wed, except in Jul and Aug*
Lively restaurant with a great service. *Paella* is a speciality, but there are plenty of other options. Live Flamenco and Gipsy Kings-style guitar music in the evenings.

SAINTES-MARIES-DE-LA-MER: L'Estelle en Camargue
Gastronomic   €€€   **Map** A4
D38 route du Petit-Rhône, 13460
Tel 04 90 97 89 01   **Closed** *Mon (except Jul & Aug); mid-Nov–Mar*
Sit in a Mediterranean garden and enjoy a feast of seasonal delicacies. The menu also includes a variety of seafood and creamy desserts.

SALON-DE-PROVENCE: La Salle à Manger
Provençal   €€   **Map** B3
6 rue du Marechal-Joffre, 13300
Tel 04 90 56 28 01   **Closed** *Sun & Mon*
Rococo dining room with a patio for summer months. Famous for delectable desserts, with over 40 varieties to choose from.

VERS-PONT-DU-GARD: La Petite Gare
Classic French   €€   **Map** A3
435 route d'Uzès, 30210
Tel 04 66 03 40 67   **Closed** *Sun & Mon*
Contemporary and creative versions of tasty classics served

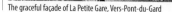
The graceful façade of La Petite Gare, Vers-Pont-du-Gard

The elegant Edouard Loubet restaurant in the Bastide de Capelongue hotel, Bonnieux

in an old train station or outside under century-old plane trees. Good value lunch menus.

VERS-PONT-DU-GARD: Les Terrasses €€
Provençal   **Map** A3
La Begude, 400 route du Pont-du-Gard, 30210
Tel *04 66 63 91 37* **Closed** *Nov–Easter*
Enjoy delicious, locally sourced food against the backdrop of the aqueduct – a spectacle by night when the bridge is illuminated.

VILLENEUVE-LÈS-AVIGNON: La Guinguette du Vieux Moulin €€
Seafood   **Map** B3
5 rue du Vieux Moulin, 30400
Tel *04 90 94 50 72* **Closed** *Sun–Wed dinner; Oct–Mar*
Lively and atmospheric riverside restaurant specializing in grilled sardines and other fish dishes. Hosts frequent events and music. Also has a summer pontoon.

VILLENEUVE-LÈS-AVIGNON: Le Prieuré €€€
Gastronomic   **Map** B3
7 pl du Chapître, 30400
Tel *04 90 15 90 15* **Closed** *Mon; Nov–Mar*
This gorgeous hotel-restaurant is set in a 14th-century priest's residence and offers sophisticated seasonal cuisine.

Vaucluse

AVIGNON: L'Epice and Love €
Provençal   **Map** B3
30 rue des Lices, 84000
Tel *04 90 82 45 96* **Closed** *Sun*
Wonderfully romantic restaurant, run with *joie de vivre* by a superb chef who bases her meals on

the market ingredients available. Reservations recommended.

AVIGNON: Le 75 €€
Classic French   **Map** B3
75 rue Guillaume Puy, 84000
Tel *04 90 27 16 00* **Closed** *Sun*
This *hôtel particulier* features Mediterranean-inspired classic dishes with a modern twist, much like the colourful decor in the 19th-century dining room.

AVIGNON: L'Essentiel €€
Gastronomic   **Map** B3
2 rue Petite Fusterie, 84000
Tel *04 90 85 87 12* **Closed** *Sun & Mon*
The minimalist beige-and-cream decor of this 17th-century building sets the scene for the authentic, skillfully-prepared food.

AVIGNON: La Fourchette €€
Provençal   **Map** B3
17 rue Racine, 84000
Tel *04 90 85 20 93* **Closed** *Sat & Sun*
Quirky, much-loved bistro with its own take on the regional classics, with lots of seafood and excellent cheeses. Booking essential.

AVIGNON: Christian Etienne €€€
Provençal   **Map** B3
10 rue Mons, 84000
Tel *04 90 86 16 50* **Closed** *Sun & Mon*
Masterchef Christian Etienne offers superb seasonal menus in a 14th-century dining room. Good value set lunch menu.

AVIGNON: La Mirande €€€
Gastronomic   **Map** B3
4 pl de la Mirande, 84000
Tel *04 90 14 20 20* **Closed** *Tue & Wed; mid-Jan–mid-Feb*
Dine indoors in an aristocratic setting or outside on the shaded terrace. Dazzling menu by a top chef and friendly service.

AVIGNON: La Vieille Fontaine €€€
Haute Cuisine   **Map** B3
12 pl Crillon, 84000
Tel *04 90 14 76 76* **Closed** *Sun & Mon; mid-Feb–mid-Mar*
Beautifully appointed restaurant in the Hotel d'Europe. Savour chef Mathieu Desmarest's creative cuisine. Excellent wines.

BONNIEUX: Un p'tit Coin de Cuisine €
Bistro   **Map** C3
Pl Gambetta, 84480
Tel *09 81 64 85 81* **Closed** *Mon, Sun lunch*
Smart bistro with a short but delicious menu. Extensive list of Côte du Rhône wines.

BONNIEUX: Edouard Loubet €€€
Haute Cuisine   **Map** C3
Les Claparèdes, chemin des Cabanes, 84480
Tel *04 90 75 89 78* **Closed** *Wed; Dec–Mar (except holiday period)*
Housed in the stunning Bastide de Capelongue hotel. The Michelin-star chef prepares delicious locally sourced dishes.

CADENET: Auberge La Fenière €€€
Haute Cuisine   **Map** C3
D943 Route de Lourmarin, 84160
Tel *04 90 68 11 79* **Closed** *Mon & Tue; Jan*
Lovely inn with superb seafood and vegetable creations from one of Provence's top chefs, Reine Sammut. Holds regular concerts.

CARPENTRAS: Chez Serge €€
Bistro   **Map** B3
90 rue Cottier, 84200
Tel *04 90 63 21 24*
Trendy decor and a creative menu featuring fresh fish, truffles and wild mushrooms. Extensive wine list with a focus on local vineyards.

For more information on types of restaurants *see page 202*

The bright entrance of La Mère Germaine, Châteauneuf-du-Pape

CAVAILLON: Restaurant Prévot €€€
Provençal Map B3
353 av du Verdun, 84300
Tel *04 90 71 32 43* **Closed** *Sun & Mon; mid-Feb–mid-Mar*
A stylish culinary treat by Chef Jean Jacques Prévot. Fabulous ingredient-based seasonal menus – asparagus (spring); melons (summer); mushrooms (autumn) and black truffles (winter).

CHÂTEAUNEUF-DU-PAPE: La Sommellerie €
Bistro Map B3
2268 route de Roquemaure, 84230
Tel *09 70 35 60 29* **Closed** *Mon from Oct–Mar, Sat lunch, Sun dinner*
Located in a 17th-century sheepfold, offers exceptional dinners focusing on regional Côtes du Rhône wines. A superlative three-course *gourmand* menu for €40.

CHÂTEAUNEUF-DU-PAPE: La Mère Germaine €€
Provençal Map B3
3 rue Commandant Lemaitre, 84230
Tel *04 90 22 78 34* **Closed** *Wed from Sep–Mar*
Surrounded by vineyard views, this restaurant features classic Provençal dishes and outstanding regional wines. Good value lunch.

GIGONDAS: Les Florets €
Bistro Map B2
Route des Dentelles, Chemin des Florets, 84190
Tel *04 90 65 85 01* **Closed** *Wed & Thu lunch*
Les Florets offers artful dishes well complimented by local wines. Diners enjoy enchanting views of the Dentelles de Montmirail from its terrace.

GORDES: Restaurant Pèir €€€
Haute Cuisine Map C3
La Bastide de Gordes, Rue de la Combe, 84220
Tel *04 90 72 12 12* **Closed** *Mon, Tue; Jan–Apr*
A luxury hotel with uninterrupted views of the Luberon, where the

famous Chef Pierre Gagnaire conjures up top-level Mediterranean-style cuisine. There's also a more affordable bistro with an identical view.

DK Choice
LAGARDE D'APT: Le Bistrot de Lagarde €€
Bistro Map C3
Route Départemental 34, 84400
Tel *04 90 74 57 23* **Closed** *Mon & Tue; early Dec–Mar*
A former missile bunker at 1,100 m (3,609 ft) up a switchback road is the setting for Le Bistrot de Lagarde. Chef Lloyd Tropeano creates extraordinary dishes using local saffron and other carefully sourced ingredients. The menu changes every three weeks.

LAURIS: La Cuisine d'Amélie €
Bistro Map C3
Domaine de Fontenille, 84360
Tel *04 13 98 00 00* **Closed** *Wed, Thu, Fri lunch; Jan–early Feb*
Part of a boutique hotel surrounded by a lovely park, the menu at this quirky bistro has no particular order – just choose the dishes you want and share them around. For those willing to splurge, there is also a gastronomic restaurant.

L'ISLE-SUR-LE SORGUE: Le Vivier €€
Provençal Map B3
800 cours Fernande Peyre, 84800
Tel *04 90 38 52 80* **Closed** *Mon; Fri & Sat lunch; Sun dinner*
Superb fresh food on a magical riverside terrace. Try the pigeon pie with cèpe mushrooms.

MENERBES: Café Veranda €
Bistro Map C3
Av Marcellin-Poncet, 84560
Tel *04 90 72 33 33* **Closed** *Mon lunch; Sun & Tue dinner*
A welcoming dining room and terrace with views over

the hills. Enjoy creative European cooking along with locally sourced wines. Friendly service.

PERNES-LES-FONTAINES: Coté Jardin €
Classic French Map B3
221 quai de Verdun, 84210
Tel *04 32 80 93 32* **Closed** *Oct–mid-Apr*
Enjoy generous salads and grilled meats while sitting in a pretty garden or on the terrace in the shade of plane trees. Superb home-made ice creams.

SEGURET: Le Mesclun €
Bistro Map B2
Rue des Poternes, 84110
Tel *04 90 46 93 43* **Closed** *Wed; Sun & Tue dinner (Sep–Jun)*
Charming terrace with lovely views of the Rhône valley and sophisticated fare that draws on Asian, Caribbean and Mexican cuisines. Good children's menu.

SERIGNAN-DU-COMTAT: Le Pré du Moulin €€€
Provençal Map B2
Cours Joël Esteve/ Route de Sainte-Cécile les Vignes, 84830
Tel *04 90 70 14 55* **Closed** *Mon, Sun dinner (Sep–Jun)*
Dine under giant plane trees on refined delicacies such as lobster ravioli with chicory and dill in this stylish hotel-restaurant. Vintage Rhône valley and Gigondas wines.

VAISON-LA-ROMAINE: Moulin à Huile €€€
Provençal Map B2
1 quai du Maréchal Foch, 84110
Tel *04 28 31 70 63* **Closed** *Sun dinner, Mon–Wed; mid-Dec–mid-Jan*
Housed in a 12th-century oil mill, this restaurant offers excellent Provençal cuisine, with a truffle-based menu in season and good vegetarian and vegan options as well. Alfresco dining on terrace-balcony.

Alpes-de-Haute-Provence

CASTELLANE: Auberge du Teillon €
Bistro Map D3
Route Napoléon le Garde, 04120
Tel *04 92 83 60 88* **Closed** *Mon, Sun dinner; Nov–Mar*
Pleasant country inn famed for its hand-smoked Norwegian salmon, foie gras, scallop and morel risotto, millefeuille and local cheeses. Friendly atmosphere. Book ahead.

L'Olivier restaurant, Digne-les-Bains

CHÂTEAU-ARNOUX: La Bonne Etape €€€
Haute Cuisine **Map** D2
Chemin du Lac, 04160
Tel *04 92 64 00 09* **Closed** *Mon & Tue; Jan–mid-Feb, late Nov*
Elegant inn specializing in dishes with a personal touch using fresh local produce, especially lamb and seafood. Superb wine list.

DIGNE-LES-BAINS: L'Olivier €
Bistro **Map** D2
1 rue des Monges, 04000
Tel *04 92 31 47 41* **Closed** *Sun dinner, Mon & Tue*
Delightful family-run restaurant with tasty seafood and meat main courses in a pretty alfresco setting.

DIGNE-LES-BAINS: Villa Gaïa €
Provençal **Map** D2
24 route de Nice, 04000
Tel *04 92 31 21 60* **Closed** *Nov–mid-Apr*
Simple and delicious seasonal fare with fresh vegetables from the garden – sautéed coriander and lemon lamb. By reservation only.

FORCALQUIER: Le 9 €
Bistro **Map** C3
9 av Jean Giono, 04300
Tel *04 92 75 03 29* **Closed** *Tue, Wed (in winter); Jan & Feb*
Enjoy simple, fresh dishes with lovely views from the garden and

terrace. Do not miss the venison sautéed with cranberries.

FORCALQUIER: Aux 2 Anges €
Bistro **Map** C3
3 pl Saint-Michel, 04300
Tel *04 92 75 04 36*
Closed *Mon dinner, Tue; Jan*
Friendly, unpretentious and intimate, with outdoor tables and delectable Provençal dishes. Excellent, good-value set menu.

MOUSTIERS-STE-MARIE: Ferme Ste Cécile €
Bistro **Map** D3
Rte des Gorges du Verdon
Tel *04 92 74 64 18* **Closed** *Mon, Sun dinner; Nov–Mar*
Bucolic setting and excellent value on tasty dishes using spelt, partridge, veal and seafood. Good wines. Shaded summer terrace. Book ahead.

DK Choice

MOUSTIERS-STE-MARIE: La Treille Muscate €
Provençal **Map** D3
Pl de l'Eglise, 04360
Tel *04 92 74 64 31* **Closed** *Wed, Thu (in winter); Jan*
Set under the crags, with a shaded terrace near a waterfall, this warm and welcoming restaurant is the perfect setting for some exceptional Provençal cuisine. The menu includes specialities such as lamb shank braised in honey, stuffed baby vegetables and an utterly mouthwatering penne with mushrooms and *foie gras*. Reservations recommended.

MOUSTIERS-STE-MARIE: La Bastide de Moustiers €€€
Provençal **Map** D3
Chemin de Quinson, 04360
Tel *04 92 70 47 47* **Closed** *Tue & Wed; Jan–Feb*
Superb, fresh cuisine. The menu here changes daily, based on the herbs and ingredients plucked that day in the Bastide's fine vegetable garden and orchards. Book "Le salon de Amoureux" for a romantic dinner.

ROUGON: Le Mur D'Abeilles €
Crêperie **Map** D3
D955 – La route du Grand Canyon, 04120
Tel *04 92 83 76 33* **Closed** *Nov–Mar*
Great stop for lunch while visiting the Grand Canyon. Spectacular views, delightful picnic tables and delicious, generous-sized savoury and sweet crêpes. Drinks and ice cream are served as well.

STE-CROIX DU VERDON: Le Comptoir €
Classic French **Map** D3
Le Village, 04500
Tel *04 92 73 74 62* **Closed** *Nov–Easter*
This traditional restaurant boasts a beautiful terrace overlooking the lake. Serves huge salads, grilled fish and meats, and *moules-frites*. Perfect for lunch. Good children's menu.

VALENSOLE: Hostellerie de la Fuste €€
Provençal **Map** D3
Route d'Oraison, 04210
Tel *04 92 72 05 95* **Closed** *Mon, Sun dinner*
Elegant country inn featuring dishes prepared from home-grown vegetables, seafood and succulent meats on a terrace shaded by plane trees.

The magnificent dining room of La Bonne Etape, Château-Arnoux

For more information on types of restaurants *see page 202*

Cafés, Bars and Casual Eating

In rural areas the world over the local bar is the centre of village life, and nowhere is this more true than in Provence. Everywhere you go you will find lively watering holes, often with outside terraces or gardens. Most bars and cafés double as lunchtime restaurants, serving straightforward daily specials at reasonable prices. Snacks are not really a part of French life but nearly all bars will make you a traditional *baguette* sandwich or a *croque monsieur* (toasted ham and cheese sandwich). Drinking is a subject close to Provençal hearts – *pastis*, the aniseed spirit synonymous with Marseille, is the region's lifeblood. In many country towns, you will see the locals sitting outside sipping *pastis* from the early morning onwards, along with strong black coffee. Lunchtime tipples include ice-cold rosé, which makes the perfect accompaniment to a sun-filled day.

Cafés

There is little distinction between cafés and bars in Provence and most serve alcohol all day. In the country, village cafés will often close around 8pm. In larger towns, many places stay open much later – popular Marseillais and Niçois bars close when the last person leaves. Many stay open all night, serving breakfast to the diehards as dawn breaks. A lot of cafés are also *tabacs* (tobacconists) selling cigarettes, tobacco, sweets and stamps.

While most Provençal cafés are simple places, where decor is restricted to the local fire brigade calendar and fashion to a hunting jacket and boots, there are several stylish exceptions. No visit to Aix is complete without an hour or two spent sipping coffee on the cours Mirabeau, one of the places in Provence to see and be seen. On the Côte d'Azur, chic cafés abound. In Cannes, **Restaurant Carlton** is the place to spot film stars during the festival. In Nice, the cafés on the cours Saleya are the hub of day- and nightlife, while Monaco boasts the crème de la crème, **La Brasserie du Café de Paris**.

What to Eat

Most Provençal cafés serve breakfast although, in village establishments, this will just be a couple of slices of *baguette* and coffee. More elaborate affairs are served in towns, with fresh orange juice, warm croissants and jam. Café lunches usually include a *plat du jour* (dish of the day) and a dessert, along with a quarter litre of wine. These can be great bargains, costing little more than €17. For more basic lunches, sandwiches, omelettes and salads can be ordered. Evening meals are usually the reserve of restaurants, although in rural areas, the local bar will also serve dinner, normally a variant on the lunchtime menu.

What to Drink

Since Roman days, when the legionnaires introduced wine to the region, drinking has been a favoured pastime in Provence. Cold beer seems to surpass the fruit of the vine in the hearts of most farmers, as village bars are filled with locals downing *pressions* (half-pint glasses of beer). More potent tipples include *pastis*, a 90 per cent proof nectar flavoured with aniseed, vanilla and cinnamon, and *marc*, a brandy distilled from any available fruits. Soft drinks such as *un diabolo* (fruit syrup mixed with lemonade) and *orange pressée* (freshly squeezed orange juice) are also popular. As in most Mediterranean lands, coffee is a way of life – *un café* is a cup of strong and black espresso. If you want white coffee, ask for *un café crème*. For filter or instant coffee order *un café filtre* or *un café américain*. Tea is served black unless you ask for milk or lemon. Herbal teas are also available, known as *tisanes* or *infusions*.

Bars

In most towns you will find a handful of bars that only serve beer and miscellaneous alcohol, rather than the more diverse range offered by cafés. These bars are lively in true Mediterranean style. Student centres such as Nice, Marseille and Aix contain British-style pubs, offering a large selection of European bottled and draught beer. Some have live bands, such as **Wayne's Bar** and **De Klomp** in Nice.

More upmarket bars are found in the plush hotels of the Côte d'Azur. Here, in *belle époque* splendour, you can sip champagne listening to jazz piano, string quartets or opera singers. Among the most impressive are the bars of the Carlton and Martinez hotels in Cannes, Le Négresco in Nice, **Le Bar** at the Grand Hôtel in St-Jean-Cap-Ferrat and the Hermitage in Monte-Carlo (*see* Where to Stay, *pp194–201*).

Picnic and Take-Away Food

You are never far from food in Provence. The traditional street food of Provence is the *pan bagnat*, a thick bun filled with crisp salade Niçoise and doused in olive oil. Pizza is a local favourite, and every small town has its pizza van, where your choice is cooked to order. A particularly Provençal form of pizza is *pissaladière*, an onion pizza coated with anchovies and olives. In Nice, the number one snack is *socca,* thick crêpes made from chickpea flour (*see pp204–5*).

The French love picnics, and the *Provençaux* are no exception. French alfresco eating is often complex – families set out tables, chairs, barbecues and portable fridges.

WHERE TO EAT AND DRINK | 219

To service this penchant for portable dining, Provençal villages have specialist shops offering ready-to-eat food. *Boulangeries* and *pâtisseries* serve everything from fresh croissants to quiches and a dazzling array of cakes and tarts. Nearly all *boulangeries* provide delicious, freshly made baguette sandwiches.

In the main towns, specialist butchers called *traîteurs* pro-vide ready-made dishes, such as salads, cold meats and roast chicken, sold in cartons according to weight. **Au Flan Coco** in Nîmes and **Bataille** in Marseille are fine examples. Most supermarkets also have similar delicatessen counters. *Charcuteries* specialize in pork dishes, particularly pâtés and sausages. For traditional spicy sausages much prized in the Camargue, head to the **Maison Genin** in Arles.

The best place to buy picnic food is the local market. Every town in Provence has its market, some daily, like Aix-en-Provence, some just once or twice a week. No Provençal picnic is complete without French bread – the *baguette* is the mainstay of the country and Provence is no exception. The only difference is that the region boasts numerous local breads, incorporating traditional ingredients. *Pain aux olives* is found almost everywhere, often in the form of *fougasse*, a flat, lattice-like loaf. Alternatively, this may contain anchovies (*pain aux anchois*), or spinach (*pain aux épinards*) and there is a sweet version flavoured with almonds. Wholemeal or brown bread is an anathema to the traditional Provençaux, although many bakeries now produce it – ask for *pain aux*

céréales. The nearest to healthy bread is *pain de campagne*, a sturdier baguette made with unrefined white flour. One of the finest *boulangeries* in the region is **Le Four à Bois**, in the old quarter of Nice, where the same recipes have been used for generations.

Boulangeries are found in every village and usually have a good selection of *pâtisseries*, cakes and tarts. Provençal ingredients are combined to make these delights, such as honey, almonds and fruit – try those at **Béchard** in Aix-en-Provence. For those with an even sweeter tooth, these same ingredients are used in the handmade chocolates and candied fruit. *Calissons* (an almond-paste sweet) and *suce-miel* (honey-based candy) are very popular. Two of the best shops are **Puyricard** in Aix and **Auer** in Nice.

DIRECTORY

Cafés

AIX-EN-PROVENCE

Brasserie Les Deux Garçons
53 cours Mirabeau.
Tel 04 42 26 00 51.

CANNES

Restaurant Carlton
58 la Croisette.
Tel 04 93 06 40 06.

EZE

Château Eza
Rue de la Pise.
Tel 04 93 41 12 24.

MONACO

La Brasserie du Café de Paris
Le Casino, place du Casino.
Tel 00 377 98 06 76 23.

NICE

Le Grand Café de Turin
5 place Garibaldi.
Tel 04 93 62 29 52.

NÎMES

Le Café Olive
22 blvd Victor Hugo.
Tel 04 66 67 89 10.

ST-PAUL DE VENCE

Café de la Place
1 place du Général de Gaulle.
Tel 04 93 32 80 03.

ST-TROPEZ

Brasserie des Arts
5 place des Lices.
Tel 04 94 40 27 37.

Le Café de Paris
Le Port, 15 quai de Suffren.
Tel 04 94 97 00 56.

Senequier
Quai Jean Jaurès.
Tel 04 94 97 20 20.

Bars and Pubs

AVIGNON

Pub Z
58 rue de la Bonneterie.
Tel 04 88 07 20 16.

CANNES

3.14
5 rue François Einesy.
Tel 04 92 99 72 09.

JUAN-LES-PINS

Pam-Pam
137 blvd Wilson.
Tel 04 93 61 11 05.

MARSEILLE

Le Bar de la Marine
15 quai de Rive Neuve.
Tel 04 91 54 95 42.

La Part des Anges
33 rue Sainte.
Tel 04 91 33 55 70.

MONACO

Flashman's
7 ave Princesse Alice.
Tel 00 377 93 30 09 03.

NICE

De Klomp
6 rue Mascoinat.
Tel 09 82 34 14 21.

Les Trois Diables
2 cours Saleya.
Tel 06 62 27 47 17.

Wayne's Bar
15 rue de la Préfecture.
Tel 04 93 13 46 99.

NÎMES

La Grande Bourse
2 blvd des Arenes.
Tel 04 66 67 68 69.

ST-JEAN-CAP-FERRAT

Le Bar
Grand Hôtel de Cap–Ferrat, 71 blvd du Général de Gaulle.
Tel 04 93 76 50 50.

VILLEFRANCHE-SUR-MER

Le Cosmo Bar
11 pl Amélie Pollonais.
Tel 04 93 01 84 05.

Picnic and Take-Away Food

AIX-EN-PROVENCE

Béchard
12 cours Mirabeau.

Puyricard
7–9 rue Rifle-rafle.

ARLES

Maison Genin
11 rue des Porcelets.

MARSEILLE

Bataille
18 rue Fontange.

Le Four des Navettes
136 rue Sainte.

NICE

Auer
7 rue St-François- de-Paule.

Le Four à Bois
35 rue Droite.

NÎMES

Au Flan Coco
21 rue du Grand Couvent.

SHOPS AND MARKETS

Shopping in Provence is one of life's great delights. Even the tiniest village may be home to a potter or painter, or you may arrive on market day to find regional produce – artichokes, asparagus, wild mushrooms – still fresh with the dew from the surrounding fields. Larger towns are packed with individual boutiques selling anything from dried flowers to chic baby clothes, and the fashion-conscious will always be able to find an avenue or two of famous names in which to window-shop. If the idea of cramming fresh foodstuffs into your luggage to take back home proves too daunting, Provence has perfected the fine art of packaging its produce, with the bottles, jars and boxes often works of art in themselves. This section provides guidelines on opening hours and the range of goods with a Provençal flavour to be found in the many stores and markets.

A butcher and a store selling household goods in a village in Provence

Opening Hours

Food shops open at around 8am and close at noon for lunch, a break that may last for up to three hours. After lunch, most shops stay open until 7pm, sometimes even later in big towns. Bakers often stay open until 1pm or later, serving tasty lunchtime snacks. Most supermarkets and hypermarkets stay open throughout lunchtimes.

Non-food shops are open 9am–7pm Mon–Sat, but most will close for lunch. Many are closed on Monday mornings.

Food shops and newsagents open on Sunday mornings but almost every shop is closed on Sunday afternoon. Small shops may close for one day a week out of high season.

Larger Shops

Hypermarkets (*hypermarchés* or *grandes surfaces*) can be found on the outskirts of every sizeable town: look out for the signs indicating the *Centre Commercial*. Among the largest are Casino, Auchan, E.LeClerc and Carrefour. Discount petrol is usually sold at 24-hour petrol pumps where you need a pin card and chip to pay.

Supermarkets selling clothes and sundries (*supermarchés*), such as Monoprix and Champion, are usually found in town centres. Most of the upscale department stores (*grands magasins*), such as Galeries Lafayette and Printemps are located in cities.

Specialist Shops

One of the great pleasures of shopping in Provence is that specialist food shops still flourish despite the presence of large supermarkets. The bread shop (*boulangerie*) is usually combined with the *pâtisserie* selling cakes and pastries. The cheesemonger (*fromagerie*) may also be combined with a shop selling other dairy produce (*laiterie*), but the *boucherie* (butcher) and the *charcuterie* (delicatessen) tend to be separate shops. A *traiteur* sells prepared foods. For dry goods and general groceries, you will need to go to an *épicerie*.

Cleaning products and household goods are sold at a *droguerie* and hardware at a *quincaillerie*. Booksellers (*libraries*) in the main towns sometimes sell English books.

Markets

This guide gives the market days for every town featured. To find out where the market is, ask a passer-by for *le marché*. Markets are morning affairs, when the produce is super-fresh – by noon the stall-holders will already be packing up and the best bargains will have sold out hours ago. By French law, price tags must state the origin of all produce: *du pays* means local.

Les marchés de Provence were immortalized in song by Gilbert Bécaud, and rightly so. In a country famed for its markets, these are among the best. Some are renowned – cours Saleya (*see p88*) in Nice and the food and flower markets of Aix (*see p152*), for example, should not be missed. Others take more searching out, such as the truffle markets of the Var. Try Aups (*see p108*) on a Thursday during truffle season, from November to February.

Enjoying a drink next to a flower shop in Luberon, Vaucluse

Bags of dried herbs on display in the market of St-Rémy-de-Provence

Regional Specialities

The sunshine of Provence is captured in its distinctive, vividly coloured fabrics, known as *indiennes*. Many shops sell them by the metre; others, such as **Mistral – Les Indiennes de Nîmes** and **Souleïado** also make them into soft furnishings, cowboy shirts and boxer shorts.

Throughout Provence, working olive mills churn out rich, pungent oil, which is also used to make the chunky blocks of soap, *savon de Marseille*. Tins and jars of olives, often scented with *herbes de Provence*, are widely available, as are bags of the herbs themselves. Bags of lavender, and honey from its pollen, are regional specialities; local flowers appear in other forms too, from dried arrangements to scented oils, or perfumes from Grasse *(see p71)*.

Traditional sweets *(confiseries)* abound, using regional fruits and nuts: almond *calissons* from Aix, fruity *berlingots* from Carpentras and *fruits confits* from Apt are just a few.

Local Wines

Provence is not one of the great wine regions of the world, but its many vineyards *(see pp206–7)* produce a wide range of pleasant wines and you will see plenty of signs inviting you to a *dégustation* (tasting). You will usually be expected to buy at least one bottle. Wine co-operatives sell the wines of numerous smaller producers. Here you can buy wine in five- and ten-litre containers *(en vrac)*. This wine is "duty free" but, with vineyards such as Châteauneuf-du-Pape and Beaumes-de-Venise, wise buyers will drink *en vrac* on holiday and pick up bargains in fine wine to bring home.

Marseille's anise-flavoured aperitif *pastis* is an evocative, if acquired, taste.

Arts and Crafts

Many of the crafts now flourishing in Provence are traditional ones that had almost died out 50 years ago. The potters of Vallauris owe the revival in their fortunes to Picasso *(see pp76–7)* but, more often, it is the interest of visitors that keeps a craft alive. From the little pottery *santons* of Marseille to the flutes and tambourines of Barjols, there is plenty of choice for gifts and mementos. Many towns have unique specialities. Biot *(see p78)* is famous for its bubbly glassware, Cogolin for pipes and carpets and Salernes for hexagonal terracotta tiles.

Works by local artists sold on the harbour at St-Tropez

DIRECTORY

Regional Specialities

AVIGNON

Souleïado
19 rue Joseph Vernet.
Tel 04 90 86 32 05.
One of several branches.

GRASSE

Huilerie Ste-Anne
138 route de Draguignan.
Tel 04 93 70 21 42.

Parfumerie Fragonard
20 blvd Fragonard.
Tel 04 92 42 34 34.
w fragonard.com

Parfumerie Galimard
73 route de Cannes.
Tel 04 93 09 20 00.
w galimard.com

NICE

Alziari
14 rue St-François-de-Paule.
Tel 04 93 62 94 03.
Olive press.

NÎMES

Mistral – Les Indiennes de Nîmes
2 blvd des Arènes.
Tel 04 66 21 69 57.

Arts and Crafts

COGOLIN

Fabrique de Pipes Courrieu
58–60 ave G Clemenceau.
Tel 04 94 54 63 82.

Manufacture des Tapis de Cogolin
Tel 04 94 55 70 65.

MARSEILLE

Ateliers Marcel Carbonel
47–49 rue Neuve Ste-Catherine.
Tel 04 91 54 26 58.
w santonsmarcel carbonel.com
Workshop and museum.

VALLAURIS

Céramiques Dominique N B
Ave Maréchal Juin.
Tel 04 93 64 02 36.

English Language Bookshops

ANTIBES

Antibes Books
13 rue Georges Clemenceau.
Tel 04 93 61 96 47.

AIX-EN-PROVENCE

Book in Bar
4 rue Joseph Cabassol.
Tel 04 42 26 60 07.

CANNES

Cannes English Bookshop
11 rue Bivouac Napoléon.
Tel 04 93 99 40 08.

MARSEILLE

Librarie Internationale Maurel
95 rue de Lodi.
Tel 04 91 42 63 44.

MONTPELLIER

Le Bookshop
8 rue du Bras de Fer.
Tel 04 67 66 22 90.

What to Buy in Provence

Best buys to be found in Provence are those that reflect the character of the region – its geographical blessings of bountiful produce and its historic traditions of arts and crafts. While the chic boutiques of St-Tropez or Cannes may rival Paris in predicting the latest fashion trend, your souvenirs of Provence should be far more timeless. The evocative scents, colours and flavours they offer will help to keep your holiday memories alive throughout the darkest winter months, and longer – at least until your next visit.

Lavender, one of the perfumes of Provence

The Scents of Provence

Provençal lavender is used to perfume a wide range of goods, but most popular are pretty fabric sachets full of the dried flowers. Bath times can be heady with the scent of local flowers and herbs, captured in delightful bottles, and Marseille's famous olive oil soaps.

Olive oil savons de Marseille

Orange water from Vallauris

Linden-scented bubble bath

Dried lavender, packed in Provençal fabrics

Mallow-scented bubble bath

Glassware

Glassblowing is a modern Provençal craft. At Biot (*see p78*) you can watch glassblowers at work, as well as buy examples of their art to take home.

Pottery

Look for traditional tiles, cookware and storage jars made from *terre rouge*, formal china of Moustiers faïence (*see p190*) or art-works of *grès* clay.

Terracotta Santons

Provençal Christmas cribs are peopled with these gaily painted traditional figures. Most crafts shops offer a good choice of characters.

Olive Wood

As rich in colour and texture as its oil, the wood of the olive can be sculpted into works of art or turned into practical kitchenware.

Hunting Knives

The huntsmen's shops of Provence are an unexpected source for the perfect picnic or kitchen knife, safe yet razor sharp.

Provençal Fabrics

Using patterns and colours dating back centuries, these traditional prints are sold by the metre or made up into fashionable items.

The Flavours of Provence

No-one should leave Provence without at least a jar of olives or a bottle of olive oil, but consider also easy-to-pack tins, jars and boxes of preserved fruits, scented honey or savoury purées – prettily packaged, they make ideal gifts.

Almond sweetmeats, the speciality of Aix-en-Provence

Candied chestnuts or *marrons glacés*

Goats' cheese, wrapped in chestnut leaves

Tuna packed in olive oil

Basil flavoured olive oil

Virgin olive oil

Puréed salt cod or *brandade de morue*

Almond and orange conserve

Lavender honey and hazelnut *confit*

ENTERTAINMENT IN PROVENCE

Provence offers a wealth of cultural options to visitors. Barely a month goes by without some major festival *(see pp36–9 & pp228–9)*. Events take place all year round, with first-class dance, opera and jazz in Nice and Marseille, rock concerts in Toulon, theatre in Avignon and blockbuster art shows in Nice, Antibes, Monaco and Aix-en-Provence. Nightlife tends to be restricted to the fashionable coastal resorts, like Juan-les-Pins and St-Tropez, where clubs and bars often stay open all night. In winter, things are quieter, but the small bars and cafés of Marseille, Nîmes and Nice remain open and full of life. Provence's most common entertainment is free – locals spend much of their time enjoying the fresh air, walking and playing *pétanque*, or Provençal bowls.

Practical Information

Information about what's on in Provence is fairly localized, with tourist offices providing listings of various events. Most large towns publish a weekly paper that outlines the best of each week's events. Local papers can also provide details of important festivals and sporting events. *Le Provençal* serves western Provence, while *Nice Matin* and its derivatives cover the east of the region. You can purchase regional newspapers and magazines at newsagents and *tabacs*.

The large English-speaking community in Provence has its own radio station, Riviera Radio, which broadcasts from Monte-Carlo in English on 106.3 FM and 106.5 FM. English-language publications such as *The Riviera Times* and *The Riviera Reporter* include event listings and websites.

Buying Tickets

Depending on the event, most tickets can be bought on the door, but for blockbuster concerts, particularly during the summer months, it is best to reserve in advance. Tickets can be purchased at branches of the **FNAC** and **Carrefour** chains in major towns.

Theatre box offices are open from approximately 11am until 7pm seven days a week and will usually accept credit card bookings over the telephone.

As a last resort, if you haven't booked in advance, tickets to popular concerts can be bought from touts at the venue doors on the night. However, they will be much more expensive and possibly counterfeit.

Opera and Classical Music

Music is everywhere in Provence, from small village churches to the *belle époque* opera houses of Marseille, Toulon and Nice. The **Opéra de Nice** is one of the best in France, and the **Monte-Carlo Philharmonic Orchestra** features many illustrious conductors. Classical and jazz festivals are held throughout the summer in major cities.

Every year on 21 June, the Fête de la Musique is held throughout France. Amateur and professional musicians alike set up their stages in villages and towns and perform. Take in as many different "concerts" as you can to enjoy an impressive range of genres.

Classical cello

Rock and Jazz

These days Provence is a major venue on most world tours, with big stadium performances at Toulon's **Zenith-Omèga** or Marseille's soccer stadium, **Le Nouveau Stade-Vélodrome**. The **Nice Festival du Jazz** in the Cimiez arena *(see p88)* is one of the world's best. It was here that Miles Davis gave one of his last performances among the Roman walls and olive groves. Also popular is the **Jazz à Juan** festival in Juan-les-Pins, which has included Ray Charles and the jazz debut of classical violinist Nigel Kennedy.

Theatre

Going to the theatre in Provence can be as formal or as relaxed as you choose. A trip to a big theatre can involve dressing up, special *souper* (late dinner) reservations at a nearby restaurant and pricey champagne during the interval. On the other hand, a visit to a smaller theatre can be cheap and casual, with a real feeling of intimacy and immediacy.

Leonard Cohen performing at the Nice Festival du Jazz

Marseille is the centre of theatre in Provence and boasts one of France's top theatrical companies, the **Théâtre National de la Criée**. Various smaller companies stage innovative plays, many of which end up in Paris. Avignon is also famous for its **Théâtre des Carmes**, the main venue for the **Festival d'Avignon** (see p229). There is also a "fringe" festival, the **Avignon Le Off**, with its own directors and box office.

Spectator Sports

With its superb weather and glamorous reputation, the regions of Provence and the Côte d'Azur are ideal venues for some of France's top sporting events. The gruelling **Tour de France** passes through the area each July, while the Monte-Carlo and Nice tennis tournaments attract the best players. The **Grand Prix de Monaco** (see p36) is one of the highlights of the Formula 1 motor-racing season, and horse-racing enthusiasts can visit the **Hippodrome de la Côte d'Azur** track at Cagnes-sur-Mer between December and March.

Provence boasts two of the top soccer teams in France – **Olympique de Marseille** and **AS Monaco FC**, known as the millionaires' club. Rugby is also popular in Provence, with top-class clubs in Nice and Toulon.

Dance

Marseille's eclectic mixture of nationalities and styles has led

The Open Tennis Championships in Monte-Carlo

to highly original and powerful dance productions.

The National Ballet Company is based at the Ecole de Danse in Marseille. Companies such as the **Bernardines** sometimes take their productions to Paris, while **La Friche La Belle de Mai**, located in an old tobacco

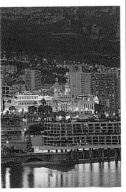

View over the harbour in Monaco to the glittering casino

factory, is a popular venue for experimental performance and music.

The new **Centre Choré-graphique National** in Aix-en-Provence is an exciting addition to the Provençal dance scene.

Gambling

The French Riviera is famed for its opulent casinos. If you are 18 and over you can play in most resorts. Monaco has the coast's most popular casino – **Le Casino** – where you have to pay an entrance fee and show an ID card before you can start gambling. Other casinos worth visiting for architecture and atmosphere are Cannes' **Casino Croisette** and **Casino Ruhl** in Nice. Even if you are not a high-roller, there is always a dazzling array of slot machines.

Bullfighting

The annual *ferias*, or bullfighting festivals, are always dramatic occasions. The traditional bullfight of Provence is the *course à la cocarde*, which starts with an *abrivado* when the bulls are chased through the town to the local arena. The bull enters the ring with a red *cocarde*, or rosette, tied to its horns, which the *razeteurs*, or matadors, try to snatch, providing riveting but goreless entertainment. At the end of the season, the bullfighter with the most rosettes receives fame and adulation, as well as cash.

Sometimes bullfights will end in death in the full-blooded Spanish-style *corrida*, but this is usually only in the main arenas in Nîmes and Arles (see p36), and it will always be advertised first. In one session there are usually six bullfights, of which two may be advertised as *mise à mort* (to the death).

Bullfighting poster for the 1992 Nîmes *feria* by Francis Bacon

Cinema

The small port of La Ciotat is where Louis Lumière shot the world's first motion picture, and Marcel Pagnol *(see p157)* laid the foundations for modern French cinema from his studios in Marseille. The French are very supportive of *la Septième Art*, as they refer to film, and there are plenty of local, independent cinemas. If your language skills won't stretch to watching a French film, look out for cinemas that show films in their *V.O. (Version Original)* – that is, screened in their original language. *V.F. (Version Française)* denotes a dubbed screening in French.

Popcorn or other snacks are available, but it tends to be the foreigners that snack their way through a movie. However, there are some French cinemas that have bars and restaurants attached, so that you may dissect the movie while enjoying a meal or a drink afterwards.

As the fame of Cannes *(see pp72–3)* reflects, film festivals are taken seriously by the French. Cannes itself is a maelstrom of media hype, old-school glamour and shiny new cash. It is an amazing experience if you can get tickets to any of the films or parties, but these are notoriously difficult to get as they are by invitation only.

Discotheques and Nightclubs

During the summer, the main towns of Provence boogie all night long. The music is far from trend-setting, usually following styles set the previous year in New York and London, but the dancers are chic and the prices high. A handful of clubs such as **Jimmy'Z** in Monaco and **Les Caves du Roy** in St-Tropez cater for the jet set, while **Kiss Club** in Juan-les-Pins and **Gotha Club** in Cannes serve a younger crowd. The dress code is usually smart, and trainers are almost always forbidden.

Children's Entertainment

Provence offers the traditional attractions of beach and sea, although small children may better appreciate them in smaller resorts. Alternatives include aqua parks like **Marineland** and **Aqualand**, zoos and aquariums. There are also numerous adventure parks for rock-climbing, cycling and zip-lining, such as the **Canyon Forest** at Villeneuve-Loubet and **Coudou Parc** at Six-Fours-les-Plages. Marseille has **Préau des Accoules**, the only children's museum in the region. In the bigger towns, museums and theatres may organize activities (ask at the tourist office). Smaller towns and villages will have playgrounds or a square where your offspring can play with other children while you relax in a café. For more action, there are plenty of sporting activities, such as biking, canoeing, tennis, horse-riding and fishing.

DIRECTORY

Buying Tickets

Carrefour
ⓦ spectacles.carrefour.fr

Marseille
Carrefour Tasso, 4 pl du 4 sept.

Nice
Carrefour Nice Notre-Dame, 17–19 ave des Embrois.

FNAC
Tel 08 92 68 36 22.
ⓦ fnacspectacles.com

Avignon
19 rue de la République.

Marseille
Centre Commercial Bourse, 12 cours Belsunce.

Nice
40–46 ave Jean Médecin.

Opera and Classical Music

AIX-EN-PROVENCE

Grand Théâtre de Provence
380 ave Max Juvénale.
Tel 04 42 91 69 70.
ⓦ lestheatres.net

MARSEILLE

Opéra Municipal
2 rue Molière.
Tel 04 91 55 11 10.
ⓦ opera.marseille.fr

MONACO

Monte-Carlo Philharmonic Orchestra
Auditorium Rainier III, Blvd Loius II, BP 197
Tel 00 377 98 06 28 28.
ⓦ opmc.mc

NICE

Forum Nice Nord
10 blvd Comte de Falicon.
Tel 04 93 84 24 37.
ⓦ forumnicenord.com

Opéra de Nice
4–6 rue St-François-de-Paule. **Tel** 04 92 17 40 00.
ⓦ opera-nice.org

Salle-Grapelli – CEDAC de Cimiez
49 ave de la Marne.
Tel 04 97 13 55 13.
ⓦ salle-grapelli-nice.org

TOULON – OLLIOULES

Châteauvallon
Tel 04 94 22 02 02.
ⓦ chateauvallon.com

Festival de Musique Classique
Tel 04 94 93 55 45.
ⓦ festivalmusique toulon.com

Opéra de Toulon
Blvd de Strasbourg.
Tel 04 94 93 03 76.
ⓦ operadetoulon.fr

Rock and Jazz

AIX-EN-PROVENCE

Hot Brass Club
1857 chemin d'Eguilles-Célony. **Tel** 04 42 21 05 57.

Le Scat
11 rue de la Verrerie.
Tel 04 42 23 00 23.

JUAN-LES-PINS

Jazz à Juan
Office de Tourisme, 60 chemin des Sables, Antibes.
ⓦ jazzajuan.com

MARSEILLES

Espace Julien
39 cours Julien.
Tel 04 91 24 34 10.
ⓦ espace-julien.com

L'Intermédiaire
63 pl Jean-Jaurès.
Tel 06 87 87 88 21.

Le Nouveau Stade Vélodrome
3 blvd Michelet.
Tel 04 86 09 50 34.

Le Pelle-Mêle
8 pl aux Huiles.
Tel 04 91 54 85 26.

NICE

Festival du Jazz
Pl Massena, Theatre de Verdure **Tel** 04 97 13 40 42.
ⓦ nicejazzfestival.fr

Theatre des Oiseaux
6 rue d'Abbaye.
Tel 04 93 80 21 93.

TOULON

Zenith-Oméga
Blvd Commandant Nicolas.
Tel 04 94 22 66 77.
ⓦ zenith-omega-toulon.com

DIRECTORY

Theatre

AVIGNON

Avignon Le Off
Tel 04 90 85 13 08.
W avignonleoff.com

Festival d'Avignon
Espace St-Louis, 20 rue
Portail Boguier.
Tel 04 90 27 66 50.
W festival-avignon.com

Théâtre des Carmes
6 place des Carmes.
Tel 04 90 82 20 47.
W theatredescarmes.com

MARSEILLE

Théâtre du Merlan
Avenue Raimu. Tel 04 91
11 19 20. W merlan.org

**Théâtre National
de la Criée**
30 quai de Rive-Neuve.
Tel 04 91 54 70 54.
W theatre-lacriee.com

NICE

Théâtre de l'Alphabet
19 rue Delille.
Tel 06 60 89 10 04.
W theatrenice.fr

Théâtre de la Semeuse
2 montée Auguste Kerl.
Tel 04 93 92 85 08.
W lasemeuse.asso.fr

Spectator Sports

CAGNES-SUR-MER

**Hippodrome de la
Côte d'Azur**
Tel 04 92 02 44 44.
W hippodrome-
cotedazur.com

MARSEILLE

ASPTT Tennis
Tel 04 84 25 56 03.
W marseille.asptt.com

Olympique de Marseille
W om.net

MONACO

AS Monaco FC
W asmonaco.com

Grand Prix de Monaco
W acm.mc

NICE

**Ligue de la Côte
d'Azur Tennis**
Tel 04 97 25 76 80.

Tour de France
W letour.fr

Dance

AIX-EN-PROVENCE

**Centre Chorégraphique
National**
530 ave Mozart.
Tel 04 42 93 48 00.

MARSEILLE

Bernardines
17 blvd Garibaldi. Tel 04
91 24 30 40. W theatre-
bernardines.org

**La Friche la
Belle de Mai**
41 rue Robin. Tel 04 95 04
95 95. W lafriche.org

Gambling

CANNES

Casino Croisette
1 espace Lucien Barriere.
Tel 04 92 98 78 00.
W lucienbarriere.com

MONACO

Le Casino
Place du Casino.
Tel 00 377 98 06 21 21.
W casinomontecarlo.com

NICE

Casino Ruhl
1 promenade des Anglais.
Tel 04 97 03 12 22.

Bullfighting

ARLES

Arènes d'Arles
Rond-point des Arènes.
Tel 08 91 70 03 70.
W arenes-arles.com

NÎMES

Les Arènes
Blvd des Arènes.
Tel 08 91 70 14 01.
W arenesdenimes.com

Cinema

AIX-EN-PROVENCE

Le Mazarin
6 rue Laroque.
Tel 04 42 38 78 82.

AVIGNON

Utopia Cinéma
4 rue des Escaliers Sainte
Anne. Tel 04 90 82 65 36.

CANNES

Cannes Film Festival
W festival-cannes.com/fr

MARSEILLE

Cinéma Le Chambord
283 ave du Prado.
Tel 04 91 25 70 06.

MONTE-CARLO

Le Sporting d'Hiver
Place du Casino.
Tel 00 377 98 06 17 17.

NICE

Cinémathèque
3 esplanade Kennedy.
Tel 04 92 04 06 66.

Mercury Cinéma
16 place Garibaldi.
Tel 04 93 55 37 81.

NÎMES

Le Sémaphore
25a rue Porte de France.
Tel 04 66 67 83 11.

Discotheques and Nightclubs

AIX-EN-PROVENCE

Le Mistral
3 rue Frédéric Mistral.
Tel 04 42 38 16 49.

AVIGNON

Les Ambassadeurs Club
27 rue Bancasse.
Tel 04 90 86 31 55.

CANNES

Gotha Club
Palm Beach Point Croisette,
Pl Franklin Roosevelt.
Tel 04 93 45 11 11.

Le Bâoli
Port Canto, La Croisette.
Tel 04 93 43 03 43.

HYÈRES

Le Gossip
15 ave du Docteur Robin,
Hyères. Tel 04 94 48 84 53.

L'Instant
RD 559, Quartier St Nicholas,
La Londe-les-Maures.
Tel 06 42 59 18 67.

JUAN-LES-PINS

Kiss Club
5 ave George Gallice.
Tel 06 30 71 46 18.

Le Village
Carrefour de la nouvelle
orleans. Tel 04 92 93 90 00.

MARSEILLE

The Trolleybus
24 quai de Rive-Neuve,
Vieux Port. Tel 04 91 54
30 45.

MONACO

Jimmy'Z
26 ave Princesse Grace.
Tel 00 377 98 06 36 36.
W fr.jimmyzmonte
carlo.com

La Rascasse
Quai Antoine 1er.
Tel 00 377 98 06 16 16.

NICE

High Club/Studio 47
45 promenade des Anglais.
Tel 07 81 88 42 04.

ST-RAPHAËL

La Réserve
Promenade René Coty.
Tel 06 27 13 88 99.

ST-TROPEZ

Les Caves du Roy
Palace de la Côte d'Azur,
Ave du marechal foch.
Tel 04 94 56 68 00.
W lescavesduroy.com

Papagayo
Résidence du Port.
Tel 04 94 97 95 96.

Children's Entertainment

Aqualand
RN 98, 83600 Fréjus.
Tel 04 94 51 82 51.
W aqualand.fr

Canyon Forest
Parc des Rives du Loup,
26 rte de Grasse Villeneuve-
Loubet. Tel 04 92 02 88 88.
W canyonforest.com

Coudou Parc
34 rue de la République,
Six-Fours-les-Plages.
Tel 06 63 77 02 06.
W coudouparc.com

Marineland
RN 7, 06600 Antibes.
Tel 08 92 42 62 26.
W marineland.fr

**Museum of
Oceanography and
Aquarium**
Ave St Martin, Monte-Carlo.
Tel 00 377 93 15 36 00.

**Park Zoologique de
Fréjus**
Le Capitou, Fréjus.
Tel 04 98 11 37 37.

**Préau des Accoules
(Children's Museum)**
29 montee des Accoules,
Marseille. Tel 04 91 91 52 06.

Festivals in Provence

Festivals in Provence are very much part of the way of life. They are not staged purely for the benefit of visitors and tourism, but more to continue the seasonal celebrations that are deeply rooted in tradition. Many *fêtes* are based on pagan rites while others are celebrations of historic occasions – only a few have been hijacked by fun-loving holiday-makers on the coast. Here is a selection of the best festivals from each of the *départements*.

One of the spectacular floats in the procession at the Nice Carnival

The Riviera and the Alpes Maritimes

The brilliant explosion of fireworks at the Carnaval de Nice above the Baie des Anges is one of the most popular images of Nice *(see pp84–9)*. It is the largest pre-Lent carnival in France, and crescendos on Shrove Tuesday with fireworks and the immolation of King Carnival, *Sa Majesté Carnaval.*

Carnival festivities, held in all Catholic countries, are based on the pagan celebrations of the death of winter and the birth of spring and life. It is a time of feasting (*mardi gras* means "fat Tuesday") before the fasting of Lent (*carne vale* is Latin for "farewell to meat").

Festivities begin three weeks before Mardi Gras, when the king is wheeled out into the streets. During the two weekends between then and his departure, the colourful, flower-decked floats of the procession parade along the 2-km (1-mile) route round Jardin Albert I, amid confetti battles, bands and mounted escorts.

Carnival characters in the streets of Nice

By the 19th century, the Nice Carnival had developed into little more than a chalk and flour battle. The floats did not appear until 1873, inspired by the local artist, Alexis Mossa, who also resurrected the figure of King Carnival. Since then, great effort and time has been put into making the costumes.

Meanwhile, the whole town is *en fête*, and parties and balls are held in hotels and public venues all night long. Visitors should book well in advance to secure accommodation.

The Var and the Iles d'Hyères

A number of festivals in the region feature the firing of muskets, reminiscent of ancient witch-scaring rites. Spectacular volleys are set off into the air in St-Tropez *(see pp122–6)* for the biannual *bravade*, commemorating two significant events.

The first one takes place on 16–18 May and is a religious procession devoted to the town's patron, Saint Torpès, He was a Roman soldier in the service of the emperor, Nero. In AD 68, Torpès converted to Christianity and was martyred by decapitation. His body was placed in a boat along with a hungry dog and a cockerel. Miraculously, the saint's body was untouched. The vessel was washed up onto the shores of southern France, on the spot where St-Tropez stands today.

The May *bravade* honours his arrival. Celebrations begin with the blessing of a lance by the town's priest in the Eglise de St-Tropez. From here, the saint's gilded wooden bust is taken and carried around the flag-decked town in a terrific flurry of musket volleys. The procession winds down to the beach, and the sea is blessed for safely conveying the saint.

The second *bravade* takes place on 15 June and is honoured with earth-shattering fusillades and military parades. It marks the anniversary of the day in 1637, when the local militia saw off a Spanish fleet, about 22 vessels strong, after an attempt to capture four ships of the Royal French fleet.

La bravade procession in St-Tropez, honouring the town's patron saint

Bouches-du-Rhône and Nîmes

Europe's largest Romany festival, the Pèlerinage des Gitans in Saintes-Maries-de-la-Mer *(see p142)*, is a simple yet very moving occasion. At the end of May, usually 24th–26th, Romanies from all over the continent gather to pay their respects to the patron saint of

Procession of the saints down to the sea in Saintes-Maries-de-la-Mer

gypsies, Saint Sarah, known as the Black Madonna. This takes place in the picturesque town of Saintes-Maries-de-la-Mer.

The pilgrimage is a colourful occasion, brightened by traditional Arlesian costumes and *gardian* cowboys. The object of their veneration is Saint Sarah, the Ethiopian servant. As legend has it, she arrived on the shores of the Camargue by boat. Also on board was Mary Magdalene, and the saints Mary Jacobe (sister of the Virgin Mary) and the elderly Mary Salome (mother of the apostles Saint James and Saint John). Sarah and the Marys decided to stay in the town and they built an oratory on which the fortified church of Notre-Dame-de-la-Mer was built. The saints started to preach the gospel and the town became known as the "Mecca of Provence".

Saint Sarah stands serene and excessively robed in the crypt. On the two nights and days of celebration in May, she is remembered with a Mass and all-night vigil. The next day, the statues of the saints are borne down to the sea where the Camargue cowboys take their horses, neck-deep, into the water and the Bishop of Arles blesses the sea.

After the statues have been returned to the church, the great folk festival begins, with rodeos, bull-running, horse racing, Arletan dancing and all manner of entertainment. The *gardians* return for a smaller celebration of Mary Salome in October, when there is a procession around the church.

Vaucluse

The Papal city of Avignon *(see pp170–72)* is a splendid setting for the foremost arts festival in Provence, the Festival d'Avignon. Theatre, music, dance and film are all covered in the month-long programme which runs from July to early August. More than a quarter of a million visitors travel to Avignon every year to attend the largest arts festival in France. It is advisable to reserve hotels and tickets in advance to avoid disappointment *(see pp226–7 for reservations)*.

The festival was established in 1947 by the late Jean Vilar whose aim was to bring theatre to the masses. He devised a number of productions to be staged in the courtyard of the Papal Palace and his Théâtre

National Populair still performs every year. Other venues include the theatres and cinemas, where films are shown all day, the opera house and churches.

Since the 1960s, the fringe-style Avignon Le Off, brings some 1,415 events to over 100 venues including many specially set-up theatres. Amateur performers can be seen for free in the main square outside the opera, the place de l'Horloge.

Alpes-de-Haute-Provence

Provence's most particular flower has its festival, the Corso de la Lavande, in the mountain spa town of Digne-les-Bains *(see p184)*.

Lavender from the festival in Digne

The colourful event, which lasts for four days, takes place in August and celebrates the harvesting of the crop. There are jars and pots of honey and all kinds of lavender produce for sale in the town, and events centre on the main street, boulevard Gassendi. The climax of the festival comes on the last day when the flower-decked floats, representing a variety of themes, parade through the streets, accompanied by music, dancing and cheering. Preceding the floats is a municipal truck spraying the roads with litres of lavender water leaving the whole town heady with the distinctive, sweet perfume.

Lively street performers at the summer Festival d'Avignon

SPECIALIST HOLIDAYS AND OUTDOOR ACTIVITIES

Everything is on offer from sun and sea bathing to skiing and extreme sports in this extraordinarily varied region of France. Watersports are extremely popular and sailing boats can be rented in most towns. For windsurfing, the experienced will want to head for Brutal Beach, just west of Toulon, although boards can be rented at most coastal resorts. Some of the best diving in the whole of the Mediterranean is around the Iles d'Hyères. There are also plenty of opportunities for canoeing and whitewater rafting in the Verdon and Gard inland. Opportunities for walking, cycling, mountain-biking and horse riding are endless. The Féderation Française de la Randonnée Pédestre publishes the widely available *Topo Guides*, which give descriptions of the tracks with details of overnight stops and transport.

Arts and Crafts

The **French Institute** is a good resource for courses in learning French combined with other activities. Students can undertake a French-speaking holiday by working part time on the restoration of historic sites with **Union Rempart** (Union pour la Réhabilitation et Entretien des Monuments et du Patrimoine Artistique).

You can also learn sculpting on a weekend course in a beautiful rural setting. Contact **Provence Verte** for details.

Several specialist tour operators organize dedicated painting holidays. For information, contact the **Maison de la France** tourist board.

Cookery Courses

An extensive range of gastronomic courses providing training in regional or classical cuisine is available. These courses are often combined with visits to markets to learn how to source the best

ingredients. The **Hostellerie Bérard** in La Cadière d'Azur runs excellent cookery courses and workshops.

Olive oil is the lifeblood of Mediterranean cuisine and many olive oil producers offer visits to their *moulins*, such as **Château Virant** in Lançon de Provence. The Olive Tree route in Canton de Levens takes you to see oil presses in action.

For lovers of figs, the family-run specialist, **Les Figuières du Mas de Luquet**, is the perfect place to learn about this delicious delicacy.

Lavender Fields and Vineyards

The regions of Provence most associated with the growing and processing of lavender are around Le Mont Ventoux, the Luberon and the Provençal Drôme. **Musée de la Lavande**, located in Lagarde d'Apt, organizes guided walking tours of a lavender field on a family-run lavender farm.

There are also plenty of opportunities in the whole of the region for *dégustations*. If you are looking to combine a trip to Les-Baux-de-Provence, Les Alpilles or St Rémy-de-Provence with a visit to vineyards, contact the **Les Vignerons des Baux**. For *dégustations* and tours of the wines of the Luberon, contact **Les Vins Luberon**.

A cookery course in progress at Hostellerie Bérard

Perfumery and Aromatherapy Courses

In Grasse, perfume initiation courses allow perfume lovers to create their own *eau de toilette* with the help of a "master perfumer". These courses are available at **Le Studio des Fragrances** at Galimard. The **Perfume Workshop** at Molinard also offers courses. The other major perfumery is **Fragonard**, where aroma-synergy workshops are on offer. These courses allow participants to learn the virtues and benefits of plants and essential oils. Lessons are given by professional aromatherapists and plant experts.

Extreme Sports

The exciting sport of snow-kiting is skiing with a stunt kite to help with the jumps. Join the best snow-kiters on the Col du Lautaret between the Grave, the Meije peak and Serre Chevalier. For an even more extreme sport, try a different kind of diving – under ice. Other

Beautiful, aromatic lavender fields in Châteauneuf-du-Pape

A game of *pétanque* in full swing, this is still a favourite pastime in the region

favourite sports include paragliding *(parapente)* and hang gliding *(deltaplane)*. For more information, contact the **Fédération Française de Vol Libre**. Gliding *(vol à voile)* is popular in the southern regions, where the climate is warm and the thermals are also good. For details of gliding clubs, contact the **Fédération Française de Vol à Voile**.

Bird-Watching

The Camargue is a twitcher's paradise. The information centre at the **Parc Naturel Regional de Camargue** provides detailed information on bird-watching. It also organizes walks within the area and has a glassed-in section, where it is possible to observe birds through binoculars. For more information contact the tourist board in Arles *(see pp148–50)* or the tourist office in Stes-Maries-de-la-Mer *(see p141)*.

Bee-eater, common in Provence

Petanque/Boules

An emblem of Provençal life, this favourite game of the local men is rarely played by women. Somewhat similar to bowls, it is played with small metal balls on any dusty ground surface. Although the rules are simple, it can be very competitive with a touch of ferocity, making it interesting to watch.

Canoeing

Canoeing is popular in the huge Lac de Ste-Croix in the National Regional Park of Verdon. The most famous route is the 24 km (15 miles) paddle down the Gorges du Verdon from Carrejuan Bridge to Lac de Ste Croix, which usually takes two days to cover. La Palud sur Verdon is the best base for whitewater rafting and kayaking on the rapids. For less challenging canoeing, try the River Sorgue, starting from the base of the high cliffs of Fontaine-de-Vaucluse. For more information, contact the **Fédération Française de Canoë-Kayak**.

Canyoning

The Grand Canyon du Verdon, Europe's largest canyon, can be visited by raft or on foot. It has now become a centre for adventure sports. The **Castellane Tourist Office** provides lists of companies offering canyoning, rafting and other outdoor trails.

Fishing

Fishing is a highly popular sport on permitted lakes and rivers. Local tourist offices and fishing shops can help you obtain a licence. You can experience bountiful sea-fishing in the Mediterranean, with catches that include bass, sardines, grey mullet, and crustaceans, such as crayfish and lobster. Night-fishing is becoming increasingly popular too.

Golf and Tennis

There's a great variety of golf in the area, from high-altitude courses to links facing the sea, or clinging to the fringes of cliffs. Overall, there are around 30 courses, mainly in the Bouches-du-Rhône and the Var and of these, over 20 are 18-hole courses. Some of the best are located at the Frégate course, St Cyr, St Raphaël's Golf de l'Esterel and, close to Avignon, the Golf De Châteteaublanc. Most offer lessons provided by resident experts.

The Provence Golf Pass gives access to 13 courses in the five departments, including five green fees. For golf addicts and occasional golfers alike, this is an excellent way to sample the courses available. For comprehensive information, contact the **Provence-Alpes-Côte d'Azur Regional Tourist Board** or the **Fédération Française de Golf**, which can supply a list of courses in France.

Most of the resorts and towns have their own tennis courts that are open to the public. Many of these are traditional Mediterranean clay courts.

Tennis lovers converge at Monte-Carlo in April, when the International Tennis Championships come here for the Monte-Carlo Open tournament for male players.

Canoeing in the Gorges du Verdon, an exhilarating experience

Horse Riding

Although the wetland area of Camargue is famous for its hardy white horses, said to be direct descendants of pre-historic horses (see p140), the whole region – from coast to mountain to rural areas – is extremely popular with horse lovers. For a detailed list of pony-trekking and riding opportunities, contact the **Ligue Régionale de Provence de Sports Equestres.**

Naturism

The largest and oldest naturist colony in the region is the easternmost of the Hyères islands, the Ile du Levant. It covers half the stretch of the 8-km (5-miles) long island. For more information on other locations where you can bare it all, contact the **Fédération Française de Naturisme.**

Skiing

The most important skiing areas are in the Maritime Alps, at the meeting point of the Alps and Provence. The main resorts, Auron, Isola 2000 and Valberg (see p100) are only a few hours from the coast, making it entirely possible to combine skiing and beach pleasures in a single day. In the north of the region in the Alpes de Haute-Provence are the ski resorts of Pra Loup and Chabanon. For more information, contact the **Fédération Française de Ski** in Annecy or the **Fédération Française de la Montagne et de l'Escalade.**

Spa Breaks

Set in the hilltop village of Gordes, one of France's prettiest villages, is the Daniel Jouvance spa, **La Bastide de Gordes.** It is undoubtedly an ideal spot for relaxing breaks.

In the picturesque, gastro-nomic village of Mougins, **Le Mas Candille** is an elegant, individual hotel, complemented by a Japanese-style Shiseido spa. For the ultimate in luxury, visit the **Thalazur** spa in Antibes.

Walking, Climbing and Cycling

Long-distance walking and climbing trails are known as Grandes Randonées (GR) and shorter trails as Petites Randonées (PR). Some trails are also open to mountain bikes and horses.

Parc Naturel Régional du Luberon offers some excellent cycling and walking trails. The information centre, **Maison du Parc**, provides a list of hikers' accommodation and details of two dozen walking trails. The Camargue has many trails and walking paths. "Sentier Littoral", a splendid coastal path from St-Tropez, covers 35 km (22 miles) to Cavalaire. You can even break the journey at Ramatuelle. An excellent French book, Promenez-vous à Pied – Le Golfe de St-Tropez has details of 26 walks in the area.

Perhaps the most spectacular trail in the whole of Provence is the GR 9, which crosses the Luberon range and the Monts du Vaucluse.

For tough rock climbing, try the Buoux cliffs in the Luberon, or one of the 933 routes in the Gorges du Verdon. The creeks, calanques, between Cassis and Marseille are utterly picturesque. Easier ascents can be found in the Dentelles de Montmirail, despite the craggy rock faces. The area boasts excellent vineyards, such as Gigondas, Vacqueyras and Beaumes-de-Venise in which to enjoy a dégustation after a climb.

The **Comité Departemental de la Randonnée Pédestre** located in Cagnes-sur-Mer, is equipped with detailed information. For details of trails in the region, contact the **Fédération Française de Randonnée Pédestre**.

Cycling tours of the lush green Luberon in Vaucluse are great for people of all ages. In the upper Var, Figanières is famous for mountain-biking, while the Alps of Haute-Provence boast around 1,500 km (900 miles) of marked tracks. For detailed information, contact the **Fédération Française de Cyclisme**.

Water Sports

Most coastal resorts have excellent facilities for both experienced and amateur sailors. Iles d'Hyères has some top-class sailing schools, in the tiny island of Bendor and the Porquerolles, the largest of the French Riviera islands.

For windsurfing, the reliable winds of the Bouches-du-Rhône and the Var make for favourable conditions. Other good locations include the Camargue, where the lively Mistral wind blows, at Port St-Louis and Les Saintes-Maries-de-la-Mer. The wind-surfing regatta in St-Tropez in July is a particularly glamorous event, which is always exciting and very well attended.

Scuba diving is popular, thanks to sparkling water, an ample sprinkling of underwater wrecks and a wealth of marine life. It is especially good in Marseille and the Iles d'Hyères and Cavalaire. The little island of Port-Cros has a special under-water "Discovery Trail". St Raphaël is also a leading diving centre, with several World War II ship-wrecks off the coast.

For more on scuba diving, contact the **Fédération Française d'Etudes et de Sports Sous-Marins** in Marseille.

The most picturesque stretch of the Rhône passes through Avignon and Arles, otherwise known as the "Cities of Art and History", and the Camargue – home to wild horses, bulls and flamingos. Several companies organize boat trips or river cruises in floating hotels. For details, contact the tourist information centres in Arles, Avignon, Les Stes-Maries-de-la-Mer or Port St Louis du Rhône.

The calanques can be visited by boats from Marseille and Cassis. Contact **Les Amis de Calanques** for more details.

Many beaches are privately owned and entry is by fee. Catamarans, dinghies, water-skiing and surfing equipment are all on offer.

For detailed information, contact the national sailing school, **Fédération Française de Voile**.

DIRECTORY

Arts and Crafts

French Institute
17 Queensberry Place,
London SW7 2DT.
Tel 020 7871 3515.
W institut-francais.
org.uk

Maison de la France
Lincoln House, 300 High
Holborn, London WC1V
7JH. **Tel** 020 70 616 600.
W au.france.fr

Provence Verte
Office de Tourisme,
83170 Brignoles.
Tel 04 94 72 04 21.
W la-provence-
verte.net

Union Rempart
1 rue des Guillemites,
75004 Paris. **Tel** 01 42 71
96 55. W rempart.com

Cookery

Château Virant
Route de St Chamas, 13680
Lançon de Provence.
Tel 04 90 42 44 47.
W chateauvirant.com

Hostellerie Bérard
83740 La Cadière d'Azur.
Tel 04 94 90 11 43.
W hotel-berard.com

**Les Figuières du
Mas de Luquet**
Chemin du Mas de la
Musique, Mas de Luquet,
13690 Graveson.
Tel 04 90 95 72 03.
W lesfiguieres.com

Lavender Fields and Vineyards

**Les Vignerons
des Baux**
Tel 04 90 92 25 01.
W lesvinsdesbaux.com

Les Vins Luberon
Blvd de Rayol, 84160
Lourmarin.
Tel 04 90 07 34 40.
W vins-luberon.fr

Musée de la Lavande
Route de Gordes,
84220 Coustellet.
Tel 04 90 76 91 23.
W museedela
lavande.com

Perfumery and Aromatherapy

Fragonard
Blvd Fragonard, 06130
Grasse.
Tel 04 92 42 34 34.
W fragonard.com

**Le Studio des
Fragrances**
5 rte de Pegomas,
06131 Grasse.
Tel 04 93 09 20 00.
W galimard.com

Perfume Workshop
60 blvd Victor Hugo,
06130 Grasse.
Tel 04 92 42 33 21.
W molinard.com

Extreme Sports

**Fédération
Française de
Vol Libre**
4 rue de Suisse,
06000 Nice.
Tel 04 97 03 82 82.
W federation.ffvl.fr

**Fédération
Française de
Vol à Voile**
55 rue des Petites Ecuries,
75010 Paris.
Tel 01 45 44 04 78.
W ffvv.org

Bird-Watching

**Parc Naturel
Régional de
Camargue**
Mas du Pont de Rousty,
13200 Arles.
Tel 04 90 97 10 82.
W parc-camargue.fr

Canoeing

**Fédération Française
de Canoë-Kayak**
87 quai de la Marne,
94340 Joinville-le-Point.
Tel 01 45 11 08 50.
W ffck.org

Canyoning

**Castellane Tourist
Office**
Rue Nationale, Castellane.
Tel 04 92 83 61 14.
W castellane.org

Golf and Tennis

**Fédération
Française de Golf**
68 rue Anatole France,
92300, Levallois Perret.
Tel 01 41 49 77 00.
W ffgolf.org

**Provence-Alpes-Côte
d'Azur Regional
Tourist Board**
62–64 le Canabière,
Marseille. **Tel** 04 91 56 47
00. W tourismepaca.fr

Horse Riding

**Ligue Régionale de
Provence de Sports
Equestres**
298 avenue du Club
Hippique, 13090 Aix-en-
Provence. **Tel** 04 42 20 88 02.
W provence-
equitation.com

Naturism

**Fédération
Française de
Naturisme**
5 rue Regnault, 93500
Pantin. **Tel** 01 48 10 31 00.
W ffn-naturisme.com

Skiing

**Fédération Française
de la Montagne et de
l'Escalade**
8 quai de la Marne, 75019
Paris. **Tel** 01 40 18 75 50.
W ffme.fr

**Fédération Française
de Ski**
50 avenue des Marquisats,
Annecy. **Tel** 04 50 51 40
34. W ffs.fr

Spa Breaks

Hôtel Baie des Anges
770 chemin des Moyennes
Bréguières, 06600 Antibes.
Tel 04 92 91 82 00.
W thalazur.fr

La Bastide de Gordes
Le Village, 84220 Gordes.
W bastide-de-
gordes.com

Le Mas Candille
Boulevard Clément
Rebuffet, 06250 Mougins.
Tel 04 92 28 43 43.
W lemascandille.com

Walking, Climbing and Cycling

**Comité
Departemental
de la Randonnée
Pédestre**
7 rue de l'Hotel de Ville,
Cagnes-sur-Mer.
Tel 09 51 05 19 23.
W cdrp06.org

**Fédération
Française de
Cyclisme**
1 rue Laurent Fignon,
78180 Montigny les
Brettonneux.
Tel 08 11 04 05 55.
W ffc.fr

**Fédération
Française de
Randonnée Pédestre**
64 rue du Dessous des
Berges, 75013 Paris.
Tel 01 44 89 93 93.
W ffrandonnee.fr

**Maison du Parc
Naturel Régional
du Luberon**
60 place Jean Jaurès,
84404 Apt.
Tel 04 90 04 42 00.
W parcduluberon.fr

Water Sports

**Fédération Française
d'Etudes et de Sports
Sous-Marins**
24 quai Rive-Neuve,
13284 Marseille.
Tel 04 91 33 99 31.
W ffessm.fr

**Fédération
Française de Voile**
17 rue Henri Bocquillon,
75015 Paris.
Tel 01 40 60 37 00.
W ffvoile.com

**Les Amis de
Calanques**
4 quai Amiral Canteaume,
La Ciotat.
Tel 06 09 33 54 98.
W visite-calanques.fr

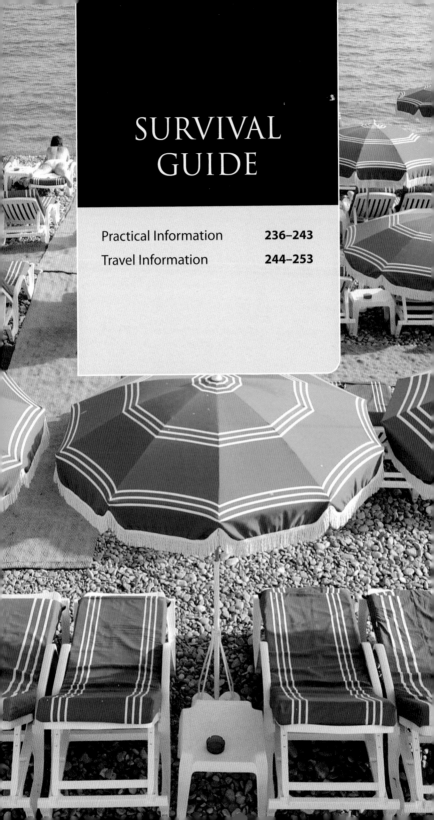

SURVIVAL GUIDE

PRACTICAL INFORMATION

The peak holiday period for Provence runs from the middle of June until the end of August. During this time, the coastal areas in particular are very crowded. However, the region offers a range of activities throughout the year to suit all tastes: skiing slopes in the winter, golden beaches in the summer, excellent modern art museums, fine Roman ruins, traditional festivals and superb food and wine. Tourist offices are excellent sources of general information and accommodation advice (see also pp194–5). The main branches in Provence are listed opposite. Shops and banks tend to close between noon and 3pm, so take advantage of this to enjoy a long, leisurely lunch, bearing in mind an old local saying: "Slow in the mornings, and not too fast in the afternoons."

Enjoying a relaxed lunch on a vine-shaded terrace

When to Go

During high season in Provence, local businesses in tourist areas hope to make their whole year's profit, and set their prices higher accordingly. The coast in particular can get very busy so to avoid the crowds, head for the wilds of upper Provence or the hills of the Var and Vaucluse.

Provence is at its best in May and September when the weather is still warm, but there are fewer visitors. The winter months can offer some sunny days, but beware of the cold mistral wind that can sweep through the area. A few festivals, such as the Nice Carnival and the Lemon Festival in Menton, are cleverly timed so as to attract off-season tourists, and skiing is usually possible between mid-November and April (see p100).

What to Take

Apart from prescription drugs, you should find everything you need in local shops. People dress quite casually, but you should take care to be respectful when visiting churches, and some restaurants have a more formal dress code.

Visas and Passports

Currently there are no visa requirements for EU nationals or for tourists from the US, Canada, Australia or New Zealand staying in France for under three months. After that a residency permit (carte de séjour) is required. Visitors from other countries should ask for visa information from their local French authorities. Like most EU countries (but not the UK and Ireland) France is part of the Schengen agreement for shared border controls. When you enter the Schengen area through any of the member states, your 90-day stay will be valid for all of them, even if you travel between several countries.

Travel Safety Advice

Visitors can get up-to-date travel safety information from the **Foreign and Commonwealth Office** in the UK, the **State Department** in the US and the **Department of Foreign Affairs and Trade** in Australia.

Customs Information

Visitors from outside the European Union can claim back the sales tax (TVA) levied on French goods if they spend more than €175 in one shop on the same day. To claim your refund, obtain an export sales form (bordereau de vente à l'exportation) and take your goods out of the EU within three months of the date of purchase. The form should be signed by both the retailer and

yourself. Hand it in to customs officials when you leave the EU, and they will give you a set of forms that you should send back to the shop. The refund will then be sent on to you or credited to your bank card. Exceptions for this détaxe rebate are food and drink, medicines, tobacco, cars and motorbikes.

There are no restrictions on the quantities of duty-paid and VAT-paid goods one is allowed to take from one EU country to another as long as they are for personal use and not for resale; you may be asked to prove this if your goods exceed the recommended amounts: 10 litres of spirits, 90 litres of wine, 110 litres of beer and 800 cigarettes.

Non-EU nationals arriving in the European Union may bring in the following: up to 4 litres of wine and 1 litre of spirits (or 2 litres of drink less than 22° proof); up to €430 worth of perfume, coffee or tea and up to 200 cigarettes. Visitors under 17 may not import or export duty-free alcohol or tobacco, even as gifts. In general, personal goods (such as a car or a bicycle)

The tourist office at Monieux, Vaucluse

◀ Sun loungers on the beach, Nice

may be imported to France free of duty and without any paperwork as long as they are for personal use and not for resale. A brochure called *Voyagez en Toute Liberté*, available from the **Centre des Renseignements des Douanes**, has further details.

Special rules apply for the import and export of plants, medicines, animals, weapons and art objects. Be sure to consult your own or French customs before travelling.

Tourist Information

Most large towns have a tourist office (*Office de Tourisme* or *Syndicat d'Initiative*); in smaller villages, it is the town hall (*mairie*) that provides information. Tourist offices will supply free maps and details of local events and accommodation; they will also book hotel rooms on your behalf.

Etiquette

The French rituals of politeness apply in Provence too. When introduced to a new person, it is correct to shake hands. In shops, say *bonjour* before asking what

you want, *merci* when you receive your change and *au revoir* when you depart. In supermarkets, the cashier will not say *bonjour* to you until they have finished with the previous customer. The usual greeting among friends of both sexes is generally two or three kisses on the cheeks.

In smaller communities, any efforts made by English speakers to communicate in French and show a real interest in the area will be met with encouragement.

Opening Times

Opening hours for museums are usually 9am–noon and 2–5:30pm, but they vary according to the season, with longer hours being kept from May to September. Most museums close one day a week: national museums on Mondays and municipal ones on Tuesdays. Many museums also close for all of November.

Most businesses open from 8 or 9am until noon and from 2 or 3pm to 6 or 7pm. Banks are open 8:30am–noon and 1:30–4:30pm Monday to Friday and sometimes on Saturday mornings. Department stores,

The beautifully decorated façade of the Musée Matisse in Nice

supermarkets, tourist offices and some sights may remain open during the lunch break.

Restaurants often close one day a week, usually Monday; many will also close on Sunday evenings.

In winter, much of seaside Provence shuts down. Phone ahead to check what is open, because some establishments may be closed for months. Transport services may also be restricted out of season.

DIRECTORY

French Tourist Offices Abroad

Australia
25 Bligh St, Level 13, Sydney, NSW 2000.
Tel (2) 9210 5400.
W au.france.fr

Canada
1800 Ave MacGill College, Suite 1010, Montreal H3A 3J6. **Tel** (514) 288 2026.
W au.france.fr

United Kingdom
300 High Holborn, London WC1 VJH. **Tel** (0207) 061 6600. W au.france.fr

USA
825 Third Ave 29th Floor, New York, NY 10022.
Tel (212) 838 7800.
W au.france.fr

Tourist Offices in Provence

Aix-en-Provence
300 ave Giuseppe Verdi.

Tel 04 42 16 11 61.
W aixenprovence tourism.com

Arles
Blvd des Lices.
Tel 04 90 18 41 20.
W arlestourisme.com

Avignon
41 cours Jean-Jaurès.
Tel 04 32 74 32 74.
W avignon-tourisme.com

Cannes
Palais des Festivals, La Croisette. **Tel** 04 92 99 84 22. W cannes-destination.com

Draguignan
2 ave Lazare Carnot.
Tel 04 98 10 51 05.
W tourisme-dracenie.com

Marseille
11 La Canebière.
Tel 08 26 50 05 00.
W marseille-tourisme.com

Monte-Carlo
2A blvd des Moulins.
Tel 00 377 92 16 61 16.
W monte-carlo.mc

Nice
5 promenade des Anglais.
Tel 04 92 14 46 14.
W nicetourism.com

Nîmes
6 rue Auguste. **Tel** 04 66 58 38 00. W ot-nimes.fr

St-Tropez
Quai Jean-Jaurès.
Tel 08 92 68 48 28.
W sainttropez tourisme.com

Travel Safety Advice

Australia
W dfat.gov.au
W smartraveller.gov.au

United Kingdom
W gov.uk/foreign-travel-advice

United States
W travel.state.gov

Customs Information

Centre des Renseignements des Douanes
23 rue de l'Université, 75007 Paris. **Tel** 08 11 20 44 44. W douane.gouv.fr

Marseille
48 ave R Schuman.
Tel 09 70 27 83 83.

Useful Websites

Anglo Info
W riviera.angloinfo.com

Provence Web
W provenceweb.fr

Provence & Beyond
W beyond.fr

The striking Hôtel de Ville of Aix-en-Provence

Admission Prices

Museum admission prices range from around €3 to €12. National museums are free the first Sunday of the month, and nearly all municipal museums offer free or discounted entry on Sundays.

The Carte Musée Côte d'Azur, which allows unlimited access to more than 50 museums in the region, can be purchased from participating museums, FNAC stores (see p226) and certain tourist offices (see p237). There is also the French Riviera Pass, which offers free access to many sights and has various discounts available; see http://en.french rivierapass.com for more details.

All permanent collections of national museums and monuments are free for EU card holders under 26 years of age.

Churches normally offer free admission, but a small charge may be levied to visit cloisters and chapels.

Tipping and Taxes

Most restaurants include a service charge of 10–15 per cent as part of the bill, so there is no need to tip. In a bar or café, leave some small change. A small amount is usually given to taxi drivers, despite service being included. Hotel porters, hairdressers and tour guides will expect a tip of around €3.

Travellers with Disabilities

Provence's narrow streets can make it a difficult area for travellers with limited mobility. On the plus side, disabled parking spaces are plentiful (remember to bring your international orange disc with you), and wheelchairs and other useful equipment can be hired at pharmacies. Wheelchair access is still rather limited, although newer buildings will have ramps and other facilities.

The train company SNCF has carriages designed to accommodate wheelchair users (see pp246–7), and taxi drivers are also obliged to take disabled people and guide dogs.

For more information, visit Access-Able Travel Source (www.access-able.com).

International Student Identity Card

Travelling with Children

Many hotels have family rooms, but if they don't you can ask them to add a cot or an extra bed. There may be an additional charge for this. If you are hiring a car and need child seats, be sure to book them in advance and ask for them to be fitted for you. Children are eligible for discounted train travel.

Gay and Lesbian Travellers

There is a strong network of gay and lesbian venues in Provence; this includes bars, discos and beaches. For listings of gay-friendly hotels and activities, visit the websites listed in the directory on the opposite page.

Travelling on a Budget

Provence is not the cheapest region in France, but prices are much more reasonable out of season. Staying inland rather than in a seaside resort will also save money. Ask the local tourist office for advice on affordable accommodation, such as hostels and campsites. Travelling by public transport is cheaper than hiring a car, and along the coast this is a perfectly adequate option (see pp246–8 and p252). Buying carnets of tickets for travel on public transport in major towns will also save money. Visiting attractions doesn't have to be costly either, as most museums have free days. Check to see if there are cheaper family tickets too. However, most of the real pleasure of Provence can be experienced for free and consists of admiring the spectacular views of the Mediterranean and mountains, swimming in the sea, walking on the beach and hiking in the hills and national parks.

Student Travellers

Students carrying a valid International Student Identification Card (ISIC) benefit from discounts of between 25 and 50 per cent at museums, theatres, cinemas and many of the public monuments.

The region's main university is split between Aix-en-Provence and Marseille; other large universities are located in Avignon and Nice. You will find the **Bureau Information Jeunesse** (BIJ) and the **Centre Régional Information Jeunesse** (CRIJ) in all university towns. These organizations can provide a great deal of information about student life and a list of inexpensive accommodation options. For information on hostels in the main towns see page 196.

Provence Time

Provence is one hour ahead of Greenwich Mean Time (GMT). It is in the same time zone as Italy, Spain and other western European countries. Standard time differences between Provence and other areas of the world may vary according to local summer alterations to the time.

The French use the 24-hour military clock rather than "am" and "pm".

Electrical Adaptors

The voltage in France is 220 volts. British appliances of 240 volts can be used with an adaptor, while American 110 volts appliances will need a transformer (*transformateur*).

Plugs have two small round pins; heavier-duty installations have two large round pins. Some of the more upmarket hotels offer built-in adaptors for shavers. Multi-adaptors, useful because they have both large and small pins, can be bought at most airports before departure; standard adaptors can be purchased from department stores.

Façade of the Russian Orthodox church in Nice

Religious Services

Provence is a strong Catholic region, with many religious services and festivals dating back 500 years. In recent decades, immigrants have brought increasing religious diversification. Regular services in English are held at the Anglican churches in Nice and Marseille.

Responsible Travel

Throughout France there has been a rapid growth in environmental awareness. **Echoway** is one of the leading French ecotourism organizations, which encourages responsible travel. Provence has a long-running rural tourism network, with farmhouse accommodation available through the central **Gîtes de France**. There are also smaller organizations with a more defined ecological stance such as **Accueil Paysan**, which is a network of small-scale farmers practising low-impact, sustainable agriculture. Finally there are hundreds of fully equipped campsites throughout Provence (*see pp196–7*).

Information on local green tourism (*tourisme vert* or *eco*) initiatives and activities can be found through *département* and local tourist offices. Many towns have weekly markets selling only organic and traditional produce (usually called a *marché bio*), which allow visitors to give back to the local community. If a town does not have a separate market dedicated to organic produce, there are often stalls within the main market that are exclusively *bio*, as is the case at Nice's market on the cours Saleya. Market days have been provided throughout the guide.

Conversion Chart

Imperial to metric
1 inch = 2.54 centimetres
1 foot = 30 centimetres
1 mile = 1.6 kilometres
1 ounce = 28 grams
1 pound = 454 grams
1 pint (UK) = 0.6 litre
1 gallon (UK) = 4.6 litres

Metric to imperial
1 millimetre = 0.04 inch
1 centimetre = 0.4 inch
1 metre = 3 feet 3 inches
1 kilometre = 0.6 mile
1 gram = 0.04 ounce
1 kilogram = 2.2 pounds

DIRECTORY

Travellers with Disabilities

Federation des Malades et Handicapes
17 blvd du General Leclerc, 95100 Argenteuil.
Tel 01 39 82 45 73.

Federation of the Blind & Visually Handicapped
Paris.
Tel 01 44 42 91 91.
W aveuglesdefrance.org

Groupement pour l'Insertion des Personnes Handicapées Physiques
61 rue du Faubourg Poissonniere, 75009 Paris.
Tel 01 43 95 66 36.
W gihpnational.org

Le soutien aux Parents d'Enfants Déficients Visuels
W apedv.fr

Gay and Lesbian Travellers

La France Gaie et Lesbienne
W france.qrd.org

Gay Provence
W gayprovence.org

International Gay & Lesbian Travel Association
W iglta.org

Student Information

Aix-en-Provence
BIJ, 37 bis blvd Aristide-Briand.
Tel 04 42 91 98 01.

Marseille
CRIJ, 96 La Canebière.
Tel 04 91 24 33 50.
W crijpa.fr

Nice
CRIJ, 19 rue Gioffredo.
Tel 04 93 80 93 93.
W ijca.fr

Responsible Travel

Accueil Paysan
W accueil-paysan.com

Echoway
W echoway.org

Gites de France
W gites-de-france.com

Personal Security and Health

On the whole Provence is a fairly safe place for visitors, however, it is wise to take a few precautions. Extra caution is required in the larger cities and along the Côte d'Azur, especially in Nice, which has a higher crime rate than Marseille. Car crime is prevalent along the coast, so make sure you never leave your valuables in a vehicle. You should also avoid groups of innocent-looking children who may, in fact, be skilled in the art of pickpocketing. Consular offices can be good sources of help in the event of an emergency (see the directory box opposite). Rural areas are usually very safe.

Policeman   Fireman

Personal Property

Pickpockets are common in the tourist areas of the Côte d'Azur and in larger towns. In Nice, bag snatching is on the rise, but fortunately muggings are still rare. Take care of your belongings at all times. Do not carry much cash at any one time, and avoid carrying valuables with you when sightseeing.

Try not to park your car in remote areas, and use multi-storey car parks if you can. These are monitored by video cameras, and parking there will also remove the risk of being towed away, which is a greater everyday issue than most car crime.

It is not advisable to sleep on the beach, since robberies and attacks have been known to take place there at night.

In the event of a theft, go to the nearest police station (*gendarmerie*) with your identity papers (and vehicle papers, if relevant). The report process (*procès-verbal*, or *PV*) may take time, but you will need a police statement for any insurance claim you make. If your passport is stolen, contact the police and your nearest consulate (see opposite).

Police car

Fire engine

Ambulance

Personal Safety

Certain train routes – for example the Marseille-Barcelona and Marseille-Ventimiglia (Italy) lines – have dubious reputations. Stay alert and keep the compartment door shut and your valuables close to you, especially if you are travelling at night.

Some tourists visiting the area during the summer, have been victims of road piracy, with their vehicle being rammed on the motorway to force them to stop. There are police stations at most motorway exits, so if you encounter any trouble, try to stay calm and keep going until the next exit.

Legal Assistance

If your insurance policy is comprehensive (including a legal service in France), they will be able to help with legal advice on claims, such as accident procedure. If you are not insured, call your nearest consulate office.

Women Travellers

Women should take the usual precautions: wearing their bag strapped across the body; being careful after dark; avoiding quiet, unfamiliar areas; locking the car doors when driving; and taking care on trains, especially sleepers.

For contraceptive advice, go to a GP or a gynaecologist (no referral is necessary); to find one, ask at a pharmacy or look in the Yellow Pages (Pages Jaunes). Pharmacies are also excellent sources of advice and can dispense the morning-after pill without a prescription.

Outdoor Hazards

Forest fires are a major risk in Provence. High winds and dry forests mean that fire spreads rapidly, so be vigilant about putting out cigarette butts. Camp fires are banned in the region. If you witness a fire, contact the emergency services at once and keep well away.

The Mediterranean Sea is safe for swimming, although there can be strong currents off the Cap d'Antibes and the Camargue. Public beaches usually have a lifeguard and indicate safe areas for swimming; some display European blue flags as a sign of cleanliness. If you are stung by a jellyfish or sea urchin, seek advice from a pharmacy. If you are sailing, keep up to date with the weather reports, and carry ID and a radio or mobile phone.

Weather conditions in the mountains can change very quickly and without warning. In winter, be sure to advise the local authorities of your projected route; in summer, pack warm clothes and some provisions in case of sudden storms. Altitude sickness can occur in the southern Alps, so climb slowly, pausing regularly to acclimatize.

In the mountains behind Nice and Cannes, you may encounter the grey-brown Montpellier snake. Despite its size (up to 1.5 m/5 ft), it is very shy and will likely flee. Vipers also live in the region. Mosquitoes are common, and repellents and antidotes can be bought from supermarkets or pharmacies. The local lavender oil is an excellent repellent and a good

antiseptic treatment for mosquito bites and wasp stings if applied immediately. Occasionally hornets and scorpions can be a problem, so get into the habit of always checking shoes and clothing before getting dressed. Also check your bedding before going to sleep. Beware of the heat, especially with children, and seek immediate medical advice for heat stroke.

During the hunting season (Sep–Feb, especially on Sundays), wear brightly coloured clothes when out walking. Signs on trees usually denote hunting areas (reserve du chasse).

Travel and Health Insurance

Check that your travel insurance is valid in France, and note that you will need extra insurance to cover winter sports. EU residents are entitled to medical treatment with the European Health Insurance Card. You will need the doctor's and pharmacy receipts (feuille de soins) to apply for reimbursements.

Medical Treatment

Pharmacists can diagnose and suggest treatments for simple conditions; they can be recognized by the green cross outside. There is usually one pharmacy open at night and at weekends. Hospital accident-and-emergency units will deal with accidents and unexpected illnesses. In rural areas, the pompiers (firefighters) are also trained paramedics and can be called in an emergency. In major cities, a 24-hour doctor service (médecin de garde) is available.

Public Toilets

Modern automatic toilets are widely available in cities. You may also come across public toilets of the squat variety, in which case you might prefer to use the services in a café or department store.

Fire-hazard poster

Banks and Local Currency

Visitors to Provence may change currency in a variety of locations, but it is always wise to arrive with at least a few euros. Credit cards are widely accepted for purchases and in restaurants, but if in doubt, ask in advance. Credit cards and bank cards can also be used to withdraw money, but check the charges levied by the credit card company first.

Banks and Currency Exchange

Banks in big towns usually open from 8:30am to noon and from 1:30 to 4:30pm Monday to Friday and Saturday morning. They are closed during public holidays.

There is no limit to the amount of money you may bring into France, but if you wish to take more than €10,000 back to the UK, you should declare it on arrival. It is wise to carry large sums of money as travellers' cheques.

You will need your four-digit PIN code (code confidentiel) to withdraw money from ATMs (but check the charges levied for this service) and for payment in shops and restaurants. ATM instructions are usually given in French, English and Italian. Note that ATMs may run out of notes just before the weekend.

Travellers' cheques can be obtained from American Express, Thomas Cook or your bank. It is recommended that you have them issued in euros. American Express cheques are accepted in France; if they are exchanged at an AmEx office, no commission is charged. In the event of theft, travellers' cheques are replaced at once.

The most common credit cards in France, accepted even at motorway tolls, are Carte Bleue/Visa and Eurocard/MasterCard. Because of the high commissions charged, some Provençal businesses do not accept American Express.

DIRECTORY

Foreign Banks

Cannes
Barclays, 8 rue Frédéric Amouretti.
Tel 04 92 99 68 00.
W barclays.fr

Fréjus
Barclays, 68 Place de la Porte d'Hermès, Port Fréjus.
Tel 04 94 17 63 40.

Marseille
Barclays, 112–114 rue de Rome.
Tel 04 91 13 98 28.

Menton
Barclays, 39 avenue Félix Faure.
Tel 04 93 28 60 00.

Nice
Barclays, 2 rue Alphonse Karr.
Tel 04 93 82 68 00.

Lost Cards and Travellers' Cheques

Visa
Tel 0800 90 1179.

MasterCard
Tel 0800 901 387.

American Express Cards and Cheques
Tel 0800 917 8047.

Banknotes and Coins

Euro bank notes have seven denominations. The €5 note is grey, the €10 is pink, the €20 is blue, the €50 is orange, the €100 is green, the €200 is yellow and the €500 is purple. There are eight coin denominations: €1 and €2 coins are silver and gold; those worth 50 cents, 20 cents and 10 cents are gold, while the 5-, 2- and 1- coins are bronze.

€5 note

€10 note

€20 note

€50 note

€100 note

€200 note

€500 note

€2 coin

€1 coin

50 cents

20 cents

10 cents

5 cents

2 cents

1 cent

Communications and Media

The main telephone company is France Télécom, while postal services are run by La Poste. Post offices (bureaux de postes) are identified by the blue-on-yellow "La Poste" sign. In small villages, the post office may be in the town hall (mairie). Internet access is readily available via Internet cafés, hotels and Wi-Fi.

Mail boxes throughout France are a distinctive yellow

Mobile Phones

A mobile phone from another European country can be used in France, though you may need to inform your network in advance so that it can be enabled. US-based mobiles need to be tri-band to work in France.

International calls on mobile phones are expensive. As an alternative, replace your SIM card with a French card and number or pre-paid mobile and Internet cards, although you may need to get your phone unlocked to be able to do this. The main local providers are Orange France, Bouygues Télécom, SFR and Free. Note, however, that French top-up vouchers have strict expiry periods.

An easier and cheaper option is to use VoIP services such as Skype from your laptop, tablet or smartphone, which allow you to place a call or send messages using only an Internet connection.

With the rise in the use of mobile phones, public phone boxes (cabines téléphoniques) are becoming obsolete and are rarely found.

Internet Access

Internet facilities are readily available. Most hotels offer Wi-Fi, while Wi-Fi hotspots can also be found in many cafés and restaurants. The larger towns such as Marseille and Nice provide for no-cost access in public places and may also have a few Internet cafés, although these have never been very popular in France. The major ports in Provence are all equipped with Wi-Fi. Airports usually offer complimentary Wi-Fi access as well.

Postal Services

Postage stamps (timbres) can be purchased singly or in books (carnets) of ten, 12 or 20 from post offices or tabacs.

Post office hours vary. The maximum hours are around 9am–5pm on weekdays, with a lunch break (noon–2pm), and 9am–noon on Saturdays.

To send letters from France, drop them into the yellow mail boxes. These often have two slots: one for the town you are in; the other for the surrounding département and other destinations.

Newspapers and Magazines

In main cities and airports, international papers can often be bought on the day of publication. The Connexion is a monthly newspaper devoted to France, and Provence also has its own English-language publications. Most major towns have an English bookshop (see p221), often an invaluable source of information.

Television and Radio

The subscription channel Canal+ broadcasts ABC American evening news at 7am daily. Sky News and CNN are available in many hotels. The Franco-German channel ARTE broadcasts programmes and films from all over the world, often in the original language with French subtitles. Listings indicate VO or VF (Version Originale or Version Française) for non-French films.

Riviera Radio broadcasts in English throughout the South of France on 106.3 and 106.5 FM stereo from Monte-Carlo. The station offers music and current affairs, including BBC World Service programmes. France Musique (92.2 FM in Nice and 94.7 in Marseille) specializes in classical music, while France Info (105.2–105.8 FM) is a national rolling-news station.

DIRECTORY

Dialling Codes

Operator
Tel 12.

International calls
Tel 00 + country code.

Mobile phones
Tel 06 and 07 + number.

Mobile phone services
W bouyguetelecom.fr
W free.fr
W orange.fr
W sfr.fr

Internet Cafés

Cannes
The Bird Phone,
75 rue Georges Clemenceau.
Tel 04 93 99 80 34.

Digne-les-Bains
48 rue de l'Hubac.
Tel 04 92 32 00 19.

Nice
Cyber Massena, 9 rue Massena.
Tel 06 06 70 42 35.

Postal Services

La Poste
W laposte.fr

TRAVEL INFORMATION

Situated at the crossroads between France, Spain and Italy, Provence is well served by international motorway and rail links. Nice airport is the most modern and the busiest of French airports outside Paris, handling 4 million visitors from all over the world annually. Marseille airport also welcomes daily direct flights from most major European cities. For travelling across France, the TGV train is swift *(see p246)*, while the motorail journey from channel ports takes 12 hours, but is effortless and dispenses with motorway tolls. The autoroutes are excellent, but do become crowded in mid-summer.

Arriving by Air

The two main airports in Provence – Marseille and Nice, Côte d'Azur, which is the second biggest airport in France – are comfortable and modern. **Marseille Provence** (or **Marseille-Marignane**) has national and international flights serving mainly business travellers, and a low-cost air terminal, MP2. It is useful for destinations in western Provence, such as Avignon and Aix-en-Provence.

Airport taxis to the centre of Marseille cost around €40 (€50 at night and on Sundays). There is also an airport bus to the main train station in Marseille (St-Charles), which leaves every 20 minutes. Car hire companies at the airport include Ada, Avis, Budget, Citer, Europcar and Hertz.

Nice, Côte d'Azur has two terminals, both of which take international and domestic flights. There is a shuttle bus between the buildings, but it is best to make sure you know which terminal you will be using. Taxis to the centre of town cost €25–€30. Airport buses – No. 90 and No. 98 – run to and from the city centre station every 10 minutes. The No. 98 stops along the promenade des Anglais and the port, while the No. 99 turns off the promenade by Hotel Négresco and continues to the mainline train station. From May to October there are buses to Cannes and Vallauris every half hour, and to Monaco and Menton every hour. **Héli-Air Monaco** offers regular helicopter transits to Monaco, St-Tropez and Cannes, while **Azur Hélicoptère** also has many daily flights to these three cities. There are several car hire companies at Nice airport, including Avis, Budget, Enterprise, Europcar, Hertz and Sixt.

There are four other airports in or near Provence which operate international flights; these are Montpellier, Avignon, Nîmes and Toulon.

Airline Details

Provence is the most easily accessible place by air in France after Paris. The vast majority of major European cities have daily direct flights to Provence. The British carriers – **British Airways**, **easyJet** and **Ryanair** – all run daily flights from London Heathrow, London Gatwick, Luton, Stansted or Manchester to Nice, Nîmes, Marseille, Montpellier or Toulon. A good option among low-cost airlines is **Flybe**, which flies to Nice from Manchester, Birmingham, Southampton and Exeter. The French national airline, **Air France**, has daily flights to and from Nice to Britain, Spain, Germany, Italy and North Africa.

There is a **Delta** flight from Nice to New York several times a week, and **Emirates** also flies to Nice from Dubai five times a week. From all other international departure

The main international terminal at Nice, Côte d'Azur airport

Departure hall at Marseille airport

points you will be required to change planes in Paris to reach Provence.

Fares and Deals

The large number of low-cost airlines flying to Provence mean that there is a wide range of prices on offer. Fares are at their highest over the Easter period and in July and August. Make sure you check which airport you are flying to when booking, as some low-cost airlines use smaller airports that may be some distance from the city centre.

Fly-Drive and Fly-Rail Package Holidays

Air France and SNCF offer combined fares for flight and train. You fly into Paris and then catch the train south. Good deals are available for the main destinations such as Avignon, Arles, Nice and Marseille. For notes on fly-drive packages see page 250.

There are also a wide variety of companies offering tailor-made package holidays in Provence, with flight, car hire and accommodation included in the cost.

Green Travel

Travelling in France without using high-impact flights or long car drives is easier than in many countries thanks primarily to the high quality of public transport, and above all the SNCF rail network.

The French government has introduced an "Ecomobility" programme, which aims to encourage a reduction in car use by making it easier to transfer from SNCF trains to local buses, bikes or other transport (for more details, see www.sncf.com). This includes free-cycle schemes like the *LeVélo* in Marseille, *V'hello* in Aixen-Provence and *Vélopop* in Avignon. There are cycle-hire shops in many towns and local tourist offices will be able to provide more information on cycle hire and routes in their area. There are also facilities for taking your bikes on SNCF trains *(see p248)*. If you don't hike or cycle, however, exploring the country-side will still be difficult without a car, as local buses are often slow and infrequent.

DIRECTORY

Airport Information

Avignon-Provence
Tel 04 90 81 51 51.
Airport to city 10 km
(6 miles). Taxi €24.
W avignon-aeroport.fr

Marseille Provence
Tel 0820 811 414.
Airport to city 25 km
(17 miles). Shuttle bus
€10, taxi €40.
W marseille-aeroport.fr

**Montpellier
Méditerranée**
Tel 04 67 20 85 00.
Airport to city 7 km
(4 miles). Shuttle bus €8,
taxi €15–€20.
W montpellier.
aeroport.fr

Nice, Côte d'Azur
Tel 0820 423 333.
Airport to city 6 km (4 miles).
Shuttle bus €4, taxi €25–€30.
W nice.aeroport.fr

**Nîmes/Arles/
Camargue/ Cevennes**
Tel 04 66 70 49 49.
Airport to city 15 km
(9 miles).
Shuttle bus €5,
taxi €25.
W aeroport-nimes.fr

Toulon-Hyères
Tel 08 25 01 83 87.
Airport to city 23 km
(15 miles).
Shuttle bus €1.40,
taxi €40.
W toulon-hyeres.
aeroport.fr

Airline Details

Air France
UK **Tel** 0871 66 33 777.
France **Tel** 3654.
W airfrance.com

British Airways
France **Tel** 0825 825 400.
UK **Tel** 0844 493 0787.
W britishairways.com

Delta
France **Tel** 0892 702 609.
US **Tel** 0800 221 1212.
W delta.com

easyJet
France **Tel** 0820 420 315.
UK **Tel** 0330 365 5000.
W easyjet.com

Emirates
France **Tel** 0157 32 49 99.
UK **Tel** 844 800 2777.
W emirates.com

Flybe
UK **Tel** 0371 700 2000.
W flybe.com

Ryanair
France **Tel** 0892 562 150.
UK **Tel** 0871 246 0000.
W ryanair.com

Helicopter Services

Azur Hélicoptère
Tel 04 93 90 40 70.
W azurhelico.com

Héli-Air Monaco
Tel 00 377 92 05 00 50.
W heliairmonaco.com

Discount Travel Agencies

Jancarthier Voyages
7 cours Sextius.
Tel 04 42 93 48 48.
W voyages-jancarthier.fr

**Thomas Cook
Canebiere**
9 rue du jeune.
Tel 04 96 11 26 26.
W thomascook.fr

Trailfinders
194 Kensington High St,
London W8 7RG.
Tel 020 7938 3939.
W trailfinders.com

Getting Around by Train

Travelling to Provence by train is fast and efficient. The French state railway, Société Nationale des Chemins de Fer (**SNCF**), is one of Europe's best equipped and most comfortable. The train journey from Paris to Avignon is almost as quick as by air – the TGV (*Train à Grande Vitesse*) takes only four hours. The Channel Tunnel provides a fast rail link via Calais between Provence and the UK, although not all of the route is high-speed.

The interior of Avignon TGV train station

Train Stations

The main stations in the region are Marseille Gare St-Charles, Nîmes and Nice (Nice Ville av Thiers). All offer a range of facilities, including restaurants, shops, Wi-Fi and secure left luggage lockers. Keep in mind that trains in France are punctual and very rarely leave late.

Main Routes

The main train routes to Provence from Northern Europe pass through Lille and Paris. In Paris you have to transfer to the Gare de Lyon – the main Paris station serving the south of France. Tickets from London to Nice, Avignon and Marseille, via **Eurostar** or ferry, are all available from the **Rail Europe** office in New York or on their website. The Eurostar connects at Lille or Paris with TGVs to the rest of France. Passengers arriving by sea at Calais can catch the train to Paris and transfer on to the Corail overnight sleeper service to Nice.

From southern Europe, trains run to Marseille from Barcelona in Spain (5 hours) and Genoa in Italy (3 hours).

Within Provence and the Côte d'Azur, the coastal route between Nice and Marseille is often crowded, so it is best to reserve tickets in advance on this and other *Grandes Lignes*. In the Var and Haute Provence, railway lines are scarce, but SNCF runs bus services. The private rail service **Chemins de Fer de Provence** runs the Train des Pignes (*see p185*).

When purchasing a rail ticket – whether in France or abroad – it is also possible to pre-book a car (*Train + Auto*), bike (*Train + Vélo*) or hotel (*Train + Hôtel*) to await you at your destination.

Further information on rail travel is provided on the main SNCF website.

Booking from Abroad

Tickets to and within France can be booked in the UK and US through Rail Europe and via www.voyages-sncf.com. Rail Europe also has information on prices and departure times. Reservations made abroad can be difficult to change once in France – you may have to pay for another reservation, or claim for a refund on your return.

Booking in France

Ticket counters at all stations are computerized. There are also automatic ticket and

The TGV Train

Trains à Grande Vitesse, or high-speed trains, travel at up to 300 km/hr (185 mph). There are five versions of TGV serving all areas of France and some European destinations. The Eurostar links Paris and London, the Thalys runs to Brussels. The TGV Méditerranée to Provence leaves from Paris Gare de Lyon. Other TGVs leave from Grenoble, Geneva and Lausanne. The trains' speed, comfort and reliability make them relatively expensive. Always reserve a seat.

Paris to Marseille now takes just three hours by TGV

reservation machines (with English instructions) on the concourse of main stations. For travel by TGV, Corail and Motorail a reservation is essential but can be made as little as five minutes before the train leaves, and up to 90 days in advance. Costs rise considerably at peak times. The international ticket and reservation system at Lille Europe station allows direct booking on services throughout the continent and the UK.

Fares

TGVs have two price levels for 2nd class, normal and peak, and a single level for 1st class. The cost of the obligatory seat reservation is included in the ticket price. Tickets for other trains can be subject to a supplement and do not include the reservation charge of €3.

Discounts of 25 per cent are available for people travelling with children (Découverte Enfant+), for young people (Découverte 12–25), for the over-60s (Découverte Senior), for two people travelling together (Billet Duo), for return trips including a Saturday night (Découverte Sejour) and for advance booking (Découverte J8 and Découverte J30).

For those spending a bit more time on French railways, the SNCF issues a Carte Enfant+ and a Carte Senior giving reductions of up to 50 per cent. Rail Europe can supply these cards. **Inter-Rail** cards allow unlimited travel in European countries excluding the one of issue. (See the Inter-Rail website for more information.) **Eurail** passes are available to non-European residents and, in North America, France Railpass is another option.

Types of Train

SNCF trains are divided into several different types. TGV trains are the flagships of the network, travelling on specially built track at around 300 kph

(185 mph). The classic Intercités trains running from city to city can be a good travelling option. Both TGVs and Intercités can be overnight sleepers. Reservations are obligatory for all services and can be made through Rail Europe or SNCF.

AutoTrain trains allow drivers to travel overnight with their car. The service runs from Paris Bercy to Avignon, Marseille, Toulon and Nice. Reservations are essential.

TER trains are regional services that usually stop at every station. Reservations are not required, and tickets are not normally available in advance. Route maps and information (in French only) are available at stations and on the TER website, see the directory box for details.

Picturesque view from the Train des Pignes

Scenic Rail Routes

The private rail service **Chemins de Fer de Provence** runs the Train des Pignes, a 151-km (90-mile) ride from Nice to Dignes-les-Bains. This is a dramatic journey through tunnels and over viaducts, with magnificent views. The single-track railway from Nice to Cuneo in Italy via Peille, Sospel and Tende is also a spectacular ride through mountainous terrain. The Alpazur service runs in summer between Nice and Grenoble with a tourist steam train on the Puget-Théniers section; hikers can leave and rejoin the train after a day's walking. For more information see cccp.traindespignes.free.fr.

DIRECTORY

Information and Reservations

AutoTrain
🅦 autotrain.uk.voyages-sncf.com/en

Eurail
🅦 eurail.com

Eurostar
St Pancras International
Pancras Road,
London NW1.
Tel 08432 186 186.
Paris Gare du Nord,
rue de Dunkerque,
75010 Paris.
Tel 08 92 35 35 39.
🅦 eurostar.com

Eurotunnel
(Off junction 11a, M20, Folkestone).
Tel 08443 353 535 (France).
Tel 08 10 63 03 04.
🅦 eurotunnel.com

Inter-Rail
🅦 interrail.eu

Rail Europe USA
44 S. Broadway, White Plains,
NY 10604, US.
Tel 1-800-622-8600
(freephone in US).
🅦 raileurope.com

SNCF
Tel 3635 (France).
Tel 00 33 892 35 35 35
(Outside France).
🅦 voyages-sncf.com

TER
🅦 ter-sncf.com

Private Railway

Chemins de Fer de Provence
Tel 04 97 03 80 80.
🅦 trainprovence.com

Bicycles on Trains

Bicycles can be transported on the Eurostar, either as personal luggage if they fold to the size of a normal suitcase, or by advance reservation. You can transport your bike on nearly every single SNCF train, including the TGV. However, this service must be booked in advance, and in some cases your bicycle will be transported separately, and can take up to four days to arrive. Bikes may also be transported on local trains (indicated by a bicycle symbol in the timetable) The SNCF *train + velo* scheme allows you to reserve a rental bike at your destination station when you book your ticket, although be aware this option is only available on certain routes.

Times and Penalties

Timetables change twice a year in May and September. Leaflets for the main routes are free, and can also be checked on the SNCF website. The Provence Alpes Côte d'Azur region has an all-inclusive TER timetable, which includes coach travel.

You must time-punch your ticket in the yellow *composteur* machine at the platform entrance or pay a penalty on the train. This is very easy to do, simply insert your ticket and (if you have one) separate seat reservation face up and the machine will date-stamp them.

Motorail

Eurotunnel rail shuttles vehicles between Folkstone and Calais in around 35 minutes. Once in France, **AutoTrain** will transport your car overnight from Paris to either Avignon, Marseille, Nice or Toulon, while you relax on a passenger train. The journey is not cheap, but it is a practical, stress-free way to avoid the long drive south. Typically, you can drop off your car any time during the day and then use a separate train to reach your destination, where you can pick up the car any time the following day. The automobiles

Composteur machines are found at the platform entrance

are carried in open railcars. Tickets must be booked at least five days in advance and include free parking at the terminals for the day before departure and the day after arrival of your vehicle.

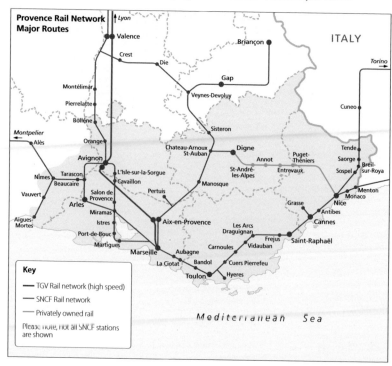

Provence Rail Network Major Routes

Key
— TGV Rail network (high speed)
— SNCF Rail network
— Privately owned rail
Please note, not all SNCF stations are shown

Travelling by Boat

There are few more enticing sights than the glittering Mediterranean of the southern Provençal coast. Almost every city along this stretch of water has a port with boats for hire. Ferry and boat companies operating to offshore islands are easy to find, and there are trips to Corsica from Marseille and Nice throughout the year. The other main waterways in Provence are the Rhône and Durance rivers, and the beautiful Camargue wetland. It is worth noting that the best way to get to St-Tropez in summer is by boat from Ste-Maxime or St-Raphaël. The town has no train station and the roads are usually very busy.

Sailing out of a rocky inlet on the Provençal coast

Mediterranean Ports

Car ferries depart all year round from Marseille to Corsica (Bastia and Ajaccio) and, in summer, from Marseille to Propriano and Ile Rousse, operated by **Corsica Linea**. **Corsica Ferries** depart from Nice and Toulon to Bastia and Ajaccio, as well as Sardinia, all year round.

Corsica Linea has crossings to North Africa every week from Marseille to Tunis or Algiers.

Regular ferries and boats to nearby islands operate from Bandol to the Ile de Bendor; from La Tour-Fondue to Porquerolles; from Port d'Hyères and Le Lavandou to Le Levant and Port-Cros; and from Cannes to the Iles de Lérins.

For a guide to all European ferry services, visit www.ferrylines.com.

Some of the smaller, local boats moored in St-Tropez

Cruises and River Trips

The Mediterranean is famous as a cruise destination, and numerous companies operate on the south coast of France, stopping at St-Tropez, Villefranche, Marseille and Monaco. **Grand Bleu** has a good range of boats for hire for weekly river trips.

River travel is also an option in Provence with several cruise lines operating luxury river trips on the Rhône between Avignon and Lyon. **Croisieres Avignon-Mireio** offers lunch, dinner or sightseeing cruises from Avignon to a range of destinations. Or you can take daily cruises through the Camargue in a converted *péniche* – a traditional river cargo boat.

Sailing

Over 70 ports along the Provence coastline welcome yachts, and mooring charges vary. The Côte d'Azur ports are particularly expensive. Contact the **Fédération Française de Voile** for information on sailing clubs and where to hire boats.

DIRECTORY

Car Ferry

Corsica Ferries
Tel 0825 09 50 95.
W corsica-ferries.fr

Corsica Linea
Marseille.
Tel 0825 88 80 88.
W corsicalinea.com

Cruises & River Trips

Croisieres Avignon-Mireio
Allée de l'Oulle, Avignon.
Tel 04 90 85 62 25.
W mireio.net

Grand Bleu
Tel 09 50 81 95 78 or
06 69 16 24 24.
W grandbleuyatching.fr

Les Péniches Isles de Stel
12 rue Amiral Courbet, 30220
Aigues-Mortes.
Tel 04 66 53 60 70.
W islesdestel.camargue.fr

Sailing

Fédération Française de Voile
Tel 01 40 60 37 00.
W ffvoile.org

A privately owned motorboat from Cannes

Getting Around by Road

France is a motorist's paradise and the main route to Provence is via an excellent, if expensive, autoroute (motorway) network. Provence is ideal for touring, with some of the most beautiful road routes in the world, including the stunning Grande Corniche above Nice, and the hilltop lanes of the Luberon *(see pp174–5)*. Popular routes, especially the motorway and coastal roads along the Côte d'Azur, are always busy in high season.

Getting to Provence

The quickest route south from Paris is the Autoroute du Soleil, the A6 motorway to Lyon, followed by the A7 to Marseille. Travellers from the UK and northern Europe should try to avoid driving through Paris, especially during the rush hour. The A26 runs from Calais to Troyes, where you can join the A5, which leads into the A6.

From Spain, the A8 motorway leads directly to Marseille and goes on to Nice and Italy.

In high season, the motorways get very crowded and if you have time it may be worth taking more minor (and attractive) roads. Try turning off the main road at Montélimar to travel to the Luberon via Nyons and Vaison-la-Romaine. Or exit

at Avignon, and head into the Luberon and on to Var.

For the adventurous, the Route Napoléon (N85) leads from Grenoble south across the Alps to Digne, and continues to Grasse. From Grasse, take the scenic D3 to Cannes, or the Route de Nice, which leads to Nice and its environs.

Car Rental

Car rental in France can be expensive so it is worth checking out your options before you go. There are numerous special offers for pre-paid car rentals in the UK and USA.

Fly-drive options work well for small groups. SNCF offers train and car-rental deals with collection from several main stations *(see pp246–7)*.

Insurance and Breakdown Services

All car insurance policies in the EU automatically include third-party insurance cover that is valid in any EU country. However, the extent of cover provided beyond the legal minimum varies between companies, so it is best to check your policy before you travel. If you are bringing your car from outside the EU, you can purchase extra insurance cover from the **AA**, **RAC** and **Europ Assistance**. While driving in France you must carry in the car your driving licence, passport, the vehicle registration document and a certificate of insurance. A sticker showing the country of registration should be displayed near the rear number plate. The headlights of right-hand drive cars must be adjusted – kits are available at most ports.

Taking out breakdown cover is advisable. It can be arranged with your European insurance cover, or through a motoring organization such as the AA or RAC. There are also local services such as **Dépannage Côte d'Azur Transports**.

Using the Autoroute Toll

When you join an autoroute, collect a ticket from the machine. This identifies your starting point on the autoroute. You do not pay until you reach an exit toll. You are charged according to the distance travelled and the type of vehicle used.

Gare de Péage
de Fresnes

2000 m

Motorway Sign
These signs indicate the name and distance to the next toll booth. They are usually blue and white; some show the tariff rates for cars, motorbikes, trucks and caravans.

Tollbooth with Attendant
When you hand in your ticket at a staffed tollbooth, the attendant will tell you the cost of your journey on the autoroute and the price will be displayed. You can pay with coins, notes or credit cards. A receipt is issued on request.

Automatic Machine
On reaching the exit toll, insert your ticket into the machine and the price of your journey is displayed in euros. You can pay either with coins or by credit card. The machine will give change and can issue a receipt.

Rules of the Road

Remember to drive on the right. The *priorité à droite* rule applies, meaning that you must give way to any vehicle coming out of a side turning on the right, unless otherwise signposted. On main roads a yellow diamond sign indicates where you have right of way. The *priorité à droite* does not apply at roundabouts, meaning you have to give way to cars already on the roundabout. Flashing headlights mean the driver is claiming right of way.

Seatbelts are compulsory for front and back seats. Children under ten are not permitted to travel in front seats apart from in baby seats facing backwards. Overtaking when there is a single solid centre line is heavily penalized. In case of breakdown it is compulsory to carry one red warning triangle and a luminous vest in the car. The autoroutes have emergency telephones every 2 km.

Speed Limits and Fines

Great efforts have been made to reduce road accidents in France, and there are now speed cameras at frequent intervals. Speed limits are:
• Motorways 130 km/hr (80 mph); 110 km/hr (68 mph) in rain.
• Dual carriageways 110 km/hr (68 mph); 50 km/hr (30 mph) in towns.
• Other roads 90 km/hr (56 mph).
Instant fines are issued for speeding and drink-driving. Driving with more than 0.5g of alcohol per litre of blood can also lead to severe fines, confiscation of your license, or even imprisonment.

Fast Through Routes

There are three main motorways in Provence: the A7 from Lyon to Marseille, the A9 from Orange to Barcelona and the A8 from Marseille to Menton. The A54 cuts across the Camargue from Aix-en-Provence to Nîmes. The A8 is the most expensive stretch of toll motorway in France, but allows you to drive from Nice to Aix-en-Provence in under two hours.

The scenic road through the Grand Canyon du Verdon

Country and Scenic Routes

One of the pleasures of touring Provence is turning off the main routes onto small country roads. The RN and D (*Route Nationale* and *Départmentale*) roads are good alternatives to motorways. *Bison futée* ("crafty bison") signs indicate alternative routes to avoid heavy traffic, and are especially helpful during the French holiday periods, known as the *grands départs*. The busiest weekends are in mid-July, and at the beginning and end of August when French holidays start and finish.

Apart from the busy coastal roads, Provence is a wonderful place to drive around. Some of the best scenic routes include the famous Corniche roads between Nice and Menton, with splendid sea views, or a tour of the back country of the Massif des Maures (*see pp120–21*). The local tourist office should be able to provide you with more information and some maps.

Maps

The best general map of Provence is the Michelin yellow map No. 245, at a scale of 1:200,000. **IGN** (Institut Géographique National) maps are more detailed. Town plans are usually provided free by tourist offices. In large towns you may need a more detailed map, published by Michelin or **Plans-Guides Blay-Foldex/Berlitz**. In the UK, **Stanfords** is famous for its range of maps.

Parking

Parking in the big towns, particularly along the coast, is strictly regulated. If you are illegally parked, you may be towed away instantly to the police pound and face a substantial fine. Most Provençal towns have pay and display machines (*horodateurs*) and parking is often time limited. Many places offer free parking from noon to 2pm – ticket machines automatically allow for this. Ensure you have enough coins for the meter or purchase a parking card, which are available from the *tabacs*.

Petrol

Petrol is relatively expensive in France, especially on autoroutes. Large supermarkets and hypermarkets sell petrol at a discount, however the pay booths may close over lunch and the automatic pumps only accept *carte bleue* (French bank cards). A map issued by French Government Tourist offices (*see p237*) indicates the cheaper petrol stations situated up to 2 km (just over a mile) from motorway exits. Unleaded petrol (*sans plomb*) and diesel fuel are found in all stations. LPG gas is also available, often on motorways. A map of locations stocking this fuel can be obtained from any LPG station in France. Note that in rural areas petrol stations can be hard to find, so ensure you have enough petrol for your journey.

As per the anti-pollution rules in place in France, Crit'Air (www.certificat-air.gouv.fr) stickers should be displayed on the windscreen of your vehicle, and

Mountain bikes are ideal for exploring the Provençal countryside

high-pollution vehicles will be banned on peak pollution days. Paris was the first city to introduce this system, with other major French cities set to follow.

Cycling

Cycling is one of the most pleasant ways to see Provence. Although there are few cycle lanes in towns in Provence, some cities, such as Arles, Avignon and Nîmes, have specified cycle routes. You can take bikes on certain trains – check the timetable first for the bike symbol (*see p248*). You can also reserve bicycles at several stations (*Train + Velo*). Rental shops can be found throughout the region, especially in the Luberon and in towns around the Camargue, which rent out mountain bikes (*VTT*). Bicycle theft is common along the Côte d'Azur – make sure you are fully insured before you go. Best of all, Provence is now following the initiative of Paris in introducing a free bike scheme in cities such as Marseille and Nice. Enquire at the tourist office for bike locations.

Taxis

Prices vary from one part of Provence to another. The charges are predictably highest along the Côte d'Azur, where it's not uncommon to pay €30 for a 20-minute journey. Elsewhere the pick-up charge is usually around €2, and €0.60 or more for every kilometre. An extra charge will be made for any luggage. All taxis must use a meter, or a *compteur*.

Hailing a taxi is not customary in Provence – you must go to a taxi rank or book by phone.

Hitchhiking and Carpooling

Hitchhiking is possible in France, although officially it is frowned upon. You are not supposed to hitch on the motorways and if you do you will be cautioned by the police. Carpooling schemes such as BlaBlaCar (www.blablacar.fr) are also becoming increasingly popular.

Coach and Bus Travel

Coach travel used to be the cheapest way of getting to Provence, but reductions in air fares have now made it a less competitive option. It is, however, one of the more environmentally friendly ways to travel and will take you directly from city centre to city centre. **Eurolines** (*see p251*) coaches depart all year round from London to Nîmes, Toulon, Marseille, Aix-en-Provence and Avignon. The journey to Marseille takes about 23 hours from London.

Larger towns have a bus station but, otherwise, the bus services are limited. SNCF runs bus lines in northern Provence, and private companies run along the major motorways between towns and on some minor routes, such as the coastal road between Toulon and St-Tropez. Local bus services are notoriously erratic.

Long distance cut-rate coach companies such as Ouibus, Isilines and FlixBus are beginning to develop domestically, and operate routes linking major cities.

Taxis lined up for business at a taxi rank, Marseille

Travelling in Cities

Apart from Marseille, which competes with Lyon for the title of second city of France, the towns and cities of Provence are small. The best way to get around is generally on foot, parking in most towns is strictly regulated, and in the summer months traffic can be very heavy. Marseille and Nice both have excellent public transport systems that are efficient and easy to use. Marseille and Nice also have bike rental schemes that are similar to the *Vélib* in Paris.

Bicycles can be hired through the Le Vélo scheme in Marseille

Metro

The fastest way to get around Marseille is by **Métro**. The system has two lines, which meet at Gare St-Charles and Castellane stations. Métro 1 goes from the hospital La Fourragère in the east to La Rose in the northeast, passing through the Vieux Port on the way. Métro 2 runs roughly north to south, connecting the shipping port with Notre-Dame-de-la-Garde and Ste-Marguerite. Tickets can be bought from Métro stations, on buses or in *tabacs*. Trains run from 5am–10:30pm daily.

Trams

The Marseille tram network consists of three lines, which together link the centre to areas to the north, south, east and west of the city. The lines meet at Noailles near Gare St-Charles. The best tickets to buy are the 24-hour or 72-hour passes, which give you unlimited travel on the metro, tram and bus.

In Nice some sections of the long-awaited tramway system are operational. The U-shaped Line 1 connects the northern and eastern neighbourhoods to the centre of the city, passing through Place Massena and the main railway station. Tickets can be bought from machines or tram operators. A new tramway to the airport from the city centre is due to open in 2018.

Buses

Although bus routes between towns in Provence can be slow and inadequate, within the towns the service is usually good. In Marseille an extensive bus network covers all of the city. Long-distance buses and airport shuttle buses leave from the *gare routière* (bus station) behind the main train station Gare St-Charles. There is a useful left-luggage facility (*consigne*) at both stations.

Nice has a good network of city buses including night buses. The Sunbus is a tourist service that runs daily and has multiple stops throughout the city. Tickets can be bought on board buses or from *tabacs*. Check the website of **Lignes d'Azur** for timetables.

Taxis

There are taxi ranks on most main squares in towns and cities. You can also telephone for taxis; enquire at the tourist office or your hotel for local numbers. It is not usual practice to hail a taxi in the street.

Cycling

Whether you bring your own bicycle or rent one, most of Provence's towns are small enough to cycle around. Marseille, Avignon and Aix-en-Provence have introduced bike-sharing schemes. Ask at a tourist office for further details and locations (*see p245*).

Walking

Explore the towns on foot as much as you can. Apart from Marseille and Nice the main city-centre sights of Nîmes, Avignon or Aix-en-Provence can easily be seen in a walking tour.

(*see p245*)

DIRECTORY

Metro

Métro (RTM) – Marseille
Ⓦ rtm.fr

Buses

Ligne d'Azur
Ⓦ lignedazur.com

Taxis

Nice Taxi Riviera
Tel 08 91 03 93 92.

Taxi Radio Marseille
Tel 04 91 02 20 20.

Cycling

Aix-en-Provence
Ⓦ aixpritvelo.com

Avignon
Ⓦ smoove-bike.com

Marseille
Ⓦ levelo-mpm.fr

Nice
Ⓦ velobleu.org

Marseille tram travelling along the Boulevard Longchamp

General Index

Acknowledgments

Dorling Kindersley would like to thank the following people whose contributions and assistance have made the preparation of this book possible.

Main Contributor
Roger Williams is a writer and editor who was for many years associated with the *Sunday Times* magazine. He has written two novels and a number of guide books, on places ranging from Barcelona to the Baltic States, and was a contributor to *Over Europe*, the first aerial record of the united continent. He visits France regularly, and has been writing about Provence for more than 30 years.

Contributors
Adele Evans, John Flower, Robin Gauldie, Jim Keeble, Anthony Rose, Martin Walters.

Additional Photography
Demetrio Carrasco, Andy Crawford, Lisa Cupolo, Franz Curzon, Philip Freiberger, Nick Goodall, Steve Gorton, Michelle Grant, John Heseltine, Andrew Holligan, Richard McConnell, Neil Mersh, Ian O'Leary, Rough Guides / Michelle Grant, Clive Streeter.

Additional Illustrators
Simon Calder, Paul Guest, Aziz Khan, Tristan Spaargaren, Ann Winterbotham, John Woodcock.

Cartographic Research
Jane Hugill, Samantha James, Jennifer Skelley, Martin Smith (Lovell Johns).

Design and Editorial
Managing Editor Georgina Matthews
Deputy Editorial Director Douglas Amrine
Deputy Art Director Gaye Allen
Production Controller Hilary Stephens
Picture Research Susan Mennell
DTP Designer Salim Qurashi
Map Co-ordinators Simon Farbrother, David Pugh
Maps Uma Bhattacharya, Kunal Singh, Jennifer Skelley, Samantha James (Lovell Johns Ltd, Oxford)
Researcher Philippa Richmond
Revisions Azeem Alam, Vincent Allonier, Michelle Arness Frederic, Rosemary Bailey, Shahnaaz Bakshi, Laetitia Benloulou, Josie Bernard, Marta Bescos Sanchez, Tessa Bindloss, Hilary Bird, Nadia Bonomally, Kevin Brown, Margaret Chang, Cooling Brown Partnership, Guy Dimond, Joy Fitzsimmonds, Lisa Fox-Mullen, Anna Freiberger, Rhiannon Furbear, Vinod Harish, Victoria Heyworth-Dunne, Jackie Grosvenor, Swati Gupta, Annette Jacobs, Stuart James, Laura Jones, Nancy Jones, Rupanki Kaushik, Sumita Khatwani, Priyanka Kumar, Rahul Kumar, Rakesh Kumar Pal, Cécile Landau, Erika Lang, Delphine Lawrance, Francesca Machiavelli, James Marlow, Sonal Modha, Sachida Nand Pradhan, Claire Naylor, Scarlett O'Hara, Lyn Parry, Helen Partington, Sangita Patel, Susie Peachey, Katie Peacock, Alice Peebles, Pure Content Ltd, Carolyn Pyrah, Ashwin Raju Adimari, Philippa Richmond, Ellen Root, Zoe Ross, Kavita Saha, Sands Publishing Solutions, Avijit Sengupta, Baishakhee Sengupta, Sailesh Sharma, Bhaswati Singh, Catherine Skipper, Amelia Smith, Priyanka Thakur, Rachel Thompson, Amanda Tomeh, Daphne Trotter, Janis Utton, Conrad van Dyk, Vinita Venugopal, Ajay Verma, Dora Whitaker, Sophie Wright, Irina Zarb.

Special Assistance
Louise Abbott; Anna Brooke, Manade Gilbert Arnaud; Brigitte Charles, Monaco Tourist Board, London; Sabine Giraud, Terres du Sud, Venasque; Emma Heath; Nathalie Lavarenne, Musée Matisse, Nice; Ella Milroy; Marianne Petrou; Andrew Sanger; David Tse.

Photographic Reference
Bernard Beaujard, Vézénobres.

Photography Permissions
Dorling Kindersley would like to thank the following for their assistance and kind permission to photograph at their establishments: Fondation Marguerite et Aimé Maeght, St-Paul de Vence; Hotel Négresco, Nice; Monsieur J-F Campana, Mairie de Nice; Monsieur Froumessol, Mairie de Cagnes-sur-Mer; Musée Ephrussi de Rothschild, St-Jean-Cap-Ferrat; Musée Jean Cocteau, Menton; Musée International de la Parfumerie, Grasse; Musée Matisse, Nice; Musée National Message Biblique Marc Chagall, Nice; Musée Océanographique, Monaco; Musée Picasso/Château Grimaldi, Antibes; Salle des Mariages, Hôtel de Ville, Menton, and all other churches, museums, hotels, restaurants, shops and sights too numerous to thank individually.

Picture Credits
a = above; b = below/bottom; c = centre; f = far; l = left; r = right; t = top.

Works of art have been reproduced with the permission of the following copyright holders:

© ADAGP, Paris and DACS, London 2011: 30tr, 31tr, 31bl, 34tr, 78tr, 80tr, 80cla, 80clb, 81tl, 81cr, 81br, 82cb, 82crb, 89bl, 103tr, 111br, 123crb, 124ca, 124bc, 125cra, 125crb, 148ca; ©ARS, NY and DACS, London 2006: 63tl, 80clb; © DACS, London 2006: 136tl; © Estate of Francis Bacon/DACS, London: 225bl; © Succession H.Matisse/DACS, London 2006: 31cr, 86tr, 86cla, 86bl, 87tc, 87cr, 87br; © Succession Miro/ADAGP, Paris and DACS, London 2006: 81cra; © Succession Picasso/DACS, London 2006: 30br, 77cl, 77cr, 77clb, 77bc, 77br.

The publisher would like to thank the following individuals, companies and picture libraries for permission to reproduce their photographs:

Alamy Images: 98br; AA World Travel Library 155clb; age fotostock 223c; Stephen Barnes 72c; blickwinkel 164bc; Christophe Boisvieux 71bc; Peter Bowater 178; Chronicle 56tc; Tor Eigeland 14cl; Derek Harris 149br; Chris Hellier 71crb; Hemis 13tl, 158, 200, 229tl; Peter Horree 57tl, 157tc; Inspiration Images 207tc; International Photobank 116c; Neil Juggins 240clb; Per Karlsson - BKWine.com 206bc, 216tl; Justin Kase zeightz 240cl; Justin Kase zfourz 58tl; Lanmas 46bc; Melvyn Longhurst 203bc; Barry Mason 247c; Megapress 109crb; Nature Photographers Ltd 118bc; john norman 206c; Pictures Colour Library 246cla, 251tc; Pixonnet.com 240bl; REDA &CO srl 195tr; Norbert Scanella 36br; Travelshots.com 238tl; Travel Pictures 122clb; WaterFrame 23br; Dave Watts 231c; Ray Wilson 23tl; Poelzer Wolfgang 118cl; Gregory Wrona 12br, 236br; **Restaurant Alexandre:** Michel Kayser/Alain Guilhot/Fédéphoto 214tc; **Alvey & Towers:** 246br; **Ancient Art and Architecture Collection:** 43t and cb, 44bl, 47tl; **Archives de l'Automobile Club de Monaco:** 56cla; **Artephot, Paris:** Plassart 31c.

Hostellerie Berard: 230cra, 211tl; **La Bonne Etape:** 197cr, 217bc; **Bridgeman Art Library:** Archives Charmet 32cl, 54tr, / Gallimard /© Antoinede Saint-Exupéry 33cla, / Bibliotheque des Arts Decoratifs, Paris, France 41b, 53t, 136cl, 164clb, / Bibliotheque Nationale, Paris, France 50cb, / Musee National des Arts et Traditions Populaires, Paris, France 50cla, 144tl; Christie's, London 51crb, 54–55; Giraudon 51tl, 52bl; Schloss Charlottenburg, Berlin 183tr.

Campagne, Campagne!, Paris: Jolyot 96br; JL Julien 35bc; Meissonnier 163cla; Meschinet 142cl; Moirenc 245tl; Pambour 175tl, 176t; Picard 163tr; **Cephas:** Mick Rock

206br, 207cra and br; **Château Val Joanis:** 207tr; **Colombe d'Or** 203tc; **Corbis:** Sophie Bassouls 33cr; Cubolmages srl 15bc; Owen Franken 231tc; Chris Hellier 101tr; Image Source 15tr; Robert Harding World Imagery/Gavin Hellier 64; **Lisa Cupolo:** 110tc; **Culture Espaces, Paris:** 90tr and cla; Véran 91tl.

Photo Daspet, Avignon: Musée du Petit Palais, Avignon 49bl; Palais des Papes, Avignon 48clb and bl; **Diaf, Paris:** J-P Garcin 37cb; J-C Gérard 228 tl and bc, 155br; Camille Moirenc 166c; Bernard Régent 30tr; Patrick Somelet 162br; **Direction Des Affaires Culturelles, Monaco:** 95cra; **Domaine de Cabasse:** 201bl; **Dreamstime.com:** Steve Allen 175bc; Carabiner 253tr Chaoss 10cla; Ciuciumama 151tr; Rene Drouyer 234–5; Evgeniy Fesenko 5cr; Fotoluminate 12tc; Wieslaw Jarek 1c; Karin59 175br; Klaus rainer Krieger 164br; Lianem 187br; Liligraphie 4tc; Magspace 39br; Mikelane45 140ca, 140c, 140cb; Nkarol 175bl; Rosamund Parkinson 27tr; Evgeny Prokofyev 155tc; Radomír Režný 18; Ribe 119c; Alex Scott 164bl; Richard Semik 60–1, 134cr; Stevanzz 4cr; Luboslav Tiles 2–3; Typhoonski 11tr.

European Commission: 242; **Mary Evans:** 32bl, crb and br, 32crb, 49br and t, 51br; **Jane Ewart:** 26clb, 27crb, 29c, 62cla, 80cla, 131b, 167cra and cr; **Explorer Archives, Paris:** cr; L Bertrand 42cb; Jean-Loup Charmet 128cl, 151crb; Coll. ES 50clb and bl; Coll. G Garde 37cra; J P Hervey 68tl; J & C Lenars 41c; M C Noailles 69br; Peter Willis 44cla; A Wolf 47cb.

Fondation Auguste Escoffier, Villeneuve-Loubet: 78c; **Fondation Maeght, Saint-Paul-de-Vence, France:** Claude Germain 81tl and cra; Coll. M et Mme Adrien Maeght 81cr; **Frank Lane Picture Agency:** N. Clark 174br; Fritz Polking 22tr.

Galerie Intemporel, Paris: Les Films Ariane, Paris 58–9; **Editions Gaud, Moisenay:** 74bl, 90br, 91bc and br, 146tl, 185cr; **Getty Images:** Peter Adams 220cla; AFP/Valery Hache 224bl; Bettmann 33cb; The Bridgeman Art Library/Gallo-Roman 148cl; Corbis Historical 32c; Culture Club 53c; DEA/G. Dagli Orti 8–9, 114clb; DEA / S.MONTANARI 118bl; julio donoso 71c, 71clb; M. Gebicki 192–3; hemis.fr/Bertrand Gardel 130; Hemis/Bertrand Rieger 20c; Hemis/Jose Nicolas 220br; Hulton Archive 54bc; Roger Hutchings 71cl; The Image Bank/Peter Adams 20tl; The Image Bank/Remi Benali 36cl; Keystone-France 33tr, 33bl; Marka 98tr; Wirelmage/ Tony Barson 59br; **Giraudon, Paris:** 31tr, bl and br, 32tr, 40, 44br, 52cla and br, 137b, 176c; Lauros-Giraudon 42cla, 49crb, 50tr (detail), 50–1, 53clb, 55cb, 57cb (all rights reserved), 77tl and tr, 114bl, 129c, 138cla, 148ca, 150tr; Musée de la Vieille Charité, Marseille 42tr; Musée de la Ville de Paris, Musée du Petit Palais/Lauros-Giraudon 30clb; Musée des Beaux-Arts, Marseille 52–3, 53bl, 156cla; Musée du Vieux Marseille, Marseille 52clb, 54cla; **Grand Grottes de St-Cézaire:** 69cl.

Hotel Eden Roc, Cap D'antibes: 195br.

Intercontinental Carlton Hotel, Cannes: 194bc; **ISIC:** 238c; **iStockphoto.com:** Anna39 141tc.

Le Jardin de la Gare: 215br; **Jardins Secret:** 196tl; **Le Julien:** 213tr.

Catherine Karnow, San Francisco: 114cla; **The Kobal Collection:** United Artists 75tl.

Edouard Loubet Restaurant: 215tc; **Louis XV, Monaco:** Bernard Touillon 209br.

Magnum Photos: Bruno Barbey 228crb; René Burri 58crb; Elliott Erwitt 95br; **Mairie de Nîmes:** Jean-Charles Blais 136t (all rights reserved); Francis Bacon 225bl (all rights reserved); **Mansell Collection:** 43b, 46br, 47bl, 55ca, 56bl; **Le Mas d'Entremont:** 212bc; **Le Mesclun:** 216bl; courtesy of SBM 55crb, 98cla; **Musée d'Art Classique de Mougins:** 13cr; **Musée De L'Annonciade, St-Tropez:** E Vila Mateu 123crb, 124–5 all; **Musée Archéologique De La Vaison-la-Romaine:** Christine Bézin 45clb; **Musée D'art Moderne Et D'art Contemporain, Nice:** 89bl; **Musée Fabre, Montpellier:** Leenhardt 139b; **Musée De La Photographie, Mougins:** 70br; **Musée Matisse, NICE:** © Service photographique, Ville de Nice 86tr, cla and bl, 87tc, cr, bc and br.

Negresco Hotel, Nice: 198br, 210bc.

L'Olivier Restaurant: 202bl, 217tl. **OTC Marseille:** 253bl.

Palais des Festivals et des Congres: 72cla, 73tl; **Pastis Hotel:** 194ca, 199tr; **Photolibrary:** 236cla; **Photo Resources:** CM Dixon 45crb.

SA Aeroports: 244bc; **Service de Presse de la Ville de Cagnes sur Mer:** 83cr; **SNCF:** 59bc, 248tr; **Superstock:** Hermis.fr 186tl, /Camille Moirenc 104; Exactostock-1491/ Tom Brakefield 34tr; **Sygma:** 79tr; Keystone 57bc.

Editions Tallendier, Paris: Bibliothèque Nationale 46–7; **Terres du Sud, Venasque:** Philippe Giraud 48cla, 49ca and bl, and br, 68br, 74bc, 85cra, 109br, 171crb, 172b; **Les Terraillers:** 208bl; **La Trattoria, Monaco:** Frédéric Ducout 209tl; **Travel Library:** Philip Enticknap 97t and br.

La Vague d'Or: 212tl.

Wallis Phototheque, Marseille: 38cra, clb and br, 39ca; Bendi 252tr; Clasen 59tl, 71cla; Constant 186br; Di Meglio 119ca; Giani 100tr, 225tr; Huet 189tr; LCI 35br, 180tr; Leroux 20br; Poulet 100c; Royer 100cr and bl; Tarta 196br; **Roger Williams:** 105, 143bl, 169tr, 174c, 185bc, 188cla.

Front endpaper: **Alamy Images:** Peter Bowater Ltr, Hemis Lcla; **Corbis:** Robert Harding World Imagery/Gavin Hellier Rtr; Getty Images: hemis.fr/Bertrand Gardel Lbc; Superstock: Hemis.fr/Camille Moirenc Rbr.

Cover images: Front & spine - Alamy Stock Photo: STOCKFOLIO®. Back - Dreamstime.com: Darius Dzinnik.

All other images © Dorling Kindersley. For further information see www.dkimages.com

Phrase Book

In Emergency

Help!	**Au secours!**	*oh sekoor*
Stop!	**Arrêtez!**	*aret-ay*
Call a doctor!	**Appelez un médecin!**	*apuh-lay uñ medsañ*
Call an ambulance!	**Appelez une ambulance!**	*apuh-lay oon oñboo-loñs*
Call the police!	**Appelez la police!**	*apuh-lay lah poh-lees*
Call the fire brigade!	**Appelez les pompiers!**	*apuh-lay leh poñ-peeyay*
Where is the nearest telephone?	**Où est le téléphone le plus proche?**	*oo ay luh tehlehfon luh ploo prosh*
Where is the nearest hospital?	**Où est l'hôpital le plus proche?**	*oo ay l'opeetal luh ploo prosh*

Communication Essentials

Yes	**Oui**	*wee*
No	**Non**	*noñ*
Please	**S'il vous plaît**	*seel voo play*
Thank you	**Merci**	*mer-see*
Excuse me	**Excusez-moi**	*exkoo-zay mwah*
Hello	**Bonjour**	*boñzhoor*
Goodbye	**Au revoir**	*oh ruh-vwar*
Good night	**Bonsoir**	*boñ-swar*
Morning	**Le matin**	*matañ*
Afternoon	**L'après-midi**	*l'apreh-meedee*
Evening	**Le soir**	*swar*
Yesterday	**Hier**	*eeyehr*
Today	**Aujourd'hui**	*oh-zhoor-dwee*
Tomorrow	**Demain**	*duhmañ*
Here	**Ici**	*ee-see*
There	**Là**	*lah*
What?	**Quel, quelle?**	*kel, kel*
When?	**Quand?**	*koñ*
Why?	**Pourquoi?**	*poor-kwah*
Where?	**Où?**	*oo*

Useful Phrases

How are you?	**Comment allez-vous?**	*kom-moñ talay voo*
Very well, thank you.	**Très bien, merci.**	*treh byañ, mer-see*
Pleased to meet you.	**Enchanté de faire votre connaissance.**	*oñshoñ-tay duh fehr votr kon-ay-sans*
See you soon.	**A bientôt.**	*a byañ-toh*
That's fine.	**Voilà qui est parfait.**	*vwalah kee ay parfay*
Where is/are…?	**Où est/sont…?**	*oo ay/soñ*
How far is it to…?	**Combien de kilomètres d'ici à…?**	*kom-byañ duh keelo-metr d'ee-see ah*
Which way to…?	**Quelle est la direction pour…?**	*kel ay lah deer-ek-syoñ poor*
Do you speak English?	**Parlez-vous anglais?**	*par-lay voo oñg-lay*
I don't understand.	**Je ne comprends pas.**	*zhuh nuh kom-proñ pah*
Could you speak slowly, please?	**Pouvez-vous parler moins vite, s'il vous plaît?**	*poo-vay voo par-lay mwañ veet seel voo play*
I'm sorry.	**Excusez-moi.**	*exkoo-zay mwah*

Useful Words

big	**grand**	*groñ*
small	**petit**	*puh-tee*
hot	**chaud**	*show*
cold	**froid**	*frwah*
good	**bon**	*boñ*
bad	**mauvais**	*moh-veh*
enough	**assez**	*assay*
well	**bien**	*byañ*
open	**ouvert**	*oo-ver*
closed	**fermé**	*fer-meh*
left	**gauche**	*gohsh*
right	**droite**	*drwaht*
straight on	**tout droit**	*too drwah*
near	**près**	*preh*
far	**loin**	*lwañ*
up	**en haut**	*oñ oh*
down	**en bas**	*oñ bah*
early	**de bonne heure**	*duh bon-urr*
late	**en retard**	*oñ ruh-tar*
entrance	**l'entrée**	*l'on-tray*
exit	**la sortie**	*sor-tee*
toilet	**les toilettes, les WC**	*twah-let, vay-see*
unoccupied	**libre**	*leebr*
no charge	**gratuit**	*grah-twee*

Making a Telephone Call

I'd like to place a long-distance call.	**Je voudrais faire un interurbain.**	*zhuh voo-dreh fehr uñ añter-oorbañ*
I'd like to make a reverse-charge call.	**Je voudrais faire une communication PCV.**	*zhuh voodreh fehr oon kom-oonikah-syoñ peh-seh-veh*
I'll try again later.	**Je rappelerai plus tard.**	*zhuh rapeleray ploo tar*
Can I leave a message?	**Est-ce que je peux laisser un message?**	*es-keh zhuh puh leh-say uñ mehsazh*
Hold on.	**Ne quittez pas, s'il vous plaît.**	*nuh kee-tay pah seel voo play*
Could you speak up a little please?	**Pouvez-vous parler un peu plus fort?**	*poo-vay voo par-lay uñ puh ploo for*
local call	**la communication locale**	*komoonikah-syoñ low-kal*

Shopping

How much does this cost?	C'est combien s'il vous plaît?	say kom-byañ seel voo play
Do you take credit cards?	Est-ce que vous acceptez les cartes de crédit?	es-keh voo zaksept-ay leh kart duh-kreh dee
Do you take travellers' cheques?	Est-ce que vous acceptez les chèques de voyage?	es-kuh voo zaksept-ay leh shek duh vwayazh
I would like …	Je voudrais…	zhuh voo-dray
Do you have?	Est-ce que vous avez?	es-kuh voo zavay
I'm just looking.	Je regarde seulement.	zhuh ruhgar suhlmoñ
What time do you open?	A quelle heure vous êtes ouvert?	ah kel urr voo zet oo-ver
What time do you close?	A quelle heure vous êtes fermé?	ah kel urr voo zet fer-may
This one	Celui-ci	suhl-wee-see
That one	Celui-là	suhl-wee-lah
expensive	cher	shehr
cheap	pas cher, bon marché	pah shehr, boñ mar-shay
size, clothes	la taille	tye
size, shoes	la pointure	pwañ-tur
white	blanc	bloñ
black	noir	nwahr
red	rouge	roozh
yellow	jaune	zhohwn
green	vert	vehr
blue	bleu	bluh

Types of Shop

antique shop	le magasin d'antiquités	maga-zañ d'oñteekee-tay
bakery	la boulangerie	booloñ-zhuree
bank	la banque	boñk
book shop	la librairie	lee-brehree
butcher	la boucherie	boo-shehree
cake shop	la pâtisserie	patee-sree
cheese shop	la fromagerie	fromazh-ree
chemist	la pharmacie	farmah-see
dairy	la crémerie	krem-ree
department store	le grand magasin	groñ maga-zañ
delicatessen	la charcuterie	sharkoot-ree
fishmonger	la poissonnerie	pwasson-ree
gift shop	le magasin de cadeaux	maga-zañ duh kadoh
greengrocer	le marchand de légumes	mar-shoñ duh lay-goom
grocery	l'alimentation	alee-moñta-syoñ
hairdresser	le coiffeur	kwafuhr
market	le marché	marsh-ay
newsagent	le magasin de journaux	maga-zañ duh zhoor-no
post office	la poste, le bureau de poste, les PTT	pohst, booroh duh pohst, peh-teh-teh
shoe shop	le magasin de chaussures	duh show-soor
supermarket	le super-marché	soo pehr-marshay
tobacconist	le tabac	tabah
travel agent	l'agence de voyages	l'azhoñs duh vwayazh

Menu Decoder

l'agneau	l'anyoh	lamb
l'ail	l'eye	garlic
la banane	banan	banana
le beurre	burr	butter
la bière	bee-yehr	beer
le bifteck, le steack	beef-tek, stek	steak
le boeuf	buhf	beef
bouilli	boo-yee	boiled
le café	kah-fayle	coffee
le canard	kanar	duck
le citron pressé	see-troñ press-eh	fresh lemon juice
les crevettes	kruh-vet	prawns
les crustacés	kroos-ta-say	shellfish
cuit au four	kweet oh foor	baked
le dessert	deh-ser	dessert
l'eau minérale	l'oh meeney-ral	mineral water
les escargots	leh zes-kar-goh	snails
les frites	freet	chips
le fromage	from-azh	cheese
les fruits frais	frwee freh	fresh fruit
les fruits de mer	frwee duh mer	seafood
le gâteau	gah-toh	cake
la glace	glas	ice, ice cream
grillé	gree-yay	grilled
le homard	omahr	lobster
l'huile	l'weel	oil
le jambon	zhoñ-boñ	ham
le lait	leh	milk
les légumes	lay-goom	vegetables
la moutarde	moo-tard	mustard
l'oeuf	l'uf	egg
les oignons	leh zonyoñ	onions
les olives	leh zoleev	olives
l'orange pressée	l'oroñzh press-eh	fresh orange juice
le pain	pan	bread
le petit pain	puh-tee pañ	roll
poché	posh-ay	poached
le poisson	pwah-ssoñ	fish
le poivre	pwavr	pepper
la pomme	pom	apple
les pommes de terre	pom-duh tehr	potatoes
le porc	por	pork
le potage	poh-tazh	soup
le poulet	poo-lay	chicken
le riz	ree	rice
rôti	row-tee	roast
la sauce	sohs	sauce
la saucisse	sohsees	sausage, fresh
sec	sek	dry
le sel	sel	salt
le sucre	sookr	sugar
le thé	tay	tea
le toast	toast	toast
la viande	vee-yand	meat
le vin blanc	vañ bloñ	white wine
le vin rouge	vañ roozh	red wine
le vinaigre	veenaygr	vinegar

Eating Out

Have you got a table?	**Avez-vous une table libre?**	avay-voo oon tahbl leebr
I want to reserve a table.	**Je voudrais réserver une table.**	zhuh voo-dray rayzehr-vay oon tahbl
The bill, please.	**L'addition, s'il vous plaît.**	l'adee-syoñ seel voo play
I am a vegetarian.	**Je suis végétarien.**	zhuh swee vezhay-tehryañ
Waitress/ waiter	**Madame, Mademoiselle/ Monsieur**	mah-dam, mah-dem wah zel/muh-syuh
menu	**le menu, la carte**	men-oo, kart
fixed-price menu	**le menu à prix fixe**	men-oo ah pree feeks
cover charge	**le couvert**	koo-vehr
wine list	**la carte des vins**	kart-deh vañ
glass	**le verre**	vehr
bottle	**la bouteille**	boo-tay
knife	**le couteau**	koo-toh
fork	**la fourchette**	for-shet
spoon	**la cuillère**	kwee-yehr
breakfast	**le petit déjeuner**	puh-tee deh-zhuh-nay
lunch	**le déjeuner**	deh-zhuh-nay
dinner	**le dîner**	dee-nay
main course	**le plat principal**	plah prañsee-pal
starter, first course	**l'entrée, le hors d'oeuvre**	l'oñ-tray, or-duhvr
dish of the day	**le plat du jour**	plah doo zhoor
wine bar	**le bar à vin**	bar ah vañ
café	**le café**	ka-fay
rare	**saignant**	say-noñ
medium	**à point**	ah pwañ
well done	**bien cuit**	byañ kwee

Staying in a Hotel

Do you have a vacant room?	**Est-ce que vous avez une chambre?**	es-kuh voo-zavay oon shambr
double room	**la chambre pour deux personnes, avec**	shambr ah duh pehr-sonavek
with double bed	**un grand lit**	un groñ lee
twin room	**la chambre à deux lits**	shambr ah duh lee
single room	**la chambre pour une personne**	shambr ah oon pehr-son
room with a bath, shower	**la chambre avec salle de bains, une douche**	shambr avek sal duh bañ, oon doosh
porter	**le garçon**	gar-soñ
key	**la clef**	klay
I have a reservation.	**J'ai fait une réservation.**	zhay fay oon rayzehrva-syoñ

Sightseeing

abbey	**l'abbaye**	l'abay-ee
art gallery	**la galerie d'art**	galer-ree dart
cathedral	**la cathédrale**	katay-dral
church	**l'église**	l'aygleez
garden	**le jardin**	zhar-dañ
library	**la bibliothèque**	beebleeo-tek
museum	**le musée**	moo-zay
railway station	**la gare (SNCF)**	gahr (es-en-say-ef)
bus station	**la gare routière**	gahr roo-tee-yehr
tourist information	**les renseignements touristiques, le syndicat d'initiative**	roñsayn-moñ office too-rees-teek, sandee-ka d'eenee-syateev
town hall	**l'hôtel de ville**	l'ohtel duh veel
private mansion	**l'hôtel particulier**	l'ohtel partikoo-lyay
closed for public holiday	**fermeture jour férié**	fehrmeh-tur zhoor fehree-ay

Numbers

0	**zéro**	zeh-roh
1	**un, une**	uñ, oon
2	**deux**	duh
3	**trois**	trwah
4	**quatre**	katr
5	**cinq**	sañk
6	**six**	sees
7	**sept**	set
8	**huit**	weet
9	**neuf**	nerf
10	**dix**	dees
11	**onze**	oñz
12	**douze**	dooz
13	**treize**	trehz
14	**quatorze**	katorz
15	**quinze**	kañz
16	**seize**	sehz
17	**dix-sept**	dees-set
18	**dix-huit**	dees-weet
19	**dix-neuf**	dees-nerf
20	**vingt**	vañ
30	**trente**	tront
40	**quarante**	karoñt
50	**cinquante**	sañkoñt
60	**soixante**	swasoñt
70	**soixante-dix**	swasoñt-dees
80	**quatre-vingts**	katr-vañ
90	**quatre-vingts-dix**	katr-vañ-dees
100	**cent**	soñ
1,000	**mille**	meel

Time

one minute	**une minute**	oon mee-noot
one hour	**une heure**	oon urr
half an hour	**une demi-heure**	oon duh-mee urr
Monday	**lundi**	luñ-dee
Tuesday	**mardi**	mar-dee
Wednesday	**mercredi**	mehrkruh-dee
Thursday	**jeudi**	zhuh-dee
Friday	**vendredi**	voñdruh-dee
Saturday	**samedi**	sam-dee
Sunday	**dimanche**	dee-moñsh

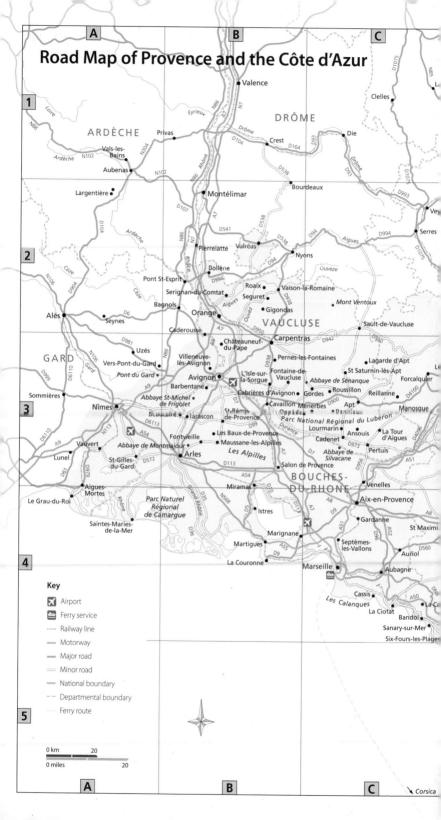